DEFIANT VOICES

DEFIANT VOICES

RUSSIAN SHORT STORIES FROM THE 19TH
TO THE 21ST CENTURIES • SELECTED BY

SERGEI LEBEDEV

An Apollo Book

First published in the UK in 2026 by Head of Zeus,
part of Bloomsbury Publishing Plc

The moral right of Sergei Lebedev to be identified as the editor of this work
has been asserted in accordance with the Copyright,
Designs and Patents Act of 1988.

The moral right of the contributing authors and translators of this anthology to be
identified as such is asserted in accordance with the Copyright,
Designs and Patents Act of 1988.

The list of individual titles and respective copyrights to be found on pages 843–847
constitutes an extension of this copyright page.

All rights reserved. No part of this publication may be: i) reproduced or transmitted
in any form, electronic or mechanical, including photocopying, recording or by means of any
information storage or retrieval system without prior permission in writing from the publishers;
or ii) used or reproduced in any way for the training, development or operation of artificial
intelligence (AI) technologies, including generative AI technologies. The rights holders expressly
reserve this publication from the text and data mining exception as per Article 4(3)
of the Digital Single Market Directive (EU) 2019/790.

All excerpts have been reproduced according to the styles found
in the original works. As a result, some spellings and accents
used can vary throughout this anthology.

9 7 5 3 1 2 4 6 8

A catalogue record for this book is available from the British Library.

ISBN (HB): 9781801104128
ISBN (E): 9781801104142

Typeset by Siliconchips Services Ltd UK

Cover design: Matt Mondou-Bray | Head of Zeus

Printed and bound in Great Britain by Clays Ltd, Elcograf S.p.A.

Bloomsbury Publishing Plc
50 Bedford Square, London, WC1B 3DP, UK
Bloomsbury Publishing Ireland Limited,
29 Earlsfort Terrace, Dublin 2, D02 AY28, Ireland

HEAD OF ZEUS LTD
5–8 Hardwick Street
London, EC1R 4RG

To find out more about our authors and books
visit www.headofzeus.com
For product safety related questions contact productsafety@bloomsbury.com

CONTENTS

Introduction ix

Alexander Pushkin	*The Shot*	1
Nikolai Gogol	*The Lost Dispatch*	14
Mikhail Lermontov	*The Fatalist*	26
Ivan Turgenev	*Yermolaï and the Miller's Wife*	37
Mikhail Saltykov-Shchedrin	*How a Muzhik Fed Two Officials*	49
Leo Tolstoy	*After the Ball*	57
Nikolai Leskov	*The Small Mistake*	67
Vsevolod Garshin	*The Bears*	76
Vladimir Gilyarovsky	*Tankard with Eagle*	93
Anton Chekhov	*Ionych*	101
Fyodor Sologub	*The White Dog*	119
Maxim Gorky	*Twenty Six Men and A Girl. A Poem*	125
Alexander Kuprin	*A Clump of Lilacs*	140
Ivan Bunin	*The Dreams of Chang*	146
Leonid Andreev	*The Silence*	163
Nadezhda Teffi	*Solovki*	176
Mikhail Kuzmin	*Father Gervasy's Secret*	192
Mikhail Prishvin	*The Blue Banner*	201
Valery Bryusov	*In the Mirror*	209
Mikhail Osorgin	*The Flora of Penza*	219
Andrei Bely	*The Yogi*	226
Boris Zaytsev	*Avdotya-Death*	242

Alexei Tolstoy	*The Marie Antoinette Tapestry*	255
Yevgeny Zamyatin	*The Cave*	268
Velimir Khlebnikov	*Nikolai*	278
Vladislav Khodasevich	*Pompeii*	284
Mark Aldanov	*The Darkness*	292
Sigizmund Krzhizhanovsky	*Quadraturin*	303
Mikhail Bulgakov	*The Steel Windpipe*	313
Leonid Dobychin	*Kozlova*	322
Isaac Babel	*The King*	329
Mikhail Zoshchenko	*A Victim of the Revolution*	336
Boris Pilnyak	*The Old House*	340
Yury Tynyanov	*Lieutenant Kijé*	359
Irina Odoyevtseva	*Epilogue*	391
Valentin Kataev	*Knives*	404
Ilf & Petrov	*Blue Devil*	415
Yury Olesha	*Liompa*	419
Vladimir Nabokov	*The Return of Chorb*	424
Andrey Platonov	*Nikita*	433
Nadezhda Mandelstam	*The Last Letter*	441
Lidya Ginzburg	*Excerpts from a Siege Day*	445
Gaito Gazdanov	*The Mistake*	454
Mikhail Sholokhov	*Shibalok's Family*	467
Daniil Kharms	*The Fate of the Professor's Wife*	473
Varlam Shalamov	*Major Pugachiov's Last Battle*	476
Georgii Demidov	*The Intellectual (The Cauchy Principle)*	491
Aleksandr Solzhenitsyn	*The Right Hand*	504
Daniil Granin	*The House on the Fontanka*	515
Vyacheslav Kondratiev	*At Freedom Station*	528
Yury Trifonov	*A Short Stay in the Torture Chamber*	550
Strugatsky brothers	*Six Matches*	562
Yuly Daniel	*Hands*	580
Yury Kazakov	*Autumn in the Oak Woods*	585

Fazil Iskander	*The Cock*	602
Vasily Shukshin	*Tough Guy*	609
Yuri Rytkheu	*A Dream in Polar Fog*	617
Vladimir Voinovich	*The Novel*	629
Nina Katerli	*The Monster*	633
Asar Eppel	*Red Caviar Sandwiches*	641
Eduard Kochergin	*The Ballad of the Wooden Plane*	654
Ludmilla Petrushevskaya	*Milgrom*	661
Svetlana Aleksievich	*It Wasn't Me*	666
Elena Makarova	*Herbs from Odessa*	675
Irina Ratushinskaya	*A Tale of Three Heads*	694
Vladimir Sorokin	*The Swim*	697
Anna Politkovskaya	*It's Nice to be Deaf*	704
Mikhail Shishkin	*Of Saucepans and Star-Showers*	711
Viktor Pelevin	*Friedmann Space*	723
Maxim Osipov	*The Cry of the Domestic Fowl*	735
Julia Kissina	*The Lithuanian Hand*	740
Linor Goralik	*Something Like That*	744
Anna Starobinets	*The Agency*	753
Dmitry Glukhovsky	*Sulfur*	770
Sergei Lebedev	*Whoooo*	781
Natalya Meshchaninova	*Mom*	791
Ksenia Buksha	*There is No Night*	800
Liza Aleksandrova-Zorina	*Alesha's Homecoming*	810
Polina Zherebtsova	*Zaina*	821
Alisa Ganieva	*A Village Fest*	830
Alla Gorbunova	*Oy Oy Oy*	841
Acknowledgements		843

INTRODUCTION

Sergei Lebedev

Translated by Antonina W. Bouis

This anthology was planned and substantially compiled before Russia's full-scale invasion of Ukraine in February 2022. Russia's unjust and brutal war against an independent neighbouring country, a war against its people, culture and language made the word 'Russian' toxic and forced us, those who write in Russian, to try to rethink and radically question the very foundations of what is known as Russian culture.

So, what can these voices, from the 19th to the 21st centuries, tell us now, when Russian language once again has become the language of hatred, chauvinism and violence?

They cannot excuse or redeem anything, nor serve as evidence that Russia's culture is a sort of separate entity, celestial and non-complicit in an earthly matters. Actually, from my point of view, Russian culture is complicit – because of its inbuilt complex of superiority, arrogance towards its closest neighbours, imperial and colonial tendencies, which it failed to recognize and reflect on.

The Russian language and its voices was (and still is) a major vehicle of assimilation and colonization, instrumentalized by the state and misused. When Ukrainians topple the monuments of Pushkin, they are reclaiming their cultural space, which was taken from them and *branded* by Russian cultural symbols.

But what still can be heard in these voices, different in temperament, tone, epoch – is, above all, *defiance*.

None of these authors lived (or live) in a democratic country, ruled by law and respecting human rights. Tsarist Russia, Soviet Russia, Putin's Russia – none of these *habitats* have been exactly welcoming for free thought and free speech.

And yet – *defiance*.

Maybe this is the most important message these stories convey. No matter how cruel the *regime*, resistance is always possible. Struggle is always possible – first with your own prejudices and ignorance, then with darkness, silence and apathy.

...

While working on the anthology I was engaged in archival research in Vilnius, the capital of Lithuania, in the declassified archive of the former Lithuanian KGB. Among other things, I found an in-house edition of Orwell's *1984*, translated and published by the KGB so that its operatives could read it in a library.

All of sudden, this amateurish edition printed on bad paper proved for me that the power of literature and the power of words really exists. What a recognition – to be published by the secret police, so that operatives can study the "subversive text", which is literally about themselves!

Many of the authors in this anthology were haunted, harassed, executed by the *state*. Their texts were prohibited, censored, excluded from the libraries, prevented from being published, smuggled to the West... But they are here, under the cover of this book.

The living word cannot be eliminated.

This anthology came into being thanks to a fateful coincidence.

My publisher suggested this project to me just as I received a Jan Michalski Foundation literary residency in Switzerland, in the mountain village of Montricher between Geneva and Lausanne.

That invitation made the anthology project a reality, because the Jan Michalski Foundation has one of the best private libraries in Europe.

It has four floors; the library was closed to the public because of the coronavirus pandemic, and for two months I was alone with thousands and thousands of books.

The marvelous collection of Russian literature of the nineteenth, twentieth, and twenty-first centuries was at my disposal.

I spent two months reading in the morning and reading in the evening, and in between, during the day, I went up in the mountains, giving the books I read time to talk with one another. There in the mountains the intuitive selections were made.

I must add that Switzerland in particular and Europe in general are extremely important for Russian culture and literature. Russian protagonists travel there, like Prince Myshkin in Dostoevsky's *The Idiot*; Russian writers and painters went there for different air and inspiration; the Russian revolution that split the county and culture in two, expelling some and elevating others, has Swiss roots because so many revolutionaries, including Vladimir Lenin himself, spent their time of political exile there.

Thus, if I may put it this way, the subalpine Jura Range was a perfect vantage point from which to view more than two centuries of the Russian story, capture the historical connections and contradictions, and create a constellation of names.

Naturally, the anthology is a very subjective genre, which says as much about the editor and compiler as it does about the writers and their works. But I hope I was able to maintain a certain historical objectivity: in the case of Russian literature the editor's task is complicated by the fact that a single, whole Russian literature does not exist.

Essentially, this anthology presents five different, albeit interrelated – and often tragically so – Russian literatures, separated by time, space, and ideology.

First, there is the classical Russian literature of the nineteenth and early twentieth centuries, full of its own internal contradictions, friendships, feuds, reconciliations, and cycles of heritage, yet still forming a provisional whole.

Second, there is the literature of the Russian emigration of the twentieth century, the literature of refugees and exiles who wrote outside Russia and which was for the most part banned or inaccessible in the Soviet Union.

Third, there is Soviet censored literature, published and presented as part of the official Soviet culture.

Fourth, there is the uncensored literature, books written in the USSR but not published, unknown or distributed through samizdat, that was, illegally, passed from hand to hand in typewritten copies.

Fifth, there is recent Russian literature, texts written after the collapse of the USSR.

These groupings are provisional, and many writers moved from one category to another within their lifetime, for example, the early and late Soviet émigrés. That split and separation in literature, in the very language, consciousness, and historical and cultural norms and expectations is important; this makes the anthology a risky project, in some ways an act of coercion, since it is obvious that some of these writers would have never shaken hands with each other, or even remained in the same room, since they represented implacable antagonistic-to-the-death positions. I try to respect this division in my home library, for example, would never put the Ovid of the Gulag Varlam Shalamov and the bard of Soviet violence Mikhail Sholokhov on the same shelf, even though they belong there alphabetically.

What, then, justifies this connection?

In my opinion it is the conflict, contradiction, and incompatibility that it creates; the inability to put them in the same canon, to create the ideal unit.

Russian history, world history, live and breathe in the anthology's construction; the experience of violence, the experience of totalitarianism, the experience of attacks on culture – and the experience of witnessing. The biographies here are no less important than the texts; the reader will be surprised (as I was) to see how many Russian writers were in exile or prison, expelled, arrested, or executed, how many works were banned and destroyed.

This only proves the great power of the word, the magical power that literature in Russia has always wielded; of the great and stubborn labor and achievement of the writing human. I hope that this exploit, the sense of the connection between word and history, poet and language, what Joseph Brodsky called "this great flame that flickers together with me," will shine as a distant reflection on the pages of this anthology.

I would suggest that the story is a very Russian genre. It is not simply wonderfully elaborated in Russian literature, it is organically and deeply tied to the roots of Russian life, unchanged (alas) throughout the centuries.

The foundation of a story is an event; and in that event the hidden face of fate develops, revealing itself as if in a photograph or on a shroud. You can't say that events occurred more frequently in Russia than in other countries; however, I believe that the Russian event is more virulent, with the highest probability of proceeding to the worst-case scenario.

The Russian, existing between the immeasurable Russian space and the cruelty of Russian rule, is an emblematic figure, the ideal target for the blows of fate. They are persecuted and they are the persecutor; nothing protects them in life, neither human responsibility nor social and state institutions, and yet, there they are, still standing. For centuries, only literature nurtured and protected them, creating a second reality where anyone who could read would find temporary refuge from the first.

This idea of the connection between event and story can be examined through a smaller example. A few years ago I wrote a preface to the Swedish edition of *Kolyma Tales* by Varlam Shalamov, one of the greatest twentieth-century Russian storytellers, the writer who led Melpomene through the freezing hell of the northernmost Gulag camps, through the enfilade of icy underworlds.

Permit me to quote from the preface:

> "In the camp world, where every question is of life and death, this anatomy of events that move fate is present especially clearly. The weapons of fate, its faces, images, and ties form the unintended subject of Shalamov's investigation. Fate can appear in the form of a weakened duck that can be caught, given to the overseer, and buy off death; in a spotless penmanship that gives clerical work in a warm room; in the sudden arrest of the investigator who had recently signed an order for your arrest; in a blow by a log – they knock you out and take your last bit of bread; or in the execution of your chemistry teacher long ago, during the Civil War and the first wave of Red Terror – you missed chemistry lessons and you can't pass the paramedical exam. This fetishization of fate boils it down to an object, there is evidence of the archaic nature of camp life, the ancient tragedy of a man facing fate alone, without the protection of institutions of civilization, and fate could take on any form, making the entire world potentially dangerous.
>
> In that sense, the camp is a naked space, without defenses, handrails, or rules, constantly open to the play of fate, like an evil casino; this space is subordinated to chance, fatum, and not ratio, intellect, and not a single conscientious proposal, not a single plan can work

here, you have to live only in the present day – thereby isolating yourself and atomizing life even more."

It might seem a stretch to extend the camp metaphor to the life and history of an entire nation; but I am certain that the basis for Russian literature's obsession with stories is the mechanism I described.

That is probably why people writing in Russian are such good storytellers and the very idea of an anthology of stories written in Russian seems so self-evident.

Of course, this anthology is neither redundant nor exhaustive. Unfortunately, we were limited to stories that were already translated into English, and thus some names were excluded, for example, the great poet and equally powerful prose writer Georgy Ivanov. Alas, very few short stories by many authors have ever been translated, especially novelists like Yevgeny Zamyatin, who is known in the west primarily for his early anti-utopia *We*. Limits of word count and pagination played their censor's role, of course; because of them, we could not include the long short stories, or in Russian terminology, the short novellas of Victor Nekrasov.

I nevertheless hope that despite the constraints of the genre, the anthology is a whole, like a dramatic painting that contains the history of the country, the language, and the literature.

Of course, I cannot leave out the many people whose work, dedication, and knowledge made this anthology possible, known to me personally and not, alive or no longer with us – the translators.

As a writer whose books are published in two dozen languages, I work almost every month with people translating my texts. I have become friends with some, with others I maintain professional contacts; some I've met and raised a glass of wine to our joint work, others I've seen only on a Skype screen. The translators are first readers, tactful editors, demanding critics, and co-authors.

Once you enter the world of international publishing, you realize that the connections between great cultures and great literatures depend on a very small number of people; the intermediaries between languages. Translators are outnumbered by writers and even more so by written books; they are creatures on the endangered list, the kind magicians of our world, which was cursed by the Babelic confusion of tongues. They relieve us of that curse of incomprehension and bring us closer together, often remaining undeservedly and unjustly in the shadow of the author's name.

Anthology as a genre allows us to accord them special honors. Many of the stories in this volume would not have been translated, would not have been born in English, if not for the personal selection, stubbornness and even lobbying abilities of their translators; in Soviet times, translators, Slavists, often brought out manuscripts to the west, saving texts and giving them a new life.

I want to thank all the translators in this anthology: gratitude, gratitude, and more gratitude!

In my childhood, introductions to good adventure books, like those by Jules Verne or Arthur Conan Doyle, ended with the same phrase. Since this anthology is an adventure for the reader, a literary, stylistic, and historical trip through time and language universes, I will use it here:

    Bon voyage, reader!

THE SHOT

Alexander Pushkin (1799–1837)
Translated by T. Keane

The father of the Russian language we use now, a man who transformed it and dragged it from eighteenth century archaism to modernity in terms of grammar, vocabulary and literary genres, **Alexander Pushkin** (1799–1837) had a partial African ancestry. The child of the Napoleonic wars and liberal early years of the emperor Alexander I, Pushkin was educated in the Lyceum, the newly founded school for the future state and cultural elite. He explored and marked out for those who came after him almost all the possible literary forms, with the exception of the major realist novel. His life was a romantic and tragic inspiration for all Russian poets and would-be writers: youthful love affairs, loss of illusions, collision course with the state (Pushkin's friends were among the leading participants in the Decembrist uprising in 1825), Ovid-like exile and then an early, abrupt, tragic death in a duel. This pattern repeats itself in the destiny of Mikhail Lermontov, Pushkin's main heir as a poetic and romantic national tribune, but characteristic features of Pushkin's life can be found in almost every biography presented here.

Chapter I

We were stationed in the little town of N—. The life of an officer in the army is well known. In the morning, drill and the riding-school; dinner with the Colonel or at a Jewish restaurant; in the evening, punch and cards. In N— there was not one open house, not a single marriageable girl. We used to meet in each other's rooms, where, except our uniforms, we never saw anything.

One civilian only was admitted into our society. He was about thirty-five years of age, and therefore we looked upon him as an old fellow. His experience gave him great advantage over us, and his habitual taciturnity, stern disposition, and caustic tongue produced a deep impression upon our young minds. Some mystery surrounded his existence; he had the appearance of a Russian, although his name was a foreign one. He had formerly served in the Hussars, and with distinction, nobody knew the cause that had induced him to retire from the service and settle in a wretched little village, where he lived poorly and, at the same time, extravagantly. He always went on foot, and constantly wore a shabby black overcoat, but the officers of our regiment were ever welcome at his table. His dinners, it is true, never consisted of more than two or three dishes, prepared by a retired soldier, but the champagne flowed like water. Nobody knew what his circumstances were, or what his income was, and nobody dared to question him about them. He had a collection of books, consisting chiefly of works on military matters and a few novels. He willingly lent them to us to read, and never asked for them back; on the other hand, he never returned to the owner the books that were lent to him. His principal amusement was shooting with a pistol. The walls of his room were riddled with bullets, and were as full of holes as a honeycomb. A rich collection of pistols was the only luxury in the humble cottage where he lived. The skill which he had acquired with his favorite weapon was simply incredible: and if he had offered to shoot a pear off somebody's forage-cap, not a man in our regiment would have hesitated to place the object upon his head.

Our conversation often turned upon duels. Silvio—so I will call him—never joined in it. When asked if he had ever fought, he dryly replied that he had but he entered into no particulars, and it was evident that such questions were not to his liking. We came to the conclusion that he had upon his conscience the memory of some unhappy victim of his terrible skill. Moreover, it never entered into the head of any of us to suspect him of anything like cowardice. There are persons whose mere look is sufficient to repel such a suspicion, but an unexpected incident occurred which astounded us all.

One day, about ten of our officers dined with Silvio. They drank as usual, that is to say, a great deal. After dinner we asked our host to hold the bank for a game at faro. For a long time he refused, for he hardly ever played, but at last he ordered cards to be brought, placed half a hundred ducats upon the table, and sat down to deal.

We took our places round him, and the play began. It was Silvio's custom to preserve a complete silence when playing. He never disputed, and never entered into explanations. If the punter made a mistake in calculating, he immediately paid him the difference or noted down the surplus. We were acquainted with this habit of his, and we always allowed him to have his own way; but among us on this occasion was an officer who had only recently been transferred to our regiment. During the course of the game, this officer absently scored one point too many. Silvio took the chalk and noted down the correct account according to his usual custom. The officer, thinking that he had made a mistake, began to enter into explanations. Silvio continued dealing in silence. The officer, losing patience, took the brush and rubbed out what he considered was wrong. Silvio took the chalk and corrected the score again. The officer, heated with wine, play, and the laughter of his comrades, considered himself grossly insulted, and in his rage he seized a brass candlestick from the table, and hurled it at Silvio, who barely succeeded in avoiding the missile. We were filled with consternation. Silvio rose, white with rage, and with gleaming eyes, said: "My dear sir, have the goodness to withdraw, and thank God that this has happened in my house."

None of us entertained the slightest doubt as to what the result would be, and we already looked upon our new comrade as a dead man. The officer withdrew, saying that he was ready to answer for his offence in whatever way the banker liked. The paly went on for a few minutes longer, but feeling that our host was no longer interested in the game, we withdrew one after the other, and repaired to our respective quarters, after having exchanged a few words upon the probability of there soon being a vacancy in the regiment.

The next day, at the riding-school, we were already asking each other if the poor lieutenant was still alive, when he himself appeared among us. We put the same question to him, and he replied that he had not yet heard from Silvio. This astonished us. We went to Silvio's house and found him in the courtyard shooting bullet after bullet into an ace pasted upon the gate. He received us as usual, but did not utter a word about the event of the previous evening. Three days passed, and the lieutenant was still alive. We asked each other in astonishment: "Can it be possible that Silvio is not going to fight?"

Silvio did not fight. He was satisfied with a very lame explanation, and became reconciled to his assailant.

This lowered him very much in the opinion of all our young fellows. Want of courage is the last thing to be pardoned by young men, who usually look upon bravery as the chief of all human virtues, and the excuse for every possible fault. But, by degrees, everything became forgotten, and Silvio regained his former influence.

I alone could not approach him on the old footing. Being endowed by nature with a romantic imagination, I had become attached more than all the others to the man whose life was an enigma, and who seemed to me the hero of some mysterious drama. He was fond of me; at least, with me alone did he drop his customary sarcastic tone, and converse on different subjects in a simple and unusually agreeable manner. But after this unlucky evening, the thought that his honor had been tarnished, and that the stain had been allowed to remain upon it in accordance with his own wish, was ever present in my mind, and prevented me treating him as before. I was ashamed to look at him. Silvio was too intelligent and experienced not to observe this and guess the cause of it. This seemed to vex him; at least I observed once or twice a desire on his part to enter into an explanation with me, but I avoided such opportunities, and Silvio gave up the attempt. From that time forward I saw him only in the presence of my comrades, and our confidential conversations came to an end.

The inhabitants of the capital, with minds occupied by so many matters of business and pleasure, have no idea of the many sensations so familiar to the inhabitants of villages and small towns, as, for instance, the awaiting the arrival of the post. On Tuesdays and Fridays our regimental bureau used to be filled with officers: some expecting money, some letters, and others newspapers. The packets were usually opened on the spot, items of news were communicated from one to another, and the bureau used to present a very animated picture. Silvio used to have his letters addressed to our regiment, and he was generally there to receive them.

One day he received a letter, the seal of which he broke with a look of great impatience. As he read the contents, his eyes sparkled. The officers, each occupied with his own letters, did not observe anything.

"Gentlemen," said Silvio, "circumstances demand my immediate departure; I leave to-night. I hope that you will not refuse to dine with me for the last time. I shall expect you, too," he added, turning towards me.

"I shall expect you without fail."

With these words he hastily departed, and we, after agreeing to meet at Silvio's, dispersed to our various quarters.

I arrived at Silvio's house at the appointed time, and found nearly the whole regiment there. All his things were already packed; nothing remained but the bare, bullet-riddled walls. We sat down to table. Our host was in an excellent humor, and his gayety was quickly communicated to the rest. Corks popped every moment, glasses foamed incessantly, and, with the utmost warmth, we wished our departing friend a pleasant journey and every happiness. When we rose from the table it was already late in the evening. After having wished everybody good-bye, Silvio took me by the hand and detained me just at the moment when I was preparing to depart.

"I want to speak to you," he said in a low voice.

I stopped behind.

The guests had departed, and we two were left alone. Sitting down opposite each other, we silently lit our pipes. Silvio seemed greatly troubled; not a trace remained of his former convulsive gayety. The intense pallor of his face, his sparkling eyes, and the thick smoke issuing from his mouth, gave him a truly diabolical appearance. Several minutes elapsed, and then Silvio broke the silence.

"Perhaps we shall never see each other again," said he; "before we part, I should like to have an explanation with you. You may have observed that I care very little for the opinion of other people, but I like you, and I feel that it would be painful to me to leave you with a wrong impression upon your mind."

He paused, and began to knock the ashes out of his pipe. I sat gazing silently at the ground.

"You thought it strange," he continued, "that I did not demand satisfaction from that drunken idiot R—. You will admit, however, that having the choice of weapons, his life was in my hands, while my own was in no great danger. I could ascribe my forbearance to generosity alone, but I will not tell a lie. If I could have chastised R—without the least risk to my own life, I should never have pardoned him."

I looked at Silvio with astonishment. Such a confession completely astounded me. Silvio continued:

"Exactly so: I have no right to expose myself to death. Six years ago I received a slap in the face, and my enemy still lives."

My curiosity was greatly excited.

"Did you not fight with him?" I asked. "Circumstances probably separated you."

"I did fight with him," replied Silvio; "and here is a souvenir of our duel."

Silvio rose and took from a cardboard box a red cap with a gold tassel and embroidery (what the French call a bonnet de police); he put it on—a bullet had passed through it about an inch above the forehead.

"You know," continued Silvio, "that I served in one of the Hussar regiments. My character is well known to you: I am accustomed to taking the lead. From my youth this has been my passion. In our time dissoluteness was the fashion, and I was the most outrageous man in the army. We used to boast of our drunkenness; I beat in a drinking bout the famous Bourtsoff,* of whom Denis Davidoff† has sung. Duels in our regiment were constantly taking place, and in all of them I was either second or principal. My comrades adored me, while the regimental commanders, who were constantly being changed, looked upon me as a necessary evil.

"I was calmly enjoying my reputation, when a young man belonging to a wealthy and distinguished family—I will not mention his name—joined our regiment. Never in my life have I met with such a fortunate fellow! Imagine to yourself youth, wit, beauty, unbounded gayety, the most reckless bravery, a famous name, untold wealth—imagine all these, and you can form some idea of the effect that he would be sure to produce among us. My supremacy was shaken. Dazzled by my reputation, he began to seek my friendship, but I received him coldly, and without the least regret he held aloof from me. I took a hatred to him. His success in the regiment and in the society of ladies brought me to the verge of despair. I began to seek a quarrel with him; to my epigrams he replied with epigrams which always seemed to me more spontaneous and more cutting than mine, and which were decidedly more amusing, for he joked while I fumed. At last, at a ball given by a Polish landed proprietor, seeing him the object of the attention of

---

* A cavalry officer, notorious for his drunken escapades.

† A military poet who flourished in the reign of Alexander I.

all the ladies, and especially of the mistress of the house, with whom I was upon very good terms, I whispered some grossly insulting remark in his ear. He flamed up and gave me a slap in the face. We grasped our swords; the ladies fainted; we were separated; and that same night we set out to fight.

"The dawn was just breaking. I was standing at the appointed place with my three seconds. With inexplicable impatience I awaited my opponent. The spring sun rose, and it was already growing hot. I saw him coming in the distance. He was walking on foot, accompanied by one second. We advanced to meet him. He approached, holding his cap filled with black cherries. The seconds measured twelve paces for us. I had to fire first, but my agitation was so great, that I could not depend upon the steadiness of my hand; and in order to give myself time to become calm, I ceded to give him the first shot. My adversary would not agree to this. It was decided that we should cast lots. The first number fell to him, the constant favorite of fortune. He took aim, and his bullet went through my cap. It was not my turn. His life at last was in my hands; I looked at him eagerly, endeavoring to detect if only the faintest shadow of uneasiness. But he stood in front of my pistol, picking out the ripest cherries from his cap and spitting out the stones, which flew almost as far as my feet. His indifference annoyed me beyond measure. 'What is the use,' thought I, 'of depriving him of life, when he attaches no value whatever to it?' A malicious thought flashed through my mind. I lowered my pistol.

"'You don't seem to be ready for death just at present,' I said to him: 'you wish to have your breakfast; I do not wish to hinder you.'

"'You are not hindering me in the least,' replied he. 'Have the goodness to fire, or just as you please—the shot remains yours; I shall always be ready at your service.'

"I turned to the seconds, informing them that I had no intention of firing that day, and with that the duel came to an end.

"I resigned my commission and retired to this little place. Since then not a day has passed that I have not thought of revenge. And now my hour has arrived."

Silvio took from his pocket the letter that he had received that morning, and gave it to me to read. Someone (it seemed to be his business agent) wrote to him from Moscow, that a CERTAIN PERSON was going to be married to a young and beautiful girl.

"You can guess," said Silvio, "who the certain person is. I am going to Moscow. We shall see if he will look death in the face with as much indifference now, when he is on the eve of being married, as he did once with his cherries!"

With these words, Silvio rose, threw his cap upon the floor, and began pacing up and down the room like a tiger in his cage. I had listened to him in silence; strange conflicting feelings agitated me.

The servant entered and announced that the horses were ready. Silvio grasped my hand tightly, and we embraced each other. He seated himself in his telega, in which lay two trunks, one containing his pistols, the other his effects. we said good-bye once more, and the horses galloped off.

Chapter II

Several years passed, and family circumstances compelled me to settle in the poor little village of M—. Occupied with agricultural pursuits, I ceased not to sigh in secret for my former noisy and careless life. The most difficult thing of all was having to accustom myself to passing the spring and winter evenings in perfect solitude. Until the hour for dinner I managed to pass away the time somehow or other, talking with the bailiff, riding about to inspect the work, or going round to look at the new buildings; but as soon as it began to get dark, I positively did not know what to do with myself. The few books that I had found in the cupboards and storerooms I already knew by heart. All the stories that my housekeeper Kirilovna could remember I had heard over and over again. The songs of the peasant women made me feel depressed. I tried drinking spirits, but it made my head ache; and moreover, I confess I was afraid of becoming a drunkard from mere chagrin, that is to say, the saddest kind of drunkard, of which I had seen many examples in our district.

I had no near neighbors, except two or three topers, whose conversation consisted for the most part of hiccups and sighs. Solitude was preferable to their society. At last I decided to go to bed as early as possible, and to dine as late as possible; in this way I shortened the evening and lengthened out the day, and I found that the plan answered very well.

Four versts from my house was a rich estate belonging to the Countess B—; but nobody lived there except the steward. The Countess had only visited her estate once, in the first year of her married life, and then she had remained there no longer than a month. But in the second spring of my hermitical life a report was circulated that the Countess, with her husband, was coming to spend the summer on her estate. The report turned out to be true, for they arrived at the beginning of June.

The arrival of a rich neighbor is an important event in the lives of country people. The landed proprietors and the people of their households talk about it for two months beforehand and for three years afterwards. As for me, I must confess that the news of the arrival of a young and beautiful neighbour affected me strongly. I burned with impatience to see her, and the first Sunday after her arrival I set out after dinner for the village of A—, to pay my respects to the Countess and her husband, as their nearest neighbour and most humble servant. A lackey conducted me into the Count's study, and then went to announce me. The spacious apartment was furnished with every possible luxury. Around the walls were cases filled with books and surmounted by bronze busts; over the marble mantelpiece was a large mirror; on the floor was a green cloth covered with carpets. Unaccustomed to luxury in my own poor corner, and not having seen the wealth of other people for a long time, I awaited the appearance of the Count with some little trepidation, as a suppliant from the provinces awaits the arrival of the minister. The door opened, and a handsome-looking man, of about thirty-two years of age, entered the room. The Count approached me with a drank and friendly air; I endeavored to be self-possessed and began to introduce myself, but he anticipated me. We sat down. His conversation, which was easy and agreeable, soon dissipated my awkward bashfulness; and I was already beginning to recover my usual composure, when the Countess suddenly entered, and I became more confused than ever. She was indeed beautiful. The Count presented me. I wished to appear at ease, but the more I tried to assume an air of unconstraint, the more awkward I felt. They, in order to give me time to recover myself and to become accustomed to my new acquaintances, began to talk to each other, treating me as a good neighbor, and without ceremony. Meanwhile, I walked around the room, examining the books and pictures. I am no judge of pictures, but one of them attracted my attention. It represented some view in Switzerland, but it was not the painting that struck me, but the circumstance that the canvas was shot through by two bullets, one planted just above the other.

"A good shot that!" said I, turning to the Count.

"Yes," replied he, "a very remarkable shot. ... Do you shoot well?" he continued.

"Tolerably," replied I, rejoicing that the conversation had turned at last upon a subject that was familiar to me. "At thirty paces I can manage to hit a card without fail,—I mean, of course, with a pistol that I am used to."

"Really?" said the Countess, with a look of the greatest interest. "And you, my dear, could you hit a card at thirty paces?"

"Some day," replied the Count, "we will try. In my time I did not shoot badly, but it is now four years since I touched a pistol."

"Oh!" I observed, "in that case, I don't mind laying a wager that Your Excellency will not hit the card at twenty paces; the pistol demands practice every day. I know that from experience. In our regiment I was reckoned one of the best shots. It once happened that I did not touch a pistol for a whole month, as I had sent mine to be mended; and would you believe it, Your Excellency, the first time I began to shoot again, I missed a bottle four times in succession at twenty paces. Our captain, a witty and amusing fellow, happened to be standing by, and he said to me: 'It is evident, my friend, that your hand will not lift itself against the bottle.' No, your Excellency, you must not neglect to practise, or your hand will soon lose its cunning. The best shot that I ever met used to shoot at least three times every day before dinner. It was as much his custom to do this as it was to drink his daily glass of brandy."

The Count and Countess seemed pleased that I had begun to talk.

"And what sort of a shot was he?" asked the Count.

"Well, it was this way with him, Your Excellency: if he saw a fly settle on the wall—you smile, Countess, but, before Heaven, it is the truth—if he saw a fly, he would call out: 'Kouzka, my pistol!' Kouzka would bring him a loaded pistol—bang! and the fly would be crushed against the wall."

"Wonderful!" said the Count. "And what was his name?"

"Silvio, Your Excellency."

"Silvio!" exclaimed the Count, starting up. "Did you know Silvio?"

"How could I help knowing him, Your Excellency: we were intimate friends; he was received in our regiment like a brother officer, but it is now five years since I had any tidings of him. Then Your Excellency also knew him?"

"Oh, yes, I knew him very well. Did he ever tell you of one very strange incident in his life?"

"Does Your Excellency refer to the slap in the face that he received from some blackguard at a ball?"

"Did he tell you the name of this blackguard?"

"No, Your Excellency, he never mentioned his name, ... Ah! Your Excellency!" I continued, guessing the truth: "pardon me ... I did not know ... could it really have been you?"

"Yes, I myself," replied the Count, with a look of extraordinary agitation; "and that bullet-pierced picture is a memento of our last meeting."

"Ah, my dear," said the Countess, "for Heaven's sake, do not speak about that; it would be too terrible for me to listen to."

"No," replied the Count: "I will relate everything. He knows how I insulted his friend, and it is only right that he should know how Silvio revenged himself."

The Count pushed a chair towards me, and with the liveliest interest I listened to the following story:

"Five years ago I got married. The first month—the honeymoon—I spent here, in this village. To this house I am indebted for the happiest moments of my life, as well as for one of its most painful recollections.

"One evening we went out together for a ride on horseback. My wife's horse became restive; she grew frightened, gave the reins to me, and returned home on foot. I rode on before. In the courtyard I saw a travelling carriage, and I was told that in my study sat waiting for me a man, who would not give his name, but who merely said that he had business with me. I entered the room and saw in the darkness a man, covered with dust and wearing a beard of several days' growth. He was standing there, near the fireplace. I approached him, trying to remember his features.

"'You do not recognize me, Count?' said he, in a quivering voice.

"'Silvio!' I cried, and I confess that I felt as if my hair had suddenly stood on end.

"'Exactly,' continued he. 'There is a shot due to me, and I have come to discharge my pistol. Are you ready?'

"His pistol protruded from a side pocket. I measured twelve paces and took my stand there in that corner, begging him to fire quickly, before my wife arrived. He hesitated, and asked for a light. Candles were brought in. I closed the doors, gave orders that nobody was to enter, and again begged him to fire. He drew out his pistol and took aim. ... I counted the seconds. ... I thought of her. ... A terrible minute passed! Silvio lowered his hand.

"'I regret,' said he, 'that the pistol is not loaded with cherry-stones ... the bullet is heavy. It seems to me that this is not a duel, but a murder. I am not accustomed to taking aim at unarmed men. Let us begin all over again; we will cast lots as to who shall fire first.'

"My head went round. ... I think I raised some objection. ... At last we loaded another pistol, and rolled up two pieces of paper. He placed these latter in his cap—the same through which I had once sent a bullet—and again I drew the first number.

"'You are devilish lucky, Count,' said he, with a smile that I shall never forget.

"I don't know what was the matter with me, or how it was that he managed to make me do it ... but I was fired and hit that picture."

The Count pointed with his finger to the perforated picture; his face glowed like fire; the Countess was whiter than her own handkerchief; and I could not restrain an exclamation.

"I fired," continued the Count, "and, thank Heaven, missed my aim. Then Silvio ... at that moment he was really terrible ... Silvio raised his hand to take aim at me. Suddenly the door opens, Masha rushes into the room, and with a loud shriek throws herself upon my neck. Her presence restored to me all my courage.

"'My dear,' said I to her, 'don't you see that we are joking? How frightened you are! Go and drink a glass of water and then come back to us; I will introduce you to an old friend and comrade.'

"Masha still doubted.

"'Tell me, is my husband speaking the truth?' said she, turning to the terrible Silvio: 'is it true that you are only joking?'

"'He is always joking, Countess,' replied Silvio: 'once he gave me a slap in the face in a joke; on another occasion he sent a bullet through my cap in a joke; and just now, when he fired at me and missed me, it was all in a joke. And now I feel inclined for a joke.'

"With these words he raised his pistol to take aim at me—right before her! Masha threw herself at his feet.

"'Rise, Masha; are you not ashamed!' I cried in a rage: 'and you, sir, will you cease to make fun of a poor woman? Will you fire or not?'

"'I will not,' replied Silvio: 'I am satisfied. I have seen your confusion, your alarm. I forced you to fire at me. That is sufficient. You will remember me. I leave you to your conscience.'

"Then he turned to go, but pausing in the doorway, and looking at the picture that my shot had passed through, he fired at it almost without taking aim, and disappeared. My wife had fainted away; the servants did not venture to stop him, the mere look of him filled them with terror. He went out upon the steps, called his coachman, and drove off before I could recover myself."

The Count was silent. In this way I learned the end of the story, whose beginning had once made such a deep impression upon me. The hero of it I never saw again. It is said that Silvio commanded a detachment of Hetairists during the revolt under Alexander Ipsilanti, and that he was killed in the battle of Skoulana.

THE LOST DISPATCH
Nikolai Gogol (1809–1852)
Translated by Christopher English

Genius of two not always allied genres, the satirical and the mystical, **Nikolai Gogol** was born Nikolai Vasilyevich Gogol-Yanovsky in what is now Ukraine, brought to Russian literature the sly, vivid, ironic folklore spirit of the empire's south, where the peasants were less oppressed by serfdom than they were in the North. From this southern perspective, Gogol wrote about the people's life in the petrifying empire, with his emblematic hero always being a small yet smart man, a trickster, a cheat, a cute swindler – and the only living and breathing soul among a society of the living dead.

This type of hero will resurrect itself powerfully a century later, in *Ilf* and Petrov's famous novel *The 12 chairs*, describing the adventures of an inventive and very Gogolian charming rascal in the upside-down world of post-revolutionary Russia.

A True Story, Told by the Verger of St N's

So you want me to tell you some more about my old grandfather? By all means, why not amuse you with another of his little stories? Ah yes, the good old days! What exuberance fills the heart when you hear about the things that went on long, long ago, longer than any of us can remember! And if one of your own kin should be mixed up in the story, your grandfather, maybe, or great-grandfather—that really crowns it all: may I choke next time I try and sing an *akathistos* to the holy martyr St Barbara if I lie, but I swear it feels as though you're doing all those things yourself, as if you've crept inside your great-grandfather's soul or as if your great-grandfather's soul were getting up to its tricks inside you ...

No, the worst ones are the womenfolk, the young women and girls; the moment they catch sight of you it's all: 'Foma Grigorievich! Foma Grigorievich! Do tell us one of your scary stories about the old days! Go on! Tell us, please! ...' and on, and on, and on ... Not that I mind telling them, of course, but if only you could see them later on in their beds! I know for a fact that every one of them will be a-tremble under her blankets, just as if she's in a fever, and ready at the drop of a pin to hide her head in her sheepskin coat. All it needs is for a rat to scratch the cooking pot, or for her to stumble on the poker—and Lord help us! She's scared clean out of her wits. The next day you'd think nothing had happened, they're at it again: tell us a scary story, go on, do.

Well, what should I tell you? Maybe I won't be able to recall anything suitable ... I know, I'll tell you about the time the witches played Jackass with my old grandfather, God rest his soul. But first I must ask you, my good people, not to interrupt me; or I'll make such a hodge-podge of the telling that no one will make head nor tail of it. My late grandfather, I should tell you, was no ordinary Cossack. He knew his letters as well as any scribe. On feast-days he used to get going with the Epistles and do such a good job of them he would have shamed many a modern seminarist. Well, as you know yourselves, in those days you could get all the fellows in Baturin* who could read and write into the back of a droshky. So it was hardly surprising that everyone who met my grandfather would doff his cap.

One day the chief hetman took a notion to send the tsarina a dispatch. The regimental scribe—may I roast in hell but I just can't remember his name ... Viskryak, no, not Viskryak ... nor Motuzochka, no, nor Goloputsek either ... all I can remember is that it was the funniest sort of name—anyway, he summons Grandfather and tells him that the hetman himself is appointing him messenger to take a dispatch to the tsarina. Grandfather wasn't one for wasting time getting ready; he sewed the dispatch into his hat; led out his horse; kissed the wife and his two piglets as he called them, one of whom was yours truly's very own father; and then he was off like a thunderbolt, leaving behind him such a cloud of dust that you'd have thought at least fifteen boys had been out playing kick-the-dust in the street.

The next morning the cocks hadn't crowed more than four times before Grandfather reached Konotop. At that time a fair had come to town: there was such a crowd on the streets it was enough to make your head swim. But as the morning was still young they were mostly

---

* Village in the Ukraine; between 1669 and 1708 it served as the official seat of the Ukrainian hetman.

asleep, stretched out on the ground. Next to his cow lay a young lad with a nose as red as a bullfinch, sleeping off the effects of a big night; further on sat a merchant woman, fast asleep and snoring in the midst of all her flints, washing-blue, musket-shot, and doughnuts; a gypsy lay under his wagon; a carter lay atop his cartload of fish; a bearded Russian vagrant sprawled across the road itself, fast asleep with his hamper full of belts and fancy cuffs ... in other words, the usual riff-raff you get at all fairs. Grandfather stopped and carefully studied the scene. Meanwhile the tents were beginning to show the first stirrings of life; Jewesses started rattling and clinking bottles; puffs of smoke billowed in the air above and the smell of hot pastries carried all over the camp.

Grandfather suddenly remembered that he had no tinder or tobacco on him, so he set off into the market to buy some. He hadn't gone more than twenty paces when he met this Zaporozhian Cossack coming towards him. One look at his face and you could see he was a real carouser! Bright red trousers, a blue *zhupan*, a brightly-coloured sash, at his side a sabre and a pipe on a bronze chain, reaching to his very heels—every inch a Zaporozhian Cossack! What a race! Watch your Cossack stand up, poker straight, twist his dashing moustache, stamp his heels, and the next moment he's away! His feet flying round and round like a spindle in a woman's hands; his hand hitting the strings of the *bandura* like a whirlwind, and the next thing you knew he'd be down on his heels with arms akimbo; the air filled with song—you felt your own soul making merry! ... No, those days are gone: you won't see any more of those Zaporozhians around now!

Anyway, so they met. They exchanged a few words and the next thing they were as thick as thieves. They jawed on about this and that and got so carried away that Grandfather clean forgot about his mission. They went on a binge as hearty as a wedding the day before Lent. Finally they got tired of smashing pots and throwing money around, and anyway the fair doesn't stand for ever! So the two new friends agreed to stick together and travel on the same road. It was well into evening when they at last set off on their way. The sun had already turned in for the night; its place in the sky was taken by a few reddish strips; the cornfields were as bright and colourful as the fancy skirts of our dark-browed maidens. Our Zaporozhian friend was in cracking form. Grandfather and another reveller who had latched himself on to them were even starting to think that there was a devil in him. He really got into his stride, telling such wild and wonderful stories that the grandfather several times had to clutch his sides and almost ruptured his gut laughing. But the further they travelled in the fields the darker it got and the more topsy-turvy his jaunty tales became. Finally our story-teller fell silent altogether and would jump at the slightest little noise.

'Ha ha, countryman! You've really got yourself steamed up now! Wishing you were at home and up on the stove-bunk, no doubt!'

'There's no reason to hide it from you,' he said, turning round and staring at them fixedly. 'You know, brothers, I went and sold my soul to the devil a long time ago!'

'Well there's a thing! But who hasn't been mixed up with Old Nick in his day? So you'd better let your hair down now, while you can.'

'I would, too, lads, but tonight my hour is up! Hey, brothers!' he said, slapping their hands, 'Listen, don't give me away! Just stay awake this one night, and all my life I'll remember your friendship!'

Who would not help his fellow man in such an hour of need? Grandfather announced right away that he'd sooner have his topknot cut off than allow that dog-snouted devil to come sniffing near his Christian soul.

Our Cossacks might have ridden on if by that time the sky had not been swathed in a night as thick as black sacking, making it as dark about them as under a sheepskin coat. All that could be seen was the far-off twinkling of a window, and the horses, scenting a stall and manger nearby, quickened their pace, nervously pricking up their ears and staring fixedly into the surrounding gloom. The window seemed to rush towards them, and soon the Cossacks saw before them a tavern, keeling over to one side, like a tipsy old woman on her way home from a christening party. In those days taverns were a far cry from what you get today. Not only was there no space for your happy Cossack to spin round in a *horlitsa* or *hopak*, there wasn't even room to lie down, when the old head started to spin from drink and the legs started to weave. The yard was full of ox-carts: under their canvas covers, in the mangers, in the sheds, everywhere lay the guests, some curled up tight, others stretched out straight, and all of them snoring like tom-cats. Only the taverner was still up, sitting by his tallow lamp, and cutting notches in a stick to mark all the pints and quarts downed by the ox-cart drivers.

Grandfather ordered a third of a pailful for the three of them and then they set off for the shed. All three lay down in a row. No sooner had he turned over than he saw that his two companions were sleeping the sleep of the dead. He woke up the Cossack who had latched on to them and reminded him of the promise they had made. The man lifted himself up, rubbed his eyes and went straight back to sleep. There was nothing to be done: he had to keep watch on his own. He tried to fend off sleep by looking round all the carts, examining the horses, smoking a pipe, then came back again and sat down next to his friends. It was so still you could hear a pin drop. Suddenly he could swear that some grey creature was poking its horns out from behind the neighbouring cart ... Then his eyelids started to droop so heavily that every few seconds he had to rub his eyes with his fist and rinse his throat with the remains of the vodka. But as soon as the mist lifted from his eyes this strange apparition was gone. Then, after a little while he saw the creature re-emerge from under the cart ... Grandad strained his eyes as hard as he could; but his cursed sleepiness covered everything in a fog; his hands became limp and heavy; his head lolled to one side and he fell into such a deep sleep that he collapsed to the ground like a dead man.

He slept for a long time and only when the sun's rays beat down with full force on to his shaved pate did he leap to his feet. Stretching his limbs a few times and scratching his back he noticed that there weren't as many carts about as there had been the previous evening. The carters had obviously pulled out before daybreak. He looked at his own companions—the Cossack was asleep, but there was no sign of their Zaporozhian friend. He asked around, but no one knew a thing; all that remained was the Cossack's topcoat lying on the spot where he had been. Grandfather was seriously alarmed and pondered hard about all this. He went off to look at the horses—neither the Zaporozhian's nor his own was there! What could all this mean? Even supposing the Zaporozhian had been whisked off by the Evil One— what about the horses? Thinking it through Grandfather came to the conclusion that the devil had come along on foot, and since it was a long way to hell he'd decided to swipe the horses as well. He felt sorely troubled at having broken his Cossack's word.

'Well,' he thought, 'there's nothing for it, I'll set off on my own two feet: as likely as not I'll meet some horse-jobber on the road on his way from the fair and I can buy a horse from him.' He went to get his hat—and his hat was gone too! The old fellow, God rest his soul, slapped his knee in vexation when he remembered that he and the Zaporozhian had swapped hats for a while the day before. And who else could have stolen it but the devil! A fine messenger for the hetman! This was some way to deliver the dispatch to the tsarina! Here Grandfather gave the devil such a tongue-lashing that I reckon the evil fellow must have taken quite a sneezing fit down in his scorcher. But swearing and cursing won't get you anywhere, and hard as Grandfather scratched his head he couldn't think of a thing to do about it.

In the end he rushed off to ask for advice. He called together all the good folk he could find in the tavern, the carters and passers – by, and told them the sorry story. The carters thought about it long and hard, propping up their chins on their sticks, shook their heads and agreed that they had never heard of such a strange carry-on in this holy land as the devil stealing a hetman's dispatch. Others chipped in that if the devil or a scurvy Russian took it into his head to pinch something there was precious little could be done about it. Only the taverner sat in his corner without saying anything. Grandfather turned to him. For when a man keeps his own counsel like that it means he has his wits about him. The trouble was the taverner was none too generous with his words, and if Grandfather hadn't forked out five gold pieces he wouldn't, as likely as not, have opened his trap at all.

'I'll tell you how to find your dispatch,' he said, leading him aside. Grandfather at once felt a weight lift from his chest. 'I can see by the look of you that you're a real Cossack and no weakling. Now look! Near the tavern you'll see a turn to the right, into the forest. Make sure you're ready by nightfall. There's gypsies living in the forest and they come out of their lairs to forge iron on nights when only the witches are at large, flying around on their pokers. What they're really up to isn't for the likes of you to know. You'll hear a lot of noise in the forest, hammering and the like: but don't make for the noise; in front of you you'll see a small path, past a scorched tree, you must take that path, and walk down and down it ... The thorns will scratch you, your way will be blocked by hazel bushes but keep on going; stop only when you get to a small stream. There you'll see the fellow you're looking for; and don't forget to stuff your pockets with … You know, what pockets are made for … You know that devils go for that stuff just as much as we people.' Saying this the taverner went back into his little hut and refused to say another word.

My late grandfather was not one of your faint-hearted types; if he came across a wolf he'd grab the creature by the tail; he'd walk through a crowd of Cossacks armed with nothing more than his bare fists—and knock them to the ground like a lot of pears. All the same, he felt his skin prickle when he set off into the forest on this pitch-black night. Not so much as a star brightened the sky. It was as still and dark as a wine-cellar; all he could hear was the cold wind rustling the tops of the trees far above his head, and the trees swayed in response, mumbling drunkenly with their leaves and waving their crowns like tipsy Cossacks nodding their heads.

Suddenly a gust of icy wind reminded Grandfather of his sheepskin coat, and the forest filled with an almighty din, like the banging of a hundred hammers, which boomed and clanged in his head. For a moment the entire place was illuminated as if by a flash of lightning. At once Grandfather saw the path, leading through low bushes. There, too, he saw the scorched tree, and the thorn-bushes! So, it was all as he had been told; the innkeeper had been telling the truth. It was none too pleasant, however, making his way through the prickly bushes; never before in his life had he been so scratched and torn as by those cursed spikes and twigs: it was all he could do not to cry out at every step. He gradually made his way to a spacious clearing in the forest, and, as far as he could make out, the trees started to thin out and became larger than any he had ever seen even in his travels the other side of Poland. He discerned a stream glinting through the trees, as black as burnished steel. Standing on the bank he looked about him for a long time. On the far bank a light burned, flickering, as if about to go out, then flaring up again and reflected in the water, which trembled like a Pole held captive by Cossack hands. And there he saw the bridge! 'Ha! I bet only the devil's caboose can drive across that!' Grandfather, however, set forth boldly, and reached the other side sooner than you could have pulled out a snuff-box from your pocket. Only now did he see that there were people sitting round the fire, all with such hideous snouts that at any other time Grandfather would have given his eye-teeth to avoid making their acquaintance. But now there was nothing for it: he had to do his work.

He gave them a low bow: 'May the Lord help you, my good people!' You'd have thought at least one of them might so much as nod his head; but they sat there in silence sprinkling something on the fire. Seeing that there was one place unoccupied Grandfather went and sat down without further ado. The snouts did not so much as twitch; nor did Grandfather. For a long time they sat in silence. Grandfather soon got fed up; he took out his pipe, looked round him—but no one looked his way. 'Well now, my good friends, pray be so kind: do you see, now, as it were, that is to say …' (Grandfather had been about in the world, and knew how to turn a fine phrase and if it came to it he would have been able to hold his own with the tsar himself), 'if you see what I mean, not to forget about myself, do you take my point, and not to offend your good selves—I've got myself a pipe, but damn-all to light it with.' And did he get a response to this speech? Not a word; instead one of the charming company thrust a brand straight into Grandfather's face, and it's a good thing he jumped aside in time, or it would have been goodbye to one of his eyes.

At last, seeing that he was wasting his time, he decided to get down to business and tell his story, whether this heathen bunch were going to listen to him or not. The ugly snouts and ears turned to face him, and hands were stretched out. Grandfather got the message: he gathered up in his hand all the money he had with him and threw it in their midst like bones to a pack of dogs. The moment he threw the money pandemonium broke loose, the earth shook and it was as though—he hardly knew how to put it himself—he had landed up in hell itself. 'Saints in heaven!' he gasped, taking a good look round him: what a sight! What a collection of ugly mugs! Each one uglier than the one before. The witches were as thick on the ground as snow at Christmas: all festooned and painted like girls at a village fair. And every single one of them was dancing hell for leather, stamping out their devil's *trepak* like so many tipsy Cossacks. Heavens above, you should have seen the dust they kicked up! It would have given any God-fearing Christian the jitters just to see how high this satanical crowd were leaping. For all that he was scared stiff Grandfather couldn't help laughing to see the devils with their dog faces, strutting on their outlandish legs, wagging their devilish tails and paying court to the witches like young lads to pretty girls; the musicians pounded their cheeks with their fists like drums and whistled through their noses like trumpets.

The moment they spotted Grandfather they swarmed round him. Their horrible mugs—the faces of pigs, dogs, goats, bustards, horses—thrust forward, making ready to kiss him. Grandfather spat with disgust! Finally they grabbed hold of him and seated him at a table as long as the road from Konotop to Baturin. 'Well now, this isn't half so bad,' thought Grandfather, seeing all the ham, sausages, chopped cabbage with onions, and other good things on the table, 'these pigs of devils obviously don't keep the fast.'

I should tell you that Grandfather was never one to say no to a good tuck-in. The old man was a hearty eater, God rest his soul, so without further ado he reached for a leg of ham and a bowl of chopped bacon fat, grabbed a fork, not much smaller than the pitchfork a peasant uses on his hay, thrust it into the biggest chunk of bacon, held a piece of bread underneath and—what do you know, pushed it straight into someone else's mouth. The fork slid right past his own ear, and he could even hear this same mouth crunching and munching away, loud enough for the whole table to hear. Nothing deterred, Grandfather speared another piece of bacon, and even brushed his lips against it, but it still didn't go down his throat. He tried a third time—still no luck. At this the old man started to see red: he forgot all about being scared and about the company he was in. He let fly at the witches:

'So you thought you'd make fun of me, you devil's spawn? You give me back my Cossack hat this very minute, or as sure as I'm no Catholic I'll wring your pig's necks for you!'

No sooner had he pronounced the last word than the entire company bared their teeth and let out such an unholy cackle of laughter that it made Grandfather's flesh creep.

'Very well!' screeched one of the witches, whom Grandfather took to be their leader because her mug was the ugliest of the lot. 'We'll give you your hat, but only when you've played three games of jackass with us!'

What could he do? Was he, a Cossack, to play jackass with a lot of women? He argued and argued, but finally sat down to play. Cards were brought, as greasy a pack as the ones priests' daughters use to foretell who they're going to marry.

'Now listen!' barked the witch, 'you only have to win once and the hat's yours; but if you're jackass all three times, then sorry, but not only won't you see your hat, you won't see the light of day again!'

'Deal the cards, you old hag! What will be, will be.'

So the cards were dealt. Grandfather picked up his hand—such rubbish, he felt like flinging them down in disgust: not a single trump amongst them. His highest card was a ten, and he didn't even have a pair; meanwhile the witch kept on playing a full hand of five cards. He had to be jackass! The moment the game was over all the onlookers started barking, grunting, neighing: 'Jackass! jackass! jackass!'

'Go and rot in hell, you pack of devils!' shouted Grandfather, blocking his ears with his fingers.

'That witch must have been cheating,' he thought, 'my turn to deal now.' He dealt; turned up the trump card; looked at his own cards: as good a hand as he could have hoped for, plenty of trumps. At first things went famously; then the witch played a full house with kings! Grandfather had a hand of straight trumps; so he plonked them down and took her kings by the whiskers.

'Whoa! That's no way for a Cossack to play! What are you taking my kings with, friend?'

'Why, with my trumps, of course!'

'You may think they're trumps, but we don't!'

He looked down, and sure enough—it was an ordinary hand. Tricked by the devil! He had to be jackass again, and once again the devilish crowd struck up their chorus of 'Jackass, jackass!' until the table started to shake and the cards leapt into the air. Grandfather flushed with anger; he dealt for the last time. Once again things went fine at first. The witch played all five cards again; Grandfather covered them and drew a full hand of trumps from the pack.

'Trumps!' he shouted, banging his card down so hard that he bent it; without a word the witch covered it with an ordinary eight.

'What do you think you're playing, you hell-ridden hag?'

The witch lifted her card: under it was an ordinary six.

'Damn you, you cheating fiend!' said Grandfather and in his rage gave the table a mighty thump.

It was a good thing that the witch had a bad hand, as Grandfather had nothing but pairs. He started drawing cards from the pack, but picked up such rubbish that he dropped his hands in disgust. There were no cards left in the pack. He played any old card, without looking: an ordinary six. The witch had to take it. 'Oho? What's this?' he wondered. 'Something fishy, no doubt!' Here Grandfather quietly sneaked his cards under the table and made the sign of the cross over them—and what did he see: in his hand he had trump ace, king, and jack; and instead of a six he had played the queen.

'But what a fool I've been! How about the king of trumps? Take it? Eh? Cat's spawn! ... Would you like the ace too? Here—the ace! and the jack! ...'

There was a roll of thunder through hell, the witch started to writhe about, and, lo and behold: his hat appeared from nowhere and plonked straight into Grandfather's face.

'No, that's not enough!' he shouted, gathering courage and putting the hat on his head. 'In one second's time I want my fine horse standing right here in front of me, or may I be struck down by lightning in this hellish place if I don't make the holy sign of the cross over the lot of you!' and no sooner had he lifted his hand than he heard the rattling of horse's bones before him.

'Take your horse!'

At the sight of the bones the poor fellow burst into tears, just like a small child. What a sorry end for his trusty old steed!

'Then give me another horse, any horse, so I can get out of your foul den!'

The devil cracked his whip—a fiery, mettlesome horse pranced beneath him, and together they soared upwards.

As they flew Grandfather became alarmed, however, since the horse, which did not respond to his shouting or tugging the reins, galloped straight across marshes and ditches. The places that horse took him—it'd give you cold shivers just to hear tell of it! Once he took a look below him—and his head swam—there was a sheer drop underneath! But the satanic beast was not bothered in the least: it leapt straight across. Finally Grandfather could cling on no longer. He flew headlong over tree-stumps and hummocks and hit the ground below with such a thump that he was sure he must have knocked his soul clean out of his body. At any rate he didn't remember what happened to him after that; but when he had come round a bit and took a look about him it was broad daylight; before him he saw familiar places and he was lying on the roof of his own house.

Grandfather crossed himself and climbed down. Talk about tricks of the devil! What diabolical wonders can happen to a man! He looked at his hands—they were all bloodied; he peered into the open barrel of water—so was his face. Washing himself thoroughly so as not to frighten the children he crept quietly into the house and what did he see?—the children backed towards him, pointing in terror at something and shouting: 'Look, look, Mama is jumping about like a looney!' And it was true: the woman had fallen asleep before her loom, and, brandishing a spindle in her hand, was leaping about on the bench in her sleep.

Grandfather took her by the arm and woke her up: 'Good-day, wife! are you unwell?' She looked at him for a long time, her eyes starting from her head, and at last, when she recognized him, she told him how she had dreamt that the stove was charging round the house, driving pots and pans and the devil knows what else before it with a spade. 'Well,' said Grandfather, 'yours was a dream, but mine was real. I see we must have the house exorcized: but I can't tarry now.' Saying this, he took a small rest, then borrowed a horse and galloped day and night until he reached his destination and delivered the dispatch to the tsarina herself.

In the capital Grandfather saw such marvels that for years after he could tell of nothing else: how he was led into the palace, as high as ten houses placed one on top of the other, and even then they wouldn't reach its roof. How he looked first into one room, not there; into another, not there either; into a third, not there; not even in a fourth; he stuck his head in the fifth—and there she sat, in her golden crown, wearing a smart new smock and red boots, and eating golden dumplings. How she ordered that he be given a hatful of banknotes, how ... well, there's no remembering all the things he told. Grandfather even forgot all about the shenanigans with that evil crowd, and if by chance anyone should remind him of it he would say nothing, as if it was no business of his, and it was the devil of a job getting him to tell the story the way it was. But every year after that, I suppose as a punishment for not going straight off to have the house exorcized, on that same day of the year Grandmother would come over all strange and start dancing and prancing like mad. Whatever else she tried to do, her feet would be off on their own, pounding out the *hopak*.

THE FATALIST

Mikhail Lermontov (1814–1841)

Translated by John Swinnerton Phillimore

Military officer, exile, poet, prose writer, duelist, the Russian Byron: in his short life **Mikhail Lermontov** (1814–1841) built a long-lasting myth about himself. In this myth the author and the characters he created are intertwined; it is dominated by a fatalistic worldview and a sixth sense for an imminent and unavoidable catastrophic destiny. Serving in the Caucasus, Lermontov introduced to Russian literature European motifs of the conflict between civilization and indigenous cultures, and of the frontier life, which triggers the inner transformation of the person previously entangled in the unreal life of the beau monde and reveals his real identity.

Shot dead in a tragic and unnecessary duel, in a kind of self-fulfilling prophecy, Lermontov became (together with Alexander Pushkin) an emblem of the Russian artist seeking a dramatic passage to eternity.

It happened to me once that I had to spend a couple of weeks in a Cossack *stanitza* on the Left Front. There was a battalion of infantry quartered there, and the officers used to meet on friendly terms and exchange civilities of entertainment; in the evening there would be cards. One day we were guests of Major S. Tired of playing Boston, we had thrown the cards down on the table; we commenced a long session of talk. Contrary to our habit, this was an interesting talk. The theme of discussion was this: that the Mussulman creed, which teaches that a man's destiny is written in heaven unalterably, is a creed that numbers plenty of votaries even among us. And everybody was proceeding to instance sundry remarkable cases in support of his argument *pro* and *con*.

"Gentlemen," said the old Major, "all this stuff amounts to nothing. Have any of you ever been an eye-witness of any of these extraordinary facts which you rest your opinions upon?"

"Ah, well—no, not exactly that ..." said most of the company; "but we heard it from trustworthy persons."

"It's all nonsense," said somebody. "Where is your trustworthy person who has ever seen the scroll that registers the hour of our death? And if there is in fact Predestination, then how did we come to be endowed with Will and Reason? And why are we accountable for our actions?"

At this point an officer who was sitting in a corner of the room got up, advanced slowly to the table, and comprised the whole company with a calm, dominating survey.

Lieutenant Boulitch was a Servian by birth, as his name betrayed; his outward appearance thoroughly corresponded to his character. Tall stature, swarthy complexion, black hair, and black, penetrating eyes, big but regularly formed nose, and the peculiar attribute of his race—a cold and cheerless smile that haunts the lips long and faintly. Every detail seemed to conspire in lending him the air of a creature apart, singular, and incapable of sharing the thoughts and passions of those with whom it was his lot to be companions.

He was a brave man, chary of speech, but his tongue sharp enough when he did speak. He made nobody free of the privacy of his spiritual or family secrets; he drank hardly any wine; and he was adamant to the seductions of those Cossack girls whose charm you cannot apprehend till you see them. Gossip had it that the Colonel's wife was not indifferent to the expressive energy of his glance; but Boulitch saw no joke in this suggestion, and got angry at the mention of it.

The only passion which he made no secret of was the passion for gaming. The sight of a green board made him forget everything. He was usually a loser, but persistent bad luck only provoked his obstinacy. It used to be told of him that once on campaign he was keeping the bank, playing on a gun-carriage for table. He was having a frightful run of luck, when suddenly the alarm was given, shots were fired, and everybody jumped up and made for his arms.

"Pay up to the bank!" shouted Boulitch, without getting up, to one of the most ardent punters in the company.

"Seven!" answered the other as he hastened off. In the thick of the bustle and uproar Boulitch dealt: the card turned up.

When he took his place in the line there was already a pretty stiff fusillade going on. Boulitch took no heed of bullets or Tchetcheness sabres, but hunted out his lucky punter.

"The seven turned up," he shouted, when at last he caught sight of his man in a line of skirmishers who were beginning to dislodge the enemy from the covert of a wood; and, coming up nearer, he took out purse and pocket-book and paid the winner, in spite of his protests against the untimeliness of the settlement. This disagreeable duty accomplished, he flung himself forward, inspired his man to follow him, and blazed away at the enemy with perfect *sangfroid* till the very end of the engagement.

When Lieutenant Boulitch came up to the table there was a general silence, in expectation that he would have something original to contribute. He began in a voice pitched lower than his wont, but quite steady,—

"Gentlemen, what is the good of this unreal debate? Would you like a proof? I propose to put this question to the test in my own person: can a man dispose of his life at his free will, or has every one of us his fatally-decreed moment to die? Who will accept the challenge?"

"Not I! Not I!" resounded from every side. "The fellow's mad! What on earth is he about?"

I said in joke, "I'll offer a bet."

"What! you bet?"

"Against Predestination," I answered, and threw down a score of quarter-guinea pieces on the table—all the money that I had in my pocket.

"Done," said Boulitch in a deep voice, and then added, "Major, you shall be umpire. Look, here are fifteen pieces; the remaining five you owe me, and you shall do me the favour of putting them down there to make up the sum."

"Right!" said the Major. "But I cannot pretend to understand what you are about, or how you are going to decide the point at issue."

Boulitch said nothing, but walked into the bedroom. We followed him. He went up to the wall on which the Major's firearms were hanging, and took down at random from a nail one out of the various calibres of pistol. We still did not take his meaning. But when he cocked the trigger and primed the pan, several of us exclaimed involuntarily, and caught him by the arm. "What are you about? Listen!

... It's madness!" He disengaged his arms and answered their ejaculations by saying slowly, "Gentlemen, who would like to pay up the five guineas for me?"

General silence was the reply, and everybody drew back. Boulitch came out of the other room and sat down at the table, and again we all followed him. He made a sign inviting us to sit down in a circle round him, and we all obeyed without a word; he exercised some mysterious authority over us during those moments. I looked him steadily and hard in the face, but he met my scrutiny with a calm and unperturbed eye, and his pale lips formed a smile. Yet, notwithstanding his cool composure, I thought I read the sign-manual of death on that white face. I have observed—and many old soldiers have confirmed the observation—that upon the face of a man who is to die within a few hours there is, as it were, the imprint of inevitable doom so clearly graven that a practised eye cannot fail to recognize it.

"You are going to die to-day," I said to him.

He turned sharply towards me, but his answer was slow and unmoved,—

"Perhaps yes, perhaps no."

Then he turned to the Major and asked if the pistol was loaded. The Major could not well recollect in the confusion of the moment.

Somebody exclaimed, "Oh, that'll do, Boulitch! Of course it's loaded if it was hanging at the head of the bed. What's the point of playing the fool?"

And another said, "Come, the joke's not good enough."

A third shouted, "I bet fifty roubles to five that it's not loaded!"

The new bet was duly recorded.

I began to be tired of all this ceremony, and said, "Look here: why don't you either fire, or else hang up the pistol again where you found it, and let's all go to bed?"

"Hear, hear!" said several voices. "Hear, hear! Let's go to bed!"

Boulitch presented the muzzle of the pistol at his forehead and said, "Gentlemen, I request that none of you move from his place." Every one might have been frozen into stone. He then addressed me. "Mr. Pechorin, take a card and toss it in the air."

I picked up (I remember it well) the ace of hearts and tossed it in the air. Everybody held his breath; every eye—in horror and a kind of irrepressible curiosity too—leapt from the pistol to the fatal ace, which fluttered in the air and then slowly fell. At the moment when it touched the table Boulitch pulled the trigger—and missed fire.

"Thank God, it was not loaded!" The words were heard from more than one quarter.

"Let us have a look, though," said Boulitch.

He cocked the trigger again, took aim for a *fourajka* cap which was hanging by the window, and fired. The room was filled with smoke. When it dispersed we picked up the *fourajka*. It had a hole in it, plumb-centre, and the bullet was imbedded deep in the wall.

It was several minutes before any one could utter a word. Boulitch poured my coin into his purse with perfect unconcern.

Then the talk revived with a discussion why the pistol had missed fire the first time. Some asserted there must have been an obstruction in the priming-pan; others whispered that the powder had been damp the first time, and Boulitch had afterwards primed it with fresh; but I was positive that this latter suggestion was quite unwarrantable, because I had never taken my eyes off the pistol the whole time.

"You've the luck of the game with you," I said to Boulitch.

He answered, "For the first time in my life," with a self-complacent smile; and added, "It's better than Faro or *Stoss*."

"A bit more risky, though."

"Do tell me, though. Are you a convert to Predestination?"

"Yes, I do believe in it. But what beats me now is—why should I have had the feeling that you would infallibly die to-day?"

The man who had a few moments before aimed quite coolly at his own forehead suddenly lost his temper and his self-control at these words.

"Oh, enough of that!" he said, and got up from the table. "Our bet is finished and done with, and I consider it bad taste for you to say any more about it."

He picked up his hat and went out.

I thought this was strange behaviour, and well I might.

However, the company soon dispersed, and everybody went home, all canvassing Boulitch's mad prank in various senses, and probably all with one voice pronouncing me a cynical egoist for accepting a bet with a man who wanted to shoot himself. As if he could not have found a suitable occasion without me.

I returned home through the deserted bystreets of the village. A full moon, red as the glare of a conflagration, was beginning to show itself clear of the indented horizon of roofs; the deep-blue vault of the sky was full of the steady brilliance of stars. How ludicrous it seemed when I thought how there were once sensible people to be found who could suppose that these celestial luminaries partake in the miserable little quarrels which we wage for the sake of a scrap of land or some imaginary right. What? Did people once hold that these lamps were kindled for us, and but to light up their squabbles and triumphs? These burn still with their ancient splendour, but *their* passions and hopes have long since been quenched with them, like a little fire which some careless traveller lights at the edge of a forest. And yet what strength of will was lent to men by this belief that the whole heaven, with its innumerable inhabitants, looked down on them with sympathetic interest, speechless but unfailing. But we, their sorry descendants, we who crawl about the world without pride or conviction, without delight or fear, notwithstanding the instinctive dread which strangles the heart at the thought of an inevitable end—we are incapable any more of making a great sacrifice either for the benefit of mankind, or even for our individual happiness, because we know its hopelessness. We pass nonchalantly from one doubt to another doubt, as our ancestors flung themselves from one error to another error; but we have not either the hopes they had, or even that vague, though vast, delectation which the soul tastes in every combat, whether with men or with Fate.

My mind ran on through many musings in this strain. I did not arrest its course, because I do not care to halt and dwell upon any abstract idea. What does it lead to? ... In my earliest youth I was a visionary: I loved to gloat over the pictures, now dark and now joyful, which an eager and restless imagination limned for me. But what profit had I in the upshot? Nothing but weariness, as of a man that has fought with dreams in the night, and a perplexed recollection full of regrets. In that vain battle I squandered the ardour of soul and the resoluteness of will which are indispensable for real life. When I first entered on life I had lived it all before in imagination, and therefore I found nothing but disenchantment and boredom—like a man reading a bad imitation of a book which he knows already.

The events of the evening had struck a pretty deep impression in me, and my nerves were shaken. In truth I do not know whether I do believe now in Predestination or not, but I was firmly persuaded of it that evening. The proof had been pretty trenchant; and though I might scoff at our ancestors and their obsequious astrology, I was falling into the same net with them, willy-nilly. However, I brought myself up short in time on this perilous road, by telling myself that the best way was to deny nothing unreservedly, to commit myself to nothing blindly, to cast metaphysics aside, and just look before my own feet.

A most timely precaution; for I as near as could be tumbled headlong over a thick, soft, but apparently lifeless obstacle in my path. Stooping down, and the moon now shining full into the street, I discovered it was a pig, slashed in two by a sabre. My hasty inspection was hardly completed when I heard the sound of footsteps, and two Cossacks came running out of a side lane. One of them approached me, and asked if I had seen the drunken Cossack who had run amok at a pig. I answered that I had met no Cossack, but pointed to the unlucky victim of his misguided prowess.

"The bloody-minded scoundrel!" said the Cossack. "Give him a sup of beer, and off he goes, bent on making mincemeat of anything that he comes across. Come along—after him, Erémeitch; we must pinch him, but it's not so ..."

I heard no more. They were already far away, and I continued my walk with more circumspection, and at last gained my quarters safely.

I lived with an old Cossack sergeant, whom I liked for his good nature, and particularly for his pretty daughter Nastia.

She was waiting for me as usual at the wicket gate, wrapped up in a fur pelisse. The moon lit up her pretty lips, which were pale, almost blue, with the cold of the night. She recognized me, and greeted me with a smile; but I had no thoughts of her, and saying, "Goodnight, Nastia," I walked past her. She wanted to answer, but uttered nothing but a sigh.

I shut the door of my room behind me, lit a candle, and threw myself down on my bed; but slumber kept me waiting longer than usual. Whitish glamours were showing in the east already when I fell asleep. But manifestly it was written in heaven that I was not to have any rest that night. At four o'clock in the morning a pair of fists knocked at my window. I sprang up. "What's the matter?" I was answered by several excited voices. "Get up! dress!" I dressed with all speed and rushed out. Three officers were there. With one voice they said, "Do you know what has happened?" They were as pale as death.

"What?"

"Boulitch has been killed."

I was stupefied.

"Killed," they repeated. "We must make haste."

"But where?"

"You shall hear as we go along."

We started; and they told me the story, interspersed with sundry comments upon the strange predestination which had saved him from imminent death in one form within half an hour of his actual death. Boulitch was walking alone in a dark street, when the drunken Cossack who had slaughtered the pig came running up to him. The man might probably have passed him without notice if Boulitch had not suddenly stopped and said, "Hullo! brother, who are you looking for?"

"You!" replied the Cossack, and felled him with his sabre; the stroke laid him open from the shoulder almost to the heart. The two Cossacks whom I had met in pursuit of the butcher hurried up, and raised the wounded man; but he was already almost at the last gasp, and could not utter more than the three words, "*He was right.*"

The inner significance of these words was known to me alone; they referred to me. I had undesignedly foretold his fate to the poor fellow, and my instinct had not deceived me. The change which I had read in his countenance had been a veritable prognostic of approaching death.

The assassin had shut himself into an empty cottage at the extremity of the village; we now proceeded thither. A multitude of women in tears was hurrying in the same direction. Every now and again a belated Cossack trooper would come charging into the street, hastily fix his dagger by his saddle-side, and gallop away past us. The confusion was frightful.

At last arrived, we began to survey the scene. A crowd was assembled around the cottage, which had doors and shutters fast closed from within. Officers and Cossacks were engaged in a heated discussion together; there was an uproar of women's voices, some accusing, some giving judgment. One figure in the midst of a group caught my eye—an old woman whose face was eloquent of distraction and despair. She sat on a big balk of timber, huddled in a heap, her elbows leaning on her knees, and her head supported in her hands. She was the homicide's mother. From time to time her lips moved; was it prayer or curse, the inaudible murmur?

However, something must be resolved upon and some means made to capture the delinquent; only nobody ventured to come forward and take the brunt.

I walked up to the window and looked through a chink in the shutter. The wretched man was lying on the floor, grasping a pistol in his right hand; his bloody sword lay by his side. His quick, eager eyes kept revolving round in terror. At times he shuddered and clutched at his head, as if in a confused recollection of overnight. I did not read much of desperado in those restless eyes, and I told the Major that there was nothing to be gained by waiting; he might as well give the Cossacks orders to break in the door and fall upon the man; better now than later, when he should be completely come to himself.

Meanwhile an old native *yesaoul* went up to the door and called him by name; and an answer came from within.

The *yesaoul* said, "Brother Ephimitch, you've done wrong; there's nothing for it but you must give yourself up."

The Cossack answered, "I won't give myself up."

And the *yesaoul* continued, "Fear God, man! Come, you're not a damned Tchetchenetz, but a decent Christian. Come now; you've fallen into temptation, and there's nothing for it—you can't escape your fate."

But the other answered in a loud voice, "I will not give myself up." And we could hear the click of the trigger as he cocked his pistol.

"Hi! Gammer," said the *yesaoul* to the old woman, "you talk to your son; perhaps he'll listen to you. It's a mere provoking of God. Why, look, the gentlemen have been waiting two hours."

The old woman stared at him steadily and shook her head. Then he walked up to the Major and said, "Vassili Petrovitch, he won't surrender; I know him. If we break in the door he may kill several of our men. Don't you think it better, sir, to shoot him? There's a wide chink in the shutter."

A curious idea flashed into my mind at this moment. Like Boulitch, I had the notion to experiment on destiny. I said to the Major, "Allow me, sir; I will take him alive."

I told the *yesaoul* to engage the man in conversation, posted three Cossacks at the door, ready to break it down and come to my aid at a given signal, and then walked round the hovel and approached the fatal window. My heart was beating hard.

The *yesaoul* proceeded to vociferate, "Ah, you damned hound! What d'you want to make fools of us for, eh? Do you think we can't master you?" And he began to rap on the door with all his might. I put my eye to the chink, and followed the Cossack's movements: he was not expecting an attack on that side. Suddenly I broke down the shutter, and threw myself in at the window head foremost.

A shot went off just by my ear; the bullet carried away my epaulette. But the smoke which filled the room prevented my adversary from finding the sabre which was lying by his side. I pinned him by the arm; the Cossacks burst in, and it was not three minutes before he was handcuffed and led off under arrest. The crowd dispersed; the officers congratulated me, and really there was some cause for it.

And was not all this enough to make anybody a fatalist? But, after all, who ever really knows what he believes and what he does not? How often we mistake for belief what is but an illusion of the senses or a mere blunder of the reason! I prefer to doubt of everything; it is a temper which does not impair energy of character; on the contrary, for my part I always go ahead with a better courage when I do not know what is awaiting me. After all, nothing worse than death can befall you, and death you cannot avoid.

When I got back to the fort, I told Maxim Maximich all that had happened to me and all that I had witnessed, and tried to elicit his opinion concerning Predestination. At first the word puzzled him; but when, to the best of my power, I had explained it to him, he shook his head significantly, and observed, "Ah, well, yes; it's all very fine and very clever! All I know is that those Asiatic triggers often do miss fire, if you don't keep them properly greased, or don't press firmly enough with your finger. To tell you the truth, I don't care about the Circassian carbines either. They don't suit the Little Brother* somehow. They're so short in the butt, you may get your nose burnt off before you know

---

* The Russian private soldier.

where you are. That's why they use the sabre. However, it's only my humble opinion."

Then he was silent for a while—pensive; and at last he added, "Yes, to be sure—a pity about that poor chap! The devil must have put it into his head to accost a drunken man at night! All the same, it looks as if it had been written that it should happen to him from his birth."

This was all that I could get out of him; he is not, in general, a great fancier of metaphysical discussions.

YERMOLAÏ AND THE MILLER'S WIFE

Ivan Turgenev (1818–1883)

Translated by Constance Garnett

Famous for his writing about the fading aristocracy, about the tender and bitter loves of youth (the phrase 'Turgenev's girl' is still a symbol of purity and innocence in the Russian language), **Ivan Turgenev** (1818–1883) was also one of the first Russian writers to focus on social life. His groundbreaking novel *Fathers and Sons* examined the paradoxes of a new generational conflict, the split between progressive youngsters and their traditional elders, which haunted Russia for decades and provided fertile ground for the emerging revolutionary movements. In his *Sportsman's Sketches* Turgenev, a devoted hunter himself, wrote not so much about partridges and rifles, but about the world and people outside the aristocratic milleux and their manors, a world you can only get in touch with if you fit yourself into hunter's boots and wander country roads – guided by hunter's luck and the weather.

One evening I went with the huntsman Yermolaï 'stand-shooting.' ... But perhaps all my readers may not know what 'stand-shooting' is. I will tell you.

A quarter of an hour before sunset in spring-time you go out into the woods with your gun, but without your dog. You seek out a spot for yourself on the outskirts of the forest, take a look round, examine your caps, and glance at your companion. A quarter of an hour passes; the sun has set, but it is still light in the forest; the sky is clear and transparent; the birds are chattering and twittering; the young grass shines with the brilliance of emerald. ... You wait. Gradually the recesses of the forest grow dark; the blood-red glow of the evening sky creeps slowly on to the roots and the trunks of the trees, and keeps rising higher and higher, passes from the lower, still almost leafless branches, to the motionless, slumbering tree-tops. ... And now even the topmost branches are darkened; the purple sky fades to dark-blue. The forest fragrance grows stronger; there is a scent of warmth and damp earth; the fluttering breeze dies away at your side. The birds go to sleep—not all at once—but after their kinds; first the finches are hushed, a few minutes later the warblers, and after them the yellow buntings. In the forest it grows darker and darker. The trees melt together into great masses of blackness; in the dark-blue sky the first stars come timidly out. All the birds are asleep. Only the redstarts and the nuthatches are still chirping drowsily. ... And now they too are still. The last echoing call of the pee-wit rings over our heads; the oriole's melancholy cry sounds somewhere in the distance; then the nightingale's first note. Your heart is weary with suspense, when suddenly—but only sportsmen can understand me—suddenly in the deep hush there is a peculiar croaking and whirring sound, the measured sweep of swift wings is heard, and the snipe, gracefully bending its long beak, sails smoothly down behind a dark bush to meet your shot.

That is the meaning of 'stand-shooting.' And so I had gone out stand-shooting with Yermolaï; but excuse me, reader: I must first introduce you to Yermolaï.

Picture to yourself a tall gaunt man of forty-five, with a long thin nose, a narrow forehead, little grey eyes, a bristling head of hair, and thick sarcastic lips. This man wore, winter and summer alike, a yellow nankin coat of German cut, but with a sash round the waist; he wore blue pantaloons and a cap of astrakhan, presented to him in a merry hour by a spendthrift landowner. Two bags were fastened on to his sash, one in front, skilfully tied into two halves, for powder and for shot; the other behind for game: wadding Yermolaï used to produce out of his peculiar, seemingly inexhaustible cap. With the money he gained by the game he sold, he might easily have bought himself a cartridge-box and powder-flask; but he never once even contemplated such a purchase, and continued to load his gun after his old fashion, exciting the admiration of all beholders by the skill with which he avoided the risks of spilling or mixing his powder and shot. His gun was a single-barrelled flint-lock, endowed, moreover, with a villainous habit of 'kicking.' It was due to this that Yermolaï's right cheek was permanently swollen to a larger size than the left. How he ever succeeded in hitting anything with this gun, it would take a shrewd man to discover—but he did. He had too a setter-dog, by name Valetka, a most extraordinary creature. Yermolaï never fed him. 'Me feed a dog!' he reasoned; 'why, a dog's a clever beast; he finds a living for himself.' And certainly, though Valetka's extreme thinness was a shock even to an indifferent observer, he still lived and had a long life; and in spite of his pitiable position he was not even once lost, and never showed an inclination to desert his master. Once indeed, in his youth, he had absented himself for two days, on courting bent, but this folly was soon over with him. Valetka's most noticeable peculiarity was his impenetrable indifference to everything in the world. ... If it were not a dog I was speaking of, I should have called him 'disillusioned.' He usually sat with his cropped tail curled up under him, scowling and twitching at times, and he never smiled. (It is well known that dogs can smile, and smile very sweetly.) He was exceedingly ugly; and the idle house-serfs never lost an opportunity of jeering cruelly at his appearance; but all these jeers, and even blows, Valetka bore with astonishing indifference. He was a source of special delight to the cooks, who would all leave their work at once and give him chase with shouts and abuse, whenever, through a weakness not confined to dogs, he thrust his hungry nose through the half-open door of the kitchen, tempting with its warmth and appetising smells. He distinguished himself by untiring energy in the chase, and had a good scent; but if he chanced to overtake a slightly wounded hare, he devoured it with relish to the last bone, somewhere in the cool shade under the green bushes, at a respectful distance from Yermolaï, who was abusing him in every known and unknown dialect. Yermolaï belonged to one of my neighbours, a landowner of the old style. Landowners of the old style don't care for game, and prefer the domestic fowl. Only on extraordinary occasions, such as birthdays, namedays, and elections, the cooks of the old-fashioned landowners set to work to prepare some long-beaked birds, and, falling into the state of frenzy peculiar to Russians when they don't quite know what to do, they concoct such marvellous sauces for them that the guests examine the proffered dishes curiously and attentively, but rarely make up their minds to try them. Yermolaï was under orders to provide his master's kitchen with two brace of grouse and partridges once a month. But he might live where and how he pleased. They had given him up as a man of no use for work of any kind—'bone lazy,' as the expression is among us in Orel. Powder and shot, of course, they did not provide him, following precisely the same principle in virtue of which he did not feed his dog. Yermolaï was a very strange kind of man; heedless as a bird, rather fond of talking, awkward and vacant-looking; he was excessively fond of drink, and never could sit still long; in walking he shambled along, and rolled from side to side; and yet he got over fifty miles in the day with his rolling, shambling gait. He exposed himself to the most varied adventures: spent the night in the marshes, in trees, on roofs, or under bridges; more than once he had got shut up in lofts, cellars, or barns; he sometimes lost his gun, his dog, his most indispensable garments; got long and severe thrashings; but he always returned home, after a little while, in his clothes, and with his gun and his dog. One could not call him a cheerful man, though one almost always found him in an even frame of mind; he was looked on generally as an eccentric. Yermolaï liked a little chat with a good companion, especially over a glass, but he would not stop long; he would get up and go. 'But where the devil are you going? It's dark out of doors.' 'To Tchaplino.' 'But what's taking you to Tchaplino, ten miles away?' 'I am going to stay the night at Sophron's there.' 'But stay the night here.' 'No, I can't.' And Yermolaï, with his Valetka, would go off into the dark night, through woods and water-courses, and the peasant Sophron very likely did not let him into his place, and even, I am afraid, gave him a blow to teach him 'not to disturb honest folks.' But none could compare with Yermolaï in skill in deep-water fishing in spring-time, in catching crayfish with his hands, in tracking game by scent, in snaring quails, in training hawks, in capturing the nightingales who had the greatest variety of notes. ... One thing he could not do, train a dog; he had not patience enough. He had a wife too. He went to see her once a week. She lived in a wretched, tumble-down little hut, and led a hand-to-mouth existence, never knowing overnight whether she would have food to eat on the morrow; and in every way her lot was a pitiful one. Yermolaï, who seemed such a careless and easy-going fellow, treated his wife with cruel harshness; in his own house he assumed a stern, and menacing manner; and his poor wife did everything she could to please him, trembled when he looked at her, and spent her last farthing to buy him vodka; and when he stretched himself majestically on the stove and fell into an heroic sleep, she obsequiously covered him with a sheepskin. I happened myself more than once to catch an involuntary look in him of a kind of savage ferocity; I did not like the expression of his face when he finished off a wounded bird with his teeth. But Yermolaï never remained more than a day at home, and away from home he was once more the same 'Yermolka' (i.e. the shooting-cap), as he was called for a hundred miles round, and as he sometimes called himself. The lowest house-serf was conscious of being superior to this vagabond—and perhaps this was precisely why they treated him with friendliness; the peasants at first amused themselves by chasing him and driving him like a hare over the open country, but afterwards they left him in God's hands, and when once they recognised him as 'queer,' they no longer tormented him, and even gave him bread and entered into talk with him. ... This was the man I took as my huntsman, and with him I went stand-shooting to a great birchwood on the banks of the Ista.

Many Russian rivers, like the Volga, have one bank rugged and precipitous, the other bounded by level meadows; and so it is with the Ista. This small river winds extremely capriciously, coils like a snake, and does not keep a straight course for half-a-mile together; in some places, from the top of a sharp declivity, one can see the river for ten miles, with its dykes, its pools and mills, and the gardens on its banks, shut in with willows and thick flower-gardens. There are fish in the Ista in endless numbers, especially roaches (the peasants take them in hot weather from under the bushes with their hands); little sand-pipers flutter whistling along the stony banks, which are streaked with cold clear streams; wild ducks dive in the middle of the pools, and look round warily; in the coves under the overhanging cliffs herons stand out in the shade. ... We stood in ambush nearly an hour, killed two brace of wood snipe, and, as we wanted to try our luck again at sunrise (stand-shooting can be done as well in the early morning), we resolved to spend the night at the nearest mill. We came out of the wood, and went down the slope. The dark-blue waters of the river ran below; the air was thick with the mists of night. We knocked at the gate. The dogs began barking in the yard.

'Who is there?' asked a hoarse and sleepy voice.

'We are sportsmen; let us stay the night.' There was no reply. 'We will pay.'

'I will go and tell the master—Sh! Curse the dogs! Go to the devil with you!'

We listened as the workman went into the cottage; he soon came back to the gate. 'No,' he said; 'the master tells me not to let you in.'

'Why not?'

'He is afraid; you are sportsmen; you might set the mill on fire; you've firearms with you, to be sure.'

'But what nonsense!'

'We had our mill on fire like that last year; some fish-dealers stayed the night, and they managed to set it on fire somehow.'

'But, my good friend, we can't sleep in the open air!'

'That's your business.' He went away, his boots clacking as he walked.

Yermolaï promised him various unpleasant things in the future. 'Let us go to the village,' he brought out at last, with a sigh. But it was two miles to the village.

'Let us stay the night here,' I said, 'in the open air—the night is warm; the miller will let us have some straw if we pay for it.'

Yermolaï agreed without discussion. We began again to knock.

'Well, what do you want?' the workman's voice was heard again; 'I've told you we can't.'

We explained to him what we wanted. He went to consult the master of the house, and returned with him. The little side gate creaked. The miller appeared, a tall, fat-faced man with a bullneck, round-bellied and corpulent. He agreed to my proposal. A hundred paces from the mill there was a little outhouse open to the air on all sides. They carried straw and hay there for us; the workman set a samovar down on the grass near the river, and, squatting on his heels, began to blow vigorously into the pipe of it. The embers glowed, and threw a bright light on his young face. The miller ran to wake his wife, and suggested at last that I myself should sleep in the cottage; but I preferred to remain in the open air. The miller's wife brought us milk, eggs, potatoes and bread. Soon the samovar boiled, and we began drinking tea. A mist had risen from the river; there was no wind; from all round came the cry of the corn-crake, and faint sounds from the mill-wheels of drops that dripped from the paddles and of water gurgling through the bars of the lock. We built a small fire on the ground. While Yermolaï was baking the potatoes in the embers, I had time to fall into a doze. I was waked by a discreetly-subdued whispering near me. I lifted my head; before the fire, on a tub turned upside down, the miller's wife sat talking to my huntsman. By her dress, her movements, and her manner of speaking, I had already recognised that she had been in domestic service, and was neither peasant nor city-bred; but now for the first time I got a clear view of her features. She looked about thirty; her thin, pale face still showed the traces of remarkable beauty; what particularly charmed me was her eyes, large and mournful in expression. She was leaning her elbows on her knees, and had her face in her hands. Yermolaï was sitting with his back to me, and thrusting sticks into the fire.

'They've the cattle-plague again at Zheltonhiny,' the miller's wife was saying; 'father Ivan's two cows are dead—Lord have mercy on them!'

'And how are your pigs doing?' asked Yermolaï, after a brief pause.

'They're alive.'

'You ought to make me a present of a sucking pig.'

The miller's wife was silent for a while, then she sighed.

'Who is it you're with?' she asked.

'A gentleman from Kostomarovo.'

Yermolaï threw a few pine twigs on the fire; they all caught fire at once, and a thick white smoke came puffing into his face.

'Why didn't your husband let us into the cottage?'

'He's afraid.'

'Afraid! the fat old tub! Arina Timofyevna, my darling, bring me a little glass of spirits.'

The miller's wife rose and vanished into the darkness. Yermolaï began to sing in an undertone—

'When I went to see my sweetheart,
I wore out all my shoes.'

Arina returned with a small flask and a glass. Yermolaï got up, crossed himself, and drank it off at a draught. 'Good!' was his comment.

The miller's wife sat down again on the tub.

'Well, Arina Timofyevna, are you still ill?'

'Yes.'

'What is it?'

'My cough troubles me at night.'

'The gentleman's asleep, it seems,' observed Yermolaï after a short silence. 'Don't go to a doctor, Arina; it will be worse if you do.'

'Well, I am not going.'

'But come and pay me a visit.'

Arina hung down her head dejectedly.

'I will drive my wife out for the occasion,' continued Yermolaï 'Upon my word, I will.'

'You had better wake the gentleman, Yermolaï Petrovitch; you see, the potatoes are done.'

'Oh, let him snore,' observed my faithful servant indifferently; 'he's tired with walking, so he sleeps sound.'

I turned over in the hay. Yermolaï got up and came to me. 'The potatoes are ready; will you come and eat them?'

I came out of the outhouse; the miller's wife got up from the tub and was going away. I addressed her.

'Have you kept this mill long?'

'It's two years since I came on Trinity day.'

'And where does your husband come from?'

Arina had not caught my question.

'Where's your husband from?' repeated Yermolaï, raising his voice.

'From Byelev. He's a Byelev townsman.'

'And are you too from Byelev?'

'No, I'm a serf; I was a serf.'

'Whose?'

'Zvyerkoff was my master. Now I am free.'

'What Zvyerkoff?'

'Alexandr Selitch.'

'Weren't you his wife's lady's maid?'

'How did you know? Yes.'

I looked at Arina with redoubled curiosity and sympathy.

'I know your master,' I continued.

'Do you?' she replied in a low voice, and her head drooped.

I must tell the reader why I looked with such sympathy at Arina. During my stay at Petersburg I had become by chance acquainted with Mr. Zvyerkoff. He had a rather influential position, and was reputed a man of sense and education. He had a wife, fat, sentimental, lachrymose and spiteful—a vulgar and disagreeable creature; he had too a son, the very type of the young swell of to-day, pampered and stupid. The exterior of Mr. Zvyerkoff himself did not prepossess one in his favour; his little mouse-like eyes peeped slyly out of a broad, almost square, face; he had a large, prominent nose, with distended nostrils; his close-cropped grey hair stood up like a brush above his scowling brow; his thin lips were for ever twitching and smiling mawkishly. Mr. Zvyerkoff's favourite position was standing with his legs wide apart and his fat hands in his trouser pockets. Once I happened somehow to be driving alone with Mr. Zvyerkoff in a coach out of town. We fell into conversation. As a man of experience and of judgment, Mr. Zvyerkoff began to try to set me in 'the path of truth.'

'Allow me to observe to you,' he drawled at last; 'all you young people criticise and form judgments on everything at random; you have little knowledge of your own country; Russia, young gentlemen, is an unknown land to you; that's where it is! ... You are for ever reading German. For instance, now you say this and that and the other about anything; for instance, about the houseserfs. ... Very fine; I don't dispute it's all very fine; but you don't know them; you don't know the kind of people they are.' (Mr. Zvyerkoff blew his nose loudly and took a pinch of snuff.) 'Allow me to tell you as an illustration one little anecdote; it may perhaps interest you.' (Mr. Zvyerkoff cleared his throat.) 'You know, doubtless, what my wife is; it would be difficult, I should imagine, to find a more kind-hearted woman, you will agree. For her waiting-maids, existence is simply a perfect paradise, and no mistake about it. ... But my wife has made it a rule never to keep married lady's maids. Certainly it would not do; children come—and one thing and the other—and how is a lady's maid to look after her mistress as she ought, to fit in with her ways; she is no longer able to do it; her mind is in other things. One must look at things through human nature. Well, we were driving once through our village, it must be—let me be correct—yes, fifteen years ago. We saw, at the bailiff's, a young girl, his daughter, very pretty indeed; something even—you know—something attractive in her manners. And my wife said to me: "Kokó"—you understand, of course, that is her pet name for me—"let us take this girl to Petersburg; I like her, Kokó. ..." I said, "Let us take her, by all means." The bailiff, of course, was at our feet; he could not have expected such good fortune, you can imagine. ... Well, the girl of course cried violently. Of course, it was hard for her at first; the parental home ... in fact ... there was nothing surprising in that. However, she soon got used to us: at first we put her in the maidservants' room; they trained her, of course.

And what do you think? The girl made wonderful progress; my wife became simply devoted to her, promoted her at last above the rest to wait on herself ... observe. ... And one must do her the justice to say, my wife had never such a maid, absolutely never; attentive, modest, and obedient—simply all that could be desired. But my wife, I must confess, spoilt her too much; she dressed her well, fed her from our own table, gave her tea to drink, and so on, as you can imagine! So she waited on my wife like this for ten years. Suddenly, one fine morning, picture to yourself, Arina—her name was Arina—rushes unannounced into my study, and flops down at my feet. That's a thing, I tell you plainly, I can't endure. No human being ought ever to lose sight of their personal dignity. Am I not right? What do you say? "Your honour, Alexandr Selitch, I beseech a favour of you." "What favour?" "Let me be married." I must confess I was taken aback. "But you know, you stupid, your mistress has no other lady's maid?" "I will wait on mistress as before." "Nonsense! nonsense! your mistress can't endure married lady's maids," "Malanya could take my place." "Pray don't argue." "I obey your will." I must confess it was quite a shock, I assure you, I am like that; nothing wounds me so—nothing, I venture to say, wounds me so deeply as ingratitude. I need not tell you—you know what my wife is; an angel upon earth, goodness inexhaustible. One would fancy even the worst of men would be ashamed to hurt her. Well, I got rid of Arina. I thought, perhaps, she would come to her senses; I was unwilling, do you know, to believe in wicked, black ingratitude in anyone. What do you think? Within six months she thought fit to come to me again with the same request. I felt revolted. But imagine my amazement when, some time later, my wife comes to me in tears, so agitated that I felt positively alarmed. "What has happened?" "Arina. ... You understand ... I am ashamed to tell it." ... "Impossible! ... Who is the man?" "Petrushka, the footman." My indignation broke out then. I am like that. I don't like half measures! Petrushka was not to blame. We might flog him, but in my opinion he was not to blame. Arina. ... Well, well, well! what more's to be said? I gave orders, of course, that her hair should be cut off, she should be dressed in sackcloth, and sent into the country. My wife was deprived of an excellent lady's maid; but there was no help for it: immorality cannot be tolerated in a household in any case. Better to cut off the infected member at once. There, there! now you can judge the thing for yourself—you know that my wife is ... yes, yes, yes! indeed! ... an angel! She had grown attached to Arina, and Arina knew it, and had the face to ... Eh? no, tell me ... eh? And what's the use of talking about it. Any way, there was no help for it. I, indeed—I, in particular, felt hurt, felt wounded for a long time by the ingratitude of this girl. Whatever you say—it's no good to look for feeling, for heart, in these people! You may feed the wolf as you will; he has always a hankering for the woods. Education, by all means! But I only wanted to give you an example. ...'

And Mr. Zvyerkoff, without finishing his sentence, turned away his head, and, wrapping himself more closely into his cloak, manfully repressed his involuntary emotion.

The reader now probably understands why I looked with sympathetic interest at Arina.

'Have you long been married to the miller?' I asked her at last.

'Two years.'

'How was it? Did your master allow it?'

'They bought my freedom.'

'Who?'

'Savely Alexyevitch.'

'Who is that?'

'My husband.' (Yermolaï smiled to himself.) 'Has my master perhaps spoken to you of me?' added Arina, after a brief silence.

I did not know what reply to make to her question.

'Arina!' cried the miller from a distance. She got up and walked away.

'Is her husband a good fellow?' I asked Yermolaï.

'So-so.'

'Have they any children?'

'There was one, but it died.'

'How was it? Did the miller take a liking to her? Did he give much to buy her freedom?'

'I don't know. She can read and write; in their business it's of use. I suppose he liked her.'

'And have you known her long?'

'Yes. I used to go to her master's. Their house isn't far from here.'

'And do you know the footman Petrushka?'

'Piotr Vassilyevitch? Of course, I knew him.'

'Where is he now?'

'He was sent for a soldier.'

We were silent for a while.

'She doesn't seem well?' I asked Yermolaï at last.

'I should think not! To-morrow, I say, we shall have good sport. A little sleep now would do us no harm.'

A flock of wild ducks swept whizzing over our heads, and we heard them drop down into the river not far from us. It was now quite dark, and it began to be cold; in the thicket sounded the melodious notes of a nightingale. We buried ourselves in the hay and fell asleep.

HOW A MUZHIK FED TWO OFFICIALS

Mikhail Saltykov-Shchedrin
(1826–1889)

Translated by Thomas Seltzer

A member of the same Petrashevsky circle as Dostoevsky, **Mikhail Saltykov-Shchedrin** (1826–1889) reestablished himself as a civil servant during his eight years of forced exile in the remote Vyatka region. Later rising to the post of vice-governor of a province, Saltykov-Shchedrin knew the bureaucratic system from within. Unlike Dostoevsky, her never became a supporter of the Tsar's government: his satire is ahead of its time and looks into the future, to the world of Zamyatin's *We* and Huxley's *Brave New World*, exploring bureaucracy as a force with its own dangerous power: faceless, anonymous, eerie.

Famous for his sense of absurd, and his masterly evocation of the paralysis of one's will in the face of power, Saltykov-Shchedrin foretells the irrational horrors of Soviet totalitarianism.

Once upon a time there were two Officials. They were both empty-headed, and so they found themselves one day suddenly transported to an uninhabited isle, as if on a magic carpet.

They had passed their whole life in a Government Department, where records were kept; had been born there, bred there, grown old there, and consequently hadn't the least understanding for anything outside of the Department; and the only words they knew were: "With assurances of the highest esteem, I am your humble servant."

But the Department was abolished, and as the services of the two Officials were no longer needed, they were given their freedom. So the retired Officials migrated to Podyacheskaya Street in St. Petersburg. Each had his own home, his own cook and his own pension.

Waking up on the uninhabited isle, they found themselves lying under the same cover. At first, of course, they couldn't understand what had happened to them, and they spoke as if nothing extraordinary had taken place.

"What a peculiar dream I had last night, your Excellency," said the one Official. "It seemed to me as if I were on an uninhabited isle."

Scarcely had he uttered the words, when he jumped to his feet. The other Official also jumped up.

"Good Lord, what does this mean! Where are we?" they cried out in astonishment.

They felt each other to make sure that they were no longer dreaming, and finally convinced themselves of the sad reality.

Before them stretched the ocean, and behind them was a little spot of earth, beyond which the ocean stretched again. They began to cry—the first time since their Department had been shut down.

They looked at each other, and each noticed that the other was clad in nothing but his night shirt with his order hanging about his neck.

"We really should be having our coffee now," observed the one Official. Then he bethought himself again of the strange situation he was in and a second time fell to weeping.

"What are we going to do now?" he sobbed. "Even supposing we were to draw up a report, what good would that do?"

"You know what, your Excellency," replied the other Official, "you go to the east and I will go to the west. Toward evening we will come back here again, and, perhaps, we shall have found something."

They started to ascertain which was the east and which was the west. They recalled that the head of their Department had once said to them, "If you want to know where the east is, then turn your face to the north, and the east will be on your right." But when they tried to find out which was the north, they turned to the right and to the left and looked around on all sides. Having spent their whole life in the Department of Records, their efforts were all in vain.

"To my mind, your Excellency, the best thing to do would be for you to go to the right and me to go to the left," said one Official, who had served not only in the Department of Records, but had also been teacher of handwriting in the School for Reserves, and so was a little bit cleverer.

So said, so done. The one Official went to the right. He came upon trees bearing all sorts of fruits. Gladly would he have plucked an apple, but they all hung so high that he would have been obliged to climb up. He tried to climb up in vain. All he succeeded in doing was tearing his night shirt. Then he struck upon a brook. It was swarming with fish.

"Wouldn't it be wonderful if we had all this fish in Podyacheskaya Street!" he thought, and his mouth watered. Then he entered woods and found partridges, grouse and hares.

"Good Lord, what an abundance of food!" he cried. His hunger was going up tremendously.

But he had to return to the appointed spot with empty hands. He found the other Official waiting for him.

"Well, Your Excellency, how went it? Did you find anything?"

"Nothing but an old number of the *Moscow Gazette*, not another thing."

The Officials lay down to sleep again, but their empty stomachs gave them no rest. They were partly robbed of their sleep by the thought of who was now enjoying their pension, and partly by the recollection of the fruit, fishes, partridges, grouse and hares that they had seen during the day.

"The human pabulum in its original form flies, swims and grows on trees. Who would have thought it your Excellency?" said the one Official.

"To be sure," rejoined the other Official. "I, too, must admit that I had imagined that our breakfast rolls came into the world just as they appear on the table."

"From which it is to be deduced that if we want to eat a pheasant, we must catch it first, kill it, pull its feathers and roast it. But how's that to be done?"

"Yes, how's that to be done?" repeated the other Official.

They turned silent and tried again to fall asleep, but their hunger scared sleep away. Before their eyes swarmed flocks of pheasants and ducks, herds of porklings, and they were all so juicy, done so tenderly and garnished so deliciously with olives, capers and pickles.

"I believe I could devour my own boots now," said the one Official.

"Gloves are not bad either, especially if they have been born quite mellow," said the other Official.

The two Officials stared at each other fixedly. In their glances gleamed an evil-boding fire, their teeth chattered and a dull groaning issued from their breasts. Slowly they crept upon each other and suddenly they burst into a fearful frenzy. There was a yelling and groaning, the rags flew about, and the Official who had been teacher of handwriting bit off his colleague's order and swallowed it. However, the sight of blood brought them both back to their senses.

"God help us!" they cried at the same time. "We certainly don't mean to eat each other up. How could we have come to such a pass as this? What evil genius is making sport of us?"

"We must, by all means, entertain each other to pass the time away, otherwise there will be murder and death," said the one Official.

"You begin," said the other.

"Can you explain why it is that the sun first rises and then sets? Why isn't it the reverse?"

"Aren't you a funny man, your Excellency? You get up first, then you go to your office and work there, and at night you lie down to sleep."

"But why can't one assume the opposite, that is, that one goes to bed, sees all sorts of dream figures, and then gets up?"

"Well, yes, certainly. But when I was still an Official, I always thought this way: 'Now it is dawn, then it will be day, then will come supper, and finally will come the time to go to bed.'"

The word "supper" recalled that incident in the day's doings, and the thought of it made both Officials melancholy, so that the conversation came to a halt.

"A doctor once told me that human beings can sustain themselves for a long time on their own juices," the one Official began again.

"What does that mean?"

"It is quite simple. You see, one's own juices generate other juices, and these in their turn still other juices, and so it goes on until finally all the juices are consumed."

"And then what happens?"

"Then food has to be taken into the system again."

"The devil!"

No matter what topic the Officials chose, the conversation invariably reverted to the subject of eating; which only increased their appetite more and more. So they decided to give up talking altogether, and, recollecting the *Moscow Gazette* that the one of them had found, they picked it up and began to read it eagerly.

Banquet Given by the Mayor

"The table was set for one hundred persons. The magnificence of it exceeded all expectations. The remotest provinces were represented at this feast of the gods by the costliest gifts. The golden sturgeon from Sheksna and the silver pheasant from the Caucasian woods held a rendezvous with strawberries so seldom to be had in our latitude in winter ..."

"The devil! For God's sake, stop reading, your Excellency. Couldn't you find something else to read about?" cried the other Official in sheer desperation. He snatched the paper from his colleague's hands, and started to read something else.

"Our correspondent in Tula informs us that yesterday a sturgeon was found in the Upa (an event which even the oldest inhabitants cannot recall, and all the more remarkable since they recognised the former police captain in this sturgeon). This was made the occasion for giving a banquet in the club. The prime cause of the banquet was served in a large wooden platter garnished with vinegar pickles. A bunch of parsley stuck out of its mouth. Doctor P—who acted as toast-master saw to it that everybody present got a piece of the sturgeon. The sauces to go with it were unusually varied and delicat—"

"Permit me, your Excellency, it seems to me you are not so careful either in the selection of reading matter," interrupted the first Official, who secured the *Gazette* again and started to read:

"One of the oldest inhabitants of Viatka has discovered a new and highly original recipe for fish soup. A live codfish *(lota vulgaris)* is taken and beaten with a rod until its liver swells up with anger. ..."

The Officials' heads drooped. Whatever their eyes fell upon had something to do with eating. Even their own thoughts were fatal. No matter how much they tried to keep their minds off beefsteak and the like, it was all in vain; their fancy returned invariably, with irresistible force, back to that for which they were so painfully yearning.

Suddenly an inspiration came to the Official who had once taught handwriting.

"I have it!" he cried delightedly. "What do you say to this, your Excellency? What do you say to our finding a muzhik?"

"A muzhik, your Excellency? What sort of a muzhik?"

"Why a plain ordinary muzhik. A muzhik like all other muzhiks. He would get the breakfast rolls for us right away, and he could also catch partridges and fish for us."

"Hm, a muzhik. But where are we to fetch one from, if there is no muzhik here?"

"Why shouldn't there be a muzhik here? There are muzhiks everywhere. All one has to do is hunt for them. There certainly must be a muzhik hiding here somewhere so as to get out of working."

This thought so cheered the Officials that they instantly jumped up to go in search of a muzhik.

For a long while they wandered about on the island without the desired result, until finally a concentrated smell of black bread and old sheep skin assailed their nostrils and guided them in the right direction. There under a tree was a colossal muzhik lying fast asleep with his hands under his head. It was clear that to escape his duty to work he had impudently withdrawn to this island. The indignation of the Officials knew no bounds.

"What, lying asleep here, you lazy-bones you!" they raged at him. "It is nothing to you that there are two Officials here who are fairly perishing of hunger. Up, forward, march, work."

The Muzhik rose and looked at the two severe gentlemen standing in front of him. His first thought was to make his escape, but the Officials held him fast.

He had to submit to his fate. He had to work.

First he climbed up on a tree and plucked several dozen of the finest apples for the Officials. He kept a rotten one for himself. Then he turned up the earth and dug out some potatoes. Next he started a fire with two bits of wood that he rubbed against each other. Out of his own hair he made a snare and caught partridges. Over the fire, by this time burning brightly, he cooked so many kinds of food that the question arose in the Officials' minds whether they shouldn't give some to this idler.

Beholding the efforts of the Muzhik, they rejoiced in their hearts. They had already forgotten how the day before they had nearly been perishing of hunger, and all they thought of now was: "What a good thing it is to be an Official. Nothing bad can ever happen to an Official."

"Are you satisfied, gentlemen?" the lazy Muzhik asked.

"Yes, we appreciate your industry," replied the Officials.

"Then you will permit me to rest a little?"

"Go take a little rest, but first make a good strong cord."

The Muzhik gathered wild hemp stalks, laid them in water, beat them and broke them, and toward evening a good stout cord was ready. The Officials took the cord and bound the Muzhik to a tree, so that he should not run away. Then they laid themselves to sleep.

Thus day after day passed, and the Muzhik became so skilful that he could actually cook soup for the Officials in his bare hands. The Officials had become round and well-fed and happy. It rejoiced them that here they needn't spend any money and that in the meanwhile their pensions were accumulating in St. Petersburg.

"What is your opinion, your Excellency," one said to the other after breakfast one day, "is the Story of the Tower of Babel true? Don't you think it is simply an allegory?"

"By no means, your Excellency, I think it was something that really happened. What other explanation is there for the existence of so many different languages on earth?"

"Then the Flood must really have taken place, too?"

"Certainly, else how would you explain the existence of Antediluvian animals? Besides, the *Moscow Gazette* says——"

They made search for the old number of the *Moscow Gazette*, seated themselves in the shade, and read the whole sheet from beginning to end. They read of festivities in Moscow, Tula, Penza and Riazan, and strangely enough felt no discomfort at the description of the delicacies served.

There is no saying how long this life might have lasted. Finally, however, it began to bore the Officials. They often thought of their cooks in St. Petersburg, and even shed a few tears in secret.

"I wonder how it looks in Podyacheskaya Street now, your Excellency," one of them said to the other.

"Oh, don't remind me of it, your Excellency. I am pining away with homesickness."

"It is very nice here. There is really no fault to be found with this place, but the lamb longs for its mother sheep. And it is a pity, too, for the beautiful uniforms."

"Yes, indeed, a uniform of the fourth class is no joke. The gold embroidery alone is enough to make one dizzy."

Now they began to importune the Muzhik to find some way of getting them back to Podyacheskaya Street, and strange to say, the Muzhik even knew where Podyacheskaya Street was. He had once drank beer and mead there, and as the saying goes, everything had run down his beard, alas, but nothing into his mouth. The Officials rejoiced and said: "We are Officials from Podyacheskaya Street."

"And I am one of those men—do you remember?—who sit on a scaffolding hung by ropes from the roofs and paint the outside walls. I am one of those who crawl about on the roofs like flies. That is what I am," replied the Muzhik.

The Muzhik now pondered long and heavily on how to give great pleasure to his Officials, who had been so gracious to him, the lazy-bones, and had not scorned his work. And he actually succeeded in constructing a ship. It was not really a ship, but still it was a vessel that would carry them across the ocean close to Podyacheskaya Street.

"Now, take care, you dog, that you don't drown us," said the Officials, when they saw the raft rising and falling on the waves.

"Don't be afraid. We muzhiks are used to this," said the Muzhik, making all the preparations for the journey. He gathered swan's-down and made a couch for his two Officials, then he crossed himself and rowed off from shore.

How frightened the Officials were on the way, how sea-sick they were during the storms, how they scolded the coarse Muzhik for his idleness, can neither be told nor described. The Muzhik, however, just kept rowing on and fed his Officials on herring. At last, they caught sight of dear old Mother Neva. Soon they were in the glorious Catherine Canal, and then, oh joy! they struck the grand Podyacheskaya Street. When the cooks saw their Officials so well-fed, round and so happy, they rejoiced immensely. The Officials drank coffee and rolls, then put on their uniforms and drove to the Pension Bureau. How much money they collected there is another thing that can neither be told nor described. Nor was the Muzhik forgotten. The Officials sent a glass of whiskey out to him and five kopeks.

Now, Muzhik, rejoice.

AFTER THE BALL

Leo Tolstoy (1828–1910)

Translated by F. D. Reeve

Cadet in the Caucasian war, artillery officer during the siege of Sevastopol by the joint British-French expeditionary force, **Leo Tolstoy** (1828–1910) became not only the greatest novelist of his time and a leading figure of the Russian literary scene, but also the strongest moral voice of his generation, an advocate of pacifist ideas and a staunch critic of the ruling monarchy and orthodox church. His life exemplifies perhaps the most impressive and profound arc of change among Russian authors.

His four-volume epic *War and peace*, about Napoleon's invasion of Russia in 1812, is the major challenge for Russian schoolchildren during their literature courses. He is widely discussed in the context of his relations with his wife and family, his views on the nature of power and the state; yet his greatest achievement, besides his masterly prose, is the unsurpassed clarity and greatness of his moral stand.

"So you contend a man cannot judge independently of what is good and what is bad, that it is all a matter of environment—that man is a creature of environment. But I contend it is all a matter of chance. And here is what I can say about myself. ..."

This is what our respected friend Ivan Vasilyevich said at the conclusion of a discussion we had been having about the necessity of changing the environment, the conditions in which men live, before there could be any talk about the improvement of the individual. As a matter of fact, no one had said it was impossible to judge independently of the good and the bad, but Ivan Vasilyevich had a habit of answering thoughts of his own stimulated by a discussion, and recounting experiences from his own life suggested by these thoughts. Often he became so absorbed in the story that he forgot his reason for telling it, especially since he always spoke with great fervor and sincerity. That is precisely what happened in the present case.

"At least I can make this claim with regard to myself. My own life has been molded in that way and no other—not by environment, but by something quite different."

"By what?" we asked.

"That is a long story. If you are to understand, I must tell it all to you."

"Then do."

Ivan Vasilyevich considered a moment and shook his head.

"Yes," he said, "my whole life was changed by a single night, or rather, a morning."

"Why? What happened?"

"It happened that I was deeply in love. I had often been in love before, but never so deeply. It took place a long time ago—her daughters are married women by this time. Her name was B., Varenka B. She was still strikingly beautiful at fifty, but in her youth, when she was eighteen, she was a dream: tall, slender, graceful, and majestic—yes, majestic. She always held herself as erect as if she were unable to bend, with her head tipped slightly backward; this, combined with her beauty and height, even though she was so thin as to be almost bony, gave her a queenly air that would have been intimidating if it had not been for her gay, winning smile, her mouth, her glorious shining eyes, and her whole captivating, youthful being."

"Ivan Vasilyevich certainly does lay it on thick!"

"However thick I were to lay it on, I could not make you understand what she was really like. But that is beside the point. The events I shall recount took place in the forties.

"I was then a student at a provincial university. I don't know whether it was a good or a bad thing, but in those days there were none of your study circles, none of your theorizing, at our university; we were just young and lived in the way of young folk—studying and having a good time. I was a very gay and energetic youth, and rich in the bargain. I owned a spirited carriage horse and used to take the girls out for drives (skating had not yet become the fad); I went on drinking parties with my fellow students (in those days we drank nothing but champagne; if we were out of money, we drank nothing, for we never drank vodka as they do now); but most of all I enjoyed parties and balls. I was a good dancer and not exactly ugly."

"Come, don't be modest," put in one of the listeners. "We've all seen your daguerreotype. You were a very handsome youth."

"Perhaps I was, but that isn't what I wanted to tell you. When my love was at its height I attended a ball given on the last day of Shrovetide by the Marshal of Nobility, a good-natured old man, wealthy, and fond of entertaining. His wife, as amiable as he was, stood beside him to receive us. She was wearing a velvet gown and a diamond tiara in her hair, and her aging neck and shoulders, plump and white, were exposed, as in the portraits of Empress Yelizaveta Petrovna. The ball was magnificent. The ballroom was charming, there were famous serf singers and musicians belonging to a certain landowner who was a lover of music, the food was abundant, the champagne flowed in rivers. Much as I loved champagne, I did not drink—I was drunk with love. But I danced till I dropped. I danced quadrilles, and waltzes, and polonaises, and it goes without saying that I danced as many of them as I could with Varenka. She was wearing a white dress with a pink sash, white kid gloves that did not quite reach her thin, pointed elbows, and white satin slippers. A wretched engineer named Anisimov cheated me out of a mazurka with her. I have never forgiven him for that. He invited her the moment she entered the ballroom, while I had been delayed by calling at the hairdresser's for my gloves. And so instead of dancing the mazurka with her, I danced it with a German girl I had once had a crush on. But I am afraid I was very neglectful of her that evening; I did not talk to her or look at her, for I had eyes for no one but a tall, slender girl in a white dress with a pink sash, with radiant, flushed, dimpled cheeks and soft, gentle eyes. I was not the only one; everyone looked at her and admired her, even the women, though she outshone them all. It was impossible not to admire her.

"Formally I was not her partner for the mazurka, but as a matter of fact I did dance it with her—at least most of it. Without the least embarrassment she danced straight to me down the length of the whole room, and when I leapt up to meet her without waiting for the invitation, she smiled to thank me for guessing what she wanted. When we had been led up to her and she had not guessed my nature, she had given a little shrug of her thin shoulders as she held out her hand to another, turning upon me a little smile of regret and consolation.

"When the figures of the mazurka changed into a waltz, I waltzed with her for a long time, and she smiled breathlessly and murmured '*encore*.' And I waltzed on and on with her, quite unaware of my own body, as if it were made of air."

"Unaware of it? I'm sure you must have been very much aware of it as you put your arm about her waist—aware of not only *your* body, but of hers as well," said one of the guests.

Ivan Vasilyevich suddenly turned crimson and almost shouted:

"That may apply to you, modern youth—all you think of is the body. In our day things were different. The more deeply I loved a girl, the more incorporeal she seemed to me. Today you are aware of legs, ankles, and other things; you disrobe the ladies with whom you are in love, but for me, as Alphonse Karr has said—and a very good writer he was—the object of my love was always clad in bronze raiment. Far from exposing, we tried to hide nakedness, as did the good son of Noah. But you cannot understand this."

"Pay no attention to him. Go on with your story," said another of the listeners.

"Well, I danced mostly with her and did not notice the passage of time. The musicians were so exhausted—you know how it always is at the end of a ball—that they kept playing the mazurka; mamas and papas were rising from the card tables in the drawing room in anticipation of supper; footmen were rushing about. It was going on for three o'clock. We had to take advantage of the few minutes left us. I invited her once more, and for the hundredth time we passed down the length of the room.

"'Will I be your partner for the quadrille after supper?' I asked her as I took her back to her place.

"'Oh, yes, if they do not take me home,' she said with a smile.

"'I won't let them,' I said.

"'Give me my fan,' she said.

"'I am sorry to give it back to you,' I said as I handed her her little white fan.

"'Here, then, to keep you from being sorry,' she said, plucking a feather out of the fan and giving it to me.

"I took the feather, unable to express my rapture and gratitude except with a glance. I was not only gay and content—I was happy, I was blissful, I was benevolent, I was no longer myself, but some creature not of this earth, who knew no evil and could do nothing but good.

"I tucked the feather in my glove and stood riveted to the spot, unable to move away from her.

"'Look, they are asking Papa to dance,' she said, indicating a tall, stately man who was her father, a colonel, in silver epaulettes, standing in the doorway with the hostess and some other women.

"'Varenka, come here,' called the hostess in the diamond tiara.

"Varenka made for the door and I followed her.

"'Do talk your father into dancing with you, *ma chère*. Please do, Pyotr Vladislavich,' said the hostess to the colonel.

"Varenka's father was a tall, handsome, stately, and well-preserved old man. He had a ruddy face with a white mustache curled *à la* Nicholas I, white side whiskers that met his mustache, hair combed forward over his temples, and the same smile as his daughter's lighting up his eyes and lips. He was very well built, with a broad chest swelling out in military style and with a modest display of decorations on it, with strong shoulders and long, fine legs. He was an officer of the old type with a military bearing of the Nicholas school.

"As we came up to the door the colonel was protesting that he had forgotten how to dance, but nevertheless he smiled, reached for his sword, drew it out of its scabbard, handed it to a young man eager to offer his services, and, drawing a suede glove on to his right hand ('Everything according to rule,' he said with a smile), he took his daughter's hand and struck a pose in a quarter turn, waiting for the proper measure to begin.

"As soon as the mazurka phrase was introduced he stamped one foot energetically and swung out with the other, and then his tall heavy figure sailed round the ballroom. He kept striking one foot against the other, now slowly and gracefully, now quickly and energetically. The willowy form of Varenka floated beside him. Imperceptibly and always just in time, she kept lengthening or shortening the step of the little white satin feet to fit his.

"All the guests stood watching the couple's every movement. The feeling I experienced was less admiration than a sort of deep ecstasy. I was especially touched by the sight of the colonel's boots. They were good calfskin boots, but they were heelless and had blunt toes instead of fashionable pointed ones. Obviously they had been made by the battalion cobbler. 'He wears ordinary boots instead of fashionable ones so that he can dress his beloved daughter and take her into society,' I thought to myself, and that is why I was particularly touched by his blunt-toed boots. Anyone could see he had once danced beautifully, but now he was heavy and his legs were not flexible enough to make all the quick and pretty turns he attempted. But he went twice round the room very well, and everybody applauded when he quickly spread out his feet, then snapped them together again and fell, albeit rather heavily, on one knee. And she smiled as she freed her caught skirt and floated gracefully round him. When he had struggled back to his feet, he touchingly put his hands over his daughter's ears and kissed her on the forehead, then led her over to me, who he thought had been her dancing partner. I told him I was not.

"'It doesn't matter; you dance with her,' he said, smiling warmly as he slipped his sword back into the scabbard.

"Just as the first drop poured out of a bottle brings a whole stream in its wake, so my love for Varenka released all the love in my soul. I embraced the whole world with love. I loved the hostess with her diamond tiara, and her husband, and her guests, and her footmen, and even the wretched Anisimov, who was clearly angry with me. As for her father with his blunt-toed boots and a smile so much like hers—I felt a rapturous affection for him.

"The mazurka came to an end and our hosts invited us to the supper table. But Colonel B. declined, saying that he must be up early in the morning. I was afraid he would take Varenka with him, but she remained behind with her mother.

"After supper I danced the promised quadrille with her. And while it had seemed that my happiness could not be greater, it went on growing and growing. We said nothing of love; I did not ask her, nor even myself, whether she loved me. It was sufficient that I loved her. The only thing I feared was that something might spoil my happiness.

"When I got home, undressed myself and thought of going to bed, I realized that sleep was out of the question. I held in my hand the feather from her fan and one of her gloves, which she had given to me when I put her and her mother into their carriage. As I gazed at these keepsakes I saw her again at the moment when, choosing one of two partners, she had guessed my nature and said in a sweet voice, 'Too proud? Is that it?' then joyfully held out her hand to me; or when, sipping champagne at the supper table, she had gazed at me over her glass with loving eyes. But I saw her best as she danced with her father, floating gracefully beside him, looking at all the admiring spectators with joy and pride for his sake as well as her own. And involuntarily the two of them became merged in my mind and enveloped in one deep and tender feeling.

"At that time my late brother and I lived alone. My brother had no use for society and never went to balls. He was getting ready to take his examinations for a master's degree and was leading the most exemplary of lives. He was asleep. I felt sorry for him as I looked at his head buried in the pillow, half covered by the blanket—sorry because he did not know and did not share the happiness which was mine. Petrusha, our serf valet, met me with a candle and would have helped me undress, but I dismissed him. I was touched by the sight of the man's sleepy face and disheveled hair. Trying to make no noise, I tiptoed to my own room and sat down on the bed. I was too happy, I could not sleep. I found it hot in the room, and so without taking off my uniform I went quietly out into the hall, put on my greatcoat, opened the entrance door, and went out.

"It had been almost five o'clock when I left the ball; about two hours had passed since, so that it was already light when I went out. It was typical Shrovetide weather—misty, with wet snow melting on the roads and water dripping from all the roofs. At that time the B.'s lived on the outskirts of town, at the edge of an open field with a girls' school at one end and a space used for promenading at the other. I went down our quiet little bystreet and came out upon the main street, where I met passersby and carters with timber loaded on sledges whose runners cut through the snow to the very pavement. And everything—the horses bobbing their heads rhythmically under their lacquered yokes, and the carters with bast matting on their shoulders plodding in their enormous boots through the slush beside their sledges, and the houses on either side of the street standing tall in the mist—everything seemed particularly dear and significant.

"When I reached the field where their house stood I saw something big and black at the promenade end of it, and I heard the sounds of a fife and drum. My heart had been singing all this time, and occasionally the strains of the mazurka had come to my mind. But this was different music, harsh and sinister.

"'What could it be?' I wondered, and made my way in the direction of the sounds, down the slippery wagon road that cut across the field. When I had gone about a hundred paces I began to distinguish in the mist a crowd of people. They were evidently soldiers. 'Drilling,' I thought, and continued on my way in the company of a blacksmith in an oil-stained apron and jacket who was carrying a large bundle. A double row of soldiers in black coats were standing facing each other motionless, their guns at their sides. Behind them stood a fifer and a drummerboy who kept playing that shrill tune over and over.

"'What are they doing?' I asked the blacksmith who was standing next to me.

"'Driving a Tatar down the line for having tried to run away,' replied the blacksmith brusquely, glaring at the far end of the double row.

"I looked in the same direction and saw something horrible coming toward me between the rows. It was a man bare to the waist and tied to a horizontal gun held at either end by a soldier. Beside him walked a tall officer in a greatcoat and forage cap whose figure seemed familiar to me. The prisoner, his whole body twitching, his feet squashing through the melting snow, advanced through the blows raining down on him from either side, now cringing back, at which the soldiers holding the gun would pull him forward, now lunging forward, at which the soldiers would jerk him back to keep him from falling. And next to him, walking firmly, never lagging behind, came the tall officer. It was her father, with his ruddy face and white mustache and side whiskers.

"At every blow the prisoner turned his pain-distorted face to the side from which the blow had come, as if in surprise, and kept repeating something over and over through bared white teeth. I could not make out the words until he came closer to me. He was sobbing rather than speaking them. 'Have mercy, brothers; have mercy, brothers.' But the brothers had no mercy, and when the procession was directly opposite me I saw one of the soldiers step resolutely forward and bring his lash down so hard on the Tatar's back that it whistled through the air. The Tatar fell forward, but the soldiers jerked him up, and then another blow fell from the opposite side, and again from this, and again from that. ... The colonel marched beside him, now glancing down at his feet, now up at the prisoner, drawing in deep breaths of air, blowing out his cheeks, slowly letting the air out between pursed lips. When the procession passed the spot where I was standing I got a glimpse of the prisoner's back through the row of soldiers. It was something indescribable: striped, wet, crimson, outlandish. I could not believe it was part of a human body.

"'God in heaven!' murmured the blacksmith standing next to me.

"The procession moved on. The blows kept falling from both sides on the cringing, floundering creature, the drum kept beating, the fife shrilling, and the tall, stately colonel walking firmly beside the prisoner. Suddenly the colonel stopped and went quickly over to one of the soldiers.

"'Missed? I'll show you!' I heard him say in a wrathful voice. 'Here, take this! And this!' And I saw his strong hand in its suede glove strike the small weak soldier in the face because the man's lash had not come down hard enough on the crimson back of the Tatar.

"'Bring fresh whips!' shouted the colonel. As he spoke he turned round and caught sight of me. Pretending not to recognize me, he gave a vicious, threatening scowl and turned quickly away. I felt so ashamed that I did not know where to turn my eyes, as if I had been caught doing something disgraceful. With hanging head I hurried home. All the way I kept hearing the rolling of the drum, the shrilling of the fife, the words, 'Have mercy, brothers,' and the wrathful, self-confident voice of the colonel shouting, 'Here, take this! And this!' And the aching of my heart was so intense as to be almost physical, making me feel nauseated, so that I had to stop several times. I felt I must throw up all the horror that this sight had filled me with. I do not remember how I reached home and got into bed, but the moment I began to doze off I saw and heard everything all over again. I jumped up.

"'There must be something he knows that I do not know,' I said to myself, thinking of the colonel. 'If I knew what he knows, I would understand, and what I saw would not cause me such anguish.' But rack my brains as I might, I could not understand what it was the colonel knew, and I could not fall asleep until evening, and then only after having gone to see a friend and drinking myself into forgetfulness.

"Do you suppose I concluded that what I had seen was bad?

Nothing of the sort. 'If what I saw was done with such assurance and was accepted by everyone as being necessary, it means they know something I do not know,' was the conclusion I came to, and I tried to find out what it was. But I never did. And not having found out, I could not enter military service, as it had been my intention to do, and not only military service, but any service at all, and so I turned out to be the good-for-nothing, that you see."

"We know very well what a 'good-for-nothing' you turned out to be," said one of the guests. "It would be more to the point to say how many people would have turned out to be good-for-nothing had it not been for you."

"Now that's a foolish thing to say," said Ivan Vasilyevich with real vexation.

"Well, and what about your love?" we asked.

"My love? From that day on my love languished. Whenever we went out walking and she smiled that pensive smile of hers, I could not help recalling the colonel out in the field, and this made me feel uncomfortable and unhappy, and I gradually stopped going to see her. My love petered out.

"So that is what sometimes happens, and it is incidents like this that change and give direction to a man's whole life. And you talk about environment," he said.

THE SMALL MISTAKE
Nikolai Leskov (1831–1895)
Translated by Richard Pevear
& Larissa Volokhonsky

Having started as an investigator in the criminal court, later as an auditor, **Nikolai Leskov** (1831–1895) then switched to investigative journalism and travelled widely in provincial Russia. As a writer, he used his previous professional experience and knowledge to create a vast gallery of folk types, having a special obsession with God's fools, freaks, and those with hidden talents. Some of Leskov's heroes, like the cross-eyed lefty from Tula, became symbols of Russian truth.

His novella *Lady Macbeth of the Mtsensk District* inspired the 1934 opera by Dmitri Shostakovich and the 1962 movie adaptation by the magnificent Polish director Andrzej Waida.

A Moscow Family Secret

I

One evening, at Christmas time, a sensible company sat talking about faith and lack of faith. The talk, however, had to do not with the loftier questions of deism and materialism, but with faith in people endowed with special powers of foresight and prophecy, and perhaps even their own sort of wonderworking. Among the listeners was a staid man from Moscow, who said the following:

'It's not easy, my good sirs, to judge about who lives with faith and who is without faith, for there are various applications of that in life: it may happen in such cases that our reason falls into error.'

And after that introduction he told us a curious story, which I shall try to convey in his own words:

* * *

My uncle and aunt were both equally devoted to the late wonderworker Ivan Yakovlevich.* Especially my aunt – she wouldn't undertake anything without asking him. First she would go to him in the madhouse and get his advice, and then she would ask him to pray for her undertaking. My uncle kept his own counsel and relied less on Ivan Yakovlevich, though he also confided in him occasionally and did not hinder his wife's bringing him gifts and offerings. They were not rich people, but quite well-to-do – they sold tea and sugar from a shop in their own house. They had no sons, but there were three daughters: Kapitolina Nikitishna, Katerina Nikitishna and Olga Nikitishna. They were all quite pretty and were good at housekeeping and all sorts of handwork. Kapitolina Nikitishna was married, only not to a merchant, but to a painter – though he was a very good man and earned money enough: he took profitable commissions for decorating churches. One unpleasant thing for the whole family was that, while he worked on godly things, he was also versed in some sort of freethinking from Kurganov's *Pismovnik*.† He liked to talk about Chaos, about Ovid, about Prometheus, and was fond of comparing fables with sacred history. If not for that, everything would have been fine. Another thing was that they had no children, and my uncle and aunt were very upset about it. They had seen only their first daughter married, and suddenly she remained childless for three years. Owing to that, suitors started avoiding the other sisters.

My aunt asked Ivan Yakovlevich how it happened that her daughter did not have children: 'They're both young and handsome,' she said, 'yet there are no children?'

Ivan Yakovlevich began to mutter:

'There's a heaven of heavens, a heaven of heavens.'

His women prompters translated for my aunt: 'The dear father says

---

* Ivan Yakovlevich Koreisha (1780–1861) was in inmate of a Moscow psychiatric clinic for over forty years. His bizarre verbosity earned him the reputation of a seer, and people of all classes came to have him 'prophesy' for them. Koreisha was Dostoevsky's model for the holy fool Semyon Yakovlevich in *Demons* (1872).
† Nikolai Gavrilovich Kurganov (1726–1796), mathematician, teacher and member of the St Petersburg Academy, published his *Pismovnik*, a collection of writings for self-education in Russian language and literature, in 1793.

to tell your son-in-law to pray to God, for it must be that he's of little faith.'

My aunt simply gasped: 'Everything's revealed to him,' she said. And she started badgering the painter to go to confession; but to him it was all horsefeathers! He treated it all very lightly ... even ate meat on fast days ... and besides that, they heard indirectly, he supposedly ate worms and oysters. Yet they all lived in the same house and were often distressed that in their merchant family there was such a man of no faith.

II

So my aunt went to Ivan Yakovlevich to ask him to pray that the servant of God Kapitolina's womb be opened and that the servant of God Lary (that was the painter's name) be enlightened by faith.

My uncle and aunt asked it together.

Ivan Yakovlevich began to babble something that couldn't be understood at all, and the attendant women sitting around him explained:

'He's not very clear today,' they said, 'but tell us what you're asking, and we'll give him a little note tomorrow.'

My aunt began to tell them, and they wrote down: 'Servant of God Kapitolina to have womb opened, and servant of God Lary to have faith increased.'

The old folk left this petitionary little note and went home stepping lightly.

At home they said nothing to anyone except Kapochka alone, and then only so that she shouldn't tell her husband, the faithless painter, but simply live with him as tenderly and harmoniously as possible, and watch to see if he would get closer to faith in Ivan Yakovlevich. But he was a terrible man for cursing and as full of little sayings as a clown from Presnya.[*] Everything was jokes and quips with him. He'd come to his father-in-law of an evening: 'Let's go and read the fifty-two-page prayer book,' he'd say, meaning play cards ... Or he'd sit down and say: 'On condition that we play till the first swoon.'

---

[*] In the late eighteenth to nineteenth century, the Presnya district of Moscow was a park and picnic area with ponds and entertainments.

My aunt simply couldn't listen to such words. My uncle said to him, 'Don't upset her so: she loves you and has made a promise for you.' He started laughing and said to his mother-in-law:

'Why do you make unwitting promises? Or don't you know that because of such a promise John the Baptist had his head cut off?[*] Watch out, there may be some unexpected misfortune in our house.'

This frightened his mother-in-law still more, and every day, in her anxiety, she went running to the madhouse. There they calmed her down – said things were going well: the dear father read their note each day, and what was now written there would soon come true.

And suddenly it did come true, but how it came true I'm reluctant to say.

III

My aunt's second daughter, Katechka, comes to her, and falls right at her feet, and sobs, and weeps bitterly.

My aunt asks:

'What's wrong – has someone offended you?'

The girl answers through her tears:

'Dearest mama, I myself don't know what it is or why … it's the first and last time it's happened … Only conceal my sin from papa.'

My aunt looked at her, poked her finger right into her belly, and said:

'Is it here?'

Katechka replies:

'Yes, mama … how did you guess … I myself don't know why …'

My aunt only gasped and clasped her hands.

'My child,' she says, 'don't even try to find out: it may be that I'm guilty of a mistake, I'll go at once and find out,' and she flew off at once in a cab to Ivan Yakovlevich.

'Show me the note,' she says, 'with our request that the dear father ask the fruit of the womb for the servant of God: how is it written?'

---

[*] The tetrarch Herod Antipas was so taken with his stepdaughter Salomé's dancing that he promised to give her whatever she asked for. At the prompting of her mother, Herodias, she asked for John the Baptist's head.

The hangers-on found it on the windowsill and handed it to her.

My aunt looked and nearly went out of her mind. What do you think? It all actually came about through a mistaken prayer, because instead of the servant of God Kapitolina, who was married, there was written the servant of God Katerina, who was still unmarried, a maiden.

The women say:

'Just imagine, what a sin! The names are very similar ... but never mind, it *can be set right*.'

But my aunt thought: 'No, nonsense, you can't set it right now: Katya's been prayed for,' and she tore the note into little pieces.

IV

The main thing was their fear of telling my uncle. He was the sort of man who was hard to calm down once he got going. Besides, he loved Katya least of all, and his favourite daughter was the youngest, Olenka – it was to her he had promised the most.

My aunt thought and thought and saw that her mind alone could not think over this calamity – she invited her painter son-in-law to a council and revealed everything to him in detail, and then begged:

'Though you have no faith,' she says, 'there may be some feeling in you – please take pity on Katya, help me to conceal her maidenly sin.'

The painter suddenly scowled and said sternly:

'Excuse me, please, but first of all, though you're my wife's mother, I resent being considered a man of no faith, and, second of all, I don't understand what can be counted as Katya's sin here, if Ivan Yakovlevich has been pleading so long for her. I have all a brother's feelings for Katechka, and I'll stand up for her, because she's not to blame for anything here.'

My aunt bit her fingers and wept, saying:

'Well ... how not for anything?'

'Of course, not for anything. It's your wonderworker who made a mess of it, and he's got to answer for it.'

'How can he answer for it? He's a righteous man.'

'Well, if he's righteous, then keep quiet. Send me Katya with three bottles of champagne.'

My aunt asked him to repeat himself:

'What's that?'

And again he answers:

'With three bottles of champagne – one right now to me in my rooms, and two later, I'll tell you where, but keep them ready here at home and on ice.'

My aunt looked at him and only shook her head.

'God help you,' she said. 'I thought you only had no faith, though you paint holy images, but it turns out you have no feelings at all ... That's why I cannot venerate your icons.'

And he replied:

'No, leave off about faith: it seems it's you who have doubts and keep thinking about nature, as if Katya had her own reasons here, but I firmly believe that Ivan Yakovlevich alone is the cause of it all; and you'll see my feelings when you send Katya to my studio with champagne.'

V

My aunt thought and thought, and did send the wine to the painter with Katechka herself. She came in with the tray, all in tears, but he jumped up, seized her by the arms and wept himself.

'My little dove,' he said, 'I grieve at what's happened to you, but there's no time for nodding over it – quickly let me in on all your secrets.'

The girl confided her mischief to him, and he locked her in his studio with a key.

My aunt met her son-in-law with teary eyes and said nothing. But he embraced her and kissed her and said:

'Now, don't be afraid, don't weep. Maybe God will help.'

'Tell me,' my aunt whispered, 'who's to blame for it all?'

But the painter tenderly shook his finger at her and said:

'That's not nice: you yourself constantly reproach me with having no faith, and now, when your faith is being tested, I see you haven't any faith at all. Isn't it clear to you that there's no one to blame, and the wonderworker simply made a little mistake?'

'But where is my poor Katechka?'

'I charmed her with a fearsome painter's charm and – poof! – she disappeared.'

And he showed his mother-in-law the key.

My aunt realised that he had hidden the girl from her father's first wrath, and she embraced him.

She whispered:

'Forgive me – there are tender feelings in you.'

VI

My uncle came, had his tea as usual, and said:

'Well, shall we read the fifty-two-page prayer book?'

They sat down. And the family closed all the doors around them and went about on tiptoe. My aunt now moved away from the door, then went up to it again – listening and crossing herself.

Finally, something clanked in there ... She ran off and hid.

'He's revealed it,' she says, 'he's revealed the secret! Now there'll be a hellish performance.'

And just so: all at once the door opened, and my uncle cried out:

'My overcoat and my big stick!'

The painter holds him back by the arm and says:

'What is it? Where are you going?'

My uncle says:

'I'm going to the madhouse to give the wonderworker a thrashing!'

My aunt moaned behind the other door.

'Quick,' she says, 'run to the madhouse, have them hide our dear Ivan Yakovlevich!'

And indeed my uncle would have thrashed him for certain, but his painter son-in-law kept him from it by frightening him with his own faith.

VII

The son-in-law started reminding his father-in-law that he had one more daughter.

'Never mind,' my uncle says, 'she'll have her portion, but I want to thrash Koreisha. Let them take me to court afterwards.'

'But I'm not frightening you with court,' says the painter. 'Look at what harm Ivan Yakovlevich can do Olga. No, it's terrible, what you're risking!'

My uncle stopped and pondered:

'Well,' he says, 'what harm can he do?'

'Exactly the same harm he's done to Katechka.'

My uncle glanced up and replied:

'Stop pouring out drivel! As if he could do that!'

The painter replies:

'Well, if, as I see, you're an unbeliever, do as you know best, only don't grieve afterwards and blame the poor girls.'

My uncle stopped at that. And his son-in-law dragged him back into the room and began persuading him.

'In my opinion,' he says, 'it's better to leave the wonderworker out of it and try to set this matter straight by domestic means.'

The old man agreed, only he did not know how to set it straight himself, but his son-in-law helped him here as well. He says:

'Good thoughts must be sought not in wrath, but in joy.'

'What joy can there be, brother, in a case like this?'

'Here's what,' says the painter. 'I've got two bottles of fizzy, and until you drink them with me, I won't say a single word to you. Agree to it. You know my character.'

The old man looked at him and said:

'Go on, go on. What next?'

But all the same he agreed.

VIII

The painter marched off briskly and came back, followed by his assistant, a young artist, with a tray bearing two bottles and glasses.

As soon as they came in, the son-in-law locked the door behind him and put the key in his pocket. My uncle looked and understood everything, and the son-in-law nodded towards the assistant – the lad stood there in humble petition.

'I'm to blame – forgive me and give us your blessing.'

My uncle asks his son-in-law:

'Can I thrash him?'

The son-in-law says:

'You can, but you needn't.'

'Well, then at least let him kneel before me.'

The son-in-law whispered:

'Well, kneel before the father for the sake of the girl you love.'

The lad knelt.

The old man began to weep.

'Do you love her very much?' he asked.

'I do.'

'Well, kiss me.'

So Ivan Yakovlevich's little mistake was covered up. And it all remained safely hidden, and suitors began to pursue the youngest sister, because they saw that the girls were trustworthy.

THE BEARS
Vsevolod Garshin (1855–1888)
Translated by Rowland Smith

Considered to be Chekhov's precursor, **Vsevolod Garshin** (1855–1888), man of letters, Russian-Turkish war volunteer, wounded veteran, promoted to the rank of warrant officer for his bravery, was the great explorer of the novella. His novellas' plots were formed and twisted by the social conflicts and extreme paradoxes of contemporary society, feelings of political impotence and the guilt of the aristocracy. These emotions, formed by a turbulent family life (his mother left home with Garshin's mentor and followed him into exile) sealed Garshin's fate as a writer and as a human being: fighting social evils, he broke down and committed suicide at the age of 33 (two of his elder brothers also took their own lives).

In the Steppe the town of Bielsk nestles on the River Rokhla at a point where it makes several sharp curves linked up by branch streams, the whole forming a network which, if looked at on a clear summer day from the lofty right bank of the channel through which the river runs here, resembles a gigantic bow of blue ribbon. At this point the bank rises some three hundred and fifty feet sheer above the level of the river as if it had been cut by a huge knife. So steep is it that to clamber from the water's edge to the top, where the limitless Steppe commences, is possible only by taking hold of the bushes of spindlewood, birch, and hazel thickly covering the face of the slope. From this summit a clear view of forty versts opens out on every side. On the right to the south and on the left to the north stretch the gradients of the right bank of the Rokhla, descending abruptly into valleys such as the one from above which we are gazing. Some of the ridges show up white with their chalk tops and naked sides destitute of soil. Others are covered for the most part with short and withered grass. In front to the east stretches the illimitable undulating

Steppe, yellow with haystacks, over which some useless weed is growing thickly, or verdant with growing crops, here showing the dark purple-black of newly upturned fallow, there the silvery grey of feather-grass. Viewed from where we are standing, the Steppe appears level, and only the accustomed eye can trace on it the scarcely discernible lines of ridges, of invisible ravines and gullies. Here and there an old half-sunken tumulus meets the view, its sides scarified by the plough, and no longer possessed of its stone slab, now perhaps adorning the courtyard of the Kharkoff University, or perhaps taken away by some peasant, and now forming part of the wall of his cattle-yard.

Below, the winding river runs from north to south, alternately receding from its high bank into the Steppe or flowing immediately under its ledge, fringed at intervals with clusters of pine-trees and about the town by gardens and grazing-plots. At some distance from the bank to the side of the Steppe a strip of quicksand runs almost the entire length of the river, barely supporting the red and black shoots of small shrubs growing on it, and its thick carpet of fragrant lilac-coloured charbrets. Amongst these sands, two versts from the town, lies the cemetery, resembling from a distance a little oasis with the small wooden bell-tower of the cemetery chapel rising from its centre. The town itself presents no outstanding features, and is much like all district towns, apart from the astonishing cleanliness of its streets, due not so much to a solicitous municipal administration as to the sandy soil on which the town is built, which absorbs any moisture an incensed heaven may pour forth, and thereby places the town swine in great difficulties, compelling them to seek suitable accommodation for themselves at least two versts distance from the town in the dirty banks of the river.

In September of 1857 the town of Bielsk was in a state of unwonted excitement. The usual routine of life was disturbed. Everywhere, whether in the Club, streets, or on the benches outside the gateway entrances of courtyards, indoors and outdoors, animated conversation was being carried on. It might have been supposed that the Zemstvo elections, which were taking place at this time, were the cause of disturbance; but there had been previous Zemstvo elections, and with all their scandals they had never produced any special impression on the natives of Bielsk. On these occasions, if meeting in the street, the citizens would merely exchange brief remarks with each other.

"Have you been?" one would ask, indicating by a glance the building in which the Zemstvo offices were housed.

"Yes," would reply the other, with a gesture of his hand; and, accustomed to this mode of expression of thoughts, the interrogator would understand and simply add:

"Who?"

"Ivan Petrovich."

"Whom?"

"Ivan Parfenovich."

Then they would both smile and part.

But now it was quite different. The town was in an uproar just as at fair-time. Crowds of urchins kept running backwards and forwards in the direction of the town common grazing-ground. Respectable, sober individuals in loose summer suits of alpaca silk were also wending their way thither, and the damsels of the town, with parasols and various coloured hoop-petticoats (they wore them in those days), occupying so much of the wide street that young Rogacheff, the merchant, driving a dapple grey, was obliged to draw in almost against the walls of the houses. The ladies were accompanied by the local cavaliers in grey overcoats with black velvet collars, carrying walking-canes and wearing straw hats or caps with cockades. Among these beaux were, of course, the brothers Isotoff, the leaders of all public gaieties, who knew how during a quadrille to call out *"Grand Rond!"* and *"Au rebours!"*—that is, when they were not running through the town imparting the latest news to their lady acquaintances.

"They have arrived from the Valuinsk District, and occupy half the ground of the Common right up to the river," said Leonid, the elder brother.

"I regarded the view from the summit of the eminence," added Constantine, the younger brother, who delighted in expressing himself in the most flowery language—"an entrancing picture!"

"Eminence" was the name he gave to the hill from which a view of the town and its vicinity could be obtained.

"Ah, what a good idea! Listen! I have a splendid idea. Let us order the *lineika*, and drive out to the eminence. It will be like a picnic, and we will watch from there."

This proposal by the first lady of Bielsk, the wife of the brother of the Treasurer (almost the whole town called her husband, Paul Ivanovich, the brother of the Treasurer), who had arrived eight years ago from Petersburg, and was therefore the authority on fashions and good tone, met with general approval. The fat old bay horse was harnessed into the lineika, which is only met with in provincial capitals, and consists of long boards with two long seats so placed that the occupants, usually twelve in all, sit in two rows of six or seven a side and back to back. The party, which consisted of some dozen persons, seated themselves in the lineika, and started off through the town, overtaking mobs of boys, strings of damsels, and crowds of every description of public, all making their way to the Common. The lineika, having negotiated the sandy streets of the town, crossed the bridge and made for the steep right bank of the river. The bay, with dogged pace, wrinkling the sleek folds of his glossy haunches, clambered up the long slope, and in half an hour the picnickers were seated on the edge of the three hundred feet high ridge, with its overgrowth of bushes, gazing at the view with which we are already acquainted. Below, under their feet, immediately under this wall, the river was quietly flowing along its course, and behind it opened out the common on which the general attention was concentrated.

In the variety of colouring it resembled a huge patchwork carpet. The dull white of tents, numberless vehicles, and a motley crowd were all visible. Dark figures of men in kaftans and dirty grey shirts intermingled with the bright yellow and scarlet dresses of the women. A dense crowd surrounded the gipsy encampment which had been formed. It was a magnificent day, not too hot, and absolutely still. Above the roar of a multitudinous crowd could be heard the ring of sledgehammers on iron, the neighing of horses, and the roar of scores of tame bears—the mainstay of the gipsies who had brought them hither out of the neighbouring Districts.

Olga Pavlona gazed at this kaleidoscope through binoculars, and went into raptures.

"How interesting it all is! What a big one! Look, Leonid, what a huge bear there on the right! And the young gipsy alongside it—a perfect Adonis!"

She handed the glasses to the young man, who through them saw the figure of a well-built and exceedingly dirty youth who was standing near and petting a beast which kept shuffling about and changing from one leg on to another.

"Allow me to look," said a stout, clean-shaven man in a duck suit and straw hat. For some time he looked attentively through the glasses, and then, turning to Olga Pavlona, said with a deep sigh: "Yes, Olga Pavlona, an Adonis. But this Adonis will turn out a first-class horse-thief."

Olga Pavlona uttered an exclamation of impatience.

"Why," said she, "do you always try to turn everything poetical into prose? Why a horse-thief? I will not believe it! He looks so good!"

"That may be, but how is he going to support his beautiful body without that bear? Tomorrow they are slaughtering all these bears, and one-half of all the gipsies in this encampment will be without a living."

"They can work as blacksmiths and shoeing-smiths, tell fortunes…"

"Tell fortunes! Ilia, the horse-doctor, came to me yesterday. You go and talk with him. 'Thomas Thomasovich,' he said, 'those greys of yours are very good, only beware of our brother.' 'What!' I said; 'surely you will not steal them?' He smiled, the blackguard! Tell fortunes! Those are the sort of fortunes he is telling!"

Out of the lineika they took a large basket, from which appeared eatables and drinks, and the company began to seat themselves in groups, chatting merrily the while, and scarcely paying any attention to the picture displayed at their feet. The sun had set, and the gigantic shadow of the height quickly spread to the Common, town, and Steppe. Outlines softened, and, as happens in the South, day was quickly replaced by night. Lights began to flicker in the town, and fires were lighted in the camp, which showed up redly through the mist rising from the slumbering river below, the distant bends of which glistened in the cold moonlight. And above the river, on the height itself, Constantine and Leonid kept up a ceaseless flow of ridiculous stories, at which Olga Pavlona occasionally smiled with condescension, and the younger ladies of the party giggled or even laughed aloud. Candles protected by glass shades were lighted, and the coachman with the maid prepared the samovar in the bushes near by—a process apparently necessitating occasional, but at the same time very cautious, squeaks on the part of the maid. Portly Thomas Thomasovich alone remained silent, and finally interrupted Leonid at the most interesting point of one of his anecdotes.

"When, then, have they finally decided to have this slaughter of bears?" said he.

"Wednesday morning," said the brothers Isotoff simultaneously.

The unhappy gipsies had journeyed hither from four Districts of the Government with all their household effects, horses, bears, etc. More than a hundred of these awkward beasts, ranging from tiny cubs to huge "old men" whose coats had become grey or whitish from age, had collected on the town common. The gipsies awaited the fatal day with terror. Those who had been the first to arrive had already been encamped here more than a fortnight. The Authorities were waiting until all should arrive, so that the business of killing the bears might be carried out in one day and finished with once and for all. The gipsies had been given five years' grace from the publication of the Order prohibiting performing bears, and now this period had expired. They were now to appear at specified places and themselves destroy their supporters.

They had completed their last round through the villages with the familiar goat and big drum—the invariable companions of the bears. For the last time, having espied them afar off coming down from the Steppe into the steep gully and bank of the river, the usual site of Little Russian villages, a crowd of boys and girls had run a verst to meet them, returning triumphantly with them, a confused rabble, back to the village, where the fun of the fair had already commenced. And what fun it was! What festivities took place! They would halt by the inn or some bigger house, or if it was an estate before the proprietor's house, and begin their performances, cures, trade, barter, fortunetelling, horseshoeing, and repairs of wagons, continuing right throughout the long summer day until the evening, when the gipsies would leave the village for the cattle-grazing ground, and, setting up their tents or simply stretching the canvas over the shafts of the wagons, would light their fires and prepare supper, whilst far into the night an inquisitive crowd would stand around the encampment.

"Come along now; it is time to go home," my father would say to me, a little boy, but no less unwilling to leave, would wait in response to my entreaties for "just a little longer—a little longer." Together we would sit in the cart, the old horse Vasia, with his head turned towards the fires and ears pricked towards the bears, standing quietly, save for an occasional snort. The fires of the camp cast dancing red lights and vague trembling shadows. A light mist was rising from the ravine to the side of us, whilst behind the camp stretched the Steppe. The dark wings of a windmill stood out as if painted against the sky, and behind it was limitless mysterious space enfolded in a silvery twilight. Amidst the din of the encampment could be heard those subdued sounds so characteristic of the Steppe at night. First from some distant pond would come the solemn reverberating chorus of frogs, then the regular but hurried chirrup of the grasshopper and the cry of the quail. Again, faint, indistinguishable harmonious sounds would be wafted to our ears—mayhap the sound of some distant bell borne on the breeze, or the voice of Nature, whose tongue we do not understand.

But in the encampment all is becoming quiet. Gradually fires are extinguished. The bears under the carts to which they are tethered growl deeply from time to time, as with a jingling of their chains they restlessly change their position. Their owners, too, are settling down to sleep. One of them in an uncultivated tenor is singing a strange song in his native language, unlike the songs of Moscow restaurant gipsies and operatic singers—a song characteristic, wild, mournful, strange to the ear. No one knows when it was composed, what Steppe, forest or mountain gave it birth. It has remained a living testimony of a land forgotten even by those who sing it now under the burning stars of a foreign sky and in alien Steppes.

"Come along," says my father. Vasia bravely starts, and the droshky wends its way along the winding road below into the valley. A thin dust rises half-heartedly from under the wheels, and then, as if also overcome with sleep, falls back on to the dewy grass.

"Papa, does anyone know gipsy?"

"The gipsies themselves, of course, do, but I have never met others who could speak to them."

"I should like to learn it. I should like to know what he was singing about. Papa, are they heathens? Perhaps he was singing about his gods, how they lived and fought."

We arrive home, and as I lie under the coverlet my imagination still works and forms strange fancies in the little head already on the pillow.

Now, bears no longer wander through the villages, and even the gipsies themselves seldom wander. The greater number of them live where they have been told to live, and only occasionally pay tribute to their century-old instincts, select some common, stretch their smoky canvas, and live whole families together, busy with the shoeing of horses, horsecuring, and dealing. I have even seen how tents have given place to hastily erected wooden shelters. This was in the provincial capital not far from the hospital and the fairground, on a piece of land as yet unbuilt on and running alongside the main road. On this plot the gipsies had built quite a little town. Only the swarthy faces, quick-glancing eyes, curly hair, and dirty clothes of the men, with the equally dirty, gaudy rags of the women and the naked bronzed children, reminded me of the former picture of a wandering gipsy encampment. The clang of iron was coming from these shelters, and I looked into one of them. An old man was making horseshoes. I looked at his work, and saw that this man was no longer a gipsy blacksmith, but an ordinary workman who had taken some order, and was working as quickly as possible to finish it so as to take up a new job. He was forging shoe after shoe, throwing them one after another into a heap in a corner of the shanty. He was working with a gloomy concentrated air, and at a great rate. This was in the daytime. Going past late that night, I went up to the shelter, and saw the old man still at the same work. It was a factory. And it was strange to see a gipsy encampment almost in the heart of the town situated between the Zemstvo hospital, the bazaar, and some kind of enclosed square where soldiers were being drilled, and from which came the sound of sharp orders given by the instructors. It was alongside a road from which the wind was raising clouds of dust, smothering with it the boarded shelters and the fires with their pots, in which the womenkind, their heads adorned with gaudy handkerchiefs, were boiling some sort of gruel.

They had gone through the villages giving their shows for the last time. For the last time the bears had displayed their histrionic talents, had danced, wrestled, showed how little boys steal the peas, imitated the mincing step of the young girl and the waddling gait of the old woman. For the last time they had received their reward in the form of a tumbler of vodka, which the bear, standing on its hind-legs, would seize with both front paws, place against his shaggy muzzle, and, throwing his head back, pour the contents down his throat, after which he would lick his jaws and express his satisfaction in a quiet rumble and strange deep sighs. For the last time old men and women were coming to the gipsies to be cured of their ailments by the true and tried process of lying on the ground under a bear, which would place his belly on the patient, spread himself out on all fours, and remain in this position until the gipsies considered the sëance had lasted long enough. For the last time they had entered huts, when, if the bear voluntarily entered, he was led into the front portion of the dwelling, and all sat there and rejoiced at his graciousness as a good omen, but if, in spite of all entreaties and caresses he refused to cross the threshold, the occupants would be sorrowful, and their neighbours would shake their heads. The greater part of the gipsies had come from the Western Districts, so that they were obliged to descend into Bielsk by a long hill nearly two versts long, and, seeing from a distance the site of their coming misfortune—this little town with its thatched and iron roofs and two or three bell-towers—the women commenced to wail, the children to cry, and the bears from sympathy, or perhaps—who knows?—understanding from their masters the bitter fate in store for them, to roar in such a way that carts which met them turned aside from the road so that the bullocks and horses should not be frightened, whilst the dogs with yelps of alarm crawled under the carts, taking refuge behind the grease and tar-pots which the peasants of these parts fasten under the body of their carts.

Several of the old men amongst the gipsies had collected at the entrance gates of the house in which the *ispravnik* of Bielsk resided. They had decked themselves out so as to present a respectable appearance before the Authorities. All wore black or dark blue under-tunics, and belts brocaded with silver and black enamel-work, silk shirts having a narrow piping of gold lace round the collar, plush trousers, high boots which in some cases were embroidered and slashed with a pattern, and the majority wore astrachan caps. This dress was worn only on the most solemn occasions.

"Is he asleep?" inquired a tall, upright gipsy, tanned from age, of a *gorodovoi* who came out of the courtyard—one of the eleven gorodovois entrusted with the preservation of law and order in the town of Bielsk.

"He is getting up—is dressing. He will send for you soon," replied the gorodovoi.

The old men, who up till now had been sitting or standing motionless, began to move and to speak in low tones amongst themselves. The senior of them drew something out of the pocket of his baggy trousers; the remainder all collected around him and looked at the object which he held in his hands.

"Nothing will come of it," he said at last. "What, indeed, can he do? It is not his doing. It is the Minister at Petersburg who has given the order. They are killing the bears everywhere."

"We will try, Ivan. Perhaps he can do something," said another of the old men.

"Of course we can try," replied Ivan dismally. "Only he will take our money and will not help in any way."

The ispravnik sent for them. They went in a crowd into the entrance-hall, and when he came out to them—a whiskered man in an unbuttoned police uniform, which exposed a red silk shirt—the old men fell at his feet. They implored his assistance, offered him money, and many of them wept.

"Your Worship," said Ivan, "will himself judge what is to happen to us. What will become of us? We had bears; we lived quietly, insulted no one. Amongst us are young men who engage in evil work, but are there not horse-thieves amongst the Russians? No one was insulted by our beasts, Your Worship; they amused all. Now what is going to happen to us, Your Worship? We must go into the world, and if not thieves, must be vagabonds. Our fathers, our grandfathers, Your Worship, led bears around. We do not know how to plough the land; we are all blacksmiths. It has been hard work travelling the wide world over as blacksmiths in search of work, and now work will not come of itself to us. Our young men will become horse-thieves—nothing else to do, Your Worship. Before God I speak frankly, concealing nothing.

A great evil has been done us and good people by taking away our bears from us. Perhaps you will help us. God will reward you for it. Kind sir, help us!"

The old man fell on his knees and prostrated himself at the feet of the ispravnik. The others followed suit. The Major stood with a gloomy expression on his face, smoothing his long moustaches with one hand and the other thrust into the pocket of his dark blue overalls.

The old man pulled out a bulging pocketbook and offered it to him.

"I will not take it," said the ispravnik surlily. "I can do nothing."

"But if you will take it, Your Worship," said the crowd, "perhaps something—if you would write."

"I will not take it," repeated the ispravnik more loudly than before. "On no account. It is useless. It is the law. You were given five years' grace. What can be done?" And he made a motion with his hands. The old men remained silent. The ispravnik continued: "I know what a misfortune this is for all of you—and to us. Now we shall have to look out for our horses, but what can I do? You, old man, put away your money. I will not take it. If I have to give you trouble through your children over horses do not be angry with me, but to take money for nothing is not one of my customs. Put it away—put it away, old man; your money will be useful to you."

"Your Worship," said Ivan, still holding the pocketbook in his hands, "be so good as to give the order for the slaughter. Please tomorrow"—the old man's voice trembled—"please tomorrow finish it. We are tired, worn out. Two weeks ago I came here with mine. We have lived quite—"

"There is still one lot to come in, old man," broke in the ispravnik. "We must wait. It must be done all at one time, and finished. The whole town has gone off its head over you all."

"They have arrived already, Your Worship. As we came to Your Excellency they were coming down the hill. Do us this kindness, sir. Do not torment us!"

"Well, if they have arrived, then tomorrow at ten o'clock I will come to you. Have you guns?"

"We have guns, but not all of us."

"All right, I will tell the Colonel to lend you some rifles. God be with you! I am sorry, very sorry for you all!"

The old men turned towards the door, but the ispravnik called them back.

"Wait a moment," he said. "I will tell you something. Go to the chemist's shop next to the church. Go and say I sent you. The chemist will buy all the bears' fat from you; he will make it into pomade. Perhaps he will buy the skins, too. He will give you a good price. He will not lose by it."

The gipsies thanked him, and in a crowd trooped off to the chemist's shop. Their hearts were torn; almost without bargaining they sold the mortal remains of their old friends. Thomas Thomasovich bought all the fat at fourteen kopecks a pood, and promised to speak about the skins later on. The young merchant, Rogacheff, who happened to be there, bought all the bear-hams at five kopecks a pound, hoping to make a good deal out of the transaction.

In the evening of that day the brothers Isotoff rushed breathless to the house of the brother of the Treasurer.

"Olga Pavlona! Olga Pavlona! they have settled it for tomorrow! All have arrived! The Colonel has already given out the rifles!" they shouted, vying against each other in their haste to tell the news. "Thomas Thomasovich has bought all the fat at fourteen kopecks a pood, and Rogacheff the hams, and—"

"Stop, stop, Leonid!" interrupted Olga Pavlona. "Why has Thomas Thomasovich bought the fat?"

"For ointment, pomade. It is a splendid thing for making the hair grow." And forthwith Constantine related an interesting anecdote of how a certain bald gentleman, through rubbing his head with bears' fat, even grew hair on his hands.

'And he was forced to shave them every two days," added Leonid; and then the two brothers burst out laughing.

Olga Pavlona smiled and pondered over the news. She had long worn a chignon, and this information about bears' grease interested her very much. When that same evening Thomas Thomasovich came round to play cards with her husband and the Treasurer, she cleverly succeeded in making him promise to send her some bears' ointment.

"Of course—of course, Olga Pavlona," he had said, "and it shall be scented. Which do you prefer—patchouli or ylang-ylang?"

* * *

The day broke cloudy and cold—a genuine September day—with an occasional slight drizzle, but this notwithstanding, numbers of both sexes and of all ages went to the Common to see the interesting spectacle. The town was almost deserted. All the vehicles the town boasted of—one carriage, several phaetons, droshkies, and lineikas—were engaged in taking out the curious. They left them at the encampment, and returned for fresh loads. By ten o'clock all were already out there.

The gipsies had lost all hopes. There was not much noise in the camp. The women were hiding in the tents with the little ones, so as not to see the massacre, and only occasionally a despairing wail was wrung from one or another of them. The men were feverishly making the last preparations. They had dragged the wagons to the edge of the camping-ground, and had tied the bears to them.

The ispravnik, with Thomas Thomasovich, passed along the rows of condemned. The bears themselves were not altogether calm. The unusual surroundings, the strange preparations, the enormous crowd, the large number of bears collected together—all this had excited them, and they tugged or gnawed at their chains, uttering occasional low growls. Old Ivan stood near his enormous bear crooked with age. His son, an elderly gipsy whose black hair was already streaked with silvery grey, and his grandson—that same Adonis whom Olga Pavlona had noticed—with ghastly faces and burning eyes were hastily tying up the bear.

The ispravnik came up level with the trio.

"Well, old man," said he, "tell them to commence."

A wave of excited expectation passed over the crowd of onlookers, conversation redoubled, but soon after all became quiet, and amidst a profound silence was heard a low but authoritative voice. Old Ivan was speaking.

"Allow me, sir, to speak." Then, turning to his fellow-gipsies, he continued: "Comrades, I beg you to let me be the first to finish. I am older than any of you. Next year I shall have seen ninety years. I have led bears from my infancy, and in the whole camp there is no bear older than mine."

He lowered his grey curly head on to his chest, shaking it sorrowfully from side to side, and wiped his eyes with his fist. Then he drew himself up, raised his head, and continued in a louder, firmer voice than before:

"Therefore I want to be the first. I thought I should not live to see such grief. I thought—that my bear, my loved one, would not live, but apparently Fate has willed otherwise. With my own hand I must kill him, my provider and benefactor. Loose him; let him be free. He will not go away; he, as with us old men, will not flee from death. Loose him, Vasia! I do not wish to kill him bound, as they kill cattle. Do not be afraid," said he, turning to the crowd, which showed signs of alarm; "he will not move."

The youth freed the huge beast, and led him a short distance away from the wagon. The bear sat on his haunches, letting his front paws hang loosely, and swayed from side to side, breathing heavily and hoarsely. He was very old, his teeth were yellow, his coat had grown a reddish colour and was falling out. He gazed in a friendly but melancholy manner at his old master with his one small eye. All around was an absolute silence, broken only by the noise of the ramrods against the barrels of the rifles as the wads were pressed home.

"Give me the gun," said the old man firmly.

His son gave him the rifle. He took it, and, pressing the muzzle against the old animal's breast, again began to address the bear:

"I am going to kill thee in a minute, Potap. God grant that my old hand may not tremble, and that the bullet may find its way into thy very heart. I do not want to torture thee. Thou dost not deserve such, my old bear, my good, my kind old mate. I caught thee a little cub. One of thy eyes had gone, thy nose was rotting from the ring, thou wert suffering from consumption. I tended thee as a son, and pitied thee, and thou grew up a big and powerful bear. There is not such another in all the camps which have collected here. And thou grew up and did not forget my kindness. Never have I had such a friend amongst men such as thou hast been. Thou hast been kind and quiet and clever, and hast learnt all. Never have I seen a beast kinder, more clever than thou. What would I have been without thee? My whole family have lived by thy labour. Thou hast bought me two troikas. It was thou who built me a hut for the winter. Thou hast done yet more for me. Thou saved my son from being a soldier. Ours is a large family, but all, from the oldest to the youngest, thou hast supported up till now. And I have loved thee greatly, and have not beaten thee too much, and if I have in any way offended against thee, forgive me. At thy feet I bow."

He threw himself at the bear's feet. The beast quietly and plaintively growled. The old man lay on the ground, his whole body quivering convulsed with sobs.

"Shoot, daddy," said his son. "Do not tear our hearts!"

Ivan rose. The tears no longer flowed. He threw back the grey mane which had fallen over his brow, and continued in a steady, resounding voice:

"And now I must kill thee. They have ordered me, an old man, to shoot thee with my own hands. Thou must no longer live on this earth. Why? May God in Heaven judge us!"

He cocked the trigger, and with a firm, steady hand aimed at the beast's heart under the left paw. And the beast understood. A pitiful, heartrending sound broke from the bear. He stood up on his hindlegs, and raised his forepaws as if to hide his face with them from the terrifying gun. A wail went up from the gipsies; in the crowd many were openly crying. With a sob the old man threw aside the rifle, and fell senseless to the ground. His son rushed forward to pick him up, and the grandson seized the gun.

"It must be," he cried in a wild, hysterical voice, with blazing eyes. "Enough! Shoot, comrades; let us end it!" And, running up to the beast, he placed the muzzle of the rifle against the bear's ear and fired. The bear fell to the ground a lifeless mass. Only his paws moved convulsively, and his jaw dropped as if yawning. Throughout the encampment rang out shots and the despairing cries of the women and children. A light breeze carried the smoke towards the river.

"One has got loose—broken loose!" resounded through the crowd, and, like a flock of frightened sheep, all rushed helter-skelter. The ispravnik, fat Thomas Thomasovich, urchins, Leonid and Constantine, young ladies—all fled, panic-stricken, running into the tents, against the carts and wagons, screeching and falling over each other.

Olga Pavlona almost fainted, but fear gave her strength, and, picking up her petticoats, she fled along the Common, regardless of the disordered state of her costume caused by such hasty flight. The horses, harnessed up in anticipation of the return of their owners to town, commenced to get out of control, and bolted in various directions. But the danger was by no means great. A still quite young brown bear, maddened by fright, with a broken chain hanging from his neck, was running away with astonishing rapidity. Everyone and everything made way in front of him, and, like the wind, he fled straight into the town. Some of the gipsies, rifles in hand, were running after him. The few pedestrians who chanced to be in the streets pressed themselves against the walls if too late to take refuge in gateways. Shutters were bolted, everything living hid, even the dogs disappeared.

Past the church went the bear, and up the main street, sometimes rushing to one or other side as if seeking a place in which to hide, but everywhere was bolted. As he flashed past the shops he was met with fiendish cries from the shopmen and boys who wished to frighten him. He fled past the bank, the school, and barracks, to the other end of the town, rushed along the road leading to the bank of the river, and stopped. His pursuers were outdistanced. But soon after a crowd, no longer composed of gipsies only, appeared from the street. The ispravnik and the Colonel were in a droshky with rifles in their hands. The gipsies and a squad of soldiers were following behind them at the double. Alongside the droshky ran Leonid and Constantine.

"There he is! there he is!" cried out the ispravnik. "The deuce take him!"

A volley of shots followed. One of the bullets grazed the bear, and in mortal fright he fled faster than ever. A verst from the town, up the Rokhla, whither the bear was running, is a large water-mill, surrounded on all sides by a small but thick wood. The animal made for this wood, but, becoming confused in the branches of the river and the dams, lost his way. A wide expanse of water separated him from the dense overgrowth, where he could perhaps find, if not safety, at least respite. But he decided not to swim. On this side there was a species of bush which grows thickly, and is only found in Southern Russia. Its long, supple, branchless stalks grow so closely together that it is impossible for anyone to make his way through it, but at its roots there are corners and bare patches into which dogs can crawl, and as they often do this to escape from the heat when the weather is warm, and widen the paths leading to them by the pressure of their flanks on the bushes, a whole labyrinth of passages is formed. It was into this undergrowth the bear rushed. The mill men, who were watching from the upper story of the mill, saw this, and when the breathless, exhausted chase arrived, the ispravnik ordered the bear's hiding-place to be surrounded.

The unfortunate animal forced its way into the very depth of the bushes. The wound made by the bullet was very painful. He rolled himself into a ball, buried his muzzle in his paws, and lay motionless, deafened by the noise, mad with fright, and deprived of the possibility of defending himself. The soldiers fired into the bushes, hoping by chance to touch him and make him roar, but to hit, firing at random, is difficult. They killed him late that evening, having smoked him out of his shelter by setting fire to the bushes. Everyone who had a rifle thought it his bounden duty to plant a bullet into the dying beast, so that when they skinned it the skin was useless.

Not long ago I chanced to be in Bielsk. The town has scarcely changed. Only the bank has smashed, and the school is now larger and of a higher grade. They have changed the ispravnik, who was given promotion as pristav in a provincial capital for zealous service. The brothers Isotoff, as of old, shout *"Grand rond!"* and *"Au rebours!"* and run about the town relating the last piece of gossip. The chemist, Thomas Thomasovich, has grown even fatter, and notwithstanding that he made a good thing out of the purchase of the bears'-fat at fourteen kopecks per pound by selling it at eighty kopecks, which brought him in all no small sum, even now speaks with disapproval of the slaughter of the bears.

"I said then to Olga Pavlona that through it her Adonis would become a horse-thief ... and what happened? Less than a week afterwards he stole my pair of greys, the blackguard!"

"And do you know it was he who stole them?"

"Who else could it have been? Last year they tried him for horse-stealing and robbery. He was sent to penal servitude."

"Ah, how sorry I was for him!" said Olga Pavlona sorrowfully.

The poor lady has grown decidedly older these last years, and notwithstanding the fact, according to Thomas Thomasovich, who told me in confidence, that she has smeared her head with four pounds of bears'-grease, her hair has not only not become thicker, but even grown thinner. But her chignon hides it so well that it is absolutely unnoticeable.

TANKARD WITH EAGLE

Vladimir Gilyarovsky (1855–1935)

*Translated by Brian Murphy
& Michael Pursglove*

> The brave archaeologist of imperial Moscow's murky underworld, **Vladimir Gilyarovsky** (1855–1935) was one of the pioneers of investigative journalism in Russia. Writing omnivorously about transport accidents, worker's strikes, fires and riots, sending reports from war zones, Gilyarovsky reserved his true passion for Moscow's criminal community, the shadowy space inhabited by thieves, pimps, hucksters and murderers. He was the first to bring to the surface the real figures of these malefactors in their dark and devilish simplicity. Not by chance his main book on the topic was banned and burnt by the police, who accused the writer of penning the solid darkness. Yet generations of Muscovites learned the ethnography and history of their city from Gilyarovsky's books.

One evening I had free I happened to go to Grachevka. I had listened to the Hungarian choir in the Crimea tavern on Trubnaya Square and there I met the card sharps (who were always at the trotting races) besides one or two of the merchants I knew. Then I set off through the thieves' dens, not the recognized ones with their red lights outside but the ones that hide in basements in dark, dirty yards and in the dank rooms of Kolosovka or Bezymyanka as it was sometimes called.

By midnight this side street, the very air of which was specifically foul, was humming with its usual noise, through which came now the strains of a broken piano, or of a violin, or of an accordion. When the doors beneath the red lights opened, drunken songs could be heard.

In one of the dark, hidden yards, the light from the windows barely penetrated; across it flitted vague shadows; whispering could be heard, then a woman's shriek or dreadful cursing.

In front of me was one such slum, to which drunks were lured and then cleaned out and thrown out on to the waste land.

Around the entrances stood women showing "live pictures" and offering their wares to drunks who had wandered in by chance, promising them all the pleasures of life for five copecks, including cigarettes for the same price...

When I crossed the yard and approached the entrance to one basement, an entrance which was deep in the depths of the yard, I heard an invitation in French, then in Russian:

"Come and see us. You can have a good time with us!"

A tall woman detached herself from the wall and dragged me by the sleeve down a staircase.

"We have vodka and beer."

We went in. A reddish light flickered before my eyes amid the smoke and soot. There was a riot of noise. Beneath the blackened vaults of a huge room stood three tables. On the wall near the door a tin lantern smoked and a stream of black smoke funnelled out beneath the vault, merging imperceptibly with the soot-blackened ceiling. On two of the tables stood the same sort of lantern and some empty bottles; bits of bread, cucumber and herring lay scattered about. At the end table, by the window, a furious game of faro was going on. A solid looking, muscular Russian was dealing; he had an imposing spade-like beard and was wearing a long coat. His rolled-up sleeves revealed huge fists which almost engulfed the pack of cards. Around him crowded pale, ragged punters with flashing eyes.

"Two copecks a pip."

"I've got that. Five copecks. I'll double you."

"Twenty-five copecks from five!" the players could be heard exclaiming.

Further on, through an open door could be seen another, similar room. It also had a table in its depths, but one with two candles, and there too a game of cards was going on...

Before me, at an unlit table, sat a pale unshaven man wearing a forage cap and embracing a drunken woman who was singing, note by note, in a falsetto voice:

Tea she dra-ank and ro-olls she ate
Then forgo-ot with whom she sa-at.

An emaciated youth, seemingly about seventeen years old, wearing patent leather boots, a hussar jacket and with a new cap perched on the back of his head, was banging the bottom of a vodka glass on the table and pointing something out emphatically to a small bedraggled man:

"Listen, you…"

"What do you mean – listen? Listen? We worked together and go halves on the loot…"

"So we have!…You helped while I did the pockets. You got a waiter's pouch and I got a watch… There were two ten-rouble notes in the pouch!.."

"The watch'll fetch fifty; even its anchor…"

"Didn't fetch much. Went for twenty-five…"

"You're kidding!"

"Honest! On my life!"

"Where's the money?"

"I've blown it all. Here are some patent-leather skates, a night-cap… Not a sausage left in my pocket!"

"Oska, look what the wind's blown in!"

The emaciated youth looked at me and I heard him whisper:

"Is he a rozzer?"

"You've got rozzers on the brain…"

"We'll find out in a minute." He turned to the "lady" who had brought me in. "Well, Mrs Colonel, have you brought one of your customers?"

"No, just some passing bloke."

The "Colonel's wife" turned her stern, plastered face to the speaker, gave a wink of her large, black, deeply sunken eyes, and shouted:

"The gent wants a drink. Sit down, sit down, je vous prie!"

"Take a seat. You'll be our guest. If you buy the wine you'll be the host!" yelled the bearded banker, shuffling the cards.

I sat down next to Oska.

"Come on, governor, get the wine in. Give the Colonel's wife a treat," said the youth in the hussar jacket.

"Certainly."

"Splash out to the tune of one rouble and treat everyone. The baron there's got a terrible hangover."

The man in the forage cap had boldly come up to me and gabbled:

"Baron Dorfhausen... Otto Karlovich... My compliments." He shuffled a foot with an old shoe on it.

"You're a baron?" I asked.

"Ma parole! I give you my word. A baron and a Provincial Secretary...*

I was born in Lithuania, studied in Berlin, got blind drunk in Moscow and gambled everything away. Lend me twenty copecks. I'll go and recoup my losses... Till our next meeting."

"Indeed."

And a minute later his powerful voice could be heard saying:

"That card wins. It's mine... It's mine..."

"It's true, sir, he is a real baron," Oska whispered to me. "Now he forges certificates of poverty and does various other fake documents. And how he puts seals on smoked glass! If you want a residence permit – go straight to him. His charge is reasonable... At present poster size, excluding forms – one and a half roubles. For life – three roubles."

"For life?"

"Yes, a nobleman's passport or permission to retire... He'll put in ranks and medals..."

"A baron... A colonel's wife," I mused.

"The colonel's wife is genuine too. She's not some lieutenant-colonel's wife. She lives with the colonel. The establishment is in her name."

At this point the colonel's wife interrupted him and, larding her speech with ungrammatical French expressions, began to relate how, as a young girl, she was married off to an old man, the colonel commanding a garrison, how she ran away abroad with a neighbouring landowner, how he abandoned her in Paris, how, as a result, she returned home and now found herself in Bezymyanka.

"Come on, you slag, you're going to wear your tongue out. Get the beer in!" yelled the banker, without looking round.

"I'll get it, you swindler. Why are you hollering, you convict?"

"Just my blasted luck! It's not going my way. Eh? What's that? No, you listen. I bet on the six – up it came! I choose a second card. One of

---

* Twelfth of the fourteen Civil Service ranks.

them wins. I take my winnings. I stick to my original stake – and lose. I try again – and lose. I bet on the seven – and lose! Loss after loss!"

"So you're out of funds?"

"Completely! If you would give me one last one – I'm Croesus! I've studied how the cards are dealt – and suddenly I've lost! Lend me some more... till we next meet. The same stake..."

Again I gave him twenty copecks.

"All right! You're a gent... Till our next meeting!.."

The colonel's wife poured beer into four glasses and, for me, into a crystal-glass tankard with a maillechort lid adorned with an eagle.

The baron tore himself away from the cards for a second and, raising his glass, proclaimed with a flourish:

"To the ladies. Cheers!"

"Why aren't you drinking? Down the hatch!" said the colonel's wife, turning to me.

"I don't drink beer..." I replied curtly.

At that moment the card game ended.

The banker thrust the cards and money into his pocket, turned down the lamp and rose to his feet,

"That's it till tomorrow! Get yourselves out of here."

The players, seemingly used to obeying him, at once stood up and left. Only the baron stayed stubbornly put. The banker threw him twenty copecks.

"Get knotted and scram! I'm fed up with you. Bet on a card, pips not suits! A pennyworth of ammunition, a pound's worth of ambition! Go away! Don't hang about!"

The banker took the baron by the shoulders and in a trice had pitched him out of the door, which he then bolted. The baron did not even have time to curse. There remained: Oska, the pickpocket in the hussar jacket, the drunk woman, the colonel's wife and the banker. He sat down beside us.

From the next room came the cries of card players. The game there must have been very serious.

The colonel's wife again filled up the glasses with beer and moved my untouched tankard towards me.

"Drink up and don't hurt our feelings."

"But I'm not alone am I? That young man isn't drinking..."

"That little thief? He can't," said Oska.

"His doctor forbids it," said the colonel's wife soothingly.

"But you, sir, why aren't you drinking? That's not how we go on. Please, drink," said the bearded banker, reaching across to clink glasses with me.

I refused.

"I consider that an insult. You're treating us with contempt! We don't behave like that. Drink! Well? Don't make me do something bad. Drink!"

"No!"

"No? Oska, pour some down his gullet!"

The banker jumped up from his chair, seized my forehead with one hand and my chin with the other, in order to force open my mouth. Oska stood with the tankard, ready to pour beer forcibly into my mouth.

That was the decisive moment. I managed to get the knuckleduster out of my pocket and bash my attacker right in the teeth. He collapsed howling on to the floor.

"What's all this then?" said a voice behind me and a man in a black overcoat emerged from the doorway; behind him two men had halted on the threshold, surveying us. The man in the overcoat turned to me and we were both stunned and surprised.

"It's you?" exclaimed the man in the overcoat and with one wave of his arm brushed aside the banker, who had jumped up from the floor and hurled himself at me, his beard covered in blood. He fell down again. Before me, confused and shaken, stood the racing "sportsman" who had given me a lift in his charabanc. Everyone else was petrified.

From the hands of Oska, who was standing by the table, he snatched the tankard of beer and poured it out on to the floor.

"Get rid of it!" he ordered the colonel's wife, who was trembling with fear. "Vladimir Alexeyevich, how did you come to be here? Let's go to my room."

"To hell with you. I'm going home..."

And, putting on my hat, I made for the door. The banker lay prone on the floor, groaning and spitting out teeth.

"No, no, I'll go with you."

Standing behind me, he took my elbow and guided me up the shattered flags of the staircase, muttering apologies.

I maintained a stubborn silence. In my head the phrases revolved: "Cover your traces, Larepland, Mickey Finn, the German, the tankard with the bird on it..."

"The sportsman" continued to offer me profuse apologies, saying, amongst other things:

"All the same, I saved you from Samson. He could have made mincemeat of you, you know."

"Well, I saved myself, because I didn't drink the Mickey Finn."

"How did you know about that?" He shuddered, then suddenly collected himself and added in a quite different tone. "What Mickey Finn was that?"

"The one in the tankard, that you poured on to the floor. I know all about it."

"You.. you..." His teeth chattered and he couldn't get the word out.

"I know everything, but I can hold my tongue."

"I can see that, sir. That's why I wanted you to come to my room. There's a separate exit. Some friends have got together to play cards. I don't live here, you know."

"I saw... I recognised Goliath the billiard marker."

"Yes, he was sitting near you. Krechinsky was dealing. There was the Heron too... Then there was Vatoshnik and..."

"Vatoshnik? Timoshka? But he's a detective!"

"To some he's a detective; to us he's a friend... Once again I ask you to be magnanimous and forgive."

"Remember: I know everything but I never show it. It's as if nothing had happened. Goodbye!" I shouted to him from the gate...

Whenever we encountered each other, the "sportsman" did his best to avoid me, but once he caught me alone near the racetrack and whispered in a trembling voice:

"You promised, Vladimir Alexeyevich, but what's this you've written in the newspaper? It's a good job no-one paid any attention to it, and it's water under the bridge. Yet it's quite clear. Everyone knows Fenka is the colonel's wife and you've given the baron's name and patronymic in full, just changing his surname. Anyway the whole police force knows him – he's even got a residence permit. The main thing is that the baron..."

"Calm down, I won't do it again."

In fact I wrote a story "Into the unknown" in which I described in detail what I had seen in the gambling den, the card game, the guest poisoned with the Mickey Finn who had been dragged off to be thrown in an underground sewer, having been taken for dead. I merely changed the name of Kolosov Lane to Bezymyanny Lane. I described the milieu in detail as I did the real-life characters. Baron Dorfhausen, Otto Karlovich – that really was his name.

The epigraph to my story was:

"While the Neglinka channel was being cleared out, bones were discovered which resembled human bones..."

IONYCH

Anton Chekhov (1860–1904)

Translated by Constance Garnett

> Russia's most celebrated playwright and storyteller, **Anton Chekhov** (1860–1904) studied medicine and practiced as a country physician. Medical experience, its rhythm, routine, sudden emergencies, glimpses of fate in everyday life, can be traced in Chekhov's writing both as a principle and a source of inspiration. An educator and a prominent civil rights advocate, Chekhov wrote more than five hundred texts (under dozens of pseudonyms). Even though he is frequently described as a bard of the everyday and the common life, this commonness is not static. Everything is changing insensibly but quickly and unavoidably, the very fabric of society, ideas, values and relationships, and Chekhov's heroes have a sixth sense, vague yet tangible, which make them vulnerable to the anxieties of the world that will soon be swept away by the storm of the 1917 revolution.

I

When visitors to the provincial town S— complained of the dreariness and monotony of life, the inhabitants of the town, as though defending themselves, declared that it was very nice in S—, that there was a library, a theatre, a club; that they had balls; and, finally, that there were clever, agreeable and interesting families with whom one could make acquaintance. And they used to point to the family of the Turkins as the most highly cultivated and talented.

This family lived in their own house in the principal street, near the Governor's. Ivan Petrovitch Turkin himself – a stout, handsome, dark man with whiskers – used to get up amateur performances for benevolent objects, and used to take the part of an elderly general and cough very amusingly. He knew a number of anecdotes, charades, proverbs, and was fond of being humorous and witty, and he always wore an expression from which it was impossible to tell whether he were joking or in earnest. His wife, Vera Iosifovna – a thin, nice-looking lady who wore a pince-nez – used to write novels and stories, and was very fond of reading them aloud to her visitors. The daughter, Ekaterina Ivanovna, a young girl, used to play on the piano. In short, every member of the family had a special talent. The Turkins welcomed visitors, and good-humouredly displayed their talents with genuine simplicity. Their stone house was roomy and cool in summer; half of the windows looked into a shady old garden, where nightingales used to sing in the spring. When there were visitors in the house, there was a clatter of knives in the kitchen and a smell of fried onions in the yard – and that was always a sure sign of a plentiful and savoury supper to follow.

And as soon as Dmitri Ionitch Startsev was appointed the district doctor, and took up his abode at Dyalizh, six miles from S—, he, too, was told that as a cultivated man it was essential for him to make the acquaintance of the Turkins. In the winter he was introduced to Ivan Petrovitch in the street; they talked about the weather, about the theatre, about the cholera; an invitation followed. On a holiday in the spring – it was Ascension Day – after seeing his patients, Startsev set off for town in search of a little recreation and to make some purchases. He walked in a leisurely way (he had not yet set up his carriage), humming all the time:

"Before I'd drunk the tears from life's goblet. ..."

In town he dined, went for a walk in the gardens, then Ivan Petrovitch's invitation came into his mind, as it were of itself, and he decided to call on the Turkins and see what sort of people they were.

"How do you do, if you please?" said Ivan Petrovitch, meeting him on the steps. "Delighted, delighted to see such an agreeable visitor. Come along; I will introduce you to my better half. I tell him, Verotchka," he went on, as he presented the doctor to his wife – "I tell him that he has no human right to sit at home in a hospital; he ought to devote his leisure to society. Oughtn't he, darling?"

"Sit here," said Vera Iosifovna, making her visitor sit down beside her. "You can dance attendance on me. My husband is jealous – he is an Othello; but we will try and behave so well that he will notice nothing."

"Ah, you spoiled chicken!" Ivan Petrovitch muttered tenderly, and he kissed her on the forehead. "You have come just in the nick of time," he said, addressing the doctor again. "My better half has written a 'hugeous' novel, and she is going to read it aloud today."

"Petit Jean," said Vera Iosifovna to her husband, "dites que l'on nous donne du thé."

Startsev was introduced to Ekaterina Ivanovna, a girl of eighteen, very much like her mother, thin and pretty. Her expression was still childish and her figure was soft and slim; and her developed girlish bosom, healthy and beautiful, was suggestive of spring, real spring.

Then they drank tea with jam, honey and sweetmeats, and with very nice cakes, which melted in the mouth. As the evening came on, other visitors gradually arrived, and Ivan Petrovitch fixed his laughing eyes on each of them and said:

"How do you do, if you please?"

Then they all sat down in the drawing-room with very serious faces, and Vera Iosifovna read her novel. It began like this: "The frost was intense. ..." The windows were wide open; from the kitchen came the clatter of knives and the smell of fried onions. ... It was comfortable in the soft deep armchair; the lights had such a friendly twinkle in the twilight of the drawing room, and at the moment on a summer evening when sounds of voices and laughter floated in from the street and whiffs of lilac from the yard, it was difficult to grasp that the frost was intense, and that the setting sun was lighting with its chilly rays a solitary wayfarer on the snowy plain. Vera Iosifovna read how a beautiful young countess founded a school, a hospital, a library, in her village, and fell in love with a wandering artist; she read of what never happens in real life, and yet it was pleasant to listen – it was comfortable, and such agreeable, serene thoughts kept coming into the mind, one had no desire to get up.

"Not badsome ..." Ivan Petrovitch said softly.

And one of the visitors hearing, with his thoughts far away, said hardly audibly:

"Yes ... truly ..."

One hour passed, another. In the town gardens close by a band was playing and a chorus was singing. When Vera Iosifovna shut her manuscript book, the company was silent for five minutes, listening to "Lutchina" being sung by the chorus, and the song gave what was not in the novel and is in real life.

"Do you publish your stories in magazines?" Startsev asked Vera Iosifovna.

"No," she answered. "I never publish. I write it and put it away in my cupboard. Why publish?" she explained. "We have enough to live on."

And for some reason everyone sighed.

"And now, Kitten, you play something," Ivan Petrovitch said to his daughter.

The lid of the piano was raised and the music lying ready was opened. Ekaterina Ivanovna sat down and banged on the piano with both hands, and then banged again with all her might, and then again and again; her shoulders and bosom shook. She obstinately banged on the same notes, and it sounded as if she would not leave off until she had hammered the keys into the piano. The drawing-room was filled with the din; everything was resounding; the floor, the ceiling, the furniture. ... Ekaterina Ivanovna was playing a difficult passage, interesting simply on account of its difficulty, long and monotonous, and Startsev, listening, pictured stones dropping down a steep hill and going on dropping, and he wished they would leave off dropping; and at the same time Ekaterina Ivanovna, rosy from the violent exercise, strong and vigorous, with a lock of hair falling over her forehead, attracted him very much. After the winter spent at Dyalizh among patients and peasants, to sit in a drawing-room, to watch this young, elegant, and, in all probability, pure creature, and to listen to these noisy, tedious but still cultured sounds, was so pleasant, so novel. ...

"Well, Kitten, you have played as never before," said Ivan Petrovitch, with tears in his eyes, when his daughter had finished and stood up. "Die, Denis; you won't write anything better."

All flocked round her, congratulated her, expressed astonishment, declared that it was long since they had heard such music, and she listened in silence with a faint smile, and her whole figure was expressive of triumph.

"Splendid, superb!"

"Splendid," said Startsev, too, carried away by the general enthusiasm. "Where have you studied?" he asked Ekaterina Ivanovna. "At the Conservatoire?"

"No, I am only preparing for the Conservatoire, and till now have been working with Madame Zavlovsky."

"Have you finished at the high-school here?"

"Oh, no," Vera Iosifovna answered for her. "We have teachers for her at home; there might be bad influences at the high-school or a boarding school, you know. While a young girl is growing up, she ought to be under no influence but her mother's."

"All the same, I'm going to the Conservatoire," said Ekaterina Ivanovna.

"No. Kitten loves her mamma. Kitten won't grieve Papa and Mamma."

"No, I'm going, I'm going," said Ekaterina Ivanovna, with playful caprice and stamping her foot.

And at supper it was Ivan Petrovitch who displayed his talents. Laughing only with his eyes, he told anecdotes, made epigrams, asked ridiculous riddles and answered them himself, talking the whole time in his extraordinary language, evolved in the course of prolonged practice in witticism and evidently now become a habit: "Badsome," "Hugeous," "Thank you most dumbly," and so on.

But that was not all. When the guests, replete and satisfied, trooped into the hall, looking for their coats and sticks, there bustled about them the footman Pavlusha, or, as he was called in the family, Pava – a lad of fourteen with shaven head and chubby cheeks.

Come, Pava, perform!" Ivan Petrovitch said to him.

Pava struck an attitude, flung up his arm, and said in a tragic tone: "Unhappy woman, die!"

And everyone roared with laughter.

"It's entertaining," thought Startsev, as he went out into the street.

He went to a restaurant and drank some beer, then set off to walk home to Dyalizh; he walked all the way singing:

"Thy voice to me so languid and caressing. ..."

On going to bed, he felt not the slightest fatigue after the six miles' walk. On the contrary, he felt as though he could with pleasure have walked another twenty.

"Not badsome," he thought, and laughed as he fell asleep.

II

Startsev kept meaning to go to the Turkins' again, but there was a great deal of work in the hospital, and he was unable to find free time.

In this way more than a year passed in work and solitude. But one day a letter in a light blue envelope was brought him from the town.

Vera Iosifovna had been suffering for some time from migraine, but now since Kitten frightened her every day by saying that she was going away to the Conservatoire, the attacks began to be more frequent. All the doctors of the town had been at the Turkins'; at last it was the district doctor's turn. Vera Iosifovna wrote him a touching letter in which she begged him to come and relieve her sufferings. Startsev went, and after that he began to be often, very often at the Turkins'. ... He really did something for Vera Iosifovna, and she was already telling all her visitors that he was a wonderful and exceptional doctor. But it was not for the sake of her migraine that he visited the Turkins' now. ...

It was a holiday. Ekaterina Ivanovna finished her long, wearisome exercises on the piano. Then they sat a long time in the dining-room, drinking tea, and Ivan Petrovitch told some amusing story. Then there was a ring and he had to go into the hall to welcome a guest; Startsev took advantage of the momentary commotion, and whispered to Ekaterina Ivanovna in great agitation:

"For God's sake, I entreat you, don't torment me; let us go into the garden!"

She shrugged her shoulders, as though perplexed and not knowing what he wanted of her, but she got up and went.

"You play the piano for three or four hours," he said, following her; "then you sit with your mother, and there is no possibility of speaking to you. Give me a quarter of an hour at least, I beseech you."

Autumn was approaching, and it was quiet and melancholy in the old garden; the dark leaves lay thick in the walks. It was already beginning to get dark early.

"I haven't seen you for a whole week," Startsev went on, "and if you only knew what suffering it is! Let us sit down. Listen to me."

They had a favourite place in the garden; a seat under an old spreading maple. And now they sat down on this seat.

"What do you want?" said Ekaterina Ivanovna drily, in a matter-of-fact tone.

"I have not seen you for a whole week; I have not heard you for so long. I long passionately, I thirst for your voice. Speak."

She fascinated him by her freshness, the naive expression of her eyes and cheeks. Even in the way her dress hung on her, he saw something extraordinarily charming, touching in its simplicity and naive grace; and at the same time, in spite of this naiveté, she seemed to him intelligent and developed beyond her years. He could talk with her about literature, about art, about anything he liked; could complain to her of life, of people, though it sometimes happened in the middle of a serious conversation she would laugh inappropriately or run away into the house. Like almost all girls of her neighbourhood, she had read a great deal (as a rule, people read very little in S—, and at the lending library they said if it were not for the girls and the young Jews, they might as well shut up the library). This afforded Startsev infinite delight; he used to ask her eagerly every time what she had been reading the last few days, and listened enthralled while she told him.

"What have you been reading this week since I saw you last?" he asked now. "Do please tell me."

"I have been reading Pisemsky."

"What exactly?"

"'A Thousand Souls,' answered Kitten. "And what a funny name Pisemsky had – Alexey Feofilaktitch!"

"Where are you going?" cried Startsev in horror, as she suddenly got up and walked towards the house. "I must talk to you; I want to explain myself. ... Stay with me just five minutes, I supplicate you!"

She stopped as though she wanted to say something, then awkwardly thrust a note into his hand, ran home and sat down to the piano again.

"Be in the cemetery," Startsev read, "at eleven o'clock tonight, near the tomb of Demetti."

"Well, that's not at all clever," he thought, coming to himself. "Why the cemetery? What for?"

It was clear: Kitten was playing a prank. Who would seriously dream of making an appointment at night in the cemetery far out of the town, when it might have been arranged in the street or in the town gardens? And was it in keeping with him – a district doctor, an intelligent, staid man – to be sighing, receiving notes, to hang about cemeteries, to do silly things that even schoolboys think ridiculous nowadays? What would this romance lead to? What would his colleagues say when they heard of it? Such were Startsev's reflections as he wandered round the tables at the club, and at half-past ten he suddenly set off for the cemetery.

By now he had his own pair of horses, and a coachman called Panteleimon, in a velvet waistcoat. The moon was shining. It was still warm, warm as it is in autumn. Dogs were howling in the suburb near the slaughter-house. Startsev left his horses in one of the side-streets at the end of the town, and walked on foot to the cemetery.

"We all have our oddities," he thought. "Kitten is odd, too; and – who knows? – perhaps she is not joking, perhaps she will come"; and he abandoned himself to this faint, vain hope, and it intoxicated him.

He walked for half a mile through the fields; the cemetery showed as a dark streak in the distance, like a forest or a big garden. The wall of white stone came into sight, the gate. ... In the moonlight he could read on the gate: "The hour cometh." Startsev went in at the little gate, and before anything else he saw the white crosses and monuments on both sides of the broad avenue, and the black shadows of them and the poplars; and for a long way round it was all white and black, and the slumbering trees bowed their branches over the white stones. It seemed as though it were lighter here than in the fields; the maple-leaves stood out sharply like paws on the yellow sand of the avenue and on the stones, and the inscriptions on the tombs could be clearly read. For the first moments Startsev was struck now by what he saw for the first time in his life, and what he would probably never see again; a world not like anything else, a world in which the moonlight was as soft and beautiful, as though slumbering here in its cradle, where there was no life, none whatever; but in every dark poplar, in every tomb, there was felt the presence of a mystery that promised a life peaceful, beautiful, eternal. The stones and faded flowers, together with the autumn scent of the leaves, all told of forgiveness, melancholy and peace.

All was silence around; the stars looked down from the sky in the profound stillness, and Startsev's footsteps sounded loud and out of place, and only when the church clock began striking and he imagined himself dead, buried there for ever, he felt as though someone were looking at him, and for a moment he thought that it was not peace and tranquillity, but stifled despair, the dumb dreariness of non-existence. ...

Demetti's tomb was in the form of a shrine with an angel at the top.

The Italian opera had once visited S——and one of the singers had died; she had been buried here, and this monument put up to her. No one in the town remembered her, but the lamp at the entrance reflected the moonlight, and looked as though it were burning.

There was no one, and, indeed, who would come here at midnight? But Startsev waited, and as though the moonlight warmed his passion, he waited passionately, and, in imagination, pictured kisses and embraces. He sat near the monument for half an hour, then paced up and down the side avenues, with his hat in his hand, waiting and thinking of the many women and girls buried in these tombs who had been beautiful and fascinating, who had loved, at night burned with passion, yielding themselves to caresses. How wickedly Mother Nature jested at man's expense, after all! How humiliating it was to recognize it!

Startsev thought this, and at the same time he wanted to cry out that he wanted love, that he was eager for it at all costs. To his eyes they were not slabs of marble, but fair white bodies in the moonlight; he saw shapes hiding bashfully in the shadows of the trees, felt their warmth, and the languor was oppressive. ...

And as though a curtain were lowered, the moon went behind a cloud, and suddenly all was darkness. Startsev could scarcely find the gate – by now it was as dark as it is on an autumn night. Then he wandered about for an hour and a half, looking for the side-street in which he had left his horses.

"I am tired; I can scarcely stand on my legs," he said to Panteleimon.

And settling himself with relief in his carriage, he thought: "Och! I ought not to get fat!"

III

The following evening he went to the Turkins' to make an offer. But it turned out to be an inconvenient moment, as Ekaterina Ivanovna was in her own room having her hair done by a hairdresser. She was getting ready to go to a dance at the club.

He had to sit a long time again in the dining-room drinking tea. Ivan Petrovitch, seeing that his visitor was bored and preoccupied, drew some notes out of his waistcoat pocket, read a funny letter from a German steward, saying that all the ironmongery was ruined and the plasticity was peeling off the walls.

"I expect they will give a decent dowry," thought Startsev, listening absent-mindedly.

After a sleepless night, he found himself in a state of stupefaction, as though he had been given something sweet and soporific to drink; there was fog in his soul, but joy and warmth, and at the same time a sort of cold, heavy fragment of his brain was reflecting:

"Stop before it is too late! Is she the match for you? She is spoiled, whimsical, sleeps till two o'clock in the afternoon, while you are a deacon's son, a district doctor. ..."

"What of it?" he thought. "I don't care."

"Besides, if you marry her," the fragment went on, "then her relations will make you give up the district work and live in the town."

"After all," he thought, "if it must be the town, the town it must be. They will give a dowry; we can establish ourselves suitably."

At last Ekaterina Ivanovna came in, dressed for the ball, with a low neck, looking fresh and pretty; and Startsev admired her so much, and went into such ecstasies, that he could say nothing, but simply stared at her and laughed.

She began saying goodbye, and he – he had no reason for staying now – got up, saying that it was time for him to go home; his patients were waiting for him.

"Well, there's no help for that," said Ivan Petrovitch. "Go, and you might take Kitten to the club on the way."

It was spotting with rain; it was very dark, and they could only tell where the horses were by Panteleimon's husky cough. The hood of the carriage was put up.

"I stand upright; you lie down right; he lies all right," said Ivan Petrovitch as he put his daughter into the carriage.

They drove off.

"I was at the cemetery yesterday," Startsev began. "How ungenerous and merciless it was on your part! ..."

"You went to the cemetery?"

"Yes, I went there and waited almost till two o'clock. I suffered ..."

"Well, suffer, if you cannot understand a joke."

Ekaterina Ivanovna, pleased at having so cleverly taken in a man who was in love with her, and at being the object of such intense love, burst out laughing and suddenly uttered a shriek of terror, for, at that very minute, the horses turned sharply in at the gate of the club, and the carriage almost tilted over. Startsev put his arm round Ekaterina Ivanovna's waist; in her fright she nestled up to him, and he could not restrain himself, and passionately kissed her on the lips and on the chin, and hugged her more tightly.

"That's enough," she said drily.

And a minute later she was not in the carriage, and a policeman near the lighted entrance of the club shouted in a detestable voice to Panteleimon:

"What are you stopping for, you crow? Drive on."

Startsev drove home, but soon afterwards returned. Attired in another man's dress suit and a stiff white tie which kept sawing at his neck and trying to slip away from the collar, he was sitting at midnight in the club drawing-room, and was saying with enthusiasm to Ekaterina Ivanovna:

"Ah, how little people know who have never loved! It seems to me that no one has ever yet written of love truly, and I doubt whether this tender, joyful, agonizing feeling can be described, and anyone who has once experienced it would not attempt to put it into words. What is the use of preliminaries and introductions? What is the use of unnecessary fine words? My love is immeasurable. I beg, I beseech you," Startsev brought out at last, "be my wife!"

"Dmitri Ionitch," said Ekaterina Ivanovna, with a very grave face, after a moment's thought – "Dmitri Ionitch, I am very grateful to you for the honour. I respect you, but ..." she got up and continued standing, "but, forgive me, I cannot be your wife. Let us talk seriously. Dmitri Ionitch, you know I love art beyond everything in life. I adore music; I love it frantically; I have dedicated my whole life to it. I want to be an artist; I want fame, success, freedom, and you want me to go on living in this town, to go on living this empty, useless life, which has become insufferable to me. To become a wife – oh, no, forgive me! One must strive towards a lofty, glorious goal, and married life would put me in bondage for ever. Dmitri Ionitch," (she faintly smiled as she pronounced his name; she thought of "Alexey Feofilaktitch") – "Dmitri Ionitch, you are a good, clever, honourable man; you are better than anyone. ..." Tears came into her eyes. "I feel for you with my whole heart, but ... but you will understand. ..."

And she turned away and went out of the drawing-room to prevent herself from crying.

Startsev's heart left off throbbing uneasily. Going out of the club into the street, he first of all tore off the stiff tie and drew a deep breath. He was a little ashamed and his vanity was wounded – he had not expected a refusal – and could not believe that all his dreams, his hopes and yearnings, had led him up to such a stupid end, just as in some little play at an amateur performance, and he was sorry for his feeling, for that love of his, so sorry that he felt as though he could have burst into sobs or have violently belaboured Panteleimon's broad back with his umbrella.

For three days he could not get on with anything, he could not eat nor sleep; but when the news reached him that Ekaterina Ivanovna had gone away to Moscow to enter the Conservatoire, he grew calmer and lived as before.

Afterwards, remembering sometimes how he had wandered about the cemetery or how he had driven all over the town to get a dress suit, he stretched lazily and said:

"What a lot of trouble, though!"

IV

Four years had passed. Startsev already had a large practice in the town. Every morning he hurriedly saw his patients at Dyalizh, then he drove in to see his town patients. By now he drove, not with a pair, but with a team of three with bells on them, and he returned home late at night. He had grown broader and stouter, and was not very fond of walking, as he was somewhat asthmatic. And Panteleimon had grown stout, too, and the broader he grew, the more mournfully he sighed and complained of his hard luck: he was sick of driving! Startsev used to visit various households and met many people, but did not become intimate with anyone. The inhabitants irritated him by their conversation, their views of life and even their appearance. Experience taught him by degrees that while he played cards or lunched with one of these people, the man was a peaceable, friendly and even intelligent human being; that as soon as one talked of anything not eatable, for instance, of politics or science, he would be completely at a loss, or would expound a philosophy so stupid and ill-natured that there was nothing else to do but wave one's hand in despair and go away. Even when Startsev tried to talk to liberal citizens, saying, for instance, that humanity, thank God, was progressing, and that one day it would be possible to dispense with passports and capital punishment, the liberal citizen would look at him askance and ask him mistrustfully: "Then anyone could murder anyone he chose in the open street?" And when, at tea or supper, Startsev observed in company that one should work, and that one ought not to live without working, everyone took this as a reproach, and began to get angry and argue aggressively. With all that, the inhabitants did nothing, absolutely nothing, and took no interest in anything, and it was quite impossible to think of anything to say. And Startsev avoided conversation, and confined himself to eating and playing *vint*; and when there was a family festivity in some household and he was invited to a meal, then he sat and ate in silence, looking at his plate.

And everything that was said at the time was uninteresting, unjust and stupid; he felt irritated and disturbed, but held his tongue, and, because he sat glumly silent and looked at his plate, he was nicknamed in the town "the haughty Pole," though he never had been a Pole.

All such entertainments as theatres and concerts he declined, but he played *vint* every evening for three hours with enjoyment. He had another diversion to which he took imperceptibly, little by little: in the evening he would take out of his pockets the notes he had gained by his practice, and sometimes there were stuffed in his pockets notes—yellow and green, and smelling of scent and vinegar and incense and fish oil—up to the value of seventy roubles; and when they amounted to some hundreds he took them to the Mutual Credit Bank and deposited the money there to his account.

He was only twice at the Turkins' in the course of the four years after Ekaterina Ivanovna had gone away, on each occasion at the invitation of Vera Iosifovna, who was still undergoing treatment for migraine. Every summer Ekaterina Ivanovna came to stay with her parents, but he did not once see her; it somehow never happened.

But now four years had passed. One still, warm morning a letter was brought to the hospital. Vera Iosifovna wrote to Dmitri Ionitch that she was missing him very much, and begged him to come and see them, and to relieve her sufferings; and, by the way, it was her birthday. Below was a postscript: "I join in mother's request. – K."

Startsev considered, and in the evening he went to the Turkins'.

"How do you do, if you please?" Ivan Petrovitch met him, smiling with his eyes only. "Bonjour."

Vera Iosifovna, white-haired and looking much older, shook Startsev's hand, sighed affectedly, and said:

"You don't care to pay attentions to me, doctor. You never come and see us; I am too old for you. But now someone young has come; perhaps she will be more fortunate."

And Kitten? She had grown thinner, paler, had grown handsomer and more graceful; but now she was Ekaterina Ivanovna, not Kitten; she had lost the freshness and look of childish naïveté. And in her expression and manners there was something new—guilty and diffident, as though she did not feel herself at home here in the Turkins' house.

"How many summers, how many winters!" she said, giving Startsev her hand, and he could see that her heart was beating with excitement; and looking at him intently and curiously, she went on: "How much stouter you are! You look sunburned and more manly, but on the whole you have changed very little."

Now, too, he thought her attractive, very attractive, but there was something lacking in her, or else something superfluous – he could not himself have said exactly what it was, but something prevented him from feeling as before. He did not like her pallor, her new expression, her faint smile, her voice, and soon afterwards he disliked her clothes, too, the low chair in which she was sitting; he disliked something in the past when he had almost married her. He thought of his love, of the dreams and the hopes which had troubled him four years before – and he felt awkward.

They had tea with cakes. Then Vera Iosifovna read aloud a novel; she read of things that never happen in real life, and Startsev listened, looked at her handsome grey head, and waited for her to finish.

"People are not stupid because they can't write novels, but because they can't conceal it when they do," he thought.

"Not badsome," said Ivan Petrovitch.

Then Ekaterina Ivanovna played long and noisily on the piano, and when she finished she was profusely thanked and warmly praised.

"It's a good thing I did not marry her," thought Startsev.

She looked at him, and evidently expected him to ask her to go into the garden, but he remained silent.

"Let us have a talk," she said, going up to him. "How are you getting on? What are you doing? How are things? I have been thinking about you all these days," she went on nervously.

"I wanted to write to you, wanted to come myself to see you at Dyalizh. I quite made up my mind to go, but afterwards I thought better of it. God knows what your attitude is towards me now; I have been looking forward to seeing you today with such emotion. For goodness' sake let us go into the garden."

They went into the garden and sat down on the seat under the old maple, just as they had done four years before. It was dark.

"How are you getting on?" asked Ekaterina Ivanovna. "Oh, all right; I am jogging along," answered Startsev. And he could think of nothing more. They were silent.

"I feel so excited!" said Ekaterina Ivanovna, and she hid her face in her hands. "But don't pay attention to it. I am so happy to be at home; I am so glad to see everyone. I can't get used to it. So many memories! I thought we should talk without stopping till morning."

Now he saw her face near, her shining eyes, and in the darkness she looked younger than in the room, and even her old childish expression seemed to have come back to her. And indeed she was looking at him with naïve curiosity, as though she wanted to get a closer view and understanding of the man who had loved her so ardently, with such tenderness and so unsuccessfully; her eyes thanked him for that love. And he remembered all that had been, every minute detail; how he had wandered about the cemetery, how he had returned home in the morning exhausted, and he suddenly felt sad and regretted the past. A warmth began glowing in his heart.

"Do you remember how I took you to the dance at the club?" he asked. "It was dark and rainy then ..."

The warmth was glowing now in his heart, and he longed to talk, to rail at life. ...

"Ech!" he said with a sigh. "You ask how I am living. How do we live here? Why, not at all. We grow old, we grow stout, we grow slack. Day after day passes; life slips by without colour, without expressions, without thoughts. ... In the daytime working for gain, and in the evening the club, the company of card-players, alcoholic, raucous-voiced gentlemen whom I can't endure. What is there nice in it?"

"Well, you have work – a noble object in life. You used to be so fond of talking of your hospital. I was such a queer girl then; I imagined myself such a great pianist. Nowadays all young ladies play the piano, and I played, too, like everybody else, and there was nothing special about me. I am just such a pianist as my mother is an authoress. And of course I didn't understand you then, but afterwards in Moscow I often thought of you. I thought of no one but you. What happiness to be a district doctor; to help the suffering; to be serving the people! What happiness!" Ekaterina Ivanovna repeated with enthusiasm. "When I thought of you in Moscow, you seemed to me so ideal, so lofty ...

Startsev thought of the notes he used to take out of his pockets in the evening with such pleasure, and the glow in his heart was quenched.

He got up to go into the house. She took his arm.

"You are the best man I've known in my life," she went on. "We will see each other and talk, won't we? Promise me. *I* am not a pianist; I am not in error about myself now, and I will not play before you or talk of music."

When they had gone into the house, and when Startsev saw in the lamplight her face, and her sad, grateful, searching eyes fixed upon him, he felt uneasy and thought again:

"It's a good thing I did not marry her then."

He began taking leave.

"You have no human right to go before supper," said Ivan Petrovitch as he saw him off. "It's extremely perpendicular on your part. Well, now, perform!" he added, addressing Pava in the hall.

Pava, no longer a boy, but a young man with moustaches, threw himself into an attitude, flung up his arm and said in a tragic voice:

"Unhappy woman, die!"

All this irritated Startsev. Getting into his carriage, and looking at the dark house and garden which had once been so precious and so dear, he thought of everything at once – Vera Iosifovna's novels and Kitten's noisy playing, and Ivan Petrovitch's jokes and Pava's tragic posturing, and thought if the most talented people in the town were so futile, what must the town be?

Three days later Pava brought a letter from Ekaterina Ivanovna.

"You don't come and see us – why?" she wrote to him. "I

am afraid that you have changed towards us. I am afraid, and *I am* terrified at the very thought of it. Reassure me; come and tell me that everything is well.

"I must talk to you.—Your E. I."

He read this letter, thought a moment and said to Pava:

"Tell them, my good fellow, that I can't come today; I am very busy. Say I will come in three days or so."

But three days passed, a week passed; he still did not go. Happening once to drive past the Turkins' house, he thought he must go in, if only for a moment, but on second thoughts ... did not go in.

And he never went to the Turkins' again.

V

Several more years have passed. Startsev has grown stouter still, has grown corpulent, breathes heavily, and already walks with his head thrown back. When stout and red in the face, he drives with his bells and his team of three horses, and Panteleimon, also stout and red in the face with his thick, beefy neck, sits on the box, holding his arms stiffly out before him as though they were made of wood, and shouts to those he meets: "Keep to the ri-i-ight!" It is an impressive picture; one might think it was not a mortal, but some heathen deity in his chariot. He has an immense practice in the town, no time to breathe, and already has an estate and two houses in the town, and he is looking out for a third more profitable; and when at the Mutual Credit Bank he is told of a house that is for sale, he goes to the house without ceremony, and, marching through all the rooms, regardless of half-dressed women and children who gaze at him in amazement and alarm, he prods at the doors with his stick, and says:

"Is that the study? Is that a bedroom? And what's here?" And as he does so, he breathes heavily and wipes the sweat from his brow.

He has a great deal to do, but still he does not give up his work as district doctor; he is greedy for gain, and he tries to be in all places at once. At Dyalizh and in the town he is called simply "Ionych": "Where is Ionych off to?" or "Should not we call in Ionych to a consultation?"

Probably because his throat is covered with rolls of fat, his voice has changed; it has become thin and sharp. His temper has changed, too: he has grown ill-humoured and irritable. When he sees his patients he is usually out of temper; he impatiently taps the floor with his stick, and shouts in his disagreeable voice:

"Be so good as to confine yourself to answering my questions! Don't talk so much!"

He is solitary. He leads a dreary life; nothing interests him.

During all the years he had lived at Dyalizh his love for Kitten had been his one joy, and probably his last. In the evenings he plays *vint* at the club, and then sits alone at a big table and has supper. Ivan, the oldest and most respectable of the waiters, serves him, hands him Lafitte No. 17, and everyone at the club – the members of the committee, the cook and waiters – know what he likes and what he doesn't like and do their very utmost to satisfy him, or else he is sure to fly into a rage and bang on the floor with his stick.

As he eats his supper, he turns round from time to time and puts in his spoke in some conversation:

"What are you talking about? Eh? Whom?"

And when at a neighbouring table there is talk of the Turkins, he asks:

"What Turkins are you speaking of? Do you mean the people whose daughter plays on the piano?"

That is all that can be said about him.

And the Turkins? Ivan Petrovitch has grown no older; he is not changed in the least, and still makes jokes and tells anecdotes as of old. Vera Iosifovna still reads her novels aloud to her visitors with eagerness and touching simplicity. And Kitten plays the piano for four hours every day. She has grown visibly older, is constantly ailing and every autumn goes to the Crimea with her mother. When Ivan Petrovitch sees them off at the station, he wipes his tears as the train starts, and shouts:

"Goodbye, if you please."

And he waves his handkerchief.

THE WHITE DOG

Fyodor Sologub (1863–1927)

Translated by John Cournos

Born in a poor peasant family and raised without a father, who died when his son was four, **Fyodor Sologub** (1863–1927) changed his common-sounding family name Teternikov to the more aristocratic Sologub (one L instead of two gives a hint that it is a pseudonym) when he started to publish his poems and short stories. He went from decadence to symbolism, explored mysteries and cast a shrewd glance towards death. He was an early supporter of revolutionary movements but became an opponent of the Bolsheviks.

For several years, until the fall of 1921, he relentlessly lobbied for permission to leave Red Russia. But, when it was finally granted, his wife committed suicide just a few days before their departure. After that he had no will to leave and died six years later, banned by the Soviets from being published in his native language.

Everything grew irksome for Alexandra Ivanovna in the workshop of this out-of-the-way town—the pattens, the clatter of machines, the complaints of the managers; it was the shop in which she had served as apprentice and now for several years as seamstress. Everything irritated Alexandra Ivanovna; she quarrelled with every one and abused the innocent apprentices. Among others to suffer from her outbursts of temper was Tanechka, the youngest of the seamstresses, who had only recently become an apprentice. In the beginning Tanechka submitted to her abuse in silence. In the end she revolted, and, addressing herself to her assailant, said, quite calmly and affably, so that every one laughed:

"You, Alexandra Ivanovna, are a downright dog!"

Alexandra Ivanovna felt humiliated.

"You are a dog yourself!" she exclaimed. Tanechka was sitting sewing. She paused now and then from her work and said in a calm, deliberate manner:

"You always whine.... Certainly, you are a dog.... You have a dog's snout. ... And a dog's ears. ... And a wagging tail. ... The mistress will soon drive you out of doors, because you are the most detestable of dogs, a poodle."

Tanechka was a young, plump, rosy-cheeked girl with an innocent, good-natured face, which revealed, however, a trace of cunning. She sat there so demurely, barefooted, still dressed in her apprentice clothes; her eyes were clear, and her brows were highly arched on her fine curved white forehead, framed by straight, dark chestnut hair, which in the distance looked black. Tanechka's voice was clear, even, sweet, insinuating, and if one could have heard its sound only, and not given heed to the words, it would have given the impression that she was paying Alexandra Ivanovna compliments.

The other seamstresses laughed, the apprentices chuckled, they covered their faces with their black aprons and cast side glances at Alexandra Ivanovna. As for Alexandra Ivanovna, she was livid with rage.

"Wretch!" she exclaimed. "I will pull your ears for you! I won't leave a hair on your head."

Tanechka replied in a gentle voice:

"The paws are a trifle short. ... The poodle bites as well as barks. ... It may be necessary to buy a muzzle."

Alexandra Ivanovna made a movement toward Tanechka. But before Tanechka had time to lay aside her work and get up, the mistress of the establishment, a large, serious-looking woman, entered, rustling her dress.

She said sternly: "Alexandra Ivanovna, what do you mean by making such a fuss?"

Alexandra Ivanovna, much agitated, replied: "Irina Petrovna, I wish you would forbid her to call me a dog!"

Tanechka in her turn complained: "She is always snarling at something or other. Always quibbling at the smallest trifles."

But the mistress looked at her sternly and said: "Tanechka, I can see through you. Are you sure you didn't begin? You needn't think that because you are a seamstress now you are an important person. If it weren't for your mother's sake—"

Tanechka grew red, but preserved her innocent and affable manner. She addressed her mistress in a subdued voice: "Forgive me, Irina Petrovna, I will not do it again. But it wasn't altogether my fault. ..."

* * *

Alexandra Ivanovna returned home almost ill with rage. Tanechka had guessed her weakness.

"A dog! Well, then I am a dog," thought Alexandra Ivanovna, "but it is none of her affair! Have I looked to see whether she is a serpent or a fox? It is easy to find one out, but why make a fuss about it? Is a dog worse than any other animal?"

The clear summer night languished and sighed, a soft breeze from the adjacent fields occasionally blew down the peaceful streets. The moon rose clear and full, that very same moon which rose long ago at another place, over the broad desolate steppe, the home of the wild, of those who ran free, and whined in their ancient earthly travail. The very same, as then and in that region.

And now, as then, glowed eyes sick with longing; and her heart, still wild, not forgetting in town the great spaciousness of the steppe, felt oppressed; her throat was troubled with a tormenting desire to howl like a wild thing.

She was about to undress, but what was the use? She could not sleep, anyway.

She went into the passage. The warm planks of the floor bent and creaked under her, and small shavings and sand which covered them tickled her feet not unpleasantly.

She went out on the doorstep. There sat the *babushka* Stepanida, a black figure in her black shawl, gaunt and shrivelled. She sat with her head bent, and it seemed as though she were warming herself in the rays of the cold moon.

Alexandra Ivanovna sat down beside her. She kept looking at the old woman sideways. The large curved nose of her companion seemed to her like the beak of an old bird.

"A crow?" Alexandra Ivanovna asked herself.

She smiled, forgetting for the moment her longing and her fears. Shrewd as the eyes of a dog, her own lighted up with the joy of her discovery. In the pale green light of the moon the wrinkles of her faded face became altogether invisible, and she seemed once more young and merry and light-hearted, just as she was ten years ago, when the moon had not yet called upon her to bark and bay of nights before the windows of the dark bathhouse.

She moved closer to the old woman, and said affably: "*Babushka* Stepanida, there is something I have been wanting to ask you."

The old woman turned to her, her dark face furrowed with wrinkles, and asked in a sharp, oldish voice that sounded like a caw: "Well, my dear? Go ahead and ask."

Alexandra Ivanovna gave a repressed laugh; her thin shoulders suddenly trembled from a chill that ran down her spine.

She spoke very quietly: *"Babushka* Stepanida, it seems to me—tell me is it true?—I don't know exactly how to put it—but you, *babushka*, please don't take offence—it is not from malice that I—"

"Go on, my dear, never fear, say it," said the old woman.

She looked at Alexandra Ivanovna with glowing, penetrating eyes.

"It seems to me, *babushka*—please, now, don't take offence—as though you, *babushka*, were a crow."

The old woman turned away. She was silent and merely nodded her head. She had the appearance of one who had recalled something. Her head, with its sharply outlined nose, bowed and nodded, and at last it seemed to Alexandra Ivanovna that the old woman was dozing. Dozing, and mumbling something under her nose. Nodding her head and mumbling some old forgotten words—old magic words.

An intense quiet reigned out of doors. It was neither light nor dark, and everything seemed bewitched with the inarticulate mumbling of old forgotten words. Everything languished and seemed lost in apathy. Again a longing oppressed her heart. And it was neither a dream nor an illusion. A thousand perfumes, imperceptible by day, became subtly distinguishable, and they recalled something ancient and primitive, something forgotten in the long ages.

In a barely audible voice the old woman mumbled: "Yes, I am a crow. Only I have no wings. But there are times when I caw, and I caw, and tell of woe. And I am given to forebodings, my dear; each time I have one I simply must caw. People are not particularly anxious to hear me. And when I see a doomed person I have such a strong desire to caw."

The old woman suddenly made a sweeping movement with her arms, and in a shrill voice cried out twice: "Kar-r, Kar-r!"

Alexandra Ivanovna shuddered, and asked: "*Babushka*, at whom are you cawing?"

The old woman answered: "At you, my dear—at you."

It had become too painful to sit with the old woman any longer.

Alexandra Ivanovna went to her own room. She sat down before the open window and listened to two voices at the gate.

"It simply won't stop whining!" said a low and harsh voice.

"And uncle, did you see——?" asked an agreeable young tenor.

Alexandra Ivanovna recognized in this last the voice of the curly-headed, somewhat red, freckled-faced lad who lived in the same court.

A brief and depressing silence followed. Then she heard a hoarse and harsh voice say suddenly: "Yes, I saw. It's very large—and white. Lies near the bathhouse, and bays at the moon."

The voice gave her an image of the man, of his shovel-shaped beard, his low, furrowed forehead, his small, piggish eyes, and his spread-out fat legs.

"And why does it bay, uncle?" asked the agreeable voice.

And again the hoarse voice did not reply at once.

"Certainly to no good purpose—and where it came from is more than I can say."

"Do you think, uncle, it may be a werewolf?" asked the agreeable voice.

"I should not advise you to investigate," replied the hoarse voice.

She could not quite understand what these words implied, nor did she wish to think of them. She did not feel inclined to listen further. What was the sound and significance of human words to *her*?

The moon looked straight into her face, and persistently called her and tormented her. Her heart was restless with a dark longing, and she could not sit still.

Alexandra Ivanovna quickly undressed herself. Naked, all white, she silently stole through the passage; she then opened the outer door—there was no one on the step or outside—and ran quickly across the court and the vegetable garden, and reached the bathhouse. The sharp contact of her body with the cold air and her feet with the cold ground gave her pleasure. But soon her body was warm.

She lay down in the grass, on her stomach. Then, raising herself on her elbows, she lifted her face toward the pale, brooding moon, and gave a long-drawn-out whine.

"Listen, uncle, it is whining," said the curly-haired lad at the gate.

The agreeable tenor voice trembled perceptibly.

"Whining again, the accursed one," said the hoarse, harsh voice slowly.

They rose from the bench. The gate latch clicked.

They went silently across the courtyard and the vegetable garden, the two of them. The older man, black-bearded and powerful, walked in front, a gun in his hand. The curly-headed lad followed tremblingly, and looked constantly behind.

Near the bathhouse, in the grass, lay a huge white dog, whining piteously. Its head, black on the crown, was raised to the moon, which pursued its way in the cold sky; its hind legs were strangely thrown backward, while the front ones, firm and straight, pressed hard against the ground.

In the pale green and unreal light of the moon it seemed enormous, so huge a dog was surely never seen on earth. It was thick and fat. The black spot, which began at the head and stretched in uneven strands down the entire spine, seemed like a woman's loosened hair. No tail was visible, presumably it was turned under. The fur on the body was so short that in the distance the dog seemed wholly naked, and its hide shone dimly in the moonlight, so that altogether it resembled the body of a nude woman, who lay in the grass and bayed at the moon.

The man with the black beard took aim. The curly-haired lad crossed himself and mumbled something.

The discharge of a rifle sounded in the night air. The dog gave a groan, jumped up on its hind legs, became a naked woman, who, her body covered with blood, started to run, all the while groaning, weeping and raising cries of distress.

The black-bearded one and the curly-haired one threw themselves in the grass, and began to moan in wild terror.

TWENTY SIX MEN AND A GIRL. A POEM

Maxim Gorky (1868–1936)

Translated by Emily Jakowleff & Dora Montefiore

The number one proletarian writer, the founding father of social realism, the man whose name was embedded in the map of the USSR like no other writer's (Gorky street, Gorky city, Gorky metro station, he even had an aircraft named after him), **Maxim Gorky**, born Alexei Maximovich Peshkov in 1868, worked from childhood on the Volga river, becoming a kind of encyclopedia of workers' and craftsmens' lives, then practiced a dozen diverse professions. He soon became a rising star of literature.

Romanticizing revolution and being seduced by its charms, Gorky engaged in a long and uneven relationship with the communist movement. This romance brought him glory, forced him into exile on the island of Capri, made him an intermediary between the old *intelligencia* and the Bolsheviks, brought about his second exile (this time from the Soviet Russia), and lured him back to the USSR. He died there under suspicious circumstances in 1936.

There were six-and-twenty of us—six-and-twenty living machines locked up in a damp basement, where from morning till night we kneaded dough and rolled it into pretzels and cracknels. Opposite the windows of our basement was a bricked area, green and moldy with moisture. The windows were protected from outside with a close iron grating, and the light of the sun could not pierce through the windowpanes, covered as they were with flour dust.

Our employer had bars placed in front of the windows, so that we should not be able to give a bit of his bread to passing beggars, or to any of our fellows who were out of work and hungry. Our employer called us crooks, and gave us half-rotten tripe to eat for our midday meal, instead of meat. It was swelteringly close for us cooped up in that stone underground chamber, under the low, heavy, soot-blackened, cobwebby ceiling. Dreary and sickening was our life within its thick, dirty, moldy walls.

Unrefreshed, and with a feeling of not having had our sleep out, we used to get up at five o'clock in the morning; and at six, we were already seated, worn out and apathetic, at the table, rolling out the dough which our mates had already prepared while we slept. The whole day, from early morning until ten at night, some of us sat round that table, working up in our hands the unyielding dough, swaying to and fro so as not to grow numb; while the others mixed flour and water. And the whole day the simmering water in the kettle, where the pretzels were being cooked sang low and sadly; and the baker's shovel scraped harshly over the oven floor, as he threw the slippery bits of dough out of the kettle on the heated bricks.

From morning till evening wood was burning in the oven, and the red glow of the fire gleamed and flickered over the walls of the bake-shop, as if silently mocking us. The giant oven was like the misshapen head of a monster in a fairy tale; it thrust itself up out of the floor, opened wide jaws, full of glowing fire, and blew hot breath upon us; it seemed to be ever watching out of its black air-holes our interminable work. Those two deep holes were like eyes—the cold, pitiless eyes of a monster. They watched us always with the same darkened glance, as if they were weary of seeing before them such slaves, from whom they could expect nothing human, and therefore scorned them with the cold scorn of wisdom.

In meal dust, in the mud which we brought in from the yard on our boots, in the hot, sticky atmosphere, day in, day out, we rolled the dough into pretzels, which we moistened with our own sweat. And we hated our work with a bitter hatred; we never ate what had passed through our hands, and preferred black bread to pretzels. Sitting opposite each other, at a long table—nine facing nine—we moved our hands and fingers mechanically during endlessly long hours, till we were so accustomed to our monotonous work that we ceased to pay any attention to our own motions.

We had all stared at each other so long, that each of us knew every wrinkle of his mates' faces. It was not long also before we had exhausted almost every topic of conversation; that is why we were most of the time silent, unless we were chaffing each other; but one cannot always find something about which to chaff another man, especially when that man is one's mate. Neither were we much given to finding fault with one another; how, indeed, could one of us poor devils be in a position to find fault with another, when we were all of us half dead and, as it were, turned to stone? For the heavy drudgery seemed to crush all feeling out of us. But silence is only terrible and fearful for those who have said everything and have nothing more to say to each other; for men, on the contrary, who have never begun to communicate with one another, it is easy and simple.

Sometimes, too, we sang; and this is how it happened that we began to sing: one of us would sigh deeply in the midst of our toil, like an overdriven horse, and then we would begin one of those songs whose gentle drawn-out melody seems always to ease the burden on the singer's heart.

At first one sang by himself, and we others sat in silence listening to his solitary song, which, under the heavy vaulted roof of the basement, died gradually away and became extinguished, like a little fire in the steppes, on a wet autumn night, when the gray heaven hangs like a leaden roof over the earth. Then another would join in with the singer, and now two soft, sad voices would break into song in our narrow, dull hole of a basement. Suddenly others would join in, and the song would surge up like a wave, would grow louder and swell upward, till it would seem as if the damp, foul walls of our stone prison were widening out and opening. Then, all six-and-twenty of us would be singing; our loud, harmonious song would fill the whole shop; the song felt cramped, it was striking, as it were, against the walls in moaning sobs and sighs, moving our hearts with a soft, tantalizing ache, tearing open old wounds, and awakening longings.

The singers would sigh deeply and heavily; suddenly one would become silent and listen to the others singing, then let his voice flow once more in the common tide. Another would exclaim in a stifled voice, "Ah!" and would shut his eyes, while the deep, full sound waves would show him, as it were, a road, in front of him—a sunlit, broad road in the distance, which he himself, in thought, wandered along.

But the flame flickers once more in the huge oven, the baker scrapes incessantly with his shovel, the water simmers in the kettle, and the flicker of the fire on the wall dances as before in silent mockery. While in other men's words we sing out our dumb grief, the weary burden of live men robbed of the sunlight, the heartache of slaves.

So we lived, we six-and-twenty, in the vault-like basement of a great stone house, and we suffered each one of us, as if we had to bear on our shoulders the whole three storys of that house.

But we had something else good, besides the singing—something we loved, that perhaps took the place of the sunshine.

In the second story of our house there was established a gold-embroiderer's shop, and there, living among the other embroidery girls, was Tanya, a little maid-servant of sixteen. Every morning there peeped in through the glass door a rosy little face, with merry blue eyes; while a ringing, tender voice called out to us:

"Little prisoners! Have you any pretzels, please, for me?"

At that clear sound we knew so well, we all used to turn round, gazing with good-natured joy at the pure girlish face which smiled at us so sweetly. The sight of the little nose pressed against the window-pane, and of the small white teeth gleaming between the half-open lips, had become for us a daily pleasure. Tumbling over each other we used to jump up to open the door, and she would step in, bright and cheerful, holding out her apron, with her head bent to one side, and a smile on her lips. Her thick, long chestnut braid fell over her shoulder and across her breast. We, ugly, dirty and misshapen as we were, looked up at her—the door was four steps above the floor—looked up at her with heads thrown back, wishing her good morning, and speaking strange, unaccustomed words, which we kept for her only. Our voices became softer when we spoke to her, our jests were lighter. For her—everything was different with us. The baker took from his oven a shovelful of the best and the brownest pretzels, and threw them deftly into Tanya's apron.

"Be off with you now, or the boss will catch you!" we warned her each time. She laughed roguishly, called out cheerfully: "Good-by, poor prisoners!" and slipped away as quick as a mouse.

That was all. But long after she had gone we talked about her to one another with pleasure. It was always the same thing as we had said yesterday and the day before, because everything about us, including ourselves and her, remained the same—as yesterday—and as always.

Painful and terrible it is when a man goes on living, while nothing changes around him; and when such an existence does not finally kill his soul, then the monotony becomes with time, even more and more painful. Generally we spoke about women in such a way that sometimes it was loathsome to us ourselves to hear our rude, shameless talk. The women whom we knew deserved perhaps nothing better. But about Tanya we never let fall an evil word; none of us ever ventured so much as to lay a hand on her, even too free a jest she never heard from us. Maybe this was so because she never remained with us for long; she flashed on our eyes like a star falling from the sky, and vanished; and maybe because she was little and very beautiful, and everything beautiful calls forth respect, even in coarse people. And besides—though our life of drudgery had made us dull beasts, oxen, we were still men, and, like all men, could not live without worshipping something or other. Better than her we had none, and none but her took any notice of us, living in the basement—no one, though there were dozens of people in the house. And then, too—most likely, this was the chief thing—we all regarded her as something of our own, something existing as it were only by virtue of our pretzels. We took on ourselves in turns the duty of providing her with hot pretzels, and this became for us like a daily sacrifice to our idol, it became almost a sacred rite, and every day it bound us more closely to her. Besides pretzels, we gave Tanya a great deal of advice—to wear warmer clothes, not to run upstairs too quickly, not to carry heavy bundles of wood. She listened to all our counsels with a smile, answered them by a laugh, and never took our advice, but we were not offended at that; all we wanted was to show how concerned we were for her welfare.

Often she would apply to us with different requests, she asked us, for instance, to open the heavy door into the cellar, to chop wood: with delight and a sort of pride, we did this for her, and everything else she wanted.

But when one of us asked her to mend his solitary shirt for him, she said, with a laugh of contempt:

"What next! A likely idea!"

We made great fun of the queer fellow who could entertain such an idea, and—never asked her to do anything else. We loved her—all is said in that. Man always wants to give his love to someone, though sometimes he crushes, sometimes he sullies, with it. We were bound to love Tanya, for we had no one else to love.

At times one of us would suddenly begin to reason like this:

"And why do we make so much of the wench? What is there in her, eh? What a to-do we make about her!"

The man who dared to utter such words we promptly and coarsely cut short—we wanted something to love: we had found it and loved it, and what we twenty-six loved must be for each of us unshakable, as a holy thing, and anyone who acted against us in this was our enemy. We loved, maybe, not what was really good, but you see there were twenty-six of us, and so we always wanted to see what was precious to us held sacred by the rest.

Our love is not less burdensome than hate, and maybe that is just why some proud souls maintain that our hate is more flattering than our love. But why do they not run away from us, if it is so?

Besides our department, our employer had also a bakery where they made rolls; it was in the same house, separated from our hole only by a wall; but the bakers—there were four of them—held aloof from us, considering their work superior to ours, and therefore themselves better than us; they never used to come into our workroom, and laughed contemptuously at us when they met us in the yard. We, too, did not go to see them; this was forbidden by our employer, for fear that we should steal the fancy rolls. We did not like the bakers, because we envied them; their work was lighter than ours, they were paid more, and were better fed; they had a light, spacious workroom, and they were all so clean and healthy—and that made them hateful to us. We all looked gray and yellow; three of us had syphilis, several suffered from skin diseases, one was completely crippled by rheumatism. On holidays and in their leisure time the bakers wore pea-jackets and creaking boots, two of them had accordions, and they all used to go for strolls in the public park—we wore filthy rags and torn leather shoes or bast slippers on our feet, the police would not let us into the public park—could we possibly like the bakers?

And one day we learned that one of their men had gone on a spree, the master had sacked him and had already taken on another, and that this other was an ex-soldier, wore a satin waistcoat and a watch and gold chain. We were anxious to get a sight of such a dandy, and in the hope of catching a glimpse of him we kept running one after another out into the yard.

But he came of his own accord into our workroom. Kicking at the door, he pushed it open, and leaving it ajar, stood in the doorway smiling, and said to us:

"God help the work! Good morning, mates!"

The frosty air, which streamed in through the open door, curled in streaks of vapor round his feet. He stood on the threshold, looked down upon us, and under his fair, twisted mustache gleamed big yellow teeth. His waistcoat was really something quite out of the common, blueflowered, brilliant with shining little red stone buttons. He also wore a watch chain.

He was a fine fellow, this soldier; tall, healthy, rosy-checked, and his big, clear eyes had a friendly, cheerful glance. He wore on his head a white starched cap, and from under his spotlessly clean apron peeped the pointed toes of fashionable, well-blacked boots.

Our baker asked him politely to shut the door. The soldier did so without hurrying himself, and began to question us about the master. We explained to him, all speaking together, that our employer was a thorough-going brute, a crook, a knave, and a slave-driver; in a word, we repeated to him all that can and must be said about an employer, but cannot be repeated here. The soldier listened to us, twitched his mustache, and watched us with a friendly, open-hearted look.

"But haven't you got a lot of girls here?" he asked suddenly.

Some of us began to laugh deferentially, others leered, and one of us explained to the soldier that there were nine girls here.

"You make the most of them?" asked the soldier, with a wink.

We laughed, but not so loudly, and with some embarrassment. Many of us would have liked to have shown the soldier that we also were tremendous fellows with the girls, but not one of us could do so; and one of our number confessed as much, when he said in a low voice:

"That sort of thing is not in our line."

"Well, no; it wouldn't quite do for you," said the soldier with conviction, after having looked us over. "There is something wanting about you all. You don't look the right sort. You've no sort of appearance; and the women, you see, they like a bold appearance, they will have a well-set-up body. Everything has to be tip-top for them. That's why they respect strength. They want an arm like that!"

The soldier drew his right hand, with its turned-up shirt sleeve, out of his pocket, and showed us his bare arm. It was white and strong, and covered with shining golden wool.

"Leg and chest, all must be strong. And then a man must be dressed in the latest fashion, so as to show off his looks to advantage. Yes, all the women take to me. I don't call to them, I don't beckon them, yet with one accord, five at a time, they throw themselves at my head,"

He sat down on a flour sack, and told at length all about the way women loved him, and how bold he was with them. Then he left, and after the door had creaked to behind him, we sat for a long time silent, and thought about him and his talk. Then we all suddenly broke silence together, and it became apparent that we were all equally pleased with him. He was such a nice, open-hearted fellow; he came to see us without any stand-offishness, sat down and chatted. No one else had ever come to us like that, and no one else had talked to us in that friendly sort of way. And we continued to talk of him and his coming triumph among the embroidery girls, who passed us by with contemptuous sniffs when they saw us in the yard, or who looked straight through us as if we had been air. But we admired them always when we met them outside, or when they walked past our windows; in winter, in fur jackets and toques to match; in summer, in hats trimmed with flowers, and carrying colored parasols. Among ourselves, however, we talked about these girls in a way that would have made them mad with shame and rage, if they could have heard us.

"If only he does not get hold of little Tanya!" said the baker, suddenly, in an anxious tone of voice.

We were silent, for these words troubled us. Tanya had quite gone out of our minds, supplanted, put on one side by the strong, fine figure of the soldier.

Then began a lively discussion; some of us maintained that Tanya would never lower herself so; others thought she would not be able to resist him, and the third group proposed to break his ribs for him if he should try to annoy Tanya. And, finally, we all decided to watch the soldier and Tanya, and to warn the girl against him. This brought the discussion to an end.

Four weeks had passed by since then; during this time the soldier baked white rolls, walked out with the gold-embroidery girls, visited us often, but did not talk any more about his conquests; only twisted his mustache and licked his lips lasciviously.

Tanya called in as usual every morning for "little pretzels," and was as gay and as nice and friendly with us as ever. We certainly tried once or twice to talk to her about the soldier, but she called him a "goggle-eyed calf," and made fun of him all round, and that set our minds at rest. We saw how the gold-embroidery girls carried on with the soldier, and we were proud of our girl; Tanya's behavior reflected honor on us all; we imitated her, and began in our talks to treat the soldier with small consideration. She became dearer to us, and we greeted her with more friendliness and kindliness every morning.

One day the soldier came to see us, a bit drunk, and sat down and began to laugh. When we asked him what he was laughing about, he explained to us:

"Why, two of them—that Lydka girl and Grushka—have been clawing each other on my account. You should have seen the way they went for each other! Ha! ha! One got hold of the other one by the hair, threw her down on the floor of the passage, and sat on her! Ha! ha! ha! They scratched and tore each others' faces. It was enough to make one die with laughter! Why is it women can't fight fair? Why do they always scratch one another, eh?"

He sat on the bench, in fine fettle, fresh and jolly; he sat there and went on laughing. We were silent. This time he made an unpleasant impression on us.

"Well, it's a funny thing what luck I have with the women-folk! Eh? One wink, and it's all over with them! It's the d-devil!"

He raised his white arms covered with golden wool, and dropped them down on his knees. And his eyes seemed to reflect such frank astonishment, as if he were himself quite surprised at his good luck with women. His fat, red face glistened with delight and self-satisfaction, and he licked his lips more than ever.

Our baker scraped the shovel violently and angrily along the oven floor, and all at once he said sarcastically:

"There's no great strength needed to pull up fir saplings, but try a real pine-tree."

"Why—what do you mean by saying that to me?" asked the soldier.

"Oh, well ..."

"What is it?"

"Nothing—it slipped out!"

"No, wait a minute! What's the point? What pine-tree?"

Our baker did not answer, working rapidly away with the shovel at the oven; flinging into it the half-cooked pretzels, taking out those that were done, and noisily throwing them on the floor to the boys who were stringing them on bast. He seemed to have forgotten the soldier and his conversation with him. But the soldier had all at once grown uneasy. He got up onto his feet, and went to the oven, at the risk of knocking against the handle of the shovel, which was waving spasmodically in the air.

"No, tell me, do—who is it? You've insulted me. I? There's not one could withstand me, n-no! And you say such insulting things to me?"

He really seemed genuinely hurt. He must have had nothing else to pride himself on except his gift for seducing women; maybe, except for that, there was nothing living in him, and it was only that by which he could feel himself a living man.

There are men to whom the most precious and best thing in their lives appears to be some disease of their soul or body. They fuss over it all their lives, and only living by it, suffering from it, they feed on it, they complain of it to others, and so draw the attention of their fellows to themselves. For that they extract sympathy from people, and apart from it they have nothing at all. Take from them that disease, cure them, and they will be miserable, because they have lost their one resource in life—they are left empty then. Sometimes a man's life is so poor, that he is driven instinctively to prize his vice and to live by it; one may say for a fact that often men are vicious out of boredom.

The soldier was offended, he went up to our baker and roared:

"No, tell me, do—who?"

"Tell you?" the baker turned suddenly to him.

"Well?"

"You know Tanya?"

"Well?"

"Well, there then! Only try."

"I?"

"You!"

"Her? Why, that's nothing to me—pooh!"

"We shall see!"

"You will see! Ha! ha!"

"She'll—"

"Give me a month!"

"What a braggart you are, soldier!"

"A fortnight! I'll prove it! Who is it? Tanya! Pooh!"

"Well, get out. You're in my way!"

"A fortnight—and it's done! Ah, you—"

"Get out, I say!"

Our baker, all at once, flew into a rage and brandished his shovel. The soldier staggered away from him in amazement, looked at us, paused, and softly, malignantly said, "Oh, all right, then!" and went away.

During the dispute we had all sat silent, absorbed in it. But when the soldier had gone, eager, loud talk and noise arose among us.

Someone shouted to the baker: "It's a bad job that you've started, Pavel!"

"Do your work!" answered the baker savagely.

We felt that the soldier had been touched to the quick, and that danger threatened Tanya. We felt this, and at the same time we were all possessed by a burning curiosity, most agreeable to us. What would happen? Would Tanya hold out against the soldier? And almost all cried confidently: "Tanya? She'll hold out! You won't catch her with your bare arms!"

We longed terribly to test the strength of our idol; we were forcibly trying to persuade each other that our divinity was a strong divinity and would come victorious out of this ordeal. We began at last to fancy that we had not worked enough on the soldier, that he would forget the dispute, and that we ought to pique his vanity further. From that day we began to live a different life, a life of nervous tension, such as we had never known before. We spent whole days in arguing together; we all grew, as it were, sharper; and got to talk more and better. It seemed to us that we were playing some sort of game with the devil, and the stake on our side was Tanya. And when we learned from the bakers that the soldier had begun "running after our Tanya," we felt a sort of delighted terror, and life was so interesting that we did not even notice that our employer had taken advantage of our preoccupation to increase our work by three hundred pounds of dough a day. We seemed, indeed, not even tired by our work. Tanya's name was on our lips all day long. And every day we looked for her with a certain peculiar impatience. Sometimes we pictured to ourselves that she would come to us, and it would not be the same Tanya as of old, but somehow different. We said nothing to her, however, of the dispute regarding her. We asked her no questions, and behaved as well and affectionately to her as ever. But even in this a new element crept in, alien to our old feeling for Tanya—and that new element was keen curiosity, keen and cold as a steel knife.

"Mates! Today the time's up!" our baker said to us one morning, as he set to work.

We were well aware of it without his reminder: but still we became alert.

"Have a good look at her. She'll be here directly," suggested the baker.

One of us cried out in a troubled voice, "Why! as though one could see anything! You need more than eyes."

And again an eager, noisy discussion sprang up among us. Today we were at last to discover how pure and spotless was the vessel into which we had poured all that was best in us. This morning, for the first time, it became clear to us that we really were playing for high stakes; that we might, indeed, through the exaction of this proof of purity, lose our divinity altogether.

All this time we had been hearing that Tanya was stubbornly and persistently pursued by the soldier, but not one of us had thought of asking her what she thought of him. And she came every morning to fetch her pretzels, and was the same toward us as ever.

This morning, too, we heard her voice outside: "You poor prisoners! Here I am!"

We opened the door hastily, and when she came in we all remained, contrary to our usual custom, silent. Our eyes fixed on her, we did not know what to say to her, what to ask her. And there we stood in front of her, a gloomy, silent crowd. She seemed to be surprised at this unusual reception; and suddenly we saw her turn white and become uneasy, then she asked, in a choking voice:

"Why are you—like this?"

"And you?" the baker flung at her grimly, never taking his eyes off her.

"What about me?"

"N-nothing."

"Well, then, give me the little pretzels quickly."

Never before had she bidden us hurry.

"There's plenty of time," said the baker, not stirring and not removing his eyes from her face.

Then, suddenly, she turned round and disappeared through the door.

The baker took his shovel and said, calmly turning away toward the oven:

"Well, that settles it! There's a soldier for you—the low cur!"

Like a flock of sheep we all pressed round the table, sat down silently, and began listlessly to work. Soon, however, one of us remarked:

"Perhaps, after all—"

"Shut up!" shouted the baker.

We were all convinced that he was a man of judgment, a man who knew more than we did about things. And at the sound of his voice we were convinced of the soldier's victory, and our spirits became sad and downcast.

At twelve o'clock—while we were eating our dinners—the soldier came in. He was as clean and as smart as ever, and looked at us—as usual—straight in the eyes. But we were all awkward in looking at him.

"Now then, honored sirs, would you like me to show you a soldier's prowess?" he said, chuckling proudly.

"Go out into the passage and look through the crack—do you understand?"

We went into the passage, and stood all pushing against one another, squeezed up to the cracks of the wooden partition of the passage that looked into the yard. We had not to wait long. Very soon Tanya, with hurried footsteps and an anxious face, walked across the yard, jumping over the puddles of melting snow and mud: she disappeared into the cellar. Then whistling, and not hurrying himself, the soldier followed in the same direction. His hands were thrust in his pockets; his mustaches were quivering.

Rain was falling, and we saw how its drops struck the puddles, and the puddles were wrinkled by them. The day was damp and gray—a very dreary day. Snow still lay on the roofs, but on the ground dark patches of mud had begun to appear. And the snow on the roofs too was covered by a layer of brownish dirt. The rain fell slowly with a depressing sound. It was cold and disagreeable for us waiting.

The first to come out of the cellar was the soldier; he walked slowly across the yard, his mustaches twitching, his hands in his pockets—the same as always.

Then—Tanya, too, came out. Her eyes—her eyes were radiant with joy and happiness, and her lips—were smiling. And she walked as though in a dream, staggering, with unsteady steps.

We could not bear this calmly. All of us at once rushed to the door, dashed out into the yard and—hissed at her, reviled her viciously, loudly, wildly.

She started at seeing us, and stood as though rooted in the mud under her feet. We formed a ring round her, and maliciously, without restraint, abused her with vile words, said shameful things to her.

We did this quietly, slowly, seeing that she could not get away, that she was hemmed in by us, and we could rail at her to our hearts' content. I don't know why, but we did not beat her. She stood in the midst of us, and turned her head this way and that, as she heard our insults. And we—more and more violently flung at her the filth and venom of our words.

The color had left her face. Her blue eyes, so happy a moment before, opened wide, her bosom heaved, and her lips quivered.

We in a ring round her avenged ourselves on her, for she had robbed us. She belonged to us, we had lavished on her our best, and though that best was beggar's crumbs, still there were twenty-six of us, she was one, and so there was no pain we could give her equal to her guilt! How we insulted her! She was still mute, still gazed at us with wild eyes, and a shiver ran through her.

We laughed, roared, yelled. Other people ran up from somewhere and joined us. One of us pulled Tanya by the sleeve of her blouse.

Suddenly her eyes flashed; deliberately she raised her hands to her head and straightening her hair she said loudly but calmly, straight in our faces:

"Ah, you miserable prisoners!"

And she walked straight at us, walked as directly as though we had not been before her, as though we were not blocking her way.

And hence none of us did actually block her way.

Walking out of our circle without turning round, she added loudly, with pride and indescribable contempt:

"Ah, you scum—brutes."

And—was gone, erect, beautiful, proud.

We were left in the middle of the yard, in the rain, under the gray sunless sky.

Then we went mutely away to our damp stone basement. As before—the sun never peeped in at our windows, and Tanya came no more. Never!

A CLUMP OF LILACS

Alexander Kuprin (1870–1938)

Translated by Rosa Savary Graham

Having experienced the harsh discipline of a military school and the routine of provincial army service, **Alexander Kuprin** (1870–1938) retired and changed cities, environments, professions: his job titles included reporter, blacksmith, actor, steel worker, teacher and many others. His prose had a perfect balance of knowledge, spirit, social life, lyricism and humor.

Supportive of the early revolutionary changes, by 1919 Kuprin had joined the White Army and after its defeat found himself in 1920 in Paris.

In 1937, in the year of the Great Terror, Kuprin was granted permission to return to the USSR – the Soviet government quite cynically concluded that the famous writer was seriously ill and probably would not write any more books, but that a rapprochement with him could bring political dividends. Kuprin lived in the USSR for an even shorter time than Maxim Gorky and passed away in 1938.

Nikolai Yevgrafovitch Almazof hardly waited for his wife to open the door to him; he went straight to his study without taking off his hat or coat. His wife knew in a moment by his frowning face and nervously-bitten underlip that a great misfortune had occurred.

She followed him in silence. Almazof stood still for a moment when he reached the study, and stared gloomily into one corner, then he dashed his portfolio out of his hand on to the floor, where it lay wide open, and threw himself into an armchair, irritably snapping his fingers together.

He was a young and poor army officer attending a course of lectures at the staff office academy, and had just returned from a class. To-day he had taken in to the professor his last and most difficult practical work, a survey of the neighbourhood.

So far all his examinations had gone well, and it was only known to God and to his wife what fearful labour they had cost him. ... To begin with, his very entrance into the academy had seemed impossible at first. Two years in succession he had failed ignominiously, and only in the third had he by determined effort overcome all hindrances. If it hadn't been for his wife he would not have had sufficient energy to continue the struggle; he would have given it up entirely. But Verotchka never allowed him to lose heart, she was always encouraging him ... she met every drawback with a bright, almost gay, front. She denied herself everything so that her husband might have all the little things so necessary for a man engaged in mental labour; she was his secretary, draughtsman, reader, lesson-hearer, and note-book all in one.

For five minutes there was a dead silence, broken only by the sorry sound of their old alarm clock, familiar and tiresome ... one, two, three-three—two clear ticks, and the third with a hoarse stammer. Almazof still sat in his hat and coat, turning to one side in his chair. ... Vera stood two paces from him, silent also, her beautiful mobile face full of suffering. At length she broke the stillness with the cautiousness a woman might use when speaking at the bedside of a very sick friend:

"Well, Kolya, what about the work? Was it bad?'

He shrugged his shoulders without speaking.

"Kolya, was it rejected? Tell me; we must talk it over together."

Almazof turned to his wife and began to speak irritably and passionately, as one generally does speak when telling of an insult long endured.

"Yes, yes. They've rejected it, if you want to know. Can't you see they have? It's all gone to the devil! All that rubbish"—he kicked the portfolio with his foot—"all that rubbish had better be thrown into the fire. That's your academy. I shall be back in the regiment with a bang next month, disgraced. And all for a filthy spot... damn it!"

"What spot, Kolya?" asked she. "I don't understand anything about it."

She sat down on the side of his chair and put her arm round his neck. He made no resistance, but still continued to stare into the corner with an injured expression.

"What spot was it, Kolya?" asked his wife once more.

"Oh, an ordinary spot—of green paint. You know I sat up until three o'clock last night to finish my drawing. The plan was beautifully done. Everyone said so. Well, I sat there last night and I got so tired that my hand shook, and I made a blot—such a big one. ... I tried to erase it, but I only made it worse. ... I thought and thought what I had better do, and I made up my mind to put a clump of trees in that place. ... It was very successful, and no one could guess there had been a blot. Well, to-day I took it in to the professor. 'Yes, yes,' said he, 'that's very well. But what have you got here, lieutenant; where have these bushes sprung from?' Of course, I ought to have told him what had happened. Perhaps he would only have laughed ... but no, he wouldn't, he's such an accurate German, such a pedant. So I said, 'There are some trees growing there.' 'Oh, no, no,' said he. 'I know this neighbourhood as well as I know the five fingers of my own hand; there can't be any trees there.' So, my word against his, we had a great argument about it; many of our officers were there too, listening. 'Well,' he said at last, 'if you're so sure that there are trees in this hollow, be so good as to ride over with me to-morrow and see. I'll prove to you that you've either done your work carelessly, or that you've copied it from a three versts to the inch map. ...'"

"But why was he so certain that no bushes were there?"

"Oh, Lord, why? What childish questions you do ask! Because he's known this district for twenty years; he knows it better than his own bedroom. He's the most fearful pedant in the world, and a German besides. ... Well, of course, he'll know in the end that I was lying and so discussed the point with him. ..."

All the time he spoke he kept picking up burnt matches from the ash-tray on the table in front of him, and breaking them to little bits. When he ceased speaking, he threw the pieces on the floor. It was quite evident that, strong man though he was, he was very near weeping.

For a long while husband and wife sat there silent. Then suddenly Verotchka jumped up from her seat.

"Listen, Kolya," said she. "We must go this very minute. Make haste and get ready."

Nikolai Yevgrafovitch wrinkled up his face as if he were suffering some intolerable pain.

"Oh, don't talk nonsense, Vera," he said. "You don't think I can go and put matters right by apologising, do you? That would be asking for punishment. Don't be foolish, please!"

"No, it's not foolishness," said Vera, stamping her toot. "Nobody wants you to go and apologise. But, don't you see, if there aren't any silly old trees there we'd better go and put some."

"Put some—trees!" exclaimed Nikolai Yevgrafovitch, his eyes staring.

"Yes, put some there. If you didn't speak the truth, then you must make it true. Come along, get ready. Give me my hat ... and coat. No, not there; in the cupboard. ... Umbrella!"

And while Almazof, finding his objections entirely ignored, began to look for the hat and coat, Vera opened drawers and brought out various little boxes and cases.

"Earrings. ... No, they're no good. We shan't get anything on them. Ah, here's this ring with the valuable stone. We'll have to buy that back some time. It would be a pity to lose it. Bracelet ... they won't give much for that either, it's old and bent. ... Where's your silver cigar-case, Kolya?"

In five minutes all their valuables were in her hand-bag, and Vera, dressed and ready, looked round for the last time to assure herself she hadn't overlooked anything.

"Let us go," she said at last, resolutely.

"But where?" Almazof tried again to protest. "It's beginning to get dark already, and the place is ten versts away."

"Stupid! Come along."

First of all they went to the pawnshop. The pawnbroker had evidently got accustomed long ago to the sight of people in distress, and could not be touched by it. He was so methodical about his work, and took so long to value the things, that Vera felt she should go crazy. What specially vexed her was that the man should test her ring with acid, and then, after weighing it, he valued it at three roubles only.

"But it's a real brilliant," said poor Vera. "It cost thirty-seven roubles, and then it was a bargain."

The pawnbroker closed his eyes with the air of a man who is frankly bored.

"It's all the same to us, madam," said he, putting the next article into the scales. "We don't take the stones into consideration, only the metals."

To Vera's astonishment, her old and bent bracelet was more

valuable. Altogether they got about twenty-three roubles, and that was more than was really necessary.

When they got to the gardener's house, the white Petersburg night had already spread over the heavens, and a pearly light was in the air. The gardener, a Tchekh, a little old man with gold eyeglasses, had only just sat down to supper with his family. He was much surprised at their request, and not altogether willing to take such a late order. He was doubtless suspicious of a practical joke, and answered dryly to Vera's insistent demands:

"I'm very sorry. But I can't send my workmen so far at night. If it will do to-morrow morning, I'm quite at your service."

There was no way out of the difficulty but to tell the man the whole story of the unfortunate blot, and this Verotchka did. He listened doubtfully at first, and was almost unfriendly, but when Vera began to tell him of her plan to plant some bushes on the place, he became more attentive and smiled sympathetically several times.

"Oh, well, it's not much to do," he agreed, when Vera had finished her story. "What sort of bushes do you want?"

However, when they came to look at his plants, there was nothing very suitable. The only thing possible to put on the spot was a clump of lilacs.

It was in vain for Almazof to try and persuade his wife to go home. She went all the way with him, and stayed all the time the bushes were planted, feverishly fussing about and hindering the workmen. She only consented to go home when she was assured that the turf under the bushes could not be distinguished from the rest of the grass round about.

Next day Vera felt it impossible to remain in the house. She went out to meet her husband. Quite a long way off she knew, by a slight spring in his walk, that everything had gone well. ... True, Almazof was covered in dust, and he could hardly move from weariness and hunger, but his face shone with the triumph of victory.

"It's all right! Splendid!" cried he when within ten paces of his wife, in answer to the anxious expression on her face. "Just think, we went together to those bushes, and he looked and looked at them—he even plucked a leaf and chewed it. 'What sort of a tree is this?' says he."

"'I don't know, your Excellency,' said I.

"'It's a little birch, I suppose,' says he.

"'Yes, probably, your Excellency.'"

Then he turned to me and held out his hand.

"'I beg your pardon, lieutenant,' he says. 'I must be getting old, that I didn't remember those bushes.' He's a fine man, that professor, and he knows a lot. I felt quite sorry to deceive him. He's one of the best professors we have. His learning is simply wonderful. And how quick and accurate he is in marking the plans—marvellous!"

But this meant little to Vera. She wanted to hear over and over again exactly what the professor had said about the bushes. She was interested in the smallest details—the expression on the professor's face, the tone of his voice when he said he must be growing old, exactly how Kolya felt. ...

They went home together as if there had been no one in the street except themselves, holding each other by the hand and laughing at nothing. The passers-by stopped to look at them; they seemed such a strange couple.

Never before had Nikolai Yevgrafovitch enjoyed his dinner so much as on that day. After dinner, when Vera brought a glass of tea to him in the study, husband and wife suddenly looked at one another, and both laughed.

"What are you laughing at?" asked Vera.

"Well, why did *you* laugh?" said her husband.

"Oh, only foolishness. I was thinking all about those lilacs. And you?"

"Oh, mine was foolishness too—and the lilacs. I was just going to say that now the lilac will always be my favourite flower. ..."

THE DREAMS OF CHANG

Ivan Bunin (1870–1953)

Translated by Bernard Guilbert Guerney

The first Russian laureate of the Nobel literature prize (1933), **Ivan Bunin** was, probably, the greatest Russian lyrical voice of the twentieth century in short prose forms. One of his short stories is called 'The grammar of love'; an outstanding explorer of sensuality and intimacy, Bunin himself was trapped in a long-lasting love triangle with his wife Vera Muromtzeva and literary protégé Galina Kuznetzova.

In 1920 Bunin, who was a strong opponent of the Bolsheviks, left Russia and established himself in France. In his late prose he tried to preserve the Russia he had lost, and the Russian language itself, occupied, distorted and enslaved by the communists.

It is worth noting that Varlam Shalamov, the martyr and the chronicler of the notorious Kolyma camps, got his third sentence in 1943 for calling Bunin a great Russian writer – informers brought his words to the ears of the camp authorities.

What does it matter of whom we speak? Any that have lived and that live upon this earth deserve to be the subject of our discourse.

Once upon a time Chang had come to know the universe and the captain, his master, to whom his earthly existence had become linked. And six entire years have run since then,—have run like the sands in a ship's hourglass.

It is again night,—dream or reality? And again comes morning,—reality or dream? Chang is old, Chang is a drunkard,—he is always dozing.

Outside, in the city of Odessa, it is winter. The weather is nasty, sullen,—far worse than that of China was when Chang and the captain met each other. Fine, stinging snow whirls through the air; it flies obliquely over the ice-covered, slippery asphalt of the desolate seaside boulevard, and painfully lashes the face of every running Jew who, with his hands shoved deep into his pockets, and with his shoulders hunched up, is zigzagging to the left and right,—awkwardly, Hebraically. Beyond the harbour, likewise deserted, beyond the bay, hazy from the snow, the barren shores, low and flat, are faintly visible. The jetty is hazy all the time with a thick, gray haze: the sea, in foamy, bellying waves, surges over it from morn till night. The wind whistles and reverberates among the telephone wires overhead. ...

On such days life in the city does not start at an early hour. Nor do Chang and the captain awake early. Six years,—is it a long time, or short? In six years Chang and the captain have grown old, although the captain is not yet forty; and their lot has harshly changed. They no longer sail the seas,—they live "on shore," as seamen say; nor are they living in the same place they lived in at one time, but in a narrow and rather dark street, in a garret; the house is redolent of anthracite, and is occupied by Jews,—of the sort that come to their families only toward evening and who sup with their hats shoved on the back of their heads. Chang and the captain have a low ceiling; their room is large and chill. Besides that, it is always gloomy and dark inside; the two windows placed in the sloping wall-roof are small and round, reminding one of port-holes. Something in the nature of a chest of drawers stands between the windows, and against the wall to the left is an old iron bed,—and there you have all the furnishings of this bleak dwelling,—unless the fireplace, out of which a fresh wind is always blowing, be included.

Chang sleeps in the nook behind the fireplace; the captain on the bed. What sort of a bed this is, sagging almost to the floor, and what kind of mattress it has, any one who has lived in garrets can easily imagine; as for the dirty pillow, it is so scanty that the captain is forced to put his jacket under it. However, the captain sleeps very peacefully even on this bed; he lies on his back, his eyes shut and his face ashen, as motionless as though he were dead. What a splendid bed had formerly been his! Well built, high, with chests underneath; the bedding was thick and snug, the sheets fine and smooth, and the snowy-white pillows were chilling! But even then, even when lulled by the rolling of the waves, he had not slept as heavily as he sleeps now: now he gets very tired during the day, and besides that, what has he to worry about now,—what can he oversleep, and with what can the new day gladden him? At one time there had been two truths in this world, that had constantly stood sentry in turns: the first was, that life is unutterably beautiful; and the second, that life holds a meaning only for lunatics. Now the captain affirms that there is, has been, and will be for all eternity but one truth,—the ultimate truth, the truth of Job the Hebrew, the truth of Ecclesiastes, the sage of an unknown tribe. Often does the captain say now, as he sits in some beer shop: "Remember now thy Creator in the days of thy youth, while the evil days come not, nor the years draw nigh, when thou shalt *say*, I have no pleasure in them!" Still the days and nights go on as before, and now there has again been a night, and again morning is coming on. And the captain and Chang are awaking.

But, having waked, the captain does not change his position and does not open his eyes. His thoughts at that moment are not known even to Chang, who is lying on the floor beside the fireless hearth from which the freshness of the sea had come all night. Chang is aware of only one thing,—that the captain will lie thus for not less than an hour. Chang, after casting a look at the captain out of the corner of his eye, again closes his lids, and again dozes off. Chang, too, is a drunkard; in the morning he, too, is befuddled, weak, and beholds the universe with that languid queasiness which is so familiar to all those travelling on ships and suffering from seasickness. And because of that, as he dozes off, in this morning hour, Chang sees a dream that is tormenting, wearisome. ...

He sees:

An old, rheumy-eyed Chinaman has clambered up onto a steamer's deck, and has squatted down on his heels; whiningly, he importunes all those who pass by him to buy a wicker-basket of spoilt small fish which he has brought with him. It is a dusty and a chill day on a broad Chinese river. In the boat with a bamboo sail, swaying in the muddy water of the river, a puppy is sitting,—a little rusty dog, having about it something of the fox and something of the wolf, with thick, coarse fur at its neck; sternly and intelligently his black eyes look up and down the high iron side of the steamer, and his ears are cocked.

"Better sell your dog!" gaily and loudly, as though to a deaf man, the young captain of the ship, who was standing idling on his bridge, yelled to the Chinaman.

The Chinaman,—Chang's first master,—cast his eyes upward;

confused, both by the yell and by joy, he began bowing and lisping: "Ve'y good dog, ve'y good."* And the puppy was purchased,—for only a single silver rouble,—was called Chang, and sailed off on that very day with his new master to Russia; and, in the beginning, for three whole weeks, he suffered so with seasickness, and was in such a daze, that he saw nothing: neither the ocean nor Singapore, nor Colombo. ...

It had been the beginning of autumn in China; the weather was bad. And Chang felt qualmish when they had barely passed into the estuary. They were met by lashing rain and mist; white-caps glimmered over the plain of waters; the gray-green swell swayed, rushed, plashed, many-pointed and senseless; meanwhile, the flat shores were spreading, losing themselves in the fog,—and there was more and more water all around. Chang, in his fur coat, silvery from the rain, and the captain, in a waterproof great-coat with the hood raised, were on the bridge, whose height could be felt now more than before. The captain issued commands, while Chang shivered and tossed his head in the wind. The water was widening, embracing all the inclement horizon, blending with the misty sky. The wind tore the spray from the great noisy swell, swooping down from any and every direction; it whistled through the sail-yards and boomingly slapped the canvas awnings below; the sailors, in the meanwhile, in iron-shod boots and wet capes, were untying, catching and furling them. The wind was seeking the best spot from which to strike its strongest blow, and just as soon as the steamer, slowly bowing before it, had taken a sharper turn to the right, the wind raised it up on such a huge, boiling roller, that it could not hold back; it plunged down from the ridge of the roller, burying itself in the foam,—and in the pilot's round-house a coffee cup, forgotten upon a little table by the waiter, shattered against the floor with a ring. ... And then the fun began!

There were all sorts of days after that: now the sun would blaze down scorchingly out of the radiant azure; now clouds would pile up in mountains and burst with peak of terrifying thunder; or raging torrents of rain descended in floods upon the steamer and the sea; or else there was rocking,—yes, rocking, even when the ship was at anchor. Utterly worn out, Chang during all the three weeks did not once

---

* In English in the orginial. *Trans*.

forsake his corner in the hot, halfdark corridor of the second-class cabins on the poop, where he lay near the high threshold of the door leading onto the deck. Only once a day was this door opened, when the captain's orderly brought food to Chang. And of the entire voyage to the Red Sea Chang's memory has retained only the creaking of the ship's partitions, his nausea, and the sinking of his heart, now flying downward into some abyss together with the quivering stern, now rising up to heaven with it; also did he remember his prickly, deathly terror whenever, with the sound of a cannon firing, a whole mountain of water would splash against this stern, after it had been raised high and had again careened to one side, with its propeller roaring in the air; the water would extinguish the daylight in the port holes, and then would run down in opaque torrents over their thick glass. The sick Chang heard the distant cries of commands, the thundering whistle of the boatswain, the tramp of sailors' feet somewhere overhead; he heard the plash and the noise of the water; he could distinguish through his half-shut eyes the semi-dark corridor filled with jute bails of tea,—and Chang went daft, became tipsy, from nausea, heat, and the strong odour of tea. ...

But here Chang's dream breaks off.

Chang starts and opens his eyes: that was no wave hitting against the stem with a sound of a cannon firing,—it was the jarring of a door somewhere below, flung back with force by somebody or other. And after this the captain coughingly clears his throat and slowly arises from his sagging couch. He puts on and laces his battered shoes, dons his black coat with the brass buttons, taking it out from under the pillow; Chang, in the meanwhile, in his rusty, worn fur coat, yawns discontentedly, with a whine, having risen from the floor. Upon the chest of drawers is a bottle of vodka, some of which has already been drunk. The captain drinks straight out of the bottle, and, slightly out of breath, wiping his moustache, he goes toward the fireplace and pours out some vodka into a little bowl standing near Chang for him as well. Chang starts lapping it greedily. As for the captain, he begins smoking and lies down again, to await the hour when it will be full day. The distant rumble of the tramway can already be heard; already, far below in the street, flows the ceaseless clamping of horses' hoofs; but it is still too early to go out. And the captain lies and smokes. Having done with his lapping, Chang, too, lies down. He jumps up onto the bed, curls up in a ball at the feet of the captain, and slowly floats away into that blissful state which vodka always bestows. His half-shut eyes grow misty, he looks faintly at his master, and, feeling a constantly increasing tenderness toward him, thinks what in human speech may be expressed as follows: "Oh, you foolish, foolish fellow! There is but one truth in this world, and if you but knew what a wonderful truth it is!" And again, in something between thought and dream, Chang reverts to that distant morning, when the steamer, after carrying the captain and Chang from China over the tormented restless ocean, had entered the Red Sea. ...

He dreams:

As they passed Perim, the steamer swayed less and less, as though it were lulling him asleep, and Chang fell into a sweet and sound sleep. And suddenly he started, awake. And, when he had become awake, he was astonished beyond all measure: it was quiet everywhere; the stern was rhythmically vibrating, without any downward plunges; the noise of the water, rushing somewhere beyond the walls, was even; the warm odour from the kitchen, creeping out on deck from underneath a door, was enchanting. ... Chang got up on his hind legs and looked into the deserted general cabin,—there, in the obscurity, was a softly radiant, aureately-lilac something: a something barely perceptible to the eye, but extraordinarily joyous; there the rear port holes were open to the sunlit blue void, open to the spaciousness, to the air, while over the low ceiling streamed sinuous rills of light reflected from mirrors,—they flowed on, without flowing away. ... And the same thing happened to Chang that had also happened more than once in those days to his master, the captain: he suddenly comprehended that there existed in this universe not one truth, but two truths: one, that to be living in this world and to sail the seas was a dreadful thing, and the other. ... But Chang did not have time to think of the other,—through the door, unexpectedly flung open, he saw the trap-ladder leading to the spar-deck, the black, glistening mass of the steamer's funnel, the clear sky of a summer morning, and, coming rapidly from under the ladder, out of the engine room, the captain. He had shaved and washed; there was the fragrance of fresh Eau-de-cologne about him; his fair moustache turned upward, after the German fashion; the glance of his light, keen eyes was sparkling, and everything upon him was tight-fitting and snowy white.

And upon beholding all this Chang darted forward so joyously that the captain caught him in the air, kissed him resoundingly on the head, and, turning him about, carrying him in his arms, with a hop, skip and a jump came out on the spar-deck, then the upper deck, and from there still higher, to that very bridge where it had been so terrible in the estuary of the great Chinese river.

On the bridge the captain entered the pilot's roundhouse, while Chang, who had been dropped to the floor, sat for a space, his fox-like brush unfurled to its full length over the smooth boards. It was very hot and radiant behind Chang, from the low-lying sun. It must also have been hot in Arabia, that was passing by so near on the right, with its shore of gold, with its blackbrown mountains, its peaks, that resembled the mountains of some dead planet, also all deeply strewn with gold dust; Arabia, its entire sandy and mountainous waste visible with such extraordinary distinctness that it seemed as if one could jump over there. And above, on the bridge, the morning could still be felt, there was still the pull of a light, fresh coolness; the captain's mate,—the very same who later on used so often to make Chang furious by blowing into his nose,—a man in white clothes, with a white helmet and wearing fearful black spectacles, was sauntering briskly back and forth over the bridge, constantly looking up at the sharp tip of the front mast that reached up to the sky, and over which was curling the flimsiest wisp of a cloud. ... Then the captain called out from the round-house: "Here, Chang! Come on and have coffee!" and Chang immediately jumped up, circled the round-house, and deftly dashed over its brass threshold. And beyond the threshold it proved to be even better than on the bridge: there was a broad leather divan, fixed to the wall; over it hung certain things like wall-clocks, their glass and hands glistening; and on the floor was a slop-bowl with a mixture of sweet milk and bread. Chang began lapping it greedily, while the captain busied himself with his work. Upon the counter, placed under the window opposite the divan, he unrolled a large maritime chart, and, placing a ruler over it, firmly drew a long line upon it with scarlet ink. Chang, having finished his lapping, with milk on his muzzle, jumped up on the counter and sat down near the very window, out of which he could see the blue turned-over collar of a sailor in a roomy blouse, who, with his back to the window, was standing at the many-horned wheel. And at this point the captain, who, as it turned out afterward, was very fond of having a chat when he was all alone with Chang, said to him:

"You see, brother, this is the Red Sea itself. You and I have to pass through it as cleverly as we can,—just see how gaily coloured it is! I have to land you in Odessa in good order, because they already know there of your existence. I have already blabbed about you to a most capricious little girl; I have bragged to her about your lordship, over a sort of long cable, d'you understand, that has been laid down by clever people over the bottom of all the seas and oceans. ... For after all, Chang, I am an awfully lucky fellow, so lucky that you can't even imagine it, and for that reason I am terribly averse to getting stuck on one of these reefs, to have no end of disgrace on my first distant cruise. ..."

And, saying this, the captain suddenly gave Chang a stern look and slapped his muzzle:

"Paws off!" he cried commandingly. "Don't you dare climb on government property!"

And Chang, with a toss of his head, growled and puckered up his face. This was the first slap he had ever received, and he was offended; it again seemed to him that to be living in this world and to be sailing the seas was an atrocious thing. He turned away, his translucently yellow eyes dimming and contracting, and with a low growl he bared his wolfish fangs. But the captain did not consider Chang's offended feelings of any importance. He lit a cigarette and returned to the divan; having taken a gold watch out of a side pocket of his *piqué* jacket, he pried back its lids with a strong nail, and looking upon a glistening, unusually animated, bustling something which ran and resoundingly whispered within the watch, again began speaking in a comradely tone. He again told Chang that he was bringing him to Odessa, to Elissavetinskaya Street; that in Elissavetinskaya Street he, the captain, had apartments, first of all; secondly, a wife who was a beauty; and, thirdly, a wonderful little daughter; and that he, the captain, was a very lucky fellow after all.

"A lucky fellow, after all, Chang!" said the captain, and then added:

"This daughter of mine, Chang, is a lively little girl, full of curiosity and persistence,—it is going to be bad for you at times, especially for your tail! But if you only knew, Chang, what a beautiful creature she is! I love her so much, brother, that at times I am even afraid of my love: she is all the world to me,—well, almost all, let us say: but is that as it should be? And, in general, should any one be loved so greatly?" he asked. "For, were all these Buddhas of yours more foolish than you and I? And yet, just you listen to what they say about this love of the universe and all things corporeal, beginning with sunlight, with a wave, with the air, and winding up with woman, with an infant, with the scent of white acacia! Or else,—do you know what sort of a thing this Tao is, that has been thought up by nobody else but you Chinamen? I know it but poorly myself, brother, but then, everybody knows it poorly; but, as far as it is possible to understand it, just what is it, after all? The Abyss, our First Mother; She gives birth to all things that exist in this universe, and She devours them as well, and, devouring them, gives birth to them anew; or, to put it in other words, It is the Path of all that exists, which nothing that exists may resist. But we resist It every minute; every minute we want to turn to our desire not only the soul of a beloved woman, let us say, but even the entire universe as well! It is an eerie thing to be living in this world, Chang," said the captain; "it's a most pleasant thing, but still an eerie one, and especially for such as I! For I am too avid of happiness, and all too often do I lose the way: dark and evil is this Path,—or is it entirely, entirely otherwise?"

And, after a silence, he added further:

"For after all, what is the main thing? When you love somebody, there is no power on earth that can make you believe that the one you love can possibly not love you. And that is just where the devil comes in, Chang. But how magnificent life is; my God, how magnificent!"

Made red hot by the now high risen sun, and quivering slightly as it ran, the steamer was tirelessly cleaving the Red Sea, now stilled in the abyss of the sultry empyrean spaciousness. The radiant void of the tropical sky was peeping in through the door of the round-house. Noonday was approaching; the brass threshold simply blazed in the sun. The glassy swell rolled more and more slowly over the side, flaring up with a blinding glitter, and lighting up the round-house. Chang was sitting on the divan, listening to the captain. The captain, who had been patting Chang on the head, shoved him to the floor: "No, it's too hot, brother!" said he; but this time Chang was not offended,—it was too fine a thing to be living in this world on this joyous noonday. And then. ...

But here again Chang's dream is interrupted.

"Come on, Chang!" says the captain, dropping his feet down from the bed. And again in astonishment Chang sees that he is not on a steamer on the Red Sea, but in a garret in Odessa, and that it really is noonday outside,—not a joyous noonday, however, but a dark, dreary, inimical one, and he growls softly at the captain who has disturbed him. But the captain, paying no attention to him, puts on his old uniform cap and his old uniform great coat, and, shoving his hands deep in his pockets and all hunched up, goes toward the door. Willy-nilly, Chang, too, has to jump down from the bed. It is a hard thing for the captain to descend the stairs and he has no heart for it, as though he were doing it under the compulsion of harsh necessity. Chang rolls along rather rapidly,—he is still enlivened by that yet unallayed irritation with which the blissful state induced by vodka always ends. ...

Yes,—it is two years now since Chang and the captain have been occupied, day in and day out, in visiting one restaurant after another. There they drink, have snacks, contemplate the other drunkards who drink and have snacks alongside of them, amid the noise, tobacco smoke, and all sorts of bad odours. Chang lies on the floor, at the captain's feet. As for the captain, he sits and smokes, his elbows firmly planted on the table,—a habit he has acquired at sea; he is awaiting that hour when it will be necessary, in accordance with some law which he had himself mentally formulated, to migrate to some other restaurant or coffee-house: Chang and the captain breakfast in one place, drink coffee in another, dine in a third, and sup in a fourth. Usually the captain is silent. But there are times when the captain meets some one of his erstwhile friends, and then he talks all day long without cease of the insignificance of life, and every minute regales with wine now himself, now his *vis à vis*, now Chang,—the last always has some bit of china on the floor before him. They would pass the present day also in precisely the same way: they had agreed to breakfast this day with a certain old friend of the captain's, an artist in a high silk hat. And that meant that at first they would sit in a certain malodorous beer-shop, among red-faced Germans,—stolid, business-like people, who worked from morn till night with, of course, the sole aim of drinking, eating, working all over again, and propagating others of their kind. Then they would go to a coffee-house filled to overflowing with Greeks and Jews, whose entire existence, likewise senseless but exceedingly perturbed, was swallowed up in ceaseless expectation of stock-exchange news; and from the coffee-house they would set out for a restaurant whither flocked all sorts of human rag-tag, and there they would sit far into the night. ...

A winter day is short, but with a bottle of wine, sitting in conversation with a friend, it is still shorter. And now Chang, the captain, and the artist had already been both in the beer-shop and in the coffee-house, and it is the sixth hour that they have been sitting and drinking in the restaurant. And again the captain, having put his elbows on the table, is ardently assuring the artist that there is but one truth in this world,—a truth evil and base. "You just look about you," he is saying, "you just recall all those that you and I see every day in the beer-shop, in the coffee-house, and out on the street! My friend, I have seen the entire earthly globe—life is like that all over! Everything that these people pretend as constituting their life is all bosh and a lie: they have neither God, nor conscience, nor a sensible purpose in existing, nor love, nor friendship, nor honesty,—there is even no common pity. Life is a dreary, winter day in a filthy tavern, no more ...

And Chang, lying under the table, hears all this in the fog of a tipsiness, in which there is no longer any exhilaration. Does he agree with the captain, or does he not? It is impossible to answer this definitely,—but since it is impossible, it means that things are in a bad vay. Chang does not know, does not understand, whether the captain is right; but then, it is only when we experience sorrow that we all say: "I do not know, I do not understand,"—whereas when joy is its portion every living being is convinced that it knows all things, understands all things. ... But suddenly a ray of sunlight seems to cut through this fog of tipsiness: there is a sudden tapping of a baton against a music stand on the band-stand of the restaurant—and a violin begins to sing, followed by a second, a third. ... They sing more and more passionately, more and more sonorously,—and a minute later Chang's soul overflows with an entirely different yearning, with an entirely different sadness. His soul quivers from an incomprehensible rapture, from some sweet torment, from a longing for something indefinite,—and Chang no longer distinguishes whether he is in a dream or awake. He yields with all his being to the music, submissively follows it into some other world—and once more he sees himself on the threshold of that beautiful world; silly, with a faith in the universe, a puppy on board a steamer in the Red Sea. ...

"Yes, but how was it?" he half-thinks, half-dreams. 'Yes, I remember: it was a good thing to be alive on that hot noonday on the Red Sea!" Chang and the captain were sitting in the round-house; later on they stood on the ship's bridge. ... Oh, how much light there was; what a deep blue the sea was, and how azure the sky! How amazingly vivid against the background of the sky were all these white, red, and yellow sailors' blouses hung cut to dry at the prow! Then, afterwards, Chang and the captain and the other men of the ship (whose faces were brick-red, with oily eyes, whereas their foreheads were white and perspiring), breakfasted in the hot general cabin of first-class, under an electric ventilator buzzing and blowing out of a corner. After breakfast Chang took a little nap; after tea he had dinner, and after dinner he was again sitting aloft, before the pilot's round-house, where a steward had placed a canvas chair for the captain, and gazing far out at the sea; at the sunset, tenderly green among the many-coloured and many-formed little clouds; at the sun, wine-red and shorn of its beams, that, as soon as it had touched the turbid horizon, lengthened out and took on the semblance of a dark-flamed mitre. ... Rapidly did the steamer run in pursuit of it; over the side the smooth, watery humps simply flashed by, giving off a sheen of blueish-lilac shagreen. But the sun hastened on and on,—the sea seemed to be absorbing it,—and kept on decreasing and decreasing, and became an elongated, glowing ember. It began to quiver and went out; and, as soon as it had gone out, the shadow of some sadness immediately fell upon all the world, and the wind, constantly blowing harder as the night came on, became still more turbulent. The captain, gazing at the dark flame of the sunset, was sitting with his head bared, his hair a-flutter in the wind, and his face was pensive, proud, and sad. And one felt that he was happy nonetheless, and that not only this entire steamer, running on at his will, but all the universe as well was in his power; because at that moment all the universe was in his soul,—and also because even then there was the odour of wine on his breath. ...

And when the night fell, it was awesome and magnificent. It was black, disquieting, with an unruly wind, and with such a vivid glow from the waves swirling up around the steamer that Chang, who was trotting behind the captain as the latter rapidly and ceaselessly paced the deck, would jump away with a yelp from the side of the ship. And the captain again picked Chang up in his arms, and putting his cheek against Chang's beating heart,—for it beat in precisely the same way as the captain's—walked with him to the very end of the deck, on to the poop, and stood there for a long time in the darkness, bewitching Chang with a wondrous and horrible spectacle: from under the towering enormous stem, from under the dully raging propeller, myriads of white-flamed needles were pouring forth with a crisp swishing; they extricated themselves and were instantly whirled away into the snowy, sparkling path that the steamer was laying down. Now, again, there would be enormous blue stars: now some sort of tightly-coiled blue globes that would explode vividly, and, fading out, smoulder mysteriously with pale-green phosphorescence within the boiling watery hummocks. The wind, coming from all directions, beat strongly and softly upon Chang's muzzle, ruffling and chilling the thick fur upon his chest; and, nestling closely to the captain, as though they were both of the same kin, Chang scented an odour that seemed to be that of cold sulphur, breathed in the air coming from the furrowed inmost depths of the sea. And the stern kept on quivering; it was lowered and lifted by some great and unutterably free force, and Chang swayed and swayed, excitedly contemplating this blind and dark, yet an hundredfold living, dully turbulent Bottomless Gulf. And at times some especially mischievous and ponderous wave, noisily flying past the stern, would illumine the hands and the silvery clothes of the captain with an eldritch glow. ...

On this night the captain for the first time brought Chang into his large and cozy cabin, softly illuminated by a lamp under a red silk shade. Upon the writing table, that was squeezed in tightly near the captain's bed, in the light and shade thrown by the lamp, stood two narrow frames, holding two photographic portraits: one of a pretty little petulant girl with curly locks, seated at her capricious ease in a deep arm-chair; and the other that of a young woman, taken almost at full length, with a white lace parasol over her shoulder, in a large lace hat, and wearing a smart spring dress,—she was stately, slender, beautiful and pensive, like some Georgian *tsarevna*. And the captain said, as he undressed to the noise of the black waves beyond the open window:

"This woman won't like you and me, Chang! There are some

feminine souls, brother, which languish eternally in a certain pensive yearning for love, and who just for that very same reason never love anybody. There are such,—and how shall they be judged for all their heartlessness, falsehood, their dreams of going on the stage, of owning an automobile, of yachting picnics, of some sportsman or other, who pretends to be an Englishman, and tortures his hair, all greasy with pomatum, into a straight parting? Who shall divine them? Everyone according to his or her lights, Chang; and are they not fulfilling the innermost secret behests of Tao Itself, even as they are being fulfilled by some sea-creature that is now freely going upon its way in these black, fiery-armoured waves?"

"Oo-oo!" said the captain, sitting down on a chair and unlacing his white shoe. "What didn't I go through, Chang, when I felt for the first time that she was not entirely mine,—on that night when for the first time she had gone alone to the Yacht Club ball and had returned toward morning, like a wilted rose, pale from fatigue and her still unabated excitement, with her eyes all dark, widened, and distant from me! If you only knew how inimitably she wanted to hoodwink me, with what artless wonder she asked: 'But aren't you asleep yet, poor dear?' Right then I could not have uttered even a word, and she understood me at once and became silent; she merely threw a quick glance at me,—and began undressing in silence. I wanted to kill her, but she dryly and calmly said: 'Help me unfasten my dress at the back,'—and I submissively approached her and began with trembling hands to unfasten all these hooks and snaps,—and just as soon as I saw her body through the open dress, saw her back between the shoulder blades, and her chemise, dropping off the shoulders and tucked into the corset; just as soon as I felt the scent of her black hair and caught a glimpse of her breasts, raised up by the corset, reflected in the bright pier glass. ..."

And, without finishing, the captain waved his hand in a hopeless gesture.

He undressed, lay down, and extinguished the light, and Chang, turning and settling in the morocco chair near the writing table, saw how the black cerement of the sea was furrowed by rows of white flame, flaring up and fading out; saw how some lights flashed up ominously upon the black horizon; saw how an awesome living wave would run up from thence and with a menacing noise would grow higher than the side of the ship, and look into the cabin,—like some serpent of fairy tale shining through and through with eyes of the natural colours of precious stones, shining through and through with translucent emeralds and sapphires. And he saw how the steamer thrust it aside and evenly kept on in its course, amid the ponderous and vacillant masses of this primordial element, now foreign and inimical to us, that is called Ocean. ...

In the night the captain emitted some sudden cry; and, frightened himself by this cry, which rang with some basely-plaintive passion, he instantly awoke. Having lain for a minute in silence, he sighed and said mockingly:

"Yes, there's a story for you! '*As* a jewel of gold in a swine's snout, *so is* a fair woman! ...' Thrice right art thou, Solomon, Sage of Sages!"

He found in the darkness his cigarette case and lit a cigarette, but, having taken two deep puffs at it, he let his hand drop,—and fell asleep so, with the little red glow of the cigarette in his hand. And again it grew quiet—only the waves glittered, swayed, and noisily rushed past the ship's side. The Southern Cross from behind the black clouds. ...

But here Chang is deafened by an unexpected thunder peal. He jumps up in terror. What has happened? Has the steamer again struck against underwater rocks through the fault of the intoxicated captain, as was the case three years ago? Has the captain again fired a pistol at his beautiful and pensive wife? No; this is not night all about them now; neither are they at sea, nor in Elissavetinskaya Street on a wintry noonday,—but in a brightly-lit restaurant, filled with noise and smoke. It is the intoxicated captain, who had struck his fist against the table, and is now shouting to the artist:

"Bosh, bosh! As a jewel of gold in a swine's snout,—that's what your Woman is! 'I have decked my bed with coverings of tapestry, with carved *works*, with fine linen of Egypt. ... Come, let us take our fill of love ... for the goodman *is* not at home. ...' Bah! Woman! 'For her house inclineth unto death, and her paths unto the dead. ...' But that is enough, that is enough, my friend. It is time to go,—they are closing up this place; come on!"

And a minute later the captain, Chang, and the artist are already in the street, where the wind and the snow make the street-lamps flicker. The captain embraces and kisses the artist, and they go in different directions. Chang, sullen and half asleep, is running sidewise over the sidewalk after the captain, who walks rapidly and unsteadily. ... Again a day has passed,—dream or reality?—and again darkness, cold, and fatigue reign over the universe. ... No, the captain is right, most assuredly right: life is simply poisonous and malodorous alcohol, nothing more. ...

Thus, monotonously, do the days and nights of Chang pass. But suddenly one morning the universe, like a steamer, runs at full speed against an underwater reef, hidden from heedless eyes. Awaking on a certain wintry morning, Chang is struck by the great silence reigning in the room. He quickly jumps up from his place, rushes toward the captain's bed,—and sees that the captain is lying with his head convulsively thrown back, with his face grown pallid and chill, with his eyelashes half-open and unmoving. And, upon seeing these eyelashes, Chang emits a howl as despairing as if he had been thrown off his feet and cut in two by a speeding automobile. ... Then, when the door of the room has been taken off its hinges, when people enter, depart, and arrive again, speaking loudly,—the most diversified people: porters, policemen, the artist in the high silk hat, and all sorts of other gentlemen who used to sit in restaurants with the captain,—then Chang seems to turn to stone. ... Oh, how fearfully the captain had said at one time: "On that day the keepers of the house shall tremble ... and those that look out of the windows be darkened ... also they shall be afraid of *that which is* high, and fears shall be in the way ... because man goeth to his long home, and the mourners go about the streets. ... For the pitcher is broken at the fountain, and the wheel broken at the cistern ..." But Chang does not feel even terror now. He lies on the floor, his muzzle toward the corner; he has shut his eyes tight that he might not behold the universe, might forget it. And the universe murmurs over him dully and distantly, like the sea over one who descends deeper and deeper into its abyss.

But when he does come to himself again, it is near the doors of a chapel, in the porch. He sits near them with drooping head; dull, half-dead,—only he is all shaking in a chill. And suddenly the chapel door is flung open,—and a wondrous scene, all mellifluously chanting, strikes the eyes and the heart of Chang. Before Chang is a semi-dark Gothic chamber, with the red stars of flames, a whole forest of tropical plants, a coffin of oak raised high upon a black scaffolding. There is a black throng of people; there are two women wondrous in their marblelike beauty and their deep mourning, who seem just like two sisters of different ages; and, over all this, reverberations, thunder peals, a choir,—of men sonorously clamorous of some sorrowful joy of the angels. Solemnity, confusion, pomp,—and chantings not of this earth, drowning all else in their strains. And Chang's every hair stands up on end from anguish and rapture before this sonorous vision. And the artist, who, with reddened eyes, stepped out of the chapel at that moment, stops in amazement:

"Chang!" he says in alarm, stooping down to him, "Chang, what is the matter with you?"

And, laying a hand that has begun to tremble upon Chang's head, he stoops still lower,—and their eyes, filled with tears, meet with such love for each other, that Chang's entire being cries out inaudibly to all the universe: "Ah, no, no,—there is upon earth some third truth, that has not been made known to me!"

That day, having returned from the cemetery, Chang moves into the house of his third master,—again up aloft, to a garret; but a garret warm, redolent of cigars, with rugs upon the floor, with antique furniture placed about it, and hung with brocaded stuffs. ... It is growing dark; the fireplace is filled with glowing, sombrely-scarlet lumps of heat; Chang's new master is seated in a chair. He had not even taken off his overcoat and his high silk hat upon returning home; he had sat down with his cigar in a deep chair, and is now smoking and gazing into the dusk of his *atelier*. As for the fatigued, tortured-out Chang,—he is lying on a rug near the fireplace, his eyes shut, his muzzle resting on his front paws. And he dreams, he sees as in a vision:

Some One is lying there, beyond the darkening city, beyond the enclosure of the cemetery, in that which is called a crypt, a grave. But this Some One is not the captain,—no. If Chang loves and feels the captain, if he sees him with the vision of memory,—that divine thing within him which he does not understand himself,—it means that the captain is still with him: in that universe, without beginning and without end, which is inaccessible to Death. In this universe there must be but one truth,—the third; but what that truth is, is known only to that last Master to whom Chang must now soon return.

THE SILENCE
Leonid Andreev (1871–1919)
Translated by W. H. Lowe

After an unsuccessful youthful suicide bid (the shot missed), and later a career as a lawyer and journalist, at the turn of the century **Leonid Andreev**, with Maxim Gorky's patronage, quickly became one of the leading voices of Russian literature. He supported the first Russian revolution (1905), helped to hide revolutionaries, was briefly arrested and forced into exile in Germany. In 1908 he returned to the Russian empire, established himself in Finland (which was then part of the empire) and abandoned his initial revolutionary idealism. In his writing he revealed the horrors of the newborn twentieth century: industrialized war, terror from below and terror from above. His best known story, 'The Seven Who Were Hanged', is based on the true story of the conspirators who planned to assassinate the Tsarist minister of justice, but were betrayed, arrested and executed.

He died in 1919 as a result of the lingering after effects of his youthful suicide attempt in the newly independent Finland. Andreev's son, Daniil Andreev, inherited his talent and mystical worldview. A field veteran of the Second World War, a detainee in the GULAG, Daniil Andreev wrote whilst in prison one of the strangest Russian texts ever written, the *Roza Mira, Rose of the World*: his own variation on Dante's descent to Hell, described with a distinctive patchwork of war and camp experience.

I

One moonlit night in May, while the nightingales sang, Father Ignatius' wife entered his chamber. Her countenance expressed suffering, and the little lamp she held in her hand trembled. Approaching her husband, she touched his shoulder, and managed to say between her sobs:

"Father, let us go to Verochka."

Without turning his head, Father Ignatius glanced severely at his wife over the rims of his spectacles, and looked long and intently, till she waved her unoccupied hand and dropped on a low divan.

"That one toward the other be so pitiless!" she pronounced slowly, with emphasis on the final syllables, and her good plump face was distorted with a grimace of pain and exasperation, as if in this manner she wished to express what stern people they were—her husband and daughter.

Father Ignatius smiled and arose. Closing his book, he removed his spectacles, placed them in the case and meditated. His long, black beard, inwoven with silver threads, lay dignified on his breast, and it slowly heaved at every deep breath.

"Well, let us go!" said he.

Olga Stepanovna quickly arose and entreated in an appealing, timid voice:

"Only don't revile her, father! You know the sort she is."

Vera's chamber was in the attic, and the narrow, wooden stair bent and creaked under the heavy tread of Father Ignatius. Tall and ponderous, he lowered his head to avoid striking the floor of the upper story, and frowned disdainfully when the white jacket of his wife brushed his face. Well he knew that nothing would come of their talk with Vera.

"Why do you come?" asked Vera, raising a bared arm to her eyes. The other arm lay on top of a white summer blanket hardly distinguishable from the fabric, so white, translucent and cold was its aspect.

"Verochka!" began her mother, but sobbing, she grew silent.

"Vera!" said her father, making an effort to soften his dry and hard voice. "Vera, tell us, what troubles you?"

Vera was silent.

"Vera, do not we, your mother and I, deserve your confidence? Do we not love you? And is there someone nearer to you than we? Tell us about your sorrow, and believe me you'll feel better for it. And we too. Look at your aged mother, how much she suffers!"

"Verochka!"

"And I ..." The dry voice trembled, truly something had broken in it. "And I ... do you think I find it easy? As if I did not see that some sorrow is gnawing at you—and what is it? And I, your father, do not know what it is. Is it right that it should be so?"

Vera was silent. Father Ignatius very cautiously stroked his beard, as if afraid that his fingers would enmesh themselves involuntarily in it, and continued:

"Against my wish you went to St. Petersburg—did I pronounce a curse upon you, you who disobeyed me? Or did I not give you money? Or, you'll say, I have not been kind? Well, why then are you silent? There, you've had your St. Petersburg!"

Father Ignatius became silent, and an image arose before him of something huge, of granite, and terrible, full of invisible dangers and strange and indifferent people. And there, alone and weak, was his Vera and there they had lost her. An awful hatred against that terrible and mysterious city grew in the soul of Father Ignatius, and an anger against his daughter who was silent, obstinately silent.

"St. Petersburg has nothing to do with it," said Vera, morosely, and closed her eyes. "And nothing is the matter with me. Better go to bed, it is late."

"Verochka," whimpered her mother. "Little daughter, do confess to me."

"Akh, mamma!" impatiently Vera interrupted her.

Father Ignatius sat down on a chair and laughed.

"Well, then it's nothing?" he inquired, ironically.

"Father," sharply put in Vera, raising herself from the pillow, "you know that I love you and mother. Well, I do feel a little weary. But that will pass. Do go to sleep, and I also wish to sleep. And to-morrow, or some other time, we'll have a chat."

Father Ignatius impetuously arose so that the chair hit the wall, and took his wife's hand.

"Let us go."

"Verochka!"

'Let us go, I tell you!' shouted Father Ignatius. "If she has forgotten God, shall we ..."

Almost forcibly he led Olga Stepanovna out of the room, and when they descended the stairs, his wife, decreasing her gait, said in a harsh whisper:

"It was you, priest, who have made her such. From you she learnt her ways. And you'll answer for it. Akh, unhappy creature that I am!"

And she wept, and, as her eyes filled with tears, her foot, missing a step, would descend with a sudden jolt, as if she were eager to fall into some existent abyss below.

From that day Father Ignatius ceased to speak with his daughter, but she seemed not to notice it. As before she lay in her room, or walked about, continually wiping her eyes with the palms of her hands as if they contained some irritating foreign substance. And crushed between these two silent people, the jolly, fun-loving wife of the priest quailed and seemed lost, not knowing what to say or do.

Occasionally Vera took a stroll. A week following the interview she went out in the evening, as was her habit. She was not seen alive again, as on this evening she threw herself under the train, which cut her in two.

Father Ignatius himself directed the funeral. His wife was not present in church, as at the news of Vera's death she was prostrated by a stroke. She lost control of her feet, hands and tongue, and she lay motionless in the semi-darkened room when the church bells rang out. She heard the people, as they issued out of church and passed the house, intone the chants, and she made an effort to raise her hand, and to make a sign of the cross, but her hand refused to obey; she wished to say: 'Farewell, Vera!' but the tongue lay in her mouth huge and heavy. And her attitude was so calm, that it gave one an impression of restfulness or sleep. Only her eyes remained open.

At the funeral, in church, were many people who knew Father Ignatius and many strangers, and all bewailed Vera's terrible death, and tried to find in the movements and voice of Father Ignatius tokens of a deep sorrow. They did not love Father Ignatius because of his severity and proud manners, his scorn of sinners, for his unforgiving spirit, his envy and covetousness, his habit of utilizing every opportunity to extort money from his parishioners. They all wished to see him suffer, to see his spirit broken, to see him conscious in his two-fold guilt for the death of his daughter—as a cruel father and a bad priest—incapable of preserving his own flesh from sin. They cast searching glances at him, and he, feeling these glances directed toward his back, made efforts to hold erect its broad and strong expanse, and his thoughts were not concerning his dead daughter, but concerning his own dignity.

"A hardened priest!" said, with a shake of his head, Karzenoff, a carpenter, to whom Father Ignatius owed five roubles for frames.

And thus, hard and erect, Father Ignatius reached the burial ground, and in the same manner he returned. Only at the door of his wife's chamber did his spine relax a little, but this may have been due to the fact that the height of the door was inadequate to admit his tall figure. The change from broad daylight made it difficult for him to distinguish the face of his wife, but, after scrutiny, he was astonished at its calmness and because the eyes showed no tears. And there was neither anger, nor sorrow in the eyes—they were dumb, and they kept silent with difficulty, reluctantly, as did the entire plump and helpless body, pressing against the feather bedding.

"Well, how do you feel?" inquired Father Ignatius.

The lips, however, were dumb; the eyes also were silent. Father Ignatius laid his hand on her forehead; it was cold and moist, and Olga Stepanovna did not show in any way that she had felt the hand's contact. When Father Ignatius removed his hand there gazed at him, immobile, two deep grey eyes, seeming almost entirely dark from the dilated pupils, and there was neither sadness in them, nor anger.

"I am going into my own room," said Father Ignatius, who began to feel cold and terror. He passed through the drawing-room, where everything appeared neat and in order, as usual, and where, attired in white covers, stood tall chairs, like corpses in their shrouds. Over one window hung an empty wire cage, with the door open.

"Nastasya!" shouted Father Ignatius, and his voice seemed to him coarse, and he felt ill at ease because he raised his voice so high in these silent rooms, so soon after his daughter's funeral. "Nastasya!" he called out in a lower tone of voice, "where is the canary?"

"She flew away, to be sure."

"Why did you let it out?"

Nastasya began to weep, and wiping her face with the edges of her calico headkerchief, said through her tears:

"It was my young mistress's soul. Was it right to hold it?"

And it seemed to Father Ignatius that the yellow, happy little canary, always singing with inclined head, was really the soul of Vera, and if it had not flown away it wouldn't have been possible to say that Vera had died. He became even more incensed at the maid-servant, and shouted:

"Off with you!"

And when Nastasya did not find the door at once he added:

"Fool!"

II

From the day of the funeral silence reigned in the little house. It was not stillness, for stillness is merely the absence of sounds; it was silence, because it seemed that they who were silent could say something but would not. So thought Father Ignatius each time he entered his wife's chamber and met that obstinate gaze, so heavy in its aspect that it seemed to transform the very air into lead, which bore down one's head and spine. So thought he, examining his daughter's music sheets, which bore imprints of her voice, as well as her books and her portrait, which she brought with her from St. Petersburg. Father Ignatius was accustomed to scrutinize the portrait in established order: First, he would gaze on the cheek upon which a strong light was thrown by the painter; in his fancy he would see upon it a slight wound, which he had noticed on Vera's cheek in death, and the source of which he could not understand. Each time he would meditate upon causes; he reasoned that if it was made by the train the entire head would have been crushed, whereas the head of Vera remained wholly untouched. It was possible that someone did it with his foot when the corpse was removed, or accidentally with a finger nail.

To contemplate at length upon the details of Vera's death taxed the strength of Father Ignatius, so that he would pass on to the eyes. These were dark, handsome, with long lashes, which cast deep shadows beneath, causing the whites to seem particularly luminous, both eyes appearing to be enclosed in black, mourning frames. A strange expression was given them by the unknown but talented artist; it seemed as if in the space between the eyes and the object upon which they gazed there lay a thin, transparent film. It resembled somewhat the effect obtained by an imperceptible layer of dust on the black top of a piano, softening the shine of polished wood. And no matter how Father Ignatius placed the portrait, the eyes insistently followed him, but there was no speech in them, only silence; and this silence was so clear that it seemed it could be heard. And gradually Father Ignatius began to think that he heard silence.

Every morning after breakfast Father Ignatius would enter the drawing-room, throw a rapid glance at the empty cage and the other familiar objects, and seating himself in the armchair would close his eyes and listen to the silence of the house. There was something grotesque about this. The cage kept silence, stilly and tenderly, and in this silence were felt sorrow and tears, and distant dead laughter. The silence of his wife, softened by the walls, continued insistent, heavy as lead, and terrible, so terrible that on the hottest day Father Ignatius would be seized by cold shivers. Continuous and cold as the grave, and mysterious as death, was the silence of his daughter. The silence itself seemed to share this suffering and struggled, as it were, with the terrible desire to pass into speech; however, something strong and cumbersome, as a machine, held it motionless and stretched it out as a wire. And somewhere at the distant end, the wire would begin to agitate and resound subduedly, feebly and plaintively. With joy, yet with terror, Father Ignatius would seize upon this engendered sound, and resting with his arms upon the arms of the chair, would lean his head forward, awaiting the sound to reach him. But the sound would break and pass into silence.

'How stupid!' muttered Father Ignatius, angrily, arising from the chair, still erect and tall. Through the window he saw, suffused with sunlight, the street, which was paved with round, even-sized stones, and directly across, the stone wall of a long, windowless shed. On the corner stood a cab-driver, resembling a clay statue, and it was difficult to understand why he stood there, when for hours there was not a single passer-by.

III

Father Ignatius had occasion for considerable speech outside his house. There was talking to be done with the clergy, with the members of his flock, while officiating at ceremonies, sometimes with acquaintances at social evenings; yet, upon his return he would feel invariably that the entire day he had been silent. This was due to the fact that with none of those people he could talk upon that matter which concerned him most, and upon which he would contemplate each night: Why did Vera die?

Father Ignatius did not seem to understand that now this could not be known, and still thought it was possible to know. Each night—all his nights had become sleepless—he would picture that minute when he and his wife, in dead midnight, stood near Vera's bed, and he entreated her: "Tell us!" And when in his recollection, he would reach these words, the rest appeared to him not as it was in reality. His closed eyes, preserving in their darkness a live and undimmed picture of that night, saw how Vera raised herself in her bed, smiled and tried to say something. And what was that she tried to say? That unuttered word of Vera's, which should have solved all, seemed so near, that if one only had bent his ear and suppressed the beats of his heart, one could have heard it, and at the same time it was so infinitely, so hopelessly distant. Father Ignatius would arise from his bed, stretch forth his joined hands and, wringing them, would exclaim:

"Vera!"

And he would be answered by silence.

One evening Father Ignatius entered the chamber of Olga Stepanovna, whom he had not come to see for a week, seated himself at her head, and turning away from that insistent, heavy gaze, said:

"Mother! I wish to talk to you about Vera. Do you hear?"

Her eyes were silent, and Father Ignatius raising his voice, spoke sternly and powerfully, as he was accustomed to speak with penitents:

"I am aware that you are under the impression that I have been the cause of Vera's death. Reflect, however, did I love her less than you loved her? You reason absurdly. I have been stern; did that prevent her from doing as she wished? I have forfeited the dignity of a father, I humbly bent my neck, when she defied my malediction and departed—hence. And you—did you not entreat her to remain, until I command you to be silent? Did I beget cruelty in her? Did I not teach her about God, about humility, about love?"

Father Ignatius quickly glanced into the eyes of his wife, and turned away.

"What was there for me to do when she did not wish to reveal her sorrow? Did I not command her? Did I not entreat her? I suppose, in your opinion, I should have dropped on my knees before the maid, and cried like an old woman! How should I know what was going on in her head! Cruel, heartless daughter!"

Father Ignatius hit his knees with his fist.

"There was no love in her—that's what! As far as I'm concerned, that's settled, of course—I'm a tyrant! Perhaps she loved you—you, who wept and humbled yourself?"

Father Ignatius gave a hollow laugh.

"There's love for you! And as a solace for you, what a death she chose! A cruel, ignominious death. She died in the dust, in the dirt—as a d-dog who is kicked in the jaw."

The voice of Father Ignatius sounded low and hoarse:

"I feel ashamed! Ashamed to go out in the street! Ashamed before the altar! Ashamed before God! Cruel, undeserving daughter! Accurst in thy grave!"

When Father Ignatius glanced at his wife she was unconscious, and revived only after several hours. When she regained consciousness her eyes were silent, and it was impossible to tell whether or not she remembered what Father Ignatius had said.

That very night—it was a moonlit, calm, warm and deathly-still night in May—Father Ignatius, proceeding on his tip-toes, so as not to be overheard by his wife and the sick-nurse, climbed up the stairs and entered Vera's room. The window in the attic had remained closed since the death of Vera, and the atmosphere was dry and warm, with a light odor of burning that comes from heat generated during the day in the iron roof. The air of lifelessness and abandonment permeated the apartment, which for a long time had remained unvisited, and where the timber of the walls, the furniture and other objects gave forth a slight odor of continued putrescence. A bright streak of moonlight fell on the window-sill, and on the floor, and, reflected by the white, carefully washed boards, cast a dim light into the room's corners, while the white, clean bed, with two pillows, one large and one small, seemed phantom-like and aerial. Father Ignatius opened the window, causing to pour into the room a considerable current of fresh air, smelling of dust, of the nearby river and the blooming linden. An indistinct sound as of voices in chorus also entered occasionally; evidently young people rowed and sang.

Quietly treading with naked feet, resembling a white phantom, Father Ignatius made his way to the vacant bed, bent his knees and fell face down on the pillows, embracing them—on that spot where should have been Vera's face. Long he lay thus; the song grew louder, then died out; but he still lay there, while his long, black hair spread over his shoulders and the bed.

The moon had changed its position, and the room grew darker, when Father Ignatius raised his head and murmured, putting into his voice the entire strength of his long-suppressed and unconscious love and hearkening to his own words, as if it were not he who was listening, but Vera.

"Vera, daughter mine! Do you understand what you are to me, daughter? Little daughter! My heart, my blood and my life. Your father—your old father—is already grey, and also feeble."

The shoulders of Father Ignatius shook and the entire burdened figure became agitated. Suppressing his agitation, Father Ignatius murmured tenderly, as to an infant:

"Your old father entreats you. No, little Vera, he supplicates. He weeps. He never has wept before. Your sorrow, little child, your sufferings—they are also mine. Greater than mine."

Father Ignatius shook his head.

"Greater, Verochka. What is death to an old man like me? But you—If you only knew how delicate and weak and timid you are! Do you recall how you bruised your finger once and the blood trickled and you cried a little? My child! I know that you love me, love me intensely. Every morning you kiss my hand. Tell me, do tell me, what grief troubles your little head, and I – with these hands – shall smother your grief. They are still strong, Vera, these hands."

The hair of Father Ignatius shook.

"Tell me!"

Father Ignatius fixed his eyes on the wall, and wrung his hands.

"Tell me!"

Stillness prevailed in the room, and from afar was heard the prolonged and broken whistle of a locomotive.

Father Ignatius, gazing out of his dilated eyes, as if there had arisen suddenly before him the frightful phantom of the mutilated corpse, slowly raised himself from his knees, and with a credulous motion reached for his head with his hand, with spread and tensely stiffened fingers. Making a step toward the door. Father Ignatius whispered brokenly:

"Tell me!"

And he was answered by silence.

IV

The next day, after an early and lonely dinner, Father Ignatus went to the graveyard, the first time since his daughter's death. It was warm, deserted and still; it seemed more like an illumined night. Following habit, Father Ignatius, with effort, straightened his spine, looked severely about him and thought that he was the same as formerly;

he was conscious neither of the new, terrible weakness in his legs, nor that his long beard had become entirely white as if a hard frost had hit it. The road to the graveyard led through a long, direct street, slightly on an upward incline, and at its termination loomed the arch of the graveyard gate, resembling a dark, perpetually open mouth, edged with glistening teeth.

Vera's grave was situated in the depth of the grounds, where the sandy little pathways terminated, and Father Ignatius, for a considerable time, was obliged to blunder along the narrow footpaths, which led in a broken line between green mounds, by all forgotten and abandoned. Here and there appeared, green with age, sloping tombstones, broken railings and large, heavy stones planted in the ground, and seemingly crushing it with some cruel, ancient spite. Near one such stone was the grave of Vera. It was covered with fresh turf, turned yellow; around, however, all was in bloom. Ash embraced maple tree; and the widely spread hazel bush stretched out over the grave its bending branches with their downy, shaggy foliage. Sitting down on a neighboring grave and catching his breath, Father Ignatius looked around him, throwing a glance upon the cloudless, desert sky, where in complete immovability hung the glowing sun disk—and here he only felt that deep, incomparable stillness which reigns in graveyards, when the wind is absent and the slumbering foliage has ceased its rustling. And anew the thought came to Father Ignatius that this was not a stillness but a silence. It extended to the very brick walls of the graveyard, crept over them and occupied the city. And it terminated only—in those grey, obstinate and reluctantly silent eyes.

Father Ignatius' shoulders shivered, and he lowered his eyes upon the grave of Vera. He gazed long upon the little tufts of grass uprooted together with the earth from some open, wind-swept field and not successful in adapting themselves to a strange soil; he could not imagine that there, under this grass, only a few feet from him, lay Vera. And this nearness seemed incomprehensible and brought confusion into the soul and a strange agitation. She, of whom Father Ignatius was accustomed to think as of one passed away forever into the dark depths of eternity, was here, close by—and it was hard to understand that she, nevertheless, was no more and never again would be. And in the mind's fancy of Father Ignatius it seemed that if he could only utter some word, which was almost upon his lips, or if he could make some sort of movement, Vera would issue forth from her grave and arise to the same height and beauty that was once hers. And not alone would she arise, but all corpses, intensely sensitive in their solemnly-cold silence.

Father Ignatius removed his wide-brimmed black hat, smoothed down his disarranged hair and whispered:

"Vera!"

Father Ignatius felt ill at ease, fearing to be overheard by a stranger, and stepping on the grave he gazed around him. No one was present, and this time he repeated loudly:

"Vera!"

It was the voice of an aged man, sharp and demanding, and it was strange that a so powerfully expressed desire should remain without answer.

"Vera!"

Loudly and insistently the voice called, and when it relapsed into silence, it seemed for a moment that somewhere from underneath came an incoherent answer. And Father Ignatius, clearing his ear of his long hair, pressed it to the rough, prickly turf.

"Vera, tell me!"

With terror, Father Ignatius felt pouring into his ear something cold as of the grave, which froze his marrow; Vera seemed to be speaking—speaking, however, with the same unbroken silence. This feeling became more racking and terrible, and when Father Ignatius forced himself finally to tear away his head, his face was pale as that of a corpse, and he fancied that the entire atmosphere trembled and palpitated from a resounding silence, and that this terrible sea was being swept by a wild hurricane. The silence strangled him; with icy waves it rolled through his head and agitated the hair; it smote against his breast, which groaned under the blows. Trembling from head to foot, casting around him sharp and sudden glances, Father Ignatius slowly raised himself and with a prolonged and torturous effort attempted to straighten his spine and to give proud dignity to his trembling body. He succeeded in this. With measured protractiveness, Father Ignatius shook the dirt from his knees, put on his hat, made the sign of the cross three times over the grave, and walked away with an even and firm gait, not recognizing, however, the familiar burial ground and losing his way.

"Well, here I've gone astray!" smiled Father Ignatius, halting at the branching of the footpaths.

He stood there for a moment and unreflecting, turned to the left, because it was impossible to stand and to wait. The silence drove him on. It arose from the green graves; it was the breath issuing from the grey, melancholy crosses; in thin, stifling currents it came from all pores of the earth, satiated with the dead. Father Ignatius increased his stride. Dizzy, he circled the same paths, jumped over graves, stumbled across railings, clutching with his hands the prickly, metallic garlands, and turning the soft material of his dress into tatters. His sole thought was to escape. He fled from one place to another, and finally broke into a dead run, seeming very tall and unusual in the flowing cassock, and his hair streaming in the wind. A corpse arisen from the grave could not have frightened a passer-by more than this wild figure of a man, running and leaping, and waving his arms, his face distorted and insane, and the open mouth breathing with a dull, hoarse sound. With one long leap, Father Ignatius landed on a little street, at one end of which appeared the small church attached to the graveyard. At the entrance, on a low bench, dozed an old man, seemingly a distant pilgrim, and near him, assailing each other, were two quarreling old beggar women, filling the air with their oaths.

When Father Ignatius reached his home, it was already dusk, and there was light in Olga Stepanovna's chamber. Not undressing and without removing his hat, dusty and tattered, Father Ignatius approached his wife and fell on his knees.

"Mother ... Olga ... have pity on me!" he wept. "I shall go mad."

He dashed his head against the edge of the table and he wept with anguish, as one who was weeping for the first time. Then he raised his head, confident that a miracle would come to pass, that his wife would speak and would pity him.

"My love!"

With his entire big body he drew himself toward his wife—and met the gaze of those grey eyes. There was neither compassion in them, nor anger. It was possible his wife had forgiven him, but in her eyes there was neither pity, nor anger. They were dumb and silent.

...

And silent was the entire dark, deserted house.

SOLOVKI

Nadezhda Teffi (1872–1952)

Translated by Robert Chandler
& Elisabeth Chandler

The queen of Russian humour, **Nadezhda Teffi** (born Nadezhda Lokhvitskaya) originally invented her pseudonym to distinguish herself from her elder sister, the poetess Mirra Lochwizkaja, and probably borrowed it from the writings of Kipling or George du Maurier.

She revived Pushkin's style of a joyful attitude towards life, engaging in "low" genres like epigrams, feuilletons, and using them as a sort of antidote to the numb and paralyzing seriousness of the literary narratives of the time. Her very name—short, vivid and foreign, is still a synonym for sharpness and irony.

She emigrated during the Civil war and lived in Paris, writing the same ironical prose and poetry with an irony that became more and more bitter.

The seagulls from the shore accompanied the steamer for a long time. After a while they grew tired and began coming down more often onto the water, barely grazing it with their breast, spinning around as if on the point of a screw—and then wearily gliding off again, leading first with one wing and then with the other, as if taking long strides.

From the stern, pilgrims threw them bread. Many of them came from far inland. It was their first encounter with the sea and they were astonished by the gulls.

"What strong birds!"

"What great big birds!"

"But people say you can't eat them."

When the boat reached open sea and the shore it had left behind was no more than a low, narrow strip of pale blue, the gulls dispersed. Three last greedy birds took a few more strides, begged again for bread, veered off somewhere to the left, called to one another, and disappeared.

The sea was now empty and free. In the sky shone two diffuse bands of crimson: one not yet extinguished, still red from the departed sun, and one now catching fire from the rising sun. The steamer, lit by their silvery-pink light that cast no shadow, was cutting aslant through the waves; from the deck it appeared to be sailing sideways, skimming weightlessly over the water. And high in the air, fastened to the mast, swaying gently against the pink clouds, a golden cross marked out the boat's path.

The *Archangel Michael*, a holy ship, was carrying pilgrims from Arkhangelsk to the Solovetsky Monastery.*

There were a lot of passengers. They sat on benches, on steps, and on the deck itself, conversing quietly and respectfully, and looking with awe at the golden cross in the sky, at the boat's steward—a monk in a faded, now greenish cassock—and at the gulls. They sighed, yawned, and made the sign of the cross over their open mouths.

Up on the bridge a monk in a sheepskin coat and a black skullcap kept coughing hoarsely, calling to the helmsman—his commands as abrupt as the gulls' cries—and then bursting out coughing again.

Waves were beating rhythmically against the hull; the crimson glow had faded; the birds had flown away. The drama of setting sail was now over and the passengers began to settle down for the night.

Peasant women hitched up the calico skirts they had starched for the holiday and this unusual journey, and then lay down on the floor, tucking in their legs and their heavy, awkward feet. The menfolk were talking quietly in separate groups.

Red-haired, thickset Semyon Rubaev came down the ladder and joined the men. His wife remained alone, sitting on one of the steps. She didn't move or even turn her head. She merely gave him a sideways look, full of mistrust and resentment.

Semyon listened for a while to the other men. A tall, curly-haired old man from White Lake was talking about the smelt they now

---

* From the second half of the nineteenth century there was a huge increase in the number of pilgrims paying short visits to Solovki. The *Archangel Michael*, acquired in 1887, was one of three steamships operated by the monastery. The journey from Arkhangelsk took seventeen hours. The pilgrimage season started late in June and the most important feast day was August 8, the name day of Saints Zosima and Savvaty, the monastery's two founders.

caught there. "We've a damage now. A damage. Engineers built it. They needed earth for this damage. They took earth of mine."

"What damage? You're not making sense."

"For the damage ... the da ... For the dam." The old man fell silent for a moment, then added, "I'm in my nineties, you know. Yes, that's how it is now."

Semyon didn't care in the least about the old man's age, nor about the smelt in the lake. He wanted to talk about his own concerns, but he didn't know how to bring them into the conversation; it was hard to find the right moment. He looked around at his wife. She was sitting sideways to him, looking away. He could barely see her broad face and the pale, taut line of her mouth.

And then nothing could hold him back. "Well, we come from near Novgorod. From the Borovichy district. Penance, a church penance—that's why I've brought'er along with me."

He stopped. But since no one asked him anything, he eventually began again: "Penance, confession an' penance.[*] Varvara, ma wife. No light matter, I'ad to take it to the district officer."

Varvara got up from the step. Baring her white teeth like a vicious cat, she moved a little farther away, then stood beside the rail, resting both elbows on it.

There was nowhere farther to go. The pilgrims sitting on the deck were densely packed. She could hardly use their heads as stepping stones.

Now at least she could no longer hear all that Semyon was saying. The odd word, however, still reached her.

"The whole village were complainin ... There weren't one lass that Vanya Tsyganov ... The officer ... Ma wife, Varvara ..."

Varvara hunched her shoulders. She was still baring her teeth. Semyon was still talking, talking, talking: "Varvara, aye, Varvara ... 'We just kissed,' she said ... A court sentence weren't possible. But a penance, a church penance ..."

For ten months Semyon had been telling this story, over and over. And now, like clockwork, all through this journey. On the iron road, at every station where they'd stopped, in the pilgrims' hostel at

---

[*] A penance would include going to all services, a prescribed number of bodily prostrations, and the repetition of additional prayers.

Arkhangelsk, wherever there were ears to be filled, he had told it once more. Since the day all this began, since their neighbor Yerokhina had run back from the fields, pulled off her kerchief, and wailed out that Tsyganov had wronged her—and then old Mitrofanikha had rushed out and yelled that her granddaughter Feklushka was being pestered by Tsyganov too, that Tsyganov wasn't giving the girl a moment's peace. Other women of all ages appeared, all white with fury, kerchiefs slipping off their heads, all cursing Tsyganov and threatening to lodge official complaints and have him driven out of the village. And then Lukina had caught sight of Varvara at her window and shouted out that Varvara had been with Tsyganov too. She'd seen them out in the rye: "Them two, walking side by side! Arms around each other!" And from then on, work had been forgotten. Semyon had done nothing but tell this story.

He went along as a witness for Yerokhina. He told the officer about Varvara and demanded that she be brought to trial and punished. He dragged Varvara around with him and wherever they went—on the road, in country inns and town lodgings—he had gone on telling this story. At first he had spoken gently, calling her "Varenka," the same as ever. "So, Varenka, tell me how all this came to happen. All o' the circumstances."

"How *wot* happened? Nowt happened."

Then he would go purple all over, his red beard seeming to fill with blood. Choking with fury, he would say, "Bitch! Snake! How dare you? How dare you speak so to yer wedded husband!"

And all day long Varvara had busied herself around the house, not exactly working, more just fussing about in one corner after another—anything to get out of earshot, anything not to hear.

As for Tsyganov, he was nowhere to be seen. He had gone off to the city to work as a cabdriver. The women began to calm down. Only on the river bank in the evening, as they beat the damp linen with their bats, the young girls sometimes sang a jokey song from Saint Petersburg:

Vanka, Vanka, wot you done wi yer conscience?
    Where be yer heart of hearts?
Wasted 'em both in the taverns
    for love o' billiards an' cards.

Their voices sounded thin, almost mosquito-like.

As for Semyon, he went on and on questioning Varvara and repeating his story. And Varvara fell more and more silent. When the officer asked her about Yerokhina, her only reply, delivered in a tone of true Novgorod obstinacy, was "Nowt to do wiv me."

And so life went on. In the daytime Varvara hardly spoke. At night she kept thinking things over, reliving that day again and again. She had heard screaming women; she had seen their white-hot, vicious fury. The devil had gotten into them. And what a lot of them there had been. Even pockmarked Mavrushka had shouted out, as if bragging, "D'ye think he didn't touch *me*? No, he touched *me* all right. Only *I* hold my tongue. But if you all speak, then *I'm* speakin too!"

Her pockmarks, evidently, had not counted against her. The lads had jeered, "Oh Mavrushka, Mavrushka! And her wi t' body of a bear!"

Yerokhina, for her part, had lamented, "Eight year, believe me, I've kept a hold o' me honor—and then ... along come this fiend an' he snatches it from me!"

All shaking in jealous rage. All shouting, as if bragging, "Me too. Aye, me too!"

A sly fellow with the nickname "Tomcat" had smirked mischievously and said, "You lassies be in a right state. What's eatin you, then? Eh?"

He seemed to have hit on something.

They reached Solovki as the bells were ringing for Matins.

On the shore to meet them were monks and seagulls.

The monks were thin, with severe faces. The gulls were large and plump, almost as big as geese. They waddled about proprietorially, exchanging preoccupied remarks.

Unloading and disembarking took a long time. Some of the pilgrims were still packing their knapsacks when the wife of the elderly fisherman returned from the Holy Lake, after bathing in its icy waters. She had put on a clean linen shirt and was smiling beatifically, her lips purple with cold.

The hosteler, a tall monk with a neatly combed beard, was dealing with the new arrivals, arranging who should sleep where. Since there were crowds of pilgrims and little space, the Rubaevs were put in part of what had once been a room for gentlefolk. This had whitewashed walls and two windows, but it was now divided into three by partitions. One part had been given to a teacher and his wife, and the biggest part—with three beds and a sofa—to a party of four.

The head of this party was an Oriental-looking abbot. Handsome and well turned out, he had chosen, for convenience while traveling, to abandon his monastic dress for that of an ordinary priest: "People, I understand, have little love for monks, and they criticize them for everything: *Why's he smoking? Why's he eating fish? Why's there sugar in his tea?* But how can a man observe the rule when he's on the road? Dress as a priest—and you don't tempt people to judge."

Together with the abbot were a merchant, a lanky young gymnasium* student, and a hypocritical old bigot of a public official. All three were family.

The remaining little cubicle, with no window, was allocated to the Rubaevs.

The pilgrims spent the rest of the day either attending church services, looking around the monastery, wandering about the forest or along the seashore, walking down the long, musty hostel corridor—with its damp and grimy, finger-marked doors, weighted to slam heavily shut—or visiting the little monastery shop and haggling over the price of icons, small cypress-wood crosses, and prayer belts for the deceased.†

There was one very tall young man whom it was hard not to notice. He was smartly dressed, with a new peaked cap and patent leather boots, and he had come for healing; he suffered from spasms that repeatedly wrenched at his mouth, forcing it open. It was as if his jaw were in the grip of a vast, insuperable yawn; he would involuntarily stick his tongue out and slobber all down his chin and neck. Then

---

* An elite secondary school for boys.
† To this day, pilgrims visiting a holy site often buy items of clothing for their burial. And it is customary for the deceased to wear a belt—into which a prayer has been woven—during an Orthodox burial, since he or she will need it when resurrected. Belts are symbolically important in Russian culture, suggesting order and dignity.

the fit would come to an end and his mouth would close, his teeth snapping together like those of a dog that has caught a fly.

Accompanying him was a short little fellow who could have passed for the impresario of an exotic theater troupe. He wore a silver chain that hung down over his round belly and he bustled about excitedly, taking evident pride in the young man's illness and proffering explanations: "Keeps on yawning, he does. Several years now, yes indeed. He's the son of rich people. Make way, make way now, if you please!"

The monastery courtyard was full of gulls. They were round and placid, like household geese. They sat between gravestones and on the track leading to the church. They weren't afraid of people and didn't get out of your way—it was for you to walk around them. And on the back of almost every one of them was a chick—like a fluffy spotted egg propped on two thin little twigs.

The gulls called out to one another in quick, curt barks. They always began loudly, then gradually quietened, as if losing hope. They sat crowded together around the monastery and did not fly anywhere. It was very cold. The small rectangular Holy Lake was swollen with gray-blue water. One gull went down to the lake and gazed for a long time, with a suspicious eye, at the violet ripples. Some way off, a chick was cheeping importantly, as if imparting advice. The gull stretched out one foot, touched the water, quickly withdrew the foot, and twitched its head a little.

"Too cold, old girl?" asked a young monk.

Against the gray sky swayed lopsided trees; their branches, reaching toward the sun like arms stretched toward a distant dream, grew only from their southern side. The northern side, gnawed by cold breaths from the throat of the Arctic Ocean, remained naked and sickly all summer, as in winter.

Down by the harbor some young men, with faded skullcaps over thick strands of curly fair hair, were throwing pebbles in the water and scuffling with one another. They were like puny young bear cubs, fighting clumsily and without anger. Pomors,* from villages along the mainland coast, they had been brought to the monastery to labor for

---

* The Russian-speaking inhabitants of the country's northern coast of European Russia. They have developed a specific culture as a result of interaction and interbreeding with the region's indigenous peoples.

a year or two in fulfillment of vows made by their mothers. "Aye,' e'll serve t' Lord—and' e'll earn' is keep too."*

And there were solitary monks wandering along the shore. Now and again they would stop and look at the water, as if waiting for something.

One after another the gray-blue waves uncoiled, splashing against the brown rocks, filling hearts with a leaden sadness.

Along with the other pilgrims, the Rubaevs went to the church and then on into the forest. Monks in faded cassocks emerged from the little chapels. They seemed to struggle to understand even the simplest questions. If someone asked, "Which church is this?" they would reply, "How?" then smile affably and withdraw to gaze at the water.†

Outside the chapel of Saint Philaret, the pilgrims took it in turn to lift the long stone that had once served Philaret as a pillow. They balanced it on their heads and walked three times clockwise around the chapel—a cure for headaches.‡

In the farthest of the little chapels, ten versts or so from the monastery, the pilgrims were met by the very oldest elders of all. They were barely able to put one foot in front of the other, barely still breathing.

"But how, good fathers, do you walk to the church?"

"We go, good people, but once a year. On Easter Sunday, yes, to Holy Matins. That day we all meet together—from cliffs, from woods, from bogs, from t' open fields. Every one of us goes—and they count us up. As for food, we get by. They bring us our bread."

The hostel was no place to sit in for long. The Rubaevs' cubicle was dark and damp. Semyon would come in, sit down on the bed, and start to drone on once again: "Mind you tell it all. As God is your

---

* Probably these women had prayed to the monastery's patron saints and vowed to send their sons to Solovki (which did not accept women except as pilgrims on short visits) if their prayer was granted. The boys would serve as laborers, also receiving some spiritual teaching. They were not trainee monks; in a year or two they would return to their homes.
† To this day, some recluse monks on Solovki keep to a rule of complete silence, living alone and devoting their lives to prayer. It seems that some of Teffi's pilgrims did not understand this. It is also possible that the mutual incomprehension resulted from people speaking different dialects.
‡ Their walk echoes the Procession of the Cross around the outside of a church on Easter Eve and certain other feast days.

witness. Each and every circumstance. Tell everything, or woe betide you!"

Varvara did not reply.

Behind the partition the merchant and the gymnasium student kept demanding more hot water for their tea. The official was sighing piously.

Behind the other partition the teacher's wife was criticizing the ways of the monastery: "They just stand there and stare at the water. Will that save their souls? And at table they defile themselves with mustard.* Will that save their souls?"

And then they would all wander up and down the shore again, or along the monastery corridors.

They looked at the paintings of the Last Judgment and the Parables of Our Lord. A huge beam planted in the eye of the sinner who so clearly beheld the mote in his brother's eye. The temptation of beauty, illustrated by a devil—with a rather appealing canine muzzle, shaggy webbed paws, a curly tail, and a modest brown apron tied around his belly†—and his charming legend: as the brothers were praying in church, this devil had slipped unseen between them, distributing the pink flowers known as house lime. Whoever received a flower found himself unable to go on praying; tempted by the spring sun and grasses, he would steal out to freedom‡—until in the end the devil was caught by the Holy Elder. And portrayals of every kind of ordeal and hardship, of sins and torments, sins and torments ...

Toward evening they were called to the refectory. The women sat in a separate room.

To one side of Varvara was a woman covered in scabs. Sitting opposite her was an old woman with a nose like a duck's beak. Before dipping her spoon into the communal bowl, she would lick it all over with her long, flaccid, rag-like tongue. They ate salt-cod soup and

---

* Mustard was considered an aphrodisiac.
† Demons in Russian iconography were usually depicted as shaggy, with webbed feet and twisting tails.
‡ Being on the west wall, the Last Judgment was the last set of images a worshiper would see as he or she left the church; this makes the monks' surrender to temptation all the more ironic.

drank bland monastery kvass* with a faint taste of mint. A monk read aloud to them in a dismal monotone—"Lechery, lechery, the devil."

There was no night. The partitions did not reach the ceiling and the Rubaevs' windowless stall was lit by a wan light that cast no shadow.

The hypocrite official got up at cockcrow and, in reproach to his companions, began bowing and crossing himself before the icon. With loud sighs—part whistle and part whisper—he repeated, "Woe is me, O Lord, O Lord—for my loins are filled with mockings."†

The abbot awoke, shamefacedly put on his clothes, and left the room. The merchant held out for a long time but couldn't get back to sleep. In a loud, clear voice, as if to the student, he said, "You get some more sleep! Yes. It's too early for church. Not even the monks have gotten up yet." He then repeated all this—really, of course, for the benefit of the hypocrite official, who was by then creating more of a disturbance than ever.

The official finished praying, looked around censoriously, sighed, and turned away. There are sights best not seen, he appeared to be saying.

Varvara had had a bad night. There was no peace anywhere and the seagulls kept calling to one another with their dismal barks. Toward morning she dozed off. She saw a field of rye and a cart. There on the cart was Vanya Tsyganov, laughing: "'Ere again, are ye? Well, there'll be no getting away this time." He got down from the cart, took her by the shoulders and looked into her eyes. "Ashamed? As if yer a maiden!"

Not a good dream, and it left her with a sense of dread.

Once again everyone went off to the church or out into the forest. After the service, Semyon sat down beside the teacher, on a bench outside the hostel, and was soon telling his same old story. Varvara went back to the room. The student was alone there, sitting at the

---

* A lightly fermented drink made from rye bread.
† The official is quoting from Psalm 37:45 (according to the Orthodox numbering), which is in the morning prayers for lay readers. In the King James Bible this is translated: "For my loins are filled with a loathsome disease: and there is no soundness in my flesh" (Psalm 38:7).

table and eating curd cheese from a large clay bowl. On his face was a look of sly embarrassment.

"Want some?" he said to Varvara. "I got it from the dairy. I'm famished. All we get in the refectory is cabbage soup seasoned with holy relics." He giggled.

"No, thank you."

The student stopped eating and looked at Varvara intently. With an awkward smile, blushing and giggling, he said, "You're quite a woman, you know. As for that husband of yours ... And your eyes—your eyes are gorgeous. But sit yourself down, for the love of God."

Varvara looked straight into his bashful but laughing eyes and felt a sense of horror. It seemed as if she was looking not at a young student but at Vanya Tsyganov—and was unable to get away from him.

"O Lord, O Lord! What is all this?"

She wanted to tear her hair, to weep and wail.

Slowly, still looking the student straight in the eye, Varvara backed toward her door.

"Is th-that where you s-sleep?" the student stammered, still blushing.

Varvara heard footsteps out in the corridor. She locked her door, sat down on the bed, and listened to her heart trembling. The merchant and the hypocrite official came back, caught sight of the curd cheese, and were incensed with rage.

"Huh! Like that, is it? Can't even last three days?[*] Well then, what's stopping you? Eat! You bought that cheese—so you eat it!"

"I've had all I want."

"Eat that cheese!"

Both men felt the same craving. And the stronger their craving, the fiercer their rage.

"Eat, I say!" hissed the official. "You bought it—so you eat it!"

"What's wrong with you?" the merchant chimed in. "If you know no shame, then eat all you want!"

The two men swallowed down their saliva, unable to take their eyes off the cheese.

---

[*] The period that these short-term visitors were allowed to stay. During those three days they were expected to avoid meat and dairy products; they were then ready to receive Communion.

* * *

During the afternoon a large-winged boat flew in, bringing Pomor women from the mainland coast. So high were the waves that no one even saw the boat draw in to the pier.

The women spilled out onto the shore. They were a bright, loquacious flock, in pink, green, lilac, and pale blue dresses, with pearl rings on their headbands. They had fair eyebrows and the eyes of seagulls or mermaids—round, yellow eyes with black rims and black dots for pupils.

The women chattered away and laughed. The pilgrims watched from a distance, the men twisting their beards between their fingers.

"Them Pomors are a rich lot. They catch fish, they shoot animals for their pelts, they gather down from eider ducks. No wonder they go around in pearls."*

A woman in a rose-lilac dress, with a yellow-eyed child on her back, was teasing a gull, holding out a piece of bread, then withdrawing it, repeating, "Bread for t' gull-bird? Bread for t' gully-bird?"

The gull, who also had a child on her back, stretched out her neck crossly.

The seagull and the woman—two of a kind, and with the same yellow-eyed children—both understood that this was a game.

"Mock away, mock away!" people called out. "But wait till she's up above yer head! See what she does to you then! Them gulls can get mighty cross."

Toward evening a gale blew up. As if through a funnel, it blew straight down the icy throat of the Arctic Ocean, shaking the trees, twisting skirts and cassocks around legs, stopping people in their tracks or knocking them to the ground, flinging sea foam against the hostel's windows. Flocking swiftly together, the Pomor women got back on board and hoisted sail. Pink, lilac, and pale blue dresses swirled in the wind. The boat had no thwarts and no gunnels—the women simply stood on the planking. Someone cast off. Two young

---

* In the mid-1880s the poet Konstantin Sluchevsky described Pomor women as "well dressed regardless of their social and economic status, wearing colourful *sarafany*, and beautifully decorated headwear. [...] A distinctive feature of women's clothing in some parts of Pomor'e was an extensive use of pearls extracted from local rivers."

lads got out their squeeze-boxes and began to play; pink, lilac, and pale blue skirts swirled and danced near the edge of the boat. The following wind filled out the sails, driving the boat on so fiercely that, for a moment, the entire stern rose high above the waves. The wind snatched the song away, brought it back, carried it off again—and then blew everything into the sea, burying both boat and song under a huge, turbid wave that smelled of fish scales. A few minutes later the pilgrims were pointing to a tiny craft now rounding a distant headland.

"Look—already there! They're a desperate lot, them Pomors."*

That evening in the refectory the old woman with the flaccid tongue was once again licking her spoon. The monk with the nasal voice read the same words about lechery, sin, and the devil. The yawning youth was once again led through the yard. A new group of pilgrims appeared—old women in black, smelling of cod and incense.

The gulls in the yard seemed cross, and something was frightening them. The gale was making their feathers stand up on end, and they were squealing shrill complaints.

Semyon took Varvara to confession. And, just as when she'd been questioned by that officer in Novgorod, her soul closed up in blank, obstinate misery. Back then, she had said, "Nowt to do wiv me." Now, in the church, she fastened her eyes on the bronze clasp of the Gospels, repeated to the priest, "I have sinned, I have sinned"—and said no more.

No one in the room slept long that night—thanks to the hypocrite official, who chose to prolong his devotions until the second cockcrow. He groaned, prostrated himself, and intoned his prayers in a noisy whisper: "Lord, Lord, who art present even in the uttermost depths of the sea. Even there thou art present." Seven beds, from seven corners, creaked angrily back.

But the official inadvertently overslept. Eventually, he got up along

---

* See note 4. In their article "The Sea Is Our Field," Masha Shaw and Natalie Wahnsiedler write: "Sluchevsky was particularly impressed by the light and skilful movements of Pomor women in their long and richly decorated dresses as they steered their boats in rough and roaring waters"; in David G. Anderson, Dimtry V. Arzyutov, and Sergei S. Alimov, eds., *Life Histories of Etnos Theory in Russia and Beyond* (Cambridge: Open Book Publishers, 2019).

with everyone else and sat down by the window, trying not to catch anyone's eye. And then, still not looking at anyone, he sidled off to church.

The church was thronged with people. There was a smell of cod, sheepskin, something sour, and melted wax. Candle flames swayed before the flat, dark faces on the ancient icons; where the saints' hands emerged from their gilt covering, the paint had long ago wrinkled and blistered from the touch of thousands upon thousands of lips. As they went past the holy relics, the pilgrims gazed with awe and horror at a deceased *skhimnik*, a monk who had followed the most extreme of the monastic rules: all that could be seen of him, poking out from a black shroud embroidered with bones, was the tip of a waxen nose, along with some wisps of gray beard and two bony hands.

High above everyone rose the head of the yawning youth, mouth suddenly gaping open with a groan and then snapping shut. The wind knocked at doors and windows, bursting into the church, then howling as it withdrew. Now and again white wings swept past the windows—and a mermaid's round yellow eye would peep in.

In the alcoves the monks' silent, shadowy figures were barely stirring, as if their prayer beads had gone stiff in their fingers. A ripple passed through the congregation as people stepped back to let the communicants through. The choir was already singing the Cherubic Hymn,* the boys' high voices soaring up to the cupola, when a woman began shrieking frenziedly, "Kuda-a-a! Ku-u-da-a-a! Ku-da-a-a!"†

Her shrieks grew ever more piercing, ever more violent.

"Possessed," whispered the peasant women. "Possessed good n' proper!"‡

Then someone else let out a scream and a wail—and began to bark like a dog, not letting up.

---

* This marks the beginning of the most solemn part of the Liturgy. It is sung as the clergy—accompanied, it is believed, by angels—enter the sanctuary through the Holy Doors. It ends, "Let us now lay aside all earthly care."
† The word means "whither." Teffi evidently chose it both for its sound and for its meaning. Unable to reproduce both, we have transliterated, reproducing the sound alone.
‡ The celebration of Christ's resurrection through the mystery of the Eucharist was believed to provoke fear among demons, which in turn could prompt fits among those in a state of demonic possession.

Varvara clenched her hands tight. The chandelier swayed, slid to one side—and she felt her legs and shoulders begin to shudder, swiftly, violently, while her whole face stretched as if clinging tight to her cheekbones, and her stomach swelled, climbing right up to her throat, and a wild scream flew out from somewhere deep and dark, twisting her whole body, tearing her body apart, smashing red lights against the crown of her head: "A-a-i-i! Da-a-a! Da-a-a!"*

A fleeting thought: *Should I stop?*

But something made her tense herself more and more powerfully, forcing her to cry out more and more loudly, to clench her whole body, to will on the convulsions. The words didn't matter. The first sounds to burst out had been "A-a-i-i!" and "Da-a-a!"—and so she had gone on. What mattered was not to stop, to expend more and more of herself in the cry, to give herself to it more intensely, yes, more and more of herself: *Oh, if only they didn't get in her way. Oh, if only they let her keep going ...* But it was so hard. Would she have the strength?

"A-a-i-i! A-a-i-i!" *If only ... if only ... How sweet ... how sweet that would be ...*

Someone's feet, next to her cheek. A strip of rug, a flax rug.

Am I lying down now? Oh, who cares? I can't keep going now. But another time. Another time, somehow ...

And suddenly she was being lifted up. She was being hoisted by hands under her shoulders—and there before her eyes was a vast golden chalice, vast as the world.

"Varvara," someone was saying beside her.

"Varvara," she heard someone else repeat.

And a sharp golden spoon, also vast, was parting her lips and knocking against her clenched teeth.† Her teeth unclenched of their

---

* Varvara's "Aida!" echoes the first woman's "Kuda!" And the word *da* means "yes."

† Varvara would not normally have received Communion before completing her penance. Now, however, she is thought to be possessed and so not responsible for her state. In the words of John Chrysostom, "They that be possest in that they are tormented of the devil are blameless and will never be punished with torment for that: but they who approach unworthily the holy Mysteries shall be given over to everlasting torments"; quoted in *The Doctrine of the Russian Church*, R. W. Blackmore, trans. (Aberdeen: A. Brown and Co., 1845), 223n. And so Varvara is given the Eucharist: a small piece of bread dipped in wine.

own accord, a gentle quiver passed through her arms and legs, and her head fell forward; she could no longer hold it up. Small beads of sweat were cooling her forehead.

How sweet! Oh, how sweet!

And her whole body became empty. As if everything heavy, swollen, and black had left with the scream.

They seated Varvara on a bench outside the hostel. She had turned suddenly thinner. She had thrown back her head, her hair uncovered, and she was smiling with a look of exhausted bliss.

Not daring to go at all close, the other pilgrim women were looking at her in fear and awe, just as they had looked at the deceased *skhimnik*. Semyon was also looking at her in speechless fear and awe. And Varvara was saying in a delirious voice, her words coming out in fits and starts, "Oh, my darlings! All of you! What sweetness! Lord God! My dearest Semyon! And now—a long, long way, on foot, to Saint Tikhon of Zadonsk.* How dear the sky is. Sweet sky, bright sky. And the gulls ... the dear gulls ..."

---

* Saint Tikhon of Zadnosk (1724–1783) was born, like Varvara and her husband, in the province of Novgorod. After serving for seven years as a bishop, he retired because of poor health to the monastery of Zadonsk, beyond the Don River. Eighty years after his death, he was canonized. Varvara imagines herself and Semyon making a pilgrimage to Zadonsk, stopping at other holy sites on the way.

FATHER GERVASY'S SECRET

Mikhail Kuzmin (1872–1936)

Translated by John A. Barnstead

> Composer, musician, poet, the first openly gay person in Russian literature, **Mikhail Kuzmin** inaugurated homosexuality as a topic in Russian prose with his novelette *The Wings*, published in 1906. As a poet he influenced, directly or indirectly, a whole generation of younger poets, including Velimir Khlebnikov.
>
> Kuzmin stayed in the USSR, more or less successfully survived the initial repressions, published poetry and earned money from translations. But after 1929, the year that the Stalinist mass repressive campaigns began, Kuzmin was excluded from public literary life and died in 1936, and most of his unpublished manuscripts and diaries disappeared.

I

People had almost forgotten the name "cow's death" first given to the large flat stone on the path running along the top of the wooded ridge, jutting far out, as if overhanging the broad valley which opened to the east. This old name had been given in time immemorial, when the Nagorno-Uspensky cloister did not yet exist; it had been given by peasants whose imagination had been fired once and for all by the spectacle of a cow that had wandered from God knows where into the forest thicket and perished there, mooing plaintively in plain sight of everyone. There were no consequences: neither hoof-and-mouth, nor drought, nor pestilences nor war followed upon this strange phenomenon; only the stone was stuck with the name "cow's death". Now it was already around ten years since the stone had been renamed "Gervasy's thought", for the new abbot of the Nagorno-Uspensky monastery, Father Gervasy, had taken a fancy to this outcropping for his long thoughts and reveries.

Below the valley spread out, almost Siberian, Transuralian, with the dark green of groves and meadows, the thick blue of the seemingly motionless river, the grey-black shadows of the clouds. There were almost no houses; everything was round, spacious, thick and darkly curling! It was as if someone had slowly poured out labrador stone by some miracle liquified, blue and primordial green, or as if a peacock had spread its tail and then just left it there.

When Father Gervasy sat on the stone, hugging his knees, his face was unusually well-suited to this congealed valley – it was stern, bold, dark, with a noble mouth set in a black beard and with "Petrine", willful, now slightly veiled eyes – "vatic orbs".

Had the Uspensky monastery been closer to the provincial seat, pious ladies would not have been slow to weave a romantic legend around the comparatively young abbot. Ten years ago Father Gervasy was not yet thirty, he was handsome, to the manor born, had loved in the world, and possessed an energetic and restrained character. Naturally it would have turned out immediately that he had been a dashing hussar, a count, that he had many high connections, that there had been a duel with a high-ranking official, that he faced the threat of exile, etc. And, doubtless, more than one of the provincial lionesses would have wished to re-enact the story of "Father Sergius".

But the Uspensky monastery was located in such a backwater that the provincial ladies did not visit it, and the simple, devout women were not interested in love legends, so that everyone readily believed that the small round portrait of a young woman with a nice face which hung in Father Gervasy's cell really did depict his supposedly dead sister. And in point of fact she had died for his heart, for his memory, and he prayed for her almost as for a sister.

The abbot was not too popular in his monastery or among the pilgrims and the pious, perhaps because in his character there were few traits of the purely Russian elder. Restrained and energetic, pious with an aggressive piety, always doing battle with himself and with the falsehood or weakness he perceived around him, he produced the impression of a stern builder, lonely and somewhat proud, far indeed from the touching mixture of simplicity and blessedness of those vernal Russian elders who sit under apple trees in the apiary and with simple, simple words which come from God knows where – from the elder's heart, from the spirit of the apple tree, from native heaven, from the buzzing of the bees, "God's labourers" – melt with a direct ray simple, desolate, spiteful, reconciled, tearful hearts, entering that most secret chamber which, even if disordered, fouled, everyone has nonetheless.

Father Gervasy was lonely, but apparently was not bothered by this, having directed all his energy to the arrangement of his soul and of the cloister entrusted to him.

The monastery was comparatively new, founded in the reign of Nicholas I for the propagation of orthodoxy among the Old Believer population. Missionary activity did not prosper, and the monastery itself declined to such an extent that by the seventies the question was even raised as to whether the Nagorno-Uspensky cloister ought not to be converted to a convent or abandoned entirely. But at this point the local merchant Maslov for some reason left his entire capital to the monastery, so that in the material sense its existence was assured. Why Maslov willed all his money to the Nagorno-Uspensky monastery remained a mystery, since although the donor's family was from the Urals, in fact from this very area, he himself had died in Moscow, having been gone from his native village fifty years or more. His body was brought from Moscow in accordance with the wishes of the deceased to the Nagorno-Uspensky cloister, and buried near the stone church which was begun at that time, where every year on the day of his death a requiem mass was celebrated. None of his near and dear ones attended the funeral, because Maslov had died childless, and by that time had no relatives.

When Father Gervasy undertook the administration of the monastery, far from all of the construction had been completed and the new abbot seemed to seek solace for his first years of a lonely and difficult life in purely administrative cares.

But beneath the facade of a stern builder the abbot had a heart, too, even an ardent one, and lofty dreams, and an unbending uprightness which he did not reveal out of proud modesty, in order to avoid seeming incomprehensible, or else so that his feelings would not be misinterpreted. But it was still difficult for him, despite the so to speak voluntary nature of his solitude, to keep all this within himself unshared and unappreciated. Therefore he was gladdened when Grisha Plotnikov, the son of a Siberian merchant, came to their monastery. It was a mystery what could have drawn a young man who had barely begun to live to monastic life, but Father Gervasy felt a rare ardour and a true vocation in him, and therefore marked him out at once from among the postulants, took him under his direct supervision, and somehow ceased to be as lonely as before. All the best that is included in the words "teacher" and "pupil" – all this was in the relations of Father Gervasy with Grisha. The latter became attached to his abbot with all the force of his dreamy heart, all the more so since he saw how little this truth-loving and, in his opinion, rare person was appreciated. After all, if you know that the treasure house of a great and lonely soul is open to you and you alone, then along with disappointment at the blindness of those around you, there is always joy as well in knowing something others do not.

II

A week before the Feast of the Assumption, or perhaps from the first Feast of the Saviour, pilgrims began to appear at the monastery despite its remoteness, to fast in preparation for communion and to meet the holiday the cloister was named for.

The short, fierce, almost Siberian summer heat had already broken, but the days were still warm and lovely. There had appeared that first distinctness which hails approaching autumn; berries were not through yet, apples rained down, mushrooms had spread from the pine forest to its very edge – a gourmet's delight during the Assumption fast! It was good to walk along the road: your legs seemed to fly by their own accord toward the bell far up ahead! ...

This evening Father Gervasy did not go to church, but read mass in his cell, as he felt a trifle ill. A knock came at the door. The abbot continued to read without answering the knock. Apparently whoever was at the door understood, for the knock was repeated only about ten minutes later, when Father Gervasy, having put aside the book, was looking out the window at the pilgrims going their separate ways after church. A feeling of slightly proud satisfaction, that it was by his energy and labours that the monastery stood firm and prosperous, passed into Father Gervasy's heart.

The servant who entered informed him that some man wanted to see the abbot.

"Who is it?"

"I don't know; one of the pilgrims, an ancient old man."

"What does he need, do you know?"

"No. He just keeps insisting he has something important to say."

The abbot frowned, thinking that the traveller would tell him about some sort of visions, dreams, portents.

"Well, then, let him come tomorrow after mass."

The servant stopped short.

"But he can't come, Father Abbot."

"What do you mean he can't come?"

"He's real sick, flat on his back. He took to his bed the moment he came, day before yesterday, and hasn't got up since. You'll have to trouble yourself to go to Father Irinarch's – he's lying there."

"Perhaps he needs to confess, is there really no one else to be found?"

"It's you he wants to tell something, Father Abbot."

"Strange. Well, all right, I'll go."

"Only, Father Abbot, don't wait too long, or else the old man may die on you."

"Why didn't you say so in the first place? Give me my cane."

The old man did not look at all like dying. Although he really was lying on a narrow bed and had even folded his hands on his breast as if preparing for departure, his face was rather animated, and his eyes glowed almost gaily. He did not speak quite as an old man from the countryside would, but rather as a man who had seen sights and been in varied company, which was of course to be expected if he were a professional traveller. He appeared to be not more than about sixty years old.

"Are you ailing, Brother?"

"Ah, Father Abbot, Your Reverence, I don't know if I'll make it to the holiday! ..."

"God is merciful!"

"Merciful, Father, merciful – he's put up with my sins for such a long time."

"Are you so old, then?"

"Eighty two."

"You're no youngster, what can I say ..."

"The thing's not youth, Your Reverence, but having a clean conscience."

"Do you want to confess?"

The old man was silent.

"Receive extreme unction, it will help you in your illness and strengthen your soul."

The old man remained silent.

"You wanted to tell me something; you called for me."

"I called, ah, I called! I have a great secret to reveal." "Reveal it, it will make it easier for you!"

Father Gervasy waved his hand for everyone to leave the room, and repeated: "Reveal it!"

"It's horrible."

"But won't it be horrible before the Lord? He knows all secrets! Perhaps your minutes are numbered and there, in the next world, it will be too late to repent."

The old man was silent for a long time, his eyes closed; finally he said quietly and calmly: "The cloister stands on blood money soaked with tears!"

"What?"

"The cloister stands on blood money!"

"What cloister? What are you saying?"

"Your cloister, this one, the Nagorno-Uspensky."

Father Gervasy even leaped from his chair, but then remembered himself and began to speak sternly: "You're raving or playing tricks! If you want to repent then tell your sins – it's no good trying to deceive me."

"I am telling my sins."

"Then tell them."

"I will ... Maslov, you know, Petr Trofimovich, how did he get his inheritance? He dispatched his brother to the next world so as not to share it with him. I knew, but I was silent, I couldn't tell. As a boy I worked in their shop – who would believe me? So I was silent. Then, when old Maslov had passed away, I said to Petr Trofimovich once (my conscience was bothering me): Petr Trofimovich, it's a big sin: I know how Viktor Trofimovich died, and he didn't meet a natural death. And he looked at me and said: You're a smart fellow, Alesha (I'm called Aleksei), smart and know what's what, but what nonsense you're spouting! If you don't have anything better to do I'll give you something!" And he made me head clerk, although I was only twenty years old. It was as if he were trying to turn my eyes away from what had happened: he made me his right hand man and hid nothing from me; I did a lot of things he ordered me to, but I was a witness to everything. He bound my conscience and made me into an unwilling evil-doer ..." Father Gervasy listened, tightly squeezing the arm of the monastery chair, never taking his eyes off the traveller, who also stared constantly at the abbot. It seemed as if it were the monk who was confessing horrible sins, and the old man who was listening to him without emotion, to such an extent did horror become ever more evident on Father Gervasy's face, and the old man's story echoed, somehow strangely indifferent and circumstantial. As the narrator unfolded the picture of deception, swindle, robberies and murders, his voice became ever duller, his story ever dryer; he seemed to be hurrying, abbreviating it – it became mere mentions, names of people and cities, sums, years – it was as though someone else, some demon were reading a scroll of accusations, a list, a notebook. Suddenly the abbot threw himself from the chair to his knees and, raising one hand toward heaven, with the other seized the hands of the dying man and loudly exclaimed: "I adjure thee by the living God, swear to me that thou art speaking the truth!" The old man squinted contemptuously and hurriedly interjected: "Why should I lie? You see I am dying." And he continued his confession. It is not known whether Father Gervasy listened any further. What he had learned about the money left by Maslov, which had so helped the monastery to flower like a rural flowering shrub, and had helped him, the abbot, to forget his bitter weaknesses in building, – that was more than enough. As if in a dream he heard: "I've told only you, Father, I've bared my soul. I bore it within myself for fifty years, now you bear it for a while!" Father Gervasy lifted his head and staggered away from the dying man, who, his eyes closed, smiled to reveal his rotten teeth. The abbot crossed himself, whispering "May God be resurrected", but the smile did not disappear, and when he touched the old man and said "What's there to be laughing at, are you crazy?" he found out, saw that the traveller was already dead. Father Gervasy remained in Father Irinarch's cell a long time, and when he came out at last he swayed slightly and said in a weak voice quite unlike his usual one: "In there ... he's dead." Grisha saw by his teacher's face that something important had happened, something that could overturn an entire life, and when the abbot put a hand on his shoulder Grisha became convinced of it. Receiving the blessing, he said fondly: "Have patience, Father Gervasy, God's truth will reveal itself!" The abbot shrank back slightly and, saying nothing in reply, bowed his head low and went to his own cell. Grisha noticed for the first time that Father Gervasy's head was trembling like an old man's.

III

Lord, Thou seest the human heart, Thou seest human weakness, Thou knowest how easily temptation enters simple souls! Thou willst not permit it: let him who is strong bear the burden! Everyone was surprised that these days the abbot was going to all the services, looking at everything attentively, finding a good word for everything, taking an interest in everything: the aviary, the barnyard, the bakery, the icon-painting studio, the bindery, as if he were a buyer, or as if he were planning to leave. He looked at everyone so pityingly and affectionately that he did not seem to be Father Gervasy at all.

Lord, Thou seest the irreparable, Thou seest their simplicity. Thou seest their light and willst not permit it. Let him who is strong keep silent and bear it. Grisha constantly followed on the heels of his teacher, as if he were waiting for him to say a word: the abbot spoke much and fondly, but it was as if these were not the words for which the youth's heart thirsted. Lord, Thou coverest the earth with snow! I shall pray! I know than everything should be revealed, that everything should be renounced, but Lord, I am not praying for myself, but for them. I shall pray! But must children be without a nest? Let it not be so! Grisha waited right up to the Assumption, but nothing changed. Father Gervasy celebrated the all night service as grandly as always, as always Father Deacon proclaimed "the founders of this holy temple", as always a requiem mass was celebrated over Maslov's grave.

When Grisha entered Father Gervasy's cell, the abbot was praying. His face was tearstained and decisive. Of course how good and noble it would be to reveal everything, to renounce the money – how easy it would be! But the cloister? These simple people, what would become of them? Let the secret be his secret, let it burden him and leave them untouched. He would lose Grisha's trust, his devotion, since he would see his struggle and be tempted, taking firmness for falsehood. He was young, ardent. But let Father Gervasy be alone once more – it would be better, more charitable for him to be silent, having taken everything on himself.

"Who takest away the sins of the world, have mercy on me!"

Grisha said: "Forgive me, Father Gervasy, I am leaving; give me leave to go."

"But why, Grisha?" They spoke as if everything between them were known already, even words weren't necessary.

"How I loved you and kept waiting for God's truth to reveal itself."

"And you couldn't wait any longer?"

"No."

"Grisha, there is no need to tell you how attached I've become to you, but is it good to save one person and tempt forty?"

"No, of course not."

"I think so, too. If you cannot remain untempted – go. I release you. Perhaps you will return."

Grisha looked up hopefully. "When God's truth reveals itself, then?"

"When you come to understand that God's charity has already revealed itself in silence, and that it is higher than His truth."

THE BLUE BANNER
Mikhail Prishvin (1873–1954)
Translated by Lisa C. Hayden

Having lost his father early, being expelled from the gymnasium because of conflicts with his teacher, the philosopher V. Rozanov, thrown out of Riga technical college for his dedication to Marxism and translation of Marxist authors, arrested and imprisoned for a year, then deported and prohibited to live in any big cities, **Mikhail Prishvin** went to learn agronomy in Germany. After his return to Russia in 1902 he worked for a while in agriculture, but then became a traveler, ethnographer, explorer of the North, reporter and a writer, forerunner of the ecological movement and advocate of responsibility towards nature.

He strongly opposed the Bolshevik coup, was briefly arrested and went into the hiding in the provinces, teaching and working as a librarian. Later Prishvin forced himself to cope with Soviet rule and found his niche: children's books about wildlife.

I

Us and Semyon Ivanych, it used to be our favourite thing chasing after tops down at the ironware row of market stalls. Clean off the ice, whittle up a top, then whip it around real good with cow tails. For Semyon Ivanych, the best-loved part was warming up, and for us little ones, it was the amusement. We're chasing that top around and old uncle Mitrofan Sergeyevich, he's right there tightening his sash around his belly, hiding his big beard behind his collar, and he spits, spits into his hand to get ready and he's warming up, too; there's the Kozhukhov brothers' stall next to our uncle's stall, then there's the Yershovs and the Abramovs and company: everybody knows each other and everybody's considered kin somehow, and in the winter everybody's chasing after tops with switches made of cow tails.

Where'd that all go! There's maybe one in ten stalls left in one piece at the ironware row, and now it's only the Cheryomukhins that's left in fish, and they don't even trade in fresh caviar and sterlet—they're on plain old salted wild carp. Compared to the others, things weren't so bad for Semyon Ivanych; the others worked in what came natural to their families; the ones trading in cheap tobacco died with cheap tobacco, the ones in the flour section came to a halt along with the windmills, but Semyon Ivanych, he kept running from one thing to another, just like a little Yid, and he only came to grief in the very last few days, when there were no goods left at all. A rumour went around that maybe the Germans had brought lots of their cheap goods into Petersburg, but Semyon Ivanych couldn't bring himself to head into that hellish pit for cheap German goods—he'd even banished the very thought as indecent. So he didn't go off to Petersburg just for his own gain: it was completely unexpected and he was beside himself, too, as it were; he was going to Lebedyan for a funeral, but landed himself in Petersburg for the cheap German goods.

As it happened, his niece Sonechka passed away during the Nativity Fast—unforeseen, like the telegram said. Semyon Ivanych had known this Sonechka as a little girl about fifteen years ago; he'd loved playing with her and he called her the Kid Goat. He hadn't seen her since then; he'd only heard rumours his Kid Goat was mixed up with actors now and had even gone off to Paris to dance. The way the rails are these days, it's hard to say why Semyon Ivanych took it into his head to go off to some half-forgotten relative's funeral; either he had nothing better to do and something strange had started brewing in his person (we'd always considered Semyon Ivanych a little strange), or maybe it's that his family was in a bad way (the eldest boy had taken to theft), or maybe it's this ruin all over the place that made the old ways unfurl like a blue banner, flying in the face of everything new, everything red, that made him want to pay back, in the old way, the ancient way, his kinship debt to the little Kid Goat, daughter of his unlucky brother who'd gone bust trading in Livny accordions. Whatever the case, Semyon Ivanych got ready fast and left for the funeral.

At the junction station where some trains go in the Petersburg direction and others to Lebedyan, a Lebedyan midwife he knew got off her train during the stop and boom—she tells him about Sonechka, that his Kid Goat'd done herself in, a shot to the heart.

There were three things Semyon Ivanych feared on this earth: the first was mountain drop-offs, something he, a steppe-dweller, had never seen but dreamt of often—he'd see himself walking up to a drop-off and the drop-off's tugging at him. He had a second fear, of magicians, that if the magicians or mesmerists did not, indeed, turn out to be the deceivers everybody said they were, and they really could do all that—well, then, it's enough to make you lose your mind: pretty scary! And the third was suicide; the thought of that tugs at you just like the drop-off, and there's only one means of salvation: run away without even thinking, as if it were a drop-off.

Semyon Ivanych found himself a place to sit at the station's little gatehouse, laid his hands on his tummy, and twiddled his thumbs as if they were a windmill: you see this all the time in merchant life, where they'll twiddle their thumbs all around and around for an hour, two hours, however long it takes, until everything's been run through the mill and a new decision comes out.

So imagine: there'd been this clear and forthright person, he'd traded, warmed up, chased after tops with cow tails, and everybody knew his value, and they took stock in what he said, and paid him due respects, too—and just you try and recognize him at that junction station, all alone, sitting for hours, twiddling his thumbs and cranking out something utterly senseless: he'd intended on going to a funeral but found out the deceased had done herself in, so he went to Petersburg for cheap German goods.

II

Semyon Ivanych arrived in Petersburg all right, but getting out proved harder: he ordered a ticket and they promised it by 15 December, so you just sit there a whole week, with nothing to do in that pit of hell. It ended up there weren't any cheap German goods, just all kinds of nonsense: bits of flint, lighters, a little cocoa—and the prices they were asking! There isn't a thing for a merchant to do. Wine cellars being looted, shooting everywhere, and the people's faces—enough to give you a fright. Things are still more or less all right during the day—but at night Semyon Ivanych's fears come together in his room, worse than any nightmare or premonition.

"Suppose," he thinks to himself, "it isn't our Russian people that's doing all this, but magicians and mesmerists."

And then Semyon Ivanych's ancient fear of magicians whispers something else: "And what if it's all the real truth, and this is the life we get all the way till the second coming?"

His second fear, the one about the drop-off, tortures him all the time in his room, too: it's all bright and warm, but then suddenly the electric light goes out with no warning at all, and you're sitting there with a thin little wax candle, just like you're over a drop-off.

And then the third fear sneaks up, the suicide fear, and you might as well go out to the pitch-black street, unbutton your hairy chest, and say, "Gun me down, lads—it's all the same in the end!"

But God forbid he go outside: soon as dusk starts falling, there goes Semyon Ivanych, run-run-running to his room, and he circles around there like a hare, all alone with his fears on a barren island with the water rising.

On the morning of the 15th, a boy brought a ticket for a train at ten in the evening. Semyon Ivanych rejoiced, left for the railway station before nightfall to economize on the tram, and put the crate of tea he'd bought at his feet, nice and careful, so it wasn't bothering anybody. For ten roubles, a soldier got him a window seat in first class—and a good, honest soldier he was, too: he held on to the crate of tea for him, used it as his seat in the lavatory.

Semyon Ivanych settled in and crossed himself: "Bring me home, Lord!"

Suddenly, at around ten in the evening, they announce: "The train's not leaving!" A blizzard was raging. Sundered Rus was snowed under, yoked into one white and boundless kingdom, just like before.

On the return tram, the number five, from Znamenskaya Square to Vasilyevsky Island, Semyon Ivanych once again put the crate of tea at his feet, nice and careful, not bothering anybody. He could hear machine guns shooting, but that wasn't scary on the tram, around people. After crossing Nikolaevsky Bridge, the number five suddenly stopped and the light shut off in the tram; and the number eighteen, which was running right behind the five, shut off, too; and all the trams in the capital, wherever they were running, stopped on the spot and their lights shut off: there was no current. They waited an hour, two—who wants to walk in a blizzard when there's shooting?! But it couldn't be helped, so the passengers scattered, disappearing one after another into the blizzard; and then, finally, the conductor left.

Semyon Ivanych with his heavy crate—fifty pounds of tea, all told—is the last to leave, and he looks around: there's no light, not even a flicker around him, and not one single person anywhere, and it seems that if someone were to appear, he'd be scarier than the fiercest beast. But lots of people would be fine. Hoping to find lots of people on Bolshoy Avenue, Semyon Ivanych hurries off like he's being chased; he's running for all he's worth, gasping for breath under the weight of the crate. It's even worse on Bolshoy Avenue, though—empty as a Siberian wasteland, even emptier: it's been that way in Siberia since the beginning of time, but here you've got an avenue and huge buildings—and nobody, not a soul!

The wind carries the sound of rapid shooting from the harbour, and it seems so close that you think you'll be left here for good, in this foreign land. And then Semyon Ivanych's Kid Goat, the deceased—his niece Sonechka—appeared plainly before him, all snow-white, and she's whimpering, asking: Why did he abandon her in Lebedyan, why did he trade in her little funeral for one so big, and no less unrighteous? The apparition wavered and flew off, and a huge grey monster appeared in the blizzard: crouching, growing, crouching, growing and waving, waving right at Semyon Ivanych.

He dropped the crate, stepped aside, crossed himself, and the huge thing hurtling out of the blizzard right at Semyon Ivanych turned out to be a little black dog.

Then three mountains emerged and walked up to Semyon Ivanych in the form of three civilians with rifles. They inspected the top of the crate and broke it open: tea!

"Marauder!"

And they led Semyon Ivanych off somewhere.

III

In a room once graced by daydreaming noble maidens, whose names were registered in a velvet book, sit two generals playing checkers; a third general is sweeping the room. New detainees are brought in every hour. Two polished little old men—they were directors of departments once—try to go to sleep but can't; they leap up from any noise, realize where they are, and lie down again, then leap up again like wind-up toys. A colonel, an elderly man with a Cross of St George on his chest, keeps muttering something about Metropolitan Antony. At midnight someone in the hallway shouts, "Caught a marauder!"

And they bring in Semyon Ivanych. This bulky, dishevelled, snow-covered man, with streaks of grey in his black hair, casts his fiery eyes around the room and sits down heavily on a stool.

Semyon Ivanych's hands are on his tummy, his thumbs tirelessly twiddling, one around the other, for one hour, two hours. The barmy colonel with the Cross of St George keeps telling him, like a friend, about his plans for the motherland's salvation: first thing tomorrow he's filing a petition with Metropolitan Antony, asking permission to go to all the hooligans' dens and hideouts and gather those roughnecks under Christ's blue banner.

"They've been led astray," he said, "but our roughnecks are godly people, I tell you!"

Semyon Ivanych is listening to the colonel carefully, but he's looking sideways at the generals playing checkers, noticing how a piece is getting forced into a dead end, getting blocked.

"The people were led astray," the colonel keeps muttering.

"That's it, blocked!" announces the general.

Then Semyon Ivanych mumbles something, gladdening the colonel very much: he'd found his voice after all.

"I," says he, "will gather all the roughnecks for the metropolitan, gather them under the blue banner, and bring them all to the metropolitan for a benediction, and Russia will be saved."

Night deepens. Where the Smolny's noble maidens, registered in the velvet book, once took their rest, now sleeps a heap of arrested generals, and a former member of the State Duma, and a member of the Constituent Assembly, and all kinds of socialists and bureaucrats—and it's only Semyon Ivanych that's awake, just twiddling his thumbs.

The Smolny Sweet Reverie makes her way through the corridors and archways into the hall with the double-height ceiling, where, as a princess, Catherine the Great danced with the last Polish king, and then she vanishes in the upper windows, which are turning a lighter blue.

The morning turns lighter, bluer. The prisoners wake up one after another, and they're all watching Semyon Ivanych: he's sitting on that same stool, just like before, and twiddling his thumbs—hasn't stirred since yesterday. The fussy general's getting ready for tea, and the department directors, socialists and deputies are getting up to relieve themselves.

The clock strikes ten, eleven, twelve ... At one, they come for Semyon Ivanych: "Questioning!"

Well, Semyon Ivanych had thought he'd be brought in for questioning, and there'd be judges sitting there—my, was he surprised: he'd seen these people before, they were familiar—oh, how familiar—he'd lived his whole life with them, these very ones, and here they were, in the afterlife.

"Hello, friends of mine!"

The sullen judges don't say a word.

"Getting mighty full of yourselves, are you? Come on, you devils—don't you recognize me?"

And he laughs—oh, does he laugh.

They ordered Semyon Ivanych be led out, but as he left, he managed to slip in, "Ah, you roughnecks, you—how godly you are!"

During his night in confinement some kind of secret was revealed to Semyon Ivanych, which had made sense of this whole mess, and all his fears fell away, as if he had outrun them, and had himself become a fright. And now he marches off into the very blaze, into the thick of it, where there's no turning back, to the wine cellars, where the Red Guards are shooting off the drunkards for the third day straight. Semyon Ivanych marches, marches right through the bullets to get to the drunkards, no fear at all.

"Cheers, lads!"

"Our Excellency!" answer the drunkards.

A red-headed, tousled, thoroughly drunk little soldier brings over some wine.

"Under the blue banner, forward march!" commands Semyon Ivanych.

"Right!" answers the redhead.

The madmen and the drunkards set out into the hail of bullets, and the bullets don't graze them: madmen and drunkards have no fear, they themselves are a fright. Sledges, trucks and automobiles move aside, trams stop to let the madman through with his troops.

And that's how it seems to Semyon Ivanych—that it isn't one drunkard drifting behind him, but all the regiments, the whole of drunken Rus marching under the blue banner. Now Semyon Ivanych doesn't fear a thing: Semyon Ivanych himself is a fright. Passers-by stand aside in horror, ordinary people watch from afar as they parade: the madman in front, the drunkard in the back, in strange, deceptive agreement.

IN THE MIRROR

Valery Bryusov (1873–1924)

Translated by Stephen Graham

Maybe the most 'French' among all Russian poets, omnivorous in his themes, from mysticism to urbanism and physics, **Valery Bryusov** also wrote prose, and was one of the first Russian science fiction authors. Bryusov explored dystopian themes, predicted the rebellion of the machines, interplanetary flights, and with this sense of the pathos of the new world to come accepted the October coup and Bolshevik rule as a way to build a new idealistic and just society.

He didn't survive for long in the Soviet Union and perished in 1924, disdained by the proletarian readership and the emerging socialist-realist authors.

I have loved mirrors from my very earliest years. As an infant I wept and trembled as I looked into their transparently truthful depths. My favourite game as a child was to walk up and down the room or the garden, holding a mirror in front of me, gazing into its abyss, walking over the edge at every step, and breathless with giddiness and terror. Even as a girl I began to put mirrors all over my room, large and small ones, true and slightly distorted ones, some precise and others a little dull. I got into the habit of spending whole hours, whole days, in the midst of intercrossing worlds which ran one into the other, trembled, vanished, and then reappeared again.

It became a singular passion of mine to give my body to these soundless distances, these echoless perspectives, these separate universes cutting across our own and existing, despite our consciousness, in the same place and at the same time with it. This protracted actuality, separated from us by the smooth surface of glass, drew me towards itself by a kind of intangible touch, dragged me forward, as to an abyss, a mystery.

I was drawn towards the apparition which always rose up before me when I came near a mirror and which strangely doubled my being. I strove to guess how this other woman was differentiated from myself, how it was possible that my right hand should be her left, and that all the fingers of this hand should change places, though certainly on one of them was—my wedding-ring.

My thoughts were confused when I attempted to probe this enigma, to solve it. In this world, where everybody could be touched, where voices were heard – I lived, actually; in that reflected world, which it was only possible to contemplate, was she, phantasmally. She was almost as myself and yet not at all myself; she repeated all my movements, but not one of these movements exactly coincided with those I made. She, that other, knew something I could not divine, she held a secret eternally hidden from my understanding.

But I noticed that each mirror had its own separate and special world. Put two mirrors in the very same place, one after the other, and there will arise two different universes. And in different mirrors there rose up before me different apparitions, all of them like me but never exactly like one another. In my small hand-mirror lived a naive little girl with clear eyes, reminding me of my early youth. In my circular boudoir mirror was hidden a woman who knew all the diverse sweetness of caresses, shameless, free, beautiful, daring. In the oblong mirrors of the wardrobe door there always appeared a stern figure, imperious, cold, inexorable. I knew still other doubles of myself—in my dressing-glass, in my folding, gold-framed triptych, in the hanging mirror in the oaken frame, in the little neck mirror, and in many other mirrors which I treasured. To all the beings hiding themselves in these mirrors I gave the possibility and pretext to develop.

According to the strange conditions of their world they must take the form of the person who stands before the glass but under this borrowed exterior they preserve their own personal characteristics.

There were some worlds of mirrors which I loved; others which I hated. In some of them I loved to walk up and down for whole hours, losing myself in their attractive expanse. Others I fled from. In my secret heart I did not love all my doubles. I knew that they were all hostile toward me, if only for the fact that they were forced to clothe themselves in my hated likeness.

But some of these mirror women I pitied. I forgave their hate and felt almost friendly to them.

There were some whom I despised, and I loved to laugh at their powerless fury; there were some whom I mocked by my own independence and tortured by my power over them. There were others, on the other hand, of whom I was afraid, who were too strong for me and who dared in their turn to mock at me, to command me. I hastened to get rid of the mirrors where these women lived, I would not look in them, I hid them, gave them away, even broke some in pieces. But every time I destroyed a mirror I wept for whole days after, conscious of the fact that I had broken to pieces a distinct universe. And reproachful faces stared at me from the broken fragments of the world I had destroyed.

The mirror with which my fate was to become linked I bought one autumn at a sale of some sort. It was a large pier-glass, swinging on screws. I was struck by the unusual clarity of its reflection. The phantasmal actuality in it was changed by the slightest inclination of the glass, but it was independent and vital to the edges. When I examined this pier-glass at the sale the woman who was reflected in it looked me in the eyes with a kind of haughty challenge. I did not wish to give in to her, to show that she had frightened me, so I bought the glass and ordered it to be placed in my boudoir. As soon as I was alone in the room, I immediately went up to the new mirror and fixed my eyes upon my rival. But she did the same to me, and standing opposite one another we began to transfix each other with our glance as if we had been snakes. In the pupils of her eyes was my reflection, in mine, hers. My heart sank and my head swam from her intent gaze. But at length by an effort of will I tore my eyes away from those other eyes, tipped the mirror with my foot so that it began to swing, rocking the image of my rival pitifully to and fro, and went out of the room.

From that hour our strife began. In the evening of the first day of our meeting I did not dare to go near the new pier-glass; I went to the theatre with my husband, laughed exaggeratedly, and was apparently light-hearted. On the morrow, in the dear light of a September day I went boldly into my boudoir alone and deliberately sat down directly in front of the mirror. At the same moment, she, the other woman, also came in at the door to meet me, crossed the room, and then she too sat down opposite me. Our eyes met. In hers I read hatred towards myself; in mine she read hatred towards her. Our second duel began, a duel of eyes—two unyielding glances, commanding, threatening, hypnotising. Each of us strove to conquer the other's will, to break down her resistance, to force her to submit to another's desire. It would have been a painful scene for an onlooker to witness; two women sitting opposite each other without moving, joined together by the magnetic attraction of each other's gaze, and almost losing consciousness under the psychical strain... Suddenly someone called me. The infatuation vanished. I got up and left the room.

After this our duels were renewed every day. I realised that this adventuress had purposely forced herself into my home to destroy me and take my place in this world. But I had not sufficient strength to deny myself this struggle. In this rivalry there was a kind of secret intoxication. The very possibility of defeat had hidden in it a sort of sweet seduction. Sometimes I forced myself for whole days to keep away from the pier-glass; I occupied myself with business, with amusements, but in the depths of my soul was always hidden the memory of the rival who in patience and self-reliance awaited my return. I would go back to her and she would step forth in front of me, more triumphantly than ever, piercing me with her victorious gaze and fixing me in my place before her. My heart would stop beating, and I, with a powerless fury, would feel myself under the authority of this gaze.

So the days and weeks went by; our struggle continued, but the preponderance showed itself more and more definitely to be on the side of my rival. And suddenly one day I realised that my will was in subjection to her will, that she was already stronger than I. I was overcome with terror. My first impulse was to flee from my home and go to another town, but I saw at once that this would be useless. I should, all the same, be overcome by the attractive force of this hostile will and be obliged to return to this room, to this mirror. Then there came a second thought—to shatter the mirror, reduce my enemy to nothingness; but to conquer her by brutal strength would mean that I acknowledged her superiority over myself; this would be humiliating. I preferred to remain and continue this struggle to the end, even though I were threatened with defeat.

Soon there could be no doubt that my rival would triumph. At every meeting there was concentrated in her gaze still greater and greater power over me. Little by little I lost the possibility of letting a day pass without once going to my mirror. She ordered me to spend several hours daily in front of her. She directed my will as a hypnotist directs the will of a sleepwalker. She arranged my life, as a mistress arranges the life of a slave. I began to fulfil her demands; I became an automaton to her wordless orders. I knew that deliberately, cautiously, she would lead me by an unavoidable path to destruction, and I already made no resistance. I divined her secret plan – to cast me into the mirror world and to come forth herself into our world – but I had no strength to hinder her. My husband and my relatives seeing me spend whole hours, whole days and nights in front of my mirror, thought me demented and wanted to cure me. But I dared not reveal the truth to them, I was forbidden to tell them all the dreadful truth, all the horror, towards which I was moving.

One of the December days before the holidays turned out to be the day of my destruction. I remember everything clearly, precisely, circumstantially. Nothing in my remembrance is confused. As usual, I went into my boudoir early, at the first beginnings of the winter dawn twilight. I placed a comfortable armchair without a back in front of the mirror, sat down and gave myself up to her. Without any delay she appeared in answer to my summons, she too placed an armchair for herself, she too sat down and began to gaze at me. A dark foreboding oppressed my soul, but I was powerless to turn my face away, and I was forced to take to myself the insolent gaze of my rival. The hours went by, the shadows began to fall. Neither of us lighted a lamp. The glass of the mirror glimmered faintly in the darkness. The reflections had become scarcely visible, but the self-reliant eyes gazed with their former strength. I felt neither terror nor ill will, as on other days, but simply an intolerable anguish and a bitter consciousness that I was in the power of another. Time swam away and on its tide I also swam into infinity, into a black expanse of powerlessness and lack of will.

Suddenly she, that other, the reflected woman, got up from her chair. I trembled all over at this insult. But something invincible, something forcing me from within compelled me also to stand up. The woman in the mirror took a step forward. I did the same. The woman in the mirror stretched forth her arms. I did so too. Looking straight at me with hypnotising and commanding eyes, she moved forward and I advanced to meet her. And it was strange—with all the horror of my position, with all my hate towards my rival, there fluttered somewhere in the depths of my soul a painful consolation, a secret joy—to enter at last into that mysterious world into which I had gazed from my childhood and which up till now had remained inaccessible to me. At moments I hardly knew which of us was drawing the other towards herself, she me or I her, whether she was eager to occupy my place or whether I had devised all this struggle in order to displace her.

But when, moving forward, my hands touched hers on the glass I turned quite pale with repugnance. And she took my hand by force and drew me still nearer to herself. My hands were plunged into the mirror as into burning-icy water. The cold of the glass penetrated into my body with a horrible pain, as if all the atoms of my being had changed their mutual relationship. In another moment my face bad touched the face of my rival, I saw her eyes right in front of my own, I was transfused into her with a monstrous kiss. Everything vanished from me in a torment of suffering unlike any other—and when I came to my senses after this swoon I still saw in front of me my own boudoir on which I gazed from out of the mirror. My rival stood before me and burst into laughter. And I – oh the cruelty of it! I who was dying with humiliation and torture was obliged to laugh too, to repeat all her grimaces in a triumphant joyful laugh. I had not yet succeeded in considering my position when my rival suddenly turned round, walked towards the door, vanished from my sight, and I at once fell into torpor, into non-existence.

Then my life as a reflection began. It was a strange, half-conscious but mysteriously sweet life.

There were many of us in this mirror, dark in soul, and slumbering of consciousness. We could not speak to one another, but we felt each other's proximity and loved one another. We could see nothing, we heard nothing clearly, and our existence was like the enfeeblement that comes from being unable to breathe. Only when a being from the world of men approached the mirror, we, suddenly taking up his form, could look forth into the world, could distinguish voices, and breathe a full breath. I think that the life of the dead is like that—a dim consciousness of one's ego, a confused memory of the past and an oppressive desire to be incarnated anew even if only for a moment, to see, to hear, to speak... And each of us cherished and concealed a secret dream – to free one's self, to find for one's self a new body, to go out into the world of constancy and steadfastness.

During the first days I felt myself absolutely unhappy in my new position. I still knew nothing, understood nothing. I took the form of my rival submissively and unthinkingly when she came near the mirror and began to jeer at me. And she did this fairly often. It afforded her great delight to flaunt her vitality before me, her reality. She would sit down and force me also to sit down, stand up and exult as she saw me stand, wave her arms about, dance, force me to repeat her movements, and burst out laughing and continue to laugh so that I should have to laugh too. She would shriek insulting words in my face and I could make no answer to them. She would threaten me with her fist and mock at my forced repetition of the gesture. She would turn her back on me and I, losing sight, losing features, would become conscious of the shame of the half-existence left to me... And then suddenly, with one blow she would whirl the mirror round on its axle and with the oscillation throw me completely into nonentity.

Little by little, however, the insults and humiliations awoke a consciousness in me. I realised that my rival was now living my life, wearing my dresses, being considered as my husband's wife, and occupying my place in the world. Then there grew up in my soul a feeling of hate and a thirst for vengeance, like two fiery flowers. I began bitterly to curse myself for having, by my weakness or my criminal curiosity, allowed her to conquer me. I arrived at the conviction that this adventuress would never have triumphed over me if I myself had not aided her in her wiles.

And so, as I became more familiar with some of the conditions of my new existence, I resolved to continue with her the same fight which she had carried on with me. If she, a shadow, could occupy the place of a real woman, was it possible that I, a human being, and only temporarily a shadow, should not be stronger than a phantom?

I began from a very long way off. At first I pretended that the mockery of my rival tormented me quite unbearably. I purposely afforded her all the satisfaction of victory. I provoked in her the secret instinct of the executioner throwing himself upon his helpless victim. She gave herself up to this bait. She was attracted by this game with me. She put forth the wings of her imagination and thought out new trials for me. She invited thousands of wiles to show me over and over again that I was only a reflection, that I had no life of my own. Sometimes she played on the piano in front of me, torturing me by the soundlessness of my world. Sometimes, seated before the mirror she would drink in tiny sips my favourite liqueurs, compelling me only to pretend that I also was drinking them. Sometimes, at length, she would bring into my boudoir people whom I hated, and before my face she would allow them to kiss her body, letting them think that they were kissing me. And afterwards when we were alone she would burst into a malicious and triumphant laugh. But this laugh did not wound me at all; there was sweetness in its keenness: my expectation of revenge!

Unnoticeably, in the hours of her insults to me, I would accustom my rival to look me in the eyes and I would gradually overpower her gaze. Soon at my will I could already force her to raise and lower her eyelids and make this and that movement of the face. I had already begun to triumph though I hid my feeling under a mask of suffering. Strength of soul grew up within me and I began to dare to lay commands upon my enemy: Today you shall do so-and-so, to-day you shall go to such-and-such a place, to-morrow you shall come to me at such a time. And she would fulfil them. I entangled her soul in the nets of my desires woven together with a strong thread in which I held her soul, and I secretly rejoiced when I noticed my success. When one day, in the hour of her laughter, she suddenly caught on my lips a victorious smile which I was unable to hide, it was already too late. She rushed out of the room in a fury, but as I fell into the sleep of my nonentity I knew that she would return, knew that she would submit to me. And a rapture of victory gushed out over my involuntary lack of strength, piercing with a rainbow shaft of light the gloom of my seeming death.

She did return! She came up to me in anger and terror, shrieked to me, threatened me. But I was commanding her to do it. And she was obliged to submit. Then began the game of a cat with a mouse. At any time I could have cast her back into the depths of the glass and come forth myself again into sounding and hard actuality. But I delayed to do this. It was sweet to me to indulge in non-existence sometimes. It was sweet to me to intoxicate myself with the possibility.

At last (this is strange, is it not?) there suddenly was aroused in me a pity for my rival, for my enemy, for my executioner. Everything in her was something of my own, and it was dreadful for me to drag her forth from the realities of life and turn her into a phantom. I hesitated and dared not do it, I put if off from day to day, I did not know myself what I wanted and what I dreaded.

And suddenly on a clear spring day men came into the boudoir with planks and axes. There was no life in me, I lay in the voluptuousness of torpor, but without seeing them I knew they were there. The men began to busy themselves near the mirror which was my universe. And one after another the souls who lived in it with me were awakened and took transparent flesh in the form of reflections. A dreadful uneasiness agitated my slumbering soul. With a presentiment of horror, a presentiment even of irretrievable ruin, I gathered together all the might of my will.

What efforts it cost me to struggle against the lassitude of half-existence! So living people sometimes struggle with a nightmare, tearing themselves from its suffocating bands towards actuality.

I concentrated all the force of my suggestion into a summons, directed towards her, towards my rival – 'Come hither!' I hypnotised her, magnetised her with all the tension of my half-slumbering will. There was little time. The mirror had already begun to swing. They were already preparing to nail it up in a wooden coffin, to take it away: whither I knew not. And with an almost mortal effort I called again and again, 'Come!' And I suddenly began to feel that I was coming to life. She, my enemy, opened the door, and came to meet me, pale, half-dead, in answer to my call, with faltering steps as men go to punishment. I fastened my eyes on hers, bound up my gaze with hers, and when I had done this I knew already that I had gained the victory.

I at once compelled her to send the men out of the room. She submitted without even making an attempt to oppose me. We were alone together once more. To delay was no longer possible.

And I could not bring myself to forgive her craftiness. In her place, in my time, I should have acted otherwise. Now I ordered her, without pity, to come to meet me. A moan of torture opened her lips, her eyes widened as before a phantom, but she came, trembling, falling – she came. I also went forward to meet her, lips curving triumphantly, eyes wide open with joy, swaying in an intoxicating rapture. Again our hands touched each other's, again our lips came near together, and we fell each into the other, burning with the indescribable pain of bodily exchange. In another moment I was already in front of the mirror, my breast filled itself with air, I cried out loudly and victoriously and fell just here, in front of the pier-glass, prone from exhaustion.

My husband and the servants ran towards me. I could only tell them to fulfil my previous orders and take the mirror away, out of the house, at once. That was wisely thought, wasn't it?

You see she, that other, might have profited by my weakness in the first minutes of my return to life, and by a desperate assault might have tried to wrest the victory from my hands. Sending the mirror out of the house, I could ensure my own quietude for a long time, as long as I liked, and my rival had earned such a punishment for her cunning. I defeated her with her own tools, with the blade which she herself had raised against me.

After having given this order I lost consciousness. They laid me on my bed. A doctor was called in. I was treated as suffering from a nervous fever. For a long while my relatives had thought me ill, and not normal. In the first outburst of exultation I told them all that had happened to me. My stories only increased their suspicions. They sent me to a home for the mentally afflicted, and I am there now. All my being, I agree, is profoundly shaken. But I do not want to stay here. I am eager to return to the joys of life, to all the countless pleasures which are accessible to a living human being. I have been deprived of them too long.

Besides – shall I say it? – there is one thing which I am bound to do as soon as possible. I ought to have no doubt that I am this I. But all the same, whenever I begin to think of her who is imprisoned in my mirror I begin to be seized by a strange hesitation. What if the real I – is there?

Then I myself who think this, I who write this, I – am a shadow, I – am a phantom, I – am a reflection. In me are only the poured forth remembrances, thoughts and feelings of that other, the real person. And, in reality, I am thrown into the depths of the mirror in nonentity, I am pining, exhausted, dying. I know, I almost know that this is not true. But in order to disperse the last clouds of doubt, I ought again once more, for the last time, to see that mirror. I must look into it once more to be convinced, that there – is the imposter, my enemy, she who played my part for some months. I shall see this and all the confusion of my soul will pass away, and I shall again be free from care – bright, happy. Where is this mirror? Where shall I find it? I must, I must once more look into its depths!

THE FLORA OF PENZA
Mikhail Osorgin (1878–1942)
Translated by Donald M. Fiene

A member of the Socialist-Revolutionary party, participant in the 1905 uprising in Moscow, **Mikhail Osorgin** (born Mikhail Ilyin) was arrested and forced into exile in Europe. In 1916 he, in a semi-legal way, returned to Russia and founded the independent Journalist's Union. After the February revolution he worked as a public investigator of the archives of the Tsarist state security, helped the relief efforts in the Volga region obliterated by famine, was arrested again, saved thanks to the influence of Fridtjof Nansen and, finally, deported from Soviet Russia in 1922 on board the so-called 'philosopher's ship', one of the hundreds of intellectuals expelled by a special decree of the Politburo.

Osorgin spent a year in Berlin and moved to Paris, where he gained his glory as a novelist and a short-story writer.

July is on the wane. The day is hot as fire. On the little porch a table is set. On the table are vodka, cucumbers and jellied fish. Father Vasily is in casual dress, the district chief of police is in full uniform. Father Vasily says to the police chief:

"You'll get all baked, friend, like an apple. At least take off your hat."

"No use, Father. That won't make my brain get bigger."

"Why so melancholy?"

"You just get sad, that's all. All my life I've toiled along, drudging for coppers and kopechs, at last worked up to be chief – but I don't understand a thing. His Excellency Lord Governor of the Province sent down a directive of the utmost urgency – but what it is he commands me to do I just can't figure out for the life of me."

The first glass burns, the second glass warms, the third goes down like water. The fish is disappearing and the cucumbers are crunching.

"Look, Father, you studied in the seminary. You understand everything. Read this paper and tell me what it means."

"From His Excellency, the Lord Governor of the Province of Penza. All district police officials upon receipt of this directive are commanded to submit without delay to the office of His Excellency all available information about the *Flora* of the district under their trust including detailed enumeration and description of existing types together with as many specimens as may feasibly be presented."

"Cease your moping, friend, this matter will soon be set straight."

The bottle is empty, the fish is all gone, but there are still plenty of cucumbers in the priest's garden. Having put on his spectacles, Father Vasily leafs through the *Academy Calendar of Saints' Days*:

"Well, here's the answer to the whole puzzle! August eighteenth is the day for both the Holy Fathers Flora and Lavra. And believe me, friend, in these matters it is better to do more rather than less! For I must say to you: Flora and Lavra are inseparable! Order our officers to gather them together."

From the district chief of police to his officers, a directive: At the earliest possible date, summon throughout the districts of Insar and Saransh all persons of the male sex who bear the given names Frol and Lavra, the which to gather first in the district seats and from there, after assigning to the task the permanent official delegate, to have them dispatched to the provincial capital for presentation, on August eighteenth of the year instant, to His Excellency Lord Governor of the Province.

An order most strict – absolute fulfilment without question. During the memorable reign [1825–1855] of Tsar Nicholas the First procrastination was impermissible and leniency unheard of: the ones on top provide the incentive, and the ones on the bottom grunt – everything functioning to perfection.

One big trouble – it is the busy season! The second crop of hay has not yet everywhere been mowed, the oats still have to be harvested, the rye is ready for the scythe, and the weather is dry for the work to begin. The muzhiks grumble, the wives howl: at such a time to drive away the workers, God knows where and for what!

The young woman Anisya has a little son; there's no way he can go by himself, since he's still nursing – so Anisya has to get ready herself to take him on the road.

"Why him? He's so little! Have mercy, dear sirs! To take a two-year-old as a result!"

"Well, see – his name is Lavra! Don't cry, foolish woman, they'll return him from the government all in one piece."

Granddaddy Frol's about a hundred years old, his eyes don't see, his ears don't hear, and he's lying on the stove. How can you get him there without a cart? And will he arrive still breathing?

"An order is an order, why all the conversation? There's good reason for it, or they wouldn't have asked it."

But the worst misfortune is when they take a young worker. Without the master, the hay will bur up and the rye will go to seed. It's two days to the district seat and not less than a week to the capital – and by the time everybody gets back it will be almost a month! Absolute ruin for the peasant households.

"And who provides the rations?"

Nothing is said in the order about food – so everybody has to take his own. Maybe, on account of it all has to do with a name day, the government will pay back the money...

Suddenly the bailiffs run into trouble: the muzhiks start hiding the Frols and Lavras and they don't give their right names. Now head counts have to be made and all the church records checked. It's not easy to manage all this for two districts in half a month, but the directive is strictly worded: without the least delay.

In the district seat of Saransh the permanent official delegate has brushed off his uniform and hung it out to air on a clothesline and is cleaning his tricorn hat. Verifying and checking in all the Frols and Lavras that keep arriving causes no end of trouble. Some have been put up at lodging houses, some were packed into the fire station, others are sleeping out under the starry sky. The biggest problem is with the women accompanying little children, and with the senile old men.

By the appointed time about two hundred Frols and Lavras had been gathered together from the two disctricts. They set off in the chill of the night – ten carts with the women, babies, old men and supplies, the remainder on foot, with the permanent delegate riding ahead in a carriage, his uniform and three-cornered hat carefully laid away in a woven basket. They arrived in the provincial capital of Penza on the very eve of August eighteenth.

During their journey and after their arrival, the peasants were diligently admonished:

"As soon as we get to the Governor's house, all the Frols stand on the right and the Lavras on the left. And if His Excellency is pleased to inquire, 'And who,' says he, 'are you?' then with all your might, each side answering for themselves, reply to him: 'Frols, Your Excellency!' – or, 'Lavras, Your Excellency!' – and you must then bow to the Lord Governor from the waist."

"And what is it that the Governor wants from us?"

"That we don't know. Perhaps he wants to congratulate you on your name day – or maybe it's something else entirely. Bow as low as you can. God grant that His Excellency will send you all back home and not keep you long. There is nothing particular to indicate that you are guilty of any wrong doing."

They slept that night wherever they could – and in the morning they made their appearance.

His Excellency the Governor of Penza Aleksandr Alekseevich Panchulidzev was an enlightened human being and an excellent administrator; not for nothing had he received from Nicholas the First, in recognition of his leadership, a golden snuff box.

His Excellency had married the maiden Zagoskina (daughter of the well-known writer), Varvara Nikolaevna. Varvara Nikolaevna had long been accustomed to the tedium of provincial life, but, because of her delicate constitution, suffered from nervousness and insomnia. She fell asleep only late at night – and then woke up at dawn, unable to sleep any longer. And in the summer time, of course, it was hot and stifling.

Among the other influential people in the city of Penza, we will mention the Venerable Marshall of Nobility, Pavel Timofeevich Morozov, the person primarily responsible for the forthcoming holiday celebration. It was Pavel Timofeevich who had conceived the idea of gathering accurate statistical data on the flora throughout the province, and it was at his urging that the Governor had sent out the decree to the district chiefs of police.

The city of Penza even at that time was not small: it measured four and a quarter versts from the Moscow Gate to the Tambov Gate, and of inhabitants there were twenty thousand souls, of which one half were engaged in peasant labour. Of industry, there were in the city three each of tanneries, soap factories and iron foundries; a snuff manufactory; and two giant mills producing coarse flour. And then as now, just below the city, the River Penza flowed into the River Sura. Logs for lumber were floated down the Penza; the Sura was fully navigable during high water.

One could not say that the province was very peaceful. At that time the peasants were often uneasy and in the city of Penza itself the factory workers would sometimes riot. His Excellency knew quite well how to deal with all this, but Varvara Nikolaevna, a fragile woman, at times became very agitated: insurrectionists will come and set the house on fire and murder everyone with axes and scythes – and the garrison won't be able to stop them! How much better it would be to live in St. Petersburg where it is safe and where one has friends…

In the evening of the seventeenth of August there appeared in the city an unknown group of people, by appearance peaceful, but who can say for certain? Upon arriving at the gate, they dispersed themselves nearby, built fires, lay down to sleep; two or three women, the rest males. They were reluctant to answer questions and would say only that tomorrow was their name day.

The Governor himself slept soundly, but Varvara Nikolaevna woke up quite early and heard a noise that sounded exactly like a crowd of people. The Governor's house stood on a hill; adjoining the house was a wide courtyard, upon which overlooked the windows of the sleeping chamber of Their Excellencies. Varvara Nikolaevna rubbed her eyes with her fist, got up, went to the window, pulled aside the curtain, looked out – and gasped: the courtyard was full of muzhiks, and some sort of person was dividing them up into two formations – one on the right and one on the left. It could only be a peasant uprising!

The Governor's Lady awakened the Governor. His Excellency also peered through the window and ascertained that in the courtyard were two detachments of muzhiks. Being, however, a man of great presence, the Provincial Governor hastened to calm his wife:

"Darling – insurrectionists always appear in an unruly crowd, with stakes, pitchforks and axes. But these, as you see yourself, are without any sort of weapons. Most likely they are elected petitioners, although no one has said a thing to me about any sort of delegates arriving – and right now is the busy season in the fields… But we'll get to the bottom of it."

And however the Governor's Lady pleaded with her husband not to go out to the courtyard but instead send secretly for the troops on garrison duty, however she explained to him that he was subjecting not only himself to mortal peril, but herself as well – should could not dissuade him. The Governor washed quickly; ordered his parade uniform to be brought – so as to overwhelm the unknown crowd with his magnificence; donned his hat with the plume; pulled on his gloves; and, having embraced his wife and bidden her to be calm, he advanced toward the door to the courtyard.

Without doubt – a man of exceptional courage! He was guided by the examples of brave men and instances of unforgettable heroism. He recalled how His Majesty Nicholas the First, having ridden out on the square that had been filled by a noisy mob, cried out loudly in an imperious voice: "On your knees!" – and the whole square fell to its knees; and then he yelled: "To your houses!" – and all the townspeople to the last man dispersed to their homes, got undressed and went to bed, quite satisfied with themselves.

The Governor of Penza comported himself in exactly the same manner. Stepping quickly from the rear porch directly into the courtyard and striding past a man in a tricorn standing importantly off to one side, he approached the peasants lined up in formation and asked them in a loud voice:

"What do you want? Who are you?"

The nearest detachment answered very nearly in unison:

"Frols, Your Excellency!"

And then they bowed from the waist.

Not having understood this answer very well, the Governor turned to the remaining men and again asked:

"Who are you?"

"Lavras, Your Excellency!"

And again everyone bowed from the waist!

Now the permanent delegate hurried up, with his hat cocked at an angle like a pie, stood directly in the Governor's gaze, and in a trembling voice pronounced his memorized speech:

"In accordance with Your Excellency's decree, I have the honor to present to Your Excellency the Frols and Lavras of the male sex of the Districts of Insar and Saransh of the Province of Penza!"

The Governor of the Province was at first quite taken aback, but he quickly recovered himself and, in a voice accustomed to command, he barked:

"Frols and Lavras – on your knees!" Then, waving his arm: "Frols and Lavras – go home!"

He did not have to repeat the command. The muzhiks broke ranks and ran, elated at having so quickly and easily been delivered from the Governor's anger.

All this is told in the Penza chronicle.

The climate in the Province of Penza is somewhat more severe than one might expect from its geographical location. At the end of August it already starts to get cold.

The table has now been placed indoors. On the table are pickled cucumbers, marinated mushrooms, and a bottle. The bottle is empty.

Father Vasily is wearing his cassock. The district police chief is in ordinary clothes; he mumbles mournfully:

"Look, Father – you studied in the seminary and you understand phi-philosophy – but here now you've gone and ruined a fellow!"

"Don't grieve, friend. Anthing is possible!" "T-true! Anyone can make a mistake. But if only I had sent just the Frols to His Excellency, then I would have been in the right. But the Lavras – why the d-devil did I send the Lavras? Eh? And you said – it's better to do more rather than less!"

"Here, have some more mushrooms."

"Mushrooms I'll take. But those Lavras, Father – with those Lavras you ruined a man!"

THE YOGI
Andrei Bely (1880–1934)
Translated by A. Kroytor

Mathematician, poet, philosopher, disciple of Rudolf Steiner, and the leading figure of Russian modernism, **Andrei Bely** (born Boris Bugaev) was labeled by Evgeny Zamyatin as the "Russian James Joyce".

Maybe only Andrei Platonov can be compared to Bely in the depth and power of his experiments with language. In his main novel *Petersburg* Bely focuses on the imperial capital, which attracted his ingenious predecessors like Pushkin, Gogol and Dostoevsky, seeing it as the symbol of power and doom, the place of destiny – and a place where the future is born, even though this particular future means the downfall of the city and the state it embodies.

Bely accepted the October coup. After his death in the USSR in 1934 Bely's brain was extracted by the emissaries of the Brain Institute, the eerie establishment founded to collect the brains of Soviet intellectuals for the future socialist *Pantheon*, which was never opened.

I

Ivan Ivanovich Korobkin has been employed in one of Moscow's museums as the head of its library department for forty years now, at least.

In summer, and during winters, autumns and springs his old, bent frame will unfailingly appear in the museum lobby. During summer – in a white, breezy jacket, wearing galoshes, carrying an overlarge umbrella; winters – in a coon-skin fur reddened with age; in a frayed overcoat in the damp autumn; and during spring – in a trench coat.

Smacking his lips and smoothing out his tufted beard, he groans his way slowly up the stairs, eventually overcoming all the 24 steps leading up to the reading hall, already packed full. He nods to the visitors racing past – he does not know them, but they have already known him a long time.

After walking into the library, he looks through memos and puts them aside – marking each off with a pencil.

Sometimes he looks a colleague over, and abruptly tears him away from his work with some worthy phrase, recalling a dictum of Lomonosov's:

Sciences sustain the young

He then rubs his palms together and leans his head back while a broad, pleased smile spreads over his face; in an instant a face severe and dry, recalling portraits of the poet and censor Maikov, becomes transparent, illuminated, simply – a child's face.

"Iconography, young man, is science!" rings out amidst the dead quiet of the rooms adjacent to the reading hall, but when that young man, torn from his work looks up, he sees: a face severe and dry, recalling portraits of the poet and censor Maikov.

They say that once, Ivan Ivanovich Korobkin, strolling through the museum's tree-lined court proclaimed:

"Paradise, gentlemen, is, in essence, a garden...
We're in a garden.
That is to say, we're in paradise..."

They say that the features of his faded visage transformed themselves suddenly; such indisputability shone through them; the museum director's assistant, walking alongside for an instant seemed to see: Ivan Ivanovich transported, enraptured to heaven's highest firmament suffers an inexpressible sweetness – as he related to Agrafina Kondrativna that evening.

"Wouldn't you know, Agrafina Kondrativna, God knows, who he is – or even – what he might be... isn't he a Mason, now; and, see, the late Ma-*yevski* gave him the job; and about Ma-*yevski* they'd say, back in the day, that he was a Mason... And he'd wear some special type of ring on his index finger."

Ivan Ivanovich Korobkin had no acquaintances; he never became close with anyone; visitors would try to come by for a visit, and – stop coming by; he was once met walking out of his home in Galosh Lane[*] with a large bronze tub, carefully covered over – and what, do you suppose, was in *that* tub? You'll never guess: *cockroaches*.

Yes!

Ivan Ivanovich Korobkin filled the tub with sugar and caught himself cockroaches; Ivan Ivanovich Korobkin had gotten cockroaches; he couldn't exterminate them (he was soft-hearted), so he caught them in the tub, and then let them out of the tub, after taking it out into the street.

Not once one or another co-worker noticed upon himself the old man's trying gaze, originating from behind an enormous pair of blue spectacles; and noticed a desire: to relate a deeply interesting yet enigmatic event; but such elderly eccentricities were ignored. It so happened many times: Ivan Ivanovich directs his attention to someone, singling them out for no reason; and suddenly – withdraws: again – for no reason.

It was also noticed that these moments of attention to whomever it may be coincided, usually, with one or another everyday misfortune of that whoever it may be – a misfortune that Ivan Ivanovich could not possibly have known about just then; quite the opposite: the circumstances of whoever it may be luckily flowed across Ivan Ivanovich's path; so, once, while N. N. Pustovalov and N. T. Kosich were having an argument, he mixed himself up right in the middle of their argument, and impolitely cutting off Pustovalov, took out his waistcoat watch, and looking at the second hand remarked:

"I'd give you, Nikolai Nikolaiovich, six minutes to explain your position... Well then, I'm listening: one minute...

"Two.

"Three."

After such an intrusion into the argument, everything was turned upside down; and – the argument dissipated; with a face recalling

---

[*] Калошный переулок is the street's name, it is pronounced approximately kaloshniy pereylok and калоши are galoshes.

the poet and censor Maikov, the respected Ivan Ivanonich laid out a weighty quote:

"Science lies in the sphere of fact: hypotheticals damage science... an argument, you see, is a game of hypotheticals, an inflation of hyperbole.

"Read *The Heuristics*, now *that* is a study on the art of matching wits."

Amazingly, one of the parties to the argument received an inheritance in forty-six days and resigned.

Bureaucrats avoided Ivan Ivanovich; essentially, they were unfamiliar with the events of his long life: he was already past seventy; he had served in the museum some forty years; he had begun work at a mature age, appearing in our parts from Tavrid;* he was given the position by the late Ma-*yevski*, a powerful influence from that long-gone epoch of czar Nicholas.

It was known only that Ivan Ivanovich himself was an epoch; and also: he resides in Galosh Lane, above the courtyard of a many-storied gray building, from which he unfailingly appears, going to work: autumns – in a coat, in summer – in a breezy canvas jacket, with an overlarge umbrella, winters – in a faded coon-skin fur.

In that old coon-skin fur he was seen running through a winter blizzard along Zhamenka Street, through a thick of snowflakes brocading the foot of the fence at the enormous Alexander institute.

II

Korobkin appears at 25 minutes to 5 on Galosh Lane, and at 5 exactly he sits in a worn, comfortable leather chair, wearing comfortable fur-lined slippers; after changing his frock-coat – for an exact (flimsier) same one – he sits at a table strewn with books and manuscripts; books of a particular kind – enormous parchment-bound folios: *Principia Rerum Naturainm, Sive Novorum Tentanium Phenomena Mundi Elementaris*. Or – rows of the *Zion Herald*'s volumes.

Charming tomes were thrown about everywhere, like: *The Letters of S. G.*, which know-how indicated authorship, but Ivan Ivanovich's hand appended *amalei* to the *G*, so *Gamalei* came out.

---

* The old name for Crimea.

On the wall, above the writing-desk, Ivan Ivanovich regularly hung out lists bearing the cursive motto of the day; every day had its own motto for Ivan Ivanovich; mornings, before setting off to work, Ivan Ivanovich selects the motto of the day; and lives by it that whole day; all else was waved aside with: "Sufficient onto the day are its own troubles."

The day's trouble was often provided by: Foma Kempeiski's dicta: "Read those books that would break your heart sooner than amuse it" ... Or Latin mottoes. And so on, and so on.

Upon waking, before choosing a motto, Ivan Ivanovich spends some 10 minutes exercising *concentration of thought*; for this he takes a very plain, very simple thought, for example – *of a pin*; fixing that *pin* before his mental gaze, he considers everything concerning a pin, wholly avoiding any desultory associations and ideas; in Ivan Ivanovich's language this exercise was called *The first rule: that of mental control*; and everything tied with the selected motto in Ivan Ivanovich's language was called *The second rule: that of initiation to action*; Ivan Ivanovich had still a third, fourth, fifth rule, but that is not worth dwelling on. They say: Ivan Ivanovich had a journal, received by inheritance, and it accompanied him throughout his life as he observed all his *rules* over the span of thirty and then some years, and observed them so subtly that his colleagues never suspected the root cause of his actions, actions that his irreproachable service in the museum but masked, concealing the wisest of rituals, practiced in the realm of pure morality: Ivan Ivanovich was, in essence, a *yogi*, not an employee.

Even today such eccentricities live among us. Upright citizens, simply – you see them daily, find yourself exchanging *hellos* with them, and unable to discern the nature of their actions you see – mere *peculiarities*.

Ivan Ivanovich's peculiarity of three and then some years' time: he did not pronounce the first-person pronoun "I", manoeuvring so delicately that none could suspect him, even were they, during those three and some years, to have to asked Ivan Ivanovich:

"Say, did you read today's paper?" – then Ivan Ivanovich would answer: "why, certainly," instead of answering: "*I* certainly read it." This rule of avoiding the personal pronoun "I" he called: *The rule of fortifying self-consciousness*. After three and some years Ivan

Ivanovich built up enormous power over the personal pronoun "I." And then, when the museum director's assistant once doubted the soundness of setting out the exhibits according to Ivan Ivanovich's plans, Ivan Ivanovich remarked to him:

"*I* know my work."

And he said it just so, so that the director's assistant saw the very walls stepping aside, and he and his plans flew right past, straight into Hades.

In the evening he proclaimed:

"Wouldn't you know, Agrafina Kondrativna, everything happens in this world... They say, there are Masons; and about Ma-*yevski* they'd say, that he was a Mason; he'd wear some special type of ring there. Maybe, right among our acquaintances – aha! – they stroll about, so calmly; but just that we don't know who they are."

The rules of his exercises brough Ivan Ivanovich into particular states of consciousness, which he divided into three areas: 1) *the concentration of thought*, 2) *meditation*, and 3) *contemplation*, adopting the terms from an order of monks in St. Victor's monastery in the middle ages.

Contemplation brought him to a state of *clarity of thought* bordering on clairvoyance; *meditation* pulled his entire soul into the circle of thought before him. And *concentration*?

Well, better we describe it.

III

Pressing his hands to his knees while stretched out in the leather chair Ivan Ivanovich grabs hold of a string of thought understandable to him alone that pierces his entire being; this string of thought evokes a sharpened state of awareness accompanied by the sensations, the recent protest of a dry, seventy-year-old body.

Fires spread around his hands, furious vibrations, furious vibrations felt by his thoughts; his thoughts poured into his hands, so that his hands thought; and – his head blossoms, the way a bud would into a luxurious, many-petaled rose, and his mind's shutters open out into sensation, like hands around his head, plucking up the thoughts of those around Ivan Ivanovich: and so it might seem that Ivan Ivanovich can swallow thoughts whole.

Ivan Ivanovich spreads out over himself *hands made of hands*; *hands of hands* that start to circle, to carry him away.

And the familiar contours of the books, shelves, wardrobe, table, room become somehow transparent, and become shot through with the approach of new, roiling life, of the *ever-seething world*; within and without his own self everything boils over, spins, trails smoke in weightless strands; all manner of spark-clusters, brocades, diaphanous and glowing films wheel and spread without limit; Ivan Ivanovich sees himself as a roiling knot of thought-strings.

Many-winged and transforming, he is pulled off himself so that he dives into the ever-seething sea of beings, presented as: spark-clusters, brocades, the diaphanous and glowing films, which all collapse through into the spark-clusters, brocades, the diaphanous and glowing films that were Ivan Ivanovich himself.

And so he could, pouring out of himself, pour into the roiling life of nearby beings; pouring out of one being into another he could clearly flow through the soul of this or that tenant in the building on Galosh Lane; and he could even flow through the soul of – well, for example: Milyukov, Vinaver, Karl Liebkhent, and maybe even: Bismark, Wikensfeld, Napoleon and Hannibal; and among these roiling, wheeling and warmly glowing forms there glimmer, of course, personages from long-gone epochs.

He could observe much in that world; but he could not bring out his illuminations, contain them in any clear words, and if he tried to contain them in a clear word, that word would shatter and open into a fan of words, and pass through a metamorphosis of lexical meanings and through the thousand thoughts and sounds secreted away within him, and emerge a clumsy muddle.

He had lived in this clumsy muddle for many years.

So, what then? A habit of keeping silent, or a habit of communicating with the help of epigrams – such were but the ordinary traces of an extraordinary life.

Ivan Ivanovich Korobkin, boiling over out of one form and into another is flung out beyond forms, and the wheeling creation of his rhythms (the wheelings of his soul) dissolve into the boundless in outwardly flowing orbits (like ripples on a pond's surface) and melt in the formless; here the stuff of his states of consciousness resembles *universal emptiness*, and he – emptiness, mute, speechless, motionless

– addresses his own exploded center of emptiness with an intimate "*you*," and this you stands acenter his soul; this *you* bears the stamp of the Unknown, and yet seems to be Known since time immemorial; and this *you*, the one who we have forgotten declares:

"The days pass by!

"Behold! I come!"

And upon returning to himself, finding himself seated (and wearing comfortable slippers), he feels a warm gladness spill out in the middle of his chest.

This is *concentration*!

Ivan Ivanovich Korobkin knew this deeply: the times – they have piled up, crowded up; *possibilities* take shape; new days come; a new era arises; with a majestic crash majestic culture bends and groans; under the skies of the old, the new ascends.

Ivan Ivanovich Korobkin loved the youth with all his heart; he knew – there will be *children* among children; clumsy rumors were spread that Ivan Ivanovich was something like a, but not quite a, confirmed mystic, but, so to say... a Gnostic – an Apocalyptic; not really a Socialist, nor really a Heliist.

IV

Among his museum co-workers he behaved like an old-fashioned gentleman, avoiding politics; he was even apprehensive of political life; more than anyone he avoided the *cadets*[*], members of the National Freedom Party who, after the rare conversation with Ivan Ivanovich Korobkin, decidedly labelled him a backward reactionary. So, once, in the museum building, a philosopher-cadet was espousing his view of the ideal government, one whose humane principles were so wide-reaching that even imprisoned convicts would be offered new and improved methods of entertaining themselves and one another.

Here Ivan Ivanovich interrupted his interlocutor:

"There will, after all, be prisons?"

To which the other responded:

"And how else?"

---

[*] Members of the Constitutional Democrat party.

"I presumed that humanity would become enlightened by a lucid understanding of the principles of fairness and humane treatment,"

"No – there'll be prisons... but those sitting locked-up in them will listen to symphonies. Right from behind the wall they'll be played Bach's fugues and Beethoven's sonatas."

But, Ivan Ivanvich, blowing his nose, and with a sour, dry face recalling the poet and censor Maikov, cut off the philosophizing:

"I prefer my prisons with bugs, and – without the sound of Beethoven."

And so he became listed with the reactionaries.

Besides that, Ivan Ivanovich Korobkin denied the need for war in the year of the war; patriotic fervor did not buoy his spirits, and he supposed, contrary to the obvious, that it wasn't worth making so much noise over a small, half-savage race; this gave everyone cause to think that he was secretly germanophiling. He kept silent about the current regime and made no remarks concerning Rasputin; the February Revolution didn't please him.

But, as Russia boiled and melted, as fragments broke off of her – Poland, Finland, Latvia, Belorussia, the Caucuses, and the Ukraine, and as the museum screamed itself hoarse, as the residents of Galosh Lane lost their appetites and sleep from anxiety, as the yellowish-brown pillars of dust swept through Moscow, eating out everyone's eyes, as a tornado of papers whirled along the avenues, boulevards and squares encrusted with invalids who appeared from God knows where, and as the trams twisted more and more out of shape, and fringes stuck out from between the bodies squeezing and shoving one another within – Ivan Ivanovich, to everyone's surprise, began to experience an unexplainable yet pleasant emotion, his eyes grew gentler, more radiant, and his elderly mouth bent more often into a smile.

What was it that was forming in Ivan Ivanovich's mind? It was difficult to say; Russia's annihilation pleased him, certainly.

Evenings, he would gaze out at the sunset from his window, and one summer (in June of 1917), he even once during a day off appeared at Agrafina Kondrativna's summer estate, the very same Agrafina Kondrativna who, or, rather: whose... but that is not the point, the point is that – strolling through the field with the museum director's assistant, Ivan Ivanovich surveyed the surroundings and then crisply remarked:

"Aha!

"Yes, yes, yes.

"How clear and bright the air!"

From then on his colleagues noticed: among the epigrams uttered by Ivan Ivanovich, new epigrams appeared.

After walking into the library, he looks through memos; and he then suddenly flashes an uncanny smile and rubs his palms together; looking at him, you would think that his spirit drank in a strange, aromatic drink, one that no one had yet drunk to the bottom – or so it seemed. After a long march of years, Ivan Ivanovich Korobkin made use of one of his days off to go spend time out in the open air.

Sometimes, sorting through his memos, he would grab his chest like one suffering from heart disorder; but this was no disorder; it was his mind intently diving into his fluttering heart; he rolled down, like a pearl, into the cup of his heart, sending ripples along the surface of his blood; you would simply say:

"My heart jumped!"

And so, with a heart that just took an untimely jump (right in the museum!), Ivan Ivanovich Korobkin addressed his colleagues not with the usual sentence, not with something like:

"Iconography, gentlemen, is a science!"

No, rather he addressed them with the strange-sounding phrase:

"Yes, yes, yes – how clear and bright the air."

Undoubtedly he spoke not of the museum air, thick with dust; nor did he mean the air over the fields; the subject of his awkward declaration was the air found in that realm of thought-feelings where he traveled evenings; that realm – of thought-feelings – was light *and* air; the composition of that air disturbed Ivan Ivanovich; he distinctly saw how before the revolution Russia was fogged up, dulled; how clouds of choking smoke escaped into the dancing light; only since the revolution did he notice a clarity of atmosphere (all the plumes of choking smoke sank, settling on the outside layer of our life, effecting an inner collapse – in the same manner that dust, packed down by rain, collects on the surfaces of objects in clumps, but the air, cleansed, shines more radiantly).

His words "How clear and bright the air" referred to that particular state of atmosphere.

When the date reached the 20's of July 1917, Ivan Ivanovich once appeared in the museum lobby with an overlarge umbrella, in a canvas jacket, but wearing galoshes, and while handing the umbrella to the doorman remarked:

"yes, yes…

"The days pass by, Feramont Semyonivich, they pass by…

"They pass by us…

"The times are piling up…"

Those were the hard days of July;[*] Russia shook.

Before the October Revolution, when Ivan Ivanovich appeared in the museum already wearing the frayed autumnal overcoat (no the trench-coat), he fixed his gaze on a young man who recently took a post in the museum, a member of one of the newly-formed parties; lifting up his glasses, Ivan Ivanovich stood before him from time to time; Ivan Ivanovich shook his gray head with a feeling of deepest sympathy; and just as if he were caught in the middle of a sigh that began long ago and that seemed to go on without end, Ivan Ivanovich thought aloud:

"And so, young man, the never-setting and limitless makes its way forward; and – oh, yes!" he interrupted himself.

And, wiping off his glasses and returning to his papers, his face changed; his face recalled in rare instants the prophet Jeremiah's face, as depicted by Michelangelo.

A few days later, that young man was killed on a sidewalk in a crossfire of machine-guns.

V

We have forgotten to mention one very important detail in Ivan Ivanovich's life: 15 minutes to 10 every night, he brings the day's affairs to a close, and views all of the day's events in reverse: from the last moment to the moment of waking; after this, his thoughts and

---

[*] The July demonstration in St. Petersburg was broken up by the forces of the temporary government.

attention gather a particular solidity and strength; 5 minutes to 11 he lays down to sleep.

He stretches out on his back, his head covered, and lies motionless. The mental screw inside his head unravels spiralwise, and its point wedges against the inside of a seventy-year old skull, and that skull cracks, and the contents of Ivan Ivanovich Korobkin's head stretch out immeasurably into sensation; at first, it seems to him that a tiara lay atop his head; the tiara then grows into his head and stretches out into an impossibly tall tower – just then, Ivan Ivanovich Korobkin's heels feel pulled by the currents of his elongating and melting legs. First, Ivan Ivanovich felt his heels at the level of, say, his knees (his legs extended beyond his heels), then in his stomach, and finally Ivan Ivanovich feels his body circumscribed into some enormous body, newly pulsing from heart to throat – in a word, he feels himself within himself a pygmy in a giant's body; so might a tired and drowsy traveler who wandered into a cavernous, empty and abandoned tower feel; Ivan Ivanovich distinctly sees that the tower's walls are stitched of the sky's daylight fabric; perceives that fabric to be none other than the skin blanketing us, or, better yet, the covering of some enormous body, from whose inside bones and skin crystallize outward; better yet – he feels himself a crystal in a glass in relation to the solution from which it precipitated.

In those minutes of transition to sleep, Ivan Ivanovich Korobkin knows that our body is a body circumscribed, folded inside of another, enormous body; and that larger body is a sky, and each of us travels under his own sky (if a chick could run inside its egg, it would roll the egg forward, stepping along the inside of the eggshell); such is the sky we walk under – an eggshell around our head. But Ivan Ivanovich Korobkin finds himself both inside and outside his own skin (inside the enormous body's skin, and outside of his regular skin).

Here with an effort of will he squeezes into himself and feels himself as a concentrated, bright, forever straining point; a shudder passes through him; the body laying between the sheets breaks into a flowing stream, and Ivan Ivanovich Korobkin is free to move within the enormous tower (from the heart to the throat, toward the shadowed portal ahead); he feels himself running inside the tower, along the staircase, step by step (organ by organ), and he runs out onto the terrace of a magnificent tower (outside his physical body and outside the elemental body).

He stands out there before a heavenly expanse glittering with stars, but these particular stars glide and fly just like birds; Ivan Ivanovich, freed from his body, reaches the terrace where he contemplates them, and they become many-feathered beings; and they pour forth fountainous flames like feathers, out of their centers; and one being – one star-bird (Ivan Ivanovich's star) descends to him and embraces him in a crackling fire of rays, or wings, and carries him away; it feels as if boiling water scalds Ivan Ivanovich's very essence; the sensation of hands becomes the sensation of the star's wings, embracing him in conflagration; Ivan Ivanovich Korobkin flew through *all* into spark-clusters, brocades, diaphanous and glowing films – into nothing, where at the core rises up our Old, Forgotten Teacher, greeting us since time immemorial – and he says:

"Behold, I come!"*

And so Ivan Ivanovich Korobkin came to clearly recognize within himself that ancient Celestial who secretly moved and filled him, exalted him with *that light* and *air*, with the stuff of his life.

Ivan Ivanovich Korobkin ordinarily drifted into unconsciousness during these sacred and hidden conversations with the Secret Teacher of life, and the most important parts of the conversation fogged over.

But, the dream conversations with the Teacher became lately edged with unusual clarity; with unusual clarity Ivan Ivanovich understood that his cloud drifts among earthly, murky ones, so that the hour, the fated moment, the foretold day may come when his cloud may rise up like a prophet above the gathered crowd; and hurl words into the crowd, not his own, but the Teacher's, spoken through him like through a horn:

"Behold, I come!

"Hurry!

"It's time…

"We'll build a grand temple…

"The times are piling up…

"Whirlwinds gather…

"Our homes – destroyed…

---

* Revelation 22:12.

"The hard soil melts,
"And the floodwaters will surround you all.
"Behold, I come!"

* * *

During one July day in 1918, when meetings gathered on the outskirts of the city, and when Mirbach's murder was being planned, everyone noticed that Ivan Ivanovich Korobkin, entering the museum, did not even touch the day's work, his face and posture recalling the prophet Jeremiah, as depicted by Michelangelo.

On finishing work at 20 to 5, Ivan Ivanovich found himself in a tram bound for the city's outskirts; the time, he felt, was ripe.

VI

A meeting was taking place under the open sky.

There was talk of freedom; of the chance to create life anew; there was talk of love and equality; of the brotherhood of man.

And then, after keeping silent all those years and awaiting in his solitary cell that shining day when the secrets of life would be distilled, and when maybe Spirit enters the heart – he stood up above the crowd.

From beneath gray and heavy brows his gaze penetrated the crowd with an inexpressible love; above the laughter, yells and gibes his inspired head turned, recalling the prophet Jeremiah's, as depicted by Michelangelo; words sounded: a swansong in crystalline time; for an instant it seemed that something drew irrevocably closer, and life itself was melted upon those words, running like rivulets down into souls, the life that flew – a gold fabric of images (a shimmer of the Spirit) – back to primeval source.

For a moment, everyone felt a relieving sigh rise from the depths of his being; an unending sigh; and he, he who had ripened for so many long years towered above the crowd.

If just then anyone's eyes could have opened up to gaze suddenly through the veil of illusions that shrouds us all, he would have seen the timeless Celestial, the Teacher taking wing like a bird from the distant spirit-world and hurling himself into the divide of Nothing; and whoever could just then have *seen*, would have *seen* the soul of

Ivan Ivanovich's words bursting into that divide of Nothing up from the fogged-over, earthly realm (bursting out from the crown of his head); and – *the unity of man and spirit*, all while an earthly seventy year old body stood above the crowd and uttered words, not its own, but the Teacher's, who spoke through him, like through a horn:

"Hurry!

"It's time...

"We'll build a grand temple...

"The times are piling up...

"The whirlwinds gather...

"Our homes are destroyed...

"The hard soil melts,

"And the floodwaters will surround you all.

"Behold, He comes!"

VII

From the rostrum Ivan Ivanovich Korobkin clearly saw bloody passions rearing their heads like grunting leopards in the throng below; he saw: sallow faces, flushed brows, hateful eyes, lips twisted into snarls.

And he clearly understood that it isn't time for a transformation, not yet; the future rose up from the depths of a discharged atmosphere, and then stepped aside and took no guests along.

There was an old, worn-out man with blank, dim eyes fixed straight ahead, his eyes ringed with the feathery cinders of lightning burning itself away; so does a still smoldering coal grow gray with cold ash on its surface; eyes like scattered ash swept about the droning crowd, and the enfeebled body, crawling off the rostrum, fell, as if into deep night, seen off by gibes.

An enfeebled body trudged home, mashing its mouth; it walked along the sleeping city's alleys and streets with a rumpled brimmed hat pulled down on its forehead, and from under the gray, rumpled hat, eye-whites helplessly stared into a puddle and turned in their orbits; they were set in a thing cast of flesh – a face recalling the censor and poet A. Maikov's – in his grave.

But then: the true Ivan Ivanovich Korobkin climbs up to the enormous tower's terrace and stands, leaning against the railing, contemplating the world of those stars, changing places in that sky; *his star speeds toward him*, to… take him away to the Teacher awaiting him.

* * *

In the beginning of July 1918, a funeral procession moved toward the Novodevichy Monastery.[*] Ivan Ivanovich was being buried. His co-workers carried the coffin, and the museum director's assistant thoughtfully remarked to the charming lady he accompanied:

"Wouldn't you know, Agrafina Kondrativna, everything happens in this world… They say, there are Masons; and about Ma-*yevski* they'd say, that he was a Mason…and I know for sure that our dear departed here was a mason."

---

[*] Andrei Bely rests there as well.

AVDOTYA-DEATH

Boris Zaytsev (1881–1972)

Translated by Temira Pachmuss

> Bunin's longtime friend and ally, a protégé of Chekhov and Andreev, **Boris Zaytsev** was throughout his life a little overshadowed by his brilliant contemporaries. But probably it was also the side effect of his talent: Zaytsev avoided controversial topics, loud public discussions, and tried to penetrate spiritual matters with subtlety and seriousness. Perhaps the very nature of his literary gifts provided him with a safe passage between the Scylla and Charybdis that swallowed or crushed so many others. Zaytsev emigrated to Europe in 1922, having received permission to go abroad for medical treatment, kept his ethical clarity during the Second World War, and died in the seventies, the last surviving figure of the Russian Silver Age.

I

The snowfall made it seem brighter indoors. Instead of going over bumpy, frozen ground, the wide sledges slipped along through the now whitening chill. The scent of snow pierced the air so sharply that it brought tears to the eye, and the leadlike distances seemed painfully mournful. Two days after the snowfall an old woman appeared in the small village of Kochki at the house of Commissar Lev Golovin. Lev, a huge man, flabby, with a hernia, a big nose, and a reddish beard, was no longer surprised by anything whatsoever. He was puttering around by the low, wide sledge, arranging its shaft in a different way, when a tall skinny peasant woman called to him.

"That's me all right," Lev answered, with effort, tugging with all his might on the loops of the rope. "And who might you be?"

"What's this, dearie, don't ya recognize me? Matyushkin's widow, he was one of yours, from Kochki. And seein' as I'm now without any support, and besides havin' a blind grandma in my care—Lord bust her—and dumb little Mishka too, we got nothing to shove in our mouths; you struggle like a little fish just to survive ..."

This woman hardly resembled a little fish; she spoke with a husky, almost masculine voice, but sobbed with sincerity ...

"That's why I moved here and dropped by ..."

"So that's how it is ..." Lev scratched himself indifferently. "Matyushkin's widow? Did he really live in our village? I don't think he lived in our village. He was always bummin' around in town."

"What do ya mean bummin' around? You've forgotten everything, dearie; ya don't even recognize me, Auntie Avdotya ..."

"What do you want?"

A knapsack hung from Avdotya's shoulders. She was extremely thin. Leaning on a long stick, she struck the ground with it and moved a few steps closer.

"What d'ya mean? No doubt ya all took the master's land, but I'm a part o' this place too, strugglin' like a little fish, just to survive, with a blind grandma and dumb little Mishka ..."

The situation was clear, despite the profusion of unnecessary words. She wanted him to parcel out a plot of land for her. Lev realized this right away, but at first gave the impression that he didn't understand. However, when it became impossible to misunderstand any longer, he commenced explaining half-heartedly that, although it was true that they had confiscated the land from the master, the amount available had by now become even smaller. Lev Golovin was deeply convinced of the truth of his words. But still, it wasn't easy to impress this on Avdotya. For his every word she had ten: her pale lips would tremble, her masculine voice would wheeze its own variation; she'd whack her stick and press against Lev more closely.

"Well then, we'll need a 'comminity' meeting ... whatever the 'comminity' decides, so be it."

Lev understood this "then" to mean: "If you're going to be such a bastard that I can't get rid of you, then let the community convince you."

And no matter how melancholy, indifferent, and slowed by his aching hernia Commissar Lev Golovin was, toward evening he still had to call a meeting and present the situation. No one was overjoyed at the prospect. But Matyushkin actually had once lived in Kochki. They even discovered some relatives of his. Like a stray dog, Avdotya sat on the steps and gnawed a piece of crust.

"There I am, adjusting the shaft," the Commissar related slowly and sadly, "and there she is … Where'd she come from? Popped right outta the ground! Or maybe she got blown to our town by the wind, down the road right along with the first fall of snow?"

"You just try and blow her," a crooked little fellow, Kuz'ka, said. "She looks to be a pretty good walker. I saw her. I spoke with her, too. Gosh … she sure breathes fire. She's a regular racehorse."

"Since her late husband was actually from our Kochki, we cannot avoid giving her a small plot of land. We must take action now, at this meeting," briskly stated a puffy man with a scarf around his neck, the former steward, now a well-to-do peasant, Fyodor Matveevich. And with that the affair was decided.

It was resolved to give her just enough land for a single person. She would be settled in the former dairy of the manor. When Avdotya found out, she crossed herself and bowed deeply to the peasants. Taking her stick, she walked, taking gigantic steps along the newly snow-covered road to the station—to get Mishka and the grandma.

"See how she gallops," said Kuz'ka. "You couldn't catch her on a gelding." Avdotya quickly disappeared into the haze.

II

"The former dairy of the manor" designated a rather small dirt-floored hut where once the separator had hummed. Its handle was then turned by Masha Golovin. She also filled Nikolay Stepanovich's containers and sent them to the station. From these past endeavors, as from the romance between Masha and Permyakov, little remained except the hut itself. The peasants of the tiny village of Kochki had long ago collected the master's cows, and with great distress they, too, had been obliged to surrender them to the village soviet. The separator was sold somewhere. Nikolay Stepanovich, so enamored of propriety and order, up and died, still wearing his spectacles and the old double-breasted jacket of his uniform. And out of the large main house, from the second floor of which could be seen the pond, a corner of the linden grove, and the hillock blocking the horizon before one's eyes, Varvara Andreevna (not by her own choosing) moved into what had formerly been the guest wing. Yet it was precisely she who had changed the least. Although she controlled only a strip of land (being considered a member of the Kochki community), she still ceremoniously and calmly received Commissar Lev Golovin in the kitchen just as before, addressed him in the familiar, and with her beaver hat, fur coat, and cane slowly and commandingly went about her former properties, dropping in to the granary, half of which—as a reward for military services—Red Army soldier Fil'ka had carried off in the spring. She continued feeding the chickens and the hungry old men who had taken over a part of the main house, selling some of her old possessions to the neighboring miller, and ruling, as before, with unquestioned authority. During this time Liza had lost her husband. She returned to the refuge of her birthplace, and in the tiny room of her former youth taught the children of Kochki. Every thing remained as of old.

When one fine day Avdotya with her blind grandma, Mishka, two cocks, a trunk, and various pitiful bags and boxes burst onto the estate, Varvara Andreevna was not surprised. She was generally reserved. During these last years her old, once very beautiful eyes had become used to accepting everything as a necessity.

"We've received yet another bawder," she said to Liza, surrendering the key to the hut to the Commissar. "She'll be living in the dairy." Varvara Andreevna pronounced "border" with a French accent, as she had once been taught in Petersburg, at the *pension* of Mme Cheminée. But Avdotya possessed little resemblance to Varvara Andreevna's former associates.

"Just think, perhaps even this Avdotya was once young ... Perhaps she loved someone and considered marrying ..."

"Well, that means nothing whatsoever. You know how men are—they just need a worker in the house. It's the bride who looks to see what kind of property the groom has."

Varvara Andreevna was generally skeptical. She treated most of what excited or enraptured Liza with indifference. Liza had grown so accustomed to her mother's continual living for others—for her father, for Liza herself—and it was so clear to her that this rather small old woman was an irreproachable model—that she had long since accepted her characteristic coldness. Likewise (although it saddened her), she had grown used to her mother's indifference to faith.

Avdotya, however, did not indulge in subtleties or niceties. She seethed. It didn't matter to her whether her blind grandma believed in God or not. But the old woman's "gorging" grieved her, drove her crazy.

"Hey you, the braggart tear you up, the devil eat you," she screamed in her masculine voice. "Why should I worry about you, why should I run around collectin' charity for an old mare? I run here, run there, beggin' from decent people. I've run my legs off, and all she does is gobble and gobble, you know, she shovels it in, oo-o you poisonous bastard ..."

Without answering, the bastard sat on the dirt stoop, stared with her tearful cataract-blinded eyes, and waited for her daughter to box her ears. In this she was not disappointed. Avdotya only pulled Mishka by the ears, but she beat the old woman with her fists, and sometimes with a stick, right across the face. The old woman groaned—because of her age she couldn't cry out loudly. The next day her face was covered with green blotches.

Liza happened to stumble upon one of these beatings. As she had done as a child when confronted with the sight of such cruelties and outrages, she turned white and immediately felt nauseous.

"What are you doing, Avdotya ..."

Turning around, Avdotya saw the "young mistress"—and herself became frightened: not by the threat of what this mistress could do, but by the fact that, in spite of everything, she was still "the mistress."

And she jumped away from the old woman.

"But, dearie, I was only doin' it a little ... just to teach her ... ooo, she's poisonous ... ya don't know her, mistress."

"But she's your mother ..."

"All she does is gobble from morning 'til night, and I've worn off my poor little feet ... Hey creep, whadda ya lookin' at," she shouted at Mishka, who was staring with curiosity at his grandmother's "lesson." "I'll tan your bottom, you'll bounce 'round here like a wheel, ya bitch's cat ..."

"Bitch yourself ..." Mishka dared to say, being beside Liza, and, sniveling, made a beeline for the wing of the manor house.

Liza felt she could no longer speak or else she might weep—and in disgust she went to the guest wing.

Varvara Andreevna approached the matter much more calmly.

"You're very tenderhearted, and have always been so. You must control your nerves better with them. They're all like this. Do you think the others are different? They don't feel things the way you do …"

"Ah, mama … the woman is old, blind. She beats her with such fury…"

"Indeed, that is so! Indeed, no one would condone this! When she comes to me, I'll give her such a reprimand …"

Avdotya came that very day, at dusk. A burst of steam and cold rushed into the kitchen when, abruptly pulling open the door with her long arm, she came in from the frost. In her hand she had a long stick. As always, she wore a tattered sheepskin coat; her eyes were whitish from the frost, and uneasy.

"I appeal to your kindness, my benevolent mistress. The thing is, behind your wing here there's one little teeny birch … what use is it to you? And I'm simply freezin', I ain't got the teensiest bit of strength left, the floor's cold, the old woman's complainin'."

Varvara Andreevna was standing in the middle of the kitchen near the wooden stove and watching the kasha boil.

"No, no, I won't allow you to take the little birch. That's just spoiling you. Cut down the brushwood in the ravine. There's as much as you could want. And there's something else—if you continue to brawl on my estate, you better watch out …"

"What are ya talkin' about, kind mistress, what brawlin', I never brawled since I was born, I'm a peace-lovin' gal."

"If you continue to cause a scandal with your old mother, don't show your face around here …"

Avdotya continued to assure her that she was a most peaceful gal. But in deference to the mistress, she was even prepared to abstain from "teaching" her bastard. And in the ravine, of course; one could certainly go and cut brushwood in the ravine …

Varvara Andreevna's tone had its effect. Possibly it seemed to Avdotya that if the mistress spoke so commandingly, it meant she also had the power to have her evicted from the dairy. She couldn't imagine that it would be far easier to chuck Varvara Andreevna and Liza out of the guest wing, than to remove her from the dairy. However that may be, whether due to a vestige of fear, or in the hope of some paltry handouts—they gave them in the kitchen all the time—Avdotya left submissively.

She humbly made her way home with her gigantic steps. Lost in thought, Liza looked out the window in gloomy disbelief.

After dinner her mother dealt out Patience in the dining room under the hanging lamp. Liza said:

"You know, when she walks like that, with that stick ... well, she looks just like Death. Like a skeleton, with its bones rattling, and a scythe over its shoulders."

From behind her pince-nez Varvara Andreevna raised her stern, beautiful eyes to her daughter.

"How can she be Death? She's just a beggar. Everything seems like something else to you."

III

Nikolay Stepanovich lay in the graveyard beyond the church under a white birch cross. The winter evening fluttered the delicate peels of birch bark, built up a snowdrift, covered over the dry flowers, and with its light snowy dust sang an eternal song full of sadness and the transience of things. Liza sometimes visited her father. With difficulty, she'd make her way along the tiny path half-covered with snow; she would stand there, rake around the flowers, fix the crosspiece, cross herself, and just as devoutly and slowly walk home. There was a hint of something monastic in her.

Near the fence of the park, from behind the gate, a long thin figure emerged as if from the bottom of the sea, with a stick and a knapsack on its shoulders.

"Ah, benevolent mistress, I'm runnin' to Alenkino, they say they brought materials, they're dolin' out pieces over a yard long ... I'll get there in a flash, be back by dinner ..."

"To Alenkino ..." Liza slowly walked home. "Ten *versts* there, ten back, back by dinner ..." And the usual depression and heaviness caused by such a meeting with Avdotya weighed on her heart.

At the same time, as if she were on stilts, Avdotya clambered up the hill behind the river from which could be seen the church, the park, and the two-story "manor" house. If she had turned around, she would also have seen the cross of Nikolay Stepanovich. But she had no time to turn around—before her lay the fields, white and cold, distant, with piercing grounds winds flying and howling along the frozen snow-crest in icy streams. She saw how they twisted, first blowing a drift around a little fir tree, then sweeping everything away from the icy bald spots till they were completely bare! One minute she'd be walking, almost gliding, along the road; the next she'd suddenly sink in practically up to her knees. There'd be little enough time to return before nightfall, but along the road in Kuneev you can get a bit of bread ... although only a crust; she was hungry, not to mention Mishka's complaining all the time, and the grandma ...

"O Lord, take them from me, those cursed devils! They've made me a prisoner, those accursed ones!"

After Varvara Andreevna's "reprimand," Avdotya behaved more quietly. But then she grew clever, beating the old woman no less enthusiastically, but silently, and locking her in the hut until the bruises were gone. She beat her for everything—for the cup she broke because she was blind, for wetting herself, for not closing the door. In these actions a certain strength emerged, which had nestled itself in Avdotya's wry body—the same strength which drove her ten *versts* through the snow for a tiny bit of chintz, or a chunk of bread for that same "bastard." She fought, rushed about, pestered everyone—this constant seething was life.

Then came the day ordained for the old woman to rest from war and battle. Avdotya was, at the time, roving far away. Mishka, though, listened curiously, in solitude, to the old woman's groaning, moaning, and absurd hiccupping. Taking advantage of his mother's absence, Mishka flew out of the dairy barefoot with a shout of victory, marching back and forth along the road. This seemed to him daring, outstanding.

When finally he burst into the hut, the old woman no longer was hiccupping. Mishka touched her sleeve; she didn't move. He became frightened and ran to the mistress.

Early the next morning Avdotya came to Varvara Andreevna.

"Mistress, allow that little pine there, ma'am, above the pond, to be cut down by the peasants. That'll make a good coffin for my old one—oh, she was born long, Lord forgive me ..."

Avdotya was gloomy and anxious and again dissatisfied—indeed it was true, the old woman had grown so "long," practically half a pine would be needed for the coffin ... Also, she worried whether the peasants would cut it down, and then about getting the priest ... Ah, life is backbreaking!!

"Yes-ss," Lev Golovin said that evening with his eternal lethargy and melancholy, to the carpenter Grigory "the Softy," who was sawing boards for the coffin with Kuz'ka. "She's gotten rid of the old lady. Now she'll be after us. First it'll be give her a cart, then cut her some wood, then they'll start dying, and you won't have enough trees to make coffins for 'em."

"I reckon you're right," said "the Softy," gloomily.

"You wait, spring'll come, you'll have enough of plowing her place. You'll hafta give her more land, let her use the horse to till ... you'll give her everything, but she'll keep twirlin' you just like an evil spirit. Here today, tomorrow in Alenkino, and then watch out—she'll reach all the way to Strakhovo ..."

Lev Golovin sighed.

"How was it she came, like she'd popped up out of the ground ... Or like the wind blowed her in?"

The hungry priest performed the old woman's funeral quickly in the unheated church. The old woman lay frozen in the coffin. The bruises on her forehead and cheek had yellowed. And what had once carried the name Elena and sung songs, and perhaps loved, was now all shrunken, bony, and very long. On pieces of torn gray Holland cloth her body was lowered deep into the earth, next to Nikolay Stepanovich's. Liza was the first to throw a clump of earth on her. And Avdotya began to howl—that was the custom in the village, and perhaps she did it not only because of the custom ...

Mishka was completely absorbed in where they were putting the old woman, but since early morning he had been bothered by a cough. Mishka felt chilled and trembled. Returning from the burial, he dozed off on the stove-perch, where the old woman used to warm herself.

"Oo-o, parasite, look how he's clambered up on the stove-perch!"

Avdotya rattled the dishes, scrubbed, cleaned them, apparently greatly upset, as though she herself wasn't sure whether she should curse or cry. Just in case, she gave Mishka a slap so he wouldn't cough. But he hacked quite loudly all night. Avdotya at times heard his cough even through her dreams and with rage she would turn over—won't he let a person sleep, the devil! The whole thing was somehow depressing and nasty. She dreamt about the cold—the fields, the whistling of the wind, the white serpents of the blizzard ... The wind blew fiercely into the hut from the windows and the floor.

The next day Mishka didn't get up. Avdotya was about to get angry, but when she noticed that he was all feverish, coughing, and his eyes were dull, she didn't touch him. She covered him with the grandmother's sheepskin coat and went herself "to the mistress" for help.

"He runs barefoot in the street—what did you expect?" Varvara Andreevna said sternly. "Watch out that pneumonia doesn't set in."

"What can I do, mistress dear, what can I do with the little bastard? I've already told him: 'I'll lock ya in, ya bitch's cat; stay home, I'll tear off your ears' ..."

"No, no, you will please be quiet. This is not a tavern."

Liza visited Mishka several times.

"How horrible it is in their hut," she said to her mother afterward. "The air ... the filth, a kind of gloominess, the cold ... I'm actually afraid of this Avdotya."

"You were always such a nervous person. But especially now, after the death of your husband ... Fear Avdotya!? She's a despicable peasant woman, nothing more."

Liza decided that was true—it was shameful to fear rather than love. She ought to pray for her. And from that day she began, in every one of her prayers, while naming those near and distant, to add the name Evdokiya. When, kneeling in the darkness, she mentally named her, it seemed that Avdotya was not entirely the same person. Evdokiya was somehow better, finer looking, than Avdotya-Death. And later on, when she'd thought it over, Liza was even embarrassed that she had called her Death. "Lord, the saints have kissed the lepers ..." She shuddered. Imagine kissing Avdotya's white lips, the bony bared teeth with their smell of decay, of the grave, with the phosphorescent sparkle of her half-starved eyes ... No, it was clear that she, Liza, was unworthy!

They gave Mishka what they could find in the old pharmacy—quinine and aspirin. But he coughed continuously. He would toss about, wheeze, and even Avdotya suddenly became downcast and walked more quietly on her stilt-like legs. Still she connived to "run off" to the neighbors, over two *versts* to the miller, to Kozlovka, to see Aksyusha "the Kind One."

Once, on a cold night before the Christmas holidays, after covering six *versts*, she was returning home at twilight, dragging some kind of food on her shoulders in a knapsack. As usual, the dogs in Kochki barked at her; as usual, the birches rustled along the ditch around the estate. The only thing which seemed strange was a tiny weak flicker in the dairy window. "I hope you're not burning it, you devil ..." And she quickened her pace. With a bony hand, she quickly opened the door. Mishka was lying on his back, very still, his little red hands crossed over his chest. A small candle burned near his head. And Liza, a Psalter in her hands.

Avdotya did not comprehend the scene immediately. A cold gust ripped in behind her—she hadn't managed to slam the door. She stopped and stared vacantly at Mishka's sharp little nose, at Liza— pale, with a moist gleam in her eyes—and suddenly, as she stood, a howl, hoarse and wordless, pierced the stinking air. Avdotya collapsed with her stick and her knapsack onto the cold little hands of her son.

"You—my handsome falcon, my golden eagle, my beloved child ..."

IV

Her child departed having tasted little in life. The coffin was not large, made from the very same pine tree, the work of those same old hands of Grigory "the Softy." Mishka was laid beside the old woman, several steps from Nikolay Stepanovich.

"Well, now she'll be a little more 'freed,'" Lev Golovin said, when he had returned from the cemetery, "she doesn't have two extra mouths now. That's a lot more 'freed'!"

But the little old peasant Kuz'ka remarked with skepticism:

"You'll see, Uncle Leon. Now she'll be so lonely, she'll hang 'round us all the time. You'll have to take the cart to town for her; in the spring, you'll have to plow her place ... No, we'll have no peace from her ..."

Avdotya, it was true, was now more free. She no longer had her two devils—nor anyone else in this world. No reason to worry, no one to beat, no one to complain about. But also no one to say a word to at home.

One time, meeting Liza, Avdotya snivelled:

"Mistress dear, this is all I got now ... I been cleaned out all at once ..."

At home Liza, sitting with her mother at dinner, suddenly said:

"Still, I feel sorry for Avdotya."

Varvara Andreevna turned her delicate profile toward her and looked at her with those dark, beautiful eyes:

"But that's just what she wanted. How many times did she say so? Besides, in reality, she slaughtered the old woman."

"Yes, but still ..."

Liza persisted.

"You were always, since childhood, softhearted ..."

The conversation was just a conversation; it vanished without a trace, like everything else, into time's abyss. The days ran by, flew. The men of Kochki worked; the women were busy with their pots and stoves. Liza taught; Varvara Andreevna managed her affairs; Avdotya, as before, rushed everywhere. Seeing this wiry peasant woman with her knapsack and stick tirelessly marching through the snow, it sometimes seemed the wind itself carried her ...

The New Year came. The icy sun arose in a milky-rose mist; from the east came the wind, burning like a flame; the snow in mounds glistened like fish scales, piercing one's eyes—you hadn't the strength to look, but could only cover your eyes and turn your head into the calm of your raised collar. But what a squeal the sledges make! Such a melody of swishing, squeaks, and whistling!

The melody is different during days when there are blizzards. Then a mighty bass drones, and echoes, and beats. Against the guest wing, where Liza and her mother were sheltered, a whole mad horde would suddenly charge, knock, rattle the roof, bang in the chimney. The blast would die down for a moment, giving way to the following one, and by morning would pile such a drift at the stoop that the door could not be opened. They'd have to dig out.

On such a day Avdotya was returning from Alenkino. She had left right after dinner. It was white, snowy-misty, though not very cold—she had set out on her stilt-like legs, but in an hour she started to tire. She dropped in on auntie Agafya in Vyselki to warm herself a little and rest. Agafya even gave her tea. When she had drunk it, she felt revived. And even though it was getting dark, she decided to go on.

"I'll get there in one try, dearie … I'll run through the little grove, then it's easier to run down the hill, and the wind'll help me."

It was fairly easy to get through the little grove, which had been recently cut down and was now overgrown with delicate little asps, nut trees, and oaks. The blizzard raged along the treetops; it tore and scattered the little brown leaves (which had survived on the oaks) across the whole field. It whistled in the bare branches; it piled drifts by the stacks of firewood in the clearing. But in the open field it showed no mercy. Avdotya, still frisky and stubborn, walked downhill. There, two *versts* below, was Kochki. The tiny forest quickly disappeared, and the wind somehow beat on her from several directions. The snow glued her eyes shut and at times even took her breath away. Suddenly it came up to her knees; the next step was up to her waist. She tried to turn around. Several solid steps—and again she lost the path. Here, there, everywhere it was really deep. She tried a while longer, but couldn't find the path and decided to take the way completely to the right, to the small ravine. And from the ravine straight to Kochki.

She got as far as the bush and was pleased—well, now the ravine, and everything would be clear. She fell into the ravine beyond the bush—that's as it should be, perfect. It became somewhat calmer, but there was so much snow …

That same night, before going to bed, Liza stood praying. It was dark; the blizzard roared outside the window. Liza bowed and prayed for her murdered husband, her mother, herself. She prayed for both Mishka and the old woman. Coming to Evdokiya, she suddenly saw—a small hollow entirely covered with snow, and white whirlwinds and serpents, a tall figure, emaciated, with a stick in its hand, a knapsack on its shoulders, desperately fighting, wading through the snow in the ravine. And in white, surrounded by such an unusual light, Mishka and the old woman suddenly appeared. They took the figure by the arms and all went off somewhere … Lord, intervene and save!

This time Kuz'ka complained in vain. The citizens of the village of Kochki no longer had any worries, and no more trouble with Matyushkin's widow Avdotya.

THE MARIE ANTOINETTE TAPESTRY

Alexei Tolstoy (1882\83–1945)

Translated by Helen Altschuler

The Red Count, the gemstone in the Soviet collection of tamed authors, **Alexei Tolstoy,** may not have been a *count* in the juridical sense (there are certain doubts as to his nobility), but certainly he cultivated himself as such, and the Soviet government assisted him with all the might of its propaganda machine, publicising him as a member of the vast *Tolstoy* family who had joined the communist cause and an aristocrat who willingly transformed himself into a faithful socialist writer.

Initially Tolstoy refused to accept Bolshevik rule and emigrated, but then returned to the USSR and got a warm welcome. Being a gifted author, he sold his pen for a very high price (three Stalin prizes included), wrote novels praising the necessary cruelties of the Russian imperial rulers and reformers like Peter the Great, or the imminent collapse of the capitalist system, but his life itself was a novel of the twentieth century with all its moral twists and traps.

Sheepskins, padded jackets, long-skirted peasant coats—the last of the sightseers file out of the palace, now a museum. Off in the west the sun is sinking, crimson, into the winter murk. The day is short, here in the north. But I can still see the leaf designs that the frost has traced on the lofty windows, as though in memory of the leafy forests that once covered the earth.

Now the tracery begins to fade, and blue-grey dusk gathers over all. A door bangs in the distance. The watchman's felt boots crunch down the path. A wintry hush spreads through the palace and the snow-blanketed park.

Sometimes, from her fearful height, the moon shines palely in at an uncurtained window. But that is not often. Most of the time it is fog, fog, fog over the park, and a storm wind whistling through the bare branches of the trees. Cold and desolate. I try to amuse myself by looking back over the years of my life. They are many, those years—some of them bright with fetes and pageantry; others, grim and tragic.

Time does not touch me, does not age me as it did the women who pass through my memories; as it did those two queens to whom I belonged. I am beautiful still as I was a hundred and fifty years ago, in my powdered wig and my rich, blood-red gown. I hang in a spacious drawing-room, by a window to the left of the door. Over the mantelpiece, opposite the windows, hangs a portrait of my mistress, painted at full length—young and proud and rather too erect, almost like a soldier—as she looked in the first years after her marriage.

Often, when the moon shines in, and the gilded chairs gleam in its light, I try to look into my mistress's face. But her eyes are turned stubbornly, angrily away from me. She always thought me the cause of all her troubles, for she was darkly superstitious as a woman of the Middle Ages.

It was not a very tactful gift, in any case, for President Loubet to have brought the Tsaritsa, Empress of the Russians, on his battleship a tapestry portrait of the guillotined French Queen. They took me out of my zinc-lined box and brought me here to this drawing-room, unrolled me, and laid me down on the rug.

"What is that?" the Tsaritsa asked, for she was no great connoisseur of the arts. (She stood looking down at me, stiff and straight as a governess, her clean, cold hands clasped before her.)

Fat little Loubet bowed low, and his starched shirt rustled. He answered glibly:

"It is a Gobelin, Your Majesty, and a very rare one. A portrait of Marie Antoinette, preserved by pure chance through the Revolution. France lays at your feet one of her national treasures."

At these words red spots came out on the Tsaritsa's faded cheeks, and she pressed her thin lips together to hide her fear. But I saw it—the look of insane horror that flashed in that instant in her round, blue German eyes.

"Why is her gown so red?" she asked.

To this Loubet could find no answer. He only bowed again, with a creaking of his boots.

They hung me on the wall, by one of the windows. The Tsaritsa never, that I can recall, looked long at me. The red of my gown annoyed her. Vague, misty, watery tones were the only ones that did not offend her taste. Marie Antoinette, too, detested vivid colours— all but the softest, the most soothing pastel tints. The bright red of my gown? Ah, but there is a story behind that. Here it is.

A hundred and fifty years ago there lived in Paris a beautiful girl named Elisabeth Roche. Elisabeth's father was a weaver at the royal tapestry manufactory, and the finest master of his trade in all of France. Old Roche might weave no more than a quarter of an inch a day; but such was his taste, his feeling for line and colour, that the tapestries that came off his loom rivalled and even excelled the living hues of nature.

Elisabeth, too, had worked at the manufactory from the age of eight; and she had inherited her father's taste and feeling for colour. When she was nineteen she was put to work in the model room, where, with bits of wool and silk, it was her task to prepare for the weavers working models of the paintings they were to copy on their looms.

For all her hot, young blood, Elisabeth lived very strictly.

Her only hope for a better lot in life lay in her maiden beauty. But fourteen hours of exhausting labour every day were enough to suppress all youthful longings. Yes—so it was, everywhere in France. The whole land was condemned to back-breaking toil, to insufferable poverty, so that the King, the Queen, the princes and the Court might spend their days in unceasing festivity: balls and ballets, fireworks and royal hunts that trampled out many a field of grain, and fantastic battles by night at the card tables, by the light of hundreds of wax candles. Futile revelry—it could not altogether still their dread of the fate that was alredy nearing. The Treasury was bare. The country was sinking deeper and deeper into destitution. The nobility could not pay their debts. The people of Paris growled ever louder after the gilded carriages, and the bourgeois circulated insolent lampoons against the Queen and the debauchery at Court. Usurers, crafty entrepreneurs, manufacturers of luxuries—only for such were the times profitable.

From the offices of the Court came an urgent order to the royal manufactory for a tapestry portrait of the Queen, after an original by the great Boucher.

The Queen, at that time, was very occupied with her toy farm in the Versailles park. There was the gilt-horned, patchouli-scented cow that she must milk with her own hands; and the mushroom omelettes to be prepared for luncheon; and the Chinese fish in the pond to be caught for dinner; yes, and, in between, she must join her ladies in pastoral dances beside the brook. What with all these cares, Boucher could only catch the Queen long enough to sketch her face, and that but hastily. The gown he designed himself—cream-coloured, in the taste of the period. He was not too satisfied with the result.

When the portrait was brought to the manufactory, Elisabeth Roche was ordered to make a working model of it for the weavers. Her frame lay on the floor, and she worked on her knees, only now and again getting up to view the result from the top of a ladder. As the weather was hot, she wore but a short, thin frock that exposed her neck and her shapely legs.

Thus was she found by the head of the manufactory—a ruined nobleman, fat and slovenly and, though far from young, only too sensible to feminine charms. Planting his ill-gartered legs wide apart, he stood goggling at her, and the sweat came trickling from under his little wig and down his shaven cheeks. The day was blazing hot; flies were buzzing against the grimy windows; and that girl—she was tempting as a luscious apple. He sat down beside the easel and got out his snuff-box. The snuff sprinkled over his lace jabot. His eyes were almost starting from their sockets. Elisabeth, preoccupied with her work, crawled about at his feet—now stretching out a hand for the scissors, now bending low to snip a thread with her teeth. Watching, he experienced almost a gourmand's greedy pleasure. His nostrils quivered in anticipation. Her hair got into her eyes, and she straightened up in annoyance and lifted her bare arms to pin it back. At this, he was seized by something in the order of a stroke. His veins were on the point of bursting. Relief must be had quickly. He let himself fall heavily from his chair upon the girl, seized her in his arms, and covered her face, her neck, her breast with kisses.

Elisabeth screamed. Never before had any man dared touch her. She struggled desperately. Getting her right arm free, she struck him in the face. After that the only sounds were a few thuds of the man's fist, and a faint moan from the girl.

When the door slammed shut, and his shuffling steps died away down the hall, the women of the manufactory came in. They found Elisabeth unconscious, her frock all torn, lying across the model she had been making; and the cream-coloured gown in the model was stained with blood. Elisabeth's face was beaten black and blue. They carried her away. She was discharged from the manufactory immediately.

The incident would hardly have been noticed—but there lay the ruined model, and when Boucher saw it he was furious. The tip of his turned-up nose flushed scarlet under its coat of powder, and he stormed and raged at the manufactory administration. Then he looked again at the model, screwed up his eyes, and snapped his fingers. An idea had struck him. He had been dissatisfied with his portrait from the first, as I have said; and it now occurred to him that these spots of blood were of a very striking colour. He had the ruined gown in the model replaced with blood-red silk, declared the result charming, and sent it on to old Roche in the weaving-room.

And that was how I came to be. Old Roche worked on me day and night. Often bitter tears ran down his wrinkled cheeks; but what had become of Elisabeth, I did not know. He began weaving me from the head, so that for many months I hung head downward in his loom. They kept hurrying him, and he worked on in gloomy silence.

At length I was ready. Boucher was accorded the honour of presenting me to the Queen. My story had become known at Court, so that he easily justified the unusual colour of my gown. The blush of virginity, he called it. That was a jest entirely in the spirit of the times, and the Queen rewarded him with an airy smile.

I was hung in the royal bedchamber in the Trianon—a little palace that the royal family used for its amours. There was some truth, unquestionably, in the lampoons. The Queen was frivolous. Her beauty had begun to fade, and the King did not often visit her bedchamber. And when he did come—fat and soft and double-chinned, in his Chinese dressing-grown and slippers—his talk was rather of his exploits in the hunt, or his achievements at the lathe, than of the subtleties of love. After such platonic visits the Queen would call for her Venetian mirror and—lying back among her frills and laces, alluring still by candlelight—would look awhile in wondering unbelief at her reflection in the glass. At length her lower lip—for she was a

Hapsburg!—would began to pout. And at this point the merry ladies who circled her broad bed would begin some new nocturnal revel, after which the Queen would go peacefully to sleep.

From very morning, every day at Versailles was a holiday, ushered in with a rumbling of carriage wheels and a clamour of merry voices. Ladies in spreading skirts, fragrant with perfume, clustered like living flowers in the Queen's bedchamber, twittering and chirping like so many song-birds. Other ladies flitted seductively to and fro among the trees of the park. Fountains murmured and tinkled; swans beat their wings; gilded boats rocked on the artificial lake. Here picturesque ruins in the Greek style, there a group of marble statues gleaming in the sun, carried empty minds away to Arcady. The effeminate cavaliers, drenched in perfume to kill their natural odour, seemed more like creatures from some imagined world than earthly noblemen with debt-ridden castles, their hands outstretched for the King's bounty.

Nature was kind to this artificial life. The lawns were odorous with sun-warmed hay, and bright with butterflies; fleecy cloudlets, floating over the lake, were reflected in its waters; even the breezes seemed to ask pardon as they rustled through the trees. And so the days flew by—brilliant, dewdecked, gossamer. The Queen shut her mind to all sad thoughts. The King, hard at work on a new set of tortoise-shell snuff-boxes, would think to himself that, in the end, things would all come to rights: the lampooners would be locked up in the Bastille; the Treasury would find money—somewhere, somehow; the honest bourgeois would learn once more to love their King; the honest peasantry would give up worrying over the taxes; and, God willing, a war might turn up to bring back his wasted wealth ...

We all know how it ended, this thoughtless merriment at Versailles. They came down the road from Paris, crying, "Bread! Bread! Bread!"—some thirty thousand women from the city outskirts; and at their head, a sabre in her hand, rode that fierce beauty, the courtesan Theroigne de Mericourt, in a scarlet gown and a scarlet hat adorned with scarlet plumes.

The King smiled down at them from his balcony, and the Queen, too, with the little Prince in her arms, tried hard to smile. The King, the Queen and the Prince were put into a carriage and taken off to Paris. No one was in the mood for smiles any longer.

Now there was no sound in the park but the autumn rain, tapping at the lofty windows of the Trianon. The trees lost their summer finery, and the dead leaves lay rotting on the paths, for there was no one to clear them away. Through the bare branches the marble gods and goddesses gleamed nude and shameless. Soon the winter fogs began. Only the watchman's footsteps broke the hush of the abandoned bedchamber. A spot came out on the ceiling of the bedchamber, and soon it was drip-dripping on to the parquet floor.

The first days of spring brought pleasure-seekers staring curiously at the whimsies of the royal park: men in dark ugly clothing of thick cloth, wearing no wigs; and women in plain woollen gowns, with modest kerchiefs on their heads, leading their children by the hand. They carried baskets of food, and ate their lunches right there on the grass, leaving behind them greasy bits of lampoons that they had used to wrap the food in. These decent bourgeois women would turn their eyes quickly away from the nude statues. Looking in at the palace windows, they would cry out in wonder at the sight of the Queen's great bed. At me, they would glare angrily, shielding their eyes from the sun with their hands, their noses pressed flat against the glass; and some of them would shake their parasols in my face.

Summer ended. A winter storm smashed several windows in the palace. But at last April came again. Once more the blackbirds ran about among the bushes. Burdock sprang up, unchecked, on the park paths; the fountains were dead, and their pools overgrown with duckweed. Cows wandered freely over the grass, leaving droppings at the feet of the statues. More and more people came on a holiday. But it was not the decorous bourgeois, now. These were a different sort: strange young men, their chests bared, their sleeves rolled up, their trousers all the way down to their ankles; and with them red-cheeked, laughing girls in scant cotton frocks. They romped like children, and when they grew tired went to sleep on the haystacks. They laughed and kissed, quarrelled and made peace again. They dived into the lake, scattering rainbow spray, and their tanned bodies did not yield in beauty to the chipped marble gods. When evening began to gather they would heap up blazing bonfires of the remnants of the gilded boats, and in the fire-light, like untamed savages, dance the fiery Carmagnole.

But this summer, too, passed and was gone. Faces grew grimmer, sterner; and in men's darkened eyes I saw the pangs of hunger, and a mad determination. Many trees in the park were felled that winter for fuel. Both cows disappeared. The watchman must have eaten them. Then the watchman, too, disappeared. One day two people stopped to look in at my window—a broad-shouldered youth, with the dark down just showing on his cheeks, and a young woman. Both were barefoot. He had his arm flung lovingly over her shoulders, which her ragged clothing barely covered. She was beautiful, straight and strong, with flowing hair. She whispered something, and the youth jerked at the window. The rotting frame splintered, sending the glass panes crashing to the floor. The two young people came into the room. Now I recognized the ragged beauty: Elisabeth Roche. She stood there awhile, looking up at me, then rose on tiptoes and spat in my face. And then the youth tore me down from the wall and threw me on to the bed.

There I lay, in the desolate chamber, until one day I was picked up as a useful bit of property by a respectable bourgeois from Paris—a sausage dealer who had made the trip to Versailles in the hope of finding some broken-kneed old nag fit for nothing but slaughter. I was folded up neatly and thrust under the wagon box, and my new master sat on top. Behind us, under a length of sacking, lay a flayed horse. That was the manner of my journey to Paris, where my master hung me up in the bullet-riddled window of his shop, to keep the wind out. And it was there, on the Place de la Revolution, that I saw the Queen for the last time—but in how pitiful a plight!

Since that day, a hundred and fifty years have passed. It would be a weary task to recount all the twists and turns of fate that I experienced. When, one misty, windy day, the black banner of the Commune was raised over the *Hôtel de Ville*, my sausage dealer was hanged in the doorway of his shop, with the slogan "We demand fixed prices" fastened to his breast. A gunpowder-blackened hand tore me down from my window, and I became a cloak on the bare shoulders of a big, husky young fellow who brandished a lance with a red cap on its point. All that day, through the whine of bullets, my blood-red gown blazed on his shoulders. When evening came, he made his way to the *Hôtel de Ville*—torchlit below, but its pointed turrets wrapped in fog. In the midst of a great crowd bristling with sabres and pistols, we burst into a vast hall, hazy with the smoke of wicks burning in oil. Here, on boards and boxes, sat the members of the Paris Commune, in endless session, their faces sallow with lack of sleep. Workers and craftsmen from the sections were demanding the heads of aristocrats and bourgeois, roaring, "Break up the Convention! Death to the traitors! All power to the Commune! Bread and fixed prices!"

My master curled up by one of the windows and tried to go to sleep, using me as a blanket. But—woven to please the eye—I must have proved poor comfort that windy night, for he got up and hurled me on to a heap of rubbish in a corner of the hall. And there I lay until someone picked me up, shook me out, and laid me on the pine table at which the leaders sat, in place of a cloth. From that time on I was littered with papers, and goosequill pens, and stale hunks of bread. Trembling with fury, a man sat at the table, his ragged-sleeved elbows pressing down on my breast. Black curls, limp with perspiration, hung over his long face and pale, bulging forehead. His name, if I remember correctly, was Hebert, and he personified the will of those half-naked people who crowded to the *Hôtel de Ville* every evening, after work, to shout of Justice, and their demands, and their hatred, and Liberty.

Like all the *Enragés*, he was beheaded. That day the sullen folk from the sections were addressed by a little man with a sharp, bony nose, neatly dressed and wearing a white wig. He stood with his head thrown slightly back and pressed down between his shoulders, his cold fingertips resting lightly on my gown, and spoke in a grating voice of moderation and of virtue. He swore that he would strike off the heads of all who led immoral lives, of all who plotted counter-revolution, yes, and of all who might think him, Robespierre, insufficiently revolutionary and patriotic. The shopkeepers, in their liberty caps, applauded. But, alas, the bourgeois were weary, sick unto death of revolutions, of the madness of the mob, of rags and paper money.

And an hour came when a group of five, wearing tricoloured sashes, gathered hastily at the table which I still covered. One of the five was Robespierre. He laid on the table before him a pistol, ready cocked. They sat in silence, staring unblinkingly at the dark windows. Outside, in the square, the mob was roaring. There was only one candle on the table, and its flickering light could not dispel the shadows that filled the huge, empty hall.

That night the Revolution ended. The roar of the mob on the square subsided. There was a thunder of cannon wheels—shouted commands—and then the footfalls of the National Guard marching implacably up the steps of the *Hôtel de Ville*. They entered.

The eyes of the five terrorists, still motionless at the table, flashed menace. But an ominous shout rose from the ranks of the National Guard. Saint-Just, youthful, effeminate, rose calmly to yield himself prisoner. Palsied Couthon buried his face in his hands. Lebas, always afire, seized the pistol and thrust it into Robespierre's hand. The little man raised it reluctantly to his temple—but a guardsman sprang forward and jerked his elbow. A shot rang out, and Robespierre, his lower jaw smashed, dropped his head on my breast. His hand closed on some sheets of paper that were lying on the table. He tried to stop the blood with them, but only smeared it over his face.

Further, my recollections drag through dreary years among the dusty rubbish in an antiquary's shop. No one would give so much as a hundred francs for me, while Napoleon was scattering the landowners' armies all over Europe. But he bled the honest bourgeois too hard, and—when it became more profitable to abandon the sword for the ledger—they betrayed him. The Revolution swung round at breakneck speed, and for a moment paused—back at its starting point. Louis XVIII ascended the French throne; and I was given a thorough cleaning and hung, as a sacred relic, in the Tuileries. The halls of the palace were freshly gilded. And in those halls, with oh! what returned ardour, danced the ladies I had known at Versailles—only faded, now with twenty years of exile. As they danced the powder sifted in white clouds from their rouged and wrinkled cheeks. A melancholy sight!

The revolutions and restorations that followed did not affect me. I hung quietly through them all in the Louvre Museum. And that is the story of my life, up to the day when I was brought to the Alexandrovsky Palace, in Tsarskoye Selo, and hung in the drawing-room of Tsaritsa Alexandra Fyodorovna, ruler over countless millions of men and women.

After all I had been through, I found my new home dreadfully dull. The Tsar and the Tsaritsa had no liking for large gatherings. They were company enough for themselves. Except on affairs of state, they had few visitors. A favoured maid of honour might drop in, to kiss her mistress' hand. Or there might be a telephone call from that tramp and horsethief, their spiritual *muzhik*,* when he wanted to come and see them. And he would come, in his peasant coat and patent leather

---

* Rasputin Grigory (1871–1916). Favourite of Emperor Nicholas II and his wife, Alexandra Fyodorovna.

boots, kiss them on the cheeks, and then sit down, screw up his crafty eyes, and lie away as fast as he could invent, while the Tsar and the Tsaritsa stared reverently at his greasy beard, afraid to miss a word.

When the urge for drink came on the Tsar, he would go to the officers' club. The regimental trumpeters would be sent for, and to their blaring the drink would flow. Next day the Tsar would groan and clutch his aching head—but not when the Tsaritsa was in the room. True, he did not make snuffboxes, like the French Louis, but he killed time quite successfully at amateur photography. The hours passed pleasantly, too, when he played his right hand against his left at billiards, humming contentedly to himself; and another pastime was reading—Averchenko, for instance, whose stories made him laugh aloud. When evening was gathering, he liked to stand at the window, smoking, and watch the autumn rain drizzle down over the trees and bushes. Behind the bushes crouched freckled secret-service agents, their hard hats pulled down over their ears, afraid to move lest they be noticed.

The Tsaritsa, in her rooms, would work at endless embroidery, thinking, thinking all the time, with knitted brows, of her innumerable enemies—of the hidden intrigues against her family—of the ungrateful, undisciplined, unruly people it had fallen to her lot to rule—of her weak-willed husband, who could not make his people respect and fear him. At times, dropping her embroidery, she would tap angrily with her thimble on the arm of her chair, and her unseeing eyes would darken. On a little table behind a screen stood a wonder-working icon, with a bell attached to it. Often, kneeling before this icon, the Tsaritsa would pray long and earnestly, in hope of the miracle that would set the bell to ringing.

And so the years slipped by—none too gaily, you will agree. But things became worse than ever when the Tsar and the Crown Prince went away to the war, and the Tsaritsa began to wear a grey dress with a blood-red cross on her breast and a linen kerchief. In Versailles, at least, they enjoyed themselves before they died. There was something to look back to, when the executioner tied their arms behind them and clipped the hair at the napes of their necks. But here—why, had I flesh-and-blood jaws, I'd have dislocated them with yawning! Coronation, anointment—what good had they brought these people, if they spent their lives so cheerlessly, surrounded by such universal hate!

Well, and then I noticed that the Tsaritsa had begun to scowl at me in the wildest way. She would stop in front of me, her hands clasped before her, and her low forehead would crease in wrathful lines—as though there were something she was trying her utmost to understand and overcome. Outside the windows, the December snow was sifting down. It collected in white heaps on the hard hats of the secret-service agents, who kept breathing on their hands to warm them as they crouched beneath the bushes. And the Tsaritsa paced up and down, up and down, her nostrils dilating in helpless rage. Alas, she had not the power to hang her foes—no, not so much as the Chairman of the State Duma. Enemies everywhere. Everyone against her.

During one such moment, tidings came that seemed to break her. The spiritual *muzhik*, her only friend and guide, had been discovered dead—bound hand and foot, his head smashed in—in a hole chopped in the ice under a bridge. The news was brought by the Tsaritsa's favourite maid of honour, who dropped sobbing to the floor as she told it. The Tsaritsa turned deathly pale. She staggered, and leaned against my blood-red gown for support.

"We are lost," she said. 'There is no one now to intercede for us with God."

That evening, dressed all in black, with a black shawl over her head, she stole furtively past the secret-service agents, and for a long time I could make out her dark figure moving away across the snow. She had gone to weep over her spiritual *muzhik*, brought out secretly from the city to a little wooden chapel in a lonely part of the park.

The last time I saw the Tsaritsa was one dark night when a distant crimson glow hung over the trees and shone in at the frosted windows. Something, somewhere, was on fire.

The drawing-room was dark and warm. The palace lay sunk in sleep. Suddenly the door squeaked, and the Tsaritsa came in, wrapped in a white dressing-gown.

"What's burning? What's burning?" she asked of the empty room, in German.

She went to the window. The frosted leaves on the glass, now blue-black, now lit up with that crimson glow, made a fantastic design.

Her face was distorted, her eyes wide with superstitious fear. She and I were haunted, at that moment, with one and the same recollection.

...Tens of thousands of heads, a roaring, surging sea, all along the railing and the terraces of the Tuileries and flooding the broad

Place de la Revolution, where, behind a picket of bayonets, loomed the scaffold—and over the scaffold the triangular blade, poised high between its two supports. From my sausage-shop window I could see the pointed turrets of the Conciergerie, and the two-wheeled cart that was moving past them. Now the cart turned off to the bridge, and crossed to my side of the river. The heads turned to watch, rolling like waves in a storm. And now the cart, with its guard of soldiers and drummers, entered the sea of heads. The roar of the mob drowned out the rattle of the drums. The cart passed by my window, and in it I saw the Queen. She sat with her back to the horse. Her arms were tied behind her, and that made her seem very stiff and straight. She had no corset on, and her withered breasts were outlined through the rumpled black wool of her gown. Court poets had once written madrigals in praise of those breasts, and an amber goblet had been made in their shape for the King to drink from. Her sallow neck was bare. Her head was bowed, and her lower lip pursed in proud loathing and contempt. A lock of hair hung from under her high cap. "Death to the cursed Austrian!" chanted the bareheaded old women who followed, in rows of four, behind the cart, working incessantly on woollen socks for the Army—Robespierre's famed knitters. The cart stopped. A hush fell over the crowd. There was a swift bustling on the scaffold, and the gleam of a white cap. The drums beat louder, louder, in desperate, ear-rending clamour. And the blade slid down between its supports, a triangular flash of light. Someone lifted the Queen's severed head and held it up over the crowd...

"Accursed maniacs! Devils, devils!" the Tsaritsa whispered hoarsely, in Russian, still peering out through the frosted, flame-lit window. And she began to cross herself, quickly, quickly, stiffly bowing her head. Her lower lip stretched, and slightly sagged.

That night her children came down with the measles. Never again did she enter the drawing-room where I hang to this day, by a window to the left of the door. Sightseers, in huge canvas slippers over their felt boots, pause a moment before me in their tour of the palace, now a museum, and the guide says:

"Here you see an example of serf production, dating to the earliest period of the struggle between agricultural capital and commercial and industrial capital."

THE CAVE

Yevgeny Zamyatin (1884–1937)

Translated by Mirra Ginsburg

Twice arrested for revolutionary activities, and living for a while as an illegal, **Yevgeny Zamyatin** got an education as a shipbuilding engineer, and during WWI was sent to England to supervise the building of the icebreakers ordered by the Russian Navy (one of the icebreakers was the future *Krasin*, sent by the Soviets to rescue the arctic expedition of Umberto Nobile in 1927).

Returning home, he was given the nickname *Englishman* for his newly acquired stylishness. Industrial England also gave him inspiration and material for the world-famous novel *WE*, (finished in 1920) the first great dystopia of the 20th century. Ironically, the communist censors immediately suspected that the novel described Soviet Russia and banned the text.

Zamyatin left the USSR in 1931 with Stalin's special permission and died in Paris.

Glaciers, mammoths, wastes. Black nocturnal cliffs, somehow resembling houses; in the cliffs, caves. And no one knows who trumpets at night on the stony path between the cliffs, who blows up white snow-dust, sniffing out the path. Perhaps it is a grey-trunked mammoth, perhaps the wind. Or is the wind itself the icy roar of the king of mammoths? One thing is clear: it is winter. And you must clench your teeth as tightly as you can, to keep them from chattering; and you must split wood with a stone axe; and every night you must carry your fire from cave to cave, deeper and deeper. And you must wrap yourself into shaggy animal hides, more and more of them.

A grey-trunked mammoth roamed at night among the cliffs, where Petersburg had stood ages ago. And cave-men, wrapped in hides, blankets, rags, retreated from cave to cave. On the Feast of the Intercession of the Holy Virgin, Martin Martinych and Masha closed up the study; a few weeks later they fled from the dining-room and huddled in the bedroom. There was nowhere else to retreat; here they must last out the seige or die.

In the Petersburg bedroom-cave things were much as they had been in Noah's ark not long ago: a confusion of beasts, clean and unclean, thrown together by the flood. A mahogany desk; books, Stone Age pancakes that seemed to have been made of potter's clay; Scriabin, Opus 74; a flat-iron; five potatoes, scrubbed lovingly to gleaming whiteness; nickel bedsteads; an axe; a chiffonier; firewood. And in the centre of this universe – its god, the short-legged, rusty-red, squat, greedy cave god: the cast-iron stove.

The god hummed mightily. A great fiery miracle in the dark cave. The people – Martin Martinych and Masha – worshipfully, silently, gratefully stretched their hands to it. For a single hour it was spring in the cave; for one hour the animal hides, claws, fangs were discarded, and green shoots – thoughts – struggled up through the ice-crusted cortex of the brain.

'Mart, you've forgotten that tomorrow ... No, I see you have forgotten!'

In October, when the leaves have yellowed, withered, drooped, there are sometimes blue-eyed days; you throw back your head on such a day, so as not to see the earth, and you can almost believe that joy, that summer are still here. And so with Masha now: if you close your eyes and only listen to her voice, you can still believe she is the same, the old Masha; in a moment she will laugh, jump out of bed, throw her arms around you. And what you heard an hour ago – a knife rasping on glass – was not her voice at all, it was not she ...

'Mart, Mart! Just as always now ... You never used to forget. The twenty-ninth: St Mary's day, my name day ...'

The cast-iron god still hummed. As usual, there was no light; the light came on at ten. The shaggy, dark vaults of the cave swayed overhead. Martin Martinych, squatting on his heels, all of him drawn into a knot – tighter, tighter! – still stared, with head thrown back, at the October sky in order not to see the faded, withered lips. And Masha –

'You know, Mart – what if we lit the stove the first thing in the morning? To make the whole day – just as now! What? How much do we have? There must still be about a cord left in the study?'

It was a long, long time since Masha had been able to get herself as far as the arctic study; she did not know there was no longer any ... But pull the knot more tightly, still more tightly!

'A cord? Much more! I think there must be ...'

Suddenly, the light: exactly ten o'clock. And, breaking off, Martin Martinych shut his eyes, turned away. It was harder in the light than in the dark ... And in the light it could be clearly seen – his face was crumpled, claylike (many people had clay faces now – back to Adam). And Masha –

'And, you know, Mart, I would try – perhaps I could get up ... if you lit the stove in the morning.'

'Of course, Masha, of course ... On such a day ... Of course, the first thing in the morning.'

The cave god was running down, shrinking. It was quiet now, crackling faintly. Downstairs, at the Obertyshevs, a stone axe was chopping the knotty logs of an old barge – a stone axe was splitting Martin Martinych into pieces. One piece of Martin Martinych smiled a clayey smile at Masha and ground dried potato peelings in the coffee mill for pancakes. Another piece – like a bird that has flown into a room from out of the open – dashed itself blindly, stupidly against the ceiling, the windows, the walls: Where can I get some wood – some wood?

Martin Martinych put on his coat, buckled on a leather belt (there is a myth among the cave-dwellers that a belt will keep them warmer), and clattered with the pail in the corner near the chiffonier.

'Where are you going, Mart?'

'Only a moment, downstairs, for some water.'

On the dark staircase, ice-crusted from splashed water, Martin Martinych stood awhile, swaying, sighing. Then, the pail clanking like a prisoner's chain, he went downstairs, to the Obertyshevs: they still had running water. The door was opened by Obertyshev himself, in a coat held together with a rope, his face, long unshaven, a wasteland overgrown with rusty, dusty weeds. Through the tangle of weeds – yellow stony teeth, and between the stones, a flick of a lizard's tail – a smile.

'Ah, Martin Martinych! Some water? Come in, come in, come in!'

Impossible to turn with the pail in the narrow passageway between the outer and the inner door – the passageway is full of Obertyshev's firewood. The clay Martin Martinych painfully struck his side against the wood – a deep dent formed in the clay. Then a still deeper one, from the corner of the chest of drawers in the dark hallway.

They crossed the dining-room. In the dining-room was the Obertyshev female and three Obertyshev cubs; the female quickly hid a bowl under a napkin: a man had come from another cave – who knows, he may suddenly rush and seize it.

In the kitchen Obertyshev turned on the faucet, grinning with stony teeth.

'Well, and how's the wife? How's the wife?'

'The same, Alexey Ivanych, the same. In bad shape. And then, tomorrow is her name day, and I have no more wood.'

'Use the chairs, Martin Martinych, and the chests ... The books too: books make an excellent fire, excellent, excellent ...'

'But you know yourself – all the furniture in the apartment is the landlord's, all but the piano ...'

So, so ... Too bad, too bad!

And now, in the kitchen, the strayed bird could be heard fluttering up, rustling, darting left, right – and suddenly, desperately, it dashed its breast against the wall: 'Alexey Ivanych, I wanted ... Alexey Ivanych, could you ... only five, six pieces ...'

Yellow stony teeth through tangled weeds, yellow teeth staring out of the eyes; all of Obertyshev was sprouting teeth and they grew longer and longer.

'Martin Martinych, how can you! We haven't got enough ourselves ... You know yourself how things are, you know yourself, you know yourself ...'

Pull the knot harder! Still harder! Twisted tight, Martin Martinych lifted the pail – and back through the kitchen, the dark hallway, the dining-room. On the dining-room threshold Obertyshev thrust out a slippery, lizard-quick hand: 'Well, good-bye ... But see that you slam the door, Martin Martinych, don't forget. Both doors, both – one cannot keep the house warm enough!'

Out on the dark icy landing Martin Martinych set down the pail, turned, and shut the first door. He listened, but he heard only the dry, bony tremor inside himself, and his gasping breath – a broken line of dots and dashes. In the narrow passageway between the doors he stretched his hand and touched a log of wood, another, and another

... No! He quickly thrust himself out onto the landing and closed the door. Now he must only slam it to, so that the lock will click ...

But he could not do it. He had no strength to slam the door on Masha's tomorrow. And on the faint dotted line traced out by his breath, two Martin Martinychs locked in mortal combat: the old one, who had loved Scriabin and who knew he must not, and the new one, the cave-dweller, who knew – he must. Gritting his teeth, the cave-dweller knocked down, throttled the old one, and Martin Martinych, breaking his nails in his haste, pulled open the door and plunged his hand into the woodpile ... one piece, a fourth, a fifth, under his coat, inside his belt, into the pail. He slammed the door and bounded upstairs with great, animal leaps. When he was halfway up the stairs, he suddenly halted on an icy step and pressed himself against the wall. The door had clicked again below, and the dusty Obertyshev voice cried out, 'Who is it? Who's there? Who?'

'It is I, Alexey Ivanych. I ... I had forgotten to close the door ... I wanted ... I came back to shut it better ...'

'You? Hm ... How could you? One must be more careful. With everybody thieving nowadays, you know it yourself. How could you?'

The twenty-ninth. From early morning – a low, ragged, cotton sky, breaking ice through the gaps. But the cave-god had filled its belly in the morning, and began to hum benignly: never mind the torn sky, never mind the toothy Obertyshev counting his logs. It does not matter, it's all the same. 'Tomorrow' is a word unknown in the cave. It will take centuries before men know 'tomorrow' and 'the day after tomorrow'.

Masha got up and, swaying from an unseen wind, she combed her hair in the old way: over her ears, with a part in the middle. And this was like a last, shrivelled leaf fluttering on a naked tree. From the middle drawer of his desk, Martin Martinych pulled out papers, letters, a thermometer, a small blue phial (he hurriedly pushed it back, so Masha would not see it), and finally, from the farthest corner, a black lacquered box: on the bottom of it there was still some real – yes, yes! – real tea. Tilting his head back, Martin Martinych listened to the voice, so much like the voice of old.

'Do you remember, Mart: my blue room, and the piano with the covered top, and the little wooden horse, the ashtray, on the piano? I played, and you came up to me from behind ...'

The universe had been created that evening, and the astonishing, wise mask of the moon, and the nightingale song of the bell, trilling out in the hallway.

'Do you remember, Mart – the open window, the green sky, and below, out of another world, the hurdy-gurdy man?'

Hurdy-gurdy man, miraculous hurdy-gurdy man, where are you?

'And on the quay ... Remember? The branches still bare, the rosy water, and a last ice-floe, like a coffin, floating by. And the coffin only made us laugh, for we would never, never die. Remember?'

Downstairs they began to split wood with a stone axe. Suddenly they stopped. Someone was running, shouting. And, split in two, Martin Martinych saw with one half of him the deathless hurdy-gurdy man, the deathless wooden horse, the deathless ice-floe; and with the other half, his breath a broken, dotted line, he was with Obertyshev, counting logs of wood. Now Obertyshev had finished counting. Now he was putting on his coat, all of him overgrown with teeth, now he furiously slammed the door, and ...

'Wait, Masha, I think there's someone at the door.'

No. No one. Not yet. It was still possible to breathe, to tilt one's head and listen to the voice – so much like the old.

Twilight. The twenty-ninth of October was growing old, peering with the intent, dim eyes of an ancient crone – and everything shrivelled, hunched up, shrank under the insistent stare. The vaults of the ceiling settled lower, the armchair, the desk, Martin Martinych, the bed, everything flattened out, and on the bed – an altogether flat, a paper Masha.

Into the twilight came Selikhov, the house chairman. Once he had weighed two hundred and forty pounds; now half of him had ebbed away, and he knocked about loosely inside the shell of his coat like a nut in a rattle. But he still had his old booming laugh.

'Well, then Martin Martinych, in the first place. And in the second place, congratulations to your spouse on her name day. Of course, of course! Obertyshev told me ...'

'Some tea? ... a moment – just a moment ... We have real tea today. You know what it means – real tea! I have just ...'

'Tea? Well, I would prefer champagne. You have none? You don't say! Haw-haw-haw! The other day a friend of mine and I, we made ourselves a brew out of some Hoffman drops. It was a howl! We got stewed … "I am Zinoviev," he says: "Down on your knees!" A howl! And then, as I was going home across the Martian Field, I met a man in nothing but his vest, I swear to God! "What's wrong?" I asked him. "Oh, nothing much," he says, "they've stripped me out there just now, I'm running home to Vasilievsky." A howl!'

Flattened, paper-thin, Masha was laughing on the bed. All of him tied into a knot, Martin Martinych laughed louder and louder – to give more fuel to Selikhov, to throw in a few more logs; if only he wouldn't stop, if only he wouldn't stop, if only he went on about something else …

But Selikhov was running down; after a few last quiet snorts, he was silent. He dangled right, left inside his coat-shell and got up.

'Well, my dear lady, your little hand. Yos! Don't you know? Your obedient servant – Y-O-S, as they would say it nowadays. A howl!'

The floor was rocking, turning under Martin Martinych's feet. With a clay smile Martin Martinych held onto the door post. Selikhov was puffing, ramming his feet into his huge snow boots.

In his boots and fur coat, mammothlike, he straightened up and caught his breath.

Then silently he took Martin Martinych by the elbow, silently he opened the door into the arctic study and silently sat down on the sofa.

The floor in the study was icy; the ice cracked faintly, broke from the shore, and floated whirling downstream with Martin Martinych, and from the distance, from the sofa, from the shore, Selikhov's voice was scarcely audible.

'In the first place, and in the second place, my dear sir, I must tell you: I would crush this Obertyshev like a louse, I swear to God … But you understand: if he makes an official complaint, if he says, – "Tomorrow I'll report it to the police …" Such a louse! I can only advise you: go to him today, right now, and shove those damned logs down his throat.'

The ice-floe rushed faster and faster. Tiny, flattened, barely visible – no more than a splinter – Martin Martinych answered – Speaking to himself, and not about the firewood … What's firewood? No, about something else: 'Yes, very well. Today. Right now.'

'Excellent, excellent! Such a louse, such a louse, I tell you …'

It was still dark in the cave. Cold, blind, made of clay, Martin Martinych stumbled dully against the things piled in confusion, out of the flood. For a moment he was startled: a voice, sounding like Masha's voice, out of the past ...

'What were you talking about with Selikhov? What? Ration cards? And I was lying here, Mart, and thinking: If it were possible to get up some energy and go away somewhere, to let the sun ... Oh, how you clatter! As if to spite me. You know, you know I can't stand it, I can't, I can't!'

Like a knife on glass. But it was all the same now. His hands and feet had become mechanical. To lift them and to lower them he needed chains, winches ... And one man could not turn the winch; you needed three. Straining at the chains, Martin Martinych put a tea-kettle and a saucepan on the fire, and threw in the last of Obertyshev's logs.

'Do you hear what I'm saying to you? Why don't you answer? You hear me!'

Of course, this was not Masha, this was not her voice. Martin Martinych moved more and more slowly, his feet sank in the shifting sand, it was harder and harder to turn the winch. Suddenly the chain slipped from the block, the arm shot down, clumsily catching at the kettle and the pan. Everything crashed to the floor. The cave-god hissed like a snake. And from the distant shore, the bed – an alien, shrill voice: 'You're doing it on purpose! Get out! Get out at once. I don't need anybody, I don't need anything – I want nothing, nothing! Get out!'

October twenty-ninth had died, and the deathless hurdy-gurdy man, and the ice-floes in the sunset-rosy water, and Masha. And that was right and necessary. There must be no impossible tomorrow, no Obertyshev, no Selikhov, no Masha, and no Martin Martinych. Everything must die.

The mechanical, faraway Martin Martinych was still going through some motions. He may have tended to the fire in the stove, picked up the pan, put the kettle on once more to boil. Masha may have said something again. He did not hear. There was nothing but the dull ache of the dents in the clay, made by words, by the corners of the chiffonier, the chairs, the desk.

Martin Martinych slowly drew out of the desk drawer bundles of letters, the thermometer, some sealing-wax, the box of tea, more letters. And finally, from somewhere at the very bottom, the dark-blue phial.

Ten o'clock: the light went on. Electric light – barren, harsh, plain, cold, like life and death in the cave. And just as plain, beside the flat-iron, Opus 74, and the pancakes, the small blue phial.

The cast-iron god hummed benignly, devouring the paper of the letters, parchment yellow, bluish, white. The tea-kettle tapped its lid, gently calling attention to itself. Masha turned, 'Is the tea boiling? Mart dear, give me …'

And then she saw it. An instant, pierced through by the clear, naked, cruel electric light: Martin Martinych, crouching before the stove; the letters glowing pink like the river at sunset; and, over there, the blue phial.

'Mart! You … you want to … already …'

Silence. Indifferently devouring the deathless, bitter, tender, white and pale-blue words, the cast-iron god purred softly. And Masha – as simply as she had asked for tea: 'Mart, darling! Mart, give it to me!'

Martin Martinych smiled from far away. 'But you know, Masha, there is only enough for one.'

'Mart, but there is nothing left of me, anyway. This is no longer I – I'll soon be … anyway … Mart, but you understand – Mart, have pity on me … Mart!'

Ah, the same, the old voice … And if you tilt your head …

'I lied to you, Masha. We do not have a single piece of wood left in the study. And I went to Obertyshev, and there, between the doors … I stole, you understand. And Selikhov said … I must take it back at once – but I burnt everything, everything! I don't mean the wood – what's wood! – you understand me?'

The iron god was dozing off indifferently. Houses, cliffs, mammoths, Masha flickered, going out.

'Mart, if you still love me … Mart, remember! Mart, darling, give it to me!'

The deathless wooden horse, the hurdy-gurdy man, the icefloe. And that voice … Martin Martinych slowly rose from his knees. Turning the winch slowly, with great effort, he took the blue phial from the table and gave it to Masha.

She threw off the blanket and sat up on the bed, rosy, quick, deathless – like the river at sunset long ago. She seized the phial and laughed.

'Well, now, you see: it wasn't for nothing that I lay here, dreaming of going away. Light another lamp, that one, on the table. So. Now put something else into the stove. I want the fire …'

Without looking, Martin Martinych swept out some papers from the desk and threw them into the stove.

'Now … Go, take a little walk. I think the moon must be out – *my* moon, remember? Don't forget to take the key, or you will shut the door and there won't be…'

No, there was no moon outside. Low, dark, thick clouds like a vaulted ceiling, and everything – one vast, silent cave. Narrow, endless passages between the walls; and houselike, dark, icy cliffs; and in the cliffs – deep, red-lit hollows. There, in those hollows, people were squatting by the fires. A light icy draught was blowing white dust underfoot, and over the white dust, the boulders, the caves, the crouching men, unheard by anyone, went the huge, measured tread of some unknown monster mammoth.

NIKOLAI
Velimir Khlebnikov (1885–1922)
Translated by Clarence Brown

Born in the middle of the Kalmyk steppes, within the territory of the nomadic tribes of the Buddhist faith (his father was an ornithologist and a silviculturist), **Velimir Khlebnikov** (born Viktor Khlebnikov) was marked by the foreignness of his origin throughout his life, becoming probably the most avant-garde of the avant-garde figures in Russian futurist poetry, conducting linguistic experiments with sounds, abandoning ordinary syntax and grammar to escape the limits of conventional speech and culture.

However, Khlebnikov was also a talented (and far more traditional) storyteller, even though this side of his writing was overshadowed by his linguistic and philosophic escapades. In 1916 he proclaimed himself (and 316 other persons) to be the Chairmans of the World Globe and was clownishly crowned as such in 1920. During the Civil war he conducted research on the rules of time, aiming to find the general formulae of human history, became a vagabond and died of gangrene in a remote village.

Strange peculiarity of an event, it leads you indifferent past what has been awarded the name terrible and, on the contrary, you look for depths and secrets behind a trivial event. I was walking down the street and stopped when I saw a crowd assembling around some carts. "What is going on here?" I asked a man who happened to be walking by. "Look," answered he, laughing. Indeed, in the gravelike silence an old black horse was stomping his hoof with a measured beat against the pavement. Other horses were listening, their heads inclined in a deep bow, taciturn and immobile. In the pounding of the hoof one heard thought, fate descried, a command, and the other horses, miserably hanging their heads, gave ear. The crowd was collecting quickly until the driver arrived from somewhere, yanked the reins of the horse, and drove off.

But the old black horse with its vague reading of fortune and its dreary comrades remained in my memory.

The vicissitudes of a vagrant life are redeemed by magical events. Among these I number my meetings with Nikolai. If you met him you would probably pay no attention. Only his slightly swarthy forehead and chin would betray him. And his eyes, which, with an excess of honesty, expressed nothing at all, might have told you that you had to do with an apathetic hunter who found people tiresome.

But this was a solitary volition, having its own path and its own end of life.

He was not with people. He was like those estates that are cordoned off from the highway by a fence and turned by the fence in the direction of a dirt track.

He seemed taciturn and simple, cautious and miserable.

His disposition seemed even poor. Drunk, he would become rude and insolent with his acquaintances, would insistently demand money of them but—strange thing—would feel a flood of tenderness toward children: Wasn't it because they had not yet turned into people? I've known this same trait in other people, too. He would gather round him a crowd of children and spend all the money in his pocket on the wretched candies, cookies, and cakes adorning the shelves of the shopkeepers. Whether or not he meant to say, "Look, people, treat others as I am treating them," still, since such tenderness was hardly his normal occupation, his silent sermon had a greater impact on me than the sermon of some teacher with a loud and universal fame.

But who in any case is going to decipher the soul of a solitary gray hunter, a stern chaser of wild boars and wild geese? I recall in this connection the harsh sentence passed on the whole of life by a certain defunct Tatar, who left behind a deathbed note with the brief but arresting message: "I spit on the entire world."

To the Tatars he seemed an apostate and traitor, and to the Russian authorities a dangerous firebrand. I confess that I have more than once wished to add my signature to that note dictated by apathy and despair. But this silent exhibition of freedom from the iron laws of life and its stern truth, this hazel tree gathering wild flowers at its feet, these are nevertheless symptoms of a profound trait; they conceal a simple and stern thought preserved by his, in the face of all odds, honest eyes.

In a certain old album, many years old, amongst the faded old men bending with age, with a decoration on their chest, amongst the finicky old women with a gold chain in their hand and eternally reading an open book, you might also happen upon the modest yellow likeness of a man with hardly remarkable facial features, with a straight beard, and with a double-barreled shotgun on his lap; his hair was divided by a simple part.

If you ask who this faded photograph is, you will be briefly informed that it is Nikolai. But detailed explanations will most probably be avoided. A slight cloud passing over the face of your informant will indicate that he was not treated as a complete outsider.

I knew this hunter. One might treat people in general as varying interpretations of one and the same white head with white curls. Then the contemplation of forehead and eye in various interpretations will present you with an endless variety, as a struggle of light and shadow on one and the same stone head, replicated in old men and children, in businessmen and dreamers, an infinite number of times.

And he, of course, was merely one of the interpretations of this white stone with eyes and curls. But can anyone not be that?

Much has been told of his feats as a hunter. When he was asked to bring in some game he would ask, with his distinguished taciturnity, "How many?" And disappear. God knows by what stratagems, but he would reappear carrying what had been ordered. Wild boars knew him as a silent and terrible enemy.

Cherni—that place where rushes grow at the edges of the shallow sea—he had learnt by heart. Who knows, if only it were possible to penetrate into the soul of the winged tribe peopling the mouth of the Volga, how the image of that terrible hunter had been imprinted upon it? When they filled with their moan those desert shores, could one not hear in their sobbing the news that the bark of Avian Death had come ashore? Did he not seem to them, with the shotgun over his shoulder and the gray cap on his head, a terrifying creature with otherworldly powers?

The terrible merciless deity would also appear among the desolate sands: The white or black flock would bruit abroad with lengthy shrieks the death of their comrades. One small corner of this soul, however, knew pity: He always spared nests and the young, who knew only the sound of his retreating steps.

He was secretive and taciturn, more frequently reticent; and those only to whom he had disclosed the bare periphery of his soul might have surmised that he condemned life and harbored "the contempt of a savage" for the whole of human fate. One might, however, understand this state of the soul best of all by saying that the soul of "nature" was obliged thus to condemn innovation, if that soul had to pass via this hunter's life from the world of the "perishing" to the world of those coming to replace it, gleaming with valedictory eye at the snowstorms of ducks, at unpeopled wastelands, at the world of blood spilt by red geese across the surface of the sea, if it had to pass over to the land of white stone piles driven into the streambed, the fine lacework of iron bridges, of anthill cities, a strong but ungracious twilight world!

He was simple, straightforward, even crudely stern. He was a good nurse, tending his sick comrades; and this tenderness toward the weak and readiness to be their shield might have been the envy of a medieval cuirassier in a plumed helmet.

He set off for the hunt as follows: He would get into his skiff, where two dogs that he had raised from puppies awaited him, fasten the sail to the grommet, and set off downriver, using sometimes the towrope and sometimes the oars. I should add that on the Volga there is a tricky wind that will fly offshore in moments of utter quietness and capsize any careless fisherman who can't manage to strike his sail.

At the campsite the boat was turned over to make a shelter, iron rods were driven into the ground, and by the fire the hunter began his twenty-four-hour days before leaving for the feast. The intelligent, taciturn dogs were fed in the boat, which had absorbed the smells of all the game known to the Volga region; black cormorants and the big leg of a boar lay here beside partridges and bustards.

The wolves howl softly: "There they come," "There they go."

His wish was to die far from the company of men, concerning whom his disenchantment was immense. He wandered about among men while denying them. Cruel by profession, he settled among the hunted nonpeople, to whom he appeared as a cruel prince, the bearer of death; but he was on their side in the fight between people and nonpeople. Thus Melnikov, the scourge of the Old Believers, could still write *In Mountains and Forests*.

No, he could not be imagined as anything other than a sort of Perun of the Birds—cruel, but faithful to his subjects, in whom he perceived a kind of beauty.

There were people whom he might call his friends; but the more his soul emerged from its "shell," the more powerfully he upset the balance between himself and them to his own advantage; he would become arrogant, and the friendship a temporary ceasefire between two belligerents. The rupture might arise from the most trivial of causes, and his gaze would say, "No, you are not one of us," and he would become dour and distant.

Only to a few was it clear that this man did not in fact belong to humankind at all. With his meditative eyes, his taciturn mouth, he had already been, for two or three decades, the chief priest in the temple of Murder and Death. Between the city and the wilderness there exist the same axes, the same difference, as between devil and demon. Intelligence takes its origin at that point where one is capable of choosing between evil and good. The hunter had made this choice on the side of the demon, the great unpeopled void. He stated emphatically that he did not wish to be buried in a cemetery; why did he not want a quiet cross? was he a stubborn heathen? and what did he learn from that book which he alone had read and the ashes of which no one now would ever read?

But death did not go against his wishes.

Once the local newspaper printed a report that the boat and body of an unknown man had been found in the region known to the local inhabitants as "Horses Gate." The report added that a double-barreled shotgun lay beside the body. Since this was the year of the Black Death and the ground squirrels, those pretty denizens of the steppe, were dying by the thousands, forcing the nomads to strike their tents and flee in terror, and since the hunter was already a week overdue and nowhere to be seen, people who knew him sent out a search party full of alarmed expectation and grim foreboding. When the party returned, they confirmed that the hunter was dead. Their story, heard from some fishermen, ran as follows.

When they'd already passed several nights in a fishing camp that they had set up on a deserted island, a strange black dog would appear every evening, station herself near the hut, and set up a forlorn howl. Beating and shouting had no effect on her. They drove her off, though not without a presentiment as to what these visits from a strange black dog on a uninhabited island might portend. But she never failed to reappear the following night, howling gruesomely and poisoning the fishermen's sleep.

Finally a kindhearted watchman went out to her: She gave a yelp of pleasure and led him to the overturned boat: Nearby, his gun in his hand, lay the remains of a man totally picked clean by the birds, there being flesh left only in his boots. A cloud of birds were wheeling above him. A second dog, half dead, lay at his feet.

Whether he died of fever or the plague was not known. Waves lapped the shores in measured rhythm.

Thus he died having achieved his strange dream—to come to his last end far away from people.

But friends nevertheless placed a modest cross over his grave. Thus died the wolfslayer.

POMPEII

Vladislav Khodasevich (1886–1939)
Translated by Bryan Karetnyk

> Able to be precise and expressive without being too poetical or too acrobatic with words, **Vladislav Khodasevich** was the son of a professional photographer, who photographed, among others, Leo Tolstoy. Maybe this unconscious heritage somehow shaped his way of writing: modern and sharp, yet organically connected with the past.
>
> Emigrating from Soviet Russia in 1922 with his second wife Nina Berberova, he moved from Berlin to Paris, wrote memoirs, poetry, and prose, divorced Berberova in 1932 and died in 1939. His third wife, Olga Margolina, was deported from France as a Jew and was murdered in Auschwitz.

To live two hours from Pompeii for six months and leave without seeing it is indecent, unthinkable. But still, I'd been putting it off for some reason, as if I felt some sort of foreboding. Finally, I settled on it. But it was 13 April, and a Monday at that – a day that was doubly onerous.*

By tram to Castellammare, by train to Torre Annunziata, then by cab. The day is cloudy, with only occasional sunshine, though the atmosphere is leaden. The road is white, dusty, covered in weeds. On both sides: vegetable gardens, water channels, gullies. The occasional house built of porous limestone, flat roofs with no eaves, windows without glass – those Italian houses that from the very day of their creation look like ruins. Everything is bare, flat, dusty, stony, scorched by the sun and eroded by the winds: the valley of Pompeii. The ennui of antiquity hangs above the road. The ash of Vesuvius seems to have eaten into everything here.

Vesuvius rises up on the left, rust-brown, its summit obscured by

---

* According to Russian superstition, Mondays are considered inauspicious for travelling.

smoke. Almost black at the crater, it lightens and disperses into a whitish cloud, stretching out south-eastward.

At the entrance to Pompeii there is a little square, jammed with motor cars and open carriages. It is enclosed at one end by a modest hotel, the Hotel Suisse. This lively establishment by the gates of the dead city immediately recalls those stalls selling crosses, wreaths and memorials that like to live near cemeteries.

A little curved road, strewn neatly with sand and bordered with lush verdure, leads from the entrance towards the excavations. Here, after the bustle of the square, the noise immediately fades away, leaving only the crunch of sand underfoot. And the little road looks like a path in a graveyard.

There are calico sedan chairs dotted around on both sides – for those who are too ill or too rich to go on foot. Now and then they bear people – 'That way!' – farther down the path. It looks like a cemetery.

Presently we enter through the gate: Porta della Marina. To the right, beneath an archway, there is a door to a little museum. Oh, what horror! In a cemetery office you're told only who lies where – while here you're shown inside the grave, what transpires within. On display is a collection of household implements uncovered during the excavations: dishes, bowls, tools, pots of rouge, padlocks, door locks, statuettes. And here we have the inhabitants themselves: casts of people buried by the ash. One, a writhing skeleton in rags, its mouth agape, full of teeth; another covering its head with a toga – a last gesture of desperation; a third, naked, lies on its back, bow-legged, in a glass grave. A dog in a broad collar, reduced to convulsions, curled up, like a caterpillar. Here, the 'secrets of the grave' are revealed. Here, the virtue of the grave is outraged, its only right – the right to secrecy.

We leave and enter the 'city'. There is something quite marvellous about its deathly silence and order. What with the number of streets, squares and walls still intact, it's impossible to think of it as a heap of ruins. Indeed it is a city, but a city from whose face everything temporary, accidental, transient, has been erased: Pompeii has been wiped clean, tidied up, 'decked out', like a corpse.

The windowless backs of the houses, giving on to the streets, are almost identical. Evidently the building work here was uniform even when the city was alive. Denuded by time, deprived of their rendering, they are now no different from tombstones in a cemetery.

Narrow but straight regular streets reveal the simplest of vistas, intersecting at right angles. They are far straighter than the streets of any modern Italian city. Uniform plaques with numbered areas and districts are nailed to the corner buildings. Each building has its own number, too; at the crossroads, by the pavements, plaques that are a little bigger – with street names – have been affixed with iron nails: a useful fabrication, necessary even for the tourists' orientation. Glancing at the numbers and names, however, one is constantly reminded that resurrected Pompeians would now find themselves resultantly lost in their own city: they are all approximate, arbitrary designations, bestowed in our time at the tyranny of scholars – just as it is in a cemetery, where the living, for their own convenience, name avenues after the dead.

Tourists here go about like visitors to a cemetery, never blending into the scenery. Like flocks of birds, small groups of young, gaily dressed English girls flit about. Occasionally, from behind a low wall, as if from behind a mausoleum, the ginger-moustached head of a German peeps out. Everyone moves in an erratic way. Only the keepers and guides walk and talk here with any certainty. For them alone, as for sextons and grave-diggers, is the dead existence of Pompeii a routine, a way of life.

Yet still, for all Pompeii's many similarities to a graveyard, there is always a sense of some important, essential difference, too. And suddenly it begins to dawn on you.

A cemetery is idyllic. Peace reigns there. Those who have trodden their path on earth we bear to a cemetery, to a city of *peace and those at peace* ... What is the grave to us? *Parva domus, magna quies.** But in these little houses there is no great peace at all. There is reconciliation in a graveyard; here there is just horror. Everybody died, yet none was reconciled with anything. Here the people were buried, taken by death not only in the midst of their earthly journey, but also, one might say, with one foot poised to take its next step. Everyone here died in terror, in frenzy, in passion, in rage. It was a thousand times worse than on the field of battle. Violent deaths befall those, too, but

---

* 'Little abode, great peace' (Latin).

every man is in part prepared for it; he sees in it even the littlest bit of sense: on the field of battle one man may be moved by patriotism, another by the thrill of glory and heroic poses, a third by a sense of duty. A fourth – at worst – goes because he has been given the order. No one here saw any sense in what happened. They perished in nonsensical terror and, according to Pliny's testimony, offended the gods – doubtless because they were sitting drinking, eating, measuring, weighing, fighting, embracing. And now, all of a sudden, you die, without the time to finish your drinking, eating, measuring, weighing, fighting, embracing …

… And when, sans strength, the lovers came to rest,
And sleep invincible subdued them, masses
Of cinerous dust then fell upon the city,
And the city was buried under ash.

The centuries passed – and, as from avid jaws,
We tore the past out from the earth, and found
Two bodies there, symbolic of immortal passion,
So incorruptible in their embrace.

O, raise on high this sacred monument,
This living sculpture of eternal forms,
So that the universe shall ne'er forget
That passion which transcended every bound.*

Lord, what soulless decadence! 'O, raise on high …'! No, for the love of God, hide it away, show it to no one, bury it again!

Death passed through here, touching everyone, delivering none from his earthly mask, purging none of his meagre, wretched horror. When a man dies of illness, of his body's exhaustion, his earthly cares leave him by degrees; the accidental and temporal fade away – anxieties, troubles, all the marks of his profession. The mask falls – and a face is revealed. It isn't a cobbler, a doctor, an actor who dies – but a man, a servant of God. It's the same when the death is

---

* An inexact quotation from the poem 'The Pompeian Girl' (*Pompeianka*) by the Symbolist poet Valery Bryusov (1873–1924).

sudden, if the sense of it is in some way deliberate: through heroism, sacrifice, perhaps even suicide, the desire to 'return the ticket'. There is a moment of purification, of catharsis in each of these deaths. At Pompeii there was none of that. They died just as they were: not men, but bakers, cobblers, prostitutes, actors. Thus it was that they 'crossed the great divide' – in their filthy, earthly guises, covered in the sweat of fear, of greed, of passion. At Pompeii, every step reveals a terror – of a death 'without repentance', of a transfiguration into an 'otherworldly' baker, an 'otherworldly' owner of a tavern or lupanar.

That is why Pompeii resembles not only a cemetery, but also something far worse than that: a house where the robbers have rushed in and slaughtered the residents in one fell swoop. They were boiling, frying, eating, breathing in the reek of onions – and right there, they were slain. We see the scattered remains of food, shreds of garments, broken crockery, traces of a brief, desperate scramble. The sight is terrible, and yet it inspires no awe, as is always the case in places of senseless catastrophe.

At Pompeii terror envelops you not on account of the number of victims. Here a modern man may startle a good few thousand Plinys with his tales. Here, it is not the quantity, but the quality of death.

Since the buildings and the houses here are turned with their backs to the street, each time you go inside one, you feel some thievish notion, as if you are not simply entering, but creeping, stealing into it. You go in, and it's as if at any moment, from this little room or that one, from some pit, the master of the house will crawl out into the light of day, disturbed by your presence. Perhaps he's that same bow-legged man lying in the glass grave. You go in, and it takes your breath away – not the fires of hell, but the onion, the eighteen-and-a-half-centuries-old onion. The pungent smells of Roman cookery seem to have spread over Pompeii. The city was small, artisanal, practical; here they knew the value of money and every kind of 'productivity', the emblems of which are strewn everywhere, in the form of various bulls, goats, swine, boars – and far more suggestive images, too. There were once many brothels and public houses here; the population had a robust love of eating, drinking and sleeping their fill. Pompeii was destroyed at supper time.

Here, a dreadfully uncouth, greasy, sticky life passed into an equally uncouth and ignominious death. And one knows not what would be more distressing: that the city were better preserved, or that it had been more violently ruined. The former bears traces of a suffocating life; the latter of a suffocating death. Here people lived and died in dingy, cramped quarters, with no windows and only a single door.

I imagine it would feel strange and unsettling to walk here in bare feet. And to touch something with your hand – no, not for all the world. There was once a terrible incident in my youth. On returning home from school one day, I found on the window sill a little round parcel. The newspaper on it was crumpled and full of holes. I stuck a finger into a hole – and recoiled in terror and disgust: coarse hairs and dry skin. Lying on my window sill was … a human head. Yes, yes, a real severed human head: a mummy brought as a gift. Pompeii reminded me of this incident at my every step.

The little rooms in the brothel are the most suffocating of all, the most cramped. They haven't been properly cleaned: the black remnants of ash have eaten into everything, probably along with the remains of ancient filth and human sweat. There is a black, ever so slightly greasy film covering everything: the wide stone beds, each occupying half the darkened box room; the thin partition walls; the posts of the doorways, from which the curtains have disappeared (or perhaps they were never really there to begin with?); in the cracks of the chipped paintings depicting the *what* and the *how*, the sight of which immediately brings on nausea and shortness of breath; and, finally, forgive me, in the round-holed board of the latrine (right there between the little rooms), which, not without a certain pride, our guide indicates to us: indeed, perhaps this is the only surviving example from antiquity. And when you manage to get out into the street – the exclamations of Petronius' characters seem to fly after you: true, the base, tedious, eternally vulgar, impenetrable (like the Pompeian night) events of the *Satyricon* unfolded a little later – though it was in these very parts.[*]

---

[*] The *Satyricon* is a work of Latin Silver Age literature, most likely written by Gaius Petronius Arbiter (c.AD 27–66), an advisor to the emperor Nero. The work is picaresque in nature and recounts the adventures of rhetor Encolpius and his companions, in racy and often ribald detail, as they travel around southern Italy, particularly in the environs of Cumae. While the work is now dated from AD 63 to 65, in the early twentieth century the dating of the work was

And so, a tour around the different buildings, the different rooms, contemplating the tasteless Pompeian artwork, with its insipid drawings and discordant colours on oil-cloth – each time you pray to God that the room be smaller, so as to pay homage to culture and snobbery all the more quickly. Even those that are somewhat better (for example, the little naumachia on one of the walls, completely out of keeping with the local style) bring no joy. How pleasant it is to examine this naumachia; yet it would be pleasanter still to run away from here.

Just for an instant, somewhere in the distance, beyond the railings, an image of Orpheus flits past – the only hint of a ghost in this city of people buried alive. Yet it passes – and again there is nothing to breathe amid the ancient twilight.

In schoolbooks, it is written that Christianity brought the Gothic spire into the world – an ascent upwards. Here you can witness this simple truth for yourself. The leaden, inert, squat cube of the Pompeian home – what inescapability, what flatness, what tedium! And these million-*pood** weights, falling like deceptively light ash from the rationalistic heavens of the Latin world – oh, what inescapability! Now you can believe and you can see how great, probably, was the yearning for the Saviour in some of these souls – from the suffocating heat, from the flesh, from the ash.

It's hot. There are still a couple of buildings to inspect. The street's vista ends in the great mass of Vesuvius, as though cutting into it. I raise my eyes, and I see: playing in the black puffs of smoke, there are flickers of lilac, the colour of wine. This isn't fire; this is only its reflection in the clouds of steam. But all the same! There, high above Pompeii, the mouth of the dragon is breathing. I recall 'the wicked flame of earthly fire'.† And the ground seems to grow hotter beneath my feet. Away from here!

O dear, spirited, jovial cabby, riding to Castellammare! O dear,

---

still hotly contested, with claims ranging from the first century BC to the third century AD; this accounts for Khodasevich's erroneous comment that the novel postdates the eruption that destroyed Pompeii, which occurred in AD 79.

* A Russian unit of weight, equivalent to approximately thirty-six pounds.

† Words taken from Vladimir Solovyov's (1853–1900) poem 'All in azure today …' (*Vse v lazuri segodnia iavilas* …).

spirited, unfossilized little galloping horse, bearing me swiftly along – with every second farther and farther hence!

The cabby, it so happens, spotted me in Sorrento. He turns around, engages me in all manner of conversation about my nationality, my domestic situation. At any other time, I would perhaps have demurred, pretending to be an Englishman. But now, I muster all my knowledge of Italian and reply to each of his questions, so that he should feel well disposed towards me and crack the whip all the more often. And how cheery, how beautiful: somewhere off to the left, in the distance, is a tall, white belfry.

THE DARKNESS
Mark Aldanov (1886–1957)
Translated by Joel Carmichael

Writer, critic and journalist, **Mark Aldanov** (born Mark Landau) was born in Kiev into a family of wealthy Jewish industrialists. He graduated from the physical-mathematical and law departments of Kiev University and initially oscillated between two avocations, his first major literary work being two volumes of *Armageddon*, fictionalized dialogue of Chemist and Writer.

Aldanov left Russia during the Civil War and became a successful novelist, publishing several historical novels on topics ranging from the Napoleonic Wars to the Russian Revolution.

He lived in Germany and France, managed to escape to the US in 1940 and went back to France in 1947.

Aldanov was also a staunch anti-Communist, researcher and critic of revolutionary movements and terror (especially in his 1947 novel *Before the Deluge*). Therefore, his books were first published in the USSR in 1987.

I

The restaurant had been in existence for several hundred years. At least that's what the guidebooks said about it: every guidebook listed it as one of the historical and gastronomical landmarks of Paris. Casual tourists seldom visited the restaurant, which was located in an unfashionable part of town, far away from the center of things. In the old days its patrons had been Parisian connoisseurs—mostly wealthy or titled people, or else people who wanted others to believe that they were wealthy or titled. Occasionally the restaurant bestowed a posthumous mark of distinction on a famous regular patron by naming some complicated dish after him as though he had been the first one to concoct it.

Year in and year out the guests were met at the door by an old maître d'hôtel who was known to the regulars as Albert. He pointed out to the novices who deserved special attention the autographs under the portraits on the walls, and he exhibited to them the "golden book" and the "historical tables" which were the creation of his inspiration or of the inspiration of his predecessors. He even persuaded himself that Napoleon had been one of the frequent guests, and that he always had had dinner at the large round table in the right corner. A suggestion had been made that "Napoleon's table" be separated from the others by a chain, but the board of directors of the corporation which owned the restaurant refused to consider any notion that was certain to curtail the revenue.

The prices in the restaurant even in the old days had made people who were wealthy enough to afford frankness shrug their shoulders as they glanced at their bill. Now everybody shrugged shoulders—the new fashion required it. On one occasion a group of German officers who appreciated everything *echt Pariser* had made an issue of the price they had been charged for an *Homard à l'Armoricaine* (the ancient argument among gourmets about the terms *à l'Armoricaine* and *à l'Américaine* had been settled in favor of the first, possibly out of consideration for the new masters of the city, who had no fondness for America, though they considered themselves above such pettiness, and even did not frown at the wine list which, among others, mentioned a famous wine that bore the name of the Jewish owner of the vineyard).

Nothing came of it because an extremely important personage—some people said it was Göring—issued orders that the restaurant was not to be disturbed. This personage frequently condescended to visit the restaurant, and whenever he was present "Napoleon's table" was surrounded by a group of unpleasant-looking men in civilian clothes whom the other patrons and waiters watched out of the corners of their eyes, now and then exchanging a whispered remark. The important personage was always on his best behavior and showed great tolerance: he volubly praised the wines, including the one that bore the Jewish name, he was not above admitting his admiration for the beauties of Paris, and he told in an atrocious French—"things like that simply cannot be told in German"—Parisian stories which invariably delighted his companions.

German officers patronized the restaurant frequently, though even with the fixed value of the mark they found the prices very high. Among them were a number of regulars who already knew the maître d'hôtel by name. But for the most part the new patrons were civilians whom Monsieur Albert never had seen before. No matter how forcefully they shrugged their shoulders when they paid their bills, no matter with how much feeling they exclaimed: "Non, tout de même!" the maître d'hôtel knew that the prices of the foods and wines made little difference to them because daily they made hundreds of thousands dealing with the Germans. Monsieur Albert was polite to them, but inwardly he despised them, though they were much more generous with their tips than his old patrons had been.

The old patrons dropped in very seldom now, and with them he exchanged sighs and bitter smiles. They looked in amazement at the menu: "Good Lord! Where do you get all these things?" The maître d'hôtel smiled sadly and with an expressive gesture of his hand indicated that the secret could not be revealed even to them.

II

That evening there were no Germans in the restaurant (their presence was no longer a novelty, but the other patrons still felt more comfortable without them). Not all the tables were occupied. The early autumn day was dreary and cold. By dinnertime darkness had settled, and at seven-thirty on the dot Monsieur Albert began the superfluous but regularly observed ritual of preparing for the night. Blue paper and diagonal white strips had been pasted on the windows at the beginning of the war. The curtains in the main dining room had to be lowered and adjusted carefully. Monsieur Albert went through this routine every evening with a sense of satisfaction, and the patrons assisted him as though these warlike precautions somehow vindicated their collective and undisputable security. The plunderers who occupied the large table at the right window, eager to demonstrate their willingness to do their bit for their country, rose from their seats to make Monsieur Albert's task easier. He exchanged a few appropriate pleasantries with them while he was performing his duty.

Next he disturbed a solitary gentleman who since seven o'clock had been reading his paper at a table by another window. In Monsieur Albert's mind this gentleman with a yellow, tired face and a black arm band did not belong among the old or among the new patrons. He never had been in the restaurant in the old days, and he was not one of the new crowd. As a rule he ordered a cutlet, a bottle of mineral water, and a cup of coffee. The maître d'hôtel assumed that the gentleman suffered with some internal disease and had to be on a strict diet which now could be observed only in a first-class restaurant. Though a cutlet and a bottle of mineral water were not enough to hold a table at this restaurant, Monsieur Albert showed utmost respect for this visitor who had become one of the regulars—perhaps because of the black arm band, or perhaps because of the unconcealed distaste with which he looked at the other patrons. Like most civilians he came to the restaurant on a bicycle. The coatroom boy in a blue jacket with gold buttons never ceased admiring his new machine, which was of a famous make.

Some new guests arrived with gay exclamations which involuntarily escaped them as they came out of the darkness into the brightly lighted, comfortable room and saw tables covered with white tablecloths and buckets holding bottles with gilded corks. Monsieur Albert anxiously seated them at a table and expressed his gloomy view of the weather (he did this in a way that implied that even the weather was not what it had been in the old days).

Precisely at seven-fifty-five the sound of clinking spurs came from the coatroom. The boy in the blue jacket threw open the doors, and two German officers entered. A tall, broad-shouldered, cleanshaven colonel—one of the new regulars who once or twice had visited the restaurant in the retinue of the important personage—followed by Monsieur Albert, made straight for "Napoleon's table." The maître d'hôtel could not distinguish the German insignia of rank, and as a rule addressed all elderly officers as "Votre Excellence," which did not evoke any protestations on their part. In this particular instance he knew that the patron was a colonel, but he could not force himself to address a German as "Mon colonel."

In age and appearance the second officer was very much like the first one: they both were large, strong, red-faced men with square heads and with folds of fat at the back of their necks; they both had the same manner and wore the same expressions which since time immemorial all over the world have simplified the work of cartoonists hostile to Germany, and which even in peacetime were responsible for a universal dislike of everything German. The only difference was that the second officer had a mustache, lacked two fingers on his white, puffy left hand, looked a shade more good-natured, and had different shoulder straps. "Probably a lieutenant colonel," the maître d'hôtel thought as with respectful dignity he helped him to a chair, inwardly wishing cancer of the stomach to both the colonel and the lieutenant colonel.

III

The colonel ordered dinner without glancing at the menu, or at the maître d'hôtel; he did it with an air of delivering a speech from the throne. The lieutenant colonel, on the other hand, buried his nose in the menu. Monsieur Albert's trained eye immediately noticed that he was concerned chiefly with the right column of the page.

The lieutenant colonel had arrived in Paris only yesterday from a distant battle front. He had been given his new assignment as a rest after his wound. He had little work, and for two days he had been sight-seeing with the aid of a German guidebook. He had come to the famous restaurant at the invitation of his colleague, but he had not understood clearly whether it was an outright invitation or a Dutch treat. The guidebook described the restaurant as: "Very famous. Prices in keeping." In discussing Paris restaurants in general, the same book offered advice: "The Paris cuisine is considered the best in the world. In the best restaurants the portions are very large. Two or three people should dine together. One portion of soup is sufficient for two; two portions of steak, for three; one portion of anything else, for three. In this way variety can be obtained without overeating. Gourmets seldom dine alone."

But the gourmet with whom he was dining had not suggested that they divide their portions. When among the resounding array of French dishes he found a humble and more modestly priced *Choucroute garnie*, the lieutenant colonel was relieved and with a brisk smile carefully enunciated:—

"Choucroute garnie. ... No wine. ... Some beer. ..."

The boy came in from the coatroom and, almost imperceptibly nodding in the colonel's direction, whispered something in the maître d'hôtel's ear. Monsieur Albert, treading noiselessly on the soft rug, hurriedly approached "Napoleon's table."

"Your car is outside, Votre Excellence. The driver asks whether he should wait," he said in a solemn tone, as if he were imparting a state secret, and glanced angrily at the red-nosed wine waiter who, with an expression of contempt, was bringing on a silver platter the beer for the lieutenant colonel. In the old days this beverage never had been served in the restaurant.

The colonel, keeping his eyes at a seventy-degree angle from the floor, gazed into space and did not answer.

"People call this beer!" having taken one sip the lieutenant colonel said bitterly. For a second his digestive memory brought back a vision of real *Pschorrbräu* with which in Munich he had accompanied the music of the *Niebelungen* and the varied assortment of *Bockwurst, Blutwurst, Rotwurst, Weisswurst, Knackwurst,* and *Leberwurst.* The angle between the colonel's gaze and the floor reduced itself to sixty degrees. Monsieur Albert, waiting for an answer, stood in the same respectfully dignified attitude.

"Tell him to wait!" Monsieur Albert, except for the accent like an echo, hurriedly repeated the order to the boy and glanced at the clock. It was two minutes past eight. With a respectfully dignified smile he looked at the German officers and at the other guests, and turned the knob on the radio. This was another innovation. During all the long years of its existence the restaurant never had had any music. The radio had been installed at the outbreak of the war. In thirty seconds an inhuman voice which seemed to rise out of an abyss on a half-finished sentence began to speak words which did not contain a particle of truth. Smiles instantly disappeared, and all the faces in the room became anxious and taut.

"The bill," the man with the black arm band said abruptly. People at adjoining tables involuntarily glanced in his direction. He finished his coffee, paid the bill, walked out into the coatroom, and, putting his foot on a chair, slipped a metal band around the bottom of his trouser—a procedure which no longer surprised anyone. The boy who enviously was holding his new bicycle noticed that his hands were trembling. Having turned off the light in the coatroom, the boy with obvious admiration switched on his new-type flashlight—one with a blue lens—and opened the door. The gentleman gave him a tip and walked outside.

"We hope you will be with us tomorrow, Monsieur," the boy said, switching off the flashlight (new batteries were difficult to get).

"What? ... Oh, yes. ... Tomorrow," the gentleman with the black arm band answered.

IV

A single green-gray, weather-beaten car stood in front of the entrance. It had a number and the initials "W. M." on it, a red flag with a black swastika, and a solitary headlight which was dimmed, but which still gave sufficient light. Ten feet away the darkness was impenetrable. The gentleman with the black arm band quickly glanced at the car, led his bicycle away from the bright streak on the sidewalk, and rolled down the street at the uncomfortably low speed which was observed by all cyclists at night. Under a lantern on the next corner an old woman, wearing a dress made of a curtain, was digging in a half-empty garbage can. The streets became completely deserted. Contrary to the regulations, some of the city lights were on. For the most part they were in front of buildings decorated with swastika flags, and guarded by helmeted German soldiers who stood like statues hewn out of stone. In this quarter of Paris such buildings were less frequent, but even here they were not uncommon.

The impenetrable, silent, heavy darkness was momentarily rent by a car with a flag which instantly disappeared from view. Nothing else could be seen or heard, except for an occasional lonesome pedestrian whose wooden shoes clattered distinctly and hurriedly on the sidewalk. Suddenly the noiseless darkness was filled with light and the clanging hubbub and uproar of a motorbus filled with young Germans returning from a pleasure and educational tour of the Paris landmarks, from Notre Dame to Montmartre. The bus stopped in front of a small, very ancient church. A bell rang imperiously inside the bus, the laughter ceased instantly, and a domineering, full-blooded voice that sounded as if it had been soaked in beer launched into a long tirade: "This is one of the oldest ..." The church door opened, and outlined against its pale light appeared the bent figure of a priest who, with a nervous gesture, pressed his fingers to his forehead.

"Quare tristis es anima mea? Et quare conturbas me?" the gentleman with the black arm-band thought. "Ages ago in Spain they said a messe pour la mort des ennemis; later Rome discarded it, but it should be revived now, at the end of a thousand-year-old civilization which groundlessly persists in wanting to go down in history as Christian. ..."

"In this church Dante Alighieri, 1265 to 1321, that great poet whose memory is justly treasured by our brave allies, the Italians ..." (there was an outburst of laughter instantly interrupted by the bell, which this time had an angry ring).

"... The finest passage in that book is: 'Moriatur anima mea cum Philistiim.' That is so true, so clear, and so fine. ..."

Almost imperceptibly he increased his speed. About fifty feet ahead two dim lights flickered in the darkness and came to meet him; they were joined by a third light just above them, as two French policemen on bicycles went by slowly, going in the opposite direction. One of them leaned forward and, holding a flashlight in his outstretched hand, looked suspiciously at the gentleman with the arm band. A little further, opposite the house behind which was an alley leading to the next street, only three feet away someone suddenly cursed in German, not angrily, but with a hearty coarseness. A high-pitched female voice repeated the curse in its briefer French form. The gentleman put on the brake and lifted his left hand, in which he held a flashlight. Right in front of the bicycle a helmeted soldier was leading a woman across the street.

"... Non, mais des fois! T'es soûl! Alors quoi! J't'enfoutrai!" the streetwalker was shouting, eager to show her companion that in a conversation of this sort she could hold her own. "Saukerl! Schweinehund!" the soldier growled.

V

At "Napoleon's table" dinner was drawing to a close. It turned out to be an outright invitation and not a Dutch treat; the lieutenant colonel realized it as soon as the colonel, without consulting him, ordered a bottle of champagne. The wine was delicious, and it tasted even better because he knew that he was not drinking a Henckell, but the best French champagne in existence. "He really is not a bad fellow.

... I wonder who is responsible for all the rumors that he is so brutal, and all that sort of thing?" the lieutenant colonel wondered. He also thought about the neat little sum he had saved; considering the price of the *Choucroute*, the beer, and his share of the tip the amount was quite sizable; even considering the price of any dinner in a medium-priced restaurant. He could afford to buy some perfume for his wife: some of the stores still had perfume for sale.

These pleasant reveries were soon dispelled by a less agreeable thought: he would have to reciprocate and ask the colonel out for dinner. But this occurred to him only for a brief moment, and even while he was thinking about it he very well knew that he had no intention of reciprocating. "I could not bring him here. This would be silly and ridiculous—he knows my financial circumstances only too well. To ask him to a cheap restaurant will not do, and, strictly speaking, it would not be reciprocating. Besides, it's definitely bad manners to extend a return invitation immediately. Sometime, when the occasion arises. ..."

Over the champagne the colonel began to talk about his successful career, and about his friends among the influential people, and the lieutenant colonel's cordiality waned. A long time ago they had been stationed in the same small town, but they had not seen each other for eight years; by birth they belonged to different social circles, and they never had been very close. "Perhaps he invited me so that he could tell me how far ahead of me he has progressed in the service? ... But with all of that he is very polite, and quite generous. ..."

At that very moment the colonel was casting his eye over the bill. Having paused for just a fraction of a second over the total, he did not say a word, and added an eight per cent tip (in Berlin he tipped ten per cent, but here his position was an assurance of proper attention). Monsieur Albert thanked him respectfully and thought that, perhaps, cancer of the liver would be even more painful than cancer of the stomach. The colonel looked at his watch and emitted an exclamation: it seemed that a most important personage was expecting him for an informal evening of conversation and bridge.

"He will not sit down at a card table without me. But first I will take you wherever you are going."

"No, no! It's out of your way, and it's not at all necessary." The lieutenant colonel was slightly embarrassed. He had hoped that the colonel would drive him home, because he still was not too familiar with the subways.

"Then allow me at least to take you to the subway station opposite my house. From there you can take a train without having to change. And this will not take me out of my way. We can be there in seven minutes."

"In seven minutes? What precision!"

"I follow the same route every night. If it were not for this miserable bridge I should be going home now. We still have time to finish the bottle."

"Our forefathers always had one before the last one," the lieutenant colonel responded with an old German saying.

VI

In the car the colonel continued to talk about his career and to air his views on army administration. The gratefully polite smile began to disappear from the lieutenant colonel's face. "The usual story: he is a headquarters man, and I am a front line officer. He receives decorations, while I receive wounds. ... I suppose I should be grateful that I only lost two fingers!" (His left wrist began to ache as soon as he remembered it.) "Perhaps there is some truth in what they say about him." The lieutenant colonel's thoughts became less and less pleasant. But he managed to keep up his end of the conversation, for the most part asking questions which gave his companion no opportunity to elaborate on his successes.

When the car presently came to a stop in front of a blue street light, the lieutenant colonel said: "I hope we see each other soon again." He deliberately refrained from being more definite, smiled hospitably, and repeated how much he had enjoyed himself. "A delightful evening. ..." He firmly shook the colonel's hand and stepped out of the car, leaning cautiously against the door in order not to jar his wounded hand.

The car rolled away and left the lieutenant colonel standing in the square. Only a few feet away everything faded into a thick darkness which had a peculiar effect on him, even though only recently he had been at a distant front, in villages which had not known a street light since the beginning of time. The lieutenant colonel remembered that

Paris had been known as the "city of light," and smiled. "As usual we have gone too far: the English have no intention of bombing us here. Probably this is the only safe place left in the world. So safe that it is positively boring. ... That must be the entrance to the subway, but I suppose one cannot smoke down there. I will have just one more smoke—the last one tonight."

Frowning with pain, he took a cigarette case out of his pocket, turned his back to the wind, and, puckering his lips which held the cigarette, tried to light it. A tiny blue dot flashed at the other end of the square. "Thank God! At least one other live human being!" The lieutenant colonel had no lighter—he had to set an example of saving lighting fluid—but he had a system of his own: he lined three matches so that the head of one protruded slightly beyond the others; if the first match went out, the other two had time to catch on. "Here is hoping that the English flyers will not take advantage of my matches, or of that blue light over there. ... Why is he traveling so fast? Is he trying to break his neck?" The blue dot, rushing straight at him, suddenly began to slow down. A quick thought stabbed the lieutenant colonel's mind. "What is this? Who is this man? What does he want? He must be ..."

The air was rent by several shots. The other two matches flared up, illuminating the lower part of a face, the puckered lips, and the graying mustache. A fleeting expression of horror passed over the cyclist's face; he dropped his hand, pressed on the pedals, and instantly was swallowed by the darkness. The lieutenant colonel clamped his teeth on the cigarette, dropped it, took several uncertain steps, swayed, and, striking the light post with his skull, fell heavily, face down, on the pavement.

QUADRATURIN

Sigizmund Krzhizhanovsky (1887–1950)

Translated by Joanne Turnbull

A literary journeyman, editor, librettist, screenwriter, historian and theorist of literature, **Sigizmund Krzhizhanovsky** wrote intellectual short fiction, but he was very rarely published during Soviet times, even though he was not openly anti-communist.

Rediscovered in the late *perestroika* period of the 1980s, Krzhizhanovsky's prose can be considered a buried treasure of the twenties and the thirties, the letter in the bottle which escaped the jaws of history and time.

I

From outside there came a soft knock at the door: once. Pause. And again – a bit louder and bonier: twice.

Sutulin, without rising from his bed, extended – as was his wont – a foot towards the knock, threaded a toe through the door handle, and pulled. The door swung open. On the threshold, head grazing the lintel, stood a tall, grey man the colour of the dusk seeping in at the window.

Before Sutulin could set his feet on the floor the visitor stepped inside, wedged the door quietly back into its frame and, jabbing first one wall, then another, with a briefcase dangling from an apishly long arm, said, 'Yes: a matchbox.'

'What?'

'Your room, I say: it's a matchbox. How many square feet?'

'Eighty-six and a bit.'

'Precisely. May I?'

And before Sutulin could open his mouth, the visitor sat down on the edge of the bed and hurriedly unbuckled his bulging briefcase. Lowering his voice almost to a whisper, he went on, 'I'm here on business. You see, I, that is, we, are conducting, how shall I put it ... well, experiments, I suppose. Under wraps for now. I won't hide the fact: a well-known foreign firm has an interest in our concern. You want the electric-light switch? No, don't bother: I'll only be a minute. So then: we have discovered – this is a secret now – an agent for biggerizing rooms. Well, won't you try it?'

The stranger's hand popped out of the briefcase and proffered Sutulin a narrow dark tube, not unlike a tube of paint, with a tightly screwed cap and a leaden seal. Sutulin fidgeted bewilderedly with the slippery tube and, though it was nearly dark in the room, made out on the label the clearly printed word: **Quadraturin**. When he raised his eyes, they came up against the fixed, unblinking stare of his interlocutor.

'So then, you'll take it? The price? Goodness, it's gratis. Just for advertising. Now if you'll' – the guest began quickly leafing through a sort of ledger he had produced from the same briefcase – 'just sign this book (a short testimonial, so to say). A pencil? Have mine. Where? Here: column III. That's it.'

His ledger clapped shut, the guest straightened up, wheeled round, stepped to the door ... and a minute later Sutulin, having snapped on the light, was considering with puzzledly raised eyebrows the clearly embossed letters: **Quadraturin**.

On closer inspection it turned out that this zinc packet was tightly fitted – as is often done by the makers of patented agents – with a thin transparent paper whose ends were expertly glued together. Sutulin removed the paper sheath from the Quadraturin, unfurled the rolled-up text, which showed through the paper's transparent gloss, and read:

DIRECTIONS

Dissolve 1 teaspoon of the Quadraturin essence in 1 cup of water. Wet a piece of cotton wool or simply a clean rag with the solution; apply this to those of the room's internal walls designated for proliferspansion. This mixture leaves no stains, will not damage wallpaper, and even contributes – incidentally – to the extermination of bedbugs.

Thus far Sutulin had been only puzzled. Now his puzzlement was gradually overtaken by another feeling, strong and disturbing. He stood up and tried to pace from corner to corner, but the corners of this living cage were too close together: a walk amounted to almost nothing but turns, from toe to heel and back again. Sutulin stopped short, sat down and, closing his eyes, gave himself up to thoughts, which began: Why not ...? What if ...? Suppose ...? To his left, not three feet away from his ear, someone was driving an iron spike into the wall. The hammer kept slipping, banging and aiming, it seemed, at Sutulin's head. Rubbing his temples, he opened his eyes: the black tube lay in the middle of the narrow table, which had managed somehow to insinuate itself between the bed, the windowsill and the wall. Sutulin tore away the leaden seal, and the cap span off in a spiral. From out of the round aperture came a bitterish gingery smell. The smell made his nostrils flare pleasantly.

'Hmm ... Let's try it. Although ...'

And, having removed his jacket, the possessor of Quadraturin proceeded to the experiment. Stool up against door, bed into middle of room, table on top of bed. Nudging across the floor a saucer of transparent liquid, its glassy surface gleaming with a slightly yellowish tinge, Sutulin crawled along after it, systematically dipping a handkerchief wound round a pencil into the Quadraturin and daubing the floorboards and patterned wallpaper. The room really was, as that man today had said, a matchbox. But Sutulin worked slowly and carefully, trying not to miss a single corner. This was rather difficult since the liquid really did evaporate in an instant or was absorbed (he couldn't tell which) without leaving even the slightest film; there was only its smell, increasingly pungent and spicy, making his head spin, confounding his fingers and causing his knees, pinned to the floor, to tremble slightly. When he had finished with the floorboards and the bottom of the walls, Sutulin rose to his strangely weak and heavy feet and continued to work standing up. Now and then he had to add a little more of the essence. The tube was gradually emptying. It was already night outside. In the kitchen, to the right, a bolt came crashing down. The apartment was readying for bed. Trying not to make any noise, the experimenter, clutching the last of the essence, climbed up onto the bed and from the bed up onto the tottering table: only the ceiling remained to be quadraturinized. But just then someone banged on the wall with his fist, 'What's going on? People are trying to sleep, but he's ...'

Turning round at the sound, Sutulin fumbled: the slippery tube spurted out of his hand and landed on the floor. Balancing carefully, Sutulin got down with his already drying brush, but it was too late. The tube was empty, and the rapidly fading spot around it smelled stupefyingly sweet. Grasping at the wall in his exhaustion (to fresh sounds of discontent from the left), he summoned his last bit of strength, put the furniture back where it belonged and, without undressing, fell into bed. A black sleep instantly descended on him from above: both tube and man were empty.

II

Two voices began in a whisper. Then by degrees of sonority – from piano to mf, from mf to fff – they cut into Sutulin's sleep.

'Outrageous. I don't want any new tenants popping out from under that skirt of yours ... Put up with all that racket?!'

'Can't just dump it in the garbage ...'

'I don't want to hear about it. You were told: no dogs, no cats, no children ...' at which point there ensued such fff that Sutulin was ripped once and for all from his sleep; unable to part eyelids stitched together with exhaustion, he reached – as was his wont – for the edge of the table on which stood the clock. Then it began. His hand groped for a long time, grappling air: there was no clock and no table. Sutulin opened his eyes at once. In an instant he was sitting up, looking dazedly round the room. The table that usually stood right here, at the head of the bed, had moved off into the middle of a faintly familiar, large but ungainly room.

Everything was the same: the skimpy, threadbare rug that had trailed after the table somewhere up ahead of him, and the photographs, and the stool, and the yellow patterns on the wallpaper. But they were all strangely spread out inside the expanded room cube.

'Quadraturin,' thought Sutulin, 'is terrific!'

And he immediately set about rearranging the furniture to fit the new space. But nothing worked: the abbreviated rug, when moved back beside the bed, exposed worn, bare floorboards; the table and the stool, pushed by habit against the head of the bed, had disencumbered an empty corner latticed with cobwebs and littered with shreds and tatters, once artfully masked by the corner's own crowdedness and the shadow of the table. With a triumphant, but slightly frightened smile, Sutulin went all round his new, practically squared square, scrutinizing every detail. He noted with displeasure that the room had grown more in some places than in others: an external corner, the angle of which was now obtuse, had made the wall askew; Quadraturin, apparently, did not work as well on internal corners; carefully as Sutulin had applied the essence, the experiment had produced somewhat uneven results.

The apartment was beginning to stir. Out in the corridor, occupants shuffled to and fro. The bathroom door kept banging. Sutulin walked up to the threshold and turned the key to the right. Then, hands clasped behind his back, he tried pacing from corner to corner: it worked. Sutulin laughed with joy. How about that! At last! But then he thought: they may hear my footsteps – through the walls – on the right, on the left, at the back. For a minute he stood stock-still. Then he quickly bent down – his temples had suddenly begun to ache with yesterday's sharp thin pain – and, having removed his boots, gave himself up to the pleasure of a stroll, moving soundlessly about in only his socks.

'May I come in?'

The voice of the proprietress. He was on the point of going to the door and unlocking it when he suddenly remembered: he mustn't. 'I'm getting dressed. Wait a minute. I'll be right out.'

'It's all very well, but it complicates things. Say I lock the door and take the key with me. What about the keyhole? And then there's the window: I'll have to get curtains. Today.' The pain in his temples had become thinner and more nagging. Sutulin gathered up his papers in haste. It was time to go to the office. He dressed. Pushed the pain under his cap. And listened at the door: no one there. He quickly opened it. Quickly slipped out. Quickly turned the key. Now.

Waiting patiently in the entrance hall was the proprietress.

'I wanted to talk to you about that girl, what's her name. Can you believe it, she's submitted an application to the House Committee saying she's …'

'I've heard. Go on.'

'It's nothing to you. No one's going to take your eighty-six square feet away. But put yourself in my …'

'I'm in a hurry,' he nodded his cap, and flew down the stairs.

III

On his way home from the office, Sutulin paused in front of the window of a furniture dealer: the long curve of a couch, a round extendable table ... it would be nice – but how could he carry them in past the eyes and the questions? They would guess, they couldn't help but guess ...

He had to limit himself to the purchase of a yard of canary-yellow material (he did, after all, need a curtain). He didn't stop by the café: he had no appetite. He needed to get home – it would be easier there: he could reflect, look round and make adjustments at leisure. Having unlocked the door to his room, Sutulin gazed about to see if anyone was looking: they weren't. He walked in. Then he switched on the light and stood there for a long time, his arms spread flat against the wall, his heart beating wildly: *this he had not expected* – not at all.

The Quadraturin was *still* working. During the eight or nine hours Sutulin had been out, it had pushed the walls at least another seven feet apart; the floorboards, stretched by invisible rods, rang out at his first step – like organ pipes. The entire room, distended and monstrously misshapen, was beginning to frighten and torment him. Without taking off his coat, Sutulin sat down on the stool and surveyed his spacious and at the same time oppressive coffin-shaped living box, trying to understand what had caused this unexpected effect. Then he remembered: he hadn't done the ceiling – the essence had run out. His living box was spreading only sideways, without rising even an inch upwards.

'Stop. I have to stop this quadraturinizing thing. Or I'll ...' He pressed his palms to his temples and listened: the corrosive pain, lodged under his skull since morning, was still drilling away. Though the windows in the house opposite were dark, Sutulin took cover behind the yellow length of curtain. His head would not stop aching. He quietly undressed, snapped out the light and got into bed. At first he slept, then he was awoken by a feeling of awkwardness. Wrapping the covers more tightly about him, Sutulin again dropped off, and once more an unpleasant sense of mooringlessness interfered with his sleep. He raised himself up on one palm and felt all around him with his free hand: the wall was gone. He struck a match. Um hmm: he blew out the flame and hugged his knees till his elbows cracked. 'It's growing, damn it, it's still growing.' Clenching his teeth, Sutulin crawled out of bed and, trying not to make any noise, gently edged first the front legs, then the back legs of the bed toward the receding wall. He felt a little shivery. Without turning the light on again, he went to look for his coat on that nail in the corner so as to wrap himself up more warmly. But there was no hook on the wall where it had been yesterday, and he had to feel around for several seconds before his hands chanced upon fur. Twice more during a night that was long and nagging as the pain in his temples, Sutulin pressed his head and knees to the wall as he was falling asleep and, when he awoke, fiddled about with the legs of the bed again. In doing this – mechanically, meekly, lifelessly – he tried, though it was still dark outside, not to open his eyes: it was better that way.

IV

Towards dusk the next evening, having served out his day, Sutulin was approaching the door to his room: he did not quicken his step and, upon entering, felt neither consternation nor horror. When the dim, sixteen candlepower bulb lit up somewhere in the distance beneath the long low vault, its yellow rays struggling to reach the dark, ever-receding corners of the vast and dead, yet empty barrack, which only recently, before Quadraturin, had been a cramped but cozy, warm and lived-in cubbyhole, he walked resignedly towards the yellow square of the window, now diminished by perspective; he tried to count his steps. From there, from a bed squeezed pitifully and fearfully in the corner by the window, he stared dully and wearily through deep-boring pain at the swaying shadows nestled against the floorboards, and at the smooth low overhang of the ceiling. 'So, something forces its way out of a tube, and can't stop squaring: a square squared, a square of squares squared. I've got to think faster than it: if I don't outthink it, it will outgrow me and ...' And suddenly someone was hammering on the door, 'Citizen Sutulin, are you in there?'

From the same faraway place came the muffled and barely audible voice of the proprietress, 'He's in there. Must be asleep.'

Sutulin broke into a sweat: 'What if I don't get there in time, and they go ahead and ...' And, trying not to make a sound (let them think he was asleep), he slowly made his way through the darkness to the door. There.

'Who is it?'

'Oh, open up! Why's the door locked? Re-measuring Commission. We'll remeasure and leave.'

Sutulin stood with his ear pressed to the door. Through the thin panel he could hear the clump of heavy boots. Figures were being mentioned, and room numbers.

'This room next. Open up!'

With one hand Sutulin gripped the knob of the electric-light switch and tried to twist it, as one might twist the head of a bird: the switch spattered light, then crackled, spun feebly round and drooped down. Again someone hammered on the door, 'Well!'

Sutulin turned the key to the left. A broad black shape squeezed itself into the doorway.

'Turn on the light.'

'It's burned out.'

Clutching at the door handle with his left hand, and the bundle of wire with his right, he tried to hide the extended space from view. The black mass took a step back.

'Who's got a match? Give me that box. We'll have a look anyway. Do things right.'

Suddenly the proprietress began whining, 'Oh, what is there to lock at? Eighty-six square feet for the eighty-sixth time. Measuring the room won't make it any bigger. He's a quiet man, home from a long day at the office – and you won't let him rest: have to measure and remeasure. Whereas other people, who have no right to the space, but ...'

'Ain't that the truth,' the black mass muttered and, rocking from boot to boot, gently and even almost affectionately drew the door to the light. Sutulin was left alone on wobbling, cottony legs in the middle of the four-cornered, inexorably growing and proliferating darkness.

V

He waited until their steps had died away, then quickly dressed and went out. They'd be back, to remeasure or check they hadn't undermeasured or whatever. He could finish thinking better here – from crossroad to crossroad. Towards night a wind came up: it rattled the bare frozen branches on the trees, shook the shadows loose, droned in the wires and beat against walls, as if trying to knock them down.

Hiding the needle-like pain in his temples from the wind's buffets, Sutulin went on, now diving into the shadows, now plunging into the lamplight. Suddenly, through the wind's rough thrusts, something softly and tenderly brushed against his elbow. He turned round. Beneath feathers batting against a black brim, a familiar face with provocatively half-closed eyes. And barely audible through the moaning air: 'You know you know me. And you look right past me. You ought to bow. That's it.'

Her slight figure, tossed back by the wind, perched on tenacious stiletto heels, was all insubordination and readiness for battle.

Sutulin tipped his cap. 'But you were supposed to be going away. And you're still here? Then something must have prevented ...'

'That's right – this.'

And he felt a chamois finger touch his chest then dart back into the muff. He sought out the narrow pupils of her eyes beneath the dancing black feathers, and it seemed that one more look, one more touch, one more shock to his hot temples, and it would all come unthought, undone and fall away. Meanwhile she, her face nearing his, said, 'Let's go to your place. Like last time. Remember?'

With that, everything stopped.

'That's impossible.'

She sought out the arm that had been pulled back and clung to it with tenacious chamois fingers.

'My place ... isn't fit,' he looked away, having again withdrawn both his arms and the pupils of his eyes.

'You mean to say it's cramped. My God, how silly you are. The more cramped it is ...' The wind tore away the end of her phrase. Sutulin did not reply. 'Or, perhaps you don't ...'

When he reached the turning, he looked back: the woman was still standing there, pressing her muff to her bosom, like a shield; her narrow shoulders were shivering with cold; the wind cynically flicked her skirt and lifted up the lappets of her coat.

'Tomorrow. Everything tomorrow. But now ...' And, quickening his pace, Sutulin turned resolutely back.

'Right now: while everyone's asleep. Collect my things (only the necessaries) and go. Run away. Leave the door wide open: let *them*. Why should I be the only one? Why not let *them*?'

The apartment was indeed sleepy and dark. Sutulin walked down the corridor, straight and to the right, opened the door with resolve and, as always, wanted to turn the light switch, but it spun feebly in his fingers, reminding him that the circuit had been broken. This was an annoying obstacle. But it couldn't be helped. Sutulin rummaged in his pockets and found a box of matches: it was almost empty. Good for three or four flares – that's all. He would have to husband both light and time. When he reached the coat pegs, he struck the first match: light crept in yellow radiuses through the black air. Sutulin purposely, overcoming temptation, concentrated on the illuminated scrap of wall and the coats and jackets hanging from hooks. He knew that there, behind his back, the dead, quadraturinized space with its black corners was still spreading. He knew and did not look round. The match smouldered in his left hand, his right pulled things off hooks and flung them on the floor. He needed another flare; looking at the floor, he started towards the corner – if it was still a corner and if it was still there – where, by his calculations, the bed should have fetched up, but he accidentally held the flame under his breath – and again the black wilderness closed in. One last match remained: he struck it over and over: it would not light. One more time – and its crackling head fell off and slipped through his fingers. Then, having turned around, afraid to go any further into the depths, the man started back towards the bundle he had abandoned under the hooks. But he had made the turn, apparently, inexactly. He walked – heel to toe, heel to toe – holding his fingers out in front of him, and found nothing: neither the bundle, nor the hooks, nor even the walls. 'I'll get there in the end. I must get there.' His body was sticky with cold and sweat. His legs wobbled oddly. The man squatted down, palms on the floorboards: 'I shouldn't have come back. Now here I am alone, nowhere to turn.' And suddenly it struck him: 'I'm waiting here, but it's growing, I'm waiting, but it's ...'

In their sleep and in their fear, the occupants of the quadratrures adjacent to citizen Sutulin's eighty-six square feet couldn't make head or tail of the timbre and intonation of the cry that woke them in the middle of the night and compelled them to rush to the threshold of the Sutulin cell: for a man who is lost and dying in the wilderness to cry out is both futile and belated: but if even so – against all sense – he does cry out, then, most likely, *thus*.

THE STEEL WINDPIPE
Mikhail Bulgakov (1891–1940)
Translated by Michael Glenny

The second most famous doctor of Russian literature after Chekhov, **Mikhail Bulgakov** worked as a military physician on the front line during the First World War, became a drug addict, fought for the Whites in the Civil war, caught severe typhus and therefore was not able to leave the country with the retreating White forces.

In the twenties Bulgakov reflected on the just ended bloody conflict in prose and drama, attracting attention and acknowledgement as well as the eerie and unstable patronage of Stalin himself.

In the thirties Bulgakov wrote prose which later brought him world fame (*The Master and Margarita*), and worked as a theater director, torn between sharp criticism by the communist bureaucracy and rare luck, and died in 1940.

So I was alone, surrounded by November gloom and whirling snow; the house was smothered in it and there was a moaning in the chimneys. I had spent all twenty-four years of my life in a huge city and thought that blizzards only howled in novels. It appeared that they howled in real life. The evenings here are unusually long, and I fell to daydreaming, staring at the reflection on the window of the lamp with its dark green shade. I dreamed of the nearest town, thirty-two miles away. I longed to leave my country clinic and go there. They had electricity, and there were four doctors whom I could consult. At all events it would be less frightening than this place. But there was no chance of running away, and at times I realised that it would be cowardly. It was for precisely this, after all, that I had been studying medicine.

'Yes, but suppose they bring me a woman in labour and there are complications? Or, say, a patient with a strangulated hernia? What shall I do then? Kindly tell me that. Forty-eight days ago I qualified "with distinction"; but distinction is one thing and hernia is another.

Once I watched a professor operating on a strangulated hernia. He did it, while I sat in the amphitheatre. And I only just managed to survive ...'

More than once I broke out in a cold sweat down my spine at the thought of hernia. Every evening, as I drank my tea, I would sit in the same attitude: by my left hand lay all the manuals on obstetrical surgery, on top of them the small edition of Döderlein. To my right were ten different illustrated volumes on operative surgery. I groaned, smoked and drank cold tea without milk.

Once I fell asleep. I remember that night perfectly – it was 29 November, and I was woken by someone banging on the door. Five minutes later I was pulling on my trousers, my eyes glued imploringly to those sacred books on operative surgery. I could hear the creaking of sleigh-runners in the yard – my ears had become unusually sensitive. The case turned out to be, if anything, even more terrifying than a hernia or a transverse foetus. At eleven o'clock that night a little girl was brought to the Muryovo hospital. The nurse said tonelessly to me:

'The little girl's weak, she's dying ... Would you come over to the hospital, please, doctor ...'

I remember crossing the yard towards the hospital porch, mesmerised by the flickering light of a kerosene lamp. The lights were on in the surgery, and all my assistants were waiting for me, already dressed in their overalls: the *feldsher* Demyan Lukich, young but very capable, and two experienced midwives, Anna Nikolaevna and Pelagea Ivanovna. Only twenty-four years old, having qualified a mere two months ago, I had been placed in charge of the Muryovo hospital.

The *feldsher* solemnly flung open the door and the mother came in – or rather she seemed to fly in, slithering on her ice-covered felt boots, unmelted snow still on her shawl. In her arms she carried a bundle, from which came a steady hissing, whistling sound. The mother's face was contorted with noiseless weeping. When she had thrown off her sheepskin coat and shawl and unwrapped the bundle, I saw a little girl of about three years old. For a while the sight of her made me forget operative surgery, my loneliness, the load of useless knowledge acquired at university: it was all completely effaced by the beauty of this baby girl. What can I liken her to? You only see children like that on chocolate boxes – hair curling naturally into big ringlets the colour of ripe rye, enormous dark blue eyes, doll-like cheeks. They used to draw angels like that. But in the depths of her eyes was a strange cloudiness and I recognised it as terror – the child could not breathe. 'She'll be dead in an hour,' I thought with absolute certainty, feeling a sharp twinge of pity for the child.

Her throat was contracting into hollows with each breath, her veins were swollen and her face was turning from pink to a pale lilac. I immediately realised what this colouring meant. I made my first diagnosis, which was not only correct but, more important, was given at the same moment as the midwives' with all their experience: 'The little girl has diphtherial croup. Her throat is already choked with membrane and soon it will be blocked completely.'

'How long has she been ill?' I asked, breaking the tense silence of my assistants.

'Five days now,' the mother answered, staring hard at me with dry eyes.

'Diphtheria,' I said to *the feldsher* through clenched teeth, and turned to the mother:

'Why have you left it so long?'

At that moment I heard a tearful voice behind me:

'Five days, sir, five days!'

I turned round and saw that a round-faced old woman had silently come in. 'I wish these old women didn't exist,' I thought to myself. With an aching presentiment of trouble I said:

'Quiet, woman, you're only in the way,' and repeated to the mother: 'Why have you left it so long? Five days? Hmm?'

Suddenly with an automatic movement the mother handed the little girl to the grandmother and sank to her knees in front of me.

'Give her some medicine,' she said and banged her forehead on the floor. 'I'll kill myself if she dies.'

'Get up at once,' I replied, 'or I won't even talk to you.'

The mother stood up quickly with a rustle of her wide skirt, took the baby from the grandmother and started rocking it. The old woman turned to the doorpost and began praying, while the little girl continued to breathe with a snake-like hiss. *The feldsher* said:

'That's what they're all like. These people!' And he gave a twitch of his moustache.

'Does that mean she's going to die?' the mother asked, staring at me with what looked like black fury.

'Yes, she'll die,' I said quietly and firmly.

The grandmother picked up the hem of her skirt and wiped her eyes. The mother shouted in an ugly voice:

'Give her something! Help her! Give her some medicine!'

I could see what was in store for me and remained firm.

'What medicine can I give her? Go on, you tell me. The little girl is suffocating, her throat is already blocked up. For five days you kept her ten miles away from me. Now what do you want me to do?'

'You're the one who's supposed to know,' the old woman whined by my left shoulder in an affected voice which made me immediately detest her.

'Shut up!' I said to her. I turned to the *feldsher* and ordered the little girl to be taken away. The mother handed her to the midwife and the child started to struggle, evidently trying to cry, but her voice could no longer make itself heard. The mother made a protective move towards her, but we kept her away and I managed to look into the little girl's throat by the light of the pressure-lamp. I had never seen diphtheria before except for mild, forgettable cases. Her throat was full of ragged, pulsating, white substance. The little girl suddenly breathed out and spat in my face, but I was so absorbed that I did not flinch.

'Well now,' I said, astonished at my own calm. 'This is the situation: it's late, and the little girl is dying. Nothing will help her except one thing – an operation.'

I was appalled, wondering why I had said this, but I could not help saying it. The thought flashed through my mind: 'What if she agrees to it?'

'How do you mean?' the mother asked.

'I'll have to cut open her throat near the bottom of her neck and put in a silver pipe so that she can breathe, and then maybe we can save her,' I explained.

The mother looked at me as if I was mad and shielded the little girl from me with her arms, while the old woman started muttering again:

'The idea! Don't you let them cut her open! What – cut her throat?'

'Go away, old woman,' I said to her with hatred. 'Inject the camphor!' I ordered the *feldsher*.

The mother refused to hand over the little girl when she saw the syringe, but we explained to her that there was nothing terrible about it.

'Perhaps that will cure her?' she asked.

'No, it won't cure her at all.'

Then the mother burst into tears.

'Stop it,' I said. I took out my watch, and added: 'I'm giving you five minutes to think it over. If you don't agree in five minutes, I shall refuse to do it.'

'I don't agree!' the mother said sharply.

'No, we won't agree to it,' the grandmother put in.

'It's up to you,' I said in a hollow voice, and thought: 'Well, that's that. It makes it easier for me. I've said my piece and given them a chance. Look how dumbfounded the midwives are. They've refused and I'm saved.' No sooner had I thought this than some other being spoke for me in a voice that was not mine:

'Look, have you gone mad? What do you mean by not agreeing? You're condemning the baby to death. You must consent. Have you no pity?'

'No!' the mother shouted once more.

I thought to myself: 'What am I doing? I shall only kill the child.' But I said:

'Come on, come on – you've got to agree! You must! Look, her nails are already turning blue.'

'No, no!'

'All right, take them to the ward. Let them sit there.'

They were led away down the half-lit passage. I could hear the weeping of the women and the hissing of the little girl. The *feldsher* returned almost at once and said:

'They've agreed!'

I felt my blood run cold, but I said in a clear voice:

'Sterilise a scalpel, scissors, hooks and a probe at once.'

A minute later I was running across the yard, through a swirling, blinding snowstorm. I rushed to my room and, counting the minutes, grabbed a book, leafed through it and found an illustration of a tracheotomy. Everything about it was clear and simple: the throat was laid open and the knife plunged into the windpipe. I started reading the text, but could take none of it in – the words seemed to jump before my eyes. I had never seen a tracheotomy performed. 'Ah well, it's a bit late now,' I said to myself, and looked miserably at the green lamp and the clear illustration. Feeling that I had suddenly been burdened with a most fearful and difficult task, I went back to the hospital, oblivious of the snowstorm.

In the surgery a dim figure in full skirts clung to me and a voice whined:

'Oh, sir, how can you cut a little girl's throat? How can you? She's agreed to it because she's stupid. But you haven't got my permission – no you haven't. I agree to giving her medicine, but I shan't allow her throat to be cut.'

'Get this woman out!' I shouted, and added vehemently: 'You're the stupid one! Yes, you are. And she's the clever one. Anyway, nobody asked you! Get her out of here!'

A midwife took a firm hold of the old woman and pushed her out of the room.

'Ready!' the *feldsher* said suddenly.

We went into the small operating theatre; the shiny instruments, blinding lamplight and oilcloth seemed to belong to another world ... for the last time I went out to the mother, and the little girl could scarcely be torn from her arms. She just said in a hoarse voice: 'My husband's away in town. When he comes back and finds out what I've done, he'll kill me!'

'Yes, he'll kill her,' the old woman echoed, looking at me in horror.

'Don't let them into the operating theatre!' I ordered.

So we were left in the operating theatre, my assistants, myself, and Lidka, the little girl. She sat naked and pathetic on the table and wept soundlessly. They laid her on the table, strapped her down, washed her throat and painted it with iodine. I picked up the scalpel, still wondering what on earth I was doing. It was very quiet. With the scalpel I made a vertical incision down the swollen white throat. Not one drop of blood emerged. Again I drew the knife along the white strip which protruded between the slit skin. Again not a trace of blood. Slowly, trying to remember the illustrations in my textbooks, I started to part the delicate tissues with the blunt probe. At once dark blood gushed out from the lower end of the wound, flooding it instantly and pouring down her neck. The *feldsher* started to staunch it with swabs but could not stop the flow. Calling to mind everything I had seen at university, I set about clamping the edges of the wound with forceps, but this did no good either.

I went cold and my forehead broke out in a sweat. I bitterly regretted having studied medicine and having landed myself in this wilderness. In angry desperation I jabbed the forceps haphazardly into the region of the wound, snapped them shut and the flow of blood stopped immediately. We swabbed the wound with pieces of gauze; now it faced me clean and absolutely incomprehensible. There was no windpipe anywhere to be seen. This wound of mine was quite unlike any illustration. I spent the next two or three minutes aimlessly poking about in the wound, first with the scalpel and then with the probe, searching for the windpipe. After two minutes of this, I despaired of finding it. 'This is the end,' I thought. 'Why did I ever do this? I needn't have offered to do the operation, and Lidka could have died quietly in the ward. As it is she will die with her throat slit open and I can never prove that she would have died anyway, that I couldn't have made it any worse …' The midwife wiped my brow in silence. 'I ought to put down my scalpel and say: I don't know what to do next.' As I thought this I pictured the mother's eyes. I picked up the knife again and made a deep, undirected slash into Lidka's neck. The tissues parted and to my surprise the windpipe appeared before me.

'Hooks!' I croaked hoarsely.

The *feldsher* handed them to me. I pierced each side with a hook and handed one of them to him. Now I could see one thing only: the greyish ringlets of the windpipe. I thrust the sharp knife into it – and froze in horror. The windpipe was coming out of the incision and the *feldsher* appeared to have taken leave of his wits: he was tearing it out. Behind me the two midwives gasped. I looked up and saw what was the matter: the *feldsher* had fainted from the oppressive heat and, still holding the hook, was tearing at the windpipe. 'It's fate,' I thought, 'everything's against me. We've certainly murdered Lidka now.' And I added grimly to myself: 'As soon as I get back to my room, I'll shoot myself.' Then the older midwife, who was evidently very experienced, pounced on the *feldsher* and tore the hook out of his hand, saying through her clenched teeth:

'Go on, doctor …'

The *feldsher* collapsed to the floor with a crash but we did not turn to look at him. I plunged the scalpel into the trachea and then inserted a silver tube. It slid in easily but Lidka remained motionless. The air did not flow into her windpipe as it should have done. I sighed deeply and stopped: I had done all I could. I felt like begging someone's forgiveness for having been so thoughtless as to study medicine. Silence reigned. I could see Lidka turning blue. I was just about to give up and weep, when the child suddenly gave a violent convulsion, expelled a fountain of disgusting clotted matter through the tube, and the air whistled into her windpipe. As she started to breathe, the little girl began to howl. That instant *the feldsher* got to his feet, pale and sweaty, looked at her throat in stupefied horror and helped me to sew it up.

Dazed, my vision blurred by a film of sweat, I saw the happy faces of the midwives and one of them said to me:

'You did the operation brilliantly, doctor.'

I thought she was making fun of me and glowered at her. Then the doors were opened and a gust of fresh air blew in. Lidka was carried out wrapped in a sheet and at once the mother appeared in the doorway. Her eyes had the look of a wild beast. She asked me:

'Well?'

When I heard the sound of her voice, I felt a cold sweat run down my back as I realised what it would have been like if Lidka had died on the table. But I answered her in a very calm voice:

'Don't worry, she's alive. And she'll stay alive, I hope. Only she won't be able to talk until we take the pipe out, so don't let that upset you.'

Just then the grandmother seemed to materialise from nowhere and crossed herself, bowing to the doorhandle, to me, and to the ceiling. This time I did not lose my temper with her, I turned away and ordered Lidka to be given a camphor injection and for the staff to take turns at watching her. Then I went across the yard to my quarters. I remember the green lamp burning in my study, Döderlein lying there and books scattered everywhere. I walked over to the couch fully dressed, lay down and was immediately lost to the world in a dreamless sleep.

A month passed, then another. I grew more experienced and some of the things I saw were rather more frightening than Lidka's throat, which passed out of my mind. Snow lay all around, and the size of my practice grew daily. Early in the new year, a woman came to my surgery holding by the hand a little girl wrapped in so many layers that she looked as round as a little barrel. The woman's eyes were shining. I took a good look and recognised them.

'Ah, Lidka! How are things?'

'Everything's fine.'

The mother unwound the scarves from Lidka's neck. Though she was shy and resisted I managed to raise her chin and took a look. Her pink neck was marked with a brown vertical scar crossed by two fine stitch marks.

'All's well,' I said. 'You needn't come any more.'

'Thank you, doctor, thank you,' the mother said, and turned to Lidka: 'Say thank you to the gentleman!'

But Lidka had no wish to speak to me.

I never saw her again. Gradually I forgot about her. Meanwhile my practice still grew. The day came when I had a hundred and ten patients. We began at nine in the morning and finished at eight in the evening. Reeling with fatigue, I was taking off my overall when the senior midwife said to me:

'It's the tracheotomy that has brought you all these patients. Do you know what they're saying in the villages? The story goes that when Lidka was ill a steel throat was put into her instead of her own and then sewn up. People go to her village especially to look at her. There's fame for you, doctor. Congratulations.'

'So they think she's living with a steel one now, do they?' I enquired.

'That's right. But you were wonderful, doctor. You did it so coolly, it was marvellous to watch.'

'Hm, well, I never allow myself to worry, you know,' I said, not knowing why. I was too tired even to feel ashamed, so I just looked away. I said goodnight and went home. Snow was falling in large flakes, covering everything, the lantern was lit and my house looked silent, solitary and imposing. As I walked I had only one desire – sleep.

KOZLOVA

Leonid Dobychin (1894–1936)

Translated by Richard C. Borden
with Natalia Belova

He left no writer's archive, no grave or place of death can be found, there is no common understanding of which literature circle or movement he belonged to and if he belonged to any at all – **Leonid Dobychin** is a figure of absence, the man lost in the blurred prelude of the Great Terror.

The archeologist of ordinary soviet life, Dobychin was severely criticised in the Leningrad Writer's Union assembly for the anti-Soviet attitude of his novel *The city N*. Next day Dobychin left his house, sent a farewell telegram to Korney Chukovsky, and disappeared forever.

I

Electricity burned in the three church chandeliers. Forty-eight Soviet office workers were singing in the choir. The newly arrived preacher prophesied that soon God would rise again and his enemies would be scattered.

Kozlova kissed the icon and, rubbing the oil on her forehead, jostled her way through to the exit. She barely squeezed her way across the square: they were setting off rockets, shoving one another, yelling something, burning a cardboard God the Father with his head in a triangle, music was playing "The International."

"Scoundrels," whispered Kozlova, "persecutors…" Snow crunched underfoot. The places oiled by sledge runners shone greasily. Over the Karl Liebknecht and Rosa Luxemburg School stood a little greenish moon. Kozlova sighed: here Monsieur Poincaré had taught French.

She slowed. Pleasant pictures of friendship with Monsieur arose in memory.

Here is—tea.

Monsieur is telling about Our Lady of Lourdes. Avdotya opens the door and spies. Kozlova points to her with her eyes. "Affable woman," says Monsieur. Then he takes up his hat, Kozlova rises, and they are reflected in the mirror: he—tidy, gray, taking his leave; she—erect, wearing a long dress, fingers of the left hand in fingers of the right, a refined nose slightly aslant, on tight lips, an old-fashioned smile. "Do come again, Monsieur …"

And here they are—at the cinematograph. A violin is playing. Monsieur is leaving tomorrow. Leaves fall slowly from a slender little tree in a green tub. "How sad, Monsieur …" A maiden in a red knit jacket draws back the curtain and admits them. Along the sides of the canvas hang Lenin and Trotsky … A comical mother-in-law smashes crockery and breaks furniture, Swiss lakes show off their beauty, and six portions of a sumptuous drama are glimpsed fleetingly: Clotilda poisoned herself, Janna threw herself from a window, and Charles slowly sailed away on the steamship *Republic*, and it begins to seem to him that everything that had happened was but a dream.

"And so too will you, Monsieur, forget us, like a dream."

"Oh, Mademoiselle!"

The return voyage is replete with effusions. In beautiful France Monsieur will think of her. He will keep up with politics.

"But whomsoever could one call the Sibyl of our times, if not Madame de Thèbes," he will write, when something of the sort could be expected …

II

Kozlova sat through her evenings on the stove bench, darning linen or reading the supplement to *The Cornfield*. Tuesday was women's day: she would go with Avdotya to the baths, where children bawled, washbasins rattled, fat-paunched peasant women with their hair let down, steaming, lashed themselves with birch twigs. On Sunday they'd each take a basket and set off for the market. "Citizen, dear citizen," the market women pressed, thrusting themselves out of the stalls. "Lady dear!" or "Little miss!"

Sometimes Suslova would come over, and they'd drink tea for a long time: the hostess—decorous, with a courteous smile; the guest—disheveled, fat, with elbows on the table and noisy sighs. They'd talk of the difficult life and of olden times. Avdotya would listen, standing in the doorway.

"In Petersburg I saw someone," the round-cheeked Suslova would relate, staring pensively at the teacups (one had on it the Winter Palace, the other, the Admiralty). "Don't know, maybe the Empress herself. I'm walking past the palace, suddenly a carriage drives up, out jumps a lady and flies up the porch."

"Perhaps the housekeeper with the shopping," Kozlova would answer ...

Winter passed. On the first of May, Kozlova laundered two jackets and a half-dozen shawls: let them choke on that. Through the open windows flew the sounds of orchestras ... The icon of Saint Kuksha had been brought from the monastery. They went to meet it. Returned agitated.

"Scoundrels, persecutors ..."

"Good Lord, when will we be spared them? ... Does Moussiour not write?"

Later the moon rose, and their spirits eased ... A peal was rung in the cathedral. A waltz played in "Red October" Park. They encountered Demeshchenko, Garashchenko, and Kalegaeva, pensive, with bird cherry twigs.

They stopped above the river and looked awhile at the moon's stripe and a boat with a balalaika.

"Venezia," whispered Kozlova.

"*Venezia e Napoli*," Suslova answered. Falling silent for a while, softly and dreamily she said, "When the cooperative store was on fire, the perfumes began to burn, and it smelled so good ..."

Toward morning someone coughed by the bed. Kozlova turned and saw Saint Kuksha, wearing a dark blue ecclesiastical stole, as on the icon. He handed her a charter, and she read what had been written there: "But whomsoever could one call the Sibyl of our times, if not Madame de Thèbcs."

She awoke agitated and left a bit earlier in order to stop by the cathedral before going to the office. The door was locked. Kozlova jogged the gate and sat down to wait in the garden.

A column with a transfiguration and a green dome stood over the maples. Loose flesh-colored clouds were melting away, and a blue glimmered through them in places. A door creaked, the bishop came out of the lodge—bareheaded, with a bucket of slops. He stood awhile, counting the strokes of the clock on the watchtower, and turned over his bucket beneath the column with the transfiguration.

"Won't be tormented long," thought Kozlova joyfully, following him with her eyes.

She ate dinner hastily—wanted to see Suslova, but, rising from the table, grew languid and barely made it to bed. Upon awaking she felt too lazy to go to Suslova's. Dispatched Avdotya to meet the cow and went into the vegetable garden. The sun was setting, and the sunset was unpretentious: one little stripe reddish and one greenish. Kozlova was a lover of watering. "When you're watering," she would say, "the soul rests and sinks into a sweet state."

She was pouring the twelfth watering can and the moon was glittering in the rapidly disappearing little puddles. An orchestra began to thunder, and Kozlova rushed to the gates.

Sneezed from the dust. Smoky fires fluttered on torches and reflected in the copper trumpets. Curzon dangled on the gallows. Light flitted across the marchers' faces.

"Hut, two! Left! Long live the Communist Party! Hurrah!"

Gaping, Suslova was marching.

Avdotya came running from out of the darkness. "England's joined the war."

They illuminated the little lights before the icon cases and, by the brightness of two lamps, drank real tea. It reeked of kerosene and soot.

With a radiant face, Kozlova got a little jar of raspberries from the medicine cabinet. "Easter," Avdotya delighted. That fool Suslova was roundly abused.

III

They were sitting doing overtime. Flies were biting. A big bell droned, and, tinkling, the windowpanes joined in.

Demeshchenko had bent over the table and was scratching out "Comrade Lenin."

Garashchenko and Kalegaeva, lounging on chairs, were gnawing sunflower seeds and gawking at the new one.

"Tomorrow's John the Warrior," said the new one, a fussy old lady with red cheeks. "Whenever you quarrel with someone, pray to John the Warrior. I always do, and, you know, she was taken away and sentenced to three years."

"A good woman," thought Kozlova, "religious ... Sutyrkina, I think."

She passed her papers and inkpot to Sutyrkina. "Where do you live?"

They left together: Kozlova—staid, wearing a dark blue gauze scarf with indistinct yellow circles; Sutyrkina—fidgety, wearing an old straw hat with feathers.

By gates cavaliers were putting on airs before maidens. Little boys were bawling, "Boldly to battle we shall go." The dust raised during the day was settling. The debris of trees planted on "Tree Day" was sticking up. Carrion wafted.

"My canvas coat," Sutyrkina was saying, "I received from the *finkotrud* union. In the year nineteen I guarded their garden, lived in a straw hut. Acquaintances would come by, and, I'll tell you, without boasting, we spent evenings full of poetry."

Kozlova listened with an expression such as though she had candy in her mouth: evenings full of poetry!

"You say, in the year nineteen," she said in an amiable and pleasing voice. "Remember, everyone then would sigh—I'd like to eat this, like to eat that. But I had one dream: to have a drink of good coffee with a little Easter cake."

They became friends. Often they would drink tea at each other's place and, when there was no rain, take a stroll out of town. They'd converse about their superiors, about the regeneration of icons, about former vogues.

"You didn't happen to be at the provincial olympiad?" Sutyrkina would sometimes ask. "Almost completely naked! Ugh, what indecency." And, smiling, for a long time would remain silent and gaze into the distance.

Once or twice they encountered Suslova, and she would stop and, turning, look at them until they'd disappeared from view ...

Sun glittered in the looking-glass crosses. Maples shone brightly yellow. The rowan trees with their red clusters reminded Kozlova of little bouquets of wild strawberries. She stopped, inclined her head to one side, and, holding her left hand in her right, picturesquely admired them.

Sutyrkina caught up with her. "Not bad weather. I'd go to the exhibition with pleasure. Very pretty, it's said, Lenin made of flowers." Kozlova pursed her lips.

"You know," Sutyrkina said to her with dignity, "I always take into consideration the spirit of the times. Right now the spirit is such that one goes to the exhibition, to supplement one's agricultural knowledge …"

Rain tapped against the glass. Black twigs rocked outside the windows. It was dark in the office. Demeshchenko, Garashenko, and Kalegaeva yawned and stood for a long time by the stove. Sutyrkina was reading the newspaper.

"Here are two interesting announcements."

Everybody looked at her, and she rose and cleared her throat. One was from Kharin: on November 7 he has an enormous assortment of bread and confectionery wares. The other was from the bishop: on November 7 there will be a ceremonial mass and a thanksgiving service in all churches.

"Understand what the spirit is now?"

IV

Kozlova was sitting on the warm stove bench reading the supplement to *The Cornfield*. Avdotya was sweeping the floor. It smelled of mice from the supplement and of wormwood from the wormwood whisk. Alexandra Nikolaevna got wedded to Pyotr Ivanovich; standing at the altar, they shone with beauty. But Alexei Yegorich would visit them every holiday and, sitting in the comfortable armchair after a substantial dinner, would heave a deep sigh from time to time.

Kozlova shut her eyes and enjoyed that pleasant ending for a few minutes. Then she took four pins from a little wooden box with lilac-colored violets and pinned up a skirt. She had painted those violets herself when she was young …

She put on her felt boots, a knitted cap, and a jacket and went to take a stroll.

Suslova came running up: red, wearing a large shawl, with a rooster under her arm.

"So, how's it going?" she muttered. "Long time since we've met ... Life is hard. Here, I bought a rooster—for two meals. In such a family ... Does Moussiour not write?"

Kozlova took her by the hands. "Come by at half past five."

Bright-eyed jackdaws hopped along the road. Storm clouds hung low. Sometimes snowflakes flew past.

Chuckling at pleasant thoughts, Kozlova wandered the streets. Turned in at the cemetery with headstones that resembled washbasins and, smiling, bowed to her parents' graves.

The Saint Kuksha Monastery was visible from the gates—little slender churches, potbellied turrets. It came back to her: the red-brown palace, the yellow Admiralty ...

This evening the sensitive Suslova will stare at the teacups, grow quiet, become pensive and tell about how she'd seen the Empress. Cozy, like in the novel from the supplement, the samovar will make a noise, the lamp will snugly smell faintly of kerosene. "You, it seems, encountered me with that woman," Kozlova will say. "She and I did not have a genuine friendship."

Electricity lit up on the poles—little yellow specks beneath the gray storm clouds. Two cartloads of firewood entered the gates of the Karl Liebknecht and Rosa Luxemburg School ... Here had taught Monsieur Poincaré.

THE KING
Isaac Babel (1894–1940)
Translated by Boris Dralyuk

Born in Odessa, the southern commercial gateway on the Black Sea, **Isaac Babel** later eulogised the rich and frivolous city and its traders, fishermen, and, especially, the notorious Odessa gangsters. He started his career just before the 1917 Revolution. Babel joined the Reds as a military correspondent and followed the 1st Cavalry Army under Semyon Buddeny in its advance and retreat from Warsaw during the Soviet-Polish war of 1920. The 1st Cavalry was notorious for cruelty and anti-Semitism, and Babel later wrote a novel *Red Cavalry*, exposing the violence and atrocity of war, even though he was hypnotized by it.

Red Cavalry turned the military old guard against Babel. In 1938 their desire for retaliation came true: Babel was arrested, accused of terrorism and espionage, tortured and executed with the personal approval of Stalin. Babel's books disappeared from the stores and libraries and returned only twenty years after, when Stalin was denounced by Khrushchev.

The wedding ceremony was over and the rabbi lowered himself into an armchair, then he stepped outside and saw the tables set up all along the courtyard. There were so many of them that they stuck their tail right through the gate onto Gospitalnaya Street. The velvet-draped tables wound through the yard like snakes with patches of every colour on their bellies, and they sang in rich voices, these patches of orange and red velvet.

The flats had been turned into kitchens. A meaty flame, a plump, drunken flame, gushed through their sooty doors. The aged faces, wobbly jowls and grimy breasts of housewives baked in its smoky rays. Sweat rosy as blood, rosy as the foam on a mad dog's lips, streamed down these piles of overgrown, sweetly stinking human flesh. Three cooks, not counting the hired help, were preparing the wedding feast, and over them reigned the eighty-year-old Reyzl—tiny, humpbacked, and traditional as a Torah scroll.

Before the feast got going, a young fellow nobody knew wormed his way into the yard. He asked for Benya Krik. He took Benya Krik aside.

"Listen, King," said the young man, "I've got a couple words for you. Aunt Hannah sent me, from Kostetskaya Street ..."

"All right," said Benya Krik, whom everyone knew as the King. "You got words? Spill."

"Aunt Hannah, she told me to tell you there's a new chief in town, took over the police station yesterday ..."

"Knew about that the day before yesterday," said Benya Krik. "Keep talking."

"The chief, he got all the cops together, gave them a speech ..."

"New broom sweeps clean," said Benya Krik. "Wants a raid. Keep talking ..."

"But *when*, King—you know *when* he wants it?"

"The raid's tomorrow."

"King, it's today."

"Who says, kid?"

"Says Aunt Hannah. You know Aunt Hannah?"

"I know Aunt Hannah. Keep talking."

"...The chief got the cops together and gave them a speech. 'We've got to stifle that Benya Krik,' he says, 'because where there's an emperor, there can't be no king. Today, when Krik's marrying off his sister and they're all in one place, that's when we raid ...'"

"Keep talking."

"...Then the coppers, they got scared. They said, if we raid today, when Benya's having a feast, he's gonna be sore, gonna waste a lot of blood. So the chief says, pride's more important ..."

"All right, get going," said the King.

"So what do I tell Aunt Hannah, raid-wise?"

"Tell her Benya knows, raid-wise."

And he left, this young man. Three of Benya's friends left too. They said they'd be back in half an hour. And they came back in half an hour. That's all there was to it.

The guests weren't seated according to seniority. Foolish old age is no less pitiful than cowardly youth. And they weren't seated according to wealth. A heavy wallet is lined with tears.

The bride and groom had first place at the table. This was their day.

Next came Sender Eichbaum, the King's father-in-law. That was his right. And Sender Eichbaum's story is worth hearing, because it isn't a simple story.

How did Benya Krik, gangster and king of the gangsters, become Eichbaum's son-in-law? How did he become the son-in-law of a man who owned no fewer than sixty milk cows? It all goes back to a shakedown. Only a year ago Benya wrote Eichbaum a letter.

"*Monsieur Eichbaum*," he wrote, "*I ask you to come to 17 Sofiyevskaya Street tomorrow morning and place twenty thousand roubles under the gate. If you do not do this, what awaits you is unheard of, and you will be the talk of all Odessa. Respectfully, Benya the King.*"

Three letters, each more direct than the last, went unanswered. So Benya took certain measures. They came at night—nine men with long sticks in their hands. The tops of the sticks were wrapped in tarred hemp. Nine blazing stars lit up over Eichbaum's stockyard. Benya knocked the locks off the shed and led the cows out, one by one. A guy with a knife stood waiting. He tipped each cow over with one blow and plunged the knife into its bovine heart. The torches blossomed like fiery roses on the blood-soaked ground, then shots rang out. Benya started shooting to drive away the milkmaids, who'd come running to the cowshed. And the other gangsters followed suit, firing shots in the air, because if you don't shoot in the air you could kill someone. And then, when the sixth cow fell at the King's feet with a dying moo, Eichbaum himself ran into the yard in nothing but his long johns and asked:

"Benya, what's this?"

"Monsieur Eichbaum, I don't get my money, you don't keep your cows. Simple as that."

"Step inside, Benya."

Inside they came to terms. The slaughtered cows were split evenly between the two of them. Eichbaum was guaranteed immunity and issued a stamped certificate to that effect. But the miracle—that came later.

During the shakedown, on that terrible night when the stabbed cows bellowed and their calves slipped and slid in maternal blood, when the torches danced like black virgins and the milkmaids squirmed and screamed before the barrels of friendly Brownings—on that terrible night, old man Eichbaum's daughter, Celia, ran out into the yard in her nightshirt. And the King's triumph proved to be his downfall.

Two days later, without any warning, Benya returned all the money he had taken from Eichbaum, and then he came calling in the evening. He had an orange suit on, a diamond bracelet gleaming beneath his cuff; he came into the room, greeted Eichbaum, and asked for his daughter Celia's hand in marriage. The old man nearly had a stroke, but he stood up. He still had a good twenty years in him.

"Listen, Eichbaum," said the King, "when you die, I'll bury you at the First Jewish Cemetery, right by the gates. I'll put up a tombstone of pink marble, Eichbaum. I'll make you an Elder of the Brodsky Synagogue. I'll abandon my profession, Eichbaum, and we'll partner up in business. We'll have two hundred cows, Eichbaum. I'll kill all the other dairymen. No thief will walk down the street where you live. I'll build you a dacha by the beach, at the sixteenth tram stop ... And remember, Eichbaum, you weren't no rabbi in your youth either. Just between us, that will didn't forge itself, did it? And you'll have the King for a son-in-law, not some snot-nosed kid—the King, Eichbaum ..."

And Benya Krik, he got his way, because he had passion, and passion rules the world. The newlyweds spent three months in fertile Bessarabia, swimming in grapes, plentiful food and the sweat of love. Then Benya returned to Odessa so as to marry off his forty-year-old sister, Dvoyra, who had a goitre that made her eyes bulge. And now, having told the story of Sender Eichbaum, we can get back to the wedding of Dvoyra Krik, the King's sister.

At this wedding they served turkey, roast chicken, goose, gefilte fish and fish soup in which lakes of lemon glimmered like mother-of-pearl. Flowers swayed above the dead goose heads like lush plumage. But does the foamy surf of Odessa's sea wash roast chickens ashore?

On that starry, that deep blue night, the noblest of our contraband, everything for which our region is celebrated across the land, did its destructive, seductive work. Wine from abroad warmed stomachs, broke legs in the gentlest way possible, numbed brains and brought up a belching as sonorous as the call of a battle horn. The black cook from the *Plutarch*, which had come in from Port Said three days earlier, smuggled in round-bellied bottles of Jamaican rum, oily Madeira, cigars from Pierpont Morgan's plantations and oranges from the environs of Jerusalem. That's what the foamy surf of Odessa's sea washes ashore; that's what Odessa's paupers can hope to get their hands on at Jewish weddings. Odessa's paupers got their hands on Jamaican rum at Dvoyra Krik's wedding, sucked up their fill like *treyf* pigs and raised a deafening clatter with their crutches. Eichbaum undid his vest, gazed at the stormy gathering with narrowed eyes and hiccupped lovingly. The orchestra played flourishes. It was like a divisional parade. Flourishes—nothing but flourishes. The gangsters, who sat in serried ranks, were at first put off by the presence of strangers, but then they loosened up. Lyova the Russkie smashed a bottle of vodka over his beloved's head. Monya the Gunner fired a shot in the air. But their enthusiasm reached its peak when, in accordance with ancient custom, the guests began to present the newlyweds with gifts. The synagogue *shammeses* leapt onto the tables and sang out the number of tendered roubles and silver spoons to the sound of the raucous flourishes. And here the King's friends showed the true worth of Moldavanka's blue blood and its yet unextinguished chivalry.* Their careless gestures filled silver trays with gold coins, jewelled rings and coral necklaces.

These aristocrats of Moldavanka were squeezed into crimson vests, rufous jackets gripped their shoulders, and their fleshy legs nearly burst through leather of the purest azure. Standing tall and sticking out their bellies, the gangsters clapped to the music, shouted "give'er a kiss" and threw the bride flowers, while she, forty-year-old Dvoyra, sister of Benya Krik, sister of the King, disfigured by disease, with an outsize goitre and bulging eyes, was perched on a mountain of pillows beside a frail boy who had been purchased with Eichbaum's money and was numb with anguish.

The rite of gift-giving was coming to a close, the *shammeses* had grown hoarse and the bass wasn't getting along with the fiddle. A faint odour of burning suddenly wafted over the courtyard.

"Benya," said Krik's papa, an old drayman who was known as a

---

* Moldavanka: A poor Jewish neighbourhood in Odessa, where Babel was born and where he chose to live in his young adulthood. The legendary ringleader of Moldavanka's gangsters, Moyshe-Yakov Volfovich Vinnitsky, alias Mishka Yaponchik (Mishka the Jap, 1891–1919), served as the model for Benya Krik.

roughneck even among other draymen. "Know what I think, Benya? What I think is the soot's burning ..." *

"Papa," the King told his drunken father. "Please, I ask you, eat a little, drink a little, and don't pay no mind to that nonsense ..."

And Papa Krik followed his son's advice. He ate a little, drank a little. But the cloud of smoke grew more and more noxious. Some patches of sky were turning pink. And a flame's tongue had already shot up into the heavens like a sword. The guests rose in their seats and began sniffing at the air, and their women squealed. The gangsters exchanged glances. Benya alone, noticing nothing, was inconsolable.

"They're spoiling my feast," he cried, full of despair. "Friends, please, I ask you, eat, drink ..."

But at that moment the same young man who'd come earlier appeared in the yard.

"King," he said. "I've got a couple words for you ..."

"All right, spill," said the King. "You're never short a couple words ..."

"King," the unknown young man said and chuckled. "Funny thing, the police station, it's burning like a candle ..."

The shopkeepers were numb. The gangsters grinned. Sixty-year-old Manya, matriarch of the Slobodka† crew, stuck two fingers in her mouth and gave a whistle so shrill it sent those around her reeling.

"Manya, you ain't on the job," Benya told her. "Cool your blood, Manya ..."

The young man who'd brought this startling news was still choking back laughter.

"They left the station, about forty of them," he said, his jaws trembling, "heading out on their raid. So they take about fifteen steps, and the fire, it's already going ... You can run over there, see for yourselves ..."

But Benya wouldn't let his guests go and look at the fire. He set out himself, with two friends. It was a proper fire, the station burning on all four sides. The policemen shimmied up and down the

---

* Draymen: In Odessa's port, the draymen, who unloaded and transported cargo, were known as tough characters and were accorded a great deal of respect. Jews dominated this field of work.

† Slobodka: A poor, predominantly Ukrainian neighbourhood on the outskirts of Odessa, home to a criminal underworld second in scale only to Moldavanka's.

smoke-clogged stairwells, their rear ends jiggling, and tossed boxes from the windows. The prisoners took advantage of the hubbub and made a break for it. The firemen were zealous, to be sure, but there wasn't a drop of water in the nearest hydrant. The chief—that very broom which sweeps clean—was standing across the street and biting his moustache, which reached into his mouth. The new broom stood motionless. Benya passed by and saluted the chief in military fashion.

"Sincerest greetings, Your Honour," he said sympathetically. "What can you say at a moment like this? A real nightmare …"

He stared at the burning building, shook his head and smacked his lips:

"Oy, what a nightmare …"

By the time Benya came home, the lanterns were going out in the courtyard and day was breaking. The guests had gone, and the musicians were dozing, their heads resting on the necks of their basses. Dvoyra alone wasn't ready for sleep. She was nudging her timid husband toward the door of their wedding chamber with both hands and leering at him like a cat that holds a mouse in its mouth, probing the creature gently with its teeth.

A VICTIM OF THE REVOLUTION

Mikhail Zoshchenko (1894–1958)

Translated by Jeremy Hicks

Highly decorated as a junior officer in the First World War, commander of a machine gun unit, wounded and gassed, **Mikhail Zoshchenko** was the ideal candidate to become Russia's Remarque, but he wrote about the peace, not war, about the eerie, comic, grotesque entanglements of the new emerging social order, about the new man praised by Bolsheviks – illiterate, malicious, narrow-minded. His self-critical narratives were to an extent officially encouraged by the Soviet state, but Zoshchenko's biting prose conveyed far more than mere humour or selective exposure. It was a grim research on the anthropological catastrophe caused by Bolshevik rule.

So it was not a coincidence that in 1946 Zoshchenko together with the poet Anna Akhmatova was scourged by the party bosses, accused of slandering 'Soviet reality', expelled from the Writer's Union, banned from publishing, and was partially rehabilitated only after the Stalin's death.

Yefim Grigoryevich took off his boot and showed me his foot. At first glance, there was nothing remarkable about it. Only a closer inspection of his toe revealed some scratches and abrasions that had now healed.

'They heal up,' said Yefim Grigoryevich. 'There's nothing you can do about it. After all it was nearly seven years ago now.'

'What are they?' I asked.

'Those?' said Yefim Grigoryevich. 'Those, esteemed comrade, are what I suffered in the October Revolution. These days, now six years have passed, everyone's trying to muscle in on it, of course: me too, they say, I took part in the Revolution, I too, they say, shed blood and sacrificed myself. But you can see the marks it left on me. Marks like that don't lie ... I, esteemed comrade, though I have never worked in any factories and by birth I am a former *meshchanin* of the town of Kronstadt, all the same, in my time I was singled out by fate: I was a victim of the Revolution. I, esteemed comrade, was crushed by the engine of revolution.'

Then Yefim Grigoryevich gave me a solemn stare and, binding up his foot, continued:

'Yes sir, I was crushed by an engine, a truck. And it wasn't as a passerby or as some petty pawn, through not paying attention or poor eyesight, on the contrary, I suffered for a reason in the Revolution itself. Did you know the former Count Oreshin?'

'No.'

'Well, it was like this ... I used to be in service with this Count. I was his floor-polisher. I had to polish their floors twice a day, whether I liked it or not. And once with wax, of course. Those Counts really loved it to be done with wax. As for me, I couldn't have cared less, it was just a waste of money. Though of course you do get a shine. But these Counts were very rich and as far as that goes, they spared no expense.

'So, you see, this is what happened: I polished their floors, say, on a Monday, and on Saturday the Revolution took place. On Monday I did their polishing, on Saturday there was the Revolution, and on Tuesday, four days before the Revolution, their doorman came running over to my place and called me over:

'"Come with me," he said, "they're shouting for you. The Count's been robbed blind, and you're the chief suspect. Look sharp about it or they'll twist your head off."

'I threw on my jacket, gobbled something to keep me going and hurried off to their place.

'I came running over to the house. Naturally I rushed into their rooms.

'I saw the former Countess herself writhing in hysterics and stamping on the carpet with her heels.

'She saw me and said through her tears:

'"Ah," she said, "Yefim, *comme-çi comme-ça*, was it you nicked my diamond-encrusted twenty-four-carat gold lady's watch?"

'"What are you talking about," I said, "What do you mean, former Countess? What do I want a lady's watch for, when I'm a man? You've got to be joking, if you'll pardon the expression."

'But she was sobbing:

'"No," she said, "it was none other than you who nicked it, *comme-çi comme-ça*."

And suddenly the former Count himself came in and contradicted to all present:

'"I," he said, "am an excessively rich man, and I could just forget about your former watch right now and be done with it, but," he said, "I'm not just going to let this go. I don't wish," he said, "to soil my hands on your gob, but I'm going to start proceedings against you, *comme-çi comme-ça*. Get out of here."

'I just looked out the window, of course, and left.

'I got home, lay down and just lay there. I was feeling really depressed. Because I hadn't taken that watch of theirs.

'I lay there for a day, for two days: I stopped eating food, all I could do was think where that encrusted watch could be.

And then suddenly, on the fifth day it hit me.

'"Now I remember," I thought, "I found that watch of theirs myself and stuffed it in a powder-container. I found it on the carpet. I thought it was a medallion, so I stuffed it in there."

'I threw on my jacket straight away and, without even having a bite to eat, I ran outside. The former Count lived on Ofitserskaya Street.

'So there I was running down the road, and I could feel something wasn't right. What's this, I thought, people are walking in a strange sideways manner and looking like they're afraid of rifle fire and artillery? Why's that, I thought.

'I asked some passers-by. They replied:

'"The October Revolution took place yesterday."

'I pressed on and came to Ofitserskaya Street.

'I ran up to the house. There was a crowd. And there was a motor vehicle standing there too. And it immediately struck me: I don't want to fall under that motor vehicle, I thought. But the vehicle was stationary ... All right then. I went nearer, and asked:

'"What's happening here?"

'"What we're doing," they said, "is putting some aristocrats in a van and arresting them. We're liquidating that class."

'And then suddenly I saw them being led out. The former Count was being led out to the motor vehicle. I pushed my way through the crowd and shouted:

'"It's in the container," I shouted, "your watch, the damned thing! It's in the powder-container."

'But the Count, the swine, didn't pay me a blind bit of notice and got in.'

'I rushed towards the motor vehicle, but the damned thing spluttered to life at that moment and the wheels threw me aside.'

'"There you go," I thought, "there's a victim for you."'

At this point Yefim Grigoryevich took off his boot and, with an air of disappointment, started inspecting the healed-over marks on his foot. Then he put his boot back on and said:

'There you are esteemed comrade, as you can see I too have suffered in my time and am, so to speak, a victim of the Revolution. I'm not making a song and dance about it, but I'm not about to let anyone take liberties with me. Which reminds me, the Chairman of the Housing Co-op is measuring my room in square metres. Right down to the place where the chest of drawers stands. He really is taking liberties. You've got about half a metre of floor-space under the chest of drawers, he said. What does he mean, half a metre – that's where the chest of drawers stands! And it's not even mine, it's the landlord's.'

THE OLD HOUSE
Boris Pilnyak (1894–1938)
Translated by Beatrice Scott

The son of a German colonist, **Boris Pilnyak** (born Boris Vogau) gained his early reputation as a short prose writer in the first years of Soviet rule, when a certain, though not very extensive, degree of literary freedom was allowed. Due to the existence of different centres of power within the party it was possible to have a personal patron and protector (Pilnyak's was, unfortunately for him, Leon Trotsky).

In 1926, probably overestimating his patron's vanishing authority, Pilnyak wrote *The tale of the unextinguished moon*, a striking novella based on a real plot: the suspicious death of the people's commissar of military affairs Mikhail Frunze on the surgeon's table (the rumors blamed Stalin for forcing Frunze to undergo an operation).

The magazine that published the novella was withdrawn from sale, Pilnyak was severely criticized, fired from his posts, performed a repentance and was forgiven – for a while. In the thirties he travelled a lot, writing travelogues, and, when he was arrested in 1937, his visit to Japan was used to accuse him of being a Japanese spy and sentence him to death.

I

On the terrace of this house there was a doorpost with a great many pencil marks, each initialed and bearing a date. Whenever the house was redecorated (in the old days, before it was pulled down), instructions were always given that these dates should not be painted over, and they are preserved to this day: K. M. APRIL 1861, K. M. APRIL 29, '62—each of the two letters representing a name and each year mounting higher. Then after twenty-five years had elapsed, the years stopped and reappeared again low down on the door. The initials K. M. stood for Katiusha Malinin, who was their grandmother, and they were written high up because in her youth

Katerina Ivanovna who was the head of the house, had been tall and well-proportioned. And it happened that the eldest girl in each generation, whose initials appeared after each quarter of a century at the bottom of the door, would reach as high as Katerina Ivanovna. And the last person—N. K. APRIL 11, 1924—was first marked near the floor on May 7 (the lilac must already have been in bloom on the terrace) in the year 1908. N. K.—Nonna Kalitinin—the last of the family; the dates of her notches appeared in the years 1914, 1917, 1919, 1920, 1924.

Katerina Ivanovna, née Malinìn, who married a Korshunov (and she was nicknamed "the Old Kite" until she died) died on October 25, 1917, by the old calendar. The family was then carried on by the Kalitinins.

This house, as the person whose dates appeared first in 1917 and 1919 remembered only vaguely, was part of Katerina Ivanovna's dowry. They lived then in the Great Moscow Road (now Lenin Street), where they owned a business, and they only came to the house to spend the summer holidays on the banks of the Volga. They moved here altogether when they lost their money and then Katerina Ivanovna's husband died. The marks on the door were made in the spring, when they first used the terrace after the winter months.

This terrace stood on posts which were about fourteen feet high. Below the terrace grew poplars, white acacia and lilacs, and for some seventy feet beyond that, as far as the embankment and the Volga, there were timber warehouses, logs bound in eights, in twelves, battens, firewood—this was the Korshunov-Kalitinin livelihood—and beyond the embankment wall flowed the Volga, wide and free each spring, sandy and chalky each autumn. It was possible to throw a pebble from the terrace into the Volga and cast out care. Stone storehouses separated the terrace from the road and in the old days they held enough stocks of salt for the whole town, and then, later, when kerosene appeared, they were full of kerosene, which was first called photogen, then photonaphthalene and only finally, kerosene. After they lost their money, before 1914, the storehouses were full of sacking and coal, an adjunct to the timber landing stage, where they traded logs in lots of five. If one glanced at the house from the sloping drive leading to the street—because houses are built along the waterway—it looked as if the house were askew. On the left, the ground came up to the windows, while on the right, under a row of windows, there was a whole floor for storage and quarters for the watchmen, and the storehouses themselves were three stories high. By 1923 the storehouse had collapsed. It looked as if the ocher-colored house had made a desperate effort to jump into the Volga and, failing, remained there, the blood-red bricks of the façade disfiguring it, while half the building crouched close to the earth, frozen in its forward leap. The house was built of stone. It was cumbersome, echoing ... Katerina Ivanovna's dowry.

The first memory of this house related to the time when Katerina Ivanovna's husband, their grandfather, lay dying. This took place in the years when the signs of this generation had only recently appeared on the door, and they remembered that their grandfather died slowly of a painful illness. In his gloomy study (the windows were always curtained) there was a stifling smell from the mahogany commode, which looked like his throne. Grandfather could not walk. He lay there, supported on high pillows, with sweets hidden under them. The memory of their sweetness in the stifling smell of the mahogany always remained and if one of them were to come across this mahogany commode throne among the rubbish of some market place even twenty years later, it would be impossible not to recognize it. But below the terrace on the little promenade, white acacia and white lilac bloomed riotously each spring, and below the terrace, below the embankment wall, the Volga—the mother of all Russian rivers—spread itself tumultuously, carrying the open spaces, the barges and steamers, their hoots, and storms and songs—the Volga boat song—and people and bargemen. The old man lay dying in the spring, and in the spring it was impossible not to absorb the violence and freedom of the earth, this earth hurrying intoxicated with bird cherry, lilacs, acacia, songs, troops of bargemen, hooting. Katerina Ivanovna walked about the house, weeping loudly for her husband in front of everyone, and she went to town with an umbrella and a bonnet, taking a pair of shaft horses, and she did the accounts, listed the securities, counted the bills of exchange, went to the landing stage with a walking stick, to see the bailiff, Mikhail Arsenteyevich.

Either the fact was remembered, or a legend grew up, that Pugachev was once in this house and that the cellars under the house (they were large and blocked up) used to shelter brigands and money forgers and had underground passages. And the boys did not care that grandmother would have to go to the bank and the law courts; for the boys, the ones whose dates began to appear in the nineties, it was essential to dig down into these cellars, to poke around them for so long that finally they themselves had to be dug out, standing on guard with kitchen knives at night (until they fell asleep at their posts), on the watch for money forgers at the door of the storehouse, wondering how to bring Pugachev to life again and each of them hoping to become a Khlopysha (Pugachev's memory was vividly alive along the Volga in those days and the boys learned about him from the bargemen). Katerina Ivanovna would come back from the bank and begin to cry on the terrace for her dead husband and because he had left all their affairs on her shoulders and she would punish the boys with her umbrella or by shutting them up in the storehouse. It was dark and damp in the storehouse, the windows were covered with wire netting, and the storehouse had two floors. There were trunks with goods in the storehouse, there were jars of jam and dried provisions, scales hung there on which you could swing, there was kvass in a barrel—swinging on the scales, the boys were not miserable in the storehouse. They ate jam and drank kvass. Once (after Easter) there were some open bottles of wine closed with glass stoppers; they drank wine and nibbled candied fruit. When girls got locked in with the boys, it was bad, because the girls took their punishment seriously, cried, and would not allow feasting and celebrating (on pain of telling tales). There were a great many girls and boys because Katerina Ivanovna had eleven children, of whom seven lived to grow up—and the boys kept aloof from the girls. Katerina Ivanovna's sons and daughters in those years were scattered all over Russia (and even abroad), and they only descended on her in the spring to leave their children with her for the summer. And sometimes when the gang of children disappeared, then those left in the house no longer discriminated between the sexes, and the story was handed down of how Boris and Nadya poisoned Andreyevna, the cook (more of Nadya later, because this was Boris' first love).

It was spring again, when houses were being redecorated all along the streets, when asphalt was smoking at the crossroads and lilac rioted beside the fences—and Boris and Nadezhda decided to be house-painters and to paint some walls with laundry bluing. Boris was in shorts with slits at the sides and no pockets and he went to get some bluing from the kitchen, which was Andreyevna's domain. He took it down from the shelf, but she came into the kitchen at just that moment. He hid the bluing bag in the slit in his shorts but Andreyevna demanded, as Granny did, "Show me your hands!" And the bluing bag fell out through the leg of his shorts. Andreyevna was not friends with Boris and said she would tell Granny. Boris returned in disgrace to Nadya, who was waiting for him with a bowl of water, in which the paint was to be mixed. Boris said, "Andreyevna's a fool. She told me to go away." Granny was not at home and it was terrible when a plan could not be carried out, so Boris said quickly:

"We'll poison Andreyevna. She'll be a martyr and go to paradise—it won't matter to her and it will be convenient for us because then she won't tell tales to Granny and we can get the bluing."

And because Granny had gone off to the courts with her companion, Darya Ermilovna, and because they really meant business, Boris soon succeeded in proving that the best thing to do was to poison Andreyevna, and in convincing Nadezhda that this would be the most convenient for all concerned. Granny had a dark, severe-looking bedroom with a whole collection of wonderful things in it and she had a little shelf there with medicines and poisons, for stomach upsets, colds, toothache, hangovers, migraine and nerves (although Katerina Ivanovna did not accept "nerves" any more than she would admit that the world was round and she herself "like a louse perched on its head"). Boris made his way to this cupboard and the plan was to tip some sort of capsule with some mysterious drops in it over the sugar which stood in the canister on the kitchen shelf. Andreyevna was not there that minute. Boris climbed onto the stove, where Ivanich the coachman was sleeping (what wonderful stories Ivanich could tell about horses and about Pugachev, and his favorite expression was: "Don't touch, child!"). Boris even enticed Nadya up there, so that they could watch Andreyevna take the poison and die. Andreyevna's fate was predestined by the stove and the stove responded to her with a flame which spread over her ugly face, already almost blue with lupus. She came into the kitchen and the children knew she drank a hundred cups of tea a day. She took down the sugar, opened the box, and the children sat quiet as mice on the stove. Andreyevna called out angrily:

"Nyushka, you wretch, what have you been splashing into the sugar?"

Nyushka, the maid, answered from the corridor:

"I haven't been near your sugar."

Then Andreyevna muttered something, poured some boiling water from the kettle into a mug and sat down at the table, still muttering. She took out a huge piece of sugar, just the one which had been moistened worse than the rest. Boris was silent; Nadya's eyes were double their usual size from tears. Andreyevna began to bring the sugar to her mouth. And then Nadya began to cry and squeaked out:

"Andreyevna dear, don't eat it, you'll die. Don't go to paradise, live with us!"

With her lupus-scarred face, Andreyevna cried furiously:

"Wh—a—at?"

"We took some poison from Granny's shelf. Don't eat it, you'll die! You wouldn't let us have the bluing bag."

Nadya was crying. Boris took the disclosure oddly: he fell on his back, kicked his legs in the air and squealed blissfully. It so happened that Katerina Ivanovna returned at this moment and Nadya and Boris, having run the gauntlet of Granny's umbrella, spent a long time in the storehouse. Boris put away the jam with gusto and Nadya endured the punishment, cried and said she was sorry. ...

Over in the house in the silence of the large rooms, the bustle of the day quietened down, candles burned under bell glasses on the terrace, moths circled them, and Granny sat alone at the samovar—Katerina Ivanovna—and in the doorway, just by the dates marking their height, stood Ivanich, the watchman, or the cook, Andreyevna. Those whose names appeared immediately below K.M., the parents, were scattered all over Russia—an engineer; a manufacturer; a city lawyer; a revolutionary and a woman revolutionary; an actress; two sons had gone over the embankment wall to rags and tatters; embittered alcoholics ...

Boris, whose dates rose along with those of the third generation, remembered this house only bit by bit—his grandfather's death, springtime, the storehouse, the money forgers. He exchanged his shorts for the long gray flannels of the highschool boy in town, hundreds of miles off, where his father whiled away his days, a halfhearted revolutionary, always forgetting, and when he remembered, sternly judging that house on the Volga. And he arrived there once again in long trousers and a jacket, in another spring when the lilac was rioting once more, caldrons of asphalt were warming and the Volga hooted with open spaces and bargemen. And from some other town in another part of Russia there arrived, as well, not a little girl with two plaits, an eternal enemy to sessions in the storehouse, but an adolescent with long plaits in a brown dress and a much higher mark on the doorpost—Nadya, a highschool girl. Boris told her he was a Social Democrat and she said she was a Socialist Revolutionary, and Boris made her a present of some poetry in a book with gold stamping and then they buried themselves in Turgenev's *Rudin* and Boris grieved for Rudin and Nadya for Natasha. They played croquet and sometimes, when they had to be on opposite sides, perhaps it was not by chance that Boris' mallet slipped and his opponent's ball, Nadya's ball, rolled into position. They played "opinions" and again perhaps only by accident, Boris always guessed whom Nadya had chosen. The grownups often went out of town by boat to the Green Island, where they drank milk, bought sterlets from the fishermen, made fish soup over a campfire, sang songs and argued (the year '05 passed over the house, over their grandmother, Katerina Ivanovna, and over this first childish love). Nadya and Boris were sitting in a boat and talking (afterward they could not remember what they were talking about), dragging their feet in the water—everyone had taken off their shoes to walk on the sand, even the grownups—and the boat heeled over. Nadya staggered and stumbled into the water. It was not deep, only knee-deep, but without thinking, Boris jumped into the water, stood in it up to his waist, picked Nadya up and carried her onto the sand. Nadya's eyes were surprised and frightened and gazed up into the sky—and Boris did not notice how his lips moved close to Nadya's cheek and how he kissed her. He realized it only when he was lost forever, with no turning back, burning with shame, bitterness and remorse.

Below the house, where the storehouses were and the cellars, half underground, there were also some prison-like, netted-off—what could one call them?—quarters, chambers that were flooded in winter, and in one of these vaulted cellars lived the carpenter, Pankrat Ivanich with his family, a man who went on strike, and then had to go hungry. Boris had a ruble, a silver one, which Granny had given him along with a purse so that he should learn how to save, and Boris ordered a little wooden bookshelf for a ruble ... Boris and Nadya sat in the drawing room, holding hands, and Granny Katerina Ivanovna passed by. Boris went with Nadya in the evening to gaze at the moon, the Volga and the silence. They sat down on a log and Boris took Nadya's hand and then Katerina Ivanovna's threatening figure appeared over the wall. And next morning, Nadya had to leave and go back to her parents and was not even allowed to say good-bye to Boris. In the drawing room, under the family portraits, striking the floor with her stick, Granny spoke to Boris and said something loathsome he could not understand about incest, and that they were not children and that she and her husband, his grandfather (the one about whom he remembered the taste of sweets in the stifling atmosphere of his dying), had lived their life together as no one had and yet had only met twice before the wedding. ...

Then Boris saw Nadya ten years later, when they were both already called by their patronymics, in Moscow, in Nikolayevsky station, where crowds of people were passing, luggage was lying about and trains kept coming and going. Nadya had a child in her arms and she was traveling to see her husband, an officer, in a far-off town where he was lying wounded at the hospital. Boris recognized her from a long way off and saw how tall, beautiful and well-built she was. She was wearing a black hat with a veil. She raised her veil to kiss her relative and began to talk about trifling things, about a porter, her trunk in the luggage van, and Boris could hear that her voice was like their Granny's had once been. They took a cab and drove past the Red Gates to the Nizhigorodsky station. ... Over there on the Volga, each spring the Volga was in a tumult of waters and lilac. The house stood over the landing stage and below the embankment wall a human crowd surged violently, along with the tons, the things, the bales, whistles, along with the burning sky, glazed like the polished whistles. Two of Katerina Ivanovna's sons had rolled down the jetty, beyond the embankment wall, into tatters, drunkenness, vodka, which could be got there by oxlike toil, expended on lugging great two-hundredweight sacks full of salt and oxhide, by that hard labor which, besides sweat, vodka and a bitter life, also gives one Caspian roach. One of them died without a trace. About the other, the police sent word after a search that it was not certain whether he was dead or not, but if not, then he must be in hiding in the south, since he had been caught with a gang of thieves and robbers that had resisted capture, leaving three unidentified corpses behind—and Katerina Ivanovna did not know whether to put his name on the side of the dead or the living in her thick Church remembrance book, bound in leather and bearing a cross. Her other children went up in the world, as things were understood in those days. One built bridges, and was a railway engineer. By the age of twenty-seven he had grown a fat stomach and his thin wife wrote that he was unfaithful to her with cabaret singers but she received her monthly housekeeping money regularly. Another went abroad to study German philosophy, returned with a patent and opened a chemical-paint factory near Petersburg. He was Katerina Ivanovna's favorite and she secretly sent him some thousands of rubles to "get started." She did not write to his wife except to send her greetings and thanks at Christmas and Easter. A third became a lawyer in Moscow, went abroad in spring, was kind and jovial—Nadya was his daughter—and his wife wrote to her mother-in-law that it was uncivilized to live as she did, to eat such rich food, that it was essential for the organism to have plenty of protein, the capitalist way of life was coming to an end, and it was dishonest to live off capital and that this year they were going to Karlsbad. One of Katerina Ivanovna's daughters remained with her for good. She left only after she got married for two years and then returned, her wings clipped, with a child in her arms, her daughter, Nonna. Katerina Ivanovna died on October 25, 1917. The last marks on the doorpost on the terrace were N. K.—Nonna Kalitinin—starting low down on May 7 (when the lilac must have been in bloom) and growing higher year by year, 1914, 1917, 1919, 1920—1924. ...

II

Nineteen fourteen and 1915 passed like a curtain before the action of 1918. In 1917 all the beliefs, the folkways, the nations of Russia were conquered. A terrible ice-encrusted thunder swept over Russia and swept everything away, even those who lived in the old house, scattered everything, froze and heated everything in heat waves and ice. Katerina Ivanovna died on October 25, 1917. Those who grew up in the generation after her were scattered over the whole world and not only over Russia. Some recalled the old house somewhere in Algiers, one spoke of it in the town of St. Petersburg in America,

Nadezhda remembered it in Blagoveschensk in eastern Siberia, where she was driven along with her husband and the remnants of Kolchak's army. Nineteen twenty-one, when cannibalism reigned in the old town, was a crossroad for these people. As streams pour from huge melting glaciers and carry with them everything that was frozen there, sometimes so that this frozen thing, preserved in the cold, flows along just as it was before—so out of the ice age of 1917 there flowed 1921. The third generation after Katerina Ivanovna, apart from Nadezhda, who remained in Russia, did not think of the old house in the old town. For this generation, the revolution was not glacial, but instead it leaped forward across Russia in action and construction, in projects and their fulfillment. And yet the glacial years must have frozen them in such a way that afterward, in the streams, something of the remembrance of life before the ice age quickened. Nineteen twenty-two and 1924 brought great misery to these people. During these years, people searched for one another and letters arrived as from the grave, letters from Algiers, from the American town of St. Petersburg, written simultaneously in another language and in Russian. And at home, it was necessary to go over and over everything that had been lived through and experienced during these glacial years, in order to build, if not afresh (since in man's life what is new comes only once), but at least for the better.

It was April, 1924, when the twilight is greenish and when the twilight takes away one's peace of mind.

It was April in a village near Moscow and it was twilight. A man whose dates appeared on the doorpost in the third generation was writing in this twilight:

> In three-quarters of an hour I shall set out for the station. I arrived in the evening and saw Katya from the street. Some boys ranged themselves in a row as I was at the outskirts of the village, let me pass their ranks and yelled something only they could understand. I felt very bitter, since in these urchin stares I recognized my estrangement from the house where all these uneasy years were lived that held more than sorrow. One loves one's children as one loves the soil and it was bitterly painful to press them to my breast. My

wife told me how Anatoly had asked her to write me a letter. He woke up one morning and asked where was Daddy and then he wanted, he insisted that Daddy must come home and asked her to write a letter at once, dictated it himself:

"Write, 'Come quickly, Daddy dear!'" My wife began to cry as she told me about this. Anatoly sat in his high chair. He had annexed *The Hunchbacked Horse* and Katya had *Tom Sawyer*. Anatoly looked at the pictures in the book, Katerina went off to bed, I sat beside her bed and she told me all about how on May 1 they would go for a ride in a car. Anatoly did not want to leave me, but his mother said, "That's enough now, or Daddy will go away again," and he cried, but went off obediently, "… only don't go away." And in the morning, in a nightshirt, his tummy bare, Anatoly lay down beside me, put an unlighted cigarette in his mouth and had a smoke. I went to the village and bought them some sweets; the children met me in the street. Anatoly took a sweet and went off with it to have a nap. …

Children are frightening. You love them as the soil, as yourself, as life itself. And it's a bitter love. Now, while I'm getting ready to leave, I feel as a man must feel who has cancer and can calculate, pencil in hand, how many weeks, hours, days he has before he dies. I walk about the house, talk, do things and eat. It's not right, I'm a stranger here.

Then this man walked through the fields and woods, the wind ruffled him, mist and darkness enveloped him … and in the mist and obscurity there was a smell of bird cherry and nightingales sang. A train crawled out of the mist and up to the stop. Then thoughts came about falsehood and truth, about how a man can never tell everything, understand and explain it to himself, so that he could be certain this was the truth. In these unhappy days of parting with his wife, neither she nor he knew how to speak the truth to one another, a truth which might dissipate their sadness, as if it really belonged to someone else, and might bring them peace of mind and some justification. The train went off in the mist and it was a good thing they did not put on the light in the carriage.

At the end of April, there was already a strong suggestion of the stifling heat of summer in Moscow, which greeted him with its lights and noisy pavements, with bursts of laughter at the crossroads.

A streetcar which had also revived after the ice age went by, creaking slowly. He unlocked the door of the house with a latchkey: the room smelled unlived in, the books were covered with dust, some bread on the windowsill was stale. The porter came and brought a batch of letters and among these there was one about money from the old town which he had quite forgotten—he had an invitation to give a lecture there. His childhood came back to him and he began to think how in all these years he had not once remembered that town and that house and how he did not know who was living there or whether any of his relatives were still there or whether the house itself had survived. He sent off a telegram that same evening agreeing to come and in two days' time the train bore him toward the steppe, the Volga and the old house.

He was in an international carriage on the train, which went along the broken sleepers and the iced-over stations, a stranger. It was spacious, unhurried and solitary and in this solitude came thoughts about the frailty of life, its transitory nature, about children like the earth. His own childhood came back to him, the landing stage on the Volga beyond the embankment wall, where you overheard the stories told about Pugachev, which the days of the year 1917 had brought back to life. And then again he thought about the soil, children, years passing and the dust of summer days. Every few miles the view from the window became more steppelike and open; the train went to the places where cannibalism had been rife. When it reached the old town, urchins at the station were selling lilies of the valley, white acacia and lilac, as they had done in his youth.

The man, whose dates were either preserved or not on the doorpost of the old house in this town, did not go to this house that evening, but to the hotel, where he took a room, both because it was a long way to the old house and because he did not know who was living there. He took a walk on the little promenade and gazed out at the Volga and at the distant stretches of the Volga below the hill.

In the morning he walked over to the old house. He went by side streets where he had once run around as a boy and where the thunderous dray horses from the quay had ridden by. Now it was empty in these places, the grass grew between the stones, and behind the fences, beyond the half-ruined gates and railings, lilac and white acacia grew riotously. There were no people about, stone storehouses and granaries stood doorless, gaping and empty, covered with last year's white weed and wormwood. The Volga opened out in a wide expanse, free and tumultuous as every spring, just beyond the old cathedral (the one where, in the porch, one of Pugachev's guns was still lying). And the Volga, like the lanes by the old cathedral, was deserted and silent. Where the barges once stood and crowds had thronged together, there was nothing now, and the embankment had been washed away by the water. As the man began to walk down the drive, he heard the Volga echo with the croaking of frogs, which had never been heard just there before, and somewhere nearby, oblivious of the daytime and crazed with night, a nightingale sang. The driveway was broken and torn by the wind.

But the house seemed to stand as before, except that the side where the storehouses used to be had collapsed and spilled over into the Volga. And then it became clear that the ashes of the passing years had scattered over the house as well. There was not a single fence around; the yard that had once held great loads of timber, descending in steps to the Volga, now lay like a lichen-covered dog, gray, overlaid with weed and wormwood. The roof over the terrace had been ripped off, but calm was wafted from the terrace, the lilac and acacia underneath had become overgrown, had penetrated into the yard, filled the empty spaces, riotously and gaily as always in spring. The steps at the main door were broken and the front door itself hung in the air—the man entered by the back way.

There on the stairs, in the chill, he met an old man, a cobbler by trade with a boot in his hand.

"Who lives here?" he asked. But before the old man could reply, a tall and strong young girl with a pail in her hand came toward them and she at once brought to mind both the old portrait of Katerina Ivanovna and Nadya as well—the Nadya of those days of their youth. The newcomer felt his heart beating fast; he remembered Nadya and his childhood and could not understand who it was standing there.

"Hullo, we've been waiting a long time for you already," she said, and her voice was Nadya's voice and Grandmother's. "Where are your things? Give them to me, I'll take them."

"Nonna, has he come?" someone called from above.

There was no roof over the terrace any longer, the lilac grew riotously down below and the Volga flowed even more widely. In the principal rooms of the house lived the carpenter, Pankrat Ivanich, who had moved up from the basement, the cobbler, a girl telephonist, two stevedores and two women students. And in the far-off rooms, where no one used to live before or only Katerina Ivanovna's hangers-on, lived her daughter, the one who had left home for just two years to have her wings clipped through love, and with her lived her daughter, Nonna. When the spring came, Nonna moved out of these rooms and made herself a dwelling on the staircase under the terrace, where only the Volga was visible from the window, and a girl friend of hers lived with her after leaving her parents' home. Nonna had her work there and it looked oddly like a scene from the contemporary theater. A bed was fixed at the bend of the staircase like a bird's nest, the rest of the floor descended in the wide steps of the stairs like an amphitheater and so there was no need for chairs. On the walls, Nonna had hung old family portraits—Katerina Ivanovna in her youth looked as Nonna did in the third generation. Nonna's toilet table hung over the drop of the stairs. A volume of Plekhanov lay open beside a saucepan filled with millet porridge.

On the terrace door where they had marked their height, the marks were still preserved. This man of the third generation found his last mark, stood beneath it and experienced a painful sensation—he had grown shorter by nearly three inches. Nonna went off with the bucket, suddenly burst merrily into a factory song, quickly returned and put the bucket down again.

"Are you measuring yourself?" she asked. "I do it every year as well." She stood by the door, straightened her back and it was clear she had grown over an inch again and so surpassed by three inches Katerina Ivanovna's last mark in 1862. She said:

"I'm the tallest in the family!"

Nonna's mother, Olga, came in and Nonna went off with the pail, singing her unfamiliar song. Olga sat at the terrace balustrade and he stood facing the Volga.

"Nonna sings well," he said.

"Yes, not bad; she studies at the conservatory and also at the VUS*—what outlandish words they use nowadays," Olga said in a dull voice.

---

* VUS, Russian initials for Higher Educational Institution.—Trans.

"How did you live?"

"Oh, well, we had our share of cannibalism. What can one say about how we lived? ... Nonna doesn't lose heart, she sings and studies, she's obstinate, takes after her Granny. But I can't understand it. Either it's youth, or the times, but she's a sort of communist, everything new attracts her, she keeps going to meetings, that's how she came to buy a ticket to hear your lecture. How did we live? It's better to forget. I keep quarreling with Nonna."

"Is there nothing of Granny's left?"

"Nothing—just junk."

"There were antiques, bead embroideries, china, utensils, books—is there nothing left?"

"Nothing—everything was swept away. Nonna collects things, ask her. I must complain to you about her: she doesn't treat me well, takes no notice of me; it's a good thing Mother died or she would have cursed her. She's a member of the Komsomol—what a word!"

Nonna came in with a samovar and said:

"I measured myself, but I didn't make a notch. I must mark the place."

He got up and began to wander around the rooms, where everything looked different and the same. The cobbler now lived in Katerina Ivanovna's room, where the shelf with the poisons had been. He went back to the terrace. Olga was asking Nonna:

"Have you been with that Pankrat again?"

Nonna said:

"You know Pankrat Ivanich lives with us now and Mother keeps going on at me because I see him and she can't forget that he used to live in our basement."

It began to feel depressing and dull, his own thoughts returned, he fell silent and began to drink his tea.

In the evening, Nonna came in the boat to fetch him and took him to the islands. They talked about trifling things; she told him about her work and her friends, about exams and student meetings. The Volga was wide and benevolent—Nonna did the rowing.

"Well, how do the students take things and what do they think? What songs do they sing?"

"They still sing the old songs about the beautiful things in life. The students are all right and we've all got to build everything up afresh, everything has broken down. I try to spend all my time at the University. At home everything is dead and dreary, wrecked, everything belongs to the past and they go on hissing away. I only go to see Pankrat Ivanich; the things he dreamed of all his life are coming about. But I shall go a different way. Do you know how we lived? The jobs I had to take? I had to buy and sell things, go up the Volga for flour, mutton, kerosene. I went on the steamers and worked in the communal association on boats. I worked on the tow-path, and chopped wood; for a month each year I lived in the forest and cut down wood for the winter. I worked as a stevedore unloading barges and wagons. I went to fetch contraband flour from beyond the Volga from the Germans—I went over there a girl and came back pregnant. I've dug trenches. Life was a stubborn struggle. This life taught me how to understand life. I'll manage to survive anywhere now! Here I am learning singing and studying law when I could command a ship! Mother is falling to pieces like the old house while I can swim three miles across the Volga. ..."

"Yes, the house has fallen to pieces."

"Do you know what I nearly did? I wanted to rent the house last spring—I've got friends—and to redecorate it through the communal association, with our own hands, of course, to fling out all the riffraff of years like summer snow, so that the house would not collapse. ... I'll take it over yet. I feel a strange tie between me and the house. I keep collecting everything that's left, old rags, useless books, oddments. I found a pair of pincers about a hundred years old for straightening out tallow candles and I treasure them, the remnants of a culture I haven't got any more. I shall take the house in hand, only there'll be no more trading on the wharf. I shall plant green trees and bushes in all the yards, so there won't be the smallest path left and no one can see what's what!"

Nonna scooped up some water in her hand and drank it.

"Why are you drinking river water?"

"It doesn't matter—one does sometimes," and she began to sing an unfamiliar song.

"What are you singing?"

"It's a robber song, supposed to have been composed in the time of Pugachev. I wrote an essay on Pugachev once, he was a good man, I like people like that. ..."

"You look very much like your grandmother, only times have changed and she used to get quite annoyed about Pugachev."

They got back late. Nonna tied up the boat, they came around the wall, she straightened up, cleared her throat and suddenly it was again quite clear that this was Nadya, a long time ago, in this same place, when the day after Granny started talking about incest. ... Nonna went on ahead out of habit, her step was firm, she was beautiful and strong. They did not go into the house but went to the hotel to fetch his things. Nonna would not hear of getting a porter and carried the case on her shoulder. Someone was lying snoring near the house. Nonna put the case down, went over and Granny's voice could be heard:

"Hey, you rascal! Drunk as a coot again. Up you get!"

Someone stirred in the gloom and Nonna reappeared, not alone but supporting the cobbler by his collar, the one who lived in her grandmother's bedroom. She picked the case up with her other hand and went on ahead again. The night was dark. Beyond the terrace, the Volga lay spread out in the gloom, silent, with just a faint splashing of water by the broken embankment wall.

And memories came back. ...

Each spring when there was a reunion in Granny's house, the marks on the door grew higher, and below the terrace the lilac grew and the Volga was in tumult beyond the wall. Beyond the wall, on the open water, stood hundreds of barges, fishing boats, steamers and every kind of craft. Under the Clock Tower Wharf there was a market on the barges, and Katerina Ivanovna herself took her grandchildren there into all the wonder of wooden painted dolls, whistles, spoons, mugs, little horses ("a horse to decorate the roof is a silent sign that we have far to go"—Kluev).

The anchor chains were like fishy whiskers going from the barges, gangways stretched across the embankment—good for swings—and hundreds of people, bargemen, tramps, women, hauled bales of flour, onions, hemp on their backs—in the powerful smell of Caspian roach, Volga water and fresh air.

Under Granny's embankment stood willow barges full of timber and firewood. Bargemen and women porters moved these loads in barrows and pushed them in wheelbarrows, one after the other, in a line, taking the wood ashore and making batches of five, whole fantastic dominoes, where they used to hide in games of hide and seek at the risk of being covered over with wood. Under the embankment, the frogs croaked all together and men and women squealed, bathing in the dull water and then drying off after their dip, eating roach, giving it a knock first on a post or a stone. In the bars and little kiosks they sold ring-shaped rolls and, since beer is bitter, sour cabbage soup. Under the terrace, on the embankment there was a riot of lilac. And over this shining water, over the stones of the jetties, over the houses and huts, over the thousandfold crowd of this semi-Asiatic town—each morning there rose a burning golden sun which decked the heavens with the same glaze that covered the clay-and-willow cockerel whistles. Along with the sun below the embankment, a human roar arose, loaders shouted and porters and hawkers shouted louder still:

Mead, co-o-old mead!
Onions, onions, green onions!

Steamers hooted and heartrending, incomprehensible yells came over the megaphones from the barges. And at night, when the water grew quiet and the sky was first painted with a slow red sunset and later when it was decked in stars, on the other side of the wall among the timber on the ground, people rested and talked, talked about the robbery that had brought a heap of money to cheer Rykavishnikov and Bugrov, told stories, talked about Emelian Ivanich Pugachev (Pugachev's gun was still lying nearby up on the hill by the old cathedral), and sometimes it seemed that Pugachev had been around just recently, say last year, and had made himself known over there on Sokolov Hill, had called the keeper of the wharf:

"Do you recognize me, Ivan Sidorov, or not?"

"I have never had the opportunity of seeing you before. I didn't recognize you," said Ivan Sidorov.

Then Emelian Pugachev took a paper from his pocket.

"I am the murdered Czar, Peter III, and it is so written in this paper here."

Ivan Sidorov first fell on his knees, then kissed his hand and said:

"I recognize you, sire, it was my foolishness, I'm old and blind."

Emelian Ivanich said:

"Stand up, Ivan Sidorov. It does not become a working man to crouch at anyone's feet," and then:

"Now tell me, who in this place is against the working man?"

"A landowner there is, our lord and master, and he is against the working man. He lives in his house and drinks our blood."

"Bring the lord here," said Emelian Pugachev.

They brought this lord, who wept and had no wish to part with his life—his life was sweet. But Emelian Pugachev said to him:

"I'm loath to hang you, since the life in you is still a human life, but there is no help for it, as you are the landowner here, the lord and master."

Emelian Pugachev frowned, his glance like a falcon's, and shouted:

"Gentlemen, hang this wretch upon the blasted aspen tree!"

Sometimes the new moon rose at night and filled the Volga reaches with mist, chilling the free Volga water. The smell of white acacia crept down the hill, the dew penetrated to one's shoulder blades, and it was rather scaring to mount the cubes of timber, with the day's warmth caught up inside one, because it felt as if Emelian Pugachev would come in a minute, stand there and say—

Nonna came, sat on the balustrade and folded her arms. And then this man whose dates had first appeared on this terrace thirty years ago suddenly realized that the truth which brings relief had come to him. He understood that life is alive with life, with the earth, with the fact that each spring the earth brings forth blossoms, cannot but do so and will do so as long as life endures. He felt the sharp pain of the wish that here on this terrace—on precisely this terrace, in this forgotten town, in this forgotten house which still held ties of family and blood—his daughter, Katya, and his son, Anatoly, should stand by this doorpost to be measured, until they grew up; even if he himself were not there, let a new life go on. And then, for a moment, in this bold and happy renunciation, came pain, because everything passes, everything flows by.

Below the terrace, just as in Grandmother's day, the lilac was in tumult, making one's head ache with its strong scent, and blending with the scent of lilac, just perceptibly, came a smell of decay because they emptied slops and garbage over the terrace balustrade.

LIEUTENANT KIJÉ

Yury Tynyanov (1894–1943)

Translated by Mirra Ginsburg

> Literary scientist, translator and critic, one of the founders of the formalist method in literary studies (the method was attacked by communist scholars as anti-Soviet), **Yury Tynyanov** wrote several novels and novellas based on themes from Russian imperial history. *Lieutenant Kijé* far outperformed the others, becoming one of the best known Russian stories of the 20th century, inspiring variations (like Varlam Shalamov's version) and symbolizing the eternal Russian conflict between the individual and the state.
>
> Stricken by sclerosis in the thirties, Tynyanov slowed down his activities, focusing more on science (probably science was also a safer place to be) and died in 1943.

I

The Emperor Paul dozed at an open window. Silence reigned in the Imperial Palace in Pavlovskoye. Disturbances were forbidden in that after-dinner hour when the food slowly grapples with the body. Paul Petrovich reclined in his high armchair, protected from behind and from the sides by a glass screen. He was dreaming his usual after-dinner dream:

> He was sitting in the trimmed little garden of his palace in Gatchina, and the plump cupid in the corner stared at him as he dined with his family. Then a creaking was heard in the distance, bouncing monotonously over the ruts and hollows of the road. Paul Petrovich discerned a three-cornered hat, galloping horses, cabriolet, dust. He hid under the table, for the three-cornered hat was a courier, coming for him from St. Petersburg.
>
> "*Nous sommes perdus* ... We're lost ..." he shouted hoarsely to his wife from under the table, so that she, too, would hide.
>
> Under the table there was not enough air, and the creaking was

now there, the cabriolet was pressing in upon him with its shafts.

The courier looked under the table, found Paul Petrovich, and reported:

"Your Majesty! Her Majesty your mother is dead."

But when Paul Petrovich began to climb out from under the table, the courier filliped him on the forehead and cried out:

"Help!"

Paul Petrovich brushed him away ... and caught a fly.

And so he sat there, goggling his gray eyes at the window of his palace, suffocating with food and anguish, listening, the buzzing fly in his hand.

Someone was shouting "Help!" under the window.

II

The old army clerk of the office of the Preobrazhensky Regiment had been deported to Siberia.

The new clerk, very young, still no more than a boy, sat at the table, writing. His hand trembled because he was late.

He was to finish transcribing the regimental order exactly by six o'clock in the morning, so that the Adjutant on duty could take it to the palace, where the Aide-de-Camp to His Majesty, adding the order to others of a similar nature, would present them to the Emperor at nine. Lateness was a major offense. The clerk had risen earlier than usual, but he had spoiled the first copy, and was writing another one. In the first copy he made two mistakes: he entered Lieutenant Sinukhayev as dead, since Sinukhayev's name followed that of the newly deceased Major Sokolov. He also made the following absurd entry: instead of "and the Second Lieutentants Steven, Rybin, and Azancheyev are appointed," he wrote "and the Second Lieuten. Nants, Steven, Rybin, and Azancheyev are appointed." An officer had come in while he was writing the word "Lieutenants," and he sprang up to salute him, leaving off at the "n." Then he returned to his work and, in confusion, wrote Lieuten. Nants."

He knew that if the order was not ready by six, the Adjutant would shout "Take him! Under arrest!" And he would be taken. Therefore his hand refused to work. He wrote more and more slowly, and suddenly squirted a large, beautiful, fountain-like blot on the order.

Only ten minutes remained.

Leaning back, the clerk looked at the clock as if it were a living person. Then his fingers, which seemed detached from his body and moving of their own volition, began to fumble among the papers for a clean sheet, although there were none on the table and he knew perfectly well that they were in the cupboard, stacked away in a neat pile.

However, as he searched in sheer desperation, simply for form's sake, he was struck anew.

Another document, equally important, was also incorrect.

According to the Emperor's Order No. 940, prohibiting the use of certain words in reports, the word *inspect* was to be used in place of "review," *fulfill* instead of "execute," and *guard* instead of "watch." Furthermore, "detail" was not to be used under any circumstances; instead, the word to be used was *detachment*.

In the case of civil statutes, it was further stated that the word *class* should be used instead of "grade," *assembly* instead of "society," and *merchant* or *burgher* instead of "citizen."

This, however, was written in small letters at the bottom of Order No. 940, which hung on the wall right before the clerk's eyes, and he had not read it. As for *inspect*, etc., he had learned it all by heart on the very first day and remembered it well.

Yet in the paper prepared for the signature of the Commander of the Regiment and addressed to Baron Arakcheyev, it was written:

"Having *reviewed*, upon the recommendation of Your Excellency, the *details* of the *watch* assigned to duty in St. Petersburg and the vicinity, I have the honor of reporting that the above has been *executed*. ..."

But that was not all.

The first line of the report, which he himself had copied, was:

"Your Excellency, Dear Sir."

Now, every child knew that a salutation written in a single line meant a command, but in the reports of a subordinate, especially to such a personage as Baron Arakcheyev, the only permissible form was two lines:

"Your Excellency,
Dear Sir"

which indicated proper subordination and courtesy.

And if he could merely be held accountable for failing to notice and pay timely attention to "having reviewed," etc., the "Dear Sir" was entirely his own mistake.

Utterly dazed and no longer aware of what he was doing, the clerk began to correct the second paper. Copying it, he instantly forgot the order, which was much more urgent.

So that when the Aide-de-Camp sent for the order, the clerk looked at the clock, then at the messenger, and suddenly handed him the page with the dead Lieutenant Sinukhayev.

Then he sat down and, still trembling, wrote:

Excellencies, detachments, guard ...

III

Exactly at nine the Emperor pulled the cord, and the bell rang in the palace. His Majesty's Aide-de-Camp entered with the daily report. Paul Petrovich sat in the same position as yesterday, at the window, behind the glass screen.

But now he neither slept nor dozed, and the expression on his face was different.

Like everyone else in the palace, the Aide-de-Camp knew that the Emperor was angry. But he also knew that anger seeks further exasperations, and the more it finds, the more it rages. Therefore, the report could under no circumstances be omitted.

He stood at attention before the glass screen and the Emperor's back, and began to read the report.

Paul Petrovich did not turn to the Aide-de-Camp. His breathing was slow and heavy. All day yesterday they had been unable to discover who it was that shouted "Help!" under his window, and at night the Emperor woke twice in anguish.

"Help!" was an absurd cry, and at first Paul Petrovich was not very angry. He simply reacted like any other man who has had a bad dream and was prevented from seeing it to the end. For the dream might have had a happy ending, and then it would still augur well. Later he became curious: who could have shouted "Help!" under his very window, and why? But when it turned out to be impossible to find the culprit in his entire frightened palace, his anger became great. The affair turned thus: in his own palace, after dinner, a man was able to cause a disturbance and remain undiscovered. Besides, there was no telling what had prompted such a cry. Perhaps it was the warning of a repentant plotter. Or, perhaps, a man was gagged and strangled in those shrubs, which were already searched three times to no avail. He seemed to have vanished from the earth. They should ... But what should they—if the man was not found?

The guard should be doubled. Everywhere.

Paul Petrovich stared without turning at the square green shrubs, so much like those in the Trianon. They were neatly trimmed. And yet it was not known who had been among them.

And, without looking at the Aide-de-Camp, he flung back his right arm. The Aide-de-Camp knew what that meant: in times of wrath the Emperor never turned. The Aide-de-Camp deftly slipped the order to the Preobrazhensky Guards Regiment into the outstretched hand, and Paul Petrovich carefully began to read it. Then the hand was flung back again, and the Aide-de-Camp quickly and silently picked up a pen from the desk, dipped it into the inkwell, shook it, and lightly placed it in the waiting hand, smearing himself with ink. All this was performed in an instant. Soon the signed sheet flew back. In that manner the Aide-de-Camp handed the Emperor all the sheets, and, signed or merely read, they flew back at him one after the other. He was beginning to grow accustomed to it, and to hope that all would yet be well, when the Emperor jumped off his elevated seat.

With little steps he ran up to the Aide-de-Camp. His face was red and his eyes dark.

He approached the Aide face to face and sniffed at him. The Emperor did this whenever he was suspicious. Then he seized the Aide-de-Camp by the sleeve with two fingers and pinched him.

The Aide-de-Camp stood at attention, holding the sheets in his hand.

"You don't know your duty, sir," said Paul Petrovich hoarsely. "Coming up from behind!"

He pinched the Aide again.

"I'll knock the Potemkin spirit out of you.* Get out!"

And the Aide-de-Camp backed out through the door, closing it silently.

As soon as he was alone, Paul Petrovich quickly unwound the scarf around his neck and slowly began to rip the shirt on his chest. His mouth twisted and his lips trembled.

The *great wrath* was beginning.

IV

The order to the Preobrazhensky Regiment, signed by the Emperor, was angrily corrected by him. The words "And the Second Lieuten. Nants, Steven, Rybin, and Azancheyev are appointed" drew his displeasure. He wrote a huge "R" after the "Lieuten." and crossed out several letters. Then he wrote over them, "Second Lieutenant Nants assigned to guard duty." The rest met with no objections.

The order was transmitted.

When the Commander of the regiment received it, he strained his memory for a long time, trying to recall the lieutenant with the strange name, Nants. He consulted the roster of all the officers of the Preobrazhensky Regiment, but found no officer of that name. Neither was the name to be found in the lists of the common soldiers. It was incomprehensible. The clerk was probably the only person in the world who knew what it was all about, but no one asked him, and he told no one. However, the Emperor's order had to be carried out. And yet it could not be carried out because Second Lieutenant Nants was not to be found anywhere in the regiment.

The Commander thought of consulting Baron Arakcheyev, but immediately abandoned the idea. Baron Arakcheyev lived in Gatchina, and the outcome was doubtful anyway.

And, since one always turns to kin when in trouble, the Commander quickly accounted himself related to His Majesty's Aide-de-Camp, Sablukov, and galloped off to Pavlovskoye.

---

* Potemkin, Grigory Alexandrovich (1739–1791). Favorite of Catherine II, the Great, and one of the most influential men at her court.

Pavlovskoye was in an uproar, and at first the Aide-de-Camp refused to admit the Commander.

Then he listened with a squeamish mien, and was just about to send him to the devil—he had troubles enough on his hands—when suddenly he frowned, flashed a glance at the Commander, and all at once the glance was transformed: it became inspired.

The Aide-de-Camp said slowly:

"The matter is not to be reported to the Emperor. Consider that Second Lieutenant Nants exists, and assign him to guard duty."

Without a second look at the distraught Commander, he turned, drew himself up to his full height, and stalked away, leaving the dazed man to his fate.

V

Lieutenant Sinukhayev was a seedy sort of a lieutenant. His father was surgeon to Baron Arakcheyev, and the Baron quietly slipped the surgeon's son into the regiment—in reward for the pills that had restored his health. The son's honest and dull-witted face pleased the Baron. In the regiment, the Lieutenant was not on intimate footing with anyone, but neither did he shun his comrades. He talked little, was fond of tobacco, did not run after women, and—scarcely a fitting diversion for a gallant officer—took pleasure in playing the oboe d'amore.

His ammunition was always spotless.

When the regimental order was being read, Sinukhayev stood stiffly upright, and his mind, as usual, was innocent of thought.

Suddenly he heard his name and pricked up his ears, like a dozing horse at the sudden crack of the whip.

"Lieutenant Sinukhayev, dead of fever, is to be considered separated from the service."

At that moment the Commander, who was reading the order, involuntarily glanced at the spot where Sinukhayev usually stood, and his hand, with the paper in it, dropped.

Sinukhayev was in his customary place. Presently, however, the Commander resumed his reading—though not quite as distinctly as before. He read about Steven, Azancheyev, and Nants, and so on to the end. Maneuvers began and Sinukhayev should have moved with the rest in figure exercises. Instead, he remained standing.

He was accustomed to regarding the words of orders as very special words, unlike ordinary human speech. What they carried was not simply meaning, but a life and power of their own. The question was not whether or not an order was obeyed. Even if it was not obeyed, an order somehow changed regiments, streets, people.

When he heard the Commander's words, he remained fixed to the spot like a man who did not trust his ears. He strained after the words. And then he ceased to doubt. The order had unquestionably referred to him. And when his column moved, he was no longer certain that he was alive.

From the sensation in his hand, which rested on the hilt of his sword, from the slight constriction caused by the tight belt, the heaviness of his pigtail, which had been freshly greased that very morning, it might be inferred that he was alive, but at the same time he knew that something was amiss, something was irreparably spoiled. The possibility of an error in the order never entered his mind. On the contrary, it seemed to him that he was alive through some oversight, some blunder on his own part. Through negligence he had failed to notice something and duly report it.

In any case, he was spoiling all the figures in the parade, standing on the square like a signpost, without thought of stirring.

As soon as the parade was over, the Commander flew at the Lieutenant. He was red. It was truly fortunate that the Emperor, who was resting at Pavlovskoye, had stayed away because of the heat. The Commander wanted to bellow: "To the guardhouse!" But he needed a more resonant sound to give full vent to his rage and was about to roar, rolling his "r"s: "Under ar-rest!"—when suddenly his jaws snapped, as if he had accidentally caught a fly in his mouth. And thus he stood before Lieutenant Sinukhayev for two or three minutes.

Then, recoiling as from the plague, he turned and strode away.

He remembered that Lieutenant Sinukhayev was separated from the service by reason of death, and restrained himself because he did not know how to speak to such a man.

VI

Paul Petrovich paced his room, stopping from time to time.

He was listening.

Since the day when, clad in dusty boots and a traveling cloak, the Emperor had thundered with his spurs out of the chamber where his mother was still gasping her last breath, and slammed the door upon her, it had been observed of the royal temper that wrath usually turned into great wrath, and great wrath ended, after two or three days, in fear or in melting sentiment.

The chimeras on the stairways in Pavlovskoye were done by the wild Brenna, and the walls and ceilings by Cameron*, lover of tender hues that swooned and languished in the sight of all. On the one hand—the open maws of rearing, half-human lions, and on the other—the most exquisite sensibility.

In addition, two lanterns hung from the ceiling in the palace hall, a gift from the recently beheaded Louis XVI. Paul had received this gift in France, when traveling abroad under the name of Count Northern.

The lanterns were of high workmanship, with walls that softened the light.

But Paul Petrovich avoided lighting them.

There was also the clock, a gift from Marie Antoinette, which stood on the jasper table. The hour hand was a golden Saturn with a long scythe, and the minute hand—a Cupid with an arrow.

When the clock struck noon or midnight, Saturn's scythe covered the Cupid's arrow. This signified that time conquers love.

However, the clock was never wound up.

And so, there was Brenna in the garden, Cameron on the walls, and overhead—in the emptiness beneath the ceiling—swayed the lanterns of Louis XVI.

In times of great wrath, Paul Petrovich assumed a certain likeness to one of Brenna's lions.

On such days, rods hailed, as from a clear sky, over entire regiments; in the dark of the night, by the flare of torchlights, heads were

---

* Brenna, Vincenzo, Italian architect, worked in Russia, 1780–1801. Cameron, Charles, Scotch architect, worked in Russia, 1779–1811.

chopped on the Don; hapless soldiers, clerks, lieutenants, generals, and governors general marched on foot to Siberia.

The usurper of the throne, his mother, was dead. He knocked out the Potemkin spirit from court and land as once Ivan the Fourth* had knocked out the Boyar spirit. He scattered Potemkin's bones upon the wind and leveled his grave. He eradicated every vestige of his mother's taste. The taste of a usurper! Gold, rooms spread with Indian silks, rooms filled with Chinese porcelain, with Dutch tile stoves, and the room of blue glass—a snuff-box. A circus! The Roman and Greek medals she had been so proud of! He ordered them melted down to gild his castle.

And yet the spirit, the scent, the tang of her remained.

He smelled it all around him. Perhaps that was why Paul Petrovich was in the habit of sniffing people.

And overhead, the French gallows-corpse, the lantern, swayed and swayed.

And the fear was rising. The Emperor felt that there was not enough air. He was not afraid of his wife, nor of his older sons, any of whom, remembering the example of their jolly mother-in-law and grandmother, might stab him to death with a fork and mount the throne.

He was not afraid of the suspiciously cheerful ministers or the suspiciously gloomy generals. Neither did he fear anyone among the fifty-million-headed rabble which squatted on the hillocks, swamps, sands, and fields of his Empire and which he never was able to envisage. He feared none of these by themselves. But together they were a sea, and he was drowning in it.

And he sent out orders to fortify his St. Petersburg castle with moats and outposts, to raise the drawbridge on its chains. But even the chains were uncertain—they were guarded by sentries.

And when the great wrath was turning to great fear, the Office of Criminal Affairs worked feverishly, and someone was hung up by the hands, and the floor collapsed under someone, while torturers awaited him below.

Therefore, when the steps heard from the Emperor's chamber were

---

* Ivan the Fourth, the Terrible. Reigned 1533–1584. Sought to centralize and consolidate the Russian state, brutally suppressing the resistance of the hereditary nobility, the Boyars.

now short, now long, now suddenly stumbling, people looked at one another in silent anguish, and few smiled.

The chamber was filled with great fear.

The Emperor walked in it.

VII

Lieutenant Sinukhayev stood on the very same spot where he had been when the Commander swooped down to reprimand him and suddenly stopped short and walked away.

There was no one around.

After drill, Lieutenant Sinukhayev usually took a deep breath and relaxed his military bearing; his arms turned limp and he walked at ease back to the barracks. All his limbs would swing loosely, as though he were a civilian.

At home, in the officers' barracks, the Lieutenant would unbutton his coat and settle down to play his oboe d'amore. Then he would fill his pipe and stare out of the window, at the large tract of wasteland that had once been a garden. The trees had been chopped down and the barren tract was now called Tsaritsa's Meadow. In the meadow there was no variety, no greenery of any kind, nothing but the tracks of horses and soldiers in the sand.

The Lieutenant liked everything about smoking: filling the pipe, tamping down the tobacco, inhaling and blowing out the smoke. A man who smokes is a solid man; he will never be lost. These activities were quite enough for him, because soon it was evening, and he would go out to visit an acquaintance or simply to take a stroll.

He enjoyed the politeness of the simple folk. Once, when he sneezed, a townsman quipped pleasantly: "A finger in the nose smells as good as a rose."

Before going to sleep he would play a game of cards with his orderly. He had taught the man a few simple games. When the orderly lost, the Lieutenant would slap him on the nose with the deck; when the Lieutenant lost, he did not slap the orderly. Before retiring, he inspected the ammunition polished by his orderly, then he curled, braided and greased his own pigtail, and went to bed.

On this day, however, he did not relax as usual after drill. His muscles seemed knotted, and no breath could be heard escaping the

Lieutenant's tightly shut lips. He looked around at the parade grounds and they were unfamiliar to him. At any rate, he had never before noticed the cornices over the windows of the red official building, or its muddy window panes.

The round cobblestones were as unlike each other as different brothers.

The military city of St. Petersburg lay before him in strict order, in gray regularity, with its barren tracts, its rivers and the bleary eyes of its pavement—an altogether unfamiliar city.

And then he understood that he was indeed dead.

VIII

Paul Petrovich heard the steps of his Aide-de-Camp. Like a cat he stole up to the armchair behind the glass screen and sat down as firmly as though he had been sitting all the time.

He knew the steps of his courtiers. Sitting with his back to them, he recognized the easy stride of the confident, the hopping tread of flatterers, and the light, airy steps of the frightened. He never heard straight, honest steps.

This time the Aide-de-Camp walked confidently, with a slight shuffle. Paul Petrovich half turned his head.

The Aide came to the center of the screen and bowed his head.

"Your Majesty, it was Second Lieutenant Nants who shouted 'Help!'"

"Who's he?"

The fear was easing; it had found a name.

But the Aide-de-Camp had not expected the question, and he stepped lightly back.

"He is the Lieutenant who was appointed to guard duty, Your Majesty."

"And why did he shout it?" The Emperor stamped his foot. "I am listening, sir."

The Aide-de-Camp was silent for a moment.

"Just out of foolishness," he replied.

"Order an inquest. Have him flogged, and on foot to Siberia."

IX

And so began the life of Second Lieutenant Nants.

When the clerk had copied the order, Second Lieutenant Nants was an error, a clerical slip, nothing more. It might have gone unnoticed and would have drowned in a sea of papers. And, since the order was in no way remarkable, later historians would not even have troubled to reproduce it.

The captious eye of Paul Petrovich extracted it, and with a firm hand invested it with dubious life: the error became a Lieutenant—without a face, but with a name.

Later, the Aide-de-Camp's quick inspiration sketched in his face as well, though faintly, as in a dream. It was he who had shouted "Help!" under the palace window.

And now this face solidified and took shape: Second Lieutenant Nants turned out to be a malefactor, who was to be sentenced to the rack or, at best, the whipping post, and then to penal exile in Siberia.

This was reality.

Until now he had been merely the anxiety of the clerk, the perplexity of the Commander, and the saving inspiration of the Aide-de-Camp.

From now on, though, the whipping post, the lashes, and the trek to Siberia were his own personal affair.

The order had to be carried out. Second Lieutenant Nants had to be separated from the military, turned over to the judicial authorities, and then marched off along the green-bordered road straight to Siberia.

And all this was done.

The Commander, facing his regiment in full formation, called out the name of Second Lieutenant Nants in the thunderous voice of a man in utter dismay.

A whipping post was ready nearby, and two guardsmen tightened leather straps around it, at the head and the foot. Two guardsmen, standing on either side of it, brought down their cats-o'-nine-tails on the smooth wood. A third man counted. And the regiment looked on.

Since the wood had been polished to a high gloss by thousands of bellies, the whipping post did not seem altogether vacant. Though no one was on it, it seemed as though someone was there all the same.

The soldiers frowned as they watched the silent whipping post, and by the end of the execution the Commander turned crimson, as he always did, and his nostrils flared.

Then the straps were loosened, and it seemed as though someone's shoulders had been freed. Two guardsmen approached and waited for the command.

They marched off down the street, away from the regiment, with even steps, their guns on their shoulders, and from time to time they glanced out of the corners of their eyes, not at each other, but at the space between them.

A young soldier, just recently recruited, stood in the ranks. He watched the execution with interest. He thought that everything he saw was quite the usual thing and that it happened frequently in military service.

In the evening, though, he began to fidget on his cot and asked the old soldier lying in the next cot:

"Say, Uncle, who is our Emperor?"

"Paul Petrovich, stupid," the old man answered in a frightened voice.

"And did you ever see him?"

"I did," the old man snapped. "And so will you."

They were silent. But the old soldier could not fall asleep. He kept twisting and turning. Ten minutes passed.

"Why do you ask?" the old man suddenly asked the boy.

"Who knows," the young man answered willingly. "They talk and talk—the Emperor! But who knows who he is? Maybe it's nothing but talk. ..."

"Stupid," the old man said, glancing uneasily around him. "You'd better keep your mouth shut, you country bumpkin."

Another ten minutes went by. The barracks were dark and silent.

"He's there all right," the old man whispered into the young man's ear, "only he's not the real one—they've slipped in someone else."

X

Lieutenant Sinukhayev attentively examined the room where he had lived until that day.

The room was spacious, with a low ceiling. On the wall there was a portrait of a man in his middle years, with eyeglasses and a small pigtail. This was the Lieutenant's father, the surgeon Sinukhayev.

The surgeon lived in Gatchina. But as he stared at the portrait, the Lieutenant was no longer certain of it. Maybe he lived there, and maybe he didn't.

Then he looked at Lieutenant Sinukhayev's belongings: the oboe d'amore in its wooden case, the curling iron, the jar with powder, the sand dish. And all those things looked back at him. He turned his eyes away.

And so he stood there in the middle of the room, waiting for something. He couldn't have been waiting for his orderly. And yet it was precisely his orderly who cautiously stepped into the room and halted in front of the Lieutenant. He opened his mouth a little and stood before the Lieutenant, staring at him.

He probably stood like that always, awaiting orders, but the Lieutenant looked at him as though seeing him for the first time, and dropped his eyes.

Death had to be concealed for a while, like a crime. In the evening a young man entered his room, sat down at the table on which lay the case with the oboe d'amore, took it out of the case, blew into it and, obtaining no sound, put it away in the corner.

Then he called the orderly and told him to bring some wine. He never once glanced at Lieutenant Sinukhayev.

The Lieutenant asked in a constricted voice:

"Who are you?"

The young man, who was sipping the wine, answered with a yawn: "Auditor of the Senate Military School." And he told the orderly to make the bed. Then he began to undress, and Lieutenant Sinukhayev watched him for a long time, nimbly pulling off his boots and dropping them with a thud, unbuttoning his clothes, covering himself with the blanket, and yawning. At last, stretching, the young man looked up at Lieutenant Sinukhayev's arm, and suddenly pulled out the linen handkerchief tucked into the cuff of the Lieutenant's sleeve. He blew his nose, and yawned once more.

At this point, Lieutenant Sinkhayev finally regained his voice and protested limply that this was against regulations.

The Auditor replied indifferently that, on the contrary, everything was strictly according to regulations. He was acting in accord with Paragraph No. 2, in view of the former Sinukhayev's recent demise. Moreover, he suggested that the Lieutenant take off his uniform, which, in his judgment, was still quite presentable, and put on a uniform no longer fit for wear.

Lieutenant Sinukhayev began to remove his uniform and the Auditor helped him, explaining that the late Sinukhayev might not do it properly himself.

Afterwards the former Sinukhayev put on a uniform no longer fit for wear, and stood a while, afraid that the Auditor might take away his gloves. He had long yellow gloves with square fingers—a part of the regulation outfit. He had heard once that losing one's gloves foretokened dishonor. A lieutenant who wore gloves was still a lieutenant, whatever else he might lack. Therefore, pulling on his gloves, the former Sinukhayev turned and walked away.

All night he wandered along the streets of St. Petersburg without even trying to direct his steps anywhere. Toward morning he felt tired and sat down on the ground near some building. He dozed off for a few minutes. Then he suddenly jumped up and strode away without looking to either side.

Soon he crossed the city limits. The sleepy clerk at the city gates absently wrote down his name.

He never returned to the barracks.

XI

The Aide-de-Camp was a wily man, and he told no one about Lieutenant Nants and his stroke of luck. Like everybody else, he had enemies. Therefore he merely told some people here and there that the man who had shouted "Help!" was found.

But this produced a strange effect in the women's quarters of the palace.

Two wings had been added to the front of the palace built by Cameron, topped by columns that were as slender as fingers striking a clavecin. These two wings were rounded like a cat's paws when the cat plays with a mouse. One of those wings was occupied by the Maid-in-Waiting Nelidova with her retinue.

Very often Paul Petrovich, guiltily slinking past the guards, made his way to this wing. And once the guards had seen the Emperor bolt out with his wig askew, a lady's slipper flying after him.

Although Nelidova was only a Maid-in-Waiting, she had her own Maids-in-Waiting as well.

And now, when the news reached the women's wing that the man who had cried "Help!" had been found, one of Nelidova's Maids-in-Waiting fell into a brief faint.

Like Nelidova, she was curly-haired and slender as a shepherd boy.

During the reign of grandmother Elizabeth,* the Maids-in-Waiting were encased in stiffly clattering brocades and rustling silks, and frightened nipples would suddenly peep out of them. Such was the fashion.

Then came amazons fond of masculine attire, with long velvet tails and stars at the nipples. They vanished with the usurper of the throne.

Now women had turned into curly-headed shepherd boys.

And so, one of them dropped into a brief faint.

Raised from the floor by her mistress and wakening from unconsciousness, she told her about the tryst she was to have had with an officer at that fateful hour. She had, however, been unable to absent herself from the upper story. Glancing out of the window she saw the enamored officer, forgetful of all caution and perhaps unaware that he was standing under the Emperor's own window, making signs to her from below.

She waved her hand at him and opened her eyes wide to indicate horror. Her lover, however, thought that he had become an object of disgust to her and cried out piteously, "Help!"

Without losing her head, she quickly flattened her nose with her finger and pointed down. At this pug-nosed gesture, the officer was aghast and vanished instantly.

She never saw him again, and since the entire amorous adventure had been so brief, she did not even know his name.

Now he had been discovered and exiled to Siberia.

Nelidova began to think.

Her own star was waning, and although she would not admit it to herself, the time for flying slippers was long past.

Her relations with the Aide-de-Camp were frigid, and she was

---

* Grandmother Elizabeth—empress of Russia. Reigned 1741–1761. Daughter of Peter the Great.

reluctant to appeal to him. The Emperor's condition was doubtful. In such cases she was now in the habit of turning to a certain civilian but powerful personage, Yury Alexandrovich Neledinsky-Meletsky.

And so she did on this occasion, sending him a note with her valet.

The brawny valet, who had carried such notes before, was always astonished at the puny size of the powerful man. Meletsky was a singer and a Secretary of State. He sang "Swift Waters" and had a sweet tooth for shepherdesses. His stature was of the smallest, his mouth was honeyed, but his eyebrows were shaggy. Besides, he was a sly fox. Looking up at the broad-shouldered valet, he said:

"Tell them not to worry. Let them wait. All this will be resolved."

However, he was himself somewhat fearful, quite unsure of how it would be resolved. And so when one of his young shepherdesses, formerly called Avdotya but now known as Selimene, opened his door, he fiercely raised his eyebrow at her.

Yury Alexandrovich's house servants were mostly young shepherdesses.

XII

The guards walked and walked.

From tollgate to tollgate, from outpost to fortress, they marched forward, glancing worriedly now and then at the important space marching between them.

This was not the first time they convoyed an exile to Siberia, but they had never before been placed in charge of such a criminal. When they had first come out of the city limits, they had some doubts. They heard no clanking chains and did not have to urge the prisoner on with their rifle butts. But later they decided that this was none of their business; it was the state's affair, and they had all the proper papers with them. They spoke little, since this was forbidden.

At the first post, the warden looked at them as though they were out of their minds, and they became confused. But the senior guard produced the order which said that the prisoner was a secret one and had no figure, after which the warden got busy and assigned to them a special cell with three cots for the night. He avoided conversing with them and was so obsequious that the guards involuntarily began to feel their own importance.

When they approached the second outpost—a much larger one—it was with confidence and an air of silent dignity. The older guard simply threw the order down on the commandant's desk, and, like the first man, he too fawned on them and bustled away to accommodate them.

Little by little they came to realize that they were escorting a most important prisoner. They became accustomed to the situation and spoke significantly to each other of their charge as "he" or "it."

They had already come deep into the heartland of the Russian Empire, along the straight, well-trodden Vladimir Road.

And the empty space which patiently marched between them changed constantly: now it was wind, now dust, now the weary, thoroughly exhausted heat of late summer.

XIII

Meanwhile, an important order followed them along the same Vladimir Road, from tollgate to tollgate, from fortress to fortress.

Yury Alexandrovich Neledinsky-Meletsky had said "Wait." And he was not mistaken.

For the great fear of Paul Petrovich was slowly but surely giving way to melting sentiment and tender pity for himself.

The Emperor had turned away from the beast-like garden shrubbery, and, after wandering for a while in emptiness, he turned his face to Cameron's delicate sensibilities.

He had broken the backs of his mother's governors and generals; he had sent them off to their estates, where they were sitting it out. He had to do it. And what was the result? A huge vacuum had formed around him.

He had put up a box for letters and complaints before his palace, for it was he and no one else who was the father of his land. At first the box remained empty, and this grieved him, for the land should speak to its father. Later an unsigned letter was found in the box; it called him pug-nosed daddy and threatened him.

He looked at himself in the mirror.

"Pug-nosed, my dear sirs, pug-nosed indeed," he wheezed and ordered the box removed.

He set out on a journey across this strange land. He exiled to Siberia the governor who had dared to build new bridges in his province for the Emperor's crossings. The journey was not like his mama's journeys: everything had to be just as it always was; nothing was to be prettied up.* However, the land was silent. Near the Volga, some peasants gathered around him. He sent a young fellow to dip some water for him from the middle of the river, so that he would have clean water to drink.

He drank the water and said gruffly to the peasants:

"Well, here I am, drinking your water. What're you gaping at?"

And the space around him became empty.

He never undertook another journey. And, instead of a complaint box, he set up strong guard units at every outpost. But he never knew whether they were loyal, and never knew who was to be feared and suspected.

He was surrounded by treason and emptiness.

He had found the secret of eradicating them: he introduced absolute precision and subordination. His many offices went to work. For himself, he assumed only executive power. But somehow it happened that the executive power threw all the offices into confusion, and therefore there was nothing around but dubious treason, emptiness, and a sly pretense at subordination. He saw himself as a chance swimmer lifting up his bare hands among raging waves; he had seen such an engraving once.

And yet, he was, after many long years, the sole legitimate Monarch.

And he was burdened with the desire to lean on his father, even a dead father. He exhumed from the grave the German imbecile† who had been murdered with a fork and who was considered to have been his father, and placed his coffin next to the coffin of the usurper of the throne. But this was done mostly to avenge himself on his dead

---

* Allusion to the pretty villages Potemkin erected along the route Catherine the Great was to travel, moving them overnight to the next stopping place. The expression "Potemkin villages" has since become proverbial.

† Reference to the erratic and mentally deficient Duke Karl-Ulrich of Holstein-Gottorp (born in 1728), half-German grandson of Peter the Great. Ascended the Russian throne in 1761 as Peter III, succeeding his aunt, the Empress Elizabeth. Assassinated, after a reign of six months, during the palace revolution of 1762, which placed on the throne his wife, a minor German princess who came to be known as Catehrine II, the Great (1729–1796), mother of Emperor Paul I (officially the son and heir of Peter III, but held to be of dubious paternity).

mother, during whose lifetime he had lived as a man condemned to momentary execution.

Besides, was she really his mother?

He knew something vaguely about the scandal attending his birth.

He was a homeless orphan, deprived of even a dead father, even a dead mother.

He never thought about all this and would have ordered any man who suspected him of such thoughts shot out of a cannon.

Yet at such moments he was ready to take pleasure in the slightest jest, the most foolish prank, and in the little Chinese houses of his Trianon. He became a simple friend of nature and wanted to be loved by everyone, or at least by someone.

This usually came upon him in fits, and then rudeness was regarded as frankness, stupidity as directness, cunning as goodness, and the Turkish orderly who shined his boots became a Count.

Yury Alexandrovich always felt the changes with some sixth sense.

He had waited a week, and then he sensed it.

With quiet but jaunty steps he approached the glass screen, shifted from foot to foot, and suddenly told the Emperor, under the guise of candor, all that he knew about Second Lieutenant Nants—with the exception, naturally, of the pug-nosed gesture.

The Emperor burst into a barking, dog-like, hoarse and broken laugh, as though he were trying to frighten someone.

Yury Alexandrovich became alarmed.

He had wanted to do Nelidova a favor, as her household friend, and also, in the meantime, to demonstrate his own importance—for, according to the German proverb current at the time, *"umsonst ist der Tod"*—only death is free. But such laughter could drive Yury Alexandrovich without delay into the grave. It could prove the instrument of his undoing.

Was the Emperor sarcastic?

But no, the Emperor was faint from so much laughter. He stretched his hand for the pen, and Yury Alexandrovich, raising himself on tiptoe, read as the Emperor's hand wrote:

"Second Lieutenant Nants, exiled to Siberia, is to be returned, promoted to Lieutenant, and married to the Maid-in-Waiting."

After he had written these words, the Emperor strode across the room, elated and inspired.

He clapped his hands and began his favorite song, singing and whistling:

"O my fir trees, my green fir trees,
 my sweet shining birch grove."

And Yury Alexandrovich echoed in a thin, small voice:

"Liushenki, lullee ..."

XIV

A bitten dog runs off into the field and cures himself there with bitter herbs.

Lieutenant Sinukhayev went on foot from St. Petersburg to Gatchina. He was going to his father—not in order to ask for help, but perhaps simply because he wanted to see for himself whether there was really a father in Gatchina. Perhaps there was no father there at all. He did not reply to his father's greeting, but looked around and prepared to leave, like a shy man, or one who liked to be asked twice.

But the surgeon, seeing his tattered clothing, made him sit down and began to question him:

"Did you lose at cards, or were you punished for something?"

"I am not alive," the Lieutenant said suddenly.

The surgeon felt his pulse, said something about leeches, and persisted with his questions.

When he learned about his son's negligence, he became agitated and spent a whole hour writing and rewriting a petition. Then he made his son sign it and took it on the following day to Baron Arakcheyev, to be submitted with his daily report. Nevertheless, he felt constrained about keeping his son at home, and placed him instead in the infirmary, where he wrote on the board above his bed:

> *Mors occasionalis*
> (Accidental death)

XV

Baron Arakcheyev was troubled by the idea of the state.

Therefore his character was difficult to define, it was elusive. The Baron was not vindictive; indeed, at times he was even gracious and condescending. When he heard a sad story, it moved him to tears, like a child. And he often gave the girl who tended his garden a kopek as he strolled along the path. Then, noticing that the paths were not well swept, he would order the girl whipped. After the punishment, he gave the child a five-kopek piece.

In the presence of the Emperor he felt a certain faintness resembling love.

He worshiped cleanliness; it was the very emblem of his temper. But he was happy only when he found faults in cleanliness and order. When there were none, he was secretly grieved. And instead of fresh roast, he always ate salt beef.

He was absent-minded like a philosopher. And, indeed, learned Germans found a certain resemblance between his eyes and the eyes of the philosopher Kant, well-known in Germany at the time: they were of a pale indefinite color, as though veiled by a transparent film. But the Baron took offense when someone spoke to him of this resemblance.

He was miserly, but he loved to make a flourish and present everything in the best light. To this end, he entered into the smallest details. He pored over plans for chapels, medals, icons, and dining tables. He was fascinated by circles, ellipses, and lines that were interlaced like strips of leather in a whip, producing patterns capable of deceiving the eye. And he was fond of hoodwinking a visitor, or even the Emperor, but pretended not to notice when anyone succeeded in fooling him as well. But then, it was not easy to put anything over on him.

He kept a detailed inventory of the belongings of each of his servants, from his chamber valet to the small boy who served as the cook's helper. He also maintained a careful check on all the infirmary inventories.

During the construction of the hospital where the father of Lieutenant Sinukhayev was employed, the Baron himself directed the placement of the beds, the benches, and the surgeon's desk; he even decided on the kind of pen to be used: it was to be bare, tuftless, like a Roman *calamus*, or reed. If the assistant surgeon failed to remove the tufts in trimming the pen, he was subject to a penalty of five strokes with a birch rod.

Baron Arakcheyev was preoccupied with the idea of the Roman state.

Therefore, he listened absently to surgeon Sinukhayev, and it was only when the latter handed him the petition that he gave it his attention and reprimanded the surgeon because the signature was illegible.

The surgeon apologized, saying that his son's hand trembled.

"Ah, my friend, you see," the Baron replied with satisfaction. "His hand trembled."

Then he glanced at the surgeon and asked:

"And when did the death occur?"

"On June 15th," the surgeon answered, somewhat taken aback.

"June 15th," the Baron drawled, thinking. "June 15th ... And today is already the 17th," he suddenly said straight into the surgeon's face. "And where was the corpse for two days?"

He grinned at the surgeon's expression, then glanced dourly at the petition and said:

"Rank mismanagement! And now good-bye, sir, be off with you."

XVI

The singer and State Secretary Meletsky took risks, and often he won, because he presented everything in the most delicate manner, matching Cameron's hues. But winnings alternated with losses, as in the game of quadrille.

Baron Arakcheyev's method was different. He took no risks and guaranteed nothing. On the contrary, in his reports to the Emperor, he pointed out abuses—there they are!—and begged for instructions on how to eliminate them. Meletsky risked disfavor. The Baron humbled himself in advance. But then, the possible winnings looming in the distance were greater, as in the game of faro.

The Baron dryly reported to the Emperor that the deceased Lieutenant Sinukhayev had arrived in Gatchina, where he was duly placed in the infirmary. He had, moreover, declared himself alive and submitted a petition for reinstatement in the rosters. Which petition was hereby transmitted, with a request for further instructions.

The Baron had meant to show his subordination by submitting this paper—like a zealous steward who consulted his master in all matters.

The reply came promptly, both to the petition and to Baron Arakcheyev himself.

The petition was marked by the resolution:

"Request of the late Lieutenant Sinukhayev, separated from the rosters by reason of death, denied for the same reason."

As for Baron Arakcheyev, he received the following note:

"Sir, Baron Arakcheyev,
"I am astonished that, though holding the rank of General, you are ignorant of the regulations, bringing directly to me the petition of the deceased Lieutenant Sinukhayev, who, moreover, does not even belong to your regiment, and which should properly have been referred first to the office of the Lieutenant's regiment, instead of troubling me directly by said petition.

"Nevertheless, I remain, favorably inclined, Paul"

The letter did not say "as ever favorably inclined."

And Arakcheyev shed some tears, since he mortally disliked receiving reprimands. He went personally to the infirmary and ordered the deceased Lieutenant turned out immediately, after issuing him a set of underwear. As for his officer's uniform, listed in the inventory, it was to be detained.

XVII

By the time Second Lieutenant Nants returned from Siberia, many people knew about him. He was the officer who had cried "Help!" under the Emperor's window, who had been punished and exiled to Siberia, and later pardoned and promoted to Lieutenant. Such were the entirely definite features of his life.

The Commander no longer felt any constraint with him and simply assigned him, now to guard duty, now to other tasks. When the regiment left town for maneuvers in camp, the Lieutenant went with it.

He was considered a good officer, for nothing wrong had ever been noted about him.

The Maid-in-Waiting whose brief faint had saved him was at first overjoyed, thinking that she was about to be reunited with her vanished lover. She pasted a beauty spot on her cheek and tightened the laces of her gown, which would not quite come together. But later, in church, she noticed that she stood alone, while an adjutant held the marriage crown over the empty space next to her. She was just about to fall into another faint, but, as her eyes were lowered and she saw her waistline, she thought better of it. Many of the guests were quite impressed with the somewhat mysterious ceremony, from which the bridegroom was absent.

Some time later, a son was born to Lieutenant Nants—an image of his father, according to rumor.

The Emperor forgot about him. He had much to occupy him.

The lively Nelidova was retired, giving place to the plump Gagarina. Cameron, the Swiss chalets, and even all of Pavlovskoye were forgotten. The soldierly St. Petersburg lay spread out in its squat, brick regularity. Suvorov[*], whom the Emperor disliked but tolerated because he had been the enemy of the late Potemkin, was disturbed out of his rustic retirement. A military campaign was in the offing, since the Emperor had plans. These plans were numerous, and often they overleaped each other with confusing rapidity. Paul Petrovich expanded in girth and seemed to have grown shorter. His face was now altogether brick-colored. Suvorov fell into disfavor once more. The Emperor laughed more and more infrequently.

One day, scanning the regimental rosters, he came across Lieutenant Nants' name and raised him to the rank of captain. Another time he promoted him to colonel. The Lieutenant was a model officer. Then the Emperor forgot about him again.

Colonel Nants' life flowed by imperceptibly, and everyone accepted this. At home he had his own study, in the barracks, his own room, and sometimes reports and orders were brought there, without too much wonder at the Colonel's absence.

---

[*] Suvorov, Alexander Vasilievich (1729–1800). Famed Russian military genius who led numerous successful campaigns under Catherine II.

He was already in command of a regiment.

But happiest of all was the Maid-in-Waiting in her huge double bed. Her husband was advancing in the service, the bed was comfortable, her son growing. On occasion, the Colonel's conjugal place was warmed by some lieutenant, captain, or civilian. This, however, was true of many a colonel's bed in St. Petersburg, whose owner was away on campaign.

Once, when the wearied lover slept, she heard a creaking in the next room. The creaking was repeated. It must have been a floor board, drying out. But she instantly shook the sleeping man awake and flung his clothes out after him through the door. When she recovered her composure, she laughed at herself.

But this too happened in many a colonel's home.

XVIII

The peasants smelled of wind, the women of smoke.

Lieutenant Sinukhayev never looked anyone in the face and distinguished people by smell.

By smell he chose his resting places at night, trying to sleep under a tree, because the rain would wet him less under its shelter.

He walked on, without stopping anywhere.

He passed through Finnish villages leaving as little trace as a flat pebble sent skimming over the surface of the water by a boy. Sometimes a Finnish woman would give him some milk. He drank it, standing, and went on. Children grew quiet, the whitish drippings under their noses glistening as they watched him. The village would close up behind him.

His gait changed little. From so much walking it became still more unstrung. But still this flabby, loose-jointed, almost toylike gait remained the gait of an officer, a military man.

He took no notice of direction. And yet the direction could be traced. Veering this way and that, zigzagging like the lightning in pictures of the Flood, he circled around and around, and these circles constantly grew smaller.

A year went by, and then the circle shrank to a dot; he reached St. Petersburg and walked around it from end to end.

Then he began to circle within the city, and sometimes would go round and round in the same path for weeks.

He walked quickly, with the same military, unstrung gait which made his hands and feet seem only loosely attached.

The shopkeepers hated him.

Whenever he passed along Gostiny Ryad, they shouted after him:

"Come yesterday!"

"Play backward!"

It was said that he brought bad luck, and the women who sold bread in the streets would slip him a bun to ward off his evil eye.

Street urchins who have ever been adept at capturing a weak point, ran after him, shouting:

"Dangle-doll!"

XIX

In St. Petersburg the guards around the castle of Paul Petrovich cried out:

"The Emperor is sleeping!"

The cry was taken up by the halberdiers at the crossings:

"The Emperor is sleeping!"

And like a windstorm, this cry caused shops to close one after the other, and pedestrians to hide in their homes.

It signaled the coming of night.

On St. Isaac's Square, the groups of peasants clad in homespun, who had been herded into the city from their villages for work, put out their bonfires and settled down on the ground where they stood, pulling their ragged jerkins over them.

After crying out that "The Emperor is sleeping!" the guards armed with halberds fell asleep themselves. A sentry paced back and forth like a clock atop the Fortress of Peter and Paul. In one of the taverns on the outskirts of town a fellow girdled with a strip of bast sat drinking royal wine with a coachman.

"The pug-nosed daddy hasn't got much time left," said the coachman. "I drove some important gentlemen. ..."

The drawbridge at the castle was raised, and Paul Petrovich looked out of the window.

For the moment he was safe on his island.

But there were looks and whispers in the palace which he understood quite well, and in the streets the people dropped to their knees before his horse with a strange expression. This was a custom he had introduced, but now people dropped into the mud differently, not as before. They dropped too hastily. His horse was tall, and he swayed in the saddle. He was reigning too fast. The castle was not sufficiently protected; it was too spacious. He must select a smaller room. However, Paul Petrovich was unable to do so—it would immediately be noticed. "If I could crawl into the snuffbox," thought the Emperor, snuffing the tobacco. He did not light the candle. He must not show where he was. He stood in the dark, in his underwear. By the window, he took account of his people. He shifted them, he crossed Bennigsen out of his memory and entered Olsufiev.

The list did not tally.

"My reckoning isn't. ..."

"Arakcheyev is a fool," he said in an undertone.

"... the vague incertitude with which he tries to please. ..."

The sentry could be faintly seen by the drawbridge.

"It's necessary," Paul Petrovich said by force of habit.

He tapped his fingers on the snuffbox.

"It's necessary," he tried to remember, tapping, and suddenly stopped.

Everything that was necessary had long been done, and proved insufficient.

"Alexander Pavlovich[*] must be imprisoned," he said hurriedly, and waved his hand.

"It's necessary. ..."

What was necessary?

He lay down and slipped under the quilt, as quickly as he did everything else.

He fell fast asleep.

At seven in the morning he awakened as though someone had jolted him, and suddenly remembered: it was necessary to elevate and

---

[*] Alexander Pavlovich, Emperor Paul's son and heir (born in 1777). The future Alexander I. Concurred in the conspiracy to depose Paul. Reigned 1801–1825.

bring close to himself some simple and modest man who would owe everything to him, and to dismiss all others.

And he fell asleep again.

XX

In the morning Paul Petrovich looked over the orders. Colonel Nants was promoted to general. He was a colonel who did not importune him with requests for land; he did not try to gain advancement on the strength of an uncle's high position; he was not a braggart or a blusterer. He did his duty without complaint or fuss.

Paul Petrovich demanded to see his service record. He halted over the paper that showed that in his early days, as a lieutenant, the Colonel had been exiled to Siberia for crying "Help!" under the Emperor's window. He recalled something vaguely and smiled. There had been some light amorous adventure.

How much he needed now a man who at the proper moment would cry "Help!" under his window. He granted General Nants an estate with a thousand serfs.

In the evening of that day General Nants' name came to the fore. It was on everybody's lips.

Someone had heard the Emperor say to Count Pahlen with a smile that had not been seen for quite some time:

"Wait to burden him with a division. I need him for more important things."

No one but Bennigsen was willing to admit that he knew nothing about the General. Pahlen squinted and kept his silence.

The First Gentleman of the Chamber Alexander Lvovich Naryshkin recalled the General:

"Oh, yes, Colonel Nants ... I remember. He ran after Sandunova. ..."

"At the maneuvers near Krasnoye. ..."

"I remember, a kinsman of Olsufiev, Fyodor Yakovlevich. ..."

"He is no kinsman of Olsufiev, Count. Colonel Nants is from France. His father was beheaded by the mob in Toulon."

XXI

Events moved quickly. General Nants was summoned to the Emperor. On the same day it was reported to the Emperor that the General had fallen dangerously ill.

He grunted with chagrin and twisted a button off the coat of Count Pahlen who had brought the news.

He muttered hoarsely:

"Take him to the hospital and have him cured.

And if they do not cure him, sir. ..."

The Emperor's *Valet de Chambre* visited the hospital twice daily to inquire about General Nants' health.

In the large ward, behind tightly shut doors, the surgeons bustled about, shivering as though they were patients themselves.

By the evening of the third day General Nants was dead.

Paul Petrovich was no longer angry. He looked at everybody with a foggy eye and withdrew to his chamber.

XXII

General Nants' funeral was long remembered by St. Petersburg, and certain memoirs preserved its details.

The regiment marched with furled flags. Thirty court carriages, empty and filled, swayed behind.

Such was the will of the Emperor. Medals and decorations were carried after the coffin on cushions.

Behind the heavy black coffin walked the General's widow, leading her child by the hand.

She was crying.

As the procession filed past the castle, Paul Petrovich slowly rode out by himself upon the bridge to watch it and raised his unsheathed sword.

"My best men are dying."

Then, after the court carriages had rolled by, he said in Latin, following them with his eyes:

"*Sic transit gloria mundi.*"

XXIII

And so General Nants was buried, having fulfilled all that can be fulfilled in life, having experienced youth and amorous adventure, punishment and exile, years of service, family life, the sudden favor of the Emperor, and the envy of the courtiers.

His name was duly entered in the "St. Petersburg Necropolis" and later mentioned in passing by several historians.

The "St. Petersburg Necropolis" contains no mention of the dead Lieutenant Sinukhayev.

He vanished without a trace, scattered to dust, to chaff, as though he had never existed.

And Paul Petrovich died in March of the same year as General Nants, of apoplexy—according to the official record.

EPILOGUE

Irina Odoyevtseva (1895–1990)

Translated by Irina Steinberg

Irina Odoyevtseva (born Iraida Heinike) married poet Georgy Ivanov, emigrated in 1922 to Berlin and then to Paris and turned to a prose, novels and short stories. She had begun as a poet, a younger member of the literary circles of the Silver Age.

Living in poverty after WWII, she wrote an extended memoir about life in Russia and her life in emigration. She was closely acquainted with the main actors of the literary scene in exile.

Odoyevtseva (an exceptional case!) managed to outlive the Soviet power that forced her into exile, returned to the USSR during perestroika in 1987, and died in 1990, less than a year before the Soviet Union ceased to exist, after seeing her books finally published at home.

"It must be snowing in Russia by now …"

Tatiana Alexandrovna shrugged.

"Well, yes, obviously. It must be snowing in Russia and it must be night-time in America. What fascinating things you come out with."

"Perhaps … But I was thinking about the time I was hiding out at our place in Sosnovka, when the Bolsheviks were searching for me. How they threatened to burn the place down. How we sat there in the dark all night, too scared even to light a candle, as the wolves howled in the park. But outside everything was white with snow. Do you remember how we wanted to escape, how we dreamt of fleeing to safety? Back then, Paris and Nice seemed like a distant paradise. Of course, now we can see that everything here is pathetic and dull. You know, Tanya, maybe we would have been happier in Russia …"

She shrugged again.

"Maybe. I don't know. We're poor, and poor people are miserable wherever they are."

"Yes, but all these Americans and Brits—they're rich, and yet I think that they, too, are …"

"Oh, stop, please. What do you know about rich people?"

They were walking along the Promenade des Anglais, struggling to weave their way through the strolling crowds. People walking towards them would stare at Tatiana Alexandrovna, which worried her. Were they staring because she was so beautiful or because of the way she was dressed? Her clothes were neat, but very plain.

She took a mirror out of her handbag.

"How dreadful. My hat has faded horribly in this sun."

"You're the prettiest girl here, isn't that enough?"

She narrowed her eyes and looked out towards the sea.

"What do I care about that! I'd rather have diamonds."

A motor car drove by them. A middle-aged woman with bright ginger hair sat inside.

"Just like hers. And her car."

He took her arm.

"Oh, but she's old and ridiculous, while you—"

She jerked her arm away.

"How many times do I have to tell you! It's uncouth to link arms here. Honestly, you'd have us look like a pair of shopkeepers."

They walked all the way back to their hotel in silence.

"Seryozha, go, buy us some bread for lunch."

The fat, self-important proprietor sat at reception. She only ever bowed if they bowed first. "Because we're Russian and you're a taxi driver," Tatiana Alexandrovna would complain to her husband.

Back in her room, she took off her dress and hung it up in the wardrobe—"God knows when I'll get the chance to have a new one made." Putting on a house gown, she got to frying a beef steak on their tiny stove. "Good grief, what has my life come to …!"

Her husband returned, carrying a loaf of bread. A large orange was sticking out of his pocket.

"Let's eat, Tanichka, I'm starving!"

She put the steak in front of him and sat down across the table.

"Where's yours?"

"I don't want any, I'm not hungry."

"No! That's not on. You must eat. You're skinny enough as it is. You'll get sick if you keep this up."

"So what if I do? I'll get sick and then I'll die. That's the best thing that can happen to me now."

"What on earth are you on about, Tanya?"

"What am I on about? Only that I'd rather die than carry on like this."

"But Tanya ... I don't understand ..."

"You don't understand? No, of course you don't. You obviously think that I'm happy enough as it is. My husband adores me and doesn't make me work. He even treats me sometimes—brings me oranges. What else could I possibly want?"

He stood in front of her, looking confused.

"But don't you remember Petersburg? We had nothing there either and you never complained."

"So? Would you have me sit around darning your socks for the rest of my life? And bring me oranges to cheer me up? In Petersburg, everyone was barely scraping by. Whereas here ... here I can't cope!"

"Look, Tanichka, if you're struggling, then I'll take on another job—a night job. Berg's already offered me something ... It'll be easy. Then I'll be earning much more and—"

"And then you'll buy me a new hat and some fake pearls. Thanks, but no thanks."

"But Tanichka—"

"Now, Johnson! Johnson promised me anything I wanted. But I'm an honest woman. I'm your wife. I will not be unfaithful. No. I would rather die of unhappiness."

He took her hand.

"Listen ... Do you ... Do you love him?"

"Love him? Are you mad? What's love got to do with it! I'm twenty-seven already. Soon I'll be old and ugly. This may be my last chance at life."

She laid her head on the table and wept loudly. He gently stroked her hair.

"Don't cry, please, don't cry. You're just tired. You're emotional. It will pass. You love me, don't you ... at least a little bit?"

She sat up.

"No. I stopped loving you long ago. Without you, I'd be rich. And happy."

"Oh. So that's how it is ... What a shame you didn't tell me this before."

He fell silent. She carried on sobbing. He passed her a glass of water.

"Have some of this, calm yourself down."

She wiped her eyes.

"Thank you. It's too late to change anything now anyway. Don't be angry, Seryozha."

"I'm not angry."

She walked over to the sink and started dabbing her face with a wet towel.

"I'm going to go and lie down for a bit now, Tanya. I need to leave early today."

"Fine. I'll go out for a walk, then, so as not to disturb you."

She stood in front of the mirror, powdering her face and painting her eyelashes. He could tell, from how meticulously she was doing it, that she was going on a date with Johnson.

She brushed back her short, black hair and put on her hat.

"You can't tell that I've been crying, can you?"

"No, not at all."

She picked up her gloves.

"Well, goodbye, Seryozha. Take care of yourself."

"Tanichka ..."

"Yes?"

"Are you leaving without even kissing me goodbye?"

"I thought you were angry. I behaved horribly and I'm ashamed of myself."

He put his arms around her.

"Tanya ..."

She sat down on the edge of the bed, looking at him guiltily.

"Forgive me, Seryozha ... Just ... forget all the stupid things I said. Make sure you eat before you go and make yourself some tea, too. Anyway, I'll be off now, or you won't get enough sleep."

She started to get up, but he held her hand.

"Wait, let me look at you for just one more minute ..."

"What's the matter with you, Seryozha?"

"Nothing, you can go now."

She kissed him again.

"Take care of yourself now. When will you be back—by twelve?"

"I love you, Tanya."

"Of course you do. I love you too. Goodbye now."

She smiled at him absent-mindedly and, so that he wouldn't detain her any longer, hurried out of the room.

Tatiana Alexandrovna looked at the clock.

"It's a quarter to ten. I must go home."

"What's the hurry? Your husband won't be back yet."

She shook her head stubbornly.

"I must."

In life, Tatiana Alexandrovna split everything into things she could do and things she couldn't do.

She could go for drives with Johnson, take tea and lunch with him, but she couldn't come home after ten—that wouldn't have been "proper," and she never did things that were not "proper."

They left the restaurant and got into a motor car.

"Must we part now? I don't want to let you go."

She looked out of the window in silence.

"Now look here, I'm bored of this game. Your reluctance is cute—every woman has her own way of flirting. But this has gone on too long. Let's be frank. If you come with me tonight, then I will get that bracelet tor you tomorrow. You know, the wide one."

"That bracelet? ..." She never could walk past the display window it was in without stopping to admire it. She felt that that wide band of diamonds contained all the happiness that was so inaccessible to her. She even had dreams about it.

"You'll get me that bracelet? Really?" she sighed. "But, no, I won't go with you ... I can't go with you ..."

"As you wish." He was clearly angry. "As you wish. I would advise you to think it over. I'll wait until midnight. Call me if you change your mind."

The car drew to a halt.

"Goodnight, I won't call you."

"But I'll still wait. And if you don't call, then I'll leave for London in the morning."

"What a pity," she tried to smile. "In that case, farewell."

* * *

Tatiana Alexandrovna walked up the stairs. "So that's that." Of course, she knew that it couldn't go on forever, but it happened so suddenly …

She opened the door, walked into her room and turned on the lights. The bed was carefully made. Sergei had tidied before he left, because she didn't like mess. It looked just like it always did—everything was in its place. But she instantly felt that something was amiss. What was it? She looked around nervously.

There was a note on top of the dresser. A note of only two lines: "I don't want to stand in your way. You're free. Farewell. Be happy."

What? Had he left? Impossible … She opened the wardrobe. Both his grey suit and his jacket were gone. The suitcase wasn't there either. So … Sergei had left …

She sat down on the bed. Tears streamed down her face. Seryozha … What am I to do now? Seryozha had left, Johnson was leaving … She threw her hat down on the floor, buried her head in a pillow and cried.

Then she got up and read the note again: "Be happy," she sobbed. "Some happiness! 'You're free.' Free?" She hadn't quite grasped the full meaning of the word, but her heart was already racing.

"Free? I'm free? Then Johnson won't leave and I'll be happy. Oh, God!" She sat down on a chair, clasping the note to her chest. "I'm free! Free!"

She suddenly had a vision of Charlie Chaplin in *La Ruée vers l'or*, jumping for joy, ecstatically tearing feathers out of a pillow. It was a shame that she couldn't do that. But what about Johnson? … Was he still waiting? She ran to the telephone.

"Hello? Hello? Is that you?"

"Yes, it's me. I knew you would call."

"No, you didn't. You didn't know anything. My husband has left … Do you understand? He's left me …"

"That's good, isn't it?"

"It's good, it's very good! I'm free now. Come and get me, quickly. Oh, I'm happy, so happy! Aren't you?"

She hung up and ran upstairs, jumping three steps at a time.

As Tatiana Alexandrovna got dressed, she thought about the lady's maid that would wait on her tomorrow. "Here are your stockings, my lady."

She put on her only pair of silk stockings and slowly rolled them up her legs: "Marie, throw these stockings away, or keep them for yourself if you like. These shoes, too."

"Thank you, my lady."

Yes, that's what the maid would say.

She put on a plain white dress. It was so simple and yet so charming. She felt like a queen dressing up as a shepherdess. How fun!

"You look lovely even in these old rags. Now, just imagine how you will look in real dresses! You're a happy woman now, Tatiana Alexandrovna!"

She smiled to herself in the mirror and glanced at her wrist: "Tomorrow, I'll be wearing the bracelet and I shan't be living here any more."

The mirror showed a reflection of the orange, which was still lying on the table. She touched it. It was a shame she couldn't keep it—it was her husband's last gift to her, after all.

Sergei's letters were infrequent and dry.

"... I arrived in London the day before yesterday and felt instantly at home. In Berlin, I had felt uneasy. It was snowing there and the snow was melting; it was altogether too similar to Petersburg. Whereas here! You wouldn't believe the traffic around the City. You have to wait a quarter of an hour just to cross the road. In London, you feel that your feet are firmly on the ground, and that has a marvellous effect on me. My affairs are going well ..."

That was his third letter.

"My dear Seryozha," Tatiana Alexandrovna wrote. "Sorry for not replying sooner. I am so happy that you don't miss me too much. It was so sensible of you to leave. We were just torturing ourselves unnecessarily. I live at the Hotel Negresco now, in that corner suite with the yellow curtains that we used to look up at so often. The carnival is on and I'm having such a fun time."

Then another letter arrived.

"... It's been three months since I left. Three months is a long time. Last night I was at a restaurant with a chance acquaintance—another

Russian, and an exofficer too. We drank a lot, reminiscing about Russia and about the Bolsheviks. At one point he suddenly turned to me with a crazed look in his eyes. "Do you realise," he said, "that there is no Russia and there are no Bolsheviks. None of that. We've made it all up in our heads." I laughed. But I was drunk then. "Maybe," I thought, "there is no Tanya either, and there was no life that we shared." All of a sudden, I felt light and happy. We drank and we laughed. And this morning I awoke happy …

"… I love Amsterdam. It's the cleanest city in the world. They wash it and scrub it all day long …

"… I went into a patisserie and saw two young ladies sitting across from me. One of them was very pretty. She had blonde hair, bright eyes, and freckles on her cheeks. I looked at her and wondered how I had even managed to notice that she was pretty. Because in all the seven years that we were together, I just hadn't looked at another woman in that way. I walked out, bought a bunch of violets from a flower girl on the street and told her to deliver them to the patisserie. The girl accepted the flowers and smiled at me. I was outside, watching her through the window. I gave her a little bow and went home.

"See, I have little romances of my own now too …"

After reading this letter, Tatiana Alexandrovna screwed up her face and wiped her brow with her hand.

"Are you in some sort of trouble?" said Johnson.

"How can I have any trouble now that I have you?"

He kissed her hand in thanks.

"So, what shall we do today? Would you like to go to Monte Carlo, my dear?"

"No, I am afraid I feel a migraine coming on. But you should go. You so enjoy playing. I should rest."

Johnson left. Tatiana Alexandrovna sat and looked out of the window for a long time—at the grey sea and the wet, rain-sodden promenade. Then she put on a waterproof cloak and went outside.

Fishermen were dragging a boat ashore. Water poured from people's umbrellas.

"This rain … It's sure to last." When she got to the bottom of the hill, she hesitated. "Maybe I should go back." But slowly she started climbing the stairs. "How steep this hill is!"

The rain battered the leaves on the trees. The fog obscured the sea from view almost entirely. The ground was wet and slippery. The park at the top was deserted and silent. Wet, grey pines and wet, grey stones. An eagle with ruffled feathers sat in a large cage. He looked at her with his indifferent, evil eyes, spread his wings noisily and flew up to sit on his perch.

Tatiana Alexandrovna came to a standstill at the white marble graveyard. "So many statues, so many crosses! And here I am, though I could have died long ago and been lying here, just like they all are." She clasped her hands to her chest before letting them fall. "What shall I do? Life is going by and I'm still not happy …"

On her way down, she took the road through the Italian quarter.

"I had it easier before. Back then, I thought that money bought you happiness, whereas now I have nothing to dream about."

The streets were very narrow, dirty, and winding. Wet clothes hung from the lines. Almost all the shutters were closed. "What is everyone up to? Not sleeping, surely? Oh, of course, it's Sunday today."

She turned a corner, walked a short distance and turned again.

"I think I'm lost!" It was almost dark, but the street lamps weren't lit. Strips of light shone through some of the shutters. Her thoughts were anxious and muddled. Then suddenly she heard a door slam somewhere behind her. A tall man in a leather coat—the kind taxi drivers wear—overtook her. He walked quickly, with wide strides.

"My God, that's Sergei!"

"Seryozha!" she shouted. She could barely breathe from excitement and joy.

The man in the leather coat turned around—a dark stranger's face stared back at her in surprise.

She stopped short. "I'm going mad. Sergei is in Amsterdam. And even if it were him—what's that to me? We're strangers now … And he got over it so quickly …"

Finally, the streets became wider and livelier. She hailed a passing cab. She was cold and uncomfortable. "Never mind, I'll be home shortly. Home?"

She thought of the large white building of the hotel, of the absurd bronze statues. "How can anyone even call that home?"

* * *

The maid fussed over Tatiana Alexandrovna, rubbing her feet with eau de cologne.

"Madame is sure to catch cold. Madame must go to bed immediately. There's so much flu going round."

"I will. You may go now. I'll get undressed myself."

This was her room ... These were her dresses and her jewellery that she had dreamt of so much, so long ago. What did she need them for? A thick carpet covered the floor, but it felt like she was standing on the bare rocks and sodden earth from that exhausting, endless walk ... The fire was blazing, but she was cold, as if she was still in the rain and the fog. "I think I've caught cold ... Oh, what does it matter ..."

She got up and switched on all the lights. "I had my own life, my own husband, after all ... Now what do I have? I have nothing. And nothing can help me. And I only have myself to blame."

The lights shone brightly. Cars drove up and down the embankment. "Is it too late? No, no, it's never too late ... It's never too late ... It's never too late if you love someone."

She wrote the letter in one go, without any corrections. "I think that's it? He will understand, regardless ..." She rang for a servant. "Send this immediately."

There was a knock at the door.

"It's me. I was told that you're ill."

"No, I just have a headache. I'll be better in the morning, don't worry. I'm sorry I can't let you in now—I'm already in bed. Did you play well?"

"Very well. I picked your age and won twice over. You bring me luck, dear."

"Goodnight."

"Goodnight. I hope you feel better in the morning."

Tatiana Alexandrovna undressed and got into bed. "It's the fourth today. He'll get the letter on the eighth. Ninth, tenth, eleventh, twelfth. Yes, he could be here by the twelfth." She put her hands behind her head. "Seryozha, my darling, come quickly ... There's nothing I want, just to be with you."

* * *

Tatiana Alexandrovna left the telegraph office. Johnson was waiting for her.

"Where shall we go for lunch? How about that little restaurant on the cliffs?"

"I don't care."

In the restaurant, sitting across from Johnson, she thought: "What a horrible, loud tie. And that pearl—so garish."

"What's the matter?" Johnson asked solicitously.

"The matter? Nothing is the matter."

"You have a strange look on your face. You're not in love, are you?"

"So what if I am?"

Her tone was confrontational and he grew serious.

"Well, my dear, I can turn a blind eye to many things ... But it would depend on who you are in love with."

She rearranged the carnations in the vase between them.

"I'm in love with my husband," she said dreamily.

"With your husband? Oh, please! He's no threat." Johnson laughed loudly.

"No threat? Why not?"

"Because he hasn't a cent!"

"Are you only threatened by the rich?"

"Of course!"

She blushed.

"I don't need your money."

"Perhaps not, but you need the things that it buys."

"Do you really think so?" She undid the clasp of her bracelet. "Watch me—I'm going to throw it into the sea."

"Don't do that. We'll have to find it. We'll have to hire divers. Let's spend that money on something else instead—some little trinket for you, how about it?"

"No, I don't want anything. Leave me alone."

"I hate all these Russian personality traits—the melancholy and the madness. You've always been so much fun, not like a Russian at all."

"Really? But I am a Russian, after all. And I hate Americans."

"Oh," he said slowly, hurt. But then he softened. "My dear, you must be unwell. All this started a week ago when you had your migraine. We must call a doctor today."

* * *

Ten days passed. There were no answers to the letters or the telegrams.

"That's just fine. Is he angry? Did he fall in love with that girl with the freckles? Has he left?"

The hotel receptionists bowed. "No, there are no letters for Madame. Madame shouldn't worry—as soon as something arrives, we'll bring it right up."

But still she checked several times a day.

"It's easier in public … The music stops you from thinking … When you dance, you almost don't feel anxious." Tatiana Alexandrovna looks at the colourless eyes of the American—her gentleman friend Johnson. "Maybe there's a letter waiting for me at home …"

"What a lively season this year, don't you think?"

She nods.

"You dance well, even compared to American girls."

She says nothing.

"Did you go to the tennis championships?"

"Yes."

"Very interesting, isn't it?"

"Yes."

"Tennis is a noble game."

"Yes."—"The letter must have arrived by now."

"How fast do you go?"

"How fast do I go?"

"Yes, I mean in the car."

"Oh that's what you mean … I haven't been counting."

The music stops and he starts again. "Do you like golf?"

In the motor car, Johnson kisses her hand.

"You haven't been this much fun for a while. I hope everything will be OK now, won't it dear?"

"Yes, it will now."

A lackey hands her an envelope.

"What a thick letter! And why is the address written in someone else's handwriting?"

Tatiana Alexandrovna runs to her room. "I knew it!"

"Don't forget that we're going to the Opéra and will take dinner early," Johnson calls after her.

"Yes, yes," she says, and slams the door.

She reads it, but it doesn't make any sense. It's in French. Typewritten ... Bright purple letters dance on the page in front of her: *"Poste privée.* Correspondence from any country. Secrecy guaranteed."

"Our client ... placed an order ... five letters ... from selected cities ... direct to you the last ... letters received from you ... pursuant to his instructions ..."

Her telegrams and letters fell out of the envelope, unopened, followed by a sheet of paper covered in Sergei's messy handwriting.

"... Dear Tanya. I think that by now you must be settled into your new life and it's time you knew the truth. I got to Marseilles and I intend to go no further. From here, I wrote several fictitious letters which will all be sent to you. Of everything I wrote only one thing is true—I met an acquaintance and we drank all night and we are still drinking now, even though day has broken. You don't like this sort of thing, but please—don't be angry, it doesn't matter now anyway. This situation came to be when an umbrella came to me! Farewell, Madame Pierpont Morgan!"

And at the bottom it said:

"My angel, if only you knew how much I don't want to die."

KNIVES

Valentin Kataev (1897–1986)

Translated by Alec Brown

A Hero of Socialist Labor, grandson of priests and generals, and the elder brother of Evgeny Petrov from the Ilf & Petrov duet, **Valentin Kataev**, born in Odessa on the Black sea, was a trickster of Soviet literature. He was shelled and gassed on the frontlines of WWI, became a student of Ivan Bunin, fought for the Whites in the Civil war, was arrested by communist secret police in 1920 – and managed not only to survive the purges, but to become a part of the Soviet literary *nomenklatura*, writing prose that was loyal to the regime and prose that verged on subversion.

In 1980, at the zenith of the period known as 'the stagnation', Kataev all of sudden published a novella revealing his participation in the White movement, provoking the head of the KGB Yury Andropov to address the CPSU Central Committee and demand a ban on the novel for slandering Soviet state security.

The Sunday stroll up and down the boulevard is a remarkable way of fixing what a man really is. Pashka Kokushkin began his Sunday stroll at Chistyé Prudy at six that evening. The first thing he did was to drop into the Moscow Country Products bar and drink a bottle of beer. That immediately made his proper approach to life clear, and gave him self-assurance.

Then he bought a couple of little measures of roasted sunflower-seeds from an old woman who kept a stall, and took his time down the main walk. On the way he met a gipsy woman who fixed on him.

'Fine gentleman, young gentleman,' she whined, 'give me your hand, I tell you all the truth, I'll tell you for whom your heart aches, young gentleman, and I'll tell you what's on your mind, I'll tell you everything, fine gentleman, I won't keep anything back from you, and you give the old gipsy-woman a penny for her pains, won't you? If I tell your fortune, it'll come all right; if I don't, you'll be sorry.'

Pashka thought it over, and said, 'Look here, mother, fortunetelling by the palm is all prejudice and twaddle, but here's something for you. Come on, tell away, it doesn't matter, it'll all be twaddle.'

The gipsy-woman slipped the coin into her gaily-coloured skirts, and bared her blackened teeth.

'Young gentleman,' she said, 'you're going to have a happy meeting, and the meeting will make your heart ache, and there's an elderly man stands in your way, but you don't be afraid, only, young gentleman, you be afraid of a knife, because you'll have a great unpleasantness through a knife, don't you be afraid of your friends, but you be afraid of your enemies, and I can see a green parrot will bring you happiness in life. Go on your way, young gentleman, and be happy.'

The gipsy stuck out her enormous belly and waddled off with a very important air, with her broad heels shuffling in the gravel of the walk.

'Damn the woman,' said Pashka to himself, 'there's something in all that she says.' Then, with a wink and a guffaw, he went on his way.

As he went, he tried all the delights that life offered him. First he pulled himself up on to a rickety weighing machine, and found he weighed four poods, fifteen pounds. A little later, squatting on his heels with the exertion, he tried his strength, and squeezed the quivering needle of the strength meter up to 'powerful adult male'.

Then came another little walk, and he tried his nerves by electric current, that is to say, he took hold of little brass handles, and ants ran in streams all over his joints, jabbing deep into him: his joints filled with soda-water, his palms stuck to the handles, but all the same, his nerves turned out to be strong.

At last, he sat down on a chair in front of a picture hung on a tree, representing a view of the Moscow Kremlin from the Kamenny Bridge, cocked one leg over the other, put on a bestial expression, and in that condition had his photograph taken. When ten minutes later they gave him the limp bit of pasteboard, Pashka examined himself at great length, and with tremendous satisfaction: there was the check cap, the familiar nose: there were his leggings, his apache shirt with open neck and his jacket, all absolutely it – he really was pleased, and could even not quite believe that he really was so handsome.

'Not so bad,' he said, rolled the still wet photo into a tube, and continued towards the lake and the boats.

To crown all these delights he had experienced, all he had to do was to find some suitable lassies and go for a boat trip with them. But, as things turned out, he went on past the boats until he came to a booth he already knew. There was a crowd in the wide-open doorway and you could hear the clink of metal and loud laughter.

'What's all this?' Pashka asked of a little Red-Army man elbowing his way in at the entrance.

'Quoits, jolly amusing. If you get a quoit on it, you can get a samovar.'

With some curiosity, Pashka peered over the heads of the audience into the booth, which was brilliantly lit inside by lamps. The whole of the end wall was stretched with canvas. There were three tiers of shelves, with knives sticking up in them. Among the knives were laid out all manner of attractive prizes. On the lower shelf were baskets of sweets and cakes: on the second, alarm clocks, pots and pans and caps, and on the third, right up under the ceiling, in halfdarkness, were really attractive presents: two balalaikas, a Tula samovar, chrome-leather knee-boots, a Tolstoy shirt, an Italian harmonica, a wall cuckoo clock and a gramophone. You got your prize according to the shelf you ringed a knife on. But it was almost impossible to ring a knife – the knives were very springy. Interesting.

Making good work with his elbows, Pashka got in. At the barrier was a little old man in silver spectacles taking in the money for the quoits, forty a shilling. A red-faced lad, with forelock wet with sweat and a stupid grin on his face, was just throwing up the last dozen. His coat flew open. The iron quoits flew from his coarse fingers, clanked among the knives, and rolled back into the sack awaiting them below. The lad grew purple. The knives rang with good steel as the quoits touched them, quivered in a sort of mist, and bent aside from the quoits.

'Blast the knives and the quoits!' the youth cried, at the end. 'I've spent a rouble and a half for nothing, I haven't even got a bag of Babaiev cakes,' and shamefaced, he made his way out.

'Last Sunday somebody got a pair of boots,' said a boy in patched trousers, 'it cost him ten roubles.'

'Well, now you let me,' said Pashka, pushing his way firmly up to the barrier. 'Now, we'll see.'

The little old man gave him some quoits.

'So,' said Pashka, in a masterful way, 'if I get a quoit on the lower row, I get some Babaiev sweets, do I?'

'That's right,' said the old man, in a bored voice.

'A bit higher, and it's an alarm-clock.'

The old man nodded.

'Interesting. Ah-ha! So I suppose, if I want a samovar, I've got to pitch one right up there, under the ceiling.'

'Look here, you get a bit of cake first, then you can cackle,' came an impatient voice from the crowd. 'Come on!'

Pashka put his photo on the barrier, elbowed the crowd away on either side of him, leant on the barrier, took aim; but then all at once his hand shook, the quoit slipped from his fingers, fell to the floor and rolled away. A wave of ice had gone through Pashka. Beside the shelves, on a chair, with her little hands neatly folded in her lap, was a smartly-dressed girl of such beauty that Pashka's eyes were clouded. The girl got up swiftly, picked up the quoit, gave it to Pashka without even looking at him, then suddenly gave a faint smile, with only the very corner of her lips, to one side – and that was Pashka's ruin.

'Come on, lad, what's the matter with ee? Come on, get your samovar! Get on with it!' shouted the onlookers behind him.

Pashka came to his senses and started tossing the quoits, one by one, blind to everything but the lowered lashes of the girl and her fine lips – like a cleanly divided cherry. When he had tossed all forty rings she gathered them together and without a word put them on the barrier, but this time did not smile at all: she only shot her grey eyes at Pashka and straightened a wisp of her auburn hair which had escaped from behind one ear.

Pashka had another set. The quoits flew, clumsily, one after the other. The crowd laughed loud and pressed on Pashka's back. The knives buzzed like bees. The old man crooked one finger and indifferently scratched his nose.

Having wasted good money, without getting a single quoit on a knife, Pashka in despair forced his way out and walked along under the lime trees and down the rose alley, away from the cascade. The lake was now covered with a faint mist. He felt a freshness over his hands. The cinema mirrored itself in the water in columns of fire. More than one pair of bobbed girls with green or blue combs in their hair scurried arm in arm past him, turned round at him, giggled and pretended to push each other – he really was a wonderful fellow! – but Pashka strode on without even noticing them and, deep in thought, continued singing:

'The gipsy woman told it, the gipsy woman told it,
The gip-sy wo-man told it, when she took my hand.'

During the night he fell in love, finally, irrevocably.

That whole month Pashka went to the booth every Sunday to throw quoits. In this way, he blew half his wages. He did not take his holiday, missed his turn, was absolutely ill with it. As always the girl lowered her eyes and gave him the quoits. There were occasions when she smiled, but as if smiling to herself. Yet it did happen that, when she suddenly caught sight of Pashka in the crowd, she went scarlet, but such a deep scarlet that it seemed even her bosom through the thin marquisette showed like swarthy peaches. But however hard Pashka tried, he simply could not find a moment to have a word with the girl; either the crowd was in the way, or there were the old man's hostile eyes peering over his spectacles, while he crooked his finger and scratched his nose, just as if warning Pashka off – 'don't you try, that girl isn't for you. Scoot!' Then one day, only a few people were there and the old man had just run out with a stick to drive some little hooligans away.

'Excuse me,' said Pashka, and his heart thumped hard. 'What is your name?'

'Liudmilla,' the girl whispered, swiftly and warmly. 'I know who you are, once you forgot your photograph on the barrier, and I took it for myself, I simply fell in love with it, it's so fine.'

She slipped her fingers in her bosom and on a locket-chain there was a crumpled little square of pasteboard. Her eyes fluttered and she went deep scarlet.

'And what is your name?'

'Pashka. Will you go to the Coliseum with me? There's an awfully interesting film on, "The Woman with Millions", it's the first instalment.'

'I can't. Daddy won't let me.'

'You slip out.'

'Heaven forbid. If I do they'd never let me back again. Mummy's worse still, she's got her own stall in the Sukharevka market. You simply don't know what severe parents I have, it's really frightful. We live in Sretenka, Prosvirny Pereoulok's our street, not far from here. Number two, in the courtyard, to the left.'

'Well, Liudmilla darling?'

'I don't know. Quick, throw your knives, there's daddy coming.'

Pashka scarce had time to begin throwing, when there the old man was, with his stick, shooting savage glances at his daughter. So Pashka had to go without any result. The next Sunday, when he came – the booth was boarded up! All it showed was a signboard saying 'Practical American Quoits, Try your Luck'. And there, in the corner, was a painting of a green parrot with a pink tail, and a quoit in its beak, while the breeze stripped yellowing lime leaves from the trees and bore them past the parrot and piled them up round the booth and the flower-beds were bedraggled and not a soul was in sight: it was autumn.

Then only Pashka recalled the fortune-teller's words: 'There's a man getting on in years stands in your way ... you will suffer great unpleasantness from knives ... a green parrot will bring you luck ...' and he felt so sick and so mad with that gipsy you couldn't have described it. He threatened the parrot with his fist and went on his way, his mind blank and the wind blowing through him whichever way he turned, straight ahead down the deserted boulevard.

Coming out on to the Sretenka, he found himself in Prosvirny Alley. It was one of those noisy, overcast, empty autumn days. And there, no doubt about it, opposite a tumble-down church, was No. 2. Pashka entered the courtyard and turned to the left, but then he was at a loss where to go next. At that instant, a hurdy-gurdy began playing, and there on the hurdy-gurdy sat a green parrot, with a green tail, watching Pashka with impudent round eyes under cherry-coloured lids.

An instant later a little window on the second floor opened, a tender hand appeared and a coin wrapped in a piece of paper fell at his feet. And through the double window, over the padded felt and stuff half way up the double winter panes and through the curtains and aspidistras, he beheld Liudmilla. She was gazing at him with delighted eyes, her bright rosy cheek pressed to the pane, making signs with her fingers, her hands, her arms, yet he could make nothing out of it all. So Pashka began waving back to her to come out, damn the parents, I can't live without you – when suddenly in front of little Liudmilla was a stout, moustached woman in a Turkish shawl, who slammed the little window, and threatened Pashka with her fist.

Pashka went home with his tail between his legs, spent a fortnight in agony, hung about Prosvirny Alley at night, got in people's way like someone without visible means of support, frayed his nerves to tatters, and the third week, when Sunday came round, cleaned up his clothes with wet tea-leaves, put on a pink tie, polished his gaiters and set off to take the bull by the horns and offer his hand and his heart. Liudmilla herself opened the door, gasped when she saw him, clutched at her heart. But Pashka made straight for the living-room, where the parents were sitting at their after-dinner tea and said, 'Good afternoon. Excuse me, Daddy, and you, Mamma, excuse me, only I simply can't live without Liudmilla. It happened the moment I saw her. You can do what you please, but here I am, for what I am, a qualified mechanic of the sixth class, plus overtime, I don't touch spirits, I've been a party member, since 1923, I don't pay any alimony, so as far as that goes, everything's straight, clean bill.'

'Look here, young fellow,' yelled the old man, in an unbelievable voice, 'I'm not daddy to you, and my wife is not mamma to you. Forget it!'

'And I'd like to know what sort of goings-on you call it,' chimed in mamma, in a deep bass voice, 'hanging about the yard, listening to the hurdy-gurdy and breaking into other people's homes. You keep that to yourself. I never heard tell. And I never saw the likes, a young man for my daughter! To think of it, sixth class mechanic! Why, last year there was a manager of a block of flats in Miasnitzka Street came after her, and I sent him away with a flea in his ear too. Get out, if you please, Citizen. And we'll keep our girl. 'She's not just anybody. We don't want any mechanics here, especially party mechanics.'

'Just by practical quoits,' interposed the father, hotly, 'I make as much as a clear thousand roubles a season. And I've got four hundred roubles' worth of prizes. Liudmilla wants a husband with a bit of capital, to expand the business a little. In other words, good day to you.'

'So you won't let me marry her?' Pashka asked, in a voice of desperation.

'Not on any account,' the old man squeaked.

'Very well, sir,' said Pashka, in terrible tones, 'if capital to expand the business is what you want, the meeting's over. You'll remember this. I'll show you ... Good-bye, Liudmilla dear, don't give in, wait for me!'

As for Liudmilla, she sat in the hall, on a chest, and wrung her hands.

Pashka set his jaw and went out into the street, where he made for the Sukharevka market and bought a sharp kitchen knife. He went home and shut himself in. Winter came and went. The blocks of ice were brought in from the lake in the park, whole loads of it. Pashka went regularly to work, never lost a minute strolling about but instead spent the long winter evenings shut in his room, and his neighbours heard sounds of vibrating metal – was he learning to play the guitar? Nobody knew. The spring breaking of the ice came. The sun began to be warm, the world grew green, the trees came out and the boats were brought out of the boathouses on the lake in the park. The park photographers hung out their Kremlins and moonlit nights. The evening life of the boulevard began again.

Every Sunday, regularly, Pashka came down by the lake – to see if the booth had opened again. It was closed. The green parrot with the pink tail still sat on the sun-faded blue ground and held a quoit in its beak, while overhead drooped the fresh lime leaves. Pashka was thin and dour. Then one fine morning he found the booth open. A crowd of idlers stood in the doorway and the lamps inside were burning fiercely. There was the sound of clinking metal and laughter.

Pashka shouldered the crowd aside and with great decorum approached the barrier. His cheek-bones stood out stark and bare and his reddened eyes burnt. Liudmilla was collecting the quoits. He had scarcely set foot in the booth when the colour left her cheeks and she became absolutely transparent; her eyes darkened, her fine lips became still more beautiful, like cherries. Papa put his spectacles straight and seemed to draw back a little.

'Excuse me, Comrade,' said Pashka grimly, and shouldered aside the lad who was throwing the quoits. Then, without so much as a glance at the old man, he nodded to the girl. Like a mechanical thing she handed him the quoits. He touched her ice-cold fingers and tossed the money on the bench.

From behind him a wave of sniggering rose. 'Hi, comrade, you'd better get a barrow to take your samovars away,' somebody shouted.

Without turning to see who had spoken, Pashka took a quoit and tossed it negligently. The knives did not even stir. There was merely a dull thud. The quoit had fallen without touching the knife at all. The old man gave his nose a quick rub and, a trifle apprehensively, handed Pashka a packet of Babaiev sweets. Pashka moved it aside, drew back, then let the second quoit go, absolutely as though not trying. Just as lightly and neatly it ringed the second knife. And the old man had not had time to reach the shelf to get the second packet of sweets before Pashka had sent three more quoits after the others, which just as lightly, just as silently, settled round three more knives. A deathly silence fell on the booth.

The old man turned to Pashka and his little eyes blinked nervously. There was a dark bead of sweat on his forehead, like a beetle. The seat of his trousers went baggy, and seemed to have grown too big. Pashka stood with his legs crossed, leaning on the bench, rattling the quoits.

'Well, what about Liudmilla?' he asked, very quietly, looking about as though the whole world was his.

'Not for you,' the old father answered.

'No?' said Pashka, sleepily. 'Very well. Here, sonny, you run down to the Pokrovska gate for a porter and barrow to take the samovar. Daddy, mind stepping aside a moment?'

Pashka's face became solid metal. A vein started up on his forehead. He drew back his taut arm a little. Lightnings flashed from his fingers. The knives buzzed as the quoits caught and ringed them round. The crowd howled, thundered, grew ever larger. There were people flocking up from all sides. Pashka scarcely looked where he was aiming. His eyes seemed to wander loosely all over the place. He was menacing. Not one quoit missed its aim. In five minutes it was all over. Pashka wiped his forehead with his sleeve. The crowd fell away from him – the barrow had arrived.

'Load up,' said Pashka.

'Here, what's going to happen now?' the old man managed to say, treading about round the shelves.

'Nowt! All this junk's going straight into the lake, and that'll be the end of that.'

'Here, what do you mean, Citizen?' whined the old man like an old woman. 'Citizen, there's four hundred roubles' worth there, not to count the enterprise.'

'That's all the same to me, even if there's a thousand roubles' worth.

The junk's mine now. I haven't stolen it. I won it in fair play. I've got witnesses. I've practised the whole winter, cut myself short of sleep. And now I'm going to do as I please. If it pleases me, I'll keep the stuff for myself; and if it pleases me, I'll throw it in the lake.'

'That's right!' shouted a delighted voice from the crowd. 'We can swear to that. Only don't throw the gramophone in, old man.'

Volunteers from among the onlookers soon piled the stuff on the porter's barrow.

'Off we go,' said Pashka.

'Here, steady on, where?' shouted the old man. 'I mean, I ... I ... citizens ... how'll I go home ... You're not really going to throw them in?'

'Not half!' said Pashka. 'Come on, down to the landing-stage.'

'You might at least have a bit of respect for Providence.'

'Providence is only a remnant of obscurity, Daddy! Just like your green parrot. Say another word, and ...' He brandished his massive clenched fist.

Surrounded by a living ring of intensely-interested people, the barrow moved off down to the landing-stage, where they halted. Pashka took a pair of chrome leather boots from the top of the pile, and threw them into the water. The crowd gasped.

'Half a mo!' cried the old man, beside himself, and clutched at the barrow. 'Stop that!'

Then Pashka laid his powerful fist on top of the pile, lowered his eyes, and said calmly, 'This is the last time, Daddy, straight. Let all these folk be witnesses. Let me marry the lass, and here's your junk back. I won't come nearer the booth from now on than one hundred paces, or I could ruin you, absolutely, Daddy! I cannot live without Liudmilla.'

'Then take her!' the old man shouted, waving his arms. And he spat in his indignation. 'Take her, quickly!'

'Liudmilla, darling!' cried Pashka, and drew back from the barrow, pale as death.

She stood at his side, shy, with her arm hiding her face from the onlookers. Even her slender arms were scarlet, she blushed so.

'The show's over, citizens. Come on, off we go,' said Pashka, and took the girl by the elbow as tenderly as if she were made of fine porcelain.

At this moment the whole boulevard was redolent of jasmine. There was jasmine everywhere, in their hair and in the water. Low down over the limes, in a dense violet-coloured sky, the moon rose like a curved knife. And its youthful light, reflected in the lake, was multiplied and subdivided in infinite betrothal rings of living gold.

And yet you assert that great passions are out of date. Not in the least, I assure you.

BLUE DEVIL

Ilf & Petrov (Ilya Ilf, 1897–1937 & Evgeny Petrov, 1902–1942)

Translated by Anne O. Fisher

The most famous duet in Soviet literature, **Ilya Ilf** and **Evgeny Petrov** (born Iehiel-Leyb Faynzilberg & Evgeny Kataev) were both born in Odessa and brought Odessa's rich and adventurous spirit to their writing. Ilf & Petrov created *The Twelve Chairs* and *Golden Calf*, two extremely popular satirical books, where the unsettled post-revolutionary Soviet world becomes an ideal landscape for the classical *picaresque novel*, even though in the end, when the issue of soviet power is finally settled, the trickster hero is no longer welcome and should be wiped out.

Ilya Ilf died of tuberculosis in 1937, quite a rare natural death in the year of the Great Terror, and Evgeny Petrov rejoined his co-author five years later, in 1942, when he was a military correspondent and his plane crashed on its way back from the Nazi-besieged Sevastopol.

Doctor Grom came back to Kolokolamsk from Moscow, where he'd gone on business, in September. He had a slight limp and, in an unusually excessive move, took a horse-cab home. The doctor usually walked home from the station.

Citizen Grom, his wife, was extraordinarily surprised at this turn of events. But when she saw the shiny, ribbed imprint of an automobile tire on her husband's left boot, her surprise increased even more.

"I got hit by a car," Doctor Grom pronounced joyously. "And I took them to court."

Then, garnishing his speech with unnecessary details, the businessman-doctor told her the saga of his good fortune.

At the Tver Gate in Moscow, Lady Luck had turned her countenance, with a screeching of tires, toward Doctor Grom. The radiance of her countenance was so blinding that the doctor fell to the ground. He only realized he'd been hit by a car once he got back to his feet.

The doctor promptly calmed down, brushed the dirt off his trousers, and shouted, "I've been killed!"

A blue Packard came to a halt and out leaped a man in a sharp little bowler and a chauffeur with a brown moustache. The colorful flag of a small adjacent nation fluttered above the ignominious automobile's radiator.

"I've been killed!" repeated Doctor Grom firmly, addressing the crowd of rubberneckers.

"I know that fellow," said a stalwart young voice. "That's the Ambassador from the country of Curstonia. The Curstonian Ambassador."

The case went to court the very next day. The court ruled that the Curstonian embassy was obliged to pay the doctor a hundred and twenty rubles a month for causing him severe personal injury.

Doctor Grom marked the occasion by celebrating with his friends in Kolokolamsk for three straight days and nights. By the end of the revelry, they noticed that Aleksey Yeliseyevich, the out-of-work confectioner, had disappeared.

The rapture over the lucky turn in Doctor Grom's fortunes hadn't even subsided before a new sensation convulsed the town. Aleksey Yeliseyevich came back. It turned out he'd gone to Moscow, where completely by accident he'd been hit by the Curstonian embassy's blue car. He returned with a court order.

This time, since the confectioner was burdened with a large family, the embassy was obliged to provide compensation of a hundred and forty rubles a month for severe personal injury.

The confectioner rolled out a barrel of beer from sheer joy. All of Kolokolamsk was wiping beer foam from its moustache and singing the traffic victim's praises.

The third victim emerged a week later. It was Sindik-Bugayevsky, the head teacher of a series of declamation and singing courses. He acted with his characteristic directness. As soon as he got to Moscow, he headed straight to the gate of the Curstonian embassy. The moment the car burst out onto the street, he stuck his foot under the wheel. Sindik-Bugayevsky got some fairly serious bruises and a hundred-ruble pension till his dying day.

Only then did the Kolokolamskians see that their town had entered into a new and fortunate era in its history. With the utmost diligence, the citizens set to mining the vein of gold Doctor Grom had discovered.

Everyone was drawn to seasonal work in Moscow: old men wise with experience, young private entrepreneurs, students from the declamation courses, and honored workers. The town's cabbies, in their long, belted blue coats, took an especial liking to it. For a while, there wasn't a single cabbie working in Kolokolamsk. They were all going out for seasonal work. With their bindles on their shoulders, they got hit by the Curstonian car, recovered in the hospital, and promptly collected the predetermined sum from the embassy.

In the meantime, an unprecedented financial crisis had erupted in Curstonia. The expense of maintaining the embassy had increased so much that the nation was forced to cut civil servants' salaries and reduce the army from three hundred soldiers to fifteen. The opposition party, the Christian Socialists, went on the move. The opposition leader, Mr. Soop, subjected the Chairman of the Council of Ministers, Mr. Edgar Parviainen, to unremitting attacks.

When Nikita Psov became the thirtieth citizen of the town of Kolokolamsk to get hit by the Curstonian car and the state opera house had to be shut down to pay for his compensation, the people's agitation hit the breaking point. Everyone expected a faction of the military to stage a putsch.

A query was issued to the Chamber: "Is the esteemed Chairman of the Council of Ministers aware that the country is teetering on the brink of ruin?"

To which the esteemed Chairman of the Council of Ministers replied, "No, he is aware of no such thing."

Still, regardless of this reassuring answer, Curstonia was forced to take on a foreign loan. But the loan only lasted a couple of months before it, too, was devoured by the citizens of Kolokolamsk.

The hopes of all Curstonia rested on the embassy's chauffeur, who performed miraculous feats of caution. But the Kolokolamskians had honed an unusual level of skill in their surprising trade and fell flawlessly under his tires. Word was that one time the chauffeur had managed to evade a certain Kolokolamsk deacon for three whole blocks, but the savvy religious worker contrived to cut through a building courtyard and throw himself under the car anyway.

The people of Kolokolamsk dragged all of Curstonia through the courts. The country was going under.

Monsieur Podlinnik, chairman of the workers' pseudo-collective "Individuwork," straggled along to Moscow from Kolokolamsk as soon as the first frost hit. He'd spent a long time hemming and hawing and complaining, but his wife was merciless. As she described the rapidity of other citizens' wealth accumulation to her husband, she concluded: "If you don't go for seasonal work, I'll throw myself under a train."

The entire town saw Podlinnik off. As soon as he got settled in his seat, Kolokolamskians who'd already done their seasonal work shouted, "Don't get hit in the head! That buggy's heavy! Just stick your foot out!"

Two days later, Podlinnik returned with his head wrapped in bandages and a great big black eye like a pool of spilled ink. He couldn't move his left arm.

"How much?" his fellow citizens asked, by which they meant the amount of the pension he'd wrested from the atrophied Curstonian treasury.

But instead of answering, the chairman of the workers' pseudo-collective burst into silent sobs. He was ashamed to admit that he'd leaped in front of the Association of Light Metals Enterprises' car by mistake, and that the chauffer, who had stopped the car in time, then got out and vigorously beat him (Podlinnikov) about the head and shoulders with a lug wrench.

The sight of Monsieur Podlinnik was so terrifying that the Kolokolamskians stopped going out for seasonal work.

This was the only thing that saved Curstonia from complete wrack and ruin.

The town of Kolokolamsk began to get bored again. Its placid, unimportant life went on as usual, until a marvelous gentleman in a pink woolen suit arrived from Argentina.

LIOMPA

Yury Olesha (1899–1960)

Translated by Aimee Anderson

Native Polish speaker, **Yury Olesha** grew up in Odessa, where he met Valentin Kataev and Ilya Ilf, and established with them and others the Odessa literary circle.

In the twenties Olesha wrote two novels *The Three Fat Men* and *Envy*, the latter considered to be the best description of the conflict between the *old* intelligencia and the new masses. In the thirties began what Olesha's brilliant biographer, Arkady Belinkov, called the surrender and doom of the Soviet intelligent: Olesha wrote no more significant fiction, but composed articles glorifying Stalin and cursing the enemies of the people.

He outlived his talent and died in the short period of the Thaw, when his books were published again.

The young boy Alexander was planing boards in the kitchen. The cuts on his fingers were covered with delectable golden scabs.

The kitchen led out into a courtyard; it was spring, doors were left open, grass was growing near the threshold, spilled water sparkled on a stone. Now and then a rat appeared in the garbage can. Finely-sliced potatoes were frying in the kitchen. The primus-stove was being lit. The life of the primus-stove began magnificently: it flared to the ceiling. Then it died down to a gentle blue flame. Eggs were jumping in boiling water. One tenant was boiling crabs. With two fingers he picked up a live crab by the waist. The crabs were greenish, the color of water-pipes. Suddenly two or three small drops of water flew by themselves from the faucet. The faucet was quietly blowing its nose. Then, above, the pipes started speaking in various voices. Then, dusk all at once began to take shape. Only a single glass continued to shine on the window-sill. It caught the last rays of the sun through the gate. The faucet talked on and on. All sorts of stirrings and cracklings were beginning around the stove.

The dusk was wonderful. People were eating sunflower seeds, singing could be heard, the yellow light from rooms fell on the pavement, the dining table was brightly lit.

In the room next to the kitchen, lay Ponomaryov, seriously ill. He lay in the room alone, a candle burned, a bottle of medicine stood above his head, a prescription hung from the bottle.

When acquaintances came to see Ponomaryov, he said:

"Congratulate me, I am dying."

Towards evening he became delirious. The bottle looked at him. The prescription stretched out, like the train of a dress. The bottle was a duchess at her wedding. The bottle was labeled "The Duchess' Name-Day." The sick man raved. He wanted to write a treatise. He conversed with the blanket.

"Now, aren't you ashamed? ..." he whispered.

The blanket sat next to him, lay down next to him, went away, reported the news.

Only a few things surrounded the sick man: the medicine, a spoon, the light, the wallpaper. All other things had gone away. When he understood that he was seriously ill and dying, then he understood, too, how huge and varied was the world of things and how few of them remained in his control. Every day the number of things decreased. Such a familiar thing as a railway ticket had already become for him irretrievably distant. At first the number of things had decreased along the periphery, far away from him; then the reduction started to draw nearer, faster and faster toward the center, toward him, toward his heart—into the yard, into the house, into the hallway, into the room.

At first the disappearance of things had not caused the sick man any anguish.

Countries disappeared, America, the possibility of being handsome or rich, a family (he was single) ... The illness had no relation at all to the disappearance of these things. They had slipped away as he had grown older—the real pain had come when it became clear to him that even those things which had constantly moved level with him were beginning to move away from him too. Thus, in a single day, the street, his work, the post office, horses had left him. And now, headlong, the disappearance had begun alongside him, close at hand; the corridor had already slipped from his power, and in his very room, before his eyes, the meaning of his coat had ceased, the door-latch, his shoes. He knew: death on its way to him was destroying things. From their vast and idle number, death had left him only a few, and they were those things which, had it been in his power, he would never have permitted into his house. He had things shoved at him. He had received the terrible visits and stares of acquaintances. He understood that he hadn't the strength to defend himself against the intrusion of these unsolicited and, as it always seemed to him, unnecessary things. But now they were the only ones, indisputable. He had lost the right to choose things.

The boy Alexander was making a model plane.

The boy was much more complex and serious than others thought. He would cut his fingers, bleed profusely, litter the floor with shavings, leave glue stains, try to get silk, cry, receive slaps on the back of the head. The grown-ups considered themselves absolutely right. But the boy behaved in a perfectly grownup manner, more than that—he behaved like only a small number of grown-ups behave; he behaved in full accordance with science. The model was constructed according to a blueprint, calculations were made—the boy knew the laws. He could have opposed the grown-ups' attacks with an explanation of the laws, a demonstration of the experiments, but he was silent because he didn't think he had a right to appear more serious than the grown-ups.

Rubber bands, wires, boards, silk, light tea-room silk cloth, the odor of glue were situated around the boy. The sky glittered. Insects walked about on a stone. A cockle-shell had petrified in the stone.

Another boy, very small, almost naked, in blue shorts, came up to the boy who was working. He touched things, got in the way. Alexander chased him away. The naked, rubber boy walked about the house, along the corridor where a bicycle stood. (The bicycle was leaning with its pedal against the wall. The pedal had made a scratch on the wallpaper. It seemed that the bicycle was holding on to the wall by this scratch.)

The little boy went into Ponomaryov's room. The youngster's head appeared indistinctly above the side of the bed. The sick man's temples were pale, like those of a blind man. The boy came up close to his head and examined it. He thought that in the world it had always been and always was like this: a bearded man lies in a room on a bed.

The boy had just entered into the recognition of things. He still did not know how to distinguish their different existences in time.

He turned away and began to walk about the room. He saw parquet tiles, dust under the skirting board, cracks in the plaster. Lines came together and spread out around him, bodies lived. Suddenly an optical illusion appeared—the boy rushed toward it, but hardly had he taken a step when the change in distance destroyed the illusion—and the boy looked around, looked up and down, looked behind the stove, searched and, not finding it, spread his hands, perplexed. Every second created something new for him. A spider was astonishing. The spider flew away at the boy's mere thought of touching it with his hand.

The vanishing things left the dying man only their names.

In the world there was an apple. It shone in the leaves, gently revolved, caught and turned in itself bits of the day, the blueness of the garden, the window sash. The law of gravity lay in wait for it under the tree, on the black earth, on the knolls. Minute ants ran among the knolls. Newton sat in the garden. In the apple were hidden a multitude of causes capable of calling forth a still greater multitude of effects. But not one of these causes was intended for Ponomaryov. The apple had become for him an abstraction. And the fact that the flesh of a thing had disappeared from him while the abstraction remained—was a torment for him.

"I thought that the external world did not exist," he mused. "I thought that my eye and my ear directed things, I thought that the world would cease to exist when I ceased to exist. But now... I see that everything is turning away from me while I am still alive. I still do exist! Why then don't things exist? I thought that my brain gave them form, weight, and color—but now they have gone away from me and only their names—useless names that have lost their owners—burrow in my brain. What are these names to me?"

In anguish Ponomaryov looked at the child. The child was walking about. Things rushed to meet him. He smiled at them, not knowing a single name. He went out, and a magnificent train of things struggled after him.

"Listen," the sick man called to the child. "Listen. You know, when I die nothing will remain. Not the courtyard, not the tree, not Papa, not Mama. I will take everything with me."

A rat had gotten into the kitchen.

Ponomaryov listened: the rat was keeping house, banging the plates, turning on the faucet, rustling in the bucket.

"Ah, it's washing the dishes," thought Ponomaryov.

Immediately the disturbing thought came into his head that the rat might have its own name, unknown to people. He began to wonder what the name could be. He was delirious. As he was thinking, fear seized him more and more powerfully. He knew that, no matter what, he must stop and not think about the rat's name—at the same time he continued, knowing that at the very instant when that singular, senseless, and terrible name was found—he would die.

"Liompa!" he cried suddenly in a terrible voice.

The house was asleep. It was early morning—just after five. The boy Alexander was not asleep. The door from the kitchen was opened onto the courtyard. The sun was still somewhere below the horizon.

The dying man was walking around the kitchen, doubled over, arms stretched out with his hands drooping down. He was seizing things.

The boy Alexander ran across the courtyard. The model flew in front of him. It was the last thing Ponomaryov saw.

He did not seize it. It flew away.

In the afternoon a blue coffin with yellow decorations appeared in the kitchen. The rubber boy watched from the corridor, his hands behind his back. For a long time they had to turn the coffin every which way to get it through the door. They grazed a shelf, a saucepan; plaster sprinkled down. The boy Alexander climbed onto the stove and helped, supporting the box from below. When the coffin finally penetrated the corridor, where it immediately became black, the little rubber boy, shuffling his sandals, ran ahead.

"Grandfather! Grandfather!" he shouted. "They've brought you a coffin."

THE RETURN OF CHORB

Vladimir Nabokov (1899–1977)

Translated by Vladimir Nabokov

His father was a lawyer and influential politician, who supported the White cause, was forced to immigrate to Germany and was murdered by an ultra-monarchist trying to assassinate someone else. His brother was arrested by the Nazis for being gay and ended up in a concentration camp. **Vladimir Nabokov** fled Russia with his family, fled Germany when the Nazis harassed his wife, fled France in 1940 on board of one of the last steamers to leave for the US, left the USA and came back to Europe in the sixties; he was the perfect émigré who never really emigrated, a person of the world, the most foreign of all Russian authors, available during the Soviet period only outside USSR or in fuzzy samizdat copies.

Entomologist, skilled chess player, Nabokov is the best Russian-speaking stylist of the twentieth century and, maybe, of all Russian literature.

The Kellers left the opera house at a late hour. In that pacific German city, where the very air seemed a little lusterless and where a transverse row of ripples had kept shading gently the reflected cathedral for well over seven centuries, Wagner was a leisurely affair presented with relish so as to overgorge one with music. After the opera Keller took his wife to a smart nightclub renowned for its white wine. It was past one in the morning when their car, flippantly lit on the inside, sped through lifeless streets to deposit them at the iron wicket of their small but dignified private house. Keller, a thick-set old German, closely resembling Oom Paul Kruger, was the first to step down on the sidewalk, across which the loopy shadows of leaves stirred in the streetlamp's gray glimmer. For an instant his starched shirt front and the droplets of bugles trimming his wife's dress caught the light as she disengaged a stout leg and climbed out of the car in her turn. The maid met them in the vestibule and, still carried by the momentum of the news, told them in a frightened whisper about Chorb's having called. Frau Keller's chubby face, whose everlasting freshness somehow agreed with her Russian merchant-class parentage, quivered and reddened with agitation.

"He said she was ill?"

The maid whispered still faster. Keller stroked his gray brush of hair with his fat palm, and an old man's frown overcast his large, somewhat simian face, with its long upper lip and deep furrows.

"I simply refuse to wait till tomorrow," muttered Frau Keller shaking her head as she gyrated heavily on one spot, trying to catch the end of the veil that covered her auburn wig. "We'll go there at once. Oh dear, or dear! No wonder there's been no letters for quite a month."

Keller punched his gibus open and said in his precise, slightly guttural Russian:

"The man is insane. How dare he, if she's ill, take her a second time to that vile hotel?"

But they were wrong, of course, in thinking that their daughter was ill. Chorb said so to the maid only because it was easier to utter. In point of fact he had returned alone from abroad and only now realized that, like it or not, he would have to explain how his wife had perished, and why he had written nothing about it to his in-laws. It was all very difficult. How was he to explain that he wished to possess his grief all by himself, without tainting it by any foreign substance and without sharing it with any other soul? Her death appeared to him as a most rare, almost unheard-of occurrence; nothing, it seemed to him, could be purer than such a death, caused by the impact of an electric stream, the same stream which, when poured into glass receptacles, yields the purest and brightest light.

Ever since that spring day when, on the white highway a dozen kilometers from Nice, she had touched, laughing, the live wire of a storm-felled pole, Chorb's entire world ceased to sound like a world: it retreated at once, and even the dead body that he carried in his arms to the nearest village struck him as something alien and needless.

In Nice, where she had to be buried, the disagreeable consumptive clergyman kept in vain pressing him for details: Chorb responded only with a languid smile. He sat daylong on the shingly beach, cupping colored pebbles and letting them flow from hand to hand;

and then, suddenly, without waiting for the funeral, he traveled back to Germany.

He passed in reverse through all the spots they had visited together during their honeymoon journey. In Switzerland where they had wintered and where the apple trees were now in their last bloom, he recognized nothing except the hotels. As to the Black Forest, through which they had hiked in the preceding autumn, the chill of the spring did not impede memory. And just as he had tried, on the southern beach, to find again that unique rounded black pebble with the regular little white belt, which she had happened to show him on the eve of their last ramble, so now he did his best to look up all the roadside items that retained her exclamation mark: the special profile of a cliff, a hut roofed with a layer of silvery-gray scales, a black fir tree and a footbridge over a white torrent, and something which one might be inclined to regard as a kind of fatidic prefiguration: the radial span of a spider's web between two telegraph wires that were beaded with droplets of mist. She accompanied him: her little boots stepped rapidly, and her hands never stopped moving, moving—to pluck a leaf from a bush or stroke a rock wall in passing—light, laughing hands that knew no repose. He saw her small face with its dense dark freckles, and her wide eyes, whose pale greenish hue was that of the shards of glass licked smooth by the sea waves. He thought that if he managed to gather all the little things they had noticed together—if he re-created thus the near past—her image would grow immortal and replace her for ever. Nighttime, though, was unendurable. Night imbued with sudden terror her irrational presence. He hardly slept at all during the three weeks of his trek— and now he got off, quite drugged with fatigue, at the railway station, which had been last autumn their point of departure from the quiet town where he had met and married her.

It was around eight o'clock of the evening. Beyond the houses the cathedral tower was sharply set off in black against a golden-red stripe of sunset. In the station square stood in file the selfsame decrepit fiacres. The identical newspaper seller uttered his hollow crepuscular cry. The same black poodle with apathetic eyes was in the act of raising a thin hindleg near a Morris pillar, straight at the scarlet lettering of a playbill announcing *Parsifal*.

Chorb's luggage consisted of a suitcase and a big tawny trunk.

A fiacre took him through the town. The cabby kept indolently flapping his reins, while steadying the trunk with one hand. Chorb remembered that she whom he never named liked to take rides in cabs.

In a lane at the corner of the municipal opera house there was an old three-storied hotel of a disreputable type with rooms that were let by the week, or by the hour. Its black paint had peeled off in geographical patterns; ragged lace curtained its bleary windows; its inconspicuous front door was never locked. A pale but jaunty lackey led Chorb down a crooked corridor reeking of dampness and boiled cabbage into a room which Chorb recognized—by the picture of a pink *baigneuse* in a gilt frame over the bed—as the very one in which he and his wife had spent their first night together. Everything amused her then—the fat man in his shirt sleeves who was vomiting right in the passage, and the fact of their having chosen by chance such a beastly hotel, and the presence of a lovely blond hair in the wash basin; but what tickled her most was the way they had escaped from her house. Immediately upon coming home from church she ran up to her room to change, while downstairs the guests were gathering for supper. Her father, in a dress coat of sturdy cloth, with a flabby grin on his apish face, clapped this or that man on the shoulder and served ponies of brandy himself. Her mother, in the meantime, led her closest friends, two by two, to inspect the bedroom meant for the young couple: with tender emotion, whispering under her breath, she pointed out the colossal eiderdown, the orange blossoms, the two pairs of brand-new bedroom slippers—large checkered ones, and tiny red ones with pompons—that she had aligned on the bedside rug, across which a Gothic inscription ran: *"We are together unto the tomb."* Presently, everybody moved toward the *hors d'œuvres*—and Chorb and his wife, after the briefest of consultations, fled through the back door, and only on the following morning, half an hour before the express train was to leave, reappeared to collect their luggage. Frau Keller had sobbed all night; her husband, who had always regarded Chorb (destitute Russian émigré and *littérateur*) with suspicion, now cursed his daughter's choice, the cost of the liquor, the local police that could do nothing. And several times, after the Chorbs had gone, the old man went to look at the hotel in the lane behind the opera house, and henceforward that black, purblind house became an object of disgust and attraction to him like the recollection of a crime.

While the trunk was being brought in, Chorb kept staring at the rosy chromo. When the door closed, he bent over the trunk and unlocked it. In a corner of the room, behind a loose strip of wallpaper, a mouse made a scuffing noise and then raced like a toy on rollers. Chorb turned on his heel with a start. The light bulb hanging from the ceiling on a cord swayed ever so gently, and the shadow of the cord glided across the green couch and broke at its edge. It was on that couch that he had slept on his nuptial night. She, on the regular bed, could be heard breathing with the even rhythm of a child. That night he had kissed her once—on the hollow of the throat—that had been all in the way of love-making.

The mouse was busy again. There exist small sounds that are more frightening than gunfire. Chorb left the trunk alone and paced the room a couple of times. A moth struck the lamp with a ping. Chorb wrenched the door open and went out.

On the way downstairs he realized how weary he was, and when he found himself in the alley the blurry blue of the May night made him dizzy. Upon turning into the boulevard he walked faster. A square. A stone *Herzog*. The black masses of the City Park. Chestnut trees now were in flower. *Then*, it had been autumn. He had gone for a long stroll with her on the eve of the wedding. How good was the earthy, damp, somewhat violety smell of the dead leaves strewing the sidewalk! On those enchanting overcast days the sky would be of a dull white, and the small twig-reflecting puddle in the middle of the black pavement resembled an insufficiently developed photograph. The gray-stone villas were separated by the mellow and motionless foliage of yellowing trees, and in front of the Kellers' house the leaves of a withering poplar had acquired the tone of transparent grapes. One glimpsed, too, a few birches behind the bars of the gate; ivy solidly muffed some of their boles, and Chorb made a point of telling her that ivy never grew on birches in Russia, and she remarked that the foxy tints of their minute leaves reminded her of spots of tender rust upon ironed linen. Oaks and chestnuts lined the sidewalk; their black bark was velveted with green rot; every now and then a leaf broke away to fly athwart the street like a scrap of wrapping paper. She attempted to catch it on the wing by means of a child's spade found near a heap of pink bricks at a spot where the street was under repair. A little way off the funnel of a workers' van emitted gray-blue smoke which drifted aslant and dissolved between the branches—and a resting workman, one hand on his hip, contemplated the young lady, as light as a dead leaf, dancing about with that little spade in her raised hand. She skipped, she laughed. Chorb, hunching his back a bit, walked behind her—and it seemed to him that happiness itself had that smell, the smell of dead leaves.

At present he hardly recognized the street, encumbered as it was with the nocturnal opulence of chestnut trees. A streetlamp glinted in front; over the glass a branch drooped, and several leaves at its end, saturated with light, were quite translucent. He came nearer. The shadow of the wicket, its checkerwork all distorted, swept up toward him from the sidewalk to entangle his feet. Beyond the gate, and beyond a dim gravel walk, loomed the front of the familiar house, dark except for the light in one open window. Within that amber chasm the housemaid was in the act of spreading with an ample sweep of her arms a snow-bright sheet on a bed. Loudly and curtly Chorb called out to her. With one hand he still gripped the wicket and the dewy touch of iron against his palm was the keenest of all memories.

The maid was already hurrying toward him. As she was to tell Frau Keller later, what struck her first was the fact that Chorb remained standing silently on the sidewalk although she had unlocked the little gate at once. "He had no hat," she related, "and the light of the streetlamp fell on his forehead, and his forehead was all sweaty, and the hair was glued to it by the sweat. I told him master and mistress were at the theater. I asked him why he was alone. His eyes were blazing, their look terrified me, and he seemed not to have shaved for quite a time. He said softly: 'Tell them that she is ill.' I asked: 'Where are you staying?' He said: 'Same old place,' and then added: 'That does not matter. I'll call again in the morning.' I suggested he wait—but he didn't reply and went away."

Thus Chorb traveled back to the very source of his recollections, an agonizing and yet blissful test now drawing to a close. All there remained was but a single night to be spent in that first chamber of their marriage, and by tomorrow the test would be passed and her image made perfect.

But as he trudged back to the hotel, up the boulevard, where on all the benches in the blue darkness sat hazy figures, Chorb suddenly understood that, despite exhaustion, he would not be able to sleep alone in that room with its naked bulb and whispery crannies. He reached the square and plodded along the city's main avenue—and now he knew what must be done. His quest, however, lasted a long while: This was a quiet and chaste town, and the secret by-street where one could buy love was unknown to Chorb. Only after an hour of helpless wandering, which caused his ears to sing and his feet to burn, did he enter that little lane—whereupon he accosted at once the first girl who hailed him.

"The night," said Chorb, scarcely unclenching his teeth.

The girl cocked her head, swung her handbag, and replied: "Twenty-five."

He nodded. Only much later, having glanced at her casually, Chorb noted with indifference that she was pretty enough, though considerably jaded, and that her bobbed hair was blond.

She had been in that hotel several times before, with other customers, and the wan, sharp-nosed lackey, who was tripping down as they were going upstairs gave her an amiable wink. While Chorb and she walked along the corridor, they could hear, from behind one of the doors, a bed creaking, rhythmically and weightily, as if a log was being sawed in two. A few doors further the same monotonous creak came from another room and as they passed by the girl looked back at Chorb with an expression of cold playfulness.

In silence he ushered her into his room—and immediately, with a profound anticipation of sleep, started to tear off his collar from its stud. The girl came up very close to him:

"And what about a small present?" she suggested, smiling.

Dreamily, absentmindedly, Chorb considered her, as he slowly grasped what she meant.

Upon receiving the banknotes, she carefully arranged them in her bag, uttered a light little sigh, and again rubbed herself against him.

"Shall I undress?" she asked with a shake of her bob.

"Yes, go to bed," muttered Chorb. "I'll give you some more in the morning."

The girl began to undo hastily the buttons of her blouse, and kept glancing at him askance, being slightly taken aback by his abstraction and gloom. He shed his clothes quickly and carelessly, got into the bed and turned to the wall.

"This fellow likes kinky stuff," vaguely conjectured the girl. With slow hands she folded her chemise, placed it upon a chair. Chorb was already fast asleep.

The girl wandered around the room. She noticed that the lid of the trunk standing by the window was slightly ajar; by squatting on her heels, she managed to peep under the lid's edge. Blinking and cautiously stretching out her bare arm, she palpated a woman's dress, a stocking, scraps of silk—all this stuffed in anyhow and smelling so nice that it made her feel sad.

Presently she straightened up, yawned, scratched her thigh, and just as she was, naked, but in her stockings, drew aside the window curtain. Behind the curtain the casement was open and one could make out, in the velvety depths, a corner of the opera house, the black shoulder of a stone Orpheus outlined against the blue of the night and a row of light along the dim façade which slanted off into darkness. Down there, far away, diminutive dark silhouettes swarmed as they emerged from bright doorways onto the semicircular layers of illumined porch steps, to which glided up cars with shimmering headlights and smooth glistening tops. Only when the breakup was over and the brightness gone, the girl closed the curtain again. She switched off the light and stretched on the bed beside Chorb. Just before falling asleep she caught herself thinking that once or twice she had already been in that room: she remembered the pink picture on its wall.

Her sleep lasted not more than an hour: a ghastly deep-drawn howl roused her. It was Chorb screaming. He had woken up some time after midnight, had turned on his side and had seen his wife lying beside him. He screamed horribly, with visceral force. The white specter of a woman sprang off the bed. When, trembling, she turned on the light, Chorb was sitting among the tumbled bedclothes, his back to the wall, and through his spread fingers one eye could be seen burning with a mad flame. Then he slowly uncovered his face, slowly recognized the girl. With a frightened mutter she was hastily putting on her chemise.

And Chorb heaved a sigh of relief for he realized that the ordeal was over. He moved onto the green couch, and sat there, clasping his hairy shins and with a meaningless smile contemplating the harlot. That smile increased her terror; she turned away, did up one last hook, laced her boots, busied herself with the putting on of her hat.

At this moment the sound of voices and footsteps came from the corridor.

One could hear the voice of the lackey repeating mournfully: "But look here, there's a lady with him." And an irate guttural voice kept insisting: "But I'm telling you she's my daughter."

The footsteps stopped at the door. A knock followed.

The girl snatched her bag from the table and resolutely flung the door open. In front of her stood an amazed old gentleman in a lusterless top hat, a pearl stud gleaming in his starched shirt. From over his shoulder peered the tear-stained face of a stout lady with a veil on her hair. Behind them the puny pale lackey strained up on tiptoe, making big eyes and gesturing invitingly. The girl understood his signs and shot out into the corridor, past the old man, who turned his head in her wake with the same puzzled look and then crossed the threshold with his companion. The door closed. The girl and the lackey remained in the corridor. They exchanged a frightened glance and bent their heads to listen. But in the room all was silence. It seemed incredible that inside there should be three people. Not a single sound came from there.

"They don't speak," whispered the lackey and put his finger to his lips.

NIKITA

Andrey Platonov (1899–1951)

*Translated by Robert & Elizabeth Chandler
and Angela Livingstone*

The son of a locomotive driver, member of the railroad revolutionary comittee and rifleman in the communist railroad militia during the Civil War, **Andrey Platonov** (born Andrey Klimentov) genuinely supported the building of a new, classless and just society, and wrote prose describing the process of transformation and rebirth of a man (*The Foundation Pit, The Chebengur*). Yet his talent was so strong that Platonov's prose became a kind of linguistic and political investigation of the foundations of totalitarian power, the bitter prophecy from the mouth of the apostle.

It is not surprising that the Soviet state did not tolerate such an approach. Platonov's major works were not published, his son Platon was arrested and sent to the GULAG; his books were widely released only in the late eighties, when the USSR was close to its end.

Early in the morning the mother would leave home to go and work in the fields. There was no father in the family; father had gone away long ago to the most important work – the war – and he had not come back. Every day the mother expected the father to come back, but he did not come and he did not come.

Five-year-old Nikita would be left on his own, master of the hut and the whole yard. As she left, his mother would tell him not to burn the hut down, to be sure to collect any eggs the hens laid beneath the fence or in the sheds, not to let any other cocks come into the yard and attack their own cock – and to eat the bread and milk she had put on the table for lunch, and in the evening she would come back and make him a hot supper.

"You haven't got a father, Nikitushka, so don't get up to mischief," his mother would say. "You're a clever boy now, and what's in the hut and yard is all we have."

"I'm clever, it's all we have, and I haven't got a father," Nikita would say. "But come back soon, Mummy, or I get frightened."

"What's there to be frightened of? The sun's shining in the sky, and the fields are full of people. Don't be frightened, you'll be all right on your own."

"But the sun's a long way away," Nikita would say, "and a cloud will cover it up."

When his mother had left, Nikita went round the whole quiet hut – the back room and the other room with its Russian stove – and then went out into the entrance. Big fat flies were buzzing there, a spider was dozing in a corner in the middle of his web, and a sparrow had crossed the threshold on foot and was looking for a grain or two on the earth floor. Nikita knew every one of them: the sparrows, and the spiders, and the flies and the hens outside; he had had enough of them, they bored him. What he wanted now was to learn something he did not know. So Nikita went on out into the yard and came to the shed, where there was an empty barrel standing in the darkness. Probably someone was living in it, some little man or other; in the daytime he slept, but at night he came out, ate bread, drank water and did some thinking, and then in the morning he would hide inside the barrel again and go to sleep.

"I know you, you live in there," said Nikita. He was standing on tiptoe and speaking down into the dark, resonant barrel. Then he gave it a knock with his fist to make sure. "Get up, you lazybones, and stop sleeping! What are you going to eat in winter? Go and weed the millet, they'll put it down as a work day!"*

Nikita listened. It was quiet in the barrel. "Maybe he's died!" Nikita thought. But there was a squeak from the wood, and Nikita got out of harm's way. He realized that whoever lived there must have turned over onto his side, or else was about to get up and chase after him.

But what was he like – this man in the barrel? Nikita pictured him at once in his mind. He was someone small but lively. He had a long beard that reached right down to the ground. Without meaning to, he

---

* Effectively a unit of payment on a collective farm. Workers were paid according to how many "work days" they completed. By working hard, it was possible to complete more than one "work day" during the day.

swept away the litter and straw with his beard when he walked about at night, leaving clean paths on the floor of the shed.

Not long ago his mother had lost her scissors. The little man must have taken them to trim his beard.

"Give us back our scissors!" Nikita said quietly. "When father comes home from the war, he'll take them anyway. He's not afraid of you. Give them back!"

The barrel remained silent. In the forest, far beyond the village, someone gave a hoot, and the little man in the barrel answered in a strange black voice: "I'm here!"

Nikita ran out of the shed into the yard. The kind sun was shining in the sky, there were no clouds in the way. Nikita was frightened and he looked at the sun, hoping it would defend him.

"There's someone there – living in a barrel!" said Nikita, looking at the sky.

The kind sun went on shining in the sky, looking back at him in return with its warm face. Nikita saw that the sun was like his dead grandfather; when he was still alive and had looked at Nikita, his grandfather had always smiled and been kind to him. Nikita thought that his grandfather had gone to live on the sun now.

"Grandpa, where are you? Do you live up there?" asked Nikita. "Stay up there then, but I'll stay here, I'll live with Mummy."

Beyond the vegetable plot, in the thickets of burdock and nettles, there was a well. It was a long time since they had taken water from it, because another well had been dug in the collective farm and the water there was better.

Deep down in this abandoned well, in its underground darkness, lay bright water with a clear sky and clouds passing below the sun. Nikita leaned over the well frame and asked: "What are you doing down there?"

Down on the bottom, he thought, lived small water people. He knew what they were like, he had seen them in dreams and wanted to catch them, but they had run away over the grass and into the well, back to their home. They were the size of sparrows, but they were fat and hairless, damp and dangerous. Nikita knew they wanted to drink up his eyes while he was asleep.

"I'll teach you!" Nikita said into the well. "What are you doing living down there?"

The water in the well suddenly went cloudy, and somebody champed their jaws. Nikita opened his mouth to scream, but nothing came out, he had lost his voice from fear; his heart just trembled and missed a beat.

"A giant and his children live here too!" Nikita realized. "Grandpa!" he shouted out loud, looking at the sun. "Are you there, Grandpa?" And Nikita ran back to his home.

Beside the shed he came to his senses. Beneath its wattle wall were two burrows in the earth. They too had their secret inhabitants. But who were they? They might be snakes. They would creep out at night, they would steal into the hut and bite his mother while she was asleep, and his mother would die.

Nikita ran quickly back inside, took two bits of bread from the table and carried them out. He put one piece by each burrow and said to the snakes: "Eat up the bread, snakes, and don't bother us at night."

Nikita looked round. There was an old tree stump in the vegetable plot. When he looked at it, Nikita saw it was the head of a man. The stump had eyes, a nose and a mouth, and the stump was quietly smiling at Nikita.

"Do you live here too?" the boy asked. "Come out and join us in the village. You can plough the earth."

The stump quacked out an answer, and its face turned angry.

"All right then, don't come out!" said Nikita, taking fright. "Stay where you are!"

It had gone quiet everywhere in the village, there was no sound of anyone. His mother was far away in the fields, he would never reach her in time. Nikita left the angry tree stump and went back into the entrance of the hut. He didn't feel frightened in there, his mother had been there not long ago. It was hot in the hut now. Nikita wanted to drink the milk his mother had left him, but when he looked at the table he noticed the table was a person too, only it had four legs and no arms.

Nikita went back out onto the porch. Far beyond the vegetable plot and the well stood the old bath hut. It was black inside from the chimney being blocked, and his mother said that his grandfather had liked to wash there when he was still alive.

The bath hut was old and covered in moss; it was a miserable little building.

"It's our grandmother, she didn't die, she turned into a bath hut!" Nikita thought in terror. "She's alive, she's alive: That's her head – it's not a chimney, it's a head: And that's her gap-toothed mouth. She's pretending to be a bath hut, but really she's still a woman. I can tell!"

Someone else's cockerel came in off the street. Its face was like the face of the thin shepherd with the short beard who had been drowned that spring in the river; he had tried to swim across the flood waters so he could go and have fun at a wedding in another village.

Nikita decided that the shepherd had not liked being dead and had become a cock; so this cock was a man – a secret man. There were people everywhere, only they seemed not to be people.

Nikita bent down over a yellow flower. Who was it? Gazing into the flower, Nikita saw that its small round face was little by little taking on a human expression, and then he could see tiny eyes, a nose and a moist open mouth that smelt of living breath.

"And I thought you really were a flower!" said Nikita. "Let me have a look inside you. Do you have insides?"

Nikita snapped the stem – the body of the flower – and saw some milk in it.

"You were a baby, you were sucking your mother!" said Nikita in surprise.

He went to the old bath hut.

"Grandma!" Nikita said to her quietly. But Grandma's pockmarked face bared its teeth at him furiously, as if he were a stranger.

"You're not Grandma, you're someone else!" thought Nikita.

The stakes looked out at Nikita from the fence like the faces of crowds of people he did not know. And every face was unfamiliar and did not love him: one was smirking angrily, another was thinking something spiteful about him, while a third stake was pushing against the fence with the withered branches that were its arms, about to climb right out of the fence to chase Nikita.

"What are you doing here?" asked Nikita. "This is our yard!"

But on every side there were strange, angry faces, looking fixedly and piercingly at Nikita. He looked at the burdocks – surely they would be kind? But now even the burdocks were sullenly shaking their big heads and not loving him.

Nikita lay down on the earth and pressed his face to it. Inside the earth were humming voices, there must be many people living there in the cramped darkness, Nikita could hear them scrabbling with their hands to climb out into the light of day. Nikita got up in terror; people were living everywhere, strange eyes were looking at him from everywhere; and if there was anyone who could not see him, they wanted to climb out after him from under the earth, from out of a burrow, from under the black eaves of the shed. He turned to the hut. The hut was looking at him like an old woman passing through on her way from some far-off village; it was whispering to him: "Oo-ooh, you useless children, there are too many of you in the world – eating good wheaten bread for free."

"Come home, Mummy!" Nikita begged his far-away mother. "Let them just put you down for half a work day. Strange people have come into our yard. They're living here. Make them go away!"

The mother did not hear her son. Nikita went behind the shed, he wanted to see if the tree-stump-head was climbing out of the earth. The tree stump had a big mouth, it would eat all the cabbages on their plot – how would his mother be able to make cabbage soup in the winter?

Keeping his distance, Nikita looked timidly at the tree stump in the vegetable plot. A gloomy, unfriendly face, grown over with wrinkly bark, looked back at Nikita with unblinking eyes.

And from far away, from the forest on the other side of the village, someone shouted loudly: "Maxim, where are you?"

"In the earth!" the tree-stump-head answered in a muffled voice.

Nikita turned round, to run to his mother in the field, but he fell over. He went numb with fear. His legs were like strange people now and they would not listen to him. Then he crept along on his stomach as if he were still little and could not walk.

"Grandpa!" Nikita whispered, and looked at the kind sun in the sky.

Then a cloud blocked out the light, and the sun could no longer be seen.

"Grandpa, come and live with us again!"

Grandpa-sun appeared from behind the cloud, as if he had immediately removed the dark shadow from his face so he could see his enfeebled grandson creeping along the earth. Grandpa was looking at him now; knowing his grandfather could see him, Nikita got up onto his feet and ran towards his mother.

He ran for a long time. He ran all the way through the village along the empty, dusty road; then he felt tired out and sat down in the shade of an outlying barn.

Nikita did not mean to sit down for long. He laid his head on the ground, however, and fell asleep, and did not wake up until evening. The new shepherd was driving the collective-farm sheep. Nikita would have gone on further, to look for his mother in the field, but the shepherd told him it was late now and his mother had long ago left the field and gone home.

When he got home, Nikita saw his mother. She was sitting at the table and gazing at an old soldier who was eating bread and drinking milk.

The soldier looked at Nikita, then got up from the bench and took him in his arms. The soldier smelt warm, he smelt of something good and peaceful, of bread and earth. Nikita felt shy and said nothing.

"Hello, Nikita," said the soldier. "You forgot me a long time ago, you were just a baby when I kissed you and went off to the war. But I remember you. I didn't forget you even when I was close to death."

"It's your father, Nikitushka, he's come home," said the mother, wiping the tears from her face with her apron.

Nikita took a good look at his father – at his face, his hands, the medal on his chest – and touched the bright buttons on his shirt.

"And you won't go away again?"

"No," said the father. "I'm going to stay with you for ever. We've destroyed the enemy, now it's time to think about you and your mother."

In the morning Nikita went out into the yard and said out loud to everyone who lived there – to the burdocks, to the shed, to the stakes in the fence, to the tree-stump-head in the vegetable plot, and to grandfather's bath hut: "Father's come home. He's going to stay with us for ever."

Everyone in the yard was silent – Nikita could see they were all afraid of a father who was a soldier – and it was quiet underground too: no one was scrabbling to get out into the light.

"Come here, Nikita. Who are you talking to out there?"

His father was in the shed. He was having a look at the tools and running his hands over them: axes, spades, a saw, a plane, a vice, a bench and all the other things he owned.

When he had finished, the father took Nikita by the hand and went round the yard with him, working out what was where, what was in good shape and what had rotted, what was needed and what was not.

Just as he had the day before, Nikita looked into the face of every creature in the yard, but now he could not see a hidden person in any of them; not one of them had eyes, a nose, a mouth or a spiteful life of its own. The fencing stakes were thick, dried-up sticks, blind and dead, and grandfathers bath hut was a tiny little house that had rotted and was slipping away into the earth from being so old. Now Nikita even felt sorry for the bath hut: it was dying, soon it would be quite gone.

His father went into the shed for an axe and began chopping up the old tree stump in the vegetable plot to make firewood. The stump began to fall apart at once, it had rotted all the way through, and from underneath his father's axe its dry dust rose into the air like smoke.

When there was nothing left of the tree-stump-head, Nikita said to his father: "But when you weren't here, he said words, he was alive. He's got legs under the ground, and a belly."

The father led his son back into the hut.

"No," he said, "it died a long time ago. It's you – you want to make everything alive because you've got a kind heart. Even a stone seems alive to you, and old grandma's living again on the moon."

"And grandpa's living on the sun!" said Nikita.

In the afternoon the father was planing boards in the shed, to make a new floor for the hut, and he gave Nikita some work too – straightening the crooked nails with a little hammer.

Nikita eagerly got down to work, just like a grown-up. When he had straightened the first nail, he saw a kind little man in it smiling at him from underneath his little iron hat. He showed it to his father and said to him: "Why were all the others so cross? The burdock was cross, and the tree stump, and the water people, but this man is kind."

The father stroked his son's fair hair and answered, "They were all people you thought up, Nikita. They're not there, they're not solid, that's what makes them cross. But you made the little nail-man by your own labour – that's why he's kind."

Nikita began to think.

"Let's make everything by our own labour. Then everything will come alive."

"Yes, let's!" agreed the father.

He was sure Nikita would remain a kind person all his life long.

THE LAST LETTER
Nadezhda Mandelstam (1899–1980)
Translated by Max Hayward

Nadezhda Mandelstam, the widow of Osip Mandelstam, a member of the Great Four of Russia's twentieth century poets (Akhmatova, Tzvetaeva, Pasternak, Mandelstam) actually started to write when her husband was arrested and disappeared in the GULAG without any notice. Nadezhda Mandelstam's prose is far more than the account of a witness. It is as if the spirit of the murdered poet blessed the lips and fingers of his wife, so she composed an outstanding and powerful judgment; there are very few texts in the Russian literature that are so ethically intense.

Mandelstam was rebuked for being too accusing or vindictive, but this is to avoid or neglect the main motive of her writing: this time it is Eurydice, not Orpheus, who descends to hell in a futile and magnificent attempt to save her partner.

In the first chapter of this book Mrs Mandelstam herself defines her purpose in writing it, but it may be helpful, particularly for readers unfamiliar with the first book,* *Hope Against Hope*, to say a little more about the relation between the two. The 'First Book' (as it was originally called by her) is essentially a narrative about the last four years in the life of her husband, Osip Mandelstam. Despite the avowedly discursive manner that frequently allows her to stray into other periods – as she says, her method is 'unchronological' – the first volume is basically contained within this limited time span. It begins abruptly with an account of the poet's first arrest in May 1934 and ends with a review of all the scraps of evidence about the circumstances of his death in a camp near Vladivostok in December 1938. Having decided there could be no compromise with a system that had reversed or traduced the cultural and ethical values he

---

* For such readers the Chronology at the end of this book may be helpful, since it recapitulates a good deal of what is told in *Hope Against Hope*.

believed in, Mandelstam consciously chose martyrdom and death by denouncing Stalin as a murderer in a poem which he then read to a few people in private – with the inevitable consequence that the text was speedily relayed to the secret police by one of his listeners. He was saved from immediate execution thanks only to the pleas of Bukharin (who at that time still had a little influence), Pasternak, and others. Through this officially arranged 'miracle', he was given a few years respite, which he spent mainly in enforced residence in the provincial town of Voronezh. Here he wrote several brilliant cycles of poems (the 'Voronezh Notebooks') before returning, at the end of his term of exile, to Moscow in 1937 – just in time for the Great Purge. Though as a 'proscribed person' he could find no work and was not allowed to live within the city limits of Moscow itself, he was at first left functionaries to whom nothing matters, neither life, nor man, nor the earth, nor anything – dimmed by their very breath – that lights our way. Heaven help them. But will they really succeed in their task of universal destruction?

Last Letter

This letter was never read by the person it is addressed to. It is written on two sheets of very poor paper. Millions of women wrote such letters – to their husbands, sons, brothers, fathers, or simply to sweethearts. But next to none of them have been preserved. If such things ever survived here, it could only be owing to chance, or a miracle. My letter still exists by chance. I wrote it in October 1938, and in January I learned that M. was dead. It was thrown into a trunk with other papers and lay there for nearly thirty years. I came across it the last time I went through all my papers, gladdened by every scrap of something that had survived, and lamenting all the huge, irreparable losses. I read it not at once, but only several years later. When I did, I thought of all the other women who shared my fate. The vast majority of them thought as I, but many dared not admit it even to themselves. Nobody has yet told the story of what was done to us by other people – by those selfsame compatriots whom I do not wish to see destroyed, lest I thereby come to resemble them. Their present-day successors, the spiritual brothers of those who murdered M. and millions of others, will curse on reading this letter – why didn't they destroy the bitch (that is, me), they will ask, while they were about it? And they will also curse those who have so 'relaxed vigilance' that forbidden thoughts and feelings have been allowed to break to the surface. Now again we are not supposed to remember the past and think – let alone speak – about it. Since the sole survivors of all the myriad shattered families are now only the grandchildren, there is in fact nobody left to remember and speak of it. Life goes on, and few indeed are those who wish to stir up the past. Not many years ago it was admitted that some 'mistakes' had been made, but now it is denied again – nothing wrong is seen with the past. But neither can I speak of the past as a 'mistake'. How can one thus describe actions that were part of a system and flowed inexorably from its basic principles?

Instead of an epilogue, then, I end my book with this letter. I shall do what I can to see that both book and letter survive. There is not much hope, even though our present times are like honey and sugar compared with the past. Come what may, here is the letter:

22/10/1938

Osia, my beloved, faraway sweetheart!

I have no words, my darling, to write this letter that you may never read, perhaps. I am writing it into empty space. Perhaps you will come back and not find me here. Then this will be all you have left to remember me by.

Osia, what a joy it was living together like children – all our squabbles and arguments, the games we played, and our love. Now I do not even look at the sky. If I see a cloud, who can I show it to?

Remember the way we brought back provisions to make our poor feasts in all the places where we pitched our tent like nomads? Remember the good taste of bread when we got it by a miracle and ate it together? And our last winter in Voronezh. Our happy poverty, and the poetry you wrote. I remember the time we were coming back once from the baths, when we bought some eggs or sausage, and a cart went by loaded with hay. It was still cold and I was freezing in my short jacket (but nothing like what we must suffer now: I know how cold you are). That day comes back to me now. I understand so clearly, and ache from the pain of it, that those winter days with all their troubles were the greatest and last happiness to be granted us in life.

My every thought is about you. My every tear and every smile is for you. I bless every day and every hour of our bitter life together, my sweetheart, my companion, my blind guide in life.

Like two blind puppies, we were, nuzzling each other and feeling so good together. And how fevered your poor head was, and how madly we frittered away the days of our life. What joy it was, and how we always knew what joy it was.

Life can last so long. How hard and long for each of us to die alone. Can this fate be for us who are inseparable? Puppies and children, did we deserve this? Did you deserve this, my angel? Everything goes on as before. I know nothing. Yet I know everything – each day and hour of your life are plain and clear to me as in a delirium.

You came to me every night in my sleep, and I kept asking what had happened, but you did not reply.

In my last dream I was buying food for you in a filthy hotel restaurant. The people with me were total strangers. When I had bought it, I realized I did not know where to take it, because I do not know where you are.

When I woke up, I said to Shura: 'Osia is dead.' I do not know whether you are still alive, but from the time of that dream, I have lost track of you. I do not know where you are. Will you hear me'! Do you know how much I love you? I could never tell you how much I love you. I cannot tell you even now. I speak only to you, only to you. You are with me always, and I who was such a wild and angry one and never learned to weep simple tears – now I weep and weep and weep.

It's me: Nadia. Where are you?

        Farewell.

                Nadia.

EXCERPTS FROM A SIEGE DAY[*]

Lidya Ginzburg (1902–1990)

Translated by Angela Livingstone

> Survivor of the Siege of Leningrad during WWII, when the second-largest Soviet city was for more than 800 days blocked from the outside world, resulting in an immensely heavy death toll from hunger, cold, diseases, **Lidya Ginzburg** (1902–1990), professional literary scientist, became a researcher of the extremes of life and death in the besieged city.
>
> In Soviet culture the Blockade was a special *taboo*, with a focus on sacrifice, with suffering minimised. So Ginzburg went into difficult and dangerous areas, finding a way to describe the indescribable: the devastating effects of hunger on morality, personality, past and future. Her *Notes from the Blockade* is probably the best prose written in Russian in the twentieth century: as profound as it is unbearable.

I

Urgency

N did not immediately understand why every day at work, around two o'clock, he was possessed by a strange sense of malaise. Then he realized what it was – urgency. This urgency was one of the guises of starvation or starvation trauma. Urgency as a mask for hunger – the ceaseless rush from one stage of eating to the next, accompanied by the fear of missing something. This urgency was particularly associated with lunch. This was given out by an indifferent government agency. That is, it had objective criteria

---

[*] These fragments originally formed part of the single "day in the life" of the hero, in the blockade-era manuscript "Otter's Day", and therefore connect with the first part of *Notes from the Blockade*.

for everything – the criteria certainly existed and they were certainly objective. But what if, suddenly, there wasn't enough? Several times during the winter there hadn't been enough porridge.

Nowadays canteens always give out everything they're supposed to. Nowadays urgency is a reflection of the mind, a race from one aimless goal to another. These goals are set in a circle, a repetitive series leading nowhere.

If the motivation were just the usual ordinary feeling of hunger, it would be something heartening, reassuring. It is at precisely that time of day that it begins to sharpen. But the traumatized person can't stand feeling hungry; that in turn gives rise to lassitude and fear. N concentrates now on the desire to go out (his working day has not been standardized). He reads his typing, moving effortlessly from line to line. The most unpleasant thing is transferring a correction from one copy to a second, then a third. A triple brake on his race. Nowadays he has to observe the decencies and he does so, meticulously slowing down his gestures. He speaks carelessly: "You give it in, then. I've got to go out just now. I'll be back before four, if anyone needs to know …"

Somebody enquires: "You off to the canteen?"

"Yes, that is I will be. I have some things to do first."

You can't reveal your hurry.

The secretary says in a bright voice: "You know it would be so nice if you signed this paper right now."

From her point of view it just means a delay of a minute or two. Sweet girl, she doesn't realize that she has cut into the internal headlong dash of a traumatized man and that it's painful.

By now N is unable to carry out a single braking movement. He can't get to his desk. He asks the secretary for a sheet of paper, although he has paper in his briefcase; it would mean snapping the lock of the briefcase again. He grabs the nearest pen, which barely works, sits himself down somewhere, and writes a few lines in an alien hand, gaining a minute that way. He writes thinking that he still has to overcome the exit to the street, the tram, the queue at the control point, the canteen queue, the deliberateness of the serving-girl … And in that series of problematic actions, the thing for the sake of which they are being carried out – a portion of soup and 200 grams of porridge – seems imperceptibly brief and ephemeral.

After the tram, there remains an extremely unpleasant stretch on foot. On the way he encounters people coming back from the canteen. It's hard to resist the question: "What is it today?" and you want to resist so as to keep all possibilities open. You can also make deductions from the way they hold their bags, lunch pails or briefcases. Round the corner he sights the entrance, always half-open. Now nothing (including air raids or shelling) will stop you going up to it and going inside. In the depths of the dark corridor there is a patch of light where the bald head of the server flickers by – the joyous sign of extra helpings. Sometimes though, the smooth surface of the counter gleams dismally.

During the winter (especially before the general evacuation) an hours-long queue used to stand here by the control point. They stood submissively. It seemed natural to employ every effort to get the lunch which saved them from starvation. Besides, people stood in a chilly corridor, not out in the freezing cold. Nowadays it was empty here – the reason being that everybody was in so much of a hurry. Getting their cards, money and passes mixed up, everybody wanted to push through the dam of the three or four slowly advancing backs; everybody had to get their tallies as soon as might be just to calm down (so long as the serving-girl hadn't lost them ...) the old trauma was still working.

Nowadays this would seem to be an apparently third-rate canteen (an imitation of normal existence) with its unwatered flowerpots on the tables, half-grimy tablecloths, almost clean serving-girls. It may not be seen at once (during the winter everything was seen at once), that people here are acting out a tragedy. You realize this if you look closely; how they lick their spoons quickly (it isn't done to lick your plate any more), scrape their plates clean, tilting it up, running the finger round the rim of the tin of porridge, how they stop talking as the food is served and study it carefully, how their heads automatically turn to follow the serving-girl.

Of all the meals, lunch bore the least resemblance to its name. The soup still gives ground for hope. It's not very tasty and there's more of it; and after all, it is the first course. At lunch the saddest thing is eating the porridge; the briefest of acts, so brief that the start touches the finish. Two swings of the spoon are enough to wreak irreparable damage on the round fluffy mass doled out on your plate, with the dimple in the middle, and 10 grams of dark-golden oil poured over it.

II

After Lunch

Gloom over the empty plate, greasy from the porridge, signals the end of the pre-lunch rush. Here begins the lull of the siege day. There is nothing unprecedented in the phenomenon of the post-lunch lull. A real midday meal (not what a man grabs during his lunch break) was always a turning point. Late dinner at seven o'clock was always the direct transition to an evening's relaxation. The earlier lunches cut across the day. Chekhov affirmed that it was only possible to work before lunch. Lunch brings with it not only indolence and drowsiness, but also a sense of the onset of decrepitude, old age, exhaustion, the dying of the day. For many, these were the empty hours dragging on somehow, until the evening eventually took shape with its own conventions and goals.

Now that people were in primitive dependence on the length of the day, the temperature and the light – the feeling of the dying day was especially concrete. In the middle of the white nights – there existed this winter trauma, terribly tenacious, like all traumas that winter. In the post-lunch depression the sense of over-satiety was now replaced by disappointment, and an exasperation brought on by the swiftness of lunch.

The siege circle consists of repeated renewed segments. Post-lunch depression occurs with the same regularity as everything else, the shelling for instance. The mind is not allowed the liberty to be depressed for long, and suddenly everything, which at other times is shrouded in mist, comes crowding in. The pointlessness of goals dawns with poignant pain, especially the repetition of the gestures accompanying the relentless race. And especially the feeling of being cut off. Cut off from those who have left the city for unoccupied Russia. They are unpicturable, their existence is unreal. Cut off from those running alongside ...

N slowly walks back from the canteen to the office. On his right is the Neva at the far end of a side street. At the hour of depression one had to walk round that, not touch it. This summer it is only when his tram crosses bridges that he sees the mighty Neva with its warships. He never once touched the granite warmed by the sun with his hand, never sat on the semicircular benches, never descended the steps down to the water, unexpectedly intimate, palpable – with sand on the bottom and the smell of fish, suddenly revealed amid the decorative riverine view.

The corner of Fontanka* with an old house. Here N used to go visiting. The people he visited had been evacuated. He always used to arrive very late, getting ready to come much later than people went to bed nowadays. There was always vodka and light refreshments there. Strange ... People sat and talked and talked. Read things to one another. Casually enquired: "Shall we have tea now or finish the reading?" "Finish, of course ..."

Visiting friends, with supper delayed by conversations. Or this wind and the constant rush of foliage along the branches – that was all part of the former life. But depression has another card to play. It doesn't want it to return. Either because that other life is quite other, utterly inconceivable, or because there is too much resemblance – like a mirage.

Engrossed in his own thoughts, N walks on from the canteen to his office without looking about him. Suddenly a familiar, heavy, shuddering sound penetrates his consciousness. He realizes at once that this is not the first such sound, there have been several, one after another. A bombardment; in another district for the moment, apparently. Now N looks about him. If it hadn't been for the noise, you wouldn't have guessed what was going on. Passers-by went about their business with the Leningrad sangfroid which had begun to dominate normal behaviour completely. They walk along the street (until driven into an entrance) carrying their briefcases, lunch pails and string bags, stand in queues, chat and light up one another's cigarettes. You hear the repartee, "I think they're our guns". "Get away – ours!" Or: "That was a bang and a half!"

The repetitive noise doesn't leave his mind now. And as always when he hears that sound N experiences a mad sensation of things being overturned, turned inside out. Confusion in the categories of space and time. The whistle of the shells overhead is more frightening but more comprehensible. It indicates a spatial presence – they are

---

* One of the great waterways which run through central Leningrad (St Petersburg) in concentric semicircles.

really here over your head at this moment – and temporal extension (the duration of the whistling). The noise of the distant explosion is something else altogether. What was the untrackable present had already become the past by the time it reached the consciousness. The reverse order: first the sound, then the fear at what had not by now happened. Then the silence and in that brief silence, the question of the life and death of a person is decided. It is decided by the fact that he has taken two extra steps towards the tram stop, or bent down to retrieve a dropped briefcase or stepped off the pavement into the roadway. A person thinks everything will happen in order – there'll be a whistling, then an explosion which he'll see from the side, then something will happen to him. He knows that's an aberration.

This is an aberration of the link between cause and effect, but there is also the aberration of security – when a person speeds up his step under bombardment, so it doesn't catch up with him. That is exactly what N does when he's annoyed at being stopped in the street and prevented from reaching the office, where there's a brew-up at this time and he could have a cup of boiled water to go with the sweet he'd got left over from lunch.

The emotion of fear is supplanted by one even more direct – exasperation, caused by hunger trauma. If this exchange of emotions did not take place, N would go into the entrance saying to himself and the others that one ought to behave sensibly – no panic and no silly carelessness.

III

Evening

The afternoon working hours were over. There remained the walk back home. In the first daylight exit from the office a nervous tension had prevailed; in the second it was torpor.

N slowly walks along the street. Now it is evening, before the onset of the white night, with a magnificent cold slanting light (even on muggy days), in which the asphalt of Nevsky Prospect glows. The usual astonishment when, after working late, you emerge from darkened rooms to find the light outside in undiminished brilliance. It is this inexhaustibility of ongoing life which real Leningraders love so much. It is a feeling of untouched reserves of life, waiting to be released each day.

Was it not from this that N had derived the dream which had occupied him when young? A dream of life made up of long days. Of days lived through and savoured in all their protracted length and in every particle of their being. But nowadays the flow of life had its own laws – the white nights notwithstanding. The circle had to close (in order to begin again – hence the circle). The flow of existence is determined by weariness, the exhaustion of the ritual gestures of the day, the imminence of the last meal-time. The circle drearily seeks its non-existent end.

There is something disorienting in the non-coincidence of the state of the day and the state of the person. The undimming light tautens the nerves and serves as a reminder that it would be possible now to take a long walk along the winding river, and do a lot more besides … The night's cruelty is revealed during the white nights. Blok understood that: "May is cruel with its white nights …" They are cruel to the person who wants to be protected by the darkness, that wants to sleep like the dead. The day is filled with a multitude of distracting, confusing things which darken the mind. At night however, freed from fuss and clutter and unsoftened by the dark, the fundamental features of life stand out. It is more fearful now than it has ever been.

There is supposed to be supper at home, the final meal, the measuring point of the evening. In the former existence, the evening used to start late for N, drag on and on, turning into a nocturnal vigil until two or three or later. It was part of the day, quite often a working day, but essentially one permitting idleness; the only part of the day when idleness was easy and allowed. And everything around filled it with amusement, love, friendly conversations over vodka. It could all be looked forward to like a sort of relaxation. Especially when the relaxation was uninterrupted, and crossed into the next unit of time. When for example one didn't have to separate until next day.

Nowadays the surrogate for all that was supper. Consciously or unconsciously, an inadequate supper, boiled beet tops for example, without bread, gave an emotional colouring to the afternoon. A proper supper on the other hand reconciled one like a happy ending.

Supper was over. N sits by the stove. There are shavings still burning out in it and the stove is giving off some smoke. With a long splinter, N stirs the brands in the confined metal space and lights up. In the former existence, the papirosa had its own typology. There was the papirosa before bed, and the morning papirosa, then the lazy after-lunch papirosa, one for business conversations, one for friendly chat. There were also papirosi which he finished off, with a squashed end and traces of lipstick.

During the siege months, the papirosa took on a multitude of new and important meanings. It became a way of physically suppressing hunger and deflecting one's thoughts from hunger. In an existence totally undesigned for pleasure, smoking a papirosa was virtually the only act of pure enjoyment unconnected with practical usefulness (like eating and sleeping were), rather the contrary. In its disinterestedly hedonistic nature, the papirosa was a kind of remnant of ordinary human life. The papirosa – especially the home-rolled type with the elaborate ritual of its preparation – was a reserve means of filling the vacuum, or some part of the emptiness. What else was there to look forward to? ... What else was in store? ... One could still have a smoke, one would reply to oneself, assuaging one's misery.

The papirosi varied during the course of the day. The hungry papirosa which N smoked just before his soup, when the serving-girl was going slow and irritation rising to a snapping point. The after-lunch papirosa had once appeared in a haze of intoxicating satiety; now it suppressed the miserable unsatisfying meal. The working papirosa. He enjoyed thinking about that on his way to the office. It was part of a communications complex with indifferent people, gossip, bureaucratic rituals and electric gadgets (economizing on matches there, they lit their cigarettes on hotplates). There was also the final, evening papirosa. With its smoke, the mind, exhausted during the day, seemed to spend itself. Despite this thematic allotment of papirosi, smoking was all the same in that existence, perhaps the freest act, the least attached to any given situation.

N digs about in an oven niche with a long splinter, finishing the evening hand-rolled papirosa, which had carried on and extended the process of eating. The last glow, shrouded in ash, glimmered at the rim of the holder. And at that moment (it had happened more than once) the feeling of the circle, the race around the circle, suddenly seemed frighteningly clear. And most terrifying of all was not so much the repetition as the absolutely precise predictability. He sees the series of movements developing now, and those of tomorrow and the day after ... He sees exactly how he picks up his briefcase, drops his key in his pocket, how he gets out of breath slightly as he climbs the office stairs, how he glances over the typist's shoulder – to see if the manuscript has got any further. Nothing can be subtracted from the linked series and nothing can be introduced which is not a predetermined, ritualized gesture.

All this is hardly new. The predictability of his future actions used to bother him in the previous existence too. He used to detach himself from his self and his double went forward into the future, automatically exact. For some reason it was particularly unpleasant when he was leaving town for a month or two. It was eerie to see in advance this alienated double getting his ticket, sitting in a carriage, opening a closed flat.

At that time they were mental mirages; in siege existence everything took on a strange literalness. Along with the gestures, the associated sensations were also predetermined. A feeling of confidence was bound to occur without fail at the moment when N proffered his pass to the guard outside the office; a feeling of relief, when the right tram appeared from round the bend; a feeling of miserable emptiness when, under the first two blows of the spoon, the porridge vanished beyond recall; a feeling of fullness, inexhaustibility, when he took out the untouched bread from his briefcase in the morning.

Absolute unfreedom of mental activity, riveted firmly to things which had once stood on the very lowest rungs of the hierarchy of values.

In the urgent race from meal to meal, there was something unconscious, the polar opposite of those long days, utterly absorbed and digested by the mind, that had once been his dream.

Today, for some reason, there is a clarity of thought not experienced for a long time, a ferment of ideas seemingly intent on breaking free. Why had he remembered those long days? It means that the dystrophic blackout is starting to lift, the bond with communal life slowly strengthening, as that life stands firm against the enemy.

THE MISTAKE

Gaito Gazdanov (1902–1971)

Translated by Bryan Karetnyk

Becoming a soldier in early youth, **Gaito Gazdanov** (born Georgii Ivanovich Gazdanov) served on an armored train, retreated with the White army to Crimea, evacuated to the Constantinople and only there, already on foreign soil, in foreign air, he wrote his first short story. He studied at the Sorbonne, worked as a taxi driver, together with his wife was a member of the Resistance movement in Nazi-occupied France, and later became a host on Radio Liberty.

Even though Gazdanov was one of the most successful writers of the young generation of the emigration, and his novels were translated into the main European languages, for the Soviet public he was not known at all, his name being discovered only in the early nineties – with an effect of a new planet being discovered in the Solar system.

(1938)

Vasily Vasilyevich had been wandering about the apartment for a whole hour, peering under tables and divans, turning on the lights everywhere—a lazy dusk had already fallen over the city—yet all his investigations had proved fruitless. He had made several tours of all the rooms, rummaging around in the divans and armchairs and poking his hand into their plush recesses, all dust and velvet, where he found scraps of paper, safety pins and the king of spades, which had fallen out of a deck of cards; what he was looking for, however, was nowhere to be seen. Undismayed, he once again set about his explorations; he was about to climb up onto the sideboard, having repositioned the armchair next to it, when suddenly he espied the black corner of his copybook poking out from under a milk-white vase standing on a small end table. He pulled the book towards him. The table shook, but the book remained firmly in place. He gave a sharp tug and then, comically toppling over, both the table and the vase came toppling down, the latter loudly hitting the parquet and shattering into little white pieces that scattered across the floor. Vasily Vasilyevich froze, breath held, listening to the silence, which was all the more surprising after such a resounding crash. It was almost completely dark; the navy-blue divan seemed black, the clock face showed a hazy yellow and the disc of the tail-like pendulum glinted dimly; on the other side of the window—still, like in a painting—were dark trees. Then, a few seconds later, the street lamps lit up and their pale radiance permeated the apartment, illuminating the table on the floor, the milky shards of glass and Vasily Vasilyevich himself, the newly uncovered copybook finally in his grasp. Vasily Vasilyevich was dressed in long breeches and a sailor's jacket. He stood there as though bewitched, his big, deep-blue eyes wide open, staring at the white, motionless debris on the floor. A long time seemed to pass before the unhurried approach of footsteps could be heard, the light came on, and a voice from the doorway said:

"What have you broken, Vasily Vasilyevich?"

Only then did Vasily Vasilyevich begin to cry, covering his face and understanding the irreparability of what he had done.

"Why ever did you touch it?"

Sobbing and incoherent with despair, Vasily Vasilyevich tried to explain that he had been searching for his copybook, that his father that morning had drawn in it a wonderful little demon for him, that the book had been under the vase, that he had tugged at it, and then the vase had accidentally fallen.

"It's all right," said his mother. "Now help me to clear up the shards. Just be careful not to cut yourself."

"Are they sharp?" asked Vasily Vasilyevich.

"Very sharp."

"But the vase wasn't sharp."

"But Vasily Vasilyevich was a very silly boy."

"Was not," said Vasily Vasilyevich.

At first there was just an armchair with a firm, well-sprung seat; then flashed a face of a cinematic beauty; next came a memory of the taste of the water in the bathhouse and the marinated fish that Natasha had prepared the previous day; then two lines from an old letter she had received: *My faith in you knows no bounds, and I hope that while I live there may be nothing to shake this belief.* Now, these lines related to something that mustn't be thought about, something that had effectively ceased to exist. Thought was to be devoted now to other things, to Italian exhibitions, to art and sculpture; however, none of those wielded its usual persuasiveness or weight any longer. And while they did not quite vanish, still, they failed wholly to engulf the attention; they became tiresome and meaningless, like the classroom exercises of yesteryear. The effort required to avoid thinking about something that has very nearly ceased to exist was akin to a physical strain reaching its limit, when the muscles ache and there is a pounding at the temples, and you want to give it all up and end it. In any case, it was unnecessary and to no avail, for life until then had been joyful, successful and proper, just like a classical schema of some abstract theory, flawless in its execution. Life had been composed—till very recently—of a great succession of sensations, memories and concerns, each of which had been a continuation of that same happy principal that was now lost in time and located somewhere far off in the past, perhaps in childhood, on the seashore. Those beginnings had grown richer, more complex, more profound—with time—and more (it seemed) certain; beyond them was just an insignificant external world, almost unreal and powerless over what constituted the very essence of life. But around eight years prior to this, a spectre of doubt had surfaced and then vanished, a stray feeling of inexplicable emptiness, as if, despite all this, something was still missing—but then Vasily Vasilyevich came along, and there could no longer be any misgivings that everything had been settled once and for all in the best and most agreeable manner possible. The days and weeks during this time were especially memorable, and they were characterized by a powerful new awareness of everything that was going on—right down to the smallest, most insignificant detail—and a recognition of the almost limitless profusion of opportunities to have as many experiences and emotions as possible. And as all this came to an end, the resulting state of happiness seemed unalterable, as did everything now in this apartment, where silence and twilight reigned. It was indeed very quiet and dark, and still; everything, it seemed, had already reverted to that classical schema, enriched by yet another day, yet another effort of imagination amid the silence—when suddenly, sharply and unexpectedly, with a desperate, almighty reverberation, the crash of broken glass tore through the apartment.

Vasily Vasilyevich had been asleep for some time, his mouth half open and his head resting on his little arm; Natasha was long gone; the armchair had traded places with the divan, at the head of which now shone a lamp with a green shade; the shards of glass had been cleared away; everything else had been dealt with, but there was still the matter of finding, among all those charming everyday objects that constituted life itself, the blind spot, the *point de départ*, beyond which things sometimes took on new meanings, shedding their former aspect. Where, when and why could this have happened? In the early years there had been cruel intentions, a couple of stolen kisses, but these could be put down to youth, not to depravity or to a lack of understanding right and wrong. Then came love and marriage, the cold stare of a mother who hated all the happy people on this earth, and a blessing from an icon as old as time, so darkened with age that it was impossible to make out the saint depicted on it; the barely distinguishable face, along with its small stern eyes, had turned black, and the nimbus around the head was yellowing, yet all this bore an arbitrary, symbolic meaning, and no one—neither those who gave nor those who received the blessing—so much as looked at the icon, which was returned to its resting place at the end of the ritual, its dried-out verdure, now brown with age, covered over. Still before that, there had been Russia, a bright apartment with enormous windows, school, lessons in foreign languages … "Like all people," scornfully said her mother, who had spent her whole life in expectation of some terrible personal tragedy or some catastrophe, and who considered her comfortable existence degrading and unworthy. She was forever planning to join a monastery or a revolutionary group and would tell her husband that to go on living as they did was shameful and that it had to stop; but she entered no monastery nor any revolutionary group, and she continued attending the theatre and receiving visitors, all the while deeply resenting this life of privilege. She came alive only when misfortune truly befell someone, when a person was at death's door; then, casting all else aside, she would set off in their direction, urging the driver on, summoning doctors, spending untold sums of money, looking after the children and generally doing a great deal of good. These deeds, however, had to be preceded by death, or at least something so severe that no amount of money or any degree of care could ever hope to cure. She did not love her daughter, or her son, or her husband; but then a constant stream of people from all walks of life would come to her—petitioners, wretched-looking individuals, cripples with their eyelids upturned, drunkards, consumptives, unfortunate and pitiful people, to whom she would give money and clothing and for whom she cared as though they were family. Later, as she entered the dining room, whereupon everyone would fall silent, she would say:

"Thanks be to God that we can eat well today."

Her husband would merely shrug his shoulders, having accustomed himself to this daily comedy over the course of thirty years.

She hated, indeed despised, everything that exhibited health, happiness, wealth and love; anything favourable would elicit from her no more than a sneer and hostility. When her daughter's future husband had approached her—this was already abroad, in Berlin, although practically nothing in the house had changed (the same poor wretches would crowd the dark stairwell as before, the only difference being that Germans had started appearing alongside the Russians)—to seek permission to ask for Yekaterina Maximovna's hand in marriage, she had just stood there, silent, staring at him wrathfully, until finally she replied that she was very happy for them; it rang with such hatred and malice that he left, perplexed and almost frightened by this inexplicable ire. On the day of the wedding, wearing a tight-fitting starched dress, she received messages of congratulation and then summoned her daughter to inform her of certain laws of nature, the reproductive instinct, the *plaisirs de la lune de miel*,* and that, when all is said and done, what will have taken place, though distressing, is perfectly normal. She advised her daughter to bear in mind the fact that there were tens of thousands of people starving in Berlin.

Only her father would occasionally say to her:

"There's nothing to be done, Katya. Your mother isn't a happy woman."

---

* Pleasures of the honeymoon.

It was so astonishing, then, that later, while living in Paris, Katya received her first letter from her mother:

My dear Katya, my darling daughter ... It was composed entirely of such tender phrases, never before employed by her; everything was so congenial and warm, so inexplicable and unexpected, that Katya wept as she read the letter and then showed it to her husband, who said that he had always held a higher opinion of his *belle-mére* than others around her, because there was undoubtedly much good in this woman and her actions had just been misinterpreted. On the day that Vasily Vasilyevich was born, the first face Katya saw was her mother's; she, however, left immediately, having ascertained—"with sorrow", as Katya's brother put it—that, regrettably, both mother and baby were well and out of harm's way. When, in the clinic, Katya's mother ran into her own son, whom she had not seen in a number of years, she said to him, "Hello," in an almost enquiring tone. "And what exactly are you doing here?"

"My sister is giving birth, Mother," he replied.

"Precisely. You have absolutely no cause to be here," she said, and sailed into the ward from which the screams of her daughter could be heard.

Later, as soon as Katya had recovered, the three of them—Katya, her husband and her brother—celebrated the birth of Vasily Vasilyevich: there was champagne, they sent telegrams to their relatives, they drank toasts to Vasily Vasilyevich, who was peacefully asleep at the other end of the apartment, snugly wrapped up in swaddling clothes. It was Katya's brother, Alexander, who had first called him Vasily Vasilyevich, saying to her:

"Just look how commanding he is. It wouldn't do to call him by his first name alone. He's got to be called Vasily Vasilyevich." Thus it became customary to call him by his first name and patronymic, and everyone later would say in all earnestness:

"Where's Vasily Vasilyevich? What's Vasily Vasilyevich up to?"

Vasily Vasilyevich was a small and chubby baby. First he crawled, then he started to walk around the apartment; he would fall over and, without saying a word, look at everyone with those serious, dazzling eyes. He loved his uncle above all others, then his mother, and then "maybe" his father—as he once said when he was asked this for the hundredth time and first used the word "maybe".

* * *

She was taking a bath late one evening, before lying down to sleep, when her husband came in. He pushed open the glass door, entered and saw Katya in the bathtub; she suddenly became terribly embarrassed by her body—overwhelmed by a sense of burning, inexplicable shame. Something had changed, something was not quite right. He said, "Forgive me, Katya, *je suis un peu dans la lune*,"[*] and walked out of the bathroom. The colour rushing to her face, she donned her bathrobe and went through to her bedroom.

He appeared a few minutes later, carrying a cup of tea on a tray. "I thought you'd care for some tea after your bath."

"Thank you. You're a darling, as always."

He sat down on the armchair and told her about the gala dinner he had just returned from; she listened to him with a feeling of detached wonderment, as though noticing for the first time how cleverly he talked about people, how he immediately grasped what was important and what was not, and how he always knew what needed to be said and done. Never yet, it seemed, had he been mistaken—either in his thoughts or in his actions; thus had it ever been, and so she had grown used to trusting him implicitly in all matters. She had doubts at first: she tested his instincts, subjected him to a huge variety of experiments, all of which confirmed only the most favourable of hypotheses—whether because he loved her more than anything in the world, as he claimed, or because he was aided by his monstrous, as she thought, intellect. A second theory had developed because the man was, or at least made himself out to be, blind in only one respect—his wife. He trusted nothing and nobody—people, ideas, relationships—and based everything on calculation. Katya was sometimes astonished by his callous estimations of people, although they were almost always proved right; he knew exactly how to talk to different sorts of people and never expressed any superfluous sentiments. He understood everything at once, and only when he was alone with Katya would he let down his guard and be transformed into as helpless a creature as little Vasily Vasilyevich, for he was certain that Katya could never be capable of any misdeed. He bid her goodnight and left the room; she again fell to thinking how it could

---

[*] "My head is a little in the clouds."

be possible that this man truly believed her incapable of any wrongdoing. Naturally, he could not account for Katya's having sudden doubts about matters that had been put to bed long ago. Kissing her hand and gazing into her eyes, he understood that he should leave, that she was in no mood for it today. Could it have been that he was just tired? No, she had sensed when he took her hand that this was not the case, and it was only after their eyes had met and his fingers had slowly and affectionately let go that he smiled, kissed her hand and silently made his exit.

His infallibility began to unnerve her sometimes—as if he were not a man, but a perfect, thinking machine. It seemed to require from him no effort whatsoever to know what would please her and what she would find disagreeable, even down to the slightest remark about a dress she was wearing for the first time. She would occasionally start to make cutting, unjust remarks, but he always kept calm and just smiled, and in his smile there was not even a shadow of derision—she would never have forgiven him for that—but only tenderness. He would smile at Vasily Vasilyevich much in the same way. It was thus that he made a complete study of Katya—her hidden desires, her unprompted, ill-reasoned ideas, all her variations. He studied her as easily as he would any problem he was addressing and was able to develop an exact formula, like an algebraic equation.

Yes, and until lately he had been right about everything. But one day, when Katya asked him what it took to know a person inside out, he replied:

"A lover's intuition."

"What about the people you don't love? The general order of things?"

"I don't think there is a general order of things."

"Then what is there?"

"The fact that every man projects a personality that can be likened to another's by casual analogy; although, this is governed not by its own set of rules, of course, but by various associations, characteristic of a certain point in time …"

"Lord, how complicated it all is! But is it actually possible to know a man through and through?"

"No, of course not. One could predict how he might act in a narrow set of circumstances, but even that would be far from certain."

"But you're so rarely mistaken."

"Oh, I make mistakes all the time," he said, smiling. "It's just that mistakes are seldom irreparable, and I try not to repeat them."

"What about me?"

"I know you intuitively, unthinkingly, because I love you."

It was after one o'clock in the morning, but she was still awake, searching, trying to understand when and how this mistake had occurred. Up to a point, it had all been clear: her life, she thought, as she lay on her back in the dark, was being played out on two stages—one on top of the other. On the first was her husband, whom she loved, Vasily Vasilyevich, her father and brother—bringing her joy to varying degrees and in different ways. The other, to which she almost never gave any thought, but which was self-evident and as distinct as the first, consisted in a sound knowledge of a number of theoretical stances: this knowledge would allow one, for example, to discern accurately whether an act was right or wrong. In the world there was disease, death, misery, hatred, resentment, deceit and betrayal, but none of this could touch her or her loved ones. These things were known to everyone, yet to her they were abstract concepts, knowledge that had never been tested, like the image of a country she had never visited. It did not occur to her that she might one day experience something in this vein. And so a change took place in this network of thoughts and feelings. Where yesterday there had been a dark, empty space, something new and repugnant—in terms of these former notions—now emerged; moreover, it had been deliberate and was nearly as vast in scope as everything that had existed for her until now—a whole new world unlike anything she had experienced before, dangerous, dark and overwhelming.

It was simple enough to establish the facts. First an evening with her husband at the theatre, then an acquaintance—a young man around five years her senior, of uncertain nationality, with a decent command of Russian, of fairly athletic build, and in no way exceptional on first appearance. For some reason he irritated her, although there seemed to be nothing to find fault with. Later he paid them a visit—a first, then a second the following week.

"Do you have much free time?" she asked.

"My whole life," he replied, smiling. "I recently came into an inheritance."

Then came the first time they stepped out together, a matinee show at the cinema, a taxi, his approaching lips and the unbearable desire to grip that mouth with her teeth—and the morning after, the pale winter's light in the window and her own naked body emerging from the bed sheets.

She went home. Her husband had gone out, and Vasily Vasilyevich was building a tower out of iron strips. Ten minutes later the telephone rang, and her husband's voice informed her that he would not dine at home, that it would be too late by the time he returned.

"Fine," she answered.

She and Vasily Vasilyevich ate together. Later her brother arrived with some amusing anecdotes and stayed until one o'clock in the morning. Gradually the deathly melancholy that had accompanied her journey home vanished, as though seeping lazily into the distant gloom; then, lifting up her bright eyes, Katya began to feel as though she was back to her usual self, that everything was in its rightful place—and that she loved everything she had previously loved just as much as before.

Three days passed. The telephone rang, and in a strange, altered, drained voice she said that, fine, she was willing—then came a repeat of the first time: first the lips and a buzzing throughout her whole body, then the slow fingers at her breast and legs, and finally that last, indescribably drawn-out motion, the glistening beads of sweat on both face and body, and the touch of firm, burning skin—the realization that she was suffocating and that it could be the most wonderful death.

After that, it became a regular occurrence. It had not the slightest bit to do with love or affection, and it was purely by chance that the young man turned out to be an impeccable, kind and decent fellow in his relations with Katya; moreover, their assignations were surrounded by such secrecy that no one apart from them knew about it. If Katya did not meet him during the course of the week, she would begin once more to feel as though nothing had happened; but all it took for her was the sound of his voice, and she would be prepared to travel anywhere; she was utterly incapable of fighting this urge. They never left a place together and were careful never to be seen in each other's company. He stopped visiting Katya's apartment altogether, and her brother, Alexander, even asked one day:

"Whatever happened to that alcoholic, Katya?"

"What alcoholic?"

"Oh, you remember, that young chap, dark-haired, I seem to recall—the rich heir."

"Yes, I remember. Only why do you call him an alcoholic? Do you know him well?"

"I don't know him from Adam. But I don't have to. Just look at him—always pristine, well dressed, cheery … That, my dear, is suspicious. Eventually it'll all come out: he's an alcoholic."

"You're such an idiot, Sasha."

"Well, I'm telling you that you don't know the first thing about psychology. My eyes never fail me. It's a crime that I'm an architect: I should have been a scientist."

"Oh, it certainly is a crime that you're an architect."

It was with some astonishment that Katya observed how seldom she spoke with her lover and that conversation with him was entirely unnecessary. Right from the very start, however, she had begun to feel, in tandem with this irresistible attraction to him, something verging on hatred. He could not fail to notice this and even said to her one day that perhaps it would be better if they put an end to their trysts—if she did not love him …

"I've never loved you," she said. "Never, do you hear? Never. But I cannot live without you."

"That is far too complicated for me."

"Yes," she said, with regret and contempt. "That's true. It *is* too complicated for you."

She was beginning to rot inside; she would fly into a rage for no good reason and, one day, in the presence of her brother and her husband, she slapped Vasily Vasilyevich right in the face—the boy was so stunned by the act that he did not even cry. Her brother shot up and shouted so loudly that his voice filled the entire apartment:

"You stupid woman!"

She looked at him, and then at her husband—for the first time she noticed his cold, foreign eyes. Without raising his voice, he said:

"Thus far I have not taken advantage of my rights, Katya. Now, however, I am compelled to do so. There are things that I cannot and will not allow."

"The older you get, the more you're like Mother," said Alexander furiously. "A pretty inheritance."

"I don't think that's the issue here, Sasha," said her husband measuredly.

It ended in hysterics, tears and Katya's lying down on her bed and not getting up until the following morning.

She became perfectly insufferable. She would scold the maid constantly, fuss bitterly, rearrange the furniture in the apartment, demand, refuse, purchase things and send them back; she lost any resemblance to the meek woman she had once been. Her husband went abroad for a month and Vasily Vasilyevich went to his uncle's "for a visit", as his uncle put it, and she was left alone. She thought she was close to suicide. She felt as though she could no longer endure such a life.

Then one day he did not show up for their assignation. She sat a whole hour in the little apartment he rented for their meetings, but he did not come. She left. She waited for the telephone to ring or for a note, thinking that some catastrophe might have befallen him. But there was no call, nor any note.

A week passed. She spent it reading books that she was unable to understand, no matter how hard she tried. She began writing letters to her husband, only to throw them away, unfinished, and await an explanation, despite outward appearances, for what had happened.

Late one evening, a week and a half to the day since their failed assignation, an unfamiliar voice informed her over the telephone that Monsieur So-and-So was very keen to see her. She brusquely hung up, but a minute later the same voice called again and explained that she had misunderstood, that she was mistaken—*monsieur* was in a very bad way and that if she did not come immediately … "I'm coming," she said. "The address, please."

Ten minutes later she entered his unfamiliar apartment. A doctor's assistant with a very grave expression—one that people have only in exceptional and usually dire circumstances—had opened the door to her, and from this she knew that he must be dying. The doctor, with a hardened, absent-minded expression on his unshaven face, walked past her, seeming not to notice her presence. A few other people had gathered in a large reception room; she knew none of them, but, looking at each one, she was able to read the situation accurately. It was warm and stuffy in the apartment, and a medicinal smell mingled with a strange, foul odour. Through the reception room, towards Katya, came another assistant, carrying a large object under her spotless white apron. A young man sitting in an armchair raised his head, glanced at Katya as one would at a table or a chair, and lowered his head, cradling it in his hands.

No sooner had Katya entered than she was hit by a palpable, chilling, almost unbearable languor. She stood for a moment, crossed herself and finally went into the room where the patient lay. At first sight of him, she felt a strange, insurmountable terror.

He lay on the bed, covered up to his waist. Instead of the torso that she knew so well, with its rippling muscles under dark, firm skin, she saw a tightly covered ribcage with angularly protruding bones. His arms were thin and his fingers too large. She leant over the unfamiliar, overgrown face. His eyes had rolled back into their sockets; in place of the irises were two frozen, jaundiced whites. His mouth lay open. The dying man's breathing was strangely shallow and quick, like a dog's after a run. He was unconscious.

She knelt before the bed and took his burning hand; he gave no sign of feeling this. Then, for a second, his eyes appeared and he looked upon Katya, failed to comprehend what was going on and wheezed in an unfamiliar voice: "Oxy … oxy …"

"He's asking for oxygen," said Katya.

"Yes, yes," came the doctor's absent-minded voice from the reception room, apparently in response to a question from his assistant. "But it's futile all the same, all the same."

Overnight his breathing grew slower and slower, and at four o'clock in the morning, without having regained consciousness, he died. Her cheeks moist, Katya left the room. The young man sitting in the chair, the deceased's brother, was crying inconsolably, sobbing like a child. Only then did it become apparent to Katya, what had long been so, but had never managed to reach her consciousness: namely, that the man who had died was the man she loved, and that she had loved only him.

She returned home, lit a cigarette and sat down to write a letter. At eight o'clock in the morning her husband arrived on the early train. He kissed her hand, looked at her much-altered face and said in French (he often switched to French):

"*Tu reviens de loin.*"[*]

"*Je ne reviens pas,*" she said. "*Je pars.*"[†]

That very day, having signed the petition for divorce, she left.

---

[*] Literally "You're coming back from afar"; metaphorically, "You've dodged a bullet."

[†] "I'm not coming back … I'm leaving."

SHIBALOK'S FAMILY
Mikhail Sholokhov (1905–1984)
Translated by H. C. Stevens

The third Russian Nobel laureate for literature after Bunin and Pasternak, author of the epic 'And Quiet Flows the Don', **Mikhail Sholokhov** was of Cossack origin and represented the so called Red Cossacks, those who accepted Bolshevik rule. The majority didn't, fought for the White army and later were subjected to de-*cossackisation*, repressive measures aimed at eliminating Cossacks as a group and a centre of power.

Sholokhov became a dedicated advocate and *troubadour* of all cruel Soviet policies, including *collectivization*, which cost millions of lives, and a conservative gatekeeper hounding dissident writers like Aleksandr Solzhenitsyn or Yuly Daniel.

"You're an educated woman, you wear glasses, and yet you can't get this into your head. ... What am I to do with him?

"Our detachment is quartered some twenty-five miles away. I've come here on foot, carrying him in my arms. You can see the skin's all rubbed off my feet. If you're the head of this children's home, take in the child. You say there's no room? But what am I to do with him? I've suffered enough through him already. I've supped of bitterness right up to my front teeth. Why, yes, he's my little son, he's my family. He's in his second year, but he hasn't any mother. There was something quite special about his mother. Oh, yes, I can tell you all about it, if you'd like to listen. The year before last I was in a company organized for special assignments. At that time we were hunting the Ignatiev bandit group through the upper districts of the Don. To be exact, I was a machine-gunner. One day we rode out of a village, the steppe all around was as bare as a baldheaded man, and the heat was unbelievable. We rode over a rise and began to drop down the hill into a little wood. I was in front on a two-wheeled cart. Suddenly I look and think I can see a woman lying on a mound close by.

I touch up the horses and make for her. She was just an ordinary sort of woman, but there she was lying mug upwards, and the edge of her skirt dragged right up to her head. I get down and could see she was alive, but breathing hard. I thrust the point of my sabre between her teeth and forced her mouth open, splashed her with water from my flask, and she came right back to life. Then the cossacks of the company galloped up and questioned her:

"'Who are you, and why are you lying so close to the road exposing yourself indecently?'

"She gave tongue as though wailing for the dead, and after a lot of hard work we got out of her that a band from the Astrakhan area had taken her on their waggon, had raped her on the spot and, as usual, flung her out on the road. I say to my fellow-cossacks:

"'Brothers, allow me to take her on my cart, seeing as she's suffered from bandits.'

"And all the company cried out:

"'Take her on your cart, Shibalok. Women are living things, the carrion; let her get a bit better and then we'll see.'

"Well, and what would you expect? Although I'm not the sort to be fond of sniffing at a woman's petticoats I felt sorry for her, and I took her on, to my own sin. She survived and grew quite used to us; she started washing the cossacks' rags, and then you'd notice that she'd patched somebody's trousers, and she did all the woman's work for the company. But we began to feel that it was a bit of a scandal to keep a woman with the company. The captain swore:

"'Take her by the tail, the hen, and turn her back to the wind.'

"But I felt sorry for her, and that to the highest and greatest degree. So I told her:

"'Clear out for your own good, Daria, or some idiotic bullet will get wedded to you, and then you'll be crying. ...'

"She burst into tears, and stormed back at me:

"'Shoot me on the spot, dear cossacks, but I'm not going to leave you.'

"Soon after that my driver was killed off, and she tries the following trick on me:

"'Take me as your driver, ah? You see, I can manage horses just a well as anyone else ...

"I hand her the reins.

"'If,' I tell her, 'we get into a fight and you can't manage to turn the cart round back to front in two shakes, lie down in the middle of the road and die: in any case, I'll flog you to death.'

"She drove to the amazement of all the serving cossacks. Even though she was a female she knew as much about horses as any cossack. There were times during a fight when she would swing the cart round so fast that the horses reared on their hind legs. And the longer we went on the more she did. And we began to get involved with her. Well, as you could expect, she got a belly. Women have to put up with a lot from the likes of us. And so for some eight months longer we hunted that bandit group. The cossacks in our company lashed out at me:

"'Shibalok, look how fat your driver's got on government rations: she's too big for the driver's seat now.'

"And then we got into a bit of a mess: we'd used up all our ammunition and supplies hadn't come up. The bandit force was holding one end of a village, we the other. We kept it a very deep secret from the villagers that we hadn't any bullets left. And then there was a spot of treachery. In the middle of the night—I was on sentry duty—I hear the ground groaning. They came streaming round the village and had in mind to encircle us. They tore into the attack, and clearly hadn't the least fear of us; they even went so far as to shout to us:

"'Surrender, you darling red cossacks, you bulletless ones. Otherwise, dear brothers, we'll finish off the lot of you.'

"Well, they hunted after us. They twisted our tail so hard that we had to run races over the rises to see who had the best horse. Next morning we reassembled in a forest some ten miles outside the village, and a good half of us failed to answer the roll-call. Some had cleared off, and those left behind were cut down. I was pretty miserable, not a house anywhere near, and Daria now fell ill. She'd galloped on horseback all night and she was changed completely, black shadows under her eyes. I see her trying to get away from us, and she goes off into the forest, into a thicket. I guessed what was up and went after her. She plunged into a ravine, among fallen logs, found a clear spot washed clean with rain, and, just like a she-wolf, scraped fallen leaves together and lay at first face downward, then turned over on to her back. She starts groaning, her labour began, but I squatted down behind a bush and didn't stir, watching her through the branches. And she groaned and groaned, then she began to scream, her tears ran down her cheeks, she went green all over, her eyes goggled, she strained until a spasm bent her double. It wasn't fitting for a cossack to do what I did, but I watched and saw that if she didn't drop the baby she'd die. I ran out from behind the bush and over to her; I could see I'd got to help her. I stooped down, rolled up my sleeve, and I felt so fearful and helpless I went all wet with sweat. I've had to kill people in my time, and I've never felt any fear then, but now what was I like? I go fussing round her, she stops howling and fires this blast at me:

"'Yasha, do you know who told the bandits we hadn't any ammunition?' And she looked at me kind of serious.

"'Well, who was it?' I asked her.

"'It was me.'

"'You fool, have you got rabies? This isn't the time for chatter; you lie quiet.'

"But she stuck to her point:

"'Death's standing at my head, I must confess to you, Yasha. You don't know what a snake you've been warming under your shirt ...

"'Well, confess away,' I said. 'The devil's in you.'

"And she told me all, beating her head against the ground; she told me:

"'I,' she says, 'was in the bandit group of my own free will and I went around with their leader, Ignatiev. ... A year ago they sent me to your company to get them any news I could, and I made up the story that I'd been raped, just for show. I shall die now, but otherwise I'd have given away the whole company sooner or later. ...'

"At that my heart went mad with fury and I couldn't stand it. I kicked her with my boot and made her mouth all bloody. But then her labour set in again, and I see the child coming between her legs. There it lay all wet, and twittering like a little hare in a fox's teeth. ... But now Daria was crying and laughing, she crawls to my feet and tries to put her arms round my knees. I turned away and went off to the company. And I told the cossacks how it had all been.

"And there was a fine row. At first they wanted to sabre me on the spot, but then they tell me:

"'You took her on, Shibalok, now you must finish her off complete with the new-born babe; for if you don't we'll shred you like cabbage.'

"I went down on my knees and said:

"'Brothers! I shall kill her not because I'm afraid of your threats but for conscience' sake, because of those brothers and comrades of ours who've lost their heads through her treachery. But have pity on the child. In it she and I have got half shares; it's my family, so let it live. You've got wives and children, but I haven't a soul except this baby.'

"I pleaded with the company and kissed the ground. And they had pity on me and said:

"'Well, all right. Let your family grow up, and may it grow up to be as fine a machine-gunner as you, Shibalok. But finish off the woman!'

"I ran back to Daria. She was sitting up; she'd come round and was holding the child in her arms.

"And I say to her:

"'I won't let you put the child to your breast. Since it's been born in a bitter year may it never taste mother's milk; and as for you, Daria, I've got to kill you because you're against our Soviet government. Stand up with your back to the ravine.'

"'Yasha, but how about the child? He's your flesh. If you kill me he'll die without milk. Let me feed him, and then kill me: I don't mind. ...'

"'No,' I say to her, 'the company's given me strict orders. I can't let you live, but don't worry about the child. I'll feed it on mare's milk; I won't let it die.'

"I stepped back a couple of paces and slipped my rifle off my shoulder. But she put her arms round my legs and kissed my boots. ...

"And afterwards I went back without looking round, my hands trembling, my knees sagging, and the child, slippery, naked, slipping out of my hands.

"Some five days later we rode back past the same spot. In the dell above the forest was a cloud of crows. ... I've known much bitterness through this child.

"'Take it by the feet and smash it against the cartwheel. What are you suffering with it for, Shibalok?' the cossacks used to ask.

"But I was sorry beyond anything I can tell for the little scamp. I would think: 'Let him grow up, he'll take on my job, my son will defend the Soviet régime. And Yakov Shibalok will leave a memory behind, I shan't die like scrub in the steppe, I shall leave my child.' You see, believe me, good woman citizen, I'd wept tears over him, though

I hadn't known tears for ages. One of our mares had a foal, we shot the foal, and so I made use of its mother's milk. Sometimes the babe wouldn't take the teat, it was a real pest; but then he grew used to it and sucked away at the teat as well as any other child at its mother's titty.

"I made him a shirt out of my old underpants. Now he's grown rather too big for it, but that doesn't matter, we'll manage.

"And now get it all clear in your head: what am I to do with him? He's too small, you say? He's intelligent and he can chew. Take him and chance it. You'll take him? Well, and thank you, citizeness. As soon as we smash the Fomin bandits I'll ride over and visit him.

"Goodbye, little son, Shibalok's family. Grow up ... Sh, you son of a bitch! What are you tugging at your daddy's beard for? Haven't I nannied you? Haven't I looked after you, and now you're trying to fight me, are you? Well, before we part, let's kiss the top of your noddle.

"Don't worry, good citizeness. D'you think he'll start screaming? Not he! He's got a little of the bolshevik in him: he can bite all right, there's no point in denying it, but you won't get any tears out of him!".

THE FATE OF THE PROFESSOR'S WIFE

Daniil Kharms (1905–1942)

Translated by Matvei Yankelevich

Born in Saint-Petersburg, the icon of Russian absurdist prose, leader of the *Oberiu*, the informal collective of futurist authors, and a dedicated and talented children's writer, **Daniil Kharms** (born Daniil Yuvachev) earned his daily bread writing for kids and won glory with his short stories circulated among his friends.

Kharms was first arrested in 1931, accused of being part of an anti-Soviet group among children's writers and exiled to the provincial city of Kursk. When he returned, Kharms created his best collections of short stories, and was arrested again in 1941, in a Leningrad soon to be blockaded by Nazi troops. Kharms was accused of 'defeatist moods', simulated madness and died of hunger in the first winter of the siege.

Kharms was buried in a mass grave like hundreds of thousands of Leningraders who starved to death that winter. But his archive was saved by his friends and kept until the Thaw, when it became possible to publish some parts of it.

Once one professor ate something not quite right and he started to vomit.

His wife comes and says, "What's with you?"

And the professor says, "Nothing." The wife goes away again.

The professor lay down on the couch, lay around a while, rested and went to work.

At work a surprise awaited him: They'd docked his pay—in place of 650 rubles, only 500 was left. The professor made a fuss, but nothing helped. He goes to the director, and the director throws him out. He goes to the bookkeeper, and the bookkeeper says, "See the director." The professor got on a train and went to Moscow.

On the way the professor caught the flu. He arrived in Moscow but couldn't get out onto the platform.

They put the professor on a stretcher and carried him off to the hospital.

The professor lay in the hospital no more than four days and died.

The body of the professor was incinerated in a crematorium. His ashes were placed in a jar and sent to his wife.

So, the wife of the professor is sitting and drinking coffee. Suddenly there's the doorbell. What is it? "You have a package."

The wife gets excited, smiles with all her teeth, presses a half-ruble into the postman's hand and hurries to open the package.

She looks inside and in the package there is a jar of ash and a note: "This is all that is left of your spouse."

The wife can't understand a thing. She shakes the jar, holds it up to the light. She read the note six times, and finally understood what was going on and got terribly upset.

The wife of the professor was very upset and cried for about three hours and then went to bury the jar of ash. She wrapped the jar up in newspaper and took it to the Park of the First Five Year Plan, previously the Tavrichesky Garden. The wife of the professor chose the most desolate path and just when she was about to bury the jar—here comes a watchman.

"Hey!" shouted the watchman. "What do you think you're doing here?"

The wife of the professor got frightened and said, "Well, I just wanted to catch some frogs in this jar."

"Alright," said the watchman, "that's fine, just watch out—walking on the grass is forbidden."

When the watchman went away, the wife of the professor buried the jar, patted down the dirt around it with her foot and went for a walk in the park.

In the park some sailor started hitting on her. Come on, let's go, he says, to sleep, and the like. She says: "Why sleep during the day?" And he goes on again talking about sleep, sleep.

And really the professor's wife was getting kind of sleepy.

She walks the streets, but she's sleepy. All sorts of people are running around, blue ones and green ones, and she's still sleepy.

She's walking along asleep. And she has a dream that Leo Tolstoy is coming towards her, holding a bedpan in his hands. She asks him, "What is that?" And he points to the bedpan and says:

"There," he says, "I've done something in here, and now I'm taking it to show the whole world. Let everyone look at it!"

The professor's wife starts looking too, and sees that it's as if it's no longer Tolstoy, but a shed, and in the shed there sits a chicken.

The professor's wife started after the chicken, but the chicken stuffed itself under the couch and now was already peeking out as a bunny rabbit.

The professor's wife crawled under the couch after the bunny and woke up.

She wakes up and looks around: She really is lying under the couch.

She crawled out from under the couch and saw that she was in her own room. And there's the table with the unfinished coffee. And on the table is a note: "This is all that is left of your spouse."

Once more the professor's wife let out a sob and sat down to finish drinking the cold coffee.

Suddenly, there's a doorbell. What is it? Some people come in saying, "Let's go for a ride."

"Where to?" the professor's wife asks.

"To the madhouse," the people answer.

The professor's wife kicked and screamed and dug her heels in, but the people grabbed her and drove her away to the madhouse.

And so here sits a perfectly normal wife of a professor on a cot in the madhouse, holding a fishing rod and catching invisible fish on the floor.

This professor's wife is only a sorry example of just how many unfortunate people there are in life, who occupy a place in life they are not meant to occupy.

MAJOR PUGACHIOV'S LAST BATTLE

Varlam Shalamov (1907–1982)

Translated by Donald Rayfield

The descendant of northern *shamans*, the grandson and son of the priests, **Varlam Shalamov** became an atheist, pacifist and leftist. First arrested in the late twenties, he witnessed the "childhood" of the GULAG, its first mass-scale camps.

His second arrest in 1937 sent Shalamov to the very East of Russia, to the notorious Kolyma camps which had one of the highest death rates because of hard labor, hunger, the harsh climate and mass killings. Shalamov survived 16 years there and later wrote *The Kolyma Tales*: the grandiose literary project equally important as a witness account, document, monument – and a bold, profound literary endeavor, because Shalamov brought writing to its very limits, into the territory of primeval, cultureless being, into the depth of inhuman experience, disintegration, and proved himself able to grasp it in the text.

Shalamov's choice to write short stories, not a novel, only underlines his creativity: existence in the Kolyma camps was not a continuity of life, it was a series of flashes, of moments of being suspended over the dark abyss. Until the end of his life this abyss haunted him and finally caught him: he died in a psychiatric hospital, ignored by the Soviet authorities and abandoned by the general public.

A lot of time must have passed between the beginning and end of these events, for months in the Far North can be counted as years, so great is the experience, the human experience, that is to be had there. Even the state recognizes this fact, since it raises the salaries and increases the privileges of those who work there. In this country of hope, but inevitably also of rumors, guesses, conjectures, and hypotheses, every event takes on a legendary quality even before some courier manages to swiftly deliver a local chief's report about that event to some "higher sphere."

There was talk that when a visiting top boss deplored the fact that cultural work in the camp was in bad shape, the cultural organizer, Major Pugachiov, told the visitor, "Don't worry, sir, we're rehearsing a show that will be the talk of all Kolyma."

The story could begin with a denunciation from the surgeon Braude, who had been posted from the central hospital to a district of military action.

It could also begin with a letter written by Yashka Kuchen, a prisoner and male nurse who was a patient in the hospital. He had written the letter with his left hand, since he had been shot in the right shoulder and the bullet had gone right through him.

Or we could start with Dr. Potanina's story: she hadn't seen a thing or heard a thing, and she'd been away on a trip when the unexpected events happened. It was this trip that the interrogator called a "false alibi," criminal inertia, or whatever the term is in the language of the law.

In the 1930s arrests happened to people by chance. They were victims of a terrible and false theory that the class struggle would intensify as socialism became established. The professors, party workers, military officers, engineers, peasants, and workers who filled the overcrowded prisons had no particular virtues except, perhaps, personal honesty or perhaps naïvety—in short, qualities that made the punitive work of the "justice system" at the time easier rather than harder. The absence of any single idea that might unite them fatally weakened the moral defenses of the prisoners. They were neither enemies of the authorities nor state criminals, and when they died, they still didn't understand why they had to die. Their self-respect or their resentment had nothing to focus on. Alienated from one another, they died in Kolyma's white desert—from hunger, from cold, from many hours of labor, from beatings, and from diseases. They immediately learned not to intercede for one another. This was what the authorities were striving to achieve. The souls of those who remained alive were subjected to complete defilement, while their bodies lacked the qualities needed for physical labor.

After the war these people were replaced by one shipload after another of repatriated Soviet citizens—from Italy, France, Germany—who were sent straight to the Far Northeast.

Among them were many men with different mindsets, with habits picked up during the war—boldness, the ability to take risks, a belief in armed strength alone. They were commanders and soldiers, pilots and reconnaissance men.

The camp administration was used to the angelic patience and servile meekness of the Trotskyists, so they weren't in the least worried and they didn't expect anything new.

The new arrivals asked those "aborigines" who were still alive, "Why do you eat your soup and porridge in the refectory, but take the bread back to the barracks? Why not eat the bread with your soup, like normal people?"

Smiling with the cracks of their blue mouths, so as to show how scurvy had removed all their teeth, the local inhabitants replied to the novices, "In two weeks every one of you will understand why, and will do the same."

How could you tell them that they had never yet in their lives known real hunger, hunger that goes on for many years, that saps your will, so that you can't fight the passionate, obsessive desire to prolong the process of eating for as long as you can, to finish eating, sucking your bread ration in the uttermost bliss in the barracks, with a mug of tasteless water made from "heated" snow.

But not all the new arrivals shook their heads in contempt before moving away.

Major Pugachiov understood quite a few things. He had no doubt that they had all been brought here to die, to replace these living corpses. They'd been brought here in autumn, with a view to winter, when there was no prospect of running away; whereas in summer, even if you couldn't get away for good, at least you would die a free man.

So there would be all winter to weave the net of this plot, the only one in twenty years.

Pugachiov realized that the only people capable of surviving the winter and then escaping would be those who didn't do manual labor at the pit face. After just a few weeks working in a brigade, nobody would be able to run away to anywhere.

Slowly, one by one, the plotters infiltrated the support jobs: Soldatov became a cook, Pugachiov became the culture organizer; there were a paramedic and two foremen, while Ivashchenko, who had been a mechanic, was repairing weapons in the guards' section.

But none of them was allowed "outside the wire" without a guard escorting them.

The dazzling Kolyma spring had begun: not a drop of rain, no cracks in the ice, no birds singing. The snow disappeared little by little, as it was burned up by the sun. Wherever the sun's rays could not reach, the snow still lay in the gullies and ravines, like silver ingots, until the following year.

The appointed day dawned.

There was a knock at the door of the tiny guardhouse by the camp gates: the guardhouse had doors leading both into and out of the camp, and the rules stated that two men always had to be on guard there. The duty guard yawned and looked at the pendulum clock. It was five in the morning. "Only five," he thought.

The duty guard lifted the hook and let in whoever was knocking. It was a prisoner, the camp cook Soldatov, who had come to get the keys to the pantry. The keys were kept in the guardhouse. Soldatov came three times a day to fetch them, and he would then bring them back.

The duty guard had to open the kitchen cupboard himself, but he knew that there was absolutely no point checking up on the cook, that no locks would stop a cook who intended to steal something. So he entrusted the cook with the keys, especially as it was five in the morning.

The duty guard had worked more than a dozen years in Kolyma; he had been getting double pay for a long time, and he had put the keys in the cook's hand thousands of times.

"Take them," he said, as he picked up a ruler and bent down to draw lines on his morning report.

Soldatov went behind the guard's back, took the key off the nail, put it in his pocket, and then seized the guard by the throat. That instant the door opened and Ivashchenko the mechanic came into the guardhouse from the camp side. Ivashchenko helped Soldatov strangle the guard and drag his corpse behind a cupboard. Ivashchenko stuffed the guard's revolver in his pocket. Looking out through the window, they could see that the other duty guard was coming back down the path. Ivashchenko hurriedly put on the murdered man's greatcoat and cap, buckled up his belt and sat at the desk, as if he were the guard. The second guard opened the door and strode into the dark, kennel-like guardhouse. Instantly he was seized, strangled, and thrown behind the cupboard.

Soldatov put on the second guard's clothes. The two plotters now had weapons and military uniforms. Everything was going exactly according to Major Pugachiov's plan. Suddenly the wife of the second guard turned up at the guardhouse. She had also come for the keys, keys her husband had accidentally taken with him.

"We shan't strangle the woman," said Soldatov. She was tied up, her mouth was stuffed with a towel, and she was placed in a corner.

One of the prisoner brigades was on its way back from work. This had been anticipated. As soon as their guard entered the guardhouse he was disarmed and tied up by the two "guardhouse" men. The fugitives now had his rifle. From then on Major Pugachiov took over command.

The area in front of the gates was a field of fire for two guard towers at each corner manned by sentries. The sentries didn't notice anything peculiar.

Slightly earlier than expected, another brigade lined up to go to work, but who can say in the north what is early and what is late? It seemed a little earlier but may have been a little later than expected.

The brigade of ten men moved off in twos down the road to the pit faces. As the rules dictated, the escort guards in their greatcoats, one of them holding a rifle, strode six meters ahead of and behind the prisoners.

The sentry in the guard tower saw the brigade turn off the road down a path that passed by the guards' section building. This was where the soldiers of the guard service lived; the squad consisted of sixty men.

The guards' sleeping quarters were at the back of the building, while the squad's duty guard's quarters and a pyramid of weapons were right by the front door. The duty guard was half asleep at his desk and dimly noticed an escort guard leading a brigade of prisoners down the path past the guards' house windows.

"It must be Chernenko," he thought, not recognizing the escort guard. "I'll definitely report him." The duty guard was an expert at causing trouble and would not miss a chance to do something nasty to somebody, as long as it conformed to regulations.

That was his last thought. The door was flung open and three soldiers ran into the barracks. Two of them rushed to the dormitory doors, while the third shot the duty guard point-blank. Prisoners came running in after the soldiers and all of them went for the pyramid: they now had rifles and automatic weapons. Major Pugachiov violently flung the barracks dormitory door open. The soldiers, barefoot and still in their underwear, tried to rush to the door, but they were stopped by two rounds of automatic fire aimed at the ceiling.

"Lie down," ordered Pugachiov; the soldiers crawled under their bunks. A man with an automatic guarded the threshold.

The "brigade" began without hurry to change into military uniform, to stack up groceries, and to supply themselves with weapons and ammunition.

Pugachiov ordered his men not to take any food except for biscuits and chocolate, but as much weaponry and ammunition as possible.

The paramedic slung a first-aid bag over his shoulder.

Those escaping now felt they were soldiers again.

The taiga lay ahead, but was that any more terrible than the Stokhod marshes in western Ukraine?

They walked out onto the highway, where Pugachiov raised an arm and stopped a truck.

"Get out," he said, opening the cab door.

"But I—"

"I told you to get out."

The driver got out. Georgadze, a tank regiment lieutenant, took the wheel, and Pugachiov got in next to him. The escaping soldiers climbed into the back of the truck and it sped off.

"There's supposed to be a turn here."

The truck turned onto one of. ...

"We're out of gas!"

Pugachiov swore.

They went into the taiga like ducks diving into water and vanished in the enormous silent forest. Using a map, they kept to the fateful path to freedom, striding straight on, through the amazing Kolyma morass of fallen timber.

Kolyma trees die lying down, like human beings. Their mighty roots resembled the giant talons of a predatory bird, caught in a rock. Thousands of fine, tentacle-like offshoots descended from these gigantic talons into the permafrost. Every summer the permafrost retreated a little, and a brown tentacle root would immediately find its way down and fix itself in each inch of newly thawed earth.

Trees here did not reach maturity until they were three hundred years old; they lifted their mighty, heavy bodies slowly on such weak roots.

Pushed over by storms, the trees fell on their backs, their crowns all facing the same way, and they died lying on a thick layer of moss, bright pink or green in color.

The men began to pitch camp for the night. They were practiced and quick.

Only Ashot and Malinin were unable to calm down.

"What are you up to?" asked Pugachiov.

"Ashot is trying to persuade me that Adam was expelled from paradise to Ceylon."

"What do you mean, Ceylon?"

"That's what the Muslims say," said Ashot.

"Are you a Tatar then?"

"I'm not, but my wife is."

"I've never heard of that," said Pugachiov with a smile.

"Quite, nor have I," Malinin joined in.

"Well, time to sleep!"

It was cold. Major Pugachiov woke up. Soldatov was sitting with his automatic over his knees, fully alert. Pugachiov lay on his back trying to catch sight of the polestar, the walker's favorite. In Kolyma the constellations had different positions from those of Europe, of mainland Russia; the map of the stars was slightly askew, and the Great Bear drifted off toward the horizon. The taiga was silent and severe. The enormous gnarled larches were widely spaced. The forest was full of a worrying silence, familiar to any hunter. But on this occasion Pugachiov was not a hunter but a wild animal being tracked down, which made the silence of the forest three times more worrying for him.

This was Major Pugachiov's first night of freedom, a first night of liberty after the long months and years of his terrible stations of the cross. As he lay there he recalled the beginning of the drama-packed film that was now being shown before his very eyes. It seemed as if Pugachiov had personally shot the film of all his twelve lives in such a way that events were flashing past with unbelievable speed instead of keeping to their slow daily unfolding. And now came the credits, the "end of film," for they were free. And it was the beginning of battle, of a game, of life.

Major Pugachiov remembered the German camp he had escaped from in 1944. The front was getting closer to the town. He worked as a sanitation truck driver inside the enormous camp. He remembered accelerating the truck to full speed and smashing through the single fence of barbed wire, ripping out the hastily erected support stakes. Shots fired by the sentries, shouts, furious driving through the town in various directions, abandoning the truck, making his way by night to the front line, and then the meeting: interrogation in the special department. Charges of spying, a sentence of twenty-five years imprisonment.

Major Pugachiov recalled the visits by emissaries of General Vlasov and he recalled Vlasov's "manifesto," his visits to starving, exhausted, tormented Russian soldiers.

"Your authorities abandoned you a long time ago. Every prisoner of war is a traitor in the eyes of your government," said Vlasov's men, who then showed them the orders and speeches in copies of the Moscow newspapers. The prisoners of war already knew about this. It was significant that Russian prisoners of war were the only ones not to be sent parcels. The French, American, English prisoners, like all the other nationalities, received parcels, letters, had their own compatriots' clubs and made friends with one another. The Russians had nothing except for starvation and angry resentment of everything in the world. No wonder that many prisoners of war left the German camps to join the Russian Liberation Army.

Major Pugachiov didn't believe Vlasov's officers until he himself reached the Red Army units. Everything Vlasov's men had said was true. The state didn't want him, the state was afraid of him.

Then came the cattle cars with their bars and escort guards, a journey of many days to the Far East, the sea, the hold of a steamship, and the gold mines of the Far North. And a hungry winter.

Pugachiov sat up. Soldatov waved an arm at him. It was Soldatov who took the credit for beginning this enterprise, although he was one of the last to be drawn into the plot. Soldatov hadn't had cold feet, he hadn't lost his head, he hadn't sold them down the river. A fine man, Soldatov!

Captain Khrustaliov lay at Pugachiov's feet. Their fate was similar. His plane had been shot down by the Germans, he'd gone through captivity, starvation, an escape, a tribunal, and the camps. Khrustaliov now turned onto his side: one cheek was redder than the other, he'd been lying on it too long. Khrustaliov was the first man that Major Pugachiov had talked to, a few months earlier, about escaping. They'd agreed that death was better than a prisoner's life, that it was better to die with a gun in your hands than to die of starvation or to die at work from the guard hitting you with a rifle butt or his boots.

Both Khrustaliov and the major were men of action, and the negligible chance of success, for which the lives of twelve men were now being gambled, had been discussed in the greatest detail. The plan was to seize an airfield and an aircraft. There were several airfields here, and they were now heading through the taiga for the nearest one.

Khrustaliov was also the foreman whom the escapees had sent for after attacking the guard squad; Pugachiov refused to leave without his closest friend. And now Khrustaliov was sleeping nearby, calmly and deeply.

Next to him was Ivashchenko, a weapons expert who had been repairing the guards' revolvers and rifles. Ivashchenko had found out everything they needed to know in order to succeed: where the weapons were kept; who of the guard squad was on duty and when; where the ammunition stores were. Ivashchenko had been a reconnaissance man.

Levitsky and Ignatovich, two pilots, Khrustaliov's comrades, were fast asleep, huddled against each other.

Poliakov the tank driver had flung both arms over the backs of his neighbors, the giant Georgadze and the bald joker Ashot, whose surname the major had momentarily forgotten. Sasha Malinin, a camp paramedic, formerly an army paramedic, and now the Pugachiov group paramedic, was asleep, with his first-aid bag under his head.

Pugachiov smiled. Each man probably had his own idea of what this escape entailed. But the fact that everything was going smoothly, that they all understood one another instantly, was, Pugachiov knew, not just down to the major. Each man knew that events were unfolding as they should. They had a commander and a goal. A confident commander and a difficult goal. They had weapons. They had freedom. They could sleep soundly, as soldiers should, even in this empty pale-lilac polar night with its strange sunless light where the trees cast no shadows.

He had promised them freedom, and they had received it. He was leading them to their death, but they didn't fear death.

"And nobody betrayed us," Pugachiov was thinking, "right to the final day." Naturally, many people in the camp had known about the plan to escape. The selection of men had been going on for several months. Many people with whom Pugachiov had spoken frankly had refused, but nobody had run to the guardhouse with a denunciation. This was a circumstance that reconciled Pugachiov with life. "Fine men, fine men," he whispered as he smiled.

They ate biscuits and chocolate, then set off in silence. They were following a barely noticeable path.

"A bear's path," said Selivanov, a Siberian hunter.

Pugachiov and Khrustaliov climbed to a pass, to the mapmaker's tripod, and began surveying the ground below them through binoculars: there were two gray stripes, a river and the highway. The river was just a river; the highway was full of trucks carrying people over a stretch of several dozen kilometers.

"Prisoners, I expect," Khrustaliov suggested.

Pugachiov took a closer look.

"No, soldiers. They're after us. We'll have to split up," said Pugachiov. "Eight men should spend the night in the haystacks, and the other four of us will follow that gully. We'll be back by morning if everything is all right."

Passing through the undergrowth, they came to a streambed. It was time to go back.

"Take a look: there are too many of them, let's go upstream."

Breathing heavily, they quickly climbed upstream, and stones flew down, rustling and rumbling, hitting the feet of the soldiers attacking them.

Levitsky turned around, swore, and fell. A bullet had hit him right in the eye.

Georgadze, stopped by a big rock, turned and fired an automatic round at the soldiers climbing the gully. It stopped them only for a short time. His automatic fell silent, and only his rifle was firing.

Khrustaliov and Major Pugachiov managed to climb much higher, right to the pass.

"Carry on alone," the major told Khrustaliov. "I'll shoot."

The major took his time, knocking out every soldier who showed his face. Khrustaliov came back, shouting, "They're coming!" and then fell. People ran out from behind the big rock.

Pugachiov dashed forward, fired at the soldiers running toward him; then he threw himself from the pass on the plateau into the narrow streambed. In midair he grabbed hold of a willow branch, clung on, and clambered to one side. The stones he had struck as he fell rumbled and crashed even before they hit the bottom.

Pugachiov walked through the pathless taiga until he was exhausted.

The sun rose over the forest clearing, and the men hiding in the haystacks could clearly see the figures in military uniform coming from all sides of the clearing.

"Is this the end?" asked Ivashchenko, jostling Ashot Khachaturian with his elbow.

"Why should it be?" replied Ashot, taking aim. A rifle shot rang out, and a soldier on the path fell.

Gunfire aimed at the haystacks then opened up from all sides.

On command, soldiers dashed across the marsh toward the haystacks; shots rang out, the wounded groaned.

The attack was beaten back. Several wounded men lay on the hummocks in the marsh.

"Stretcher-bearer, crawl forward," an officer ordered.

The stretcher-bearer, a male nurse and prisoner, Yashka Kuchen, from western Ukraine, had been brought from the hospital as a precaution. Without saying a word, Kuchen crawled to a wounded man, waving his first-aid bag as he went. A bullet hit him in the shoulder and he stopped halfway.

The guard squad officer leapt out, unafraid. He came from the squad that the escapees had disarmed. He yelled out, "Hey, Ivashchenko, Soldatov, Pugachiov, surrender, you're surrounded. You can't hide anywhere."

"Come and take my weapon," shouted Ivashchenko from his haystack.

Bobyliov, the guard squad officer, ran toward the haystacks, his boots squelching in the marsh.

When he had run half the distance, Ivashchenko's rifle crackled, and a bullet hit Bobyliov right in the forehead.

"Attaboy!" Soldatov said in praise of his comrade. "The reason the officer's so brave is that he doesn't care. He'll be shot, or he'll get prison for letting us escape."

The fugitives were fired on from all sides. Machine guns were brought up; they rattled away.

Soldatov felt both his legs burn, and then he felt Ivashchenko, who'd been killed, thrust his head into his shoulder.

No sound came from the other haystack. About a dozen corpses lay in the marsh.

Soldatov kept firing until something hit him in the head and he lost consciousness.

Nikolai Sergeyevich Braude, the hospital's senior surgeon, was sent orders by a telephoned telegram from Major General Artemiev, one of the four Kolyma generals and the head of the guards of all the Kolyma camps. Braude was told to go to the settlement of Lichan and bring, in the words of the telegram, "two paramedics, bandaging material, and instruments."

Braude made no attempt to guess what was afoot. He quickly got everything ready and the hospital's decrepit little one-and-a-half-ton truck moved off in the required direction. The hospital truck, once on the highway, was constantly overtaken by powerful Studebakers laden with armed soldiers. The distance was only forty kilometers, but because of the frequent stops and the pileup of trucks ahead of it, because of the constant checks on papers, Braude took all of three hours to get there.

Major General Artemiev was in the local camp chief's apartment, waiting for the surgeon. Both Braude and Artemiev were old Kolyma hands, and this was not the first time that they were fated to meet.

"What's going on here? War?" Braude asked the general after they exchanged greetings.

"Not exactly war, but twenty-eight men killed in the first battle. As for the wounded, see for yourself."

While Braude was washing his hands in a basin hung by the door, the general told him about the escape.

"Why didn't you call out aircraft?" asked Braude, lighting a cigarette. "Two or three squadrons, then you could bomb them and bomb them. Or just use one atom bomb."

"You think it's all a joke," said the major general. "I'm waiting for orders, and there's no joking about it. I'll be lucky if I'm just dismissed from command of the guards. I could be court-martialed. Anything could happen."

Yes, Braude knew that anything could happen. Some years previously three thousand men were sent on foot, in winter, to one of the ports, where the stores that lay on the shore had been destroyed by a storm. In the course of that journey, only three hundred men of the original three thousand survived. The deputy chief of administration who had signed the order for the party of prisoners to go was sacrificed; he was put on trial.

Braude and his paramedics were extracting bullets, amputating limbs, and bandaging wounds until evening. The only wounded men were soldiers of the guard: there was not a single escaped prisoner among them.

Toward evening on the next day more wounded men were brought in. Surrounded by officers of the guard, two soldiers carried in a stretcher, on which Braude saw his first and only escaped prisoner. The fugitive was wearing a military uniform and only his unshaven face differentiated him from the soldiers. He had gunshot fractures in both shins, a gunshot fracture of the left shoulder, and a head wound with damage to the skull. The fugitive was unconscious.

Braude carried out first aid and, at Artemiev's orders, admitted the wounded man, along with his escort guards, to the big hospital where Braude worked and where he had the right facilities for a serious operation.

Everything was over. A military truck, covered with a tarpaulin, was parked nearby, and in it the bodies of the escaped prisoners were stacked. Next to it was another truck with the bodies of the dead soldiers.

The army could have been demobilized after this victory, but for many more days truckloads of soldiers drove up and down all sections of the two-thousand-kilometer highway.

The twelfth escapee, Major Pugachiov, was missing.

Soldatov's treatment took some time, until he was well enough to be shot. Actually, his was the only death penalty out of the sixty cases—the number of the fugitives' friends and acquaintances—that were tried by a tribunal. The chief of the local camp was given ten years. The head of the health service, Dr. Potanina, was acquitted by the court, and as soon as the trial was over she found herself a new job somewhere else. Major General Artemiev seemed to have been clairvoyant: he was removed, dismissed from his post in the guard service.

Pugachiov managed with some difficulty to crawl down through the narrow opening of a cave; it was a bear's den, its winter quarters, but the bear had long since left it and was wandering about the taiga. There was bear fur here and there on the cave walls and on the stones on the ground.

"How very quickly it all ended," thought Pugachiov. "They'll bring dogs and find me. And capture me."

Lying in the cave, he recalled his life, a hard life, a man's life, which was coming to an end now on a bear's track in the taiga. He recalled people, everyone he had respected and loved, beginning with his mother. He remembered Maria Ivanovna, his schoolteacher, who wore a quilted jacket covered with black velvet that had faded to a rust color. He recalled many, many other people whom he had been destined to come across.

But best of all, finest of all were his eleven dead comrades. None of the other people in his life had endured so many disappointments, so much deceit, so many lies. Even in this northern hell they had found enough inner strength to believe in him, Pugachiov, and to reach out for freedom. And to die in battle. Yes, those were the best people in his life.

Pugachiov tore off a bunch of lingonberries: a clump of bushes grew on a rock right by the cave entrance. Last year's blue, wrinkled berries burst when his fingers touched them, and he licked his fingers.

The overripe fruit had no more taste than melted snow. The skin of the berries stuck to his dried-out tongue.

Yes, they had been the best people. And he now knew Ashot's surname: Khachaturian.

Major Pugachiov remembered them all, one after the other, and smiled at each one of them. Then he put the barrel of his pistol in his mouth and, for the last time in his life, he fired.

THE INTELLECTUAL (THE CAUCHY PRINCIPLE)

Georgii Demidov (1908–1987)

Translated by Diane Nemec Ignashev

Varlam Shalamov's fellow prisoner, hero of the two stories in the *Kolyma tales*, **Georgii Demidov** was a physicist and a disciple of Lev Landau, the future Nobel Laureate. Arrested in 1938, he spent 13 years in Kolyma, was released and worked as engineer. In the seventies Demidov started to write prose based on his camp experience, but in 1980 all his manuscripts were confiscated by the KGB and given back to the family only after Demidov's death in 1988. After the confiscation Demidov resumed writing.

His prose won the recognition it deserves only in the 21st century, making Demidov one of the most important names in GULAG literature.

(The Cauchy Criterion)

If at a critical point a function's derivative changes from positive to negative, the function has its maximum at that critical point.

"Cauchy's First Criterion"—
from a mathematics textbook

Before his arrest, the chair of the calculus department had been referred to by some (with a note of disdain) and by others (with a nod of respect) as the "Intellectual," a term which had not yet entered common usage.

The young professor's range of knowledge and interests was indeed very broad. He was both a superb mathematician and a talented cellist in the Scholars' Club amateur orchestra. He took interest in a variety of subjects, those related to mathematics as well as those at considerable remove, for example, philosophy and history. One might run into him in the gymnasium or among a group of vagabond backpackers out on the slopes. And yet some considered him "refined intelligentsia," which was a more than dubious compliment for a Soviet citizen, because the adjective *refined* not only did not exclude, it underscored another epithet virtually coterminous with *intelligentsia—flabby*. The assumption was (admittedly not without some basis in fact) that a surfeit of education could have dangerous consequences for the revolutionary cause. Indeed, unlike the proletariat, unencumbered by doubts about the revolution's historical justifiability, the Russian intelligentsia—even its most recent new members—still bore the burden of political, ethical, and various other misgivings. And although this usually in no way reflected on their day-to-day lives or their integrity as citizens, looming suspicion of them would have especially tragic consequences for the Soviet intelligentsia in the "black" year of 1937. That year many—if not all—of its best would perish.

The Intellectual would be among them. But by the time he joined the ranks of loaders and haulers working the mine on Tin Mountain, he had acquired a simpler nickname: the "Scholar."

Of all the knowledge and skills the former professor possessed, the only one now of any practical use was his ability through force of will to squeeze every ounce of strength from his ever-declining muscles when on the job. And, when off, to withstand the dehumanizing effects of camp conditions so as not to descend to the level of near-beast, which happened to just about everyone here. The Scholar felt that the best way to stave off the stultifying effects of hard labor was to engage in mental gymnastics, as indispensible here as regular gymnastics for people with desk jobs. This place had turned him into a muscle machine for loading skids with chunks of blasted rock or pushing the heavy skids down the rails or sledgehammering particularly large stones. Therefore, as he worked, the Scholar devised various problems for himself, such as what would be the formula for calculating the volume of that wedge-shaped rock over there? Or, how would you express the analytic curve of the whimsical dip in the rails at the bend in the skid-rail tracks? Usually he worked these problems in his head, but in especially difficult cases he sometimes used a piece of soft white rock to scribble intricate mathematical symbols on the granite wall of the mine gallery.

Of course, he was considered touched in the head for this, but so, for that matter, were most people with a higher education. No one, however, despised or mocked his strange behavior.

First of all, the Scholar, it turned out, could, when necessary, stand up for himself. Second, and this was the main reason, he, unlike the majority of his intelligentsia brethren, was always collected and braced, outperforming not only them, but many who had done physical labor all their lives: farmers and even former miners. He had already outlived just about everyone with whom he'd been shipped from the mainland to this camp at the foot of God-and man-forsaken Tin Mountain two years ago. What exactly had helped this former member of the "refined intelligentsia" to break so difficult a record? It was hard to say: Perhaps it was the unusually strong heart he had inherited from his peasant forebears? Perhaps it was his even more unusual will power? Or that he had grown accustomed to physical labor while still a young man? In the mid-1920s a state scholarship was hardly a regular occurrence if a student's heritage was not pristinely proletarian. For that reason many students earned their board unloading freight cars, chopping firewood, or performing similarly not-light labor. It was also not insignificant—particularly given conditions in the camp at the foot of the "hill" (as Tin Mountain was known here)—that in his former life the Scholar had done mountain climbing. In ways he'd never expected, his experience in the Caucasus and Altai mountains proved quite useful in Kolyma.

Most likely, of course, it was not any single one of the former scholar-musician-athlete's qualities and skills, but all of them combined that for so amazingly long kept him from sliding down the path of least resistance to the camp's cemetery. To the very end he preserved his conscious will for life, whereas the majority of his camp comrades had only the degradation and often counterproductivity of animal instinct left to them. Rummaging for sardine heads in garbage containers, for example, or drinking incredible quantities of water to stifle hunger sooner brought on rather than staved off death from starvation and the diseases related to it.

But there wasn't a dancing-prancing fairytale hero the steep incline known as Tin Mountain would not (more likely sooner rather than later) send sprawling to the bottom. The mountain was steep not only in the metaphorical sense of the mineshaft within its depths or the prisoners' almost unbearable living conditions in the camps that served it. The incline of the "hill" that prison mine-laborers daily ascended to its peak was steep in the direct sense of the word, and almost all the entrances and descents into the many shafts, quarries, and galleries were located at its summit or in direct proximity to it.

For an experienced climber, Tin Mountain was hardly a challenge. A somewhat elongated hummock of average height, it was a typically dismal, treeless mountain for these parts. The trail from its foot to its peak stretched barely a thousand meters. And the slope along which the camp detachment made its daily ascent was so laid-back that a cable rail system had been laid along it to the mine. But add to the height of the "hill" yet another three-hundred-meter incline on the way from the camp located three kilometers from its foot, coat its slopes with bare ice in fall and spring or pile them high with snowdrifts in the winter, whip the faces of those who daily "conquered" the hill with the hurricane-strength winds of high-altitude snowstorms, frostbite them with fifty- and sixty-degree-below-zero cold, multiply all this by the number of days in the year, and you get what will still be a far-from-comprehensive tally of the difficult conditions under which these willy-nilly alpestrians set their records. The daily ascents and descents came, of course, in addition to their fourteen-hour workday at the mine. In fact, many saw it the other way around: that the work itself was but a complement to their daily "taking of the summit." But, as we all know, the value of a summand does not vary in relation to the relative position of its addends. Under high-altitude conditions combined with exorbitant workloads even the most enduring of the accursed mountain's "conquerors" developed enlarged hearts and other related disorders, and it was these disorders that drove to the grave those alpestrians who had not already succumbed to exhaustion or starvation or perished in the innumerable accidents that occurred at the mine. (Safety precautions were at best just hearsay, and of little concern to anyone. Why waste money on measures to protect those destined to survive no more than two or three years at this place?) Almost daily one (some days, it might be two or three) of the climbers would fail to "take" the peak. Falling short of it, they collapsed, never to arise again. Nothing helped—neither the obscenities nor the threats, nor the boots, nor the butts of the convoy's rifles.

As the camp detachment made its way towards the foot of Tin Mountain—whose peak on days with low cloud cover disappeared into the gray clouds—the convoy chief shouted out the order to take a short break. He never had to repeat the command. All one thousand—sometimes it might be only three hundred, depending on how many months had passed since the last complement had been delivered to the camp—would collapse onto the snow or rocks. Although everyone knew that the break would last no more than five minutes, the majority quickly sank into sleep. Chronic sleep deficiency posed hardly less an adversity than ordinary malnutrition. Once you subtracted the number of hours spent working at the mine, time spent ascending and descending the hill, standing around for roll calls and at checkpoints, lining up for bread and watery *balanda*, and all the senseless searches and frequent frisks, those who worked "mainline production" were left no more than five or six hours a day for sleep. Days off were out of the question. Hence, the only opportunities prisoners had to compensate for perpetual sleep deficiency were sick days. But getting a sick day off from work was hardly easy. As a very not-funny camp joke went, you had to show up at the infirmary with "your head tucked in your armpit."

Thus, the prisoners' readiness to "fall out" was matched only by their loathing to emerge from the leaden torpor that momentarily overcame them. They lumbered back up to their feet, not infrequently only after a guard's kick, and resumed their excruciating trek up the hill, which cost them the larger part of their diminishing physical powers.

At this stretch of their march the convoy guards let the prisoners move on ahead and walked at the rear, rather than surrounding the column as usual. Inherently more pack-drivers than guards, when ascending the hill the convoy gave itself over entirely to the task of herding, for which it employed the most savage devices. There was no other way. As they made their way up Tin Mountain the prisoners had a malicious tendency to string themselves out along the entire length of the slope. The head of the "column" would already be approaching the summit, while its tail still trudged along a half-mile below, despite constant shoving and prodding with rifle butts. Those who fell to the ground were methodically beaten. This was done more as a lesson to the others than to force the fallen man to get back up on his feet and keep going, for there was little hope of that. You had to pelt the near-corpse (that lay panting like a spent horse) or corpse (that had already stopped breathing entirely) with kicks and rifle-butts, otherwise there would be no end to the ranks of shirkers ready to feign total exhaustion or heart attacks so as to be sent back to the infirmary. The camp's doctors would, of course, figure out whether the prisoner really couldn't move or if he were only "faking." But in either case he wouldn't get sent back out to the hill, which in itself was no small prize. However, if his good fortune were to cost him a punctured lung or broken rib, then neither he nor the other convicts would have any desire to engage in similar malingering in the future. As for those who really couldn't continue the climb, the majority of them died, and those who didn't became vegetables of absolutely no worth to the work force. Consequently, there was no real need to fuss over them either. The method had its particular logic.

For nearly a year, although he was far from the youngest of the prisoners here, the Scholar had always been one of the first to reach the place where those who had managed to complete the climb lay gasping, mouths wide-open, for the thin mountain air. But gradually the separator that was the hill had tossed him further and further back from the head of the column, so that by now he trudged along not even at the middle. His heart—about which he had used to joke that he barely knew where it was—increasingly and more frequently let itself be known. Weakness, piercing pain in his chest, and the sensation of asphyxiation got the better of him. The closer to the tail of the column he trudged up the mountain, the more often he observed someone nearby stop and clutch at his heart. The man would then fall slowly back down the slope, staring with glazed-over eyes at those who—raising heavy foot over heavy foot—kept plodding on. Usually the man's eyes expressed only physical pain, but sometimes they also held terror and a mortal sadness. Sometimes you might see foam in the corner of the man's mouth. Turning back, the Scholar would watch as the guards unhurriedly approached the fallen man. Sometimes he also overheard, as one of the guards, having first given the writhing man a swift kick in the gut, started shouting at him in an unnaturally coarse voice, like a shepherd goading some beast, "All right, stop faking already!"

The prospect of such an end did not so much frighten as enrage the Scholar with its senselessness. What was the point of having been born an exceptionally talented human being (nowadays in his current situation he felt he had the right to consider himself such), of having achieved so much and of having strived for even more, only to perish in such a ludicrous, unnatural fashion among these grim mountains somewhere at the far end of the earth? Over the past two years he had tried with every fiber of his being to stave off such an end, hoping for some miracle, the impossibility of which he also fully realized. But for human beings in dire predicaments to believe in miracles is as innate as to protect one's face from falling rock. In its naivete faith manifests itself not only in things great and small, but in the ridiculous as well. After all, when he'd gone to the camp's medical assistant, a former veterinarian, to ask for something to relieve his ever-intensifying heart failure, hadn't he known that the camp's infirmary had almost no medications? The veterinarian had not even pretended to confirm his patient's complaint by listening to his heart. He had just handed him some powder. The indifference with which the powder had been dispensed and its very familiar taste had given the patient the idea of mixing it with some diluted hydrochloric acid prescribed by the same medical assistant to the Scholar's bunkmate in the barracks. (The diluted acid and a pine-nut extract were the only medicinal preparations readily available in the camp.) The acid-powder compound had swelled into a foam. Bicarbonate of soda! Just like a Chekhovian rural Asclepius, he bet on the psychotherapeutic effect of placebos.

If psychotherapy by way of bicarbonate could have an effect, he would need his usual "distraction therapy" all the more. It would keep his mind off his real predicament and help him forget his pain and even that his physical powers were inexorably on the wane. Besides, the list of subjects to contemplate during these ascents, which lasted at least an hour, was inexhaustible. One might think about why, for example, the higher one ascended the hill, the more readily apparent it became that the surrounding mountains might be considered a chaotic formation only when viewed from below. Generally speaking, the attribution of chaos to any phenomenon is always but the product of insufficient knowledge of the nature and laws of that phenomenon. And from here it was obvious that the hills—particularly the more distant ones—were strung out in a chain, one hill seeming to roll into the next, which got him thinking about the nature of undulatory movement. This particular undulation could not be considered frozen insofar as orogenetic processes were still active, especially in this region. In fact, this undulation could even be expressed, albeit somewhat abstractly, in a mathematical formula. And, as opposed to the notion of chaos, which indicated the mind's capitulation before the unknown, the mathematical formulation of a phenomenon signified the mind's triumph. Hadn't Max von Laue said that mathematics lends us the joy of experiencing truth in its purest and most immediate form? It was merely that this truth was deprived of colors, of sounds, and of anything else connected with the real world. Take this mountainous landscape, for example. It made you think of dead planets, of things profoundly foreign and hostile to human beings. To express this you needed not a formula, but music. For if architecture is "a frozen music," as someone had said long ago, then mountains have all the more right to that claim. Only, in this particular instance, symphony necessarily alternated with cacophony. Which of the two principles dominated? That depended on the musician's perception of the world. Unlike mathematical manipulations, which are absolutely objective in their very essence, music not only allows for, it demands subjectivity. Without it, art loses its meaning.

One of the great thinkers—whose mind, likely, had turned in ways quite different from physicist von Laue's—had conceived the notion that music was good because it obstructed logical thought. Was that really so? Rather, was it always so? The father of non-Euclidian geometry, Janos Bolyai, had uncovered the laws of his geometry while playing the violin. The brain's mathematical and musical centers almost certainly lie in close proximity to one another, if they do not, in fact, overlap. True, there were no mathematicians among professional musicians. But that probably had to do with the specialized nature of mathematics and the difficulty of mastering its techniques. But there were plenty of highly qualified musicians among mathematicians. The orchestra at the Scholars' Club, for example, was comprised entirely of mathematicians and physicists. The genius physicist Albert Einstein had been a wonderful violin player. At various times in his life the cellist from the Scholars' Club orchestra could not have answered with sufficient certainty which of the two—mathematician or musician—was dominant in him. In his youth the great physicist Max Planck also had been unable to answer that question.

Since the times of the Greeks, many had attempted to uncover the mathematical laws of music. The Scholar himself, as a sort of "hobby," had tried to devise (at least in general terms) a mathematical formula for the fugue. His friends had teased him, quoting Pushkin's "I tested harmony with algebra." But the joke had struck him as insulting, because Pushkin's attribution to Salieri of an attempt to substitute formulaic music for the intuition of genius had been merely a poetic device. Mathematics itself—if we're to speak of its uncharted paths—also progressed by way of intuition. And the idea that mathematics' creative geniuses were highly rationalistic people was but the product of uninformed and two-dimensional thinking. The discovery of Truth for the sake of Truth itself could not be of a primitively rationalistic nature if for no other reason than for what we already know: all scientific breakthroughs raise more questions than they answer. Humankind's discovery of the laws of nature is often compared to a child taking apart a nested stacking doll. The Scholar found the comparison lacking. As the captivating toy comes apart, the dolls grow smaller and smaller in size. Whereas the enigmas of nature that reside within one another grow larger, more profound, and ever more difficult to solve. Perhaps in the stacking doll metaphor we would do better to replace the child with, say, a carpenter worm set inside the smallest of the dolls. As it attempted to uncover the hidden structure of the "world" around it, the worm would have to bore its way through one sturdy wooden wall after the next. In the process it would discover that the walls grew increasingly thicker, more voluminous, and more difficult to overcome. And were our worm to possess the same brooding and absolute mind as Shakespeare's Hamlet, it would, no doubt, arrive at the same conclusion as the hero of the famous tragedy: "There are more things in heaven and earth, Horatio, than are dreamt of in your philosophy."

But the Scholar's mind wearied of such abstract philosophical questions almost as quickly as his pericardium tired from physical exertion. It needed easier tasks. Like calculating the amount of energy expended by each member of the "detachment" in order to reach the hill's summit. The problem was elementary. Multiply the average weight of a prisoner—one could assume that equaled fifty kilograms, since few here now weighed more—by the distance, in meters, of the climb. The result was 50,000 kilogram-meters of mechanical labor. In order to express this in calories, divide the number of kilogram-meters by the mechanical equivalent of heat, which equaled, roughly rounded, about 400 [and multiply by gravitational force ($g = 9.80665$ m/s^2)—*trans.*]. The result: just climbing the hill, measured from the foot of the hill alone, a single prisoner expended more than 1200 calories. That was more than half the calories contained in the bread rations of workers who fulfilled production norms. As for those who failed to fulfill the daily "plan," their reduced ration barely replaced the calories they burned just climbing the hill. Which explained why the hearts of even the youngest and strongest prisoners soon began to function like motors running on near-empty gas tanks. But that was a real-life topic and off-limits.

A wooden post off to the right—one of twenty posts along the cable railway that supported power lines to the winch engine—bore the number 531, traced in thick paint. The post at the bottom of the cable railway was number 517. Almost two-thirds of the length of the slope was already behind them. However, a more appropriate measure of the correlation of distance traveled to distance remaining would have been in terms not of length but of energy expended. The result would be much less encouraging, for the hill's slope grew steeper towards the top. In fact, the most difficult sector of the climb lay between posts 533 and 534, where the slope was intersected by a rock formation resembling a cornice or barrier parallel to the hill's summit. The incline at this jut was so steep that a section of it had been cut out in order to reduce the vertical pitch of the railway. Of course, it would have been much easier for the prisoners to proceed by way of this cutaway, but when the entire detachment was on its way up the hill, they were not allowed to use it. They might hold up "train" traffic.

The accursed jut was the critical section of the ascent's curve from a purely mathematical point of view as well. The expression of the function of this curve was, of course, unknowable. What was beyond doubt, though, was that precisely at this point the function's primary derivative changed its sign from plus to minus. That is, it satisfied the mathematical criterion of the maximum of any analytical function. This criterion had been established a century earlier by the French mathematician Augustin-Louis Cauchy, and for a long time afterward it had borne his name. For the prisoner who knew mathematics and who at each climb grew ever less confident that he could surmount this maximum, the "Cauchy criterion" had of late become something of a grim symbol. Of course, this was what he got for his gloomy idle thinking. But it was also fact that the majority of deaths that accompanied their ascent of Tin Mountain occurred precisely in this sector. Possibly, the long-deceased Marquis Augustin-Louis Cauchy—had he the chance to observe the tragedies that occurred here almost daily—also would have gleaned in them more than just another superfluous illustration of his theorem. An outstanding mathematician, he had held extremely conservative political views. He considered all attempts to reform society through force—no matter how well-intended—were invariably destined to fail insofar as they violated God's own creation. Yes, it was the naive opinion of a believer and a clerical. But was that opinion really so far from the truth if considered from a less-biased position?

An unbiased position, a tendency to question in one's own mind that which must not be questioned at all, was more intrinsic to people in the intellectual professions than to others. To people like himself, for example. In authoritarian societies an unbiased point of view is considered a dangerous encroachment on the monopoly of the few to think for the whole. Hence the eternal conflict between despotic one-man dictatorships and their intelligentsias. The conflict had its origins in ancient Egypt and had coursed like a red thread through the history of imperial Rome, not to mention the medieval semi-theocracies of Europe with their Inquisition. But the first to turn this conflict into a conscious rationalistic principle had been the Chinese emperor Qin Shi Huang. To mark the beginning of his absolute autocratic rule he had had all the philosophers in the empire put to death. By means, moreover, such as drowning them in toilets, for example. This was to disincline even those burdened with an excess of intellect and knowledge from engaging in critical thinking. Qin Shi Huang had lived more than two thousand years ago. The old *bogdykhan*'s techniques were now obsolete. But not his political principles. Otherwise this professor of mathematics would not be groping his way up the side of this hill instead of studying theorems of divergent series.

Before the jut that had become increasingly difficult for him to cross there remained one more span between posts. A mere one-twentieth of the slope's total length. But the equivalent of a twelve-story building. And, what was more, they had to make their way up that building not by way of a convenient staircase, but over slippery rocks that in some places were still covered with melting snow. The end of May was one of the very worst times of the year for climbing.

The densely innervated "sack of muscle" people have for so long considered the receptacle of their souls is, generally speaking, more cowardly than the brain. The mere approach of the steep section of the slope made his heart ache and threaten to fail at the least opportune moment. He had to shift his thoughts from the maximum point of steepness that lay just ahead, which was also the point of maximum stress for his almost-failed heart, to something else. To the "music of the mountains," for example. From this height it was obvious that the local mountain chain possessed a clearly expressed, albeit quite complex, undulation. That undulation would be best captured by means of polyphonic music, of the fugue, in particular. Through a slight stretch of imagination he could invoke the powerful waves of sounds as they rolled in, one upon the next. At first those sounds should depict a collision and struggle among enormous masses of moribund material. Then a certain organizing principle should penetrate their primeval chaos. Gradually this principle should progress toward its triumph, a triumph not yet final. The struggle between forces so powerful as not even to acknowledge the presence of man raged on. Over the thunder-rolls of imaginary polyphony the tragic motif of man could barely make itself heard. For today that motif was a weak, imploring sound. Because the man had already exhausted all his strength in his struggle against hostile forces. And one of those forces, the force of gravity, had now become almost insuperable. It got in his way as he tried raising first one trembling, unsteady foot, then the other, from the slope's surface. It caused his heart to rush between frantic vibrations, when at any moment it might burst from its tight cage, to almost full stops, when his legs, his entire body, seemed to go soft, as if stuffed with cotton. The world around him was going dark. It felt as if someone were dragging a sharp scraper over his face and chest. He couldn't get enough air, although by this point he was panting, mouth wide open, like a grounded fish. Past him trudged the other men, bent in half, their legs moving only through great effort, their mouths, like his, wide open. Right, he'd made it to the point where the curve of the slope fulfilled Cauchy's criterion for the maximum. Was he really not going to make it over the maximum today? The last of the prisoners trudging up the hill passed him by. After them came the savage guards with their rifles.

Perhaps, though, through an exceptional exertion of will power he might still force himself to surmount that accursed barrier? Perhaps he might catch his second wind, like that which not rarely came to the rescue of athletes when they seemed to have lost all hope?

But no second wind came. Through the gloom that enveloped his vision he watched as the neighboring hill, considerably higher than Tin Mountain, began to sway back and forth. Someone had given this dismal bare cone the improbable name of Bacchante, and apparently today it had decided to justify the epithet. But after swaying drunkenly back and forth, it suddenly crashed to the ground. Where its brownish, red-gutted slope had just stood there now hung a sole low, ragged cloud. In early spring the clouds were always heavy and swollen. Early spring by local standards, that is. In other parts of the world lilac bushes were already shedding their blossoms, but here there were only these clouds, the snow turned to ice, and something else he couldn't remember ...

All bodies follow a path of least resistance. All bodies except biological systems, that is, as long as they are alive. He, too, was alive, because he was trying to remember what the other characteristic signs of spring in this accursed place were. Of course! Sturdy high leather boots. Just recently the guards had exchanged their felt boots for leather ...

"Come on, get up, enough faking already!" The tip of the heavy boot struck him with all the force and accuracy of an experienced soccer penalty kicker's blow. The pain permeated even his dimming consciousness. Then faded. Immediately, together with his consciousness, with the ragged black cloud above, and with the dark figures towering over him. The Scholar never felt the second blow.

THE RIGHT HAND

Aleksandr Solzhenitsyn (1918–2008)

Translated by Michael Glenny

The fourth Russian Nobel laureate of literature, **Aleksandr Solzhenitsyn** was a mathematician, artillery officer, labor camp prisoner, and the author of the *GULAG Archipelago*, a book that created its own genre, scope and significance, representing millions of the silent voices of the repressed, presenting hard evidence of Soviet crimes. The book was distributed in the USSR in samizdat copies and people were arrested for spreading it, while Solzhenitsyn was forced go abroad, stripped of his Soviet citizenship and established himself in the US.

There he wrote *The Red Wheel*, a multi-volume epic on the First World War and the Bolshevik seizure of power. He returned in Russia in 1994 and demonstrated a most impressive and sad metamorphosis, exposing his archaic nationalism and shaking hands with the former vice-colonel of the KGB Vladimir Putin, the representative of the very same organization that earlier haunted him and harassed his readers.

When I arrived in Tashkent that winter I was practically a corpse. I came there expecting to die.

But I was given another lease of life.

A month passed, then another and a third. Outside, the vivid Tashkent spring unfolded and advanced into summer; it was already very warm and lush greenery was everywhere when I started to venture out of doors on my shaky legs.

I still did not dare to admit to myself that I was getting better; in my wildest dreams I still measured my extra span of life not in years but in months. I would tread slowly along the gravel and asphalt paths in the park which was laid out between the blocks of the clinic. I would often have to sit down for a rest and sometimes, when overcome with nausea, I had to lie down with my head as low as possible.

I was like the sick people all around me, and yet I was different: I had fewer rights than they had and was forced to be more silent. People came to visit them, relatives wept for them, and their one concern, their one aim in life was to get well again. But if I recovered, it would be almost pointless; I was thirty-five years of age and yet in that spring I had no one I could call my own in the whole world. I did not even own a passport, and if I were to recover, I should have to leave this green, abundant land and go back to my desert where I had been exiled "in perpetuity." There I was under open surveillance, reported on every fortnight, and for a long time the local police headquarters had not even allowed me, a dying man, to go away for treatment.

I could not talk about all this to the free patients around me; had I done so, they would not have understood. On the other hand, I had ten years of long and careful reflection behind me and already knew the truth of the saying that the true savour of life is not to be gained by big things but from little ones – things like my ability to shuffle along hesitantly on my weakened legs; my cautious breathing, to avoid stabbing pains in the chest; and a single potato, undamaged by the frost, that I fished out of my soup.

So for me this spring was the most painful and the loveliest of my life.

I was surrounded by things I had either forgotten or had never seen, so everything interested me – even the ice-cream cart, the road-sweeper with his hose, the women selling bunches of long radishes, and especially the foal who had strayed through a gap in the wall onto the grass.

With every passing day I dared to wander farther away from the clinic, through the park, which must have been laid out at the end of the last century, when these good, sturdy buildings, with their ornamental brickwork at the corners, were also put up. From the magnificent sunrise, throughout the long southern day, and deep into the electric-yellow evening, the park was alive with movement. The healthy people would scurry around while the sick would make their unhurried promenade.

At the point where several avenues merged into the one leading to the main gates, there stood a large white alabaster Stalin, grinning sarcastically behind his stone whiskers. Other, smaller statues were spaced out evenly along the path leading to the gates.

Then there was a stationer's kiosk. It sold plastic pencils and tempting notebooks. But I decided it was better to do without them, not merely because I had to keep a strict watch on my spending but also because previous notebooks of mine had fallen into the wrong hands.

A fruit stall and a teahouse were situated right by the gates. We patients in our striped pyjamas were not allowed into the teahouse, but you could watch what was going on through the openwork fence. I had never in my life seen a real teahouse, with those individual pots of green or black tea for each person. The teahouse had a European section with small tables, and an Uzbek section with a large dais. The people at the tables ate and drank quickly, left a small payment in an empty bowl, and departed. But on the dais people sat or sprawled around for hours on end, some of them even for days. On sackcloth mats beneath a rush awning which had been put up at the beginning of the hot weather, they consumed pot after pot of tea while playing dice, as if the whole long day was completely free of cares.

The fruit stall did sell to the patients, but the few kopecks I had earned in exile shied away from the prices. I stared hard at the piles of dried apricots, raisins, and fresh cherries, then walked away.

Farther on there was a high wall; the patients were not allowed beyond the gates. Two or three times a day the strains of a band playing funeral marches would waft over this wall into the hospital grounds.

The city had a million inhabitants, but the cemetery was right next door to us. We could hear the slow funeral processions for about ten minutes, until they had passed the grounds. The sound of the drum produced an odd result: its rhythm had no effect on the crowd of mourners, whose jerky movements were always slightly faster than the beat; the healthy bystanders would hardly stop to look around before hurrying off again to wherever they had to go (and they all knew exactly where they had to go); but the patients would stop when they heard these marches, poke their heads out of the windows of the wards, and listen for a long time.

The clearer it grew that I was recovering from the disease, and the more certain I became that I would remain alive, the more wistfully I looked around: I was already sorry to be leaving all this.

In the medical students' sports ground, white figures were hitting white tennis balls to each other. All my life I had wanted to play tennis, but I had never had the chance. Beneath its steep bank, the muddy yellow water of the river Salar was gurgling furiously. Wide-branching oak trees grew in the park, shady maples and delicate Japanese acacias. The octagonal fountain was throwing up fresh, slender streams of silver as high as they could reach. And what grass on the lawns!—succulent and mercifully disregarded, unlike the grass in the prison camps, which the authorities ordered to be weeded out like an enemy, while in my place of exile grass could not grow at all. Just to lie in it face downwards, peacefully breathing in its herbal fragrance and its sun-warmed exhalation, was a taste of paradise.

I was not the only one lying there in the grass. Dotted about were students from the Medical Institute, slogging away at their bulky textbooks. Some of them, however, were absorbed in reading short stories which were not part of the examination syllabus, while others, the athletic ones, emerged from the changing rooms swinging their sports hold-alls. In the evening girls, indistinct and therefore three times more attractive, would walk round the fountain in creased or well-ironed frocks, crunching the gravel of the paths under their feet.

My heart was bursting with pity for someone: it might have been for myself and my contemporaries, frozen to death near Demiansk, burnt alive in Auschwitz, harried to exhaustion in Djezkazgan, or dying in the wastes of Siberia, because these girls would never belong to us. Or it might have been for these girls, because of the things I could never tell them and which they would never find out.

The whole day long, women – women, women! – would flow along the gravel and asphalt paths, young doctors, nurses, laboratory assistants, clerks, housekeepers, dispensers, and relatives visiting patients. They would pass me by in their austere white coats and their bright southern dresses, often semi-transparent, the richer ones in bright blues and pinks slowly twirling fashionable bamboo-handled Chinese parasols over their heads. Each one, as she flashed past, momentarily made up a complete plot for a novel: her past, the (non-existent) chance of my getting to know her.

I was a pitiful wreck. My emaciated face bore the stamp of what I had been through – the wrinkles caused by the enforced gloom of camp life, the ashen colour of death on my leathery skin, the more recent poisoning caused by a venomous disease and toxic medicines which had added a greenish tinge to my cheeks. My back was hunched from the defensive habit of submission and self-effacement. My clown-like striped jacket barely reached as far as my stomach, my striped trousers ended above my ankles, and the edges of my footcloths, brown from long wear, were hanging out of the canvas uppers of my blunt-toed prison-camp boots.

Not one of these women would have dared to walk beside me. But I could not see myself, and the world impinged upon my consciousness through eyes that were as sensitive as theirs.

One day, towards evening, I was standing by the main gates, looking around me at the usual stream of people rushing past; parasols bobbed along, silk dresses and tussore trousers with bright sashes, embroidered shirts and skullcaps flickered by. There was a buzz of voices. People were selling fruit; behind the fence, others were drinking tea and throwing dice. At the same time, leaning against the fence, a small, ungainly man who looked like a beggar was addressing the crowd from time to time in a voice gasping for breath: "Comrades … Comrades …"

The busy, gaily-coloured crowd was not listening to him. I went up to him. "What's the matter, brother?"

The man had an enormous belly, larger than a pregnant woman's, which hung down like a sack. It had burst through his dirty khaki tunic and trousers. His shoes, their soles worn away, were clumsy and dusty. His thick, unbuttoned overcoat with its soiled collar and frayed cuffs, unsuitable for this weather, weighed down his shoulders. On his head he wore an ancient, torn peaked cap, fit for a garden scarecrow. His eyes, swollen with dropsy, were glazed.

With great effort he raised one clenched hand, and I pulled a sweaty, crumpled piece of paper out of it. It was an application from citizen Bobrov, written in an angular hand with a pen that had scratched the paper, requesting admission to hospital; slanting across the application were two stamps, one in blue ink and one in red. The one in blue ink was from the Town Health Committee giving reasoned grounds for its refusal to admit him. The one in red ink, however, ordered the clinic of the Medical Institute to accept the man as an in-patient. The blue ink bore yesterday's date; the red ink—today's.

"Look," I explained to him loudly, as if he were deaf. "You've got to go to Reception, in Ward One. So just go straight on past these ... statues ..."

But then I noticed that his strength had abandoned him at the very moment that he reached the goal of his journey; not only was he incapable of asking any more questions or dragging his feet over the smooth asphalt path; he was even too weak to carry his shabby bag, which weighed no more than three or four pounds. So I made up my mind and said: "All right, old fellow, I'll take you. Let's go. Give me your bag."

He understood. He handed me his bag with relief, leaned on my proffered arm, and moved forward by dragging his shoes along the asphalt path, hardly lifting his feet off the ground. I guided him by his elbow, holding on to his coat, which was reddish-brown from the dust. His swollen stomach seemed to pull the old man forward and downwards. He frequently heaved a deep sigh.

Thus we advanced, two dishevelled figures, along the same avenue where, in my thoughts, I had linked arms with the most beautiful girls in Tashkent. For a long time we slowly dragged ourselves past the alabaster statues.

At last we turned off. Beside our path stood a bench with a back rest. My companion asked to sit down for a while. I too could feel an attack of nausea coming on, as I had been standing too long. We sat down. From here we could see the fountain.

While we were still walking along, the old man had said a few things to me, and now that he had recovered his breath, he resumed his story. He had to get to the Urals, and the residence permit in his passport was for the Urals, which was the whole trouble. He had been taken ill somewhere near Takhia-Tashem (where, I remember, they had started building a canal). At Urgench they had kept him in hospital for a month, drained the water from his stomach and legs, made him worse, and then discharged him. He had interrupted his journey at Chardzhou and then at Ursatevskaya, but wherever he went for treatment he was turned away; instead, they had sent him on to the Urals, because that was his official place of residence. He had felt too weak to go there by train, and anyway he did not have enough money for the ticket. So two days ago he had managed to get to Tashkent in the hope of being admitted to hospital.

I did not ask what he was doing down south or what had brought him here. His illness was, according to his medical certificates, "advanced," but a glance at the man was enough to tell you that it was terminal. I had seen a lot of patients and I could tell that he no longer had the will to live. He had lost control of his lips, his speech was indistinct, and his eyes had a dull lifelessness about them.

Even his cap was a burden to him. With great difficulty he pulled it off his head, down onto his knees. He struggled to raise his arm again and wiped the sweat off his forehead with his dirty sleeve. The top of his head was bald, though it was ringed by some sparse, untidy hair, still pale red under its coating of dust. It was not old age that had reduced him to this state but disease.

Folds of superfluous skin hung from his neck, which had grown pitifully thin, like a chicken's, and his triangular Adam's apple protruded visibly. I wondered how he held his head up, and we had scarcely sat down when it lolled forward onto his chest, supported by his chin.

There he collapsed, with his cap on his knees and his eyes closed. He seemed to have forgotten that we had only sat down for a moment to recover our breath and that he had to go on to Reception.

Before our eyes, the almost noiseless jet of the fountain was casting its silver thread upwards. Beyond it, two girls passed, side by side. I watched them walk away. One was wearing an orange skirt, the other a maroon one. I found both of them extremely attractive.

My neighbour sighed audibly, rolled his head across his chest, and, raising his yellowish-grey lashes, squinted up at me. "Do you happen to have a cigarette, comrade?"

"You can forget that idea, old fellow," I barked at him. "You and I haven't got a hope unless we give up smoking. Take a look at yourself in a mirror. A cigarette! Really!" (I had only just succeeded in breaking myself of the habit a month before.)

Panting for breath, he again raised his eyes and looked at me from underneath his yellow lashes, rather like a dog. "All the same, comrade, give us three roubles."

I thought about whether to give them to him or not. After all, I was still a prisoner, while he was a free man. For all the years I had worked in prison camps I had been paid nothing. And when they did start to pay me they took all of it back in deductions: for the escort, for lighting the perimeter, for police dogs, for the officers, for the prison stew.

I took my oilskin purse out of the small breast pocket of my clown's jacket and inspected the notes in it. I sighed, then handed the old man a three-rouble note.

"Thanks," he said hoarsely. Struggling to hold his arm out, he took the note and put it in his pocket; at once his arm flopped down and slapped against his knee. His chin sagged forward until his head was again resting on his chest.

We fell silent. A woman passed by, then two more girl students. I found all three of them very attractive. It had been years since I had heard girls' voices or the tapping of their stiletto heels.

"You're lucky they gave you an admission form, otherwise you might have had to hang around here for a week or so. It often happens. Lots of people have to put up with it."

He pulled his chin away from his chest and turned towards me. In his eyes a spark of sense glinted, his voice quivered, and he spoke more distinctly: "They're putting me in here, son, because I'm a deserving case. I'm a veteran of the Revolution. Sergey Mironovich Kirov personally shook me by the hand during the fighting at Tsaritsyn. I should be getting a special pension."

A slight movement of his cheeks and lips – the shadow of a proud smile – registered on his unshaven face.

I examined his rags, then looked him over once more. "Why don't you get it, then?"

"That's life," he sighed. "Now they don't even acknowledge my existence. Some of the records were burnt, others were lost. And I can't get any witnesses. Sergey Mironovich was murdered ... It's all my fault, I didn't keep my documents ... I've just one thing here ..."

He lifted his right hand and fumbled in his pocket with his round, swollen finger joints, but here his burst of activity expired, and he again dropped his arm and his head and sat stock-still.

The sun was already sinking behind the hospital buildings and we would have to hurry to Reception (it was still a hundred paces away). In my experience, getting admitted to hospital is always beset with difficulties.

I took the old man by the shoulder. "Wake up, old fellow. Look, see that door over there? See it? I'm going over there to start persuading them. Come on your own if you can, but if not, wait for me. I'll take your bag."

He nodded as if he understood.

Reception was part of a large, shabby hall, divided off by rough partitions; at one time there had been a communal bathroom, a dressing room, and a hairdresser's here. In the daytime it was always crowded with patients whiling away the long hours until they would be admitted, but now, to my surprise, there was not a soul there. I knocked at the plywood hatch, which was closed. A very young nurse with a snub nose opened it; her lips were painted not red but a thick violet.

"What do you want?" She was sitting at a table reading a spy comic, as far as I could see.

She had very lively eyes.

I gave her the application with the two stamps on it and explained: "He can hardly walk. I've just brought him in."

"How dare you bring anyone in!" she cried sharply, without even looking at the piece of paper. "Don't you know the routine? We only admit patients at nine a.m.!"

She was the one who did not know the "routine." I stuck my head through the hatch and as much of my arm as I could manage, so that she could not slam it shut on me. Twisting my lower lip and pulling a face like a gorilla, I hissed in a menacing voice: "Listen, woman. And get this into your head—I'm not going to be bossed about by you!"

She took fright, moved her chair farther back into her little room, and said: "There's no admission, citizen. Only at nine a.m."

"Look ... read this bit of paper!" I growled at her in my nastiest voice.

She read it.

"Well, so what? The normal routine applies. And there may not be any places tomorrow. There weren't any this morning."

She announced that there had been no places that morning with a sort of satisfaction, as if the remark would puncture me.

"But the man's just passing through, don't you see? He's got nowhere to go."

As I backed out of the hatch and stopped talking in my harsh prison-camp rasp, her face took on its former expression of cheerful callousness. "They're all passing through. Where can we put them? They have to wait. He'll have to find a room somewhere."

"But just come and have a look. You'll see the condition he's in."

"Whatever next? Do you expect me to go round collecting patients? I'm not an orderly, you know!"

And she proudly twitched her snub nose. Her reply was as snappy and as automatic as clockwork.

"Then what the hell are you doing sitting here?"

I banged on the plywood wall with my fist, and a thin layer of whitewash scattered like pollen. "Lock the place up!"

"No one asked for your opinion, you lout!" She exploded with anger, jumped up, ran round, and appeared out of the narrow corridor. "Who do you think you are, anyway? Don't you teach me how to do my job! The ambulance'll bring him in."

Except for her crude violet lips and her matching nail varnish, she would not have been at all bad-looking. Her nose was her attractive feature, and she made great play with her eyebrows. Because it was so stuffy, she had undone the top buttons of her white coat and I could see her nice little pink scarf and Komsomol badge.

"What? If he hadn't come here by himself but had been picked up in the street by an ambulance, you would have admitted him? Is that your rule?"

She stared haughtily at my absurd figure and I stared back at her. I had completely forgotten that my footcloths were poking out of my boots. She snorted, looked at me coldly, and continued: "Yes, *patient*. That *is* the rule."

And she went back behind the partition.

I heard a rustling sound behind me. I looked around. My companion was already standing there. He had heard and understood everything. Clutching onto the wall and hauling himself towards the large bench put there for visitors, he was scarcely able to wave his right hand, which was clutching a tattered piece of paper.

"Here you are," he appealed to me in a faint voice. "... Here you are, show her this ... let her ... here ..."

I managed to support him and lowered him onto the bench. With helpless fingers he tried to pull his only certificate out of his wallet but just could not manage it.

I took the top piece of paper from him, which was stuck down along its folds because it was falling apart, and opened it. On it were typed, in violet ink, lines with the letters dancing up and down over the creases:

WORKERS OF THE WORLD UNITE!

This certificate is presented to Comrade Bobrov N.K. for active service in 1921 in the distinguished "World Revolution" Special Detachment of _____ Province for personally eliminating large numbers of counterrevolutionary terrorists.

Signed: Commissar_____

A pale violet seal was attached to it.

Scratching my chest, I asked him quietly: "What's this 'Special Detachment'? What did it do?"

"Aha," he replied, scarcely able to keep his eyes open. "Show it to her."

I noticed his hand, his right hand – so small, with its brown, swollen veins and its round, puffed joints, practically incapable of pulling a certificate out of his wallet. And I remembered the way horsemen used to strike down men on foot with a single, sweeping backhand stroke.

Strange ... That right hand had once swung a sabre in a full arc and chopped off heads, necks, and shoulders. And now it could not even hold a scrap of paper ...

I went up to the plywood hatch and again tried to persuade her to listen. The registrar did not raise her head but continued reading her comic. On the open page I saw a handsome man in uniform leaping onto a windowsill with a pistol.

I quietly placed the torn certificate on top of her book and turned away. I kept rubbing my chest to avoid being sick as I walked towards the door. I had to lie down as quickly as possible.

"What have you put this paper here for? Take it away!" the girl shot at me through the hatch as I walked away.

The veteran shrank into the bench. His head and even his shoulders seemed to sink into his torso. His helpless fingers dangled, outspread. His unbuttoned coat hung down, his bulbous, unbelievably swollen belly sagging into the fold of his thighs.

THE HOUSE ON THE FONTANKA

Daniil Granin (1919–2017)

Translated by Margarete D'Arcy Orga

Fighting as a private on the frontline surrounding Leningrad, **Daniil Granin** (born Daniil German) became a witness to the horrors of the first blockade winter, 1941–1942. Many years later, already a celebrated, decorated and respected author in the Soviet hierarchy, he joined Belorussian writer Ales Adamovich in writing *The Book of the Blockade*, the documentary chronicle of siege, suffering and life within the encircled city. The book brought on them the wrath of the Soviet rulers, even though there were no direct juridical reprisals.

It is important to mention that Granin played a dark role in the show trial of Josef Brodsky in 1964, publicly confirming the rightness of the accusation against the poet in his capacity as an official of the Writer's Union.

Occasionally I dreamed of Vadim. Year after year it recurred—always the same dream, very clear, with hardly a variation to it: I walked along Nevsky Prospekt and suddenly ran into him, and 'Good God!' he would exclaim, 'you're alive!' He would look at me happily, unbelievingly, saying, 'So you weren't killed!' Then, half apologetically, I would tell him about myself, but for some reason I was never able to ask him what had happened; it was something I couldn't bring myself to do … yet for a long time after the war was over I refused to accept that he had died. But in my dream it was the other way round: *he* was surprised that *I* had survived.

In my dream he was as thin and pale as I had always known him, with clear, steady eyes, and the old habit of stammering slightly at the beginning of a sentence. We never mentioned Katia, but in the dream we spoke of other things: he had worked in a research institute—so secret was its name and whereabouts that I would never have been able to find him—but now, in our dream, he had found me again and we would stick together, firm pals.

In my dream I was happy. I feasted my eyes on Vadim. I was blissfully happy. I babbled all sorts of nonsense, and Vadim poked fun at me. Whatever he said was precise and irrefutable and, again, I recognised his superiority, envied and forgave him, scolded myself because of my envy. I could not imagine where he had been all these years, yet, even in my dream, I was afraid to get too inquisitive. I felt it would be wrong, something bad would happen. So we would walk along Nevsky Prospekt, I holding his arm firmly. It was today's street—tube stations, pedestrian subways, unfamiliar crowds. In the old days when we had known it together it was filled with familiar faces; we would have been sure to pass the time of day with acquaintances, old school friends, students.

After the last dream I had of Vadim, when I woke up it was some time before I realised where I was. Where was Vadim? Perhaps I had not woken up at all but fallen asleep instead; perhaps I was asleep now? Yet the dream seemed more real than this tenebraic silence. Somewhere my wife, my daughter, the neighbours, the whole house was sleeping. They lived in their dreams. They were far away and could not help me. Nothing filled the space between the me who had been walking with Vadim on the Nevsky Prospekt and the me lying in bed in a dark house. Nothing linked us, save the memory of Vadim. I, the real I, existed elsewhere and was reluctant to return to myself—to the greying self who suffered still the aftermath of shellshock, to a life filled with other people's worries. The gap was too great.

Once I told Venya about my dreams. He looked at me thoughtfully. 'You know ...' he said, 'I too ... sometimes it seems to me he's still alive.'

But we never brought up the subject again. Vadim was our past. Out of all our comrades only Venya and I remained. Boris had died in the blockade, Irina of typhoid fever, Lyuda many years ago, and Inna had moved to Moscow. Nowadays, Venya and I scarcely ever remembered that only we were left.

One Sunday Venya called to see me about noon. He was just passing, he said, and dropped in for no special reason. I wasn't in much of a mood for talking, so we played a couple of games of chess. After a while Venya said, 'Let's go for a walk.'

A light snow was falling, and the low, grey sky hung limply, like wet clothes on a line. 'All right,' I said without much enthusiasm, 'I'll see you as far as the tram stop.'

In the street we talked intermittently, idly, but when we got as far as the tram stop I said suddenly, 'Let's go to Vadim's place.'

Venya didn't seem surprised. He said nothing for a while, then he said, 'What for? You think that Elena Osipovna will get any pleasure from our visit?'

I said perhaps not, but he pressed the point. 'Or we, for that matter,' he observed. 'Do you really think we should go at all?'

'Suit yourself,' I said, not quite sure how I felt.

His tram came, but he turned away. 'Well,' he said, 'we can't not go, now. It would look as if we're afraid otherwise.'

We waited for another tram for Vadim's house. After we got off we walked along Fontanka Embankment, and we talked about the American astronauts, but a few yards from Vadim's door I stopped. 'What shall we say?' I asked Venya.

'That we'd been wanting to come for a long time, but were afraid it might be awkward.'

'And now it's stopped being awkward? You're a clever fellow!'

'Well, let's not go in,' Venya said patiently.

'Perhaps we'd better say we just happened to be passing.' We shifted from one foot to the other, irresolute and apprehensive. The truth was that I had passed this grey granite building many times through the years. I used to quicken my steps and avert my eyes, as though someone were spying on me. But little by little it had become easier. There's Vadim's house, my mind would register, and that was all, for everything else was compressed into his name: my own emotions seemed compressed, too. For why indeed had we, Vadim's closest friends, never visited his mother? Not strictly true! I had, once, but I had never told Venya. It had been terrible.

We went through the doorway. There was the little bench where Frosya used to sit. And there was the old, enamelled sign: Gate Keeper's Bell. Frosya had taken on the job during the blockade, then stayed on. She never changed. She was always the same age to us. She had been old when we were schoolboys. She had nursed Vadim and kept house for his family. When I had come here once in 1942, with a tin of condensed milk and a slice of frozen bread, Frosya was sitting on this very bench with a gas mask dangling at her side. I kissed her, and she broke into tears and led me in to Elena Osipovna. And when I came back after the war was over she was still sitting on the bench, wearing a black jacket, as straight backed as ever, with steel-rimmed glasses, and grey hair cut short. Afterwards I stopped passing Fontanka Street, preferring to make a detour so as not to meet her. And now it all seemed a long, long time ago.

The spacious, old-fashioned hall had a fireplace, and a mirror hung on the wall. We looked at ourselves in it, then walked up to the first floor. I wanted to ring the bell, but Venya said no and pointed to the door opposite. I was surprised: could he have forgotten the door? He was also surprised that I hadn't remembered it. We shuffled indecisively on the landing, then remembered that Vadim had had a balcony. We went down to have a look: there was a balcony on either side. We went up again. It had never occurred to us we could forget the door to his flat.

'Listen,' I said finally, 'I was here after the war.'

'Were you? Why didn't you tell me?'

I rang the bell before Venya could stop me. The brown, varnished door was stark—no name plates, no letter boxes, and the bell itself, which was fitted to the middle of the door, was hand operated—an old-fashioned affair hardly ever used nowadays. We heard footsteps, the lock clicked open and a pink-cheeked youth of twenty or so looked out at us. Could I have been mistaken after all? 'Excuse me,' I said, 'do the Pushkaryovs live here?'

Suddenly the words seemed strange. I realised that twenty years had gone by—no, more than that, a whole lifetime, the entire life of this young man looking at me questioningly. What Pushkaryovs, he might ask, who are they? I've never heard of them. And we would have to explain that once, long ago, they had lived here.

'Perhaps it's Olga Ivanovna you want?'

'Who's Olga Ivanovna?' I asked. I turned to Venya helplessly. 'No,' he said to my look, 'Elena Osipovna.'

The youth gave us an odd look. 'Come in,' he said. He went over to a door on the right and knocked. 'Olga Ivanovna, someone to see you,' he said.

As we went inside the large hall took shape in my mind: on the left was the study of Nikolai Ivanovich, Vadim's father, a dim room looking out on a garden. There had been a low leather-upholstered couch where we had sat leafing through a fat Bible with illustrations by Doré. Along the walls had been Swedish bookcases filled with books on mechanics, bridge building, the relative strengths of materials. On the right was the dining-room, and out of it now came a small old woman with yellowish grey short hair, a cigarette in her mouth. She looked at us inquiringly, and the youth hovered beside her with inquisitive expectancy. Something stopped us from asking for Elena Osipovna. 'We were Vadim's friends,' Venya said.

The old woman stepped back a pace and narrowed her eyes. 'Venya,' she said hesitantly, and took his hand. He beamed. Turning to me she said, 'And you are ...' and she used the name I had been called by only in this house.

Still we couldn't place her. Then, slowly, I remembered Vadim's aunt—a lively, vivacious woman with a pile of wavy hair.

I think the coat rack in the hall was the same one. I hung my coat on it as I always had, on the last hook.

We went into the dining-room. It was gloomy and cramped, cluttered with old furniture from other rooms—or as much of it as had escaped being burnt as firewood, or sold for food. An atmosphere reminiscent of the winter of the blockade still clung to it. A dirty silk lampshade hung from the grimy ceiling. The paint-peeling window sills were littered with jars, empty medicine phials and milk bottles. A glazed door led to another room—a long, narrow room with a balcony: Vadim's room. Now I recognised the sideboard. It occupied the whole wall, and dust covered the ornamental brasswork of its wooden pillars. The glass of an oil lamp glinted on top of it. In one corner stood an iron stove: I did not recall it. The sour smells of impoverished and ailing old age confused my thoughts.

We sat down at the table, Venya and I side by side, Olga Ivanovna opposite. 'You've hardly changed,' Olga Ivanovna said to me, 'except that you've turned into a big, grown-up man.'

Several fresh cigarette stubs were in the stone ashtray. There was nothing else on the table and it was impossible to determine what she had been doing before we arrived: you might think she had been sitting there smoking and waiting for us.

'Venya, your eyes have turned dark blue. They used to be sky blue, bright sky blue. And your forehead is larger!' She laughed and with a quick, young gesture lit a new fat cigarette.

I looked at Venya out of the corner of my eye: he was bald, and his eyes were pale. Still, they *had* been sky blue I remembered, and the girls had liked him. He had been, still was probably, the kindliest, most credulous of us all, holding in holy belief everything said, printed, taught. It had never been any fun pulling his leg.

'Elena Osipovna died thirteen years ago.'

Thirteen years. So long ago! I felt only a belated sense of compassion: if we'd come a little later we'd have found no one.

'She wasn't ill—simply she didn't want to live. When Nikolai Ivanovich died all her life centred on Vadim. She couldn't believe he would never come back ... she waited for him all the time, you know, she continued to hope. ...'

Oddly enough, I thought, of all the young men who had not returned, it was only Vadim's death I couldn't believe in. Venya felt the same, I knew. All the other young men were dead immediately, but Vadim ... Then I remembered the table at which we were sitting. It could be extended almost to the size of the room itself. We used to play ping-pong on it, gathered round it during the holidays, celebrated our graduation from university. Vadim's professor had sat at it, next to Elena Osipovna. They whispered to each other, shooting glances at Vadim now and then. We had thought the professor decrepit—now he was an academician, still hale and hearty. Vadim had been assigned to his Chair at the university.

One might think Vadim had had a premonition, so great was his haste. He had finished the university a year ahead of time and remained at the laboratory for that summer. In those days we met rarely, although occasionally he had asked Venya to help with a mathematical problem. I had been jealous: a three-way friendship is always a complicated thing. Elena Osipovna had said the day I called after the war: 'He should have been taking his postgraduate course now. He would have gone ahead of all of you; he knew German well.'

She had reckoned the date when he would have presented his thesis. She pictured his life year by year: his postgraduate thesis, his doctorate, marriage, the birth of his children, when they would go to school. She had asked about Venya, about Lyuda, about my daughter, and she calculated everything.

Thirteen years ... I had no idea. That meant she died soon after I stopped calling. There was no need to link the events. Perhaps it had been cruel to make her compare, to lacerate her wounds, but there was nothing I could have done to help her—so what was the use of going to see her? What purpose do we serve in visiting the wives and mothers of our perished friends? And why do we feel perpetually guilty? Because we managed to stay alive, to be capable of laughter? I noticed that Olga Ivanovna was looking at me and I felt caught red-handed: even now, after so many years, everything in this house compelled utter frankness.

'Why do you keep that oil lamp?' I asked her.

'That's Frosya's doing, she doesn't let us throw anything away.'

'Frosya? Is she still alive?'

'Yes, she will come and see us soon. But she's in a bad way, poor creature—not physically ...' Suddenly Olga Ivanovna looked away from me, upset.

'May I have a look at Vadim's room?' I asked after a small pause.

'Of course, but you'll have to excuse the untidiness there.'

I wanted to see it before Frosya came. Perhaps I was afraid of her.

Vadim's bookcases were gone—the tall bookcases where there had been the complete works of Jack London in brown covers, the supplement to the magazine *World Pathfinder*, sets of *The World of Adventures*. We had all read them avidly then carted them off to the second-hand dealers. Only Vadim's desk remained; we had prepared for our examinations there, Vadim coaching me. Vadim had coached me in school, too, and again when I was entering the Institute. He solved the most difficult problems with graceful ease. He enjoyed, and looked for, brain teasers. He solved them aloud, stuttering with excitement, and everything became elegant and terribly simple. The balcony door flew open in a gust of wind from the embankment and the curtain billowed out. I heard Vadim saying, 'When will you learn to reason logically?'

There were pictures on the walls. I recognised Nikolai Ivanovich—peaked cap at a rakish angle, linen jacket, luxuriant moustache. I had quite forgotten his face, but now I recalled how he had read *Faust* to us, how he had sung excerpts from it, how he had explained that the Bible had to be read as good literature. He had been a big man, with strange swinging gestures—already a rarity, a prominent engineer of the old Russia. He had built bridges on the Volga and the Oka—famous bridges, famous surveys, famous expeditions to remote regions. A big man in every sense of the word. A ring on his little finger. Ah, look who has called to see us—welcome, young man! He had had independence, and a pride because he was one of the intelligentsia ... yet I could hardly recall any of it, and him not at all. When we were young we were not interested in the grown-ups.

What was the appeal of Vadim's house for us? The intellectual atmosphere, the open-hearted welcomes, the heretic views? We had grown up in communal flats, accustomed to queuing for everything, with the noise of primus stoves our lullaby. Our chief asset was our social background, and the word 'intellectual' was almost an accusation, like being called a sissy. In short, we were regarded as Philistines, has-beens, something suspect. And yet we had all been drawn to this jolly, easy going, noble house. There, we were all equals and enjoyed the same rights as the noble Vadim.

On another wall was a photograph of Vadim: sharp faced, sharp nosed, cocky, wearing a necktie, already a student. The narrow tie had a modern look to it, but the padded shoulders of the jacket had an offensively old-fashioned air. No one knows that a great physicist died in Vadim, and in my mind's eye I suddenly saw this photograph printed in a magazine beside student photographs of Joffe, Joliot-Curie and Kurchatov—but his photograph exists only for Olga Ivanovna and us two. And the same for his scratched, rickety desk with the marble inkstand. To strangers old things are junk, but for Venya and me this was the only place in the world where our youth was preserved intact, untouched.

'Here is Frosya,' said Olga Ivanovna.

Frosya did not seem surprised to see us, as though she had been expecting us all these years. Frosya was one who accepted partings as temporary affairs; sooner or later one would return to the fold, to the family circle; it was the nature of things, wasn't it? I wondered what she thought about Vadim.

She gave us a worried, deprecating smile—the same smile as she had reserved for us long ago, when we used to come and see Vadim. But Frosya was old now—bent and shrivelled, only her hands the same, large, the fingers slightly crooked. We went over to greet her, but her glance expressed nothing.

'We have visitors,' Olga Ivanovna said.

'How do you do, Frosya?' I said loudly.

She nodded at me, eyes lustreless, then took several packages from her bag. 'I must make tea for the visitors,' she said.

Venya and I looked at each other, dismayed. We told her our names, almost shouting them at her in the end. She couldn't have forgotten us, we said. I had been dreading her scoldings, how she would have said that it was time we came—we had been Vadim's friends, so where had we been … Now all I longed for was her recognition.

Olga Ivanovna said into her ear: 'Frosya, they went to school with Vadim.'

'Yes, yes,' said Frosya testily. 'Here, I've got a cheesecake here.'

Olga Ivanovna took the package, slightly embarrassed by Frosya. 'She has a weakness for cheesecakes,' she explained. 'If you're not in a hurry, boys, have some tea with us. She'll be pleased.'

She said 'boys' as it had always been said in this house.

'The piano used to be over there,' Venya said to me softly.

I remembered. I think it had been Borya who had sat at the piano—we were composing something, singing: what was it we had sung? I can't remember. Too long ago. But it was a week after the war began, and we had all gathered here for the last time. I had signed up in the volunteer corps, Vadim was joining the marines, and Venya was to leave later. We refused to think of it as our last evening together. Our future would certainly be hectic—but triumphant, of course; there was too much future for us, this was only a small parting of the ways. Borya pounded out a foxtrot (arranged from Bach!), and we had crabmeat to eat, and Khvanchkara wine dark and rich to wash it down. Vadim and I were already in army tunics and puttees and terribly proud. We hardly mentioned the war once. We had no idea what it was like. Someone began to read poetry aloud, and we argued with Irina whether literary studies were a science or an art: Irina was reading philology. All right, we said, so let us define what a science is. 'Something that can be refuted,' said Vadim. He had the knack of twisting the expected, exposing another side. 'Once a thing *cannot* be refuted, then it stops developing: science is developing all the time, so it's refutable.' We thought it terribly sage, although some of us were not quite sure what he meant.

Elena Osipovna left in the middle of our light-hearted argument. Vadim went after her, and only then did a small but uneasy presentiment fall on us: she had found our thoughtlessness unbearable. But we shrugged away unease. We put out the lights and opened the window. The water in the Fontanka reflected the milky sky, the shadowless light, the night-dark windows of the Sheremetyev Palace. We stood there at the window, arms flung round each other's shoulders, gay, slightly tipsy, our girls subdued, not sharing our excitement. I remember the down on Vadim's face. He had just begun to shave, later than the rest of us. What we believed in then was wonderful.

'What made you come?' Olga Ivanovna asked gently. She was slicing the cheesecake, arranging the slices on a plate.

I said nothing.

Frosya poured the tea, her big hands shaking. Venya sighed. 'We wanted to come for a long time ... just happened to be passing ...'

Frosya moved the remains of the cheesecake towards us. 'Frosinka,' Olga Ivanovna said, 'I've already set out the cake.'

Frosya looked at her blankly, uncomprehendingly. Olga Ivanovna embraced her protectively. 'Ah, Frosya! Frosinka!' She looked at us. 'No one has any need for us, now,' she said. 'The neighbours are only waiting, but our two rooms are connected and nobody else can be moved in.' She smiled crookedly.

'You heard nothing more of Vadim?' Venya asked, still embarrassed about the lie that we were 'just passing'.

'No. They were bombed at Oranienbaum in the September. No one came out alive. We had two letters from him, that's all.'

She waited tactfully, but we didn't ask her to show us the letters. Vadim's childish handwriting floated before my eyes. I felt the muscles of my face tensing, making my expression fierce, like a mask I couldn't tear off.

'And how are you getting on, Venya?' Olga Ivanovna asked.

He was fortunate enough to have come through the war, but from this distance his fate did not fit in with the youthful image of that blue-eyed dreamy Venya. It would have been different, it seemed to me, had Vadim lived: there would have been *real* mathematics to tease the brain, not a yearly repetition of the course Venya taught at the technical school, and Vadim would probably never have let me give up my post-graduate course.

Olga Ivanovna was telling Venya of an argument she had had. I missed most of it, coming in almost at the end, '... and he said that if Pushkin had killed Dantes he would never have been Pushkin. He said Pushkin would have changed, just as our perception of him ...' I listened, bewildered, unable to judge who had been right, who wrong.

In the corner of the room stood an antiquated telephone with push buttons: group A, group B. It seemed to be speaking to me, the voices floating out of nowhere: 'Ring me at the Komsomol committee room ...' 'Operator, give me Misha. Misha, *you* know ...' 'Killed? What do you mean, *killed*? He can't be, he was here just now, writing poetry! Then where's his girl friend, Lyuda, his dark-haired Lyuda ... did she ever marry?' The operator seemed to sigh. 'Her life snapped and went out, no, she never married ...' 'Well, operator, call Borya then, Borya Abramov, the composer ... or Mitya Pavlov ... or Tolya, why doesn't Tolya answer, what has become of them all ... and ... Vadim?'

My mind strayed from the disembodied voices. I remembered that Vadim had said to me, 'I'd have made it with another six months to go ...' And then he added, 'Four even ...' Vadim needn't have gone, not then anyway, he could have had his four months, but Vadim obeyed the laws of his house, was still obeying them I am sure right up to his last moment. 'Hallo,' said the operator, 'where are you?'

Ah, indeed, where are we, and where is that operator? Does she still exist, her sleep troubled occasionally by our demanding voices? Only these two old women remain. When they die all this furniture, the photographs, portraits, the junk will be thrown away, and the rooms painted and papered for the new tenants.

Venya and I sat meekly under their searching eyes. Our sudden appearance had ruffled their lives a little, disenchanted them or made them hopeful—were we secretly the bearers of news? Olga Ivanovna began to speak about herself, about her last job as a translator in a design office, then fell silent with embarrassment, perhaps feeling we were not really interested, yet she wanted to understand why we had come. Was it Vadim? Her excitement communicated itself to Frosya, who kept looking from one to the other, and it seemed that at any moment she would recognise us, the warmth of remembrance lighting her vacant eyes.

Olga Ivanovna lit another cigarette. 'I oughtn't to smoke,' she said. She looked at us almost coolly. 'Vadim is still listed as missing,' she said.

What was she trying to say—that he had been taken prisoner? That, wounded and unconscious, he had ended up in a POW camp? That because he was listed missing he might still turn up?

We finished our tea and stood up. Olga Ivanovna was still embarrassed by our presence and did nothing to stop us. What was there to say?

Frosya said suddenly: 'The window panes remained. The windows were all stopped up with bricks.'

'During the blockade, she means,' Olga Ivanovna explained. 'She laid all the bricks herself,' she added proudly, her eyes warm for Frosya.

'Is that the same old lampshade?' Venya asked, smiling.

But no, it was a different one. The old one had been yellow, with black figures drawn on it, and I had burned it a little staging some youthful experiment, but had not confessed, and Elena Osipovna had pretended it was nothing, had said the bulb was too big for such a small shade. The youthful fear of being found out almost returned, brushing me from distance, small now.

We had to go, but we stood there, not knowing how to leave; it was even more difficult than coming here. Venya said in a choked voice, 'We're sorry, but we really have to go now.'

'Of course,' said Olga Ivanovna, 'Not at all ... we're so happy you came!' She bobbed her head ceremoniously. 'Who would have thought ... she said.

I looked down at the long-unpolished parquet floor. Olga Ivanovna suddenly put her hand on mine, her fingers trembling slightly. I wanted to bend down and kiss her hand, but it was a long time since I had kissed a woman's hand. We had given up all that. It was old-fashioned. I should have felt ridiculous.

She didn't ask us to come again. Perhaps she didn't dare, didn't want to, wouldn't hope. She stood there, holding Frosya by the arm, they both mumbled their good-byes: she had explained nothing, we had promised nothing.

Nevsky Prospekt smote our ears with its Sunday crowds. High heels tapped the pavements, cars thundered by, sounds clashed and scattered, as though pursuing someone, looking for something. Girls' eyes peered out from fur capes, swept over us swiftly, then turned from us indifferently. They reminded me of Irina, of Lyuda, of Katya.

'Old memories raked up,' Venya said. 'Hard on them, hard on us, too. What made us go, I wonder?'

'Are you sorry?'

'No,' he said. 'We were bound to go one day.'

Exactly, I thought. Sooner or later we'd have gone back, and not for Vadim's sake either—for our own. The house on the Fontanka had come into our lives again; it wasn't the same, of course, and neither were we, yet even so something of it had remained with us all these years: of course we had had to go back—needing nothing, seeking something, the dead years, perhaps?

'I wonder will someone visit us one day?'

'Who?' Venya asked. 'Me? Hardly!' He paused, then said. 'We should have asked Olga Ivanovna if we could help her, some medicine maybe ... I don't know.'

'Yes,' I agreed, knowing I would do nothing about it. And, besides, I thought, besides ... but I couldn't remember what it was I wanted to bring back.

Venya looked at his watch; he was expected home for a meal. We parted and I went on alone, full of memories, locked in the past. I wondered if Vadim would still come to me in dreams.

AT FREEDOM STATION

Vyacheslav Kondratiev (1920–1993)

Translated by Helena Goscilo

Surviving the most ferocious infantry fighting of the early period of war on Soviet territory, the battle of Rzhev, twice heavily wounded and discharged from the army in the rank of second lieutenant, **Vyacheslav Kondratiev** worked as a book designer and started to write only in his late fifties. Kondratiev become one of the most important names in the informal and fluid group nicknamed *lieutenant prose*: the former junior officers writing about their experience in the trenches, on the front lines, opposing the syrupy memoirs of the generals and marshals and the over-glorification of the war during the Brezhnev period, when the collective cult of the war heroes replaced the individual cult of the overthrown Stalin.

Kondratiev committed suicide in 1993, initially approving the collapse of communism, but probably being unable to cope with the scale of the economic collapse that followed.

> *To those of my generation who found it more difficult than the rest to fight, but who fought no worse, and perhaps even better, than the others.*

"Heading west, fellows?" Andrei asked.

"Most likely ... Why are you looking like that? Are you jealous?"

"Sure. I've still got a year left here."

"There's nothing to be jealous about. Things are getting hot in the west."

"Well, if it gets started there, it's gonna be a fine kettle of fish here too."

"That's for sure ..."

The troop train started to move. Andrei watched as at first slowly, and then faster and faster, the boxcars sailed by with wide open doors, and within Red Army men were standing behind a wooden railing—a whole military unit was heading west.

He stood a little longer, gazing after the train ... He could hardly believe that in little more than a year he too would be setting off back home to Moscow, now so distant. When the train disappeared from sight, he went into the station building.

"Where've you been wandering, my boy? Our train is coming soon," said Pogost, who was sitting on a small bench in a careless pose with his legs crossed, and displaying his enormous, ugly army shoes to general view without any embarrassment.

"I was on the platform. Two troop trains heading west passed through." Andrei sat down beside him, but he drew back his legs in their wraps, hiding them under the bench.

He felt awkward in them, especially here off post, in a crowded station where every now and then women would pass by and they seemed very beautiful, no doubt because he hadn't seen any for so long. In nine months of duty he'd got a pass to go off post only once. And now it seemed almost like a holiday to him to be traveling with Pogost on assignment to the town of Freedom with the opportunity to ride on a passenger train along with civilians.

He and Pogost were just pretty lucky. They had graduated early from regiment school, been given the rank of sergeant, and posted to a railroad checkpoint not far from a small town. And their assignment was hardly tough: to stand guard on a railroad bridge and regulate passage of the troops during maneuvers. The regiment school cadets envied them because the school would have summer camps, where, as the senior staff said, they would make it hot for them—endless marches over volcanic hills and tactical exercises.

Andrei pulled out some cigarettes with long tips and offered them to Pogost. Andrei's mother had sent him the cigarettes. She filled them herself with good Choice brand tobacco; this made it much cheaper than packs.

"Are you nervous, Andryusha?" asked Pogost.

"No, I think I know everything fine. What about you?"

Pogost started to laugh, and Andrei understood the stupidity of his question. Why should Pogost—a construction engineer—be nervous before some sort of exam for the post of bridge supervisor that they would be taking that day at the Amur Railway Directorate, the reason for their trip to Freedom? For him it was peanuts, but for Andrei the exam was important: at least it involved some specialty, and it was especially important because he didn't know if he'd get to study in an institute after the army.

As he smoked Andrei kept glancing at the shoe that Pogost was displaying for effect, and he felt as if everyone walking by was looking at that ugly shoe. He couldn't stand it:

"What are you putting that beauty on display for?"

Pogost burst out laughing again.

"Do you really care about such trifles, son? Forget about it! Look on all of this as an amusing adventure. We'll mark time for one more year and return to our own business. I still find it funny that I, the head of a proper construction bureau, am suddenly summoned to the military commissariat, ordered to show up with my things in a few days, then planted in a cattle car, hauled clear across the country to this Godforsaken hole, forced to wear this overcoat, issued these famous shoes with leg wraps, and forced to do stupid drills and to subordinate myself to our matchless platoon commander with a fourth-grade education. Isn't it funny? And for what? It's good that that's all behind us now and at least we have a job to do. It's true that for now our duty on the bridge is a real cushy job ... Well, Andryusha, I think we earned it by laboring without sparing our strength and by the sweat of our brow, amusing ourselves with the game of soldiers within the walls of our illustrious regimental school."

"A lot of trains are heading west, Pogost."

"Well, let them, and good riddance."

"I don't understand you; you're a lot older than everyone, but ..."

"But what? Finish what you started to say. I'm not easily offended, you know that. Did I take offense at your idiotic guffaws when I was hanging like a sack on the horizontal bars? Or when our company commander poked me in the stomach, which I couldn't pull up and stick somewhere, no matter how much I wanted to?"

"You weren't mad, that's true. I was even surprised."

"I just admired you young red-cheeked idiots who are incapable of understanding that the main thing in a man isn't swollen biceps but something else, even if it's the number of convolutions right in this spot"—he made circles around his head with a finger. "So finish what you were saying."

"I wanted to say that you somehow don't take anything seriously. Like the article in *Red Star* on 'The Myth of the Invincibility of the

German Army' that took up a whole page, and these trains going west ..."

"I understand, Andrei, but I don't want to think about war. I was pulled off work on a big project to do marching drills, wind on leg wraps during alerts, and do all kinds of nonsense that's completely unnecessary to me. And you want me to take all this seriously. It's incredibly stupid. I'd have been much more useful in my construction office ... And as far as *Red Star* goes, you'll recall that not very long ago it carried articles like 'The Infantry Platoon in an Offensive,' signed by Captain von Paul such-and-such. Remember?"

"Yes."

"So what do you make of that?"

"I don't know," Andrei shrugged.

"Me neither. And we won't rack our brains. Our train will be here soon." Pogost looked at his watch. "On the way back from passing the exam I'll treat you to a beer in the dining car. Any objections?"

"Of course not."

An attractive girl with a braid sat opposite them in the coach, and as soon as Andrei sat down he immediately hid his feet under the seat. Pogost, who noticed this, also refrained from displaying his shoes, as Andrei feared, but he didn't pass up the chance to smile ironically and wink at Andrei, as if to say "I hope you appreciate it—I'm doing it for your sake."

A general conversation didn't get started for a long time. Pogost gazed rather indifferently out the window, and the girl leafed through some magazine, while Andrei opened the newspaper in which he had wrapped his textbooks, put them at first on the little table so the titles would be visible (they were institute textbooks!); and then, picking up *The Strength of Materials*, opened it to a marked page and, while pretending to read, cast occasional glances at the girl. The institute textbooks had not made any impression on her; she didn't even give them a passing glance, and Pogost smiled ironically again.

"Quit cramming, Andryusha," he put his hand on the book. "You can't get your fill of breathing right before death. Better tell me how your Moscow sweetheart's getting along, and what she writes. I recall that you got a big love letter recently."

"The letter wasn't from her," Andrei answered dryly, sensing that

Pogost would now start to spout nonsense, but not having decided yet how to react to it.

"Not from her?" Pogost feigned astonishment. "Aw, too bad that it's not from her. How can that be? We're tempering ourselves unsparingly here in the rigors of army daily life, we're learning by the sweat of our brow to defend our Homeland, while there in Moscow, under the neon lights, they are starting to forget us little by little and writing less and less often." He shook his head as if stricken.

"Cut it out, Pogost," implored Andrei.

But this conversation interested the girl a great deal more than the institute textbooks that had been put out for show, and she glanced at the embarrassed Andrei. Pogost didn't let up.

"You see, miss, here we are in the rigors of daily army life, while they, there in Moscow ..."

"Under the neon lights," she continued with a smile.

"Exactly," Pogost burst out laughing.

Andrei smiled too, even though he found the conversation unpleasant.

"Tell us, miss, are you all really so forgetful? Don't you have a friend serving in the army?" Pogost asked.

"No. But if I did, I'd write him often."

"You hear, Andryusha? She'd write often. But yours ..."

Andrei stood up abruptly and headed for the platform. As he passed, he heard the girl say reproachfully to Pogost: "Why did you do that? Maybe for him it's something really serious?" Pogost burst out laughing and retorted derisively: "What can be serious at nineteen?"

The last letter from Zhenya had been a month before New Year's; Andrei remembered it by heart: "I met (imagine—on the street!) a very engaging man. He's a lot older than we are—over thirty—but he's very intelligent. You can have a very good conversation with him about literature, and just in general. Apparently I made an impression on him. But for me he's interesting only as a person. You understand? As a person! For New Year's (even though it's still some way off) he's invited me to a restaurant. To the National! I haven't been there even once! I'm asking your permission to go—may I? You understand, I'm so depressed. There are only girls in the institute, and the available boys are all rejects who weren't drafted into the army. You can't even get a group together to celebrate New Year's. So tell me, may I go? My father's given his permission!"

Of course, her father would allow anything if only she would break off with him, Andrei thought, as he stood on the car platform. He remembered very well the conversation they had before the army. Her father had summoned Andrei into his study (they had a three-room apartment) and, after seating him in a leather armchair, studied him long and silently; then he began without ceremony:

"You understand of course that I don't have anything against you personally, but I can't approve of your relationship with Zhenya due to circumstances you're aware of. So while you're in the army, while fate itself, so to speak, keeps you apart for a long time, I'm asking you to restrain your feelings and try to forget Zhenya. It will be better ... for her, and probably for you, too."

"And what does Zhenya think?" Andrei smiled wryly.

"Don't worry about her. We'll try to see that this passes more or less painlessly for her. Only you don't have to write to her from the army. Have we come to an understanding?"

Andrei shrugged and left the study without answering.

It was Zhenya, though, who wrote first to him in the army, cautioning him to reply in care of general delivery. They had been corresponding, although infrequently, but since that letter before the new year there hadn't been anything from her. And all this was serious to him, even though he was only nineteen, but he would never say anything about it to Pogost, who generally didn't take anything seriously except the work he'd left unfinished at the construction office.

When Andrei returned to his seat after having a smoke on the platform, Pogost greeted him with exaggerated joy.

"Our star pupil of combat and political training has finally returned! We were afraid you might jump off the train out of pique. By the way, Andryusha, our enchanting traveling companion's name is Nadyusha. I recommend her to you. Kindly introduce yourself."

"Shchergin ... Andrei," he said inertly, still not having put aside his painful recollections ...

Upon leaving Zhenya's father's study with a face as red as if it had been slapped, he immediately encountered her mother, who approached him apparently knowing what sort of conversation had taken place in her husband's study.

"Don't pay any attention to it, Andrei. I'm your ally. Zhenya will wait for you. As for my husband … you know his situation. But let's not go on about that," she said with a wave of her hand; and then, coming right up close to Andrei, she quietly added: "In my opinion, he's afraid … of the same thing. You understand?"

"Yes," he nodded. "But I won't come by any more, or call. Let Zhenya herself …"

"Of course, of course," she said hurriedly. "I'll tell her."

Very late that same evening Zhenya came rushing over to his place.

"You gave me up? And did you ask me?" she set upon him right from the doorway. "It turns out I don't mean anything to you?"

"I didn't give you up. I just can't come to see you."

"Rubbish! You will come! I'm grown up! And nobody, nobody can keep us from being together. You understand?—nobody! You want me to stay with you tonight?" she suddenly asked, throwing her arms around his neck. "Do you want me to? I'm not afraid of anything! You want me to?" she ardently whispered. "Just don't be a coward. I'm not afraid!"

"But my mother … Right now my mama's supposed to come," he mumbled, disengaging himself from Zhenya, who had pressed close to him.

No one knows what might have happened had his mother not returned from visiting friends. But even now he couldn't forget Zhenya's dilated, wildly-flashing eyes, her half-open mouth, her crazy words, and his heart would start at the thought that she could be like that with someone else.

"In the summer I'll be in Moscow," said Nadya meanwhile. "My papa and I travel every summer. He's a native Muscovite, but for ten years now we've been in the Far East. He doesn't want to live in Moscow; he says that in two months of vacation he gets more from the city than he got in the years he lived there. And it's true, we go to all the theaters, all the museums. If you want, Andrei, I'll stop by your girlfriend's and say that it's not good not to write letters to a person who …"

"Who in the rigors of army daily life, unsparingly and by the sweat of his brow …," chimed in Pogost, and they all burst out laughing.

"There's no need to see Zhenya, but if you would kindly stop by my mother's …"

"Gladly," Nadya quickly agreed.

"Mama's very lonely; we have few acquaintances and ..."

"What's there to explain? Of course I'll stop by," Nadya interrupted.

"And maybe, Nadyusha," Pogost began with a smile, "you'll permit my young friend to write to you? And then to hell with all those Moscow maidens there, under the neon lights ..."

"If Andrei wants to, let him ... write," she replied, somewhat embarrassed.

"As if he wouldn't want to!" Pogost guffawed and slapped Andrei on the shoulder. "Can't you see he's dying of happiness?"

Here Andrei too became embarrassed, and he mumbled:

"Well, if you allow it, if I may ... I'll write."

"Then we're agreed!" Pogost exclaimed. "Thank old Pogost, because you're a bit timid for a lad from the capital."

Nadya became curious about Pogost's surname. A *pogost* is a cemetery, so how did the name originate? Pogost explained, and she remarked that in spite of his name there was nothing morbid about him; on the contrary, he was a very cheerful fellow.

Andrei didn't participate in the conversation; he was looking at Nadya and suddenly caught himself wanting to kiss this girl. She noticed his look, apparently sensing something, and fell silent, embarrassed. Andrei became uncomfortable, for it seemed to him that the girl had guessed his wish. "I'm going to have a smoke," he said and got up.

He smoked unhurriedly on the car platform, biding his time, having concluded for some reason that Nadya would come there, and then they would talk without any witnesses, but she didn't come. And why had he thought that she would come? It was just a simple farce started by Pogost and of course it was as a joke that she talked about a correspondence and about how she would visit his mother, and he took it all seriously, now wasn't that stupid? His conjecture was confirmed upon his return when he heard animated voices and Nadya's laughter: no doubt Pogost was again making jokes about him, Andrei. He frowned and sat down on his seat.

"I was telling Nadya about our famous Captain Ivanov," Pogost said. "So don't think that we were picking you apart," he added, smiling.

Andrei smiled too—Captain Ivanov was worth telling about ...

When he and Pogost had gotten off the train at a platform marked "77th km," they were struck by a sense of wilderness and desolation: a river, hills, silence, and absence of human life. There were just two lieutenants who got off here and headed in the direction of the bridge, while on the platform near the ticket window stood some elderly captain, whom they decided to ask for directions to the railroad checkpoint.

"Will you permit an inquiry, comrade captain?" Andrei came to attention.

The captain turned around. He was bulky, and his poorly tightened wide belt hung on his bulging stomach; his face was flaccid. He glanced at them with dissatisfaction.

"Wadd'ya want?"

"How do we get to the railroad checkpoint, comrade captain?"

"Ah, I understand. So, you're reporting to me. Bridge specialists?"

"Yessir!" barked Andrei, and the captain frowned.

"Your papers, please ..." the captain kept repeating as he examined their documents. "Well, let's get going."

They set off from the platform toward the little checkpoint buildings visible not far away. After going a short distance, the captain suddenly asked:

"What's your attitude toward the female sex? Are you real skirt-chasers or not?"

The unexpectedness of the question confused not only Andrei, but Pogost, too, who shrugged in perplexity and muttered:

"In regard to me, comrade captain, I'm ... I'm probably not much of a 'skirt-chaser' as you expressed it, insofar as I've been a bachelor 'til now. And this boy"—he nodded toward Andrei—"in my opinion still has no conception of such things."

"Uh-huh," said the captain, smiling oddly. "I brought it up because I have a young wife here. Very young." It was unclear if the captain was speaking seriously or joking. "And you yourselves can see the crushing boredom here—it's an isolated spot, there's no human contact, a passenger train comes through just twice a day ... You can do yourself in."

They listened to the captain without understanding why he was baring his soul to them. Was it heartfelt candor or was he mocking them?

"You, comrade ..." he poked Pogost in the chest with his finger.

"Pogost, comrade captain."

"You, comrade Pogost—that's a strange kind of name ... I'll dispatch you to the 73rd kilometer, beyond the river. It's the same distance to the bridge as it is from here."

"Yessir, comrade captain. I'm flattered, of course, since I never thought I could pose a threat ..." Pogost began, but the captain wearily interrupted him:

"There's no room for two at the post. Get it?"

"Yessir," replied Pogost.

"Did you have breakfast at regiment headquarters?"

"No, we didn't manage to. We were afraid of missing the train."

"We'll find out from the cook if there's anything left."

They continued walking in silence while Andrei studied the captain with interest. He was somehow very civilian, with his belly, loose belt, unhurried, ambling gait, and his strange candor regarding his wife. And very unlike the commanders from the regiment school, who spit out orders crisply, with metal in their voices, and who, of course, didn't engage in heart-to-heart talks with their subordinates.

The 77th kilometer checkpoint consisted of an ordinary railroad shack of prerevolutionary construction, like the ones which stand along all our railroad tracks, and two contemporary army-style buildings—a canteen and a Red Army barracks. They approached the former along with the captain.

"Vasek!" the captain shouted, opening the door. "Anything left over from breakfast? We've got to feed two commanders."

Andrei was surprised at the address to the cook by name, the familiar tone in which it was expressed, and the cook's cheerful, informal response:

"We'll find something, comrade captain. We'll feed 'em."

"After you've eaten, come see me," the captain said casually, in response to which Andrei and Pogost came to attention and barked in unison: "Yessir! to report, sir, comrade captain!" They barked so loudly that the captain covered his ears with his palms and winced.

"A little quieter, fellows. This isn't your regiment school."

Apparently out here at the checkpoint they didn't stick all that closely to regulations and military formality.

"Well, how does the captain strike you?" asked Pogost, wolfing down kasha with meat gravy. "An interesting guy. And in spite of his simple manner, I think he's well educated, possibly from the ranks of prerevolutionary officers."

In fact they soon found out from Sashka Novikov, the platoon vice-commander, that their captain had been a staff officer in the Imperialist War,* and had commanded a regiment in the Civil War, that he had the Order of the Red Banner, but had been demobilized, and only in the 1930s had been called up from the reserves; but he had been given a minor rank then, and assigned insignificant duties. Actually it was rather insulting to be commander of a company, and a railroad security one at that, after having commanded a regiment, but the captain had been working a long time on getting a transfer to the infantry and a higher command.

Andrei saw the captain's wife the second day. She didn't seem all that young to him, for she was rather thin and pale, with frightened eyes; she certainly was no beauty. But the captain always accompanied her to the platform and the ticket window where she sold tickets before the arrival of the passenger trains; while she was there he would pace about the platform, keeping a sharp eye on the window, and as soon as some lieutenant or other would dawdle at the ticket window, he would direct his heavy steps toward it …

When Nadya learned where they were stationed from Pogost's story about Captain Ivanov, she said it was quite close to their town, and letters would take only two or three days, not like to and from Moscow, which required almost two weeks.

"So you were serious about corresponding?" asked Andrei.

"Of course."

"I thought you were joking," Andrei uttered with relief, and the thought came to him that Nadya evidently was a very fine and unpretentious girl, unaffected, and it would be splendid to correspond with her.

He glanced at her sweet, already tanned face, her honey-blond braid falling forward across her shoulder, and a feeling of tenderness toward this girl enveloped him, so that once again he felt a desire to kiss her.

---

* World War I.

"I expect that our renowned Captain Ivanov will let us come into town, and then, my boy …," Pogost broke off meaningfully.

"By the way, we don't live far from the station," Nadya remarked.

"You hear that, Andryusha? Not far from the station! That means you have tremendous prospects awaiting you, so let them there in Moscow, under the neon lights …," Pogost gestured and again started to laugh.

"Haven't we had an awful lot of the 'neon lights,' Pogost?" said Andrei with a slight laugh.

"You're right—I've overdone it," agreed Pogost good-naturedly, and he turned the conversation to another subject.

They sat and talked about this and that, about Moscow and about their "cushy job" at the 77th kilometer checkpoint … Andrei boasted of climbing to the topmost beam of the bridge superstructure and from there in good weather enjoying the view of the town where Nadya lived. She in turn said that their town was very beautiful and fairly ancient, that the Amur River on which the town stood was very broad and mighty, but through binoculars one could easily view the Manchurian settlement on the far bank, and in the recent past Manchurians and Koreans would come across in their little boats on market days and trade in the town …

When Andrei got ready to go out again for a smoke, Nadya also got up.

"It's very hot … I'll go with you onto the platform."

Andrei opened the door on the platform. The blast of air lifted Nadya's braid, ruffled her blouse, and billowed her skirt, revealing her knees. At first they didn't say anything, but after Andrei had closed the door Nadya asked:

"Have you been in the army long?"

"Less than a year … But Moscow and my former life have receded somewhere so far away, it's as if they never existed."

"Come on, that can't be."

"It can. In regiment school we were like machines; we had only twenty minutes of personal time per day, otherwise we went from reveille to taps without a breather. There wasn't even time to think about anything. But I had the good luck to wind up in the technical section."

"So that's why you have institute textbooks!"

"You did notice, then. I'd planned to master the first-year institute course work on my own during my army service, but apparently it's not going to work out. Now maybe during the second year ..."

"And which institute are you in?"

"The Moscow Railway Engineering Institute. I knew I'd be called up into the army but I took the exams anyway, although ..." he thought a moment, "although I don't know if I'll get the chance to study."

"And why not?"

"Just because of ... various circumstances." He took a last drag on the cigarette, then discarded it. "Yes, we've grown completely wild in the course of the winter. We got a pass only once. And right now it seems strange that I'm out of formation, riding in a passenger train, talking with you ... It's just that this is embarrassing." Andrei touched a hand to his close-cropped head and then pointed to his leg wraps: "I'll never get used to them."

"What nonsense," Nadya smiled. "Can that really be bothering you?"

"It's killing me," he sighed. "I asked my mother to send me boots. Maybe I'll get a package soon ..."

"Don't agonize over it," she continued to smile. "Intelligent people don't pay attention to such trifles."

"Nor do you?"

"Nor do I."

Andrei felt relieved, although he still couldn't imagine that anyone might like him in those ugly leg wraps. He decided to boast again and said that he had already been swimming.

"Wasn't the water terribly cold?"

"It was fine ... But there was a very strong current; you couldn't swim against it. A little way downstream from our checkpoint there's a small island, and when I was swimming toward it I was almost swept past. The island is completely primitive, and it was very interesting to wander around. It even seemed that some sort of prehistoric monsters would suddenly appear ..."

The sudden wish to kiss Nadya that Andrei had felt in the coach had gone now that they happened to be alone on the platform. He just found it exceptionally pleasant to be standing with her and talking ... He began to tell her about a certain evening that he couldn't forget. Captain Ivanov had invited him and platoon vice-commander Sashka

Novikov (also a Muscovite) to his quarters, treated them to the pipe tobacco that he himself smoked, and after several officers' jokes from the days of the First World War recounted by the captain and conversations of no particular significance, he suddenly frowned and asked them quite seriously, without his usual ambiguity, whether it seemed to them that this year they would have to do some fighting. That wasn't the impression they had. Then the captain sighed: "No, boys, my heart tells me we'll have to. That's why I'm not pushing you. Relax for now, gather your energies. There's going to be a hard war. The Germans will start it, of course, but then the Japs might start to stir as well."

"Is it really going to happen after all?" Nadya asked.

"I don't know. Right now in the daytime when the sun's shining you somehow can't believe it, but then at night sometimes you think about it."

"Are you afraid of war?" Nadya began, then started to laugh. "What a thing to ask! Would a man admit it? But I'm afraid, I don't want war, and I'm not ashamed to admit it, since I'm a woman."

"I'm probably not afraid of it," Andrei replied seriously, so seriously that she stopped smiling immediately. "And I'm not showing off. You understand, I can't tell you everything about myself right now; I'll just say that after a war something has to change. That's what I think."

"What has to change?"

"Oh, I don't know specifically, but something has to."

"And possible death in war? You're not afraid of it either?"

"Death? Of course I'm afraid," he smiled, "but at present I can't imagine it in reality."

They were silent a while, then Nadya asked if he liked the Far East.

"I do. Except it literally is so far. You feel a kind of wrenching separation from home that I've never experienced before ... It's very beautiful at our checkpoint: there's the river, the hills, the great breadth ..."

"Yes, there's so much space ... Really, I couldn't live in a big city ... under the neon lights ..."

"Well, I'm a city man. Big cities are beautiful, especially in the evenings. I've visited Leningrad; it's more beautiful than Moscow and somehow more historical, even though Moscow is a lot older than

Peter.* You wander along Nevsky and you find yourself thinking: this is where Pushkin walked, and Gogol, Dostoevsky, Blok, Esenin ... Cities are full of the past, full of history. I roamed around Leningrad even at night, and I imagined that suddenly on one of the white nights I would meet ... well, Raskolnikov, for instance."

"How interesting!" she exclaimed. "You probably have a great imagination."

"No, I'm more likely too rational, but Peter, the white nights ... you involuntarily start to fantasize. You just can't help fantasizing. Do you understand?"

"I do. Even though my father is a railway engineer, he's terribly imaginative and inventive."

"Where did he finish his institute studies? Not in Moscow?"

"In Moscow."

"Do you know in what year?"

"In 1920, I believe."

"And mine in 1918! It's possible our fathers were acquainted! That's great!"

"You tell me his name, and I'll ask my father. Anyway, when you get leave, come straight to see us. All right?"

"Thanks, Nadya. Of course I'll come by, if only I get leave. You know, it's so good that we got acquainted. I won't feel as lonely now in this remote Far East," Andrei said warmly and sincerely. "You can't even imagine what it means to be in a family's home after barracks life, to sit a while in a home environment. We've all developed such a longing for our homes."

"I can understand ..."

Overcome with feeling, Andrei involuntarily touched Nadya's hand, and she did not pull it away. Then he lightly squeezed her fingers. They kept standing like that, holding hands on the breezy car platform, until Pogost intruded upon their isolation.

"Are you all right, kids?"

"We're all right," Nadya smiled.

"That's very good that you're all right. I'm making myself scarce," said Pogost, and he vanished.

---

* Peter (*Piter* in Russian) is an old colloquial term of affection for St. Petersburg (later Leningrad, and in 1991 renamed St. Petersburg).

Andrei squeezed her fingers again, and blurted out: "I really like being with you!"

"Me too," she said simply, and squeezed his hand also.

The cars clattered, and the nondescript scenery of a monotonous plain floated by; only to the left of the train were there volcanic hills very far off, which appeared blue ... And the kilometer posts were flashing past, inexorably bringing the end of the journey closer, and with it also the end of their encounter. Andrei didn't want to think about it; he wished that the trip would never end, that the little town of Freedom would be somewhere at the end of the world.

"Nadya, if for some reason they won't give me a leave, can you come to see us at the checkpoint?"

"Of course I can. But how would I manage to get back? The next train isn't until the morning of the following day."

"We can go to the closest bypass and I'll put you on a freight."

"That's an idea!"

"But we'll have to arrange by letter that you don't come on a day when I'm on duty. They won't let you onto the bridge; it's under guard." He was briefly silent. "If only nothing happens that's ... unforeseen."

"And what can happen?"

"A lot of things. What if suddenly there's war?"

"I don't believe in any war. You must have read the TASS communique."

"I did, but our captain just shrugged in response to it."

"Never mind him, that captain of yours!" Nadya tossed her head. "We won't go on about it."

And indeed, why think about bad things on this day, so exceptional for him? He would be corresponding with this sweet girl, and maybe also meeting her. He began telling her that he would certainly take her by boat to the uninhabited island he had spoken about, that they would wander there like the first people on earth; he spoke of other things also. The train meanwhile was nearing the station; the drawn-out whistle of the locomotive had already sounded at the approach semaphore, the clicking of wheels had slowed, and the hissing of brakes was heard.

"We've arrived, my young friends," said Pogost, as he entered the platform and handed Andrei the textbooks wrapped in newspaper. "Are you traveling on, Nadya?"

"I am," she answered in a dejected voice, and squeezed Andrei's hand.

"Your address, Nadya," Andrei remembered to ask about the most important thing and he pulled out a pencil.

The train came to a halt. They stood silently looking at each other for several more minutes until Pogost nudged Andrei. "It's time to go, my boy."

They hopped down off the car step ... Andrei was tormented by the thought that he had not said something to the girl, and it was only when the car shuddered, the buffers clashed, and the train started to move that he shouted: "If we don't manage to meet, I'll still remember you!"

"I will too." And she started to wave her hand.

They stood a while longer on the station platform, watching the train leave.

"Is that incredibly serious also?" laughed Pogost.

"Very," Andrei replied.

"What can I say, except that I envy your nineteen years ... By the way, has standing on the car platform with an enchanting girl driven all the rules for technical utilization and instructions on signalization out of your head?"

"I guess not," Andrei smiled.

"Well, let's tramp off, then, to that famous administration. We still have to ask around where it's located."

Freedom turned out to be an uninteresting little town, gray and plain, dusty and dirty. There were wretched wooden dwellings even in the center where the railroad administration was located. As they walked around the place Andrei, filled with impressions of the unexpected acquaintance in the car, was not thinking at all about the examination facing him. He was picturing to himself future meetings and correspondence with Nadya; Pogost was not distracting him by conversation, thus giving him the opportunity to day dream. Only when they were right at the administration building did Andrei come back to reality, and the familiar chill always sensed before examinations passed through his breast.

But the exam turned out to be ridiculously easy. Andrei knew much more than was required of him, and the examiners smiled approvingly. On the whole this examination, conducted by civilians, took him back temporarily to his previous life before the army, and a feeling of calm settled over him: the year of army service would soon fly by, and then Moscow, the institute, and the beginning of a real, normal life.

Pogost remained in the building after the examination for some instructions, while Andrei went out into Freedom's little streets in an elated mood, gratified by his brilliant exam performance. He and Pogost had agreed to meet at the station.

He walked along the unappealing, village-like streets, inhaling deeply, pleasurably sensing the springiness of his steps, the strength of his well-conditioned young body, and he even felt like taking a run. He wasn't embarrassed now by his leg wraps or by the clumsy shoes on his feet, for even with them Nadya apparently had liked him a little; she wouldn't have hung about with him on the car platform if she hadn't found him interesting.

He turned off from the main street leading to the station and, whistling, walked along some dusty, unpaved alleys, past small one-story houses. The station was somewhere nearby—one could hear the engine whistles and the signals of the trainmen. Andrei had to turn left, and he looked for some passageway or cattle track leading to the rail line. Such a lane soon appeared; he turned into it, went a short way, and then ...

At first he couldn't make sense of anything. In front of him something gray spread ... Spread was the right word, because people—and these were people!—were kneeling with their backs toward him and their faces toward a long line of boxcars. And glancing in both directions, he was barely able to discern the ends of this enormous stationary rectangle that sprawled out in front of the cars ... Then he caught the sharp odor of unclean human bodies, a distinctive odor of damp padded cotton jackets that never get dried out, of dirty leg wraps, and also the smell always given off by a large number of people jammed together, dirty and hungry.

Andrei reeled ... He retreated toward the fence so that the guards wouldn't notice him. The scene began to swim before his eyes, and he couldn't tell if this gray mass was actually moving or if everything in his vision was shifting. From somewhere seemingly distant a command was heard, and the enormous gray rectangle that had been sprawled on the ground started to stir and to move toward the boxcars ... Dust boiled up, raised by shuffling knees, and it hung as a gray, hot haze over the people, making everything around spectral, indistinct, nightmarish. This movement on the knees was unnatural, and therefore terrifying ...

A shouted order rang out again, and the rectangle froze ... The front rows had already moved right up against the boxcars, the black holes of their open doors gaping. Then—another order, and at each door one person got up from his knees. At the next order they got into the car. The rest crawled again on their knees, moving toward the line of cars.

Andrei's vision went black. He pressed a hand against his mouth so that a moan or cry wouldn't escape and stood, lacking the strength to avert his gaze from that mass of dust-covered human beings ... But no, not human beings, rather some kind of unknown creature ... some astounding monster ... "A monster most ponderous, fearsome, enormous ..."—the lines of Radishchev's epigraph floated up for some reason. "My God ... Father ... Can it be that he's like that too—on his knees?" His father—and on his knees! Andrei pressed his hand even harder against his mouth, barely suppressing a moan.

"Go on, get outa here, there's nothin' here to look at," someone's voice reached him.

He raised his head. One of the convoy guards was approaching him, a young fellow with a pockmarked face.

"Go on," he repeated.

"But why ... why are they on their knees?" Andrei asked with dry lips.

"Don't you understand, or what? So that the scum don't scatter off. All right, beat it," said the guard in an almost friendly manner, and tramped off.

Andrei cast a final glance at the dirty jackets, the shorn heads, the gray winter caps, and he left, barely able to move his legs, which felt like cotton and refused to obey him. He staggered, and after a few dozen steps halted, leaning on the garden fence in front of some house. He felt sick and he bent over, trying to get rid of his nausea.

Occasional passersby looked with surprise or disapproval at Andrei doubled over, white, his hand still on his mouth. Some probably thought he was drunk. With trembling fingers he pulled out a cigarette, but couldn't light it, for the matches kept breaking. He threw it away and pressed himself even more heavily against the fence.

"Are you feeling bad, sonny?" An elderly woman in a kerchief had halted near him.

"N-no, it's o-okay," he barely managed to utter with trembling lips.

"Let's go to my place; I'll give you some water. Well, come on, let's go," she urged and took him by the sleeve of his uniform, but Andrei shook his head in refusal. "You feel bad, son, I can see that. Your face is blank, you've turned white as a sheet."

They entered the house, and Andrei sank down heavily on a chair. The woman filled a mug for him, and Andrei greedily drank some water, then pulled out his cigarettes.

"Go ahead, go ahead and smoke," she replied hastily to his questioning glance.

Andrei inhaled deeply, then again and again, but the deep draughts did nothing to help him recover. Suddenly the woman asked:

"Who do you have ... over there, dear?" and she pointed in the direction of the station.

He started at the unexpectedness of the question and didn't reply, whereupon she continued:

"I saw how you were standing there beside the tracks, and so I guessed. Looking at such a thing for the first time is horrible ... But we've seen our fill. They often drive them along our street. So who is it? Your father, probably?"

Andrei nodded.

"So that's how it is," she sighed and shook her head in grief. After a little while she quietly asked:

"How will you fight, son, if a war starts?"

He raised his head. What was she getting at? He didn't understand the connection between what he had seen and the woman's words. He frowned, trying to figure it out, but wasn't in the right frame of mind, for what he had seen loomed before his eyes.

"What am I saying ... maybe God will grant that there won't be a war." She crossed herself and offered him more water.

"Thanks, I'll be going." Andrei stood up.

He made it to the station staggering, but didn't enter the building where he had agreed to meet Pogost. He didn't care about him, or anyone else, for that matter. Pogost would wait for the train on which they were supposed to return and could get back alone. Andrei walked out onto the station tracks, sought out a freight train heading east, climbed onto the brake platform of one of the cars, sat down on the bench, and only then did the long-suppressed cry of anguish burst forth.

Soon the train set off. The cars started to clank at their couplings, and occasionally the drawn-out, melancholy whistle of the engine would jar his ears. Andrei sat hunched over, holding his head in his hands—he had never experienced such despair and hopelessness. Not even when his father was arrested. "My father ... on his knees, my father ... on his knees ..." kept pounding in his head, and the car wheels seemed to hammer out the same thing.

He thought about his father constantly. Just as constant was the pain, but until the sight he had witnessed today he had not imagined, nor could he have imagined, the full horror and nightmare of what had happened to his father ... Andrei, like everyone else, knew about the camps only from the movie *The Convicts*, where the barracks looked almost like a picture postcard, where the reeducated engineer-saboteurs were well-dressed, with neckties and silver cigarette cases, where the irresistible jailbird Kostya the Captain guzzled vodka and the romantic thief Sonka, accompanied on guitar, sang the hearttugging ditty, "My wings are all smashed and broken, my whole spirit has been gripped by quiet pain, all my roads have been buried by the silvery dust of cocaine ...," where the camp administrators were wise and charming ... There was nothing, nothing frightful in that movie. And Andrei had thought that his father, too, of course, was working in his specialty, supervising some sort of camp construction or else designing it, like those engineers in the movie. Especially since in his infrequent letters he would write that everything was fine and that he didn't need anything.

And here was that "fine" ... Again there floated before his eyes the enormous gray rectangle of a thousand people on their knees stirring in the dust ...

And he, Andrei, young, strong, was completely powerless to change anything, to help. He didn't even know who was to blame for all of this and what it was all for. He was certain that his father wasn't guilty of anything, but, then, what was going on?

Towers appeared on the right side of the track, and soon the train sped by gray barracks encircled with barbed wire ... And here Andrei remembered the woman's words: "How will you fight, son?" "Yes, how will I fight?" he repeated to himself. "How will I fight?" ...

Nine days later the war began ...

A SHORT STAY IN THE TORTURE CHAMBER

Yury Trifonov (1925–1981)

Translated by Helena Goscilo

His father Valentin Trifonov was a revolutionary, one of the leaders of the Red Cossacks, later chairman of the Military Collegium of the Supreme Court of the Soviet Union, a Soviet trade representative and diplomat, who was executed in 1938 after a direct order from Stalin.

Raised by his grandmother, **Yury Trifonov** grew up as a writer during the Thaw and became one of the pioneers of so-called 'urban prose', officially accepted yet ideologically pristine writing on the life and dramas of the emerging mass urban intelligentsia.

However, Trifonov's greatest achievement was a historical and deeply personal novella *The House on the Embankment*, analyzing the birth trauma of the same intelligentsia, the Stalinist slaughter of their parents. Trifonov focused on a real place, the so-called House of the Government, a modernist building built in front of the Kremlin to house the new ruling elite, including Trifonov's father Valentin. The edifice was renamed in his novel, and bears the nickname The House on the Embankment to this day.

In the early spring of 1964, when I was still suffering from an insatiable love of sports, when I kept charts on the champions, knew by heart the best players of the Fiorentina and the Manchester United, when I believed that you could write as seriously about sports as, say, about the tomb of Lorenzo di Medici in Florence, when I had just released my legendary film about hockey and didn't feel at all embarrassed by it, I arrived in the Tyrol with a group of sports writers, lived in a mountain village not far from Innsbruck, and each morning took the bus to the games. The Olympics were being held in Innsbruck. Who won there, who lost, I don't remember. All that nonsense has been forgotten. I don't remember the name of a single athlete from that time—what I remember is the blinding snow on the slopes, the sharp blue of the sky, the freshness in the air, the smell of coffee, and my landlord, who would squint and squeeze out, "*Morgen,*" through his dry lips.

Sometimes when I didn't feel like going to town I would stay in the hotel and watch the games on television. On a table in the empty hall lay thick books in antique-looking leather bindings: *Gästebücher.* Guest books. Having nothing to do, I leafed through them, relishing the examples of German ingenuousness. The books had been kept since 1929, when the hotel first started up in the village of Stubental. All of the comments were the same: gratitude to the proprietor, praise for the mountains, the snow, the view, the girls, the selection of records on the jukebox. I reached the Anschluss: nothing was changed, the same delight about the snow, the air, the girls. And then the war: judging from the comments, wounded German officers took time off here, but it was impossible to find out anything from them, either, except raptures over nature, girls, Italian wine, Spanish oranges. Once there flashed a patriotic entry: "*Alles wagen, England schlagen!*" that is, "Give it your all—beat England." Someone had written above in pencil in small letters, "But England really trounced you." And then still later, with a green felt-tip, "*O Sie gute arme Idioten!*" But it was unclear to whom this was addressed: to the beaten Germans or to those who rejoiced in the victory. And that was all about the war. The same comments continued: skis, sun, happiness, *Erlebnis.* The proprietor didn't care for us. We paid him money; he tolerated us. He did not enter into conversation. The only thing we heard from him through his clenched teeth was: "*Morgen!*"

But still, I liked the snowy mountains, the valley, the huge bridge across the gorge, the smell of coffee in the morning, and I liked what I was so madly and senselessly carried away with then, what filled the newspapers, what I wrote about at night, and at noon shouted by telephone to Moscow, and only one thing spoiled my mood: the presence of N. in our group. He had emerged from my distant past. Of course, I knew that he existed and I would come across his name in the newspapers, and from time to time would run into him one place or another. We both would act as if we were scarcely acquainted or, indeed, if we did bump into each other head-on, we would barely nod and would pass on by, although at one time we had been on friendly terms and had liked the same girl. But she was incidental. The girl had nothing whatever to do with the whole matter, which took place fourteen years ago—the point was this: we had lived separate lives all those years. He worked for the radio; I sat working at home. I thought I was done with him. And suddenly, he turned up in Innsbruck. N. was always far removed from sports. How the hell did he turn up in our group? The first minute we saw each other in the group gathering in Moscow, I noticed something waver in his face, like a momentarily repressed impulse to be glad, or, maybe, to nod in a friendly way, but he couldn't read this weakness in my face. I met him with a cold look and barely discernible nod which signified nothing on my part but an icy memory. That kind of relationship, I assumed, would become established between us, and somehow I would get through the twelve days.

Sometimes, when my friends would go to town and I would stay at the hotel, it would be partly because I didn't want to see the rosy-cheeked, dried-up, old-mannish N. There had been a time, I remembered, when he wore an army jacket and boots, smoked a handmade pipe and looked like a staid, patrician youth, deeply absorbed in something. Later, I found out in what. But at the time it seemed to me that his unhurriedness, his quiet, indistinct voice, and his gloomy look concealed something significant. I was engrossed in reading Blok* then, and it seemed to me that this line was about him: "Let us forgive the gloomy look,/For not here lies the hidden moving force." True, he did not resemble the lines that followed: "He was all a child of love and light,/He was all a celebration of freedom." N.'s moving force had to do with something else: N. himself alone.

But when we arrived in the Tyrol and settled in the hotel, something strange began: he behaved as if nothing had ever happened. In the morning he would greet me from afar with happy smiles, raise his hand in greeting and nod earnestly, and the nods conveyed not only the old amiability, but also a genuine esteem, the kind expressed to people you sincerely respect. I tried not to pay attention. Then it started to annoy me. Once we ran into each other in the pressbox at the stadium, face to face, and in passing he grabbed my arm above the elbow, squeezed it rather familiarly, and said, "Hi!" I pulled my arm away and muttered, "What is it?" But my mutter sounded more

---

* The Russian Symbolist poet, Alexander Blok (1880–1921).

frightened than hostile. He winked at me and passed by without saying anything else. Another time in the presence of two journalists, an Italian and a German, he launched into a conversation with me about hockey, after introducing me as an expert, the author of an excellent film, *The Hockey Players*. That's the way he said it—"excellent," and his voice sounded honest and simple, without the slightest touch of envy or irony, and, like it or not, I had to respond and talk with him. But I cut the conversation short and left.

Later, the German found me and asked me to give an interview about how the games were going, observing, "Mr. N. reads all your dispatches with delight. He said that they are genuinely *Spitze!*" I didn't know how to take this. I didn't understand him and I didn't understand myself. Can it be, I thought, that a person has completely forgotten *how he behaved fourteen years ago*? But that's impossible. It doesn't happen. He didn't forget, probably, but looks at his own past cold-bloodedly, as something natural, trivial, and worthy of oblivion. If he had acted differently—had not greeted me, had scowled, passing by without a glance and wearing a haughty look—this would not have bothered me. I would have accepted it as the way things should be. A person who has done something evil to someone else always looks at his victim with a scowl or passes him by with a haughty look. That is the nature of things. But here he was pretending *that nothing bad had ever happened!*

And the more I thought about it the more I boiled with rage and just waited for the opportunity to vent my rage on N. A fuss started about awarding the Rolex Company's "Golden Pen" award to the best journalist from each national group, and N. nominated me. This was ridiculous. I am not a professional journalist and had not earned the "Golden Pen." Someone else was nominated, and N. began to insist on me. It became so intolerable that I left the room. Our meeting was taking place in the restaurant. I was beside myself with anger. I waited for him in the hall. As soon as he appeared, I went up to him and said: "What the hell makes you keep hanging on to me? I'm not bothering you!" I probably had a malicious look on my face, for he was silent for a second, looking at me in bewilderment, and then, seemingly flustered, shrugged his shoulders and said, "Me, hanging on to you? You're off your rocker. You've lost your mind, buddy."

"I'm asking you to stop bugging me."

"You're sick," he said. "You should get help."

It was a starry night. I walked along the asphalt road in front of the hotel, breathing in the warm night air of the mountain valley, now empty and silent, and thought: is it true that I'm sick? Occasionally the headlights from cars rushing past would flash over me. I reached the turn onto the bridge and looked at the range of darkening slopes; there, far in the depths, where the now-invisible road led, Innsbruck shone weakly with a handful of lights. It flickered below like a small forest campfire that hadn't been doused. I am sick, I thought, like a person who hasn't shunted his memory aside. I remember too well: the May evening before the meeting when he came without calling, on the pretext of returning some books because he was leaving for Berdyansk. He went to Berdyansk every summer to see his relatives. But I felt that something else had caused him to come. From the start his actions were unnatural: he didn't put the books on the table, he didn't say "Thank you," or "I'm returning these," or "Here are your books," but from a distance threw them on the bed without a word. There was nervousness, a lack of decorum, and decisiveness in this gesture. He was tossing aside not books, but something which had burdened his life. As soon as the two of us were left alone, he said, breaking into a little laugh, "Want to hear a joke? Tomorrow I'm going to speak out against you!"

"Against what?" I asked stupidly, not understanding a damn thing.

"Against you. You, you!" he smiled and poked a finger at me. I thought he was drunk. Something like that could happen, I supposed, but why come and warn me? I said people play dirty tricks without giving warnings. He mumbled something about having understood the "conscious necessity" of it. And I mumbled something meaningless. Suddenly I shouted, "Why did you come here?" He said he came not of his own accord. So Nadya had made him come. She demanded that either he not speak at all, or that he go to the person and honestly warn him. "You don't know what she's like. She actually went into hysterics on me."

I had forgotten about Nadya. Nadya was the girl we both had liked earlier. She had survived the Leningrad blockade; she was pale, fragile, and anemic, with straw-colored braids and a thoughtful look; she was soft-spoken, wrote poetry, and to me as an admirer of Blok, she seemed like the mysterious stranger in Blok's poem. Her whole family had perished in the blockade. Nadya lived in a domitory. Once I had dreamed passionately of her. The summer of '47, when we moved up into the third-year class, the three of us—Nadya, N. and I—went on summer assignment to write articles about the hydroelectric stations at Lake Sevan. This was arranged through the Komsomol organization. We set out in July. At first everything was fun, poignant, intriguing, enveloped in the opiate of uncertainty and love. We had the girl right there beside us and we expected a struggle for her. We kidded around, sang songs, didn't sleep at night, and endlessly recited poetry. We had to transfer four times to get to Yerevan. In Sochi, I swam in the sea for the first time in my life. I remember how N. and I swam far out, while Nadya stayed on the shore and N. asked, "Shall we cast lots for Nadya?" That caught me off guard, and I almost choked on the salt water and blurted out, "No!"

He said, "Watch out, then, you'll have yourself to blame." This threat seemed absurd to me. I had blurted out, "No!" precisely because deep down I thought that if she had to choose between us, Nadya would choose me. I, too, wrote poetry, but N. composed articles for the Sovinform Bureau.

Our journey was becoming more and more tiring. From Sochi to Samtredia we traveled by a local train that was stifling and cramped, where all around people were shouting in a strange language. Some men made passes at Nadya. N. and I defended her, and the matter almost ended in a fight. Because of the closeness and heat everyone stripped down to his undershirt. We sat Nadya in the corner and blocked her from view with our backs. Samtredia seemed to us the Promised Land—it was quiet, peaceful, and people were selling pears and corn flat bread. But later we came to hate Samtredia: we couldn't get out of there.

As soon as the ticket counter opened, a bellowing crowd rushed over, and while were were making our way to our goal, using our elbows to help, the cashier said, "No *teekeets!*" and slammed the window shut. We went to the station guard on duty. He ignored us. N. got into an argument with him and threatened to write about him to the newspaper. He waved our assignment orders, which, signed by the provost of the institute, looked impressive, though they actually didn't mean a thing.

"Your papers mean zilch to me!" the guard said and swept them onto the floor without reading them. Then he said, "You won't get out of here alive!" We had to spend the night in Samtredia. We were afraid to spend the night in the station: that was the guard's territory and he could harass us there. N. proposed that we sleep in the square at the base of the Lenin monument, which was illuminated all night.

"Here they won't dare touch us," N. said. We were afraid that they would attack us and abduct Nadya. All this time N. kept quietly humming, "Enemy whirlwinds swirl above us ..." He had begun to annoy me. Nadya calmly lay down on my raincoat, covered up with his jacket, and went to sleep, and we guarded her, and grumbled and argued all night. I remember we swore at each other over Akhmatova. But no one attacked us.

The next day we managed to get on a train by evening and we left for Tbilisi. There our quarrels grew bitter: our money had melted away catastrophically, and I thought that we simply had to go on without delay, but he took it into his head to stay a few days in Tbilisi. He had a friend there who had served with him at the front. I objected strenuously. Suddenly, he said that if I was going to be stubborn I could go on ahead, and they would catch up with me at Lake Sevan. Something stirred up inside me and burst. As if a trench had been dug out, a mine laid, and now it exploded.

I asked Nadya, "Do you really want to stay with him in Tbilisi?"

"I don't care," she said. "I'm not rushing anywhere."

An unusual honesty set her apart. But for some reason, her honesty burst like a bomb and inflicted contusions on people. The friend from the front couldn't be located, and we went on together. In Yerevan a hundred-degree heat wave was raging—we just had to dream up a trip to Armenia in July! The heat turned us into half-corpses: our energy sapped, we lay around in a room that an old woman had offered us at the station. On the third day N. advised me to look for a room for myself.

"Somewhere nearby," he said. "Not far from us." And I left them that very evening. Just that suddenly everything ended. It was my first disappointment: in friendship, in women, and mainly, in myself. To be so self-confident and blind! But I didn't suffer for long. I was twenty-one.

Later, my relations with N. recovered, although our previous friendship was no longer possible. We became distant, but not hostile to each other. Without half-trying, I noticed that he and Nadya were going together, then they split up, and about the time we finished the institute they got back together, and for good it seemed. But this didn't affect me. I was busy with something else. I was writing a book. Other women with straw-colored braids came and went. Suddenly, I got married. Life flew by in youthful impatience. My second-rate book became famous, a fog obscured my vision, and then a mountain collapsed on me.

For four years N. had not once come to see me, and suddenly he turned up. This didn't scare me: he was only a small part of the mountain. But what was puzzling and what I cannot understand was why did he come and warn me? Although I cannot understand it now, at the time, suprisingly enough, when I heard that Nadya had made him come, for some reason I *understood* and *agreed*. The matter involved a threat of expulsion. I had finished the institute, but had remained a member of the institute Komsomol. The second-rate book suddenly received a prize. Therefore, it was sweet to expel me. And there was a reason: in my entrance application I had concealed that my father was an enemy of the people, which I had never believed. What N. had said when he came to see me at night was sheer madness. And what Nadya had demanded from him, which implied honesty and openness, was also sheer madness. Everything was sheer madness; the month of May, the prize, the expulsion, the applause, and the animosity. And perhaps the plea for remission of sins was also madness. They would have liked for me to say to them, "Go ahead!" and maybe they heard the words "Go ahead!" for I muttered something incoherent, as in a dream, yawned, and shook hands on parting. Sometimes dreams such as these do occur. All the absurd things that happen during the dream seem incredibly logical and perfectly reasonable, but when you wake up, you can't for the life of you figure out why all that hocus-pocus seemed so clear to you. So, all the speakers talked only about the entrance application. They needed more, something concrete that would confirm that I was *rotten inside*, that the case of the application was merely evidence of a general *rottenness*, the way feverish lips are evidence of a breakdown of the whole organism with a cold. N. spoke with difficulty, as if it was painful. It was hard for him. After all, he had been on friendly terms with me. He could barely put words together. He said that he had a torturously dual relationship with me: on the one hand this, on the other hand, unquestionably, that. Details are important in such things: well, for example, what I once said about Akhmatova. This was long ago, but so much the worse for me. That is, already at that time I had some faulty ideas. Once I praised so-and-so. Another time I was all upset about something. Once I teased him when he wanted to sing revolutionary songs. But I was not a hopeless case, however. Therefore he was against expulsion, and for a severe reprimand and warning. After long arguments the meeting decided just that way. But the Regional Committee expelled me; the minor details of N.'s testimony were good enough for that. Later, the City Committee reinstated me with a stiff rebuke, or as people used to say then, half-lovingly—a "stiffy."

In the Tyrol all of this seemed ancient; by now it had receded into such a biblical antiquity that you suddenly thought: did all this happen to me? Maybe I dreamed it. Maybe someone told me a pack of tall tales, and in my mind everything got turned around and upside down? Someone said that in Russia a writer has to live a long time: and it is true, you can come upon many surprises and marvels. Time darkens the past with an ever-thickening veil, and you won't see through it, for it's pitch-dark. Because the veil is in us. And the surprises also disappear behind the same veil. Chekhov could have lived to see the war. As an old man, he could have sat as an evacuee in Chistopol, have somehow lived on ration cards, read the newspapers, and listened to the radio. With a hand growing weak, he could have written something important and necessary for that moment. He could have reacted to the liberation of Taganrog, but how would he have viewed his own past, remaining behind the dusk of days? His own *Uncle Vanya*? His own chopped-down orchard? How would he have viewed Olga, who dreamed, "If only we could know! If only we could know!" As soon as we find something out, it vanishes into a fog. Indeed, Anton Pavlovich would have been able to find out before Chistopol about things that poor Olga wouldn't have dared to dream of. So, he found out—and so what? He couldn't find out the main thing—how the war would end. But we know this.

Strolling at night along the highway in front of the Stubental Hotel, I suddenly decided: I have to have it out with N. Why I had to was unclear. But I was possessed by the idea. Now, when it's all stopped hurting, and we're both free of those days, and the waves are rolling us in different directions, it's easy to ask: why did you do it? I began to wait for a convenient time. While the games were going on, we rarely met: I was watching hockey; he, figure skating. And then it was all over. The hotel proprietor smiled for the first time as he said good-bye to us, and we left by bus for Vienna, stopping along the way to have a look at this and that. The weather was warm. We were tanned, as if we had been in the south. In the bus he looked friendly and again nodded amiably, as though nothing had happened. Sometimes he would ask me something insignificant in passing: "Do you know what the next stop will be?" or, "Did you happen to notice where the bathroom is?" I always answered dryly. I thought: "Just wait, I'll ask you something altogether different. You'll stop smiling!" On the second day after lunch in Salzburg, we went on an excursion to a castle which housed a medieval torture chamber. I thought: "Here's the very place!"

Everyone was feeling a little high after lunch—we wandered through the huge castle laughing and joking, and lingered in the passages and halls of the dungeon, where in the semi-darkness, as luck would have it, instruments of torture stood on end and the two of us turned up alone in one of the rooms. I asked him, "Listen, I've been waiting a long time to ask you, just out of curiosity, why did you try to do me in then?"

He didn't understand. "When?"

"You know, during those years, the devil knows when. They were expelling me. Remember?" We were standing in front of a huge tub into which they used to place a criminal and then, with a windlass, lower him into a well of putrid water with snakes and toads. There the victim was either drowned and his corpse dragged out, or he was kept half-drowned, then tortured and forced to tell his secrets. This information was conveyed on a plaque inscribed in beautiful Gothic letters. This occurred in the sixteenth century. We looked into the depths of the well. It was now dry, but had no bottom. Our voices disappeared in a rumble below.

I knew what he would say. "I swear to you, old man, I acted sincerely! We were fools. I believed that you needed to be punished, that your father was an enemy, and that mercy shows weakness. If you like, one should feel sorry not for you, but for us sincere fools."

I would answer: "But the difference is that you fools weren't threatened by anything, but I was, of being without work, without money, and maybe, without a home, without a family. Times were grim, but that didn't trouble you fools. What could one expect from you? You acted sincerely. There's nothing nobler and more remarkable than sincerity!"

"Are you calling that into question?"

"If it means sincerely forgetting about conscience, about other people's suffering—then to hell with sincerity! You didn't give a thought to what your sincerity was turning into. You didn't give a damn what was happening to the people who ran up against your sincerity, shining with its satanic light! And you know on the day of the damned meeting, my mother ..." All of a sudden a crimson cloud of rage sailed into me.

"Your sincerity is villainy." And grabbing the puny N. below his knees, I lightly lift him over the well and throw him across the barrier. He plops into the tub. There's a inhuman scream, the windlass crank begins to turn, faster and faster, the tub crashes below, the scream dies out, the crank turns on and out of control, and I run up the stone stairway. In the bus no one notices that N. is not there. It only dawns on them two hours later. They turn back. Everyone has suddenly sobered up. They run through the castle looking for him, wailing, calling, while I sit on the porch and smoke. Gradually, the terrible truth becomes clear. "Well?" they ask each other with terrified eyes. And someone says, "*But you know, there was something out of kilter with him.*"

"Where?"

"In Innsbruck."

"What was it?"

"He stood around a lot on the street reading notices ..."

N. looked at me in fright and, shaking his head, whispered, "You've forgotten everything, old man. I didn't try to do you in. I tried to save you."

"Save me?"

"Of course, I shifted the course of the meeting. They wanted to expel you, but after my speech they gave you a 'stiffy.' You thanked me. Don't you remember?"

"I remember something else: you said something about Akhmatova, about my being two-faced."

He stared at me with wide eyes, as if I were a madman, and then grabbed me by the shoulders and shook me. "No way! I saved you! I dragged you out of the fire! Later, I caught it: why, they said, did you go out of your way to defend him? He's scum. I quarreled because of you. How strange that you've forgotten everything."

Yes, I did forget, I didn't remember, I mixed it up, everything disappeared into a fog. He stretched a tentative hand out to me, and I shook it tentatively. We climbed up out of the dungeon into the open air. The snowy white backbone of the mountain flashed in the blue sky. The alpine spring was in full swing. Music floated over from the bus—our driver had turned on Mozart. He liked to doze to music.

I thought about the thick books at the Stubental Hotel: in fact, there really is nothing else in the world but snow, sun, music, girls, and the fog which comes with time.

Fifteen years have passed since our visit to the torture chamber, and it is also covered in fog. N. died of heart disease eight years ago. I don't know what became of Nadya. I haven't been to the stadium for a long time now, and I watch hockey on television.

SIX MATCHES

Strugatsky brothers (Arkady 1925–1991 and Boris 1933–2012)

Translated by Leonard Stoklitsky

The absolute titans of Soviet science fiction, the **Strugatsky brothers** were separated twice. The first time was during the German siege of Leningrad, when the younger Boris stayed in the hunger-stricken city and the elder Boris was evacuated over the ice of lake Ladoga, losing his father in a German bomb attack. The second time was when Arkady died at the very moment of the collapse of the USSR, forever dissolving the most productive duet of Soviet literature.

The Strugatskys' writing gained them the aura of the visionaries and dystopians. They coined new notions and words, cultural constructs like *Zone* and *Stalker*, in which generations of late Soviet and post-Soviet people have interpreted themselves and their time, and inspired the best directors, like Andrei Tarkovsky and Alexei German, to make philosophical movies expanding the science fiction far beyond its limits.

I

The inspector put his notebook aside. 'A queer business, Comrade Leman,' he said. 'Deep, too.'

'I disagree,' said the director of the Institute.

'Indeed?'

'Yes. It's an open and shut case.'

The director was aloof. He gazed down at the empty, sun-flooded square. Nothing was happening there and his neck ached, but he stubbornly kept his head turned towards the window. He was protesting. The director was a proud young man. He knew perfectly well what the inspector meant but he did not think the man had any right to meddle. The inspector's calm persistence irritated him. He wants to dig – that's what he wants to do, the director thought angrily. It's as clear as daylight but he just wants to dig.

The inspector sighed. 'Well, it's not open and shut to me.'

The director shrugged, then glanced at his watch and stood up. 'You must excuse me, Comrade Rybnikov. I have a seminar in five minutes. If there's nothing else I can do for you now – '

'That's quite all right, Comrade Leman. But I'd like to have a talk with that chap – the "private" laboratory assistant. Gorchinsky is his name, isn't it?'

'Yes, Gorchinsky. He's not here now. As soon as he gets back he'll drop in to see you.'

The director nodded and went out. The inspector followed him with a quizzical look. Acting uppity, eh? he said to himself. Never fear, we'll see what makes *you* tick, too.

But first he had to get to the heart of the matter. On the surface, it did look like an open and shut case. If he wanted to, Inspector Rybnikov of the Labour Protection Office could have sat down that very minute and started writing his *Report on the Case of Andrei Komlin, Head of the Physics Laboratory, Central Brain Institute*. Andrei Komlin had carried out dangerous experiments on himself and had been in hospital three days now, in a state between coma and delirium, his round, bristly head covered with strange, ring-shaped bruises. He could not speak coherently, the doctors were giving him injections to keep up his strength, and they spoke ominously of 'acute nervous exhaustion', 'damage to memory centres' and 'damage to speech and auditory centres'.

Everything about the case that might interest the Labour Protection Office was clear to the inspector. This was not a matter of malfunctioning, negligence or inexperience. Nor had there been any infringement of the safety rules – not, at any rate, in their usual meaning. And on top of it all, Komlin had experimented on himself in the deepest secrecy. No one at the Institute had known anything about the experiments, not even Alexander Gorchinsky, Komlin's 'private' laboratory assistant. Although some of the laboratory staff suspected Gorchinsky knew something.

The inspector was more than just an inspector. An old-time scientific researcher himself, his intuition told him that behind the scraps of information he had collected about Komlin's work, and behind the strange accident that had occurred there lay the story of an unusual discovery. And the more he reviewed, in his mind, the statements made by the laboratory staff the stronger grew his conviction that he was right.

Three months before the accident the laboratory had received a new instrument, a neutrino generator, a device for producing and focusing beams of neutrinos. The arrival of the neutrino generator had set off a chain of events which had escaped the notice of those whose job it was to notice such things, and which had finally led to the accident.

Komlin had very willingly turned over all work on an unfinished project to his deputy, while he and laboratory assistant Alexander Gorchinsky had locked themselves up in the neutrino generator room and got down to what he called preparations for a series of preliminary experiments.

What they were working on had become known only two days before the accident, when Komlin (with Gorchinsky as co-author) had delivered a 'breakthrough' report on neutrino acupuncture. In the three months of his work with the generator, however, Komlin had attracted the attention of other members of the staff on three occasions.

One fine day Andrei Komlin had come to the laboratory wearing a black skull-cap on a shaven head. This, in itself, might not have made any particular impression, but an hour later Gorchinsky, pale and upset, had raced out of the neutrino room, grabbed several packets of surgical dressing from the first-aid kit and dashed back to the room, slamming the door after him. While the door was open one of the other laboratory assistants had noticed Andrei Komlin standing by the window, his clean-shaven scalp glistening. His left arm was covered with what looked like blood, and he was cradling it in his right.

Later that afternoon Komlin and Gorchinsky had quietly emerged from the neutrino room and, without a glance at anyone, walked out of the laboratory. They had both looked unhappy; Komlin's left arm was bandaged.

A month after the above occurrence a junior researcher named Vedeneyev had come across Komlin one evening in a quiet lane in Blue Park. Komlin was sitting on a bench, staring straight ahead and evidently talking to himself in a half-whisper; a large book with tattered pages lay on his knees. Vedeneyev said hullo to Komlin and sat down beside him. Komlin immediately stopped whispering and turned towards Vedeneyev, stretching his neck in a curious manner. There was something odd about Komlin's expression, and Vedeneyev had felt like bolting, but thought it would look odd, and remained seated.

'An interesting book?' he asked Komlin.

'Yes, indeed. The title is *Back-Waters*, and it's by Shih Nai-an.'

Vedeneyev, a young man who knew practically nothing about Chinese classical literature, felt more awkward than ever. All of a sudden Komlin closed the book, handed it to Vedeneyev and asked him to open it to a page at random. With a somewhat uncomfortable feeling Vedeneyev did this. Komlin glanced at the page (Vedeneyev: 'Just once, a fleeting glance'), then nodded and said, 'Follow the text.'

In his clear, ringing voice Komlin began to relate how Hu Yanchou, who attacked Ho Chen and Hsieh Pao with a whip, while Wang Ying, known as 'Short-Pawed Tiger,' and his wife, 'The Green One'... At this point Vedeneyev realized that Komlin was reciting the page from memory. He continued to the very bottom of the page without missing a single line or confusing a single name; it was all word for word and letter for letter.

'Did I slip up anywhere?' Komlin asked when he finished.

Vedeneyev, dumbfounded, shook his head. Komlin chuckled, took the book from him and walked off. Vedeneyev did not know what to make of it. He mentioned the incident to a few of his friends, who advised him to ask Komlin himself what it was all about. Komlin, however, reacted to his question with such unfeigned surprise that Vedeneyev hurried to change the subject.

What happened only a few hours before the accident was even more curious.

That afternoon Komlin, in higher spirits than anyone had ever seen him before, gave a display of conjuring skill. His audience consisted of Alexander Gorchinsky, unshaven, his eyes glowing with affection for his chief, and three young laboratory assistants, Lena, Dusya and Katya. The girls had stayed behind to get some instruments ready for the next day's experiments.

Komlin began by offering to hypnotize any member of the group, but no one volunteered.

'Very well,' he said. 'Now, Lena, I'll guess what you hide in your desk drawer.'

Two of his three guesses turned out to be right, at which Dusya remarked that he had peeked. Komlin protested that he had done nothing of the sort. When the girls laughed in disbelief he said he knew how to put out a flame just by looking at it. Dusya took a box of matches, walked over to a corner of the room, and lit a match. After burning for a moment the match went out. Everyone was much surprised. Komlin stood with arms folded on his chest and a frown on his face, in the pose of a professional conjurer.

'You must have the lungs of an ox!' exclaimed Dusya, who was standing at least ten paces away from Komlin.

At this Komlin suggested that someone should tie a handkerchief over his mouth. When this had been done, Dusya struck another match. It went out, just like the first one.

Dusya stared at him in wonder. 'Did you do it through your nose?'

Komlin removed the handkerchief, gave a chuckle and then, seizing Dusya round the waist, waltzed her about the room.

He showed them two more tricks. He dropped a match, but instead of falling straight down it floated to the right in a fairly wide arc ('You're blowing at it,' said Dusya uncertainly). Then he placed a tungsten filament on the table. Quivering, it wriggled to the edge of the table and fell to the floor. Everyone was amazed. Gorchinsky begged Komlin to tell them how he did it.

Komlin suddenly grew serious and said that now he would multiply in his head any big figures they named.

'Six hundred and fifty-four by two hundred and thirty-one and then by sixteen,' Katya suggested timidly.

'Write down the answer,' said Komlin in a queer, tense voice. 'Four, eight, one –' His voice dropped to a whisper as he finished rapidly: 'Seven, one, four, two. From right to left.'

He turned away (the girls were amazed at how he seemed to have shrunk and become stooped), shuffled over to the neutrino room and locked himself in. Gorchinsky watched him with a worried expression on his face, then announced that Komlin had multiplied the numbers correctly. Reading the figures from right to left the answer was 2,417,184.

The girls worked until ten o'clock, with Gorchinsky helping, although he was not of much use. Komlin remained in the neutrino room. They all left at ten, wishing Komlin goodnight through the door. The next morning Komlin was taken to the hospital.

Formally speaking, the result of Komlin's three months of work was neutrino acupuncture, a method of treatment based on irradiating the brain with neutrino beams. The method was extremely interesting, but what connection was there between neutrino acupuncture and Komlin's injured arm? Or his remarkable memory? Or the tricks with the matches and the filament, and the mental multiplication?

'He kept it all to himself,' the inspector muttered. 'Because he wasn't certain? Or was he afraid of endangering his comrades? A queer business. And deep, too.'

The videophone clicked. The secretary's face appeared on the screen. 'Excuse me, Comrade Rybnikov. Comrade Gorchinsky is here.'

'Send him in,' said the inspector.

II

The back of a large man in a checkered shirt with rolled-up sleeves filled the doorway. Over the broad shoulders rose a powerful neck topped by a head covered with thick black hair through which a small bald patch shone, or two bald patches, it seemed to the inspector. The man backed into the room. Before the inspector grasped what was going on the man in the checkered shirt said, 'After you, Iosif Petrovich,' and ushered the director in. Then he carefully closed the door, faced about unhurriedly, and made a short bow. The man with the checkered shirt and unusual manners had a short, fluffy moustache and wore a gloomy expression. This was Alexander Gorchinsky, Komlin's 'private' laboratory assistant.

The director sat down in an armchair and stared silently out the window. Gorchinsky stood facing the inspector.

'Take a seat,' said the inspector.

'Thank you,' Gorchinsky rumbled. He sat down, resting his hands on his knees, and stared at the inspector with cautious grey eyes.

'Are you Gorchinsky?' asked the inspector.

'Yes, Alexander Gorchinsky.'

'Glad to meet you. I'm Rybnikov, Inspector of the Labour Protection Office.'

'It's a pleasure,' Gorchinsky said.

'You're Komlin's "private" assistant, aren't you?'

'I wouldn't put it that way. I'm a laboratory assistant in the physics laboratory of the Central Brain Institute.'

The inspector glanced sideways at the director. Had he seen the flicker of a sarcastic smile on the director's face?

'What have you been working on the past three months?' he asked.

'Neutrino acupuncture.'

'Could you give me some details?'

'It's all in the report,' Gorchinsky said. 'The whole story.'

'Still, I'd like to hear some details from you,' the inspector insisted quietly.

For a few seconds they stared at each other. The inspector flushed angrily. Gorchinsky, his moustache twitching, screwed up his eyes.

'All right,' he rumbled, 'I can do that. We studied the action of focused neutrino beams on the grey and white matter of the brain as well as on the entire body of an experimental animal.'

Gorchinsky spoke in a monotone, rocking forward and backward slightly as he talked.

'While recording pathological and other changes in the body as a whole we measured the action potentials, the differential decrement and lability-instability curves of various tissues and also the relative quantities of neuroglobulin and neurostromin –'

The inspector leaned back in his chair in a mood of fury mingled with admiration. Just you wait, he thought. The director, now tapping his fingers on the table, continued to gaze out the window.

'– The latter, like the neurokeratin –' Gorchinsky boomed.

'What happened to your hands, Comrade Gorchinsky?' the inspector suddenly asked. He could not stand being on the defence. He liked to attack.

Gorchinsky looked down at his hands resting on the arms of the chair. They were covered with blue scars. He made a movement as if to hide his hands in his pockets, then slowly made them into huge fists.

'A monkey scratched me,' he said through clenched teeth. 'In the vivarium.'

'Were your experiments on animals only?'

'Yes, I experimented on animals only,' Gorchinsky put a slight stress on the 'I'.

The inspector took the bull by the horns. 'What happened to Komlin two months ago?'

Gorchinsky shrugged. 'I don't remember.'

'Let me refresh your memory. Komlin cut his hand. How did that happen?'

'He simply cut it, that's all,' Gorchinsky said abruptly.

'Gorchinsky!' the director said warningly.

'Ask Komlin himself.'

The inspector's widely-spaced grey eyes narrowed.

'You amaze me, Gorchinsky,' he said softly. 'You seem to think I want to drag something out of you that will harm Komlin, or harm you or others. That's not it at all. I'm not an expert on the central nervous system. My field is radio optics. I have no right to judge from my own impressions. My job here is to get to the bottom of what happened, not to make wild guesses. So there's no need to get all worked up. You ought to be ashamed of yourself.'

There was a long silence. The director suddenly realized the strength of this stubborn, middle-aged man. Gorchinsky evidently did too.

'What do you want to know?' he finally asked, staring at the floor.

'What is neutrino acupuncture?'

'That's Komlin's idea,' Gorchinsky said in a tired voice. 'Irradiating certain sections of the cortex with neutrino beams results in the appearance – or rather, sharply increases the body's resistance to chemical and biological poisons. Infected and poisoned dogs recovered after two or three neutrino punctures. This is something similar to the Chinese method of treatment with needles. Hence the name acupuncture. The neutrino beam plays the role of a needle. The analogy is, of course, purely superficial.'

'How is it done?'

'Neutrinic suction devices attached to the animal's shaven skull focus the neutrino beam on a layer of grey brain matter. It's very complicated, and the hardest part of it was finding the sections and spots in the cortex that stimulate phagocytic mobilization in the required direction.'

'That's extremely interesting,' said the inspector. 'What diseases can this cure?'

'Lots of them,' said Gorchinsky after a pause. 'Komlin believes that neutrino acupuncture mobilizes forces in the body about which we know nothing. Not phagocytes and not nerve stimulation, but something far more powerful. But he has not yet … He says that any disease can be cured with neutrino beams – toxic conditions, heart disease, malignant tumours.'

'Cancer?'

'Yes. Burns, too. And it may even be possible to restore lost organs. The body has enormous stabilizing powers, he says, and the key to them lies in the cortex. All you have to do is to find the places in the cortex to which the beams should be directed.'

'Neutrino acupuncture,' the inspector said slowly, as though testing the sound of the words. 'Splendid, Comrade Gorchinsky,' he said more energetically. 'Thank you very much.' (Gorchinsky gave a wry smile.) 'Now tell me about Komlin. You were the first to see him, weren't you?'

'Yes. When I came to work that morning I found Komlin sitting, or rather lying, in an armchair at the table – '

'In the neutrino room?'

'That's right, in the neutrino generator room. Suction devices were attached to his skull. The generator was switched on. I thought he was dead. I summoned a doctor. That's all.'

Gorchinsky's voice shook on those last words. This was so unexpected that the inspector paused before asking his next question. The director was still tapping his fingers, his gaze fixed on the window.

'Do you know what kind of experiment Komlin was conducting?'

'No, I don't. Laboratory scales and two matchboxes stood on the table in front of him. One of the boxes was empty.'

'Matches, you say?' The inspector glanced at the director and then back at Gorchinsky. 'Matches? What have matches to do with it?'

'Yes, matches,' Gorchinsky said. 'They were lying in a heap. Some were stuck together in twos and threes. Six matches lay in one pan of the scales. There was a sheet of paper with figures on it. Komlin was weighing the matches. I checked that.'

'Matches,' muttered the inspector. 'Why did he want to do that, I wonder? Know anything about it?'

'No,' said Gorchinsky.

The inspector rubbed his chin reflectively. 'The other laboratory assistants told me about those tricks with fire and with matches. Komlin was evidently working on something else beside neutrino acupuncture. But what?'

Gorchinsky said nothing.

'He must have experimented on himself many times. His scalp is covered with traces of those suction devices of yours.'

Gorchinsky still said nothing.

'Did you ever notice that Komlin was a wizard at mental arithmetic? I mean, before he showed you those tricks.'

'No, I never noticed anything of the sort. Well, now you know as much about it as I do. Komlin experimented on himself. He tried the neutrino beam on himself. He slashed his arm with a razor and then focused a neutrino beam on it to see how the wound would heal. It didn't work that time. He was also doing something else, on the side, about which none of us knew. Not even I. I only know it's connected with neutrino irradiation. That's all.'

'Did anyone else know about it?' asked the inspector.

'No, not a soul.'

'Do you know what kind of experiments Komlin conducted without you?'

'No.'

'That's all,' said the inspector. 'You may go.'

Gorchinsky rose and, without lifting his eyes, turned towards the door. The inspector gazed at the back of his head. Yes, the man had two bald spots, just as it had seemed to him the first time.

The director still stared out of the window. A small helicopter hovered above the square. Its silvery fuselage sparkling in the sun, it turned slowly on its axis and landed. The cabin door opened. The pilot, in a grey flying suit, jumped lightly to the ground. He walked across the square to the Institute, lighting a cigarette on the way. The director recognized the inspector's helicopter. Must have gone to refuel, he said to himself.

'Could neutrino acupuncture lead to mental disturbances?' the inspector asked.

'Hardly,' replied the director. 'Komlin says it doesn't.'

The inspector leaned back in his chair and stared up at the ceiling.

'Gorchinsky won't be in any condition to work today,' said the director in a low voice. 'You shouldn't have –'

'Yes, I should have,' the inspector insisted. 'You surprise me, Comrade Leman. How many bald spots do you think a man ordinarily has? Those scars on his hands, too. A worthy pupil of Komlin's indeed.'

'They're in love with what they are doing,' said the director.

The inspector stared at the director in silence for a few seconds, his face muscles working. 'Perhaps. But it's not the right way to be in love with it. It's the old-fashioned way. And you don't love your staff the way you should, Comrade Leman. We're a rich country – the richest in the world. We provide you with all the equipment you need and as many experimental animals as you want. Experiment and investigate to your heart's content. But why do you expend researchers so light-mindedly? Who gave you permission to treat human beings that way?'

'I—'

'Why do you think you can break laws passed by the Supreme Soviet? When will an end be put to this disgraceful state of affairs?'

'But this is the first case in our Institute,' protested the director.

The inspector shook his head. 'But what about other research institutes? Or factories? Did you know that Komlin is the eighth case in the past six months? It's barbarous! Barbarous heroism! Men climb into automatic rockets, into autobathyscaphes, into atomic reactors going critical.' He forced a crooked smile. 'They're seeking the shortest way to victory over nature. And they often pay for it with their lives. Your Komlin is the eighth. Can we tolerate this?'

The director scowled. 'There are circumstances when it's inevitable. Think of the doctors who injected themselves with cholera and plague.'

'Huh – historical analogies! But times have changed altogether.'

Both were silent for a while. Twilight was falling. Vague grey shadows appeared in the far corners of the room.

The director broke the silence. 'I ordered Komlin's safe to be opened. His notes were brought to me. You'll probably find them interesting.'

'Of course,' said the inspector.

The director smiled faintly. 'There's a great deal that is – hm, specific. I've glanced through the notes, and I'm afraid you'll find them rough going. I'll take them home with me and summarize them for you, if you wish.'

The inspector was clearly pleased.

'Only don't count too much on me. Those neutrino beams – they were like a bolt from the blue to all of us. None of us had imagined anything like them. Komlin's the world pioneer in this. It may be quite beyond me.'

The director left.

Komlin's notes might help, the inspector reflected. He very much hoped they would. He visualized Komlin with those suction devices pressed to his bare scalp, weighing matches that were stuck together. This was not acupuncture but something quite new, and Komlin must have had doubts about it himself if he conducted such frightful experiments on himself in secret.

But this was a wonderful time to be living in. The fourth generation of Communists. Bold, dedicated men with never a thought for themselves. They braved the unknown with such enthusiasm that it took tremendous effort to restrain them. The human race should gain mastery over nature not by sacrificing its best sons but by using powerful machines and precise instruments. Not simply because the living could accomplish far more than the dead but because Man was the most precious thing in the world.

The inspector rose stiffly and moved towards the door. He moved unhurriedly because it was natural to him, and also because of his age and his leg.

'Those old wounds,' he muttered as he hobbled across the floor of the empty reception room, dragging his right foot.

III

Next morning, at the very hour when the doctors, still in the dark as to the reason for Komlin's illness, were overjoyed to note that their patient was recovering his speech, the inspector and the director again sat at the long bare table in the latter's office. A notebook lay open on the inspector's knees. In front of the director lay a heap of papers – Andrei Komlin's notes, diagrams, sketches and drawings.

The director spoke rapidly, at times disjointedly; his eyes, red-rimmed from a sleepless night, were fixed on a point beyond the inspector. Every now and then he halted, as if to listen in amazement to his own words. As the inspector listened, the chain of events became more and more clear to him. Here is what he learned.

Komlin had not taken up irradiation of the brain with neutrino beams by accident. The method of obtaining conveniently compact neutrino beams had been discovered only a short time before and very little was known about it. When he got the neutrino generator Komlin decided to test it at once.

He expected a great deal from his experiments. High-energy irradiation by nucleons, electrons and gamma rays disrupts the molecular and intranuclear structure of brain protein and destroys the brain. It can only produce pathological changes in the body. Experiments have confirmed this. The neutrino, an uncharged elementary particle with zero rest mass, is a different matter. Komlin calculated that the neutrino would not call forth either explosive processes or molecular reorganization. He hoped it would arouse moderate stimulation of the nuclei of brain proteins, intensify the nuclear fields and perhaps arouse in brain matter completely new power fields, hitherto unknown to science. All of Komlin's conjectures had been brilliantly confirmed.

'There's a lot in Komlin's notes I do not understand,' said the director, 'and some things I simply cannot believe. For these reasons I'll tell you only about the main points and about anything that might shed light on those mysterious tricks.

'When he began experiments with animals Komlin immediately got the promising idea of neutrino acupuncture. A monkey injured its paw, and the wound healed remarkably fast. Spots on its lungs, traces of tuberculosis, which is common in monkeys in a temperate climate, disappeared just as fast.

'Several dogs were given various types of biological poisons. The neutrino "needle" cured them very quickly. The "Komlin needle" (as Gorchinsky named the method) cured tuberculosis in monkeys dozens of times faster than the most effective antibiotics.

'In that report of his Komlin put forward a supposition that the bodies of human beings and animals possess hidden curative powers science still knows nothing about but whose existence has been revealed by the experiments in neutrino acupuncture. He outlined a detailed programme of going over from experiments on animals to experiments on human beings, starting with the simplest and safest neutrino treatment and leading up to complex and combined forms. Large teams of doctors, physiologists and psychologists were to be drawn into the experiments. But –'

The inspector was right. Komlin had been working on something else besides neutrino acupuncture. Experiments with the neutrino generator very soon showed that a remarkable mobilization of the body's curative powers was not the only result of irradiating the brain with neutrino beams. Some of the experimental animals were behaving strangely. Those cured after short-term neutrino treatment usually behaved normally, but the 'favourites', the animals on which numerous experiments of various kinds were made, amazed the two researchers. Whereas the young Gorchinsky saw only amusing or irritating tricks of nature, Komlin's intuition told him he stood on the threshold of a significant discovery.

A dog named Gene (short for Generator) began to do circus stunts no one had ever taught him. He walked on his hind legs, and even on his front legs, and 'shook hands'. Once Gorchinsky found him doing a strange thing. He was sitting on a stool, staring fixedly in front of him and rising at regular intervals to give a short bark. He did not recognize Gorchinsky and growled at him.

Komlin was amazed by the behaviour of the baboon Cora. Immediately after being irradiated Cora sat in her cage chattering at Komlin. Suddenly a shock seemed to go through her. She stared at something in the corner, growled loudly, then piteously, and started moving backwards. Neither threats nor caresses affected her. Cora ran into a corner, curled herself into a ball and sat there a whole hour, staring fixedly at something invisible, from time to time uttering a sharp howl, always a danger signal. The symptoms passed, but Komlin noticed that now Cora looked first at the ill-starred corner whenever she entered her cage.

One day Gorchinsky came running to call Komlin to the monkey room. A young baboon was sitting in a cage eating a banana. There was nothing odd about either the baboon or the banana, but the attendant and Gorchinsky both maintained they had witnessed something altogether fantastic. They had found, they said, the baboon watching with obvious interest a piece of paper that was slowly but surely moving across the floor towards it. As the baboon stretched out a paw to the paper Gorchinsky hurried to find Komlin. The attendant said the baboon had swallowed the paper. At any rate, it could not be found. An attempt to reproduce the amazing phenomenon failed.

'Here is what Komlin wrote in this connection' said the director, handing the inspector a sheet of ruled paper.

The inspector read: 'Mass hallucination? Or something new? Mass hallucination including a baboon is amazing in itself. There's something here. We won't find out anything from monkeys or dogs. Have to try it myself.'

Komlin began experimenting on himself. Gorchinsky soon learned of this and immediately followed his chief's example. They had a brief quarrel on this score. Gorchinsky finally promised not to experiment any more, while Komlin promised to try only the simplest, shortest and safest irradiations. Not until the day of the accident did Gorchinsky learn that Komlin had dropped neutrino acupuncture.

'There is really very little information in Komlin's notes about the astounding results of his experiments,' said the director. 'The notes become more and more fragmentary and disjointed. You feel Komlin cannot find words with which to describe his sensations and impressions. His deductions are unclear.'

Komlin devoted several pages torn out of a notebook to describing the remarkable memory he acquired after one of the experiments. He wrote: 'After one glance at an object I can see it in all its details when I turn away or close my eyes. After one glance at a page of a book I can read it from the "image" imprinted in my memory. I don't believe I shall ever forget several chapters from *Back-Waters* or the entire four-place table of logarithms from the first to the last figure. What enormous possibilities!'

Among the notes there were observations of a general nature. 'Memory, thought, reflexes and habits,' Komlin wrote in a firm hand, as though meditating, 'have a definite material foundation that is not yet clear to us. That is elementary. The neutrino beam seeps into that foundation and creates a new memory, new reflexes and new habits. That is what happened to the dog Gene, to Cora and to myself (mnemogenesis – the creation of a false memory).'

The last few pages, clipped together, dealt with the most interesting and amazing of all Komlin's discoveries. The director picked them up and held them above his head.

'Here,' he said solemnly, 'is the answer to your questions. This is something in the nature of an outline or rough draft of a future paper. Shall I read it?'

'Do, please,' said the inspector.

'"You cannot will yourself to wink unless the muscle is there. The nervous system plays the role of an impulse trigger, nothing more. A tiny discharge leads to the contraction of a muscle that is capable of moving tens of kilograms, of performing an enormous amount of work compared with the energy of the nervous impulse. The nervous system is the fuse in the powder-magazine, the muscle is the powder, and the contraction of the muscle is the explosion.

'"Intensification of the process of thinking intensifies the electromagnetic field arising somewhere in the cells of the brain. These are action potentials. The very fact we are able to discover this means the process of thinking affects matter. Not directly, though. When I solve a differential equation the brain field grows stronger, and the needle of the instrument that measures it moves. Isn't that a mental motor? The field is the muscle of the brain!

'"I have acquired the ability to multiply with great speed. How I do it I cannot say. I just multiply. 1,919 multiplied by 237 equals 454,803. It took me four seconds by my stop-watch to multiply that. It's wonderful but not altogether clear. The electromagnetic field grows much stronger, but what about the other fields of the brain, if they exist? The 'muscle' is developed. But how is one to control it?

'"Eureka! A tungsten filament weighing 4.732 grams. Suspended in a vacuum on a nylon thread. I simply looked at it and it deviated from the initial position by about 15 degrees. That is already something. The generator regime . ..."'

The director read off a string of figures, then interrupted to say that Gorchinsky had seen a vacuum hood with a tungsten filament, but it had later disappeared. Komlin must have taken it apart.

He continued reading:

'"The psychodynamic field, the muscle of the brain, is functioning. I don't know how I do it. There's nothing strange about not knowing. What do you have to do to bend your arm? No one can tell you. To bend my arm I bend my arm. That's all. The bicep is a very obedient muscle. Muscles have to be trained. The field of the brain also has to be taught to work. But how?

'"There is not a single thing I can lift by a 'mental effort'. I can only move things. But not as I wish. A match or a piece of paper always moves to the right. Metal moves towards me. It works best with matches. Why?

'"The psychodynamic field operates through a glass hood but not through a newspaper. To influence an object I have to see it. I put out a candle on the other side of the neutrino room.

'"I am certain the possibilities of the brain are inexhaustible. All one needs is training and a definite activization, stimulation of the protein molecules and neurons. Some day man will be able to compute better than any computer; he will be able to read and understand a whole library in a few minutes.

'"This is terribly exhausting. My head is splitting. Sometimes I can work only under constant irradiation and at the end I am sweating. I must not break down. Am working with matches today." '

On this Komlin's notes ended.

The inspector sat with his eyes closed. Komlin's idea was probably destined to yield rich fruit, he thought. That was all in the future, though. Meanwhile, Komlin was in hospital. The inspector opened his eyes, and his glance fell on the sheet of ruled paper. 'We won't find out anything from monkeys or dogs. Have to try it myself.' Perhaps Komlin was right.

No, Komlin was wrong. Wrong as wrong could be. He shouldn't have taken such a risk, at any rate, not alone. Even where neither machines nor animals (the inspector again glanced at the sheet of ruled paper) could help, man had no right to play with death. Komlin had been doing just that. And you, Professor Leman, will not remain director of the Institute because you do not understand that and appear to be filled with admiration for Komlin. I tell you, comrades, that we shall not allow you to brave fire. In this day and age we can afford to be super-cautious. You and your lives are more precious to us than the most magnificent discoveries.

Aloud the inspector said: 'We must draw up a statement of the inquiry. The cause of the accident is clear to us.'

'Yes,' said the director. 'Komlin collapsed while lifting six matches.'

The director accompanied the inspector out of the building. They emerged into the square and moved unhurriedly towards the helicopter. The director was silent and absent-minded. He found it hard to keep in step with the inspector's shuffle. Gorchinsky, dishevelled and gloomy, caught up with them just as they reached the helicopter. The inspector, who had already said goodbye to the director, climbed into the cabin with difficulty. 'Those old wounds are acting up again,' he muttered.

'Komlin's much better now,' Gorchinsky said in a low voice. 'He'll be up and about in a month from now.'

'Yes, I know,' said the inspector. With a sigh of relief he finally settled himself in his seat.

The pilot quickly climbed into his seat.

'Will you write a report?' Gorchinsky asked.

'Yes, I will,' the inspector replied.

'I see.' Gorchinsky, his moustache twitching, looked the inspector in the eye. 'I say,' he blurted out, 'are you the Rybnikov who discharged those thingamajigs in Kustanai in '68, without waiting for the automatic machines?'

'I say, Gorchinsky,' the director snapped.

'And that was when your leg was injured, wasn't it?'

'Gorchinsky, stop it, I tell you!'

The inspector did not reply. He slammed the cabin door shut and leaned back in the soft seat.

The director and Gorchinsky stood in the square, staring up at the big silver beetle as it soared above the white and rose-coloured seventeen-storey tower of the Institute and disappeared from sight in the late afternoon sky.

HANDS

Yuly Daniel (1925–1988)

Translated by Brian James Baer

Coeval and co-defendant of Andrei Sinyavsky, poet, writer and translator, field veteran of WWII, **Yuly Daniel** also published his writings in the West under the pseudonym Nicolay Arzhak, was exposed by the KGB, accused of anti-Soviet propaganda, brought together with Sinyavsky in a celebrated show trial and sentenced to five years in labor camps.

Unlike his counterpart, Daniel was not granted an exit ticket, and reunited with Sinyavsky only when the latter came to his grave a month after the funeral ceremony, unable to arrive on time due to the obstructions of the staunch Soviet bureaucracy.

Daniel's most famous prose is a dystopian novella *This is Moscow Speaking*, tracing the murderous legacy of the Stalinist past within the upgraded Communist system.

You, Sergei, you're an educated guy, polite. And so you don't say anything; you don't ask any questions. But our guys at the factory, they'll give it to you straight: "So," they say, "is Vaska drunk to his fingertips?!" They're talking about my hands. Do you think I didn't notice how you looked at my hands then turned away? And now you're trying to avoid looking at them. I understand everything, my friend. You do that out of tact, so you don't embarrass me. But go ahead, look—it's okay. I won't get offended. And, well, you don't see something like this every day. That, my friend, isn't from drinking. I don't drink very often, mostly when I'm with pals or on special occasions—like now with you. How could we not drink to our reunion? My friend, I remember everything. How we worked together in surveillance near the frontline, how you spoke French with that White army soldier, and how we took Yaroslavl ... Do you remember how you spoke up at that political meeting, you took me by the hand—I happened to be standing next to you—and said: "With these hands ..." Ah, yes. Well, Seryozha, pour us another round. Or I'll start sniveling. I've forgotten what it's called, this shaking—the medical word for it. Well, anyway, I wrote it down; I'll show it to you later ...

So, why did this happen to me? There was an incident. If I were to tell you in order, then I'd begin with when we were demobilized in 1921, the year of victory, and I returned immediately to my factory. Well, there I was treated, needless to say, with honor and respect as a hero of the Revolution, as well as a member of the party and a politically conscious worker. It can't be denied, of course, that there were some brains that needed to be straightened out. There were all kinds of gossips running around: "So," they'd say, "we finished fighting, and this is all the food we get. There's no bread. Nothing ..." Well, I cut that business short. I was always firm. You won't lead me through their Menshevik chaff. No way. Pour yourself another. Don't wait for me.

I'd only worked there a year, no more, when—*bam!*—I'm called to the Regional Committee. "Well," they said, "here's a train ticket for you, Malinin." "The party," they said, "is mobilizing you, Vasily Semenovich Malinin, into the ranks of the valorous Extraordinary Commission to fight against counter-revolutionaries." "We wish you," they said, "success in the struggle against the international bourgeoisie, and give our humble regards to Comrade Dzerzhinsky if you should see him." Well, what was I to do? I was a member of the Party. "Yes comrade," I said, "I will fulfill the orders of the Party." I took the ticket, ran back to the factory, said goodbye to the guys, and left. On my way, I imagined how I would mercilessly fish out all those counter-revolutionaries so they couldn't defile our young Soviet state.

Well, I arrived. I really did see Felix Edmundovich Dzerzhinsky, and passed on from our Regional Committee what I'd been told to pass on. He shook my hand, thanked me, and then he ordered all of us—there were thirty of us being mobilized by the Party into formation and said, "You can't build a house on a swamp; you have to," he said, "first drain the swamp, and then," he said, "when you do that you'll have to destroy all the toads and snakes, because," he said, "it's an iron-clad necessity. And we must all," he said, "put our hands to the task ..." You see, he told us a kind of fairy tale or anecdote, and, of course, everything was understood. He was a stern one; he didn't smile.

After that, they split us up. Who, what, and where, they asked us. "Education," they said, "what kind?" "I got my education, you know, in the war with Germany and in the Civil War, and on the factory line—that's all my education. I finished two grades at our parish school ..." So they assigned me to the special service, and they told me, to put it simply, that I would be executing sentences. It wasn't such hard work, but I wouldn't call it easy either. It affects your spirit. It's one thing, as you remember, at the front: it's either him or you. But here ... Well, I got used to it, of course. I would walk behind them through the courtyard, thinking and repeating to myself: "You *have* to do it, Vasily, you *have* to. If you don't finish him off now, that bastard will destroy the whole Soviet Republic." I got used to it. I drank, of course; you need it. They gave us alcohol. As far as some kind of special rations, they say that Chekists get chocolate and white rolls, but that's all bourgeois fabrication: our rations were the usual rations, normal, soldier's rations—bread, millet, and dried roach. But they did give us alcohol. You can't do this kind of work without it, as you yourself understand. Oh, well.

I worked in that way for seven months and then suddenly the incident occurred. We were ordered to execute a group of priests. For counter-revolutionary agitation. For malicious activity. They were probably sent from Tikhon. Or they were just against socialism, I don't know. In a word—enemies. There were twelve of them. Our boss gave us orders: "You," he said, "Malinin, take three. You, Vlasenko, you, Golovchiner, and you ..." I forgot the name of the fourth guy. He was Latvian, with a foreign last name. Not one of ours. He and Golovchiner went first. Things were arranged like this: in the sentry booth—it was in the middle. On the one side, you see, was the room where the prisoners were held, and on the other was the exit to the courtyard. We took them out one at a time. We had to drag the bodies away or else when you brought out the next one, he'd see the bodies and begin to struggle and try to break free—you'll have no end of trouble, which is understandable. It's better when they're quiet. So, then, you see, Golovchiner and that Latvian finished theirs off, then it was my turn. I'd drunk some alcohol before that. It's not that I was afraid or I was attached to religion. No, I'm a Party man, strong, I don't believe in that rot—god and all that stuff, angels, and archangels. All the same, I wasn't feeling myself. It was easy for Golovchiner—he's a Jew. They say they don't even have icons. I don't know if that's true, but I'm sitting there, drinking, and all kinds of stupid stuff comes into my head: how my dead mother would take me to the village church and I'd kiss the hand of our priest, Father Vasily. He was an old man and he always called me his namesake ... Ah, yes. Well, I went, you see, for the first one, then led him out. Then I went back, had a smoke, and led out the second one. I went back again, drank a shot—but something was bothering me. "Wait a minute, guys," I said. "I'll be right back." I put my Mauser on the table and went out. I'd drunk too much, I thought. I'll stick my fingers down my throat, throw up, wash my face and hands, and everything will be back in order. So I stepped out, did all that, but, no, it didn't help. Okay, I thought, the hell with it, I'll finish up everything, then take a nap. I picked up my Mauser and went for the third one.

The third one was still young, distinguished-looking—this priest was strong, handsome. I led him down the hall, and watching how he lifted his floor-length cassock over the door jamb, I felt sick to my stomach. I couldn't say why. We walked out into the courtyard. He lifted his head and looked at the sky. "March," I said. "Father, don't look around. You," I said, "have prayed your own way into heaven." That was a joke, you see, to keep my spirits up. Why—I don't know. I'd never acted like that before—had a conversation with a condemned man. So, I let him walk three steps ahead, as arranged, placed my Mauser between his shoulder blades and fired. The Mauser—you know how it fires—like a cannon! The recoil almost rips your arm from your shoulder. I just stood there looking—the priest who'd just been shot turns around and starts walking toward me. Of course, that happens from time to time. Some fall down flat immediately, while others spin around like a top; but it sometimes happens that they start to walk, swaying like a drunk. But this one walked toward me with small steps, gliding along in his cassock.

I'd shot someone else. "What are you doing?" I said. "Father, stop!" Once again I put the Mauser up to him—up to his chest. But he tears open the top of his cossack, baring his curly-hairy chest, then goes and screams at the top of his lungs: "Shoot me," he cries, "Antichrist! Kill me! I am your Christ!" I was confused, and I shot him once more, then again. But he was still walking toward me! No wounds, no blood, and he goes and prays: "Lord, You stopped the bullet from those black hands! I take on this suffering for You! One cannot kill an immortal." And something else ... I don't remember anymore how I discharged the cartridge; I only know for sure that I couldn't have missed—at point-blank range. So he's standing in front of me, his eyes burning like a wolf's, and there's some kind of glow coming from his head—I realized later that he was blocking the sun; this was all happening at sunset. "Your hands," he cried, "are covered in blood! Look at your hands!" I threw the Mauser on the ground, ran into the sentry room, collided with someone in the doorway, then ran inside. The guys looked at me like I was crazy and broke into raucous laughter. I grabbed a rifle from the stack and shouted: "Take me this minute," I screamed, "to Dzerzhinsky or I'll bayonet you all!" Well, they took away the rifle and rushed me away. I entered his office, broke free of my comrades, and said to him, shaking all over and stammering: "Shoot me," I said, "Felix Edmundovich, I can't kill a priest!" As soon as I said that, I fell to the ground and don't remember anything more. I came to in the hospital. The doctors said: "A nervous breakdown."

They treated me, if truth be told, very well, attentively. Care and cleanliness, and food was healthy for the time. They cured everything, but my hands, you see, still shake. The breakdown should have gone away, but it went into my hands. Of course, they fired me from the Cheka. They didn't need hands like these. Needless to say, I couldn't go back to the factory line either. They assigned me to the factory warehouse. Well, so what? I do my work there. True, there are all kinds of forms, reports, that I can't fill out myself—because of my hands. I have a helper for that—she's a bright girl. So that's how I live, my friend. As for the priest, I found out later what happened. There was nothing divine about it. When I went to the latrine, the guys just took the cartridge out of the Mauser and put in a different one—with blanks. It was a joke, you see. So what. I'm not mad at them. A youthful prank. It was no picnic for them either, so they thought this up. No, I'm not offended by it. It's just that my hands ... they're not fit for work anymore.

AUTUMN IN THE OAK WOODS

Yury Kazakov (1927–1982)

Translated by Bernard Isaacs

Probably the best lyricist of Soviet prose, the direct heir of Bunin, and obsessed with Bunin's prose emerging from the oblivion of the early Soviet years, **Yury Kazakov** wrote short prose forms, and travelled a lot in the Russian North, which became his inspiration and a refuge from the hard world of Soviet literature.

In his late years Kazakov mostly abandoned writing and lived alone at his dacha in the suburbs of Moscow. Today the Kazakov prize is given annually to the author of the best short story written in Russian.

I took the pail to get some water from the spring. I was happy that night, because she was coming by the night boat. But I knew what happiness was, how fickle it could be, and so I purposely took the pail, as if I never hoped for her coming, and was just going out to get some water. Somehow things were shaping too good for me that autumn.

That late autumn night was slate-black, and I did not feel like leaving the house, but nevertheless I went out. I took a long time setting the candle in the lantern, and when I had set and lighted it, the glass misted over for a minute and the dim patch of light blinked and blinked until the candle burned up and the glass dried and became transparent.

I purposely did not put the light out indoors, and the illumined window was well in view as I descended to the Oka by the avenue of larches. My lantern threw a fluttering light in front and on the sides, and I must have looked like a pointsman. The heap of dank maple and larch leaves, which even in the pale light of the lantern looked golden, gave off a deadened sound under my boots, and the barberries glowed redly on the bare bushes.

Walking alone in the night with a lantern gave you a creepy feeling. The only sound was the rustle of your boots, you alone were illumined and in view, while everything else lay hidden, watching you.

The path dipped steeply, and the light in my window soon vanished. Then the avenue came to an end, giving place to a disarray of bushes, oakwood and firs. The last tall stalks of the daisies, the tips of fir branches and various naked twigs flipped against my pail, and a "Boom! Boom!" now muffled, now clear, could be heard a long way off in the stillness of the night. The winding footpath grew steeper, the birch-trees denser, their white stems floating out of the darkness. Then the birches, too, came to an end, the path became stony, the air freshened, and although I could see nothing beyond the lantern's patch of light, I could feel a wide-open space in front of me – I came out onto the river.

I could now see the distant buoy on the right, its red light doubled by its reflection in the water. Then the buoy on my side came into view, much nearer, faintly winking, and I saw the river.

I walked along the bank through the wet grass between the willow shrubs to the place where the boat usually put in if anybody got off on our out-of-the-way side. The spring babbled and gurgled monotonously in the dark. I put the lantern down, went to the spring, drew some water, had a drink and wiped my mouth with my sleeve. Then I put the wet pail down beside the lantern and started to look in the direction of the distant landing-stage.

The boat was already standing near the landing stage, its red and green sidelights faintly visible. I sat down and started smoking. My hands shook and were cold. It suddenly occurred to me that if she wasn't on the boat and somebody saw my lantern from there, they would think I wanted to board the boat and would come alongside. So I extinguished the lantern. It got dark immediately, and only the buoys all along the river punctured the darkness as if with needles. A vibrant silence reigned; at that late hour I must have been the only person on the bank for miles around. Up there, beyond the oak wood, lay a dark little village, with everyone in it long asleep, and only my house on the edge of it had a light burning.

I suddenly pictured to myself her whole long journey to me – how she travelled from Arkhangelsk, slept or sat by the window in the railway coach and talked with somebody. How she, like myself, was thinking all these days about our meeting. And how she was now sailing along the Oka, seeing the banks I had written her about when inviting her to come. How she went out on deck with the wind blowing in her face, wafting up the smell of damp oak woods. And what conversations all the way down, in the warmth, behind misted glass, with people explaining to her where to get off and where to spend the night if no one met her.

Then I recalled the North, my wanderings there, and how I lived at the fishery, and she and I speared lancet fish during the white nights. The fishermen were fast asleep, snoring and groaning, and we, not waiting for the tide to run out, put to sea in the *karbas*. She rowed noiselessly, while I stared into the depths, among the clumps of seaweeds, searching for the outlines of a fish. I quietly moved the spear within striking distance and plunged the white blade into the head of the lancet fish, then, with an effort, pulled it out of the water. It spattered water over us, struggling ferociously at the end of the spear, opening terrifying jaws, coiling up into a ring and then straightening like a spring and resembling a triton, and afterwards, in the bottom of the boat, slithering about, squirming and snapping rapaciously at everything within reach.

And I recalled the whole of that year, what a happy year it had been for me, what a lot of stories I had managed to write and how many more I would probably still write in the remaining quiet secluded days on this river, in the midst of this scenery, now already faded and winter-boding.

Night lay around me, and my cigarette, when I drew at it, brightly lit up my hands, my face and my boots, but did not prevent me seeing the stars – and they were such a brilliant multitude that autumn that one could see their ashy light, the starlit river, the trees, the white boulders on the bank, and the dark squares of the fields on the hillsides, and it was much darker and more fragrant in the gullies than in the fields.

This set me thinking that the most important thing in life was not how long you would live – thirty, fifty or eighty years – because it was very little anyhow and in any case it was going to be terrible dying – but how many such nights life would give you.

The boat had moved away from the landing stage. It was still too far off to catch its movement. It seemed to be standing still, but stood away from the landing stage and that meant it was now coming up the river towards me. Presently I caught the high-pitched sound of the diesel, and all of a sudden a fear fell upon me that she would not be coming, that she was not on board the boat and that I was waiting for nothing. I suddenly saw the distance and all the days she had to overcome to reach me, and realised how precarious it all was – those plans of mine for a happy life here together.

"How can it be!" I said aloud, and got up. I could not sit still, and started to walk along the bank. "How can it be!" I repeated helplessly from time to time and kept glancing at the boat, thinking how ridiculous I would look going back alone with my pail of water, and how empty my house would be. Would we be so unlucky again after all these days of waiting and frustration?

I recalled how I had left the North for home three months ago, how she had come unexpectedly to the village from the fishing place to see me off, how she had stood on the planked footway while I boarded the motor boat to take me down to the steamer standing in the distant roadstead, and how she kept repeating: "Where are you going? You don't understand anything! You don't understand! Where are you going?" And it was on the motor boat, amid the leave-takings, the women's tears, the boys' shouts and all the hubbub, that I realised I was acting childish in going away and dimly hoped to mend things somehow in the future.

The boat was now near, and I was no longer walking – I was standing on the brink, on the very edge of the cliff over the black water, staring at it fixedly, and breathing loud from excitement and hope.

The sound of the engine suddenly dropped a tone lower, a searchlight flashed on in the deck-house, and a smoky beam slashed across the bank, skipping from tree to tree. The boat was looking for a place to draw alongside. It kept bearing to the right. The searching beam struck me in the face, and I turned away, then looked back again. A sailor was standing on the upper deck, making ready to lower the gangplank. Next to him, dressed in something light, stood she.

The boat nosed deep into the bank, the sailor adjusted the gangplank and helped her down, while I snatched the suitcase, carried it a little way off and placed it next to the pail. This done, I slowly turned round. The blinding searchlight was in my eyes and I couldn't see her properly. She came towards me, throwing a gigantic wavering shadow on the wooded slope. I wanted to kiss her, but changed my mind. I didn't like doing it under that searchlight. We just stood side by side, shading our eyes with our hands, and looked at the boat with a strained smile. The boat backed water, the searchlight beam crept aside, then went out altogether, the diesel below resumed its song and the boat, with a long row of lighted windows in the lower lounges, quickly moved away up the river. We were left alone.

"Well, good evening!" I said embarrassedly.

She stood up on tiptoe, gripped my shoulders painfully and kissed my eyes.

"Come along," I said, and gave a cough. "It's so dark, damn it. Wait a minute, I'll light the lantern. ..."

I lit the lantern and it misted over again. We had to wait until the candle burned up and the glass dried and became transparent. Then we started off – I in front with the suitcase and the lantern, she behind with the pail of water.

"It isn't too heavy for you?" I asked after a minute.

"Go along!" she said huskily.

She always had a low husky voice, and generally she was hard and strong, and for a long time I had not loved her for it. I loved softness in women. But now, here, on the bank of the river, at night, when we were walking towards the house one behind the other, after all those days of anger, separation, letters and strange sinister dreams, her voice, her strong body and rough hands, her northern pronunciation, were like the breath of a bird from a different clime – a wild, grey-feathered straggler from the autumnal flock.

We turned right into the ravine, up which ran a short path, paved nobody knew by whom and when – a narrow path overgrown with walnut, pine and rowan trees. We started climbing it in the dark, barely lighting our way with the lantern, and above us flowed a narrow starry river with black pine branches floating across it, covering and uncovering the stars in turn.

We came out, panting, onto the avenue of larches and walked along side by side.

I suddenly felt a desire to show her everything and tell her about the people hereabouts, about various little incidents.

"Smell this," I said.

"Smells like wine," she said, somewhat breathless from the walk. "I smelt it long ago, while I was still on the boat."

"They're leaves. Come over here, will you!"

We left the luggage on the path, jumped over a ditch and plunged into the bushes, lighting our way with the lantern.

"It's somewhere round about here. ..." I muttered.

"Mushrooms," her astonished voice said behind me.

At last I found what I was looking for. They were the white feathers of a chicken scattered in the grass amid the pine needles and yellow leaves.

"Look," I said, turning the light on them. "We have a poultry farm here in the village. The chickens have grown up and they've been let out. Now a fox comes here every day and stalks in the bushes. When the chickens scatter about the forest he catches one of them. And gobbles it up right away."

I pictured that fox with grey on his dark muzzle, licking his chops and snorting to blow the fluff off his nose.

"He should be killed!" she said.

"I have a shotgun, you and I will take rambles in the woods, maybe we'll have luck."

We got back onto the path and continued on our way. The lighted window of my house came into view, and I started thinking of what we would do when we got there. I suddenly felt like having a drink. I had some ashberry brandy at home. I had made it myself. It was good to pick ashberries in the woods, bring them home, squash them in a juice extractor and pour the yellow frothy juice off into a bottle with vodka.

"It's winter with us," she said as if in surprise. "The Dvina has frozen, just a lane in the middle which the icebreakers have made. Everything white, and the lane black. And reeking. And when a ship goes down the black water the dogs come running out onto the ice at once. Three at a time, for some reason."

Her northern accent helped me to picture the Dvina, the steamers, Arkhangelsk, her home village by the White Sea. The tall two-storeyed empty cottages, the black walls, the silence and seclusion.

"Has the ice appeared already?" I asked. "At sea?"

"It's beginning to harden," she, too, said musingly, probably thinking of what she had left behind. "I'll have to go back by reindeer, if –"

She fell silent. I waited a bit, listening to her breathing and footsteps, then asked:

"If what?"

"Nothing," she said slowly and more huskily than ever. "If the ice thickens, that's what I meant!"

We stamped our feet on the porch and went inside.

"O-oo!" she said, looking round and taking off her shawl. She always uttered that deep slow "oo" of hers when surprised or glad.

The house was a small and old one. I had rented it from a Muscovite who lived in it only during the summer. There was hardly any furniture in it, just a couple of old cots, a table and chairs. The walls were attacked by beetles and covered with a white floury dust. But then there was a radio receiver, electric light, a stove, and several fat old books which I loved to read of an evening.

"Take your things off," I said. "We'll heat the stove in a minute."

I went outside to get some kindling for the stove. But I did not feel quite myself through happiness. There was a ringing in my ears, my hands shook, and I felt all weak somehow and wanted to sit down. The stars glittered, sharp and small. "There'll be a frost," I thought. "And by morning all the leaves will drop off. Wintertide soon!"

A melodious triple-toned horn sounded over the Oka and rolled over the hills. Somewhere down below a tugboat was chugging upstream, one of those old steam tugs which were getting rare today. The new launches and water-jet pusher boats give a short, high-pitched, twangy hoot. Awakened by the hoot, several cockerels at the poultry farm crowed in a shrill falsetto.

I chopped some kindling, gathered an armful of firewood and went indoors. She had taken her coat off and was standing with her back to me, getting something out of her suitcase amid a rustle of newspapers. She was wearing a bright-coloured frock which was too tight for her. If I had taken her out somewhere in Moscow, visiting friends or to the club, everybody would smile inwardly, yet this was probably her best dress. Then I remembered that she usually went about in slacks worn inside high boots, with an old faded skirt over them, and it was smashing.

I put the kettle on and started to light the fire. Soon the stove was roaring, the wood crackled and there was a smell of smoke and firewood.

"This is for you," she said behind me.

I turned and saw a salmon on the table – a magnificent, silvery specimen with a broad dark spine, and upturned lower jaw. A fish smell invaded the room, and the wanderlust seized me again.

She was a Pomor,* born at sea in a motor boat, on one golden summer night. But the nights left her unmoved. It was only newcomers who saw them and went crazy over the silence and solitude. Only when you are a visitor, cut off from everybody and forgotten, as it were, by the world, do you spend wakeful nights, thinking and thinking and saying to yourself: "Ah, well! It's nothing, it's just night, and you're not here for always, and what do you care about the night, let the sun creep along the edge of the sea. Sleep, sleep. ..."

And she? She slept soundly at night in the fishery huts behind a cotton curtain, because at daybreak she had to be up and rowing with the stalwart fishermen, getting the fish out of the pound and afterwards cooking fish soup and washing up. And she had done that always, every summer, until I had arrived.

And now on the Oka we were drinking ashberry brandy, eating salmon and reminiscing, chatting about this, that and the other. About how we had gone out to sea in the white nights to spear lancet fish, and how we had hauled in the stake nets with the fisherman in a gale, choking with the bitter water and feeling sick, and how we had gone to the lighthouse for bread, and how we had sat one night in the village library, divested of boots and padded jackets, and read through all the papers and magazines that had come out during the days we had spent at the fishing grounds.

I threw my coat down on the floor near the stove, fur side up, we put the teapot and sweets within reach, took our cups and lay down on the coat, glancing in turn at one another, at the rosy glow under the grating, at the coals and the tongues of flame leaping over them, and so that we might lie there as long as possible I would sometimes get up to feed more wood into the stove, which would begin to crackle and make us move away from the heat.

Round about two o'clock in the night I got up in the dark, as I could not sleep. It seemed to me that if I fell asleep she would go away and I would lose my awareness of her, for I wanted her to be with me

---

* Pomors – inhabitants of the White Sea coast, most of them descendants of ancient settlers.

all the time and to know it. "Take me into your dreams, so that I can be with you always!" I wanted to say to her. "Because we must not part for long." And then I thought that people who go away from us and whom we meet no more, these people are dead to us. And we to them. Strange thoughts come into your mind at night, when you cannot sleep through joy or heartache.

"Are you sleeping?" I said softly.

"No," she answered from the bed. "I feel good. Don't look, I'm going to dress."

So then I went into the corner where the radio set was strapped to the wall, and switched it on. Amid the crackle and mutterings of announcers I sought music. I knew it had to be there, and I found it. A deep masculine voice said something in English, then there was a pause, and I understood that in a minute the music would come on.

I started, because at the very first sound I recognised the tune. When I feel good, or, on the contrary, unhappy, I always remember that jazz tune. It's foreign to me, but it voices a secret thought, and I can't make out whether it is a sad or joyful thought. I often remembered it afterwards when I travelled anywhere, when anything gladdened me or, on the contrary, depressed me. It reminded me of that Moscow night when we had driven and driven and walked about, lonely and miserable, and I had not heard a word of rebuke from her all the night, and I felt ashamed.

She was leaving for Arkhangelsk after five empty days spent in Moscow. Everything was exactly the way it always is at Moscow's railway terminals: porters pushed their hand trolleys, motor trolleys buzzed past, everyone was in a hurry, saying goodbye, with only minutes left. She was going away, though she needn't have gone so soon – she still had time to spare, several free days. And I had been annoyed, I felt very bitter, angry both with myself and her. I was thinking how empty life would be for me without her and that I would have to start drinking again to drown my sorrows.

"Don't go away!" I had said to her.

She had only smiled wryly and looked up at me with quivering eyes. She had dark eyes with green lights in them – you couldn't tell whether they were green or black. But when she looked at me like that they were black, I remember that very well.

"It's so silly!" I said. "First I left the North without having understood anything, and now you, and again nothing. ... How silly! Don't go away!"

"What's the use of talking now," she muttered angrily.

"You shouldn't have put up at some relatives who are always at home!"

"Where else? At your place? Oh, well," she said obstinately, "what's the use of talking now. ..."

"Let's go to a hotel, you'll live there these last few days."

"The train will be starting soon," she said, turning away.

"Wait a minute, listen, just think! After so many letters we'll be together, alone. Just think!"

After a long silence during which her eyes slowly scanned my face, she said at last piteously, brokenly, biting her lip: "Will you be glad if I stay?"

I found difficulty in breathing and a lump rose in my throat. I turned, quickly went into the coach, bumping into somebody, shouldered my way through to her compartment, took her suitcase and went out. I still remember the way the conductor and everyone else who stood near the coach at that moment looked at us.

"Come on," I said.

"What about my ticket?" she said radiant-eyed.

"To hell with the ticket!" I said and took her arm. We went out into the square and got into a taxi.

"To a hotel," I said.

"Which one?" the driver asked.

"Oh, any one!"

The car moved off, racing towards the traffic lights, past the now burning neon signs, past railway stations, people and houses.

"Stop a minute, old chap," I said to the driver near some shop, jumped out and bought a bottle of wine. I came back with the bottle thrust into my side pocket. I imagined us drinking the wine alone, raising our glasses and looking into each other's eyes. I could feel the taste of it in my mouth as we drove up to the hotel and I went over to the desk.

"Full up," the receptionist said coolly.

"Any room will do. D'you understand – any old room, the worst you have or the best!"

"Full up," he repeated sourly, lifting the receiver of the incessantly ringing telephone with a gesture of annoyance.

She was waiting for me in the lobby, timidly eyeing the splendour of marble columns and mirrors. She even glanced at me timidly, as if I were lord and master of it all. We went out to the taxi stand.

"Let's go to another one," I said with chagrin.

She got into the car without a murmur, and we sped through Moscow. I called at a friend's to borrow some money and was on the point of asking him to take us in, but his sister had guests staying. I glanced at them, at the table with the wine, at the ottoman, at the drawn-up legs in narrow moccasins, and said nothing. But then I borrowed a round sum.

"Have a drink," my friend said, intercepting my glance.

"No, thanks, I've got somebody waiting downstairs."

An hour, two hours later found us still driving about, and everywhere we were told the same thing: "Full up!" Coming out into the street I surveyed the huge building of the hotel and the houses, all those multi-storeyed rows of windows, many of which were already dark, and thought of all those people who could sit or lie comfortably at home at that hour, listening to the radio, reading something in bed or embracing a woman, and my heart began to ache.

Completely worn out, we drove back to the station, handed her suitcase in to the cloak room and slowly made our way towards Sokolniki park. It was some minutes past eleven.

"What are we going to do?" I said with a laugh.

"I don't know," she said wearily. "Let's go to a restaurant, I'm hungry."

"The restaurants are closed," I said, after consulting my watch, and laughed again, a silly laugh. "Let's go to the centre, to the boulevards."

We walked at a brisk pace, the way we used to walk up North along the seashore when we were in a hurry not to be late for the film show at the club twenty kilometres away. The street-lamps were out, and only those on the other side of the road burned at intervals. There were hardly any people about. At last we came to Tverskoi Boulevard and sat down on one of the seats.

"Can't we go to your place at all?" she asked with hope.

"Would I be walking the streets with you! Father, mother – nothing doing!"

"Oh, all right," she answered. "Don't worry. I'll go away tomorrow, there's another train in the morning. And then ..." she sighed, "then you'll come up North again some time."

I put my arm round her, and she snuggled up to me and closed her eyes.

"We'll just sit like this, shan't we?" she murmured, settling herself more comfortably in the seat. "You're a good boy, I love you, stupid. I fell in love with you out there, but you didn't know it. Poor, poor boy!"

She sat motionless for a minute, then threw off her shoes and drew up her legs, pulling her skirt down over them.

"My feet hurt," she murmured sleepily. "Those shoes. ... Not used to them. ..."

Two militiamen were coming down the sidepath. Seeing us, one of them came out into the light and went up to us.

"Pass along, citizen," he said, addressing me alone for some reason. "This is not permitted."

"What is not permitted?" I asked, while she embarrassedly put the shoes on her swollen feet.

"None o' your talk, now! You've been told, pass along!"

We got up and walked away. I started looking at the houses and windows again and kept seeing a room with an ottoman in it. There was nothing else in the room, only a faint rosy light and the ottoman.

"I say, let's go into a doorway," I suggested irresolutely.

"Let's," she agreed with a wan smile. "I'll take my shoes off there and we can sit on the stairs."

We entered a dark courtyard, crossed to the farthest entrance in a corner, shut the door behind us and sat down on the stairs. She immediately took her shoes off and started to rub her feet.

"Tired?" I asked and lighted up. "Poor girl, you've had no luck in Moscow."

"Yes," she said, rubbing her cheek against my shoulder. "It's such a big city."

There came a sound of footsteps, the door opened, and the yardkeeper looked in and saw us.

"Now then, get out!" she shouted. "You people are a damned

nuisance, prowling around the dark gateways like cats! Beat it, or I'll whistle for the militia!"

Saying which, she whipped a shiny whistle out of the pocket of her apron. She was a dour-faced woman with high cheek-bones. We went back through the yard again, escorted by the swearing yard-keeper.

Out in the street we looked at each other and started laughing.

"This isn't the White Sea for you," I said.

"Never mind," she reassured me again. "Let's just walk about. Or let's go to the station, at least we can sit on the seats there, eh?"

"All right," I agreed, then suddenly livened up. "I say, let's go out of town! We'll take a taxi. I've got money, and we'll drive out some thirty kilometres – that's how it's done here."

A taxi was passing slowly down the street. Always, when coming home late, I liked to look at these nocturnal taxis. They wandered ghostlike around the sleeping city with glimmering green lights, and looking at these lights one always felt a desire to ride somewhere, somewhere far away.

We hailed the taxi.

"Out of town?" the driver queried, and immediately began to play the bully. "Seven fifty does it!"

"All right," I said. It was all the same to me now.

As we drove along I began to feel sleepy. The road was deserted, darkness still lingered in the west, but the east had lightened, day was breaking. The wind hummed steadily outside, and there was a strong smell of petrol inside.

"Will this place do?" the driver asked, slowing down near a small wood. "This is as far as we go. Are you from the provinces?" he asked, looking at us.

We got out and shivered at the cold touch of predawn.

"Will half an hour do?" the driver asked, eyeing me appraisingly. "I'll take a nap. Wake me up when you get back. Got a fag?"

He started to turn the car round into the roadside, and we walked towards the wood through the wiry grass. My only sensation was one of dampness and chilliness. My suit grew stiff and heavy, my shoes got wet, and my trousers uncreased. A sombre light stood in the wood. I glanced at her, thinking what to do next. She looked tired, her face was drawn and circles lay under her eyes. Suddenly she gave an undisguised yawn and looked round with a bored eye as if wondering what had brought us there.

"Some forest, this," she muttered and suddenly glanced at me resentfully.

I yawned too, feeling bored and angry that I was not at home in bed, but out here in the damp and cold.

"I'm fed up," she said in a low husky voice, yawning again openly. "My God! I don't want anything, let's go back."

"All right, let's go back," I said listlessly and I too yawned. "Let's have a drink first, it's weighing down my pocket."

I pulled out the bottle and tried to knock out the cork, but it was plugged in tight. So then I pushed it in with a twig.

"Have a drink," I said, offering her the warm bottle.

"I don't want it," she muttered, but took the bottle, and, began to drink. Two trickles, like blood, ran down her chin. She started coughing and handed the bottle back. I finished it and threw it away.

"Come along," I said with relief.

We trudged back through the dark ferny wood and tussocky clearing, and she kept lifting her dress not to get the skirts wetted with dew.

"Why so soon?" the taxi driver said and looked at me with amusement. "Had a tiff?"

"Get going!" I said savagely. It was all I could do to keep from hitting him.

We drove back dozing, lurching against each other at the sharp turns, and I remember the contacts with her being unpleasant to me, and to her too, no doubt. It was about five in the morning, and we had to hang about somewhere for three more hours before the train was due. I felt bad, the wine had gone to my head in a heavy, stifling sort of way.

Those three hours were agony. The worst of it was that I couldn't go away, I had to stay with her to the end. When the train did come in at last I didn't know what to say to her at parting. My head was splitting.

"Ah well, write to me," she said, taking hold of the hand-rail.

I summoned up strength to stop her.

"Don't be angry," I muttered, kissed her on the forehead, and went towards the exit. I remember feeling so relieved at parting with her that I was even surprised, but I also felt a bit sad. Somewhere deep down within me I felt a twinge of pain and shame.

I dragged the coat closer to the radio and we sat down on it side by side with our arms round each other. All these months I had been living with a sense of loss in my heart, and now I had found it all, and what I had found was even better than I could have thought.

The double-bass rumbled its elegiac way through the dark of contrapuntal passages, wandering insolubly, rising and falling, and its slow movement reminded me of a star-studded sky. And listening to it, the saxophone complained of something, the trumpet again and again rose to frenzied heights, and the piano from time to time went in among them with its quint-apocalyptic chords. And like a metronome, like Time, marshalling the rhythm into syncopes, the drummer held sway over everything with soft empty taps.

"Don't let's put the light on, eh?" she said, looking up from the floor at the greenish dial of the radio set, at its wolfish eye.

"All right," I said, thinking that I would probably never have a night like this again. It made me sad to think that three hours had already gone. I wanted it all to start again, from the beginning, with me going out again with the lantern and waiting, and with our remembering everything again and afterwards again being afraid to part with each other in the dark.

She got up for a minute, then looked through the window and said, "Snow. ..."

I sat up and looked into the darkness outside the window. Snow was falling soundlessly. The first real snow that autumn. I pictured to myself the scene we would see in the daytime – the mouse tracks around the heaps of brushwood in the forest, and the hare tracks round the acacia, which they were so fond of gnawing at night – and I thought of my shotgun with a glad thrill. How good that it was snowing, that she had come, and we were alone, with this music, with our past and future, which was perhaps better than the past, and that tomorrow I would take her to my favourite spots, show her the Oka, the fields, the hills, woods and ravines. The night wore on, but we could not fall asleep. We spoke in whispers and embraced, fearing to lose each other, then heated the stove again, gazed into its fiery maw, and the red light shone hotly in our faces. We fell asleep round about seven in the morning, when the windows were already a pale blue, and we slept a long time, because no one woke us up in our house.

While we slept the sun rose and melted the snow a little, but afterwards it froze again. Having drunk tea, I took my gun, and we left the house. For a moment it even hurt – the blinding white winter glare and the clear tingling air. The snow had thawed, leaving icy crusts everywhere. They were opaque, semi-transparent. An odorous vapour issued from the cowshed, around which the calves jostled and clattered as if treading on boardwalks. This was because the dungwash had not yet frozen under the upper crust of ice. Some of them were grazing with pleasure on the hoary winter crops and frequently urinating, sticking up their tails and with legs, curly in the groin, planted wide apart. On the spots where they urinated there appeared emerald patches of wet young rye.

We went first along the road. The ruts were covered over with a matt film, but under the ice stood clayey water, and when our boots broke through the crust it squirted brown over the ice. And in the woods, late dandelions, barely touched with yellow, stuck out from under the ice. Leaves and pine needles could be seen frozen into the ice. Late mushrooms stood stiff and frozen, and when we kicked them they snapped into pieces and went skidding over the ice. The ice sagged underfoot and crackled and snapped a long way ahead and behind and all round.

The hillside fields were smokily green from afar, as if sprinkled with flour, the haystacks had turned dark, the forest was denuded and black, relieved only by the white palisade of birches, the glossy velvety green of the asp trunks, and the last red caps of lingering leaves on the trees along the wooded hillocks. The river could be seen at a great distance through the forest, and it looked cold and empty to the eye. We descended a snowy ravine, leaving deep tracks, at first dirty, then clean, behind us, and drank from a spring beside a felled asp. Sunken, blackened maple and oak leaves lay thickly at the bottom of the still pool and the felled asp smelled bitter and cold, and the cut face was the colour of amber.

"Like it?" I said, looking at her. I was astonished – her eyes were green.

"Wonderful!" she said, gazing around eagerly and licking her lips.

"Better than at the White Sea?" I asked.

She started looking at the river again and up the slope, and her eyes grew greener.

"I don't know about the White Sea …" she said vaguely. "At our place. … But here there are oak-trees," she interrupted herself. "How did you manage to find such a spot?"

I was happy, but felt at once strange and afraid – everything had turned out so good for me that autumn. To calm myself I started smoking. I was all wreathed in smoke and vapour. A tugboat appeared on the Oka from the direction of Alexino. It pounded downstream at a brisk pace and we followed it in silence with our eyes. Heavy steam rose from its engine and shot out from its side in a jet.

When the tugboat disappeared round the bend we started climbing up, hand in hand, to the sparse trees in the thinned woods in order to have another look at the Oka from above. We walked slowly, silently, like in a white dream, in which we were at last together.

THE COCK
Fazil Iskander (1929–2016)
Translated by Robert Daglish

Born in Abkhazia on the Black Sea coast in the family of a Persian man who came to the USSR from Iran, ten years after his birth **Fazil Iskander** lost his father, who was deported in 1938, and never saw him again.

Iskander became the most important voice from the Caucasus during the Soviet period, writing about the clash of the archaic tribal cultures of the mountains and the modernist yet ruthless, and in its core even more archaic, Soviet project. His prose is full of parables, Eastern coloring, and, more important, the hidden yet evident action of honor and dignity, the qualities officially demanded from the Soviet person but severely punished in reality.

As a boy I was much disliked by all farmyard cocks. I don't remember what started it, but if a warlike cock appeared in the neighbourhood there was bound to be bloodshed.

One summer I was staying with my relatives in one of the mountain villages of Abkhazia. The whole family—the mother, two grown-up daughters, two grown-up sons—went off to work early in the morning to weed maize or pick tobacco. I was left behind in the house alone. My duties were pleasant and easy to perform. I had to feed the goats (one good bundle of rustling hazelnut branches), draw fresh water from the stream for the midday break and in general keep an eye on the house. There was nothing special to keep an eye on, but now and then I had to give a shout to make the hawks feel there was a man in the vicinity and refrain from attacking our chickens. In return for this I, as a representative of the feeble urban branch of the family, was allowed to suck a pair of fresh eggs straight from the nest, which I did both gladly and conscientiously.

Fixed along the outside wall of the kitchen there were some baskets in which the hens laid their eggs. How they knew they were supposed to lay them there was always a mystery to me. I would stand on tip-toe and grope about until I found an egg. Feeling simultaneously like a successful pearl diver and the thief of Baghdad, I would break the top by tapping it on the wall and suck the egg dry at once. Somewhere nearby the hens would be clucking mournfully. Life seemed significant and full of wonder. The air was healthy, the food was healthy, and I swelled with juice like a pumpkin on a well-manured allotment.

In the house I found two books: Mayne Reid's *The Headless Horseman* and *The Tragedies and Comedies of William Shakespeare*. The first book swept me off my feet. The very names of the characters were music to my ears: Maurice the Mustanger, Louise Pointdexter, Captain Cassius Calhoun, El Coyote, and the magnificent Doña Isidora Covarubio de los Llanos.

"'My pistol is at your head! I have one shot left—an apology, or you die!' ...

"'It's the mirage!' the Captain exclaimed with the addition of an oath to give vent to his chagrin."

I read that book from beginning to end, then from the end to the beginning, and skipped through it twice.

Shakespeare's tragedies seemed to me muddled and pointless. On the other hand, the comedies fully justified the author's efforts at composition. I realised that it was not the jesters who depended on the royal courts but the royal courts that depended on the jesters.

The house we lived in stood on a hill and the winds blew round it and through it twenty-four hours a day. It was as dry and sturdy as a veteran mountaineer.

The eaves of the small veranda were tufted with swallows' nests. The swallows dived swiftly and accurately into the veranda and hovered with fluttering wings at a nest, where their greedy, vociferous young waited open-beaked, almost falling out in their eagerness. Their gluttony was matched only by the tireless energy of their parents. Sometimes having fed its young, the father would hang for a few moments leaning back from the edge of the nest, its arrow-shaped body motionless and only the head turning warily this way and that. One more instant and it would drop like a stone, then deftly level out and soar away from the veranda.

The chickens foraged peacefully in the yard, the sparrows and chicks twittered. But the demons of rebellion were not slumbering.

Despite my preventive shouts, a hawk came over nearly every day. In a diving or low-level attack, it would snatch up a chicken and with mighty sweeps of its burdened wings make off in the direction of the forest. It was a breath-taking sight and I would sometimes let it get away on purpose and shout later just to soothe my conscience. The captured chicken hung in an attitude of terror and foolish submission. If I made enough noise in time, the hawk would either miss its prey or drop it in flight. In such cases we would find the chicken somewhere in the bushes, glassy-eyed and paralysed with fright.

"She's a goner," one of my cousins would say, cheerfully chopping off its head and marching away to the kitchen with the carcass.

The chief of this barnyard kingdom was a huge red-feathered cock, rich in plumage and cunning as an Oriental despot. Within a few days of my arrival it became obvious that he hated me and was only looking for a pretext to come openly to blows. Perhaps he had noticed that I was eating a lot of eggs and this offended his male vanity? Or was he infuriated by my half-heartedness during the hawk attacks? I think both these things had their effect on him but his chief grudge was that someone was challenging his power over the hens. Like any other despot, this he would not tolerate.

I realised that dual power could not last long and, in preparation for the forthcoming battle, kept him under close observation.

No one could deny the cock his share of personal bravery. During the hawk attacks, when the hens and chickens would flutter clucking and squawking in all directions, he alone would remain in the yard and, gobbling fiercely, try to restore order in his timid harem. He would even take a few resolute steps in the direction of the swooping foe, but since nothing that runs can overtake that which flies, this made an impression of mere bravado.

Usually he would forage in the yard or the kitchen garden accompanied by two or three of his favourite hens but without losing sight of the others. Now and then he would crane his neck and look up at the sky in search of danger.

As soon as the shadow of a gliding hawk passed over the yard or the cawing of a crow was heard, he would throw up his head belligerently and signal his charges to be on the alert. The hens would listen in a scared fashion and sometimes scuttle away for cover. More often than not it was a false alarm, but by keeping his numerous mistresses in a state of nervous tension he crushed their will and achieved complete submission.

As he scratched the ground with his horny claws he would sometimes discover a delicate morsel and summon the hens with loud cries to join in the feast.

While the hen that got there first was pecking his find, he would circle round her a few times, dragging his wing exuberantly and apparently choking with delight. This operation usually ended in rape. The hen would shake herself bemusedly, trying to recover her senses and grasp what had happened, while he looked round in victorious satisfaction.

If the wrong hen ran up in response to his call, he would guard his find or drive her away while continuing to summon his new beloved with loud grunting noises. His favourite was a neat white hen, as slim as a pullet. She would approach him cautiously, stretch out her neck, cleverly scoop up the morsel and run away as hard as she could, showing no signs of gratitude whatever.

He would pound after her humiliatedly, trying to keep up appearances though well aware of the indignity of his position. Usually he failed to catch her and would eventually come to a halt, breathing heavily and trying to look at me as though nothing had happened and his little trot had been entirely for his own pleasure.

Actually the invitations to a feast were quite often sheer deception. He had nothing worth eating and the hens knew it, but they were betrayed by their eternal feminine curiosity.

As the days went by he grew more and more insolent. If I happened to be crossing the yard he would run after me for a short distance just to test my courage. Despite the shivers going down my spine I would nevertheless stop and wait to see what would follow. He would stop, too, and wait. But the storm was bound to break and break it did.

One day, when I was eating in the kitchen, he marched in and planted himself in the doorway. I threw him a few pieces of hominy but to no avail. He pecked up my offering but I could see he had no intention of making peace.

There was nothing for it. I brandished a half-burnt log at him but he merely gave a little jump, stuck out his neck like a gander and stared at me with hate-filled eyes. Then I threw the log. It fell beside him. He jumped even higher and flung himself at me, belching a stream of barnyard abuse. A flaming red ball of hate came flying towards me. I managed to shield myself with a stool. He flew straight into it and collapsed on the floor like a slain dragon. While he was getting up, his wings beat on the earthen floor, raising spurts of dust and chilling my legs with the wind of battle.

I managed to change my position and retreat towards the door, protecting myself with the stool like a Roman legionary with his shield.

As I was crossing the yard he charged several times. Whenever he came at me I felt as if he was going to peck my eyes out. I made good use of the stool and he bounced off it regularly on to the ground. My hands were scratched and bleeding and the heavy stool was becoming ever harder to hold. But it was my only means of protection.

One more attack. With a mighty sweep of his wings the cock flew up and, instead of colliding with my shield unexpectedly perched on top of it.

I threw the stool down and in a few bounds reached the veranda, and from there darted into the room slamming the door behind me.

My chest was humming like a telegraph pole and my hands were streaming with blood. I stood and listened. I was sure that the wretched cock was lurking at the door. And so he was. After a while he moved away a little and began to march up and down the veranda, his iron claws clacking loudly on the floor. He was calling me out to do battle but I preferred to lie low in my stronghold. At length he grew tired of waiting and, perched on the railing, gave vent to a victorious cock-a-doodle-doo.

When my cousins learnt of my affray with the cock, they started holding daily tournaments. Neither of us gained any decisive advantage and we all went about with scratches and bruises.

The fleshy tomato-like comb of my opponent bore several marks of the stick and his glorious fountain of a tail showed signs of drying up, but far from losing any of his self-assurance he had become all the more insolent.

He had acquired an annoying habit of crowing from a perch on the rail of the veranda, just under the window of the room where I slept. Evidently he regarded the veranda as occupied territory.

Our battles were held in all kinds of places, in the yard, in the kitchen garden, in the orchard. If I climbed a tree for figs or for apples, he would stand and wait for me patiently beneath.

To cure him of some of his arrogance I resorted to various stratagems. I started treating the hens to extra food. He would fly into a rage when I called them but they treacherously deserted him all the same. Persuasion was useless. Here, as in any other field, abstract propaganda was easily deflated by the reality of profit. The handfuls of maize that I tossed out of the window conquered the tribal loyalty and family traditions of the valourous egg-layers. In the end the pasha himself would appear. He would reproach them indignantly but they, merely pretending to be ashamed of their weakness, went on pecking up the maize.

One day, when my aunt and her sons were working in the kitchen garden, we had another encounter. By this time I was an experienced and cold-blooded warrior. I found a forked stick and, using it like a trident, after a few unsuccessful attempts pinned the cock to the ground. His powerful body writhed frantically and its vibrations came up the stick like an electric current.

I was inspired by the madness of the brave. Without letting go of the stick or releasing its pressure, I bent down and, seizing my chance, pounced on the cock like a goal-keeper on a ball and managed to seize him by the throat. He writhed vigourously and dealt me such a blow on the head with his wing that I went deaf in one ear. Fear reinforced my courage. I squeezed his throat even tighter. Hard and sinewy, it jerked and twisted in my hand and I felt as if I were holding a snake. With the other hand I grasped his legs. His long claws worked desperately to reach my body and fasten on to some part of it.

But the trick was done. I straightened up and the cock hung suspended by his feet, emitting stifled squawks.

All this time my cousins and aunt had been roaring with laughter as they watched us from behind the fence. So much the better! Great waves of joy flowed through me. In a very short time, however, I felt rather confused. My vanquished opponent showed no signs of giving in. He was throbbing with a furious desire for revenge. If I let him go, he would come at me again, and yet I couldn't go on holding him like this forever.

"Throw him over the fence," my aunt advised.

I went up to the fence and tossed him over with leaden arms.

Curse it all! He, of course, did not fly over the fence but perched on it, spreading his massive wings. The next moment he flung himself at me. This was too much. I made a wild dash for safety and from my breast rose the ancient cry for help of all fleeing children:

"Mummy!"

One must be very foolish or very brave to turn one's back on an enemy. In my case it was certainly not bravery, and I paid the price for it.

He caught me several times while I was running till at last I tripped and fell. He sprang on top of me, he rolled on me, he gurgled with bloodthirsty glee. He might quite easily have pecked through my spine if my cousin had not run up and knocked him off into the bushes with his hoe. We decided that this had killed him, but in the evening the cock came out of the bushes, subdued and saddened.

As she bathed my wounds, my aunt said, "It doesn't look as if you two will ever get on together. We'll roast him tomorrow."

The next day my cousin and I set about catching the cock. The poor fellow sensed that fate had turned against him. He fled from us with the speed of an ostrich. He flew into the kitchen garden, he hid in the bushes. Finally he flapped into the cellar, and there we caught him. He looked persecuted and his eyes were full of mournful reproach. He seemed to be saying to me, "Yes, we were foes, you and I. But it was an honourable war, between men. I never expected such treachery from you." I felt strangely upset and turned away. A few minutes later my cousin lopped off his head. The cock's body jerked and writhed, the wings flapped and folded as if to cover the gushing throat. Life would be safer now but all the fun had gone out of it.

Still, he made us a fine dinner, and the spicy nut sauce that went with it diluted the pangs of my unexpected sorrow.

Now I realise that he was really a splendid fighting cock, but born too late. The days of cock fighting have long since passed, and fighting the human race is a lost cause from the start.

TOUGH GUY

Vasily Shukshin (1929–1974)

Translated by Laura Michael & John Givens

Another writer from the generation born in the Stalinist Soviet Union, **Vasily Shukshin** lost his father, a kolkhoz worker in a remote village in the Siberian Altai mountains, in 1938, when he was arrested and executed by an extrajudicial tribunal.

Shukshin got himself a proper proletarian biography, working as a builder, locksmith and serving in the army. With this he made his way to Moscow, to the Institute of Cinematography, and became an actor, film director and writer.

Shukshin's prose is often described by critics as 'the anatomy of the Soviet life in sixties and seventies'.

The third work brigade from the kolkhoz Giant put a new warehouse into operation. From the old warehouse, which had once been a church, they removed some empty, nasty-smelling barrels, bags of cement, sacks full of granulated sugar and salt from the village store, heaps of matting, and harnesses. (The work brigade only had five horses, but there were enough harnesses here for at least fifteen. Now that'd be just fine—can't have too much of a good thing—if it weren't for those damn mice. The harnesses had been treated with tar and sprayed with all sorts of chemicals, but the mice went on gnawing away at them just the same.) There were also brooms, rakes, and shovels ... And now the little church stood empty, of no use to anybody at all. Even though it wasn't a large church, it had livened up the village (which at one time had been attached to an estate). The church was its focal point and a showpiece that drew people's eyes from far and near.

Foreman Nikolai Sergeyevich Shurygin stood for a while in front of it, thinking ... He walked up to a wall, chipped away at a bit of the brickwork with a crowbar that happened to be lying nearby, lit a cigarette, and went home.

When he met with the chairman of the kolkhoz two days later, Shurygin said:

"That little church is all emptied out now …"

"So."

"So what're you gonna do with it?"

"Close it up and leave it be. What of it?"

"That brick's good stuff. I could put it to use makin' a pigsty, instead of haulin' bricks over from the factory."

"It'd take five men two weeks to pull it down. That's no ordinary pile of bricks—might as well be made of cast iron. Hell if I know how they laid those bricks!"

"I'll tear it down all right."

"How?"

"No sweat. I'll hook three tractors up to it—it'll fly apart like a house of cards."

"Give it a shot."

On Sunday, Shurygin gave it a shot. He called in three powerful tractors … Three thick cables were wound around the little church at different levels. Ten logs were placed under the cables—at the corners and in the center of one wall …

At first Shurygin gave orders for this job just like he did for any other—with lots of yelling and cussing. But when people started running up, when all around they started gasping and sighing and showing how sad they were about the church, Shurygin suddenly felt like some important official with unlimited powers. He stopped cussing and wouldn't look at people—as if he didn't hear them and didn't see them.

"Nikolai, you followin' orders, or what?" people asked. "You didn't go and think this up yourself, now did you?"

"What'd it ever do to you?"

Mikhailo Belyakov, the tipsy warehouse manager, crawled under the cables to get over to Shurygin.

"Kolka, why you doin' this?"

Shurygin, shaking with anger, was livid:

"Get outta here, you stinkin' drunk!"

Mikhailo backed away from the foreman in astonishment. And everybody all around fell quiet, equally surprised. Shurygin liked to hit the bottle himself, and he'd never called anybody a "stinkin' drunk" before. What was the matter with him?

Meanwhile the logs were reinforced and the cables aligned ... In a moment the tractors would begin roaring, and something unprecedented would happen in the village—the church would come down. The older folk had all been baptized in it, funeral services for their grandfathers and great-grandfathers had been held in it. They were as used to seeing it there as they were to the sun in the sky each day.

Once again voices began to sound out.

"Nikolai, who ordered it, huh?"

"*He* did! ... Can't you see how he keeps turnin' his ugly mug away, the devil!"

"Shurygin, stop bein' so pigheaded!"

Shurygin paid absolutely no attention. He just kept on, with the same look of concentration on his face and the same principled severity in his gaze. Shurygin's wife, Klanka, was nudged out from among the ranks ... Klanka saw that something incomprehensible was going on with her husband. She timidly walked up to him.

"Kol, why do you wanna tear it down?"

"Get outta here!" Shurygin ordered her as well. "Don't butt in!"

Some of the villagers walked over to the tractor drivers to try to buy time, while others ran off to call the district authorities and to fetch the village school teacher. But Shurygin had promised the tractor drivers a bottle of vodka each and extra pay for the job.

The teacher came running up. He was still a young man and was respected in the village.

"Stop that this instant! Who's responsible here? This church is from the seventeenth century! ..."

"Mind your own business," Shurygin said.

"It *is* my business! It's the people's business!" The teacher was all worked up and couldn't find words powerful and persuasive enough. He turned beet red and kept yelling: "You don't have the right! Barbarian! I'm going to write the authorities!"

Shurygin waved at the tractor drivers ... The engines roared. The cables began to tighten. The crowd gasped quietly in horror. The teacher tore loose from the crowd, ran up to the side of the church that was to be toppled, and stood under the wall.

"You'll have to answer for murder! You idiot …"

The tractor drivers stopped.

"Outta the way!" Shurygin roared. And the thick veins on his neck bulged.

"Don't you dare touch the church! Don't you dare!"

Shurygin ran up to the teacher, grabbed hold of him and carried him away from the church. The puny teacher did his best to break loose, but Shurygin's arms were like iron.

"Let's go!" he shouted to the tractor drivers.

"Everyone! Stand next to the wall!" the teacher shouted at everybody. "Hurry! … They won't dare! I'll go to the regional authorities, they'll put an end to this! …"

"Let's go, damn it all!" Shurygin yelled at the tractor drivers.

The tractor drivers slipped into their cabs and grabbed hold of the controls.

"Go stand by the wall! Everybody! Stand by the wall!"

But no one stirred. Shurygin's fury had glued them to the spot. Everybody was speechless. They all waited.

The cables strained, squeaked, cracked, rang out … One log was crunched. A cable, which had cut into a corner of the church, sang like a balalaika string. It was strange, but you could hear everything so clearly, despite the roar of the tractors as they strained with all their iron strength. The top of the church trembled … The wall opposite the one they were trying to knock down suddenly tore open, cracking all along its entire breadth … A terrible lacerated fissure, black in its depths, began to open wide on the white wall. The top of the church with its little dome bowed, bowed, and came crashing down. The earth shuddered as if struck by a shell. Everything was lost in a cloud of dust.

Shurygin let go of the teacher, who, without saying a word, walked away from the church.

Two tractors continued clawing the earth with their caterpillar treads. The cable at the middle elevation cut through a corner and was now senselessly crumbling the bricks from two walls, cutting deeper and deeper into them.

Shurygin stopped the tractors. They began to reset the cables.

Folks started going their separate ways. Only the most curious and the kids stayed on.

In three hours, everything was finished. All that was left of the church was a low shell with rough edges. The church lay in a formless heap, in ruins. The tractors drove off.

All sweaty and completely covered with dust and bits of plaster, Shurygin headed for the store to make a phone call to the chairman of the kolkhoz.

"That's it—she bit the dust!" he shouted into the mouthpiece cheerfully.

The chairman, obviously, didn't know who'd bit the dust.

"The church, that's who! She bit the dust, I said. Uh-huh. Everythin's under control. The teacher kicked up a bit of a fuss ... Yep! He may be a teacher, but he's worse than an old woman. Forget it, everythin's under control. She dropped like a rock! A lot of it crumbled, uh-huh. And they're all stuck together to boot, three or four bricks to a clump. I don't know how we'll pry'em apart. I tried with a crowbar—that damn church was tough, a real pain in the ass. You were right—it's just like cast iron! Yep. Goodbye. Don't worry about it."

Shurygin hung up. He went up to the shop girl, a woman he'd dragged out of bed during the night on more than one occasion when somebody came from the district center to do a bit of fishing and stayed afterward at the foreman's place late, till the cock crowed twice.

"Did you see us do a number on the church?" Shurygin was smiling; he was satisfied.

"Doesn't take brains to do somethin' stupid," the shop girl said, not hiding her malice.

"Why stupid?" Shurygin stopped smiling.

"What'd it do to you? It was just standin' there."

"Why should it just stand there bein' of no use? At least we'll get some brick from it ..."

"Poor you! As if you couldn't find some anywhere else! You idiot!"

"Stupid bitch!" Shurygin also became angry. "Keep your mouth shut if you don't know what you're talkin' about."

"Just try and wake me up in the middle of the night again, just try, and we'll see who wakes who! Stupid bitch, huh? I've half a mind to give it to you right in that onion dome of yours—with a five-kilo weight! Then you'll know what a stupid bitch is!"

Shurygin wanted to call that fool of a shop girl a few other names, but just then some of those ever present village women walked up.

"Gimme a bottle of vodka," he snapped.

"Sure—he's gotta wet his whistle," they started in behind him. "It's all dried out."

"Naturally—from all the dust!"

"And itchin' to do the devil's work ..."

Shurygin turned and looked sternly at the women but there were too many of them, it'd be impossible to shout them down. And their malice toward him was somehow unusual: they really hated him through and through. He picked up the bottle and went out of the store. On the threshold he turned around and said:

"I'll shut your yaps!"

And he beat a hasty retreat.

He walked, fuming with anger. "It's not like they prayed there or somethin', the parasites—but they've got to go and make a stink. Nobody gave a hang as long as it just stood there—and now they're raisin' hell."

Passing by the former church, Shurygin stopped for a long time and watched the kids rummaging around in the bricks. As he watched, he calmed down. "They'll grow up and remember how I tore down the church when they were kids. I sure remember how Vaska Dukhanin took the cross off it when I was a kid. And here the whole thing came crashin' down. 'Course they'll remember. They'll tell their kids: Uncle Kolya Shurygin fastened cables on it and ..." Shurygin suddenly remembered the shop girl. "It had no business standin' there bein' an eyesore," he thought spitefully and unrepentantly.

At home Shurygin met with open rebellion: his wife had left for the neighbors without fixing supper, and his ailing mother laid into him from her spot on the stove.

"Kolka, you're a cursed heathen, you are! What a sin you've taken on your soul! ... Didn't say a word to nobody, walked 'round real quiet, you devil ... If you'd just breathed one word maybe good folk would've talked some sense into that head of yours. And now look ... Woe and misery be on our house! Can't even show our faces to folks now. They'll curse you, you know, cu-urse you! And you won't know the hour when disaster'll overtake you, could be right here at home, could be some tree'll fall on you somewheres."

"Now why would they go and curse me? Nothin' better to do?"

"'Cause it's a s-i-n!"

"Did they curse Vaska Dukhanin? He took the cross off it. Just the opposite, he became a big shot ..."

"Them were different times. Who put you up to it, to destroy it, now, of all times? Who? 'Twas the devil made you do it ... Just you wait, the authorities'll put you on the hot seat yet. That there teacher's writin' letters, so they tell me; he knows where to write, too. You'll see. ... Little mother church, you stood your ground durin' good times and bad! And now *he* comes along ... The bug-eyed heathen!"

"Fine. Just lie there and be sick then!"

"Can't show our faces to folks ..."

"It's not like they went there to pray! It just stood there—nobody even noticed it ..."

"Who says we didn't notice it? Used to be, wherever you was comin' from, you'd see it. And no matter how tuckered out you was, when you saw it—it was good as bein' home already. It'd boost your strength."

"It'd boost your strength ... As if anybody goes around on foot these days! This is the atomic age, isn't it, and they're feelin' sorry for a church. There isn't a club in the whole village—and not a single soul gives a hoot. But take away the church and they get all upset. They'll get over it!"

"It's *you* as gots to get over it now! It's *you* as'll shrivel up and die from shame now ..."

To keep from hearing any more of her grumbling, Shurygin went into the other room, where he sat down at the table, quickly poured himself a full glass of vodka, and downed it. He lit a cigarette. "Not a one of those devils will touch the bricks now," he thought. "Well, to hell with'em! I'll shovel'em all into a pile with a bulldozer. Let the nettles grow over'em."

His wife came home late. Shurygin had already drained the bottle, felt like drinking another, but wasn't up to seeing that nasty shop girl again—it'd be too much. He asked his wife:

"Go get me a bottle."

"Go to the devil! He's a pal of yours now."

"I'm askin' you ..."

"Folks were askin' you things, too, but did you listen to 'em? So don't go askin' anybody for anythin' now. You idiot."

"Shut your trap. You're just takin' their side."

"Their side! Their side is where all the good folks are! Not your side, you ignorant slob! They asked you, the whole village did, they pleaded with you—but no! You just goggled your eyes at 'em ..."

"Shut up! Or I'll belt you one!"

"Belt away! Just try and touch me, you shameless slob! Just try and touch me!"

"No, this'll probably go on all night. Everybody's lost their mind," Shurygin thought.

Shurygin went outside and started up his motorcycle ... It was eighteen kilometers to the district center. They had a store there, the chairman of the kolkhoz was there. He could have a drink and chat for a while. And at the same time tell about the scene folks had made here ... At least have a few laughs.

As he turned out of the alley, his headlight picked up the ugly pile of bricks in the dark. It smelled musty, like a cellar that had been disturbed.

"From the seventeenth century," Shurygin remembered. "Here it is, here's your seventeenth century! He's gonna write the authorities, see! Go ahead and write!"

Shurygin stepped on the gas ... and sang loudly, so everybody would know that all those curses had put him in a wonderful mood:

You're outta, outta, outta line!
I'm a soldier from company nine.
From division thirty-one.
Boop dee boop, tiddle dee dum.

The motorcycle rolled out of the village, pierced the night with its gleaming blade of light, and took off down the dirt road in the direction of the district center. Shurygin liked going fast.

A DREAM IN POLAR FOG

Yuri Rytkheu (1930–2008)

Translated by Ilona Yazhbin Chavasse

Demiurge of the Chukchi literature, **Yuri Rytkheu** wrote in both Chukchi and Russian. Born into a family of hunters on the Chukotka peninsula, his grandfather being a shaman, Rytkheu had chosen to study at university. Before doing so, he was a sailor, a worker on a geological expedition, and a professional hunter.

He later moved to Leningrad to study and established himself as a novelist, writing about native people of the North and about ecological problems. His prose contains motifs of magical realism and sometimes plays freely with the Soviet canon.

Being almost forgotten in Russia after the collapse of the Soviet Union, Rytkheu was rediscovered and widely published in the West.

Kelena threw back the sleeve of her kerker and bared one stringy, dried-out breast, which drooped like an empty leather bag. She ordered an extra pair of braziers, so that there was enough light. The men obeyed her without question, spreading out a well-scrubbed leather rug, while Orvo sharpened the shaman-woman's knives with great concentration.

Kelena went up to the patient. Her face was long and thin. Tattoo lines disappeared into deep wrinkles like footpaths in the tundra hills. Bristly hairs sprouted from her wide nostrils. But her hands and her eyes were astonishing. Toko couldn't tear his eyes away from her fingers, marveling that a woman could have such powerful hands. Kelena's eyes burned with yellow light, as though each eye housed a blazing grease lamp. It seemed, whenever the shaman-woman cast her eyes into a shadowy corner, that she shone a torch into the darkness.

Despite her unattractive appearance, Kelena aroused neither fear nor revulsion. Perhaps it was due to the huge strength and confidence emanating from her tall, withered frame, that people inevitably felt reassured and trusting toward the big and kindly woman who could not fail to help them.

"To save this man, we must slaughter a dog," said she to Il'motch, quietly, but with authority.

"Get one from Orvo," Il'motch replied.

"But we have still got a long way to go," Orvo objected.

"Armol', go and bring a puppy from my yaranga," said Kelena, taking charge.

While Armol' was off on his errand, the sick man was moved closer to the center, and the braziers were raised high on supports, so that their light could fall from above. Kelena laid out her instruments on a clean bleached piece of sealskin: sharpened knives, needles and bones, tightly wound thread made of deer tendons, pieces of fur and long strips of clean, soft deerskin.

Armol' carried the struggling puppy into the room.

"Il'motch, Orvo, you're to help me," instructed Kelena. "The dog must be killed."

Il'motch took the puppy, and Orvo bent down to help the shaman-woman unbind John's tightly bandaged hands.

"You, young ones, don't go far off," ordered Kelena, "you may be needed. If he starts to scream and struggle, get on top of him and hold him down."

"All right," Toko nodded, feeling his mouth dry up.

Kelena shrugged off her kerker, now clad only in a narrow loincloth. As though out of nowhere, a little bottle appeared in her hands. She took out the plug with her teeth, tested the contents on the tip of her tongue and, forcing John's clenched teeth open, poured the liquid into his mouth. John thrashed and flailed his arms, but Kelena held him down with a knee.

Some time passed, and John lay still. Even his breath seemed to steady.

Then the shaman-woman carefully inspected her blades, spat down on each one, rubbing the spittle into the knife with her palm, and looked satisfied. Raising her face upward, she was motionless for a while, eyes shut, whispering charms. A strange thing, but it seemed to Toko that she was speaking in the white people's language. Was it because it was a white man she was about to heal?

Finished with her preparations, Kelena cautiously peeled back the bandages from John's broken hands. Where they were stuck to the skin and hard to lift, the shaman-woman wet them with fresh dog's blood. As the blackened skin appeared, a sweetish suppurating smell filled the room, making everyone breathe faster and harder.

The sight that awaited them could not even be called the remains of human hands. Everything was mixed together in a bloody mess—clumps of fur from the mittens, smashed finger bones, shreds of flesh and skin. Unable to stand it, Toko turned away.

"More blood, more blood," called Kelena. "Let the puppy blood wash your wounds and give you a dog's endurance."

With effort, Toko turned back to where Kelena was doing her work. She moved quickly and purposefully, as though she were handling walrus flippers or deer legs, not human hands. The blade slid over joints, separating the bones and leaving large, hanging folds of skin. Tossing aside a severed hand, Kelena picked up a needle threaded with deer tendons. A straight, beautiful seam began to stretch across the stump, and little droplets of blood marked the needle's wake.

The shaman-woman's face was covered in perspiration. Sometimes she would wipe the sweat from her forehead with an elbow and sniff impatiently. Having finished with one hand, she moved on to the other.

And then what everyone was dreading happened: John became conscious. At first he looked up, surprised, at the shaman-woman who was bent over him with her knife. Then, his face twisted in a grimace of horror and revulsion, he let out an awful scream and thrashed under her hand.

"Hold him," Kelena shouted. "Hold him tight!"

Toko and Armol' threw themselves over poor John, tried to weigh him down. But the white man was still strong and quick. More than once he managed to throw off their combined weight. But, ultimately, what can a cripple do? Orvo and Il'motch came to help.

"He mustn't move his hand!" were Kelena's orders. "You, Armol', hold his arm, and the rest of you, don't let him move."

Finally, they were able to bear down so that John couldn't move a muscle. Toko was almost lying on top of him, face to face, feeling John's hot breath on his skin.

John's large blue eyes were frozen with terror. Big tears rolled out from an overflowing blue lake, quickly running down his cheek and somewhere behind an ear into a thicket of light hair, wet with perspiration.

He was muttering something. Quickly, hurriedly. His tone conveyed pleading, horror, promises, pain, rage ...

Without having understood a single word, Toko answered him.

"Just bear it for a little while longer. All will be well. This woman is saving your life, don't fear her ... Your pain is hurting me too, but it must be borne. To go on living, it must be borne. You want to see your land, your mother, your loved ones, don't you? Maybe you have a wife? You'll come back to them alive. Without hands, but so what? White people have many jobs that don't require hands. So you'll do that kind of job. Besides, you folk are clever with gadgets and contraptions, you'll manage to fix something in place of hands. You've figured out many things; big fire-breathing boats like mountains roaming the seas, you've forced flame into a little jar, and it burns there with a noisy blue heat. Came up with guns, food in tins ... All will be well, Son."

"Grab him tighter," Toko heard the shaman-woman's voice, "I'm going to start sewing."

Toko leaned over John again and continued over his muttering.

"Kelena can sew. She'll make you a seam you'll be proud of—brag to all your friends. Deer-tendon threads are strong, they won't tear... Don't twitch, there's only a little left now. The blizzard will end, we'll drive back. It won't take two days to get to Enmyn, and you'll see your friends again. The ice has gone, it's a clearway. You'll sail off ... Just a little more, now. It's hard for me too, looking into your eyes ... "

John lost consciousness again, or else decided that resisting was useless, and Toko realized that it was easier to hold the white man down.

Through half-closed eyelashes, heavy with tears, John watched his torturers. When the terrible hag swam into view, sharp knife in hand, he had thought that they were intending to eat him. And right away he recalled tales of cannibals, devourers of human flesh, of savages who roast their prey over dying coals. He could smell his own burned flesh, the singed hairs of his beard.

He writhed and screamed, trying to reach Toko's dark, sweaty face with his teeth, trying to reach the treacherous and bloodthirsty brute that fed him from his own hands, cared for him, only to pin him down later, until each of the others had cut off a tasty morsel.

But it was an unequal battle. Toko lay on top of him like a boulder, and there was an incredible amount of weight in the young man. It was useless to fight. And it was then that John was seized by such self-pity that he couldn't restrain his tears. They rolled down his feverish cheek, calling up an overwhelming feeling of bitterness and irreparable damage. He had never been so helpless. Perhaps only somewhere in the foggy deep of childhood, in a life lost forever. Still, it was not the life he'd already lived that he grieved for, but that he'd never go home, never appear on the doorstep as the conqueror of polar seas. All the joys of the world will be for those who, at that moment, haven't an inkling of death. They will belong to Hugh Grover, his friend, the only one, maybe, who is hoping for his return. Poor, dear Hugh! Freezing in an ice-bound little ship that seemed so strong and secure, waiting for his friend.

It was as though a stone slab were weighing him down, and not a human being. A slab reeking revoltingly of sweat, rancid seal fat, and something else, filthy and unbearable.

Nausea assailed him. The pain had grown numb and, oddly, moved to his heart. But maybe he was dead, and all that was happening didn't matter. And the heavy weight—it was only the weight of the gravestone, laid over his final resting place. John closed his eyes and willed himself not to open them again, to shut out the hateful features, shiny with grease and sweat. He sensed some kind of commotion. They were doing something with his hands! But what?

John opened his eyes again. Strange—he had always been certain that the Chukchi had narrow slits for eyes, yet this one had enormous black irises, with intense sorrow and pity in their depths.

"What are you doing to me?" John shouted. "Let me go! You'll pay for this!"

"Just stick it out a little longer," he heard the voice of Orvo answer back. "Only a little while left."

"What are you doing to me?" John was howling.

"Taking care of your hands!" Orvo shouted back at him. "Taking off black flesh, saving your life!"

"Dear God," John moaned. "My hands! My hands!"

He did not feel the shaman-woman Kelena carefully tying soft deerskin strips over his stumps. But suddenly he understood that these primitives had cut off his fingers, barring the way for gangrene. What barbarism! A good surgeon could surely have rescued at least two, three fingers on each hand ... And they ... What if that horrible witch had chopped off both his hands?

John opened his eyes and saw that Toko had let go of him and was now sitting beside him, studying his face.

"He's come back!" Kelena pronounced it with joy. "He's moving his eyes."

"What have you done to me?" John asked quietly, addressing Orvo.

"Saved your life," came the old man's exhausted reply.

"What have you done with my hands?"

"It had to be done," Orvo answered. "Your flesh went black. Death stood close beside you, and you would have shut your eyes forever. There was only one way out—to take away the black flesh and black blood. And that's what she has done." Orvo nodded toward the shaman-woman, who was wearily packing a tobacco pipe with a huge convex mouthpiece.

"Oh, my Lord," John sobbed, and burst into tears, mindless of the others. "Who's going to need me without hands?"

Kelena wiped her bloody fingers with a wet cloth, smoothed her hair and looked at John with a smile.

"What's he wailing about?" she inquired of Orvo.

"Crying over his hands," said the old man.

"Understandable," the shaman-woman nodded.

She walked closer to John and softly stroked his head.

At the touch, John turned sharply and saw the old woman's hideous face. Her skin was like something baked in a roaring fire. Her burning eyes held untold tenderness. It was awful—compassion and ugliness intertwined!

He made a move to push the old woman away, but lost consciousness again, sinking back into the furs.

Kelena tucked him in, saying, "He'll sleep a long while."

Gathering her instruments neatly into a special leather bag, she began collecting what was left of the puppy and what she'd cut off with her knife, wrapping the stuff in a square of deerskin.

She looked around, hummed approvingly and called out to Orvo, "You'll help me."

There were dogs in the chottagin, curled up asleep. A fine powdery snow drifted in through the smoke-hole, and the blizzard shone down with a faint, mysterious light.

Kelena lifted the stone that held down the pelt hanging over the entrance, and instantly, the wind rushed into the yaranga, tousling the dogs' rough coats. The pelt flapped and buckled in her hands.

Orvo rushed to help the old woman.

As soon as they were outside, Orvo and Kelena were caught up in the whirlwind. Orvo followed the old woman, who had steamed forward into the wind at a clip. He was beginning to worry about going too far from the yarangas when, all of a sudden, the shaman-woman stopped dead in her tracks. She stood there like a broken-off fragment of a mountain crag, set in the face of the gale. And the blizzard's gusts passed around her, quickly raising a snow funnel around this living, motionless idol. She stood still for some time, whispering prayers and incantations, then reached down and dug a deep hole in the snow. Into the hole she lowered the puppy's remains and the severed hands of the white man.

The dogs, well-rested over the days of the blizzard, pulled well, and soon the sled caravan left the grazing camp and its welcoming valley by the foot of the mountain range far behind. John looked back for a long while, seeing the yarangas' smoke in the blue twilight. A kind of new, unfamiliar feeling trembled in his breast; it might have been gratitude toward the people he was leaving behind, people that had treated him with such warmth and compassion; or perhaps the happy expectation of seeing Hugh Grover, who waited for him at the Enmyn cape; or perhaps it was the understanding that he'd escaped the bony hand of death that had been cast over him …

Toko sat sideways on his dogsled, also glad to be going home. Even if the captain doesn't put up the reward, to hell with the Winchester, it could have been worse. What if Sson had died on the road, or after his fingers had been cut off? Then they would have had to forget the way back home and find another place; probably, they'd have to hide out in the tundra. It goes without saying, tundra folk live well, especially if their herd is as big as Il'motch's. The food is right outside the yaranga, and all you have to do is keep an eye on the deer in a blizzard and keep the wolves off. But the wandering! As soon as you're used to a spot, you've got to roll up your yaranga and go find another ... Toko considered the deer-herding life compared to the life of a sea hunter and concluded decisively that, although the shore dweller hasn't got a four-legged food supply waiting by the yaranga walls, still his life was far better. You can leave the yaranga on an early morning and look out onto the same unbroken line of the horizon.

There's nothing better than running the dogsleds in such weather, right after a long hard snowstorm, when spent nature seems to be resting after the last days' work. Silence hangs over everything, horizon to horizon, and the sound of gliding runners, the dogs' uneven breath or human voices, travels far and wanders the air, bouncing off icy crags and snowbound hummocks.

There's barely any frost. Spit, and the spittle lands on the snow, without having been frozen to an icy white lump in midflight. You can ride on top of the sled for long stretches, without having to jog alongside it for warmth.

Making nearly half the distance between the mountains and Enmyn, Orvo signaled a rest stop—to give themselves and, more importantly, the dogs a breather.

They made camp on the ice-bound river shore, putting up the tarpaulin tent. It was cramped, and only by bunching together could all four adults fit inside. Really, the tent had been meant for John, but he'd insisted strenuously on all the drivers piling in.

By some miracle, Orvo had managed to find a few dry twigs and make a fire. For a nightcap, each man received a mug of hot tea, strongly laced with vodka.

Dragging in all the deerskins he could find on the three sleds, Toko made a fluffy bed for John.

"I'm as healthy now as any of you," John declared. "I shouldn't have any special treatment."

Everyone bedded down helter-skelter.

Wriggling from side to side, John asked Orvo:

"Do you like this sort of life?"

"What sort?" At first Orvo didn't understand.

"The life that you lead out here, in the snows, in the frost?" John clarified. "There are other lands, you know, where life is more comfortable. It's warmer there, and there aren't such terrible snowstorms, like the one we've just lived through. You can weather one blizzard, at most two or three, but all your life! It's impossible! Take you, Orvo—you've seen other countries and other lands. Didn't you like them? Eh?"

"I liked them," Orvo said, uncertainly.

"You see. That means your homeland must be less comfortable," John concluded.

"Maybe so," Orvo agreed, and turned on his side with the intention of falling asleep, but John was evidently determined to make up for all the days of his silence.

"So what's the matter?" he asked. "Look here, the entire American continent is peopled with men who came over from other places. These men crossed enormous distances in search of a better life, in search of a better land."

"It's no good to us," Orvo answered. "We believe that we live on the best land in the world. That's the beauty, that no one wants it except for us ... I've seen our neighboring Eskimos forced to leave the coastline, because gold was found there."

John was quiet for a moment, then uttered thoughtfully:

"Well, maybe you're right. Maybe it's only because the Chukchi and the Eskimos settled in the worst lands that they've escaped annihilation."

Such talk chased away Orvo's desire for sleep, and no matter how he twisted and turned, on his side, on his back, still he couldn't fall asleep.

Growing sure that neither John nor Toko nor Armol' was asleep, Orvo decided to broach a worrying and important question whose gravity bore no comparison with any of John's deep and meaningful queries.

"What do you think," Orvo asked, "will the captain give us the promised reward?"

"Why wouldn't he?" John was surprised.

"Because we didn't get you to Anadyr'. And the work that the Russian doctor ought to have done, was done by the shaman-woman Kelena."

"That's no matter," John shrugged. "I only have to say the word, and Hugh will give you not only what he promised, but more besides. Have no doubt—your reward awaits you."

"Do you hear that?" Orvo couldn't hold his tongue. "He says we'll be paid in full!"

"That means I'll have a new Winchester!" exclaimed Toko.

John looked at his excited companions with a patronizing smile. How little these savages needed to be happy! No more than an old Winchester, one that's only good for the garbage heap in another world.

The reassurance that their reward would be paid in full, so agitated John's fellow travelers that for a long while there was nonstop talk inside the small tent, and Orvo himself promised John that they would do everything in their power to get him back to the ship at top speed.

John barely closed his eyes that night.

No sooner had his eyelids begun to inch down, than he could see before him the ship's silhouette against the black crags of Enmyn, Hugh's kind manly face, could hear the voices of his comrades, and good old English speech instead of this barbaric babble, where you can't tell where one word ends and another starts.

Morning came in the shape of a light crimson stripe over the eastern horizon. After a hurried snack, the travelers were under way and heading for the shore.

The drivers ran alongside their sleds, so as not to exhaust the dogs and conserve strength for the long unbroken journey ahead.

By the time the Northern Lights blazed across the sky, the dogsleds had reached the south side of the lagoon. If you listened carefully, you could already hear voices rising from the settlement, dogs' muted barking, a child's cry.

Sensing the nearness of home, the dogs ran without urging. Toko overtook Armol', then Orvo, and together with John broke into the lead position. The pack had been about to make a turn for the yarangas, but Toko shouted at them and steered them toward the seashore, to the craggy shelter where the Belinda lay.

Awakened by the barking, people were spilling out of their yarangas. They ran after the sled, shouting something, but it was impossible to make out a single word against the furious gallop of the pack.

The sled flew down the shore. Joyfully, tenderly, John looked out into the open sea that was soon lost from view over a dark horizon. Not a single piece of ice—the storm had cleared the water's expanse: Sail away to your heart's desire.

But the place where the Belinda had lain was empty. Toko held back, but John yelled something impatient and motioned ahead into the darkness, closer to the crags. Toko started the sled again, and drove slowly, wary of falling off the high shelf of fast ice and into the water.

John peered into the darkness, trying to discern the lines of a ship, until his eyes ached. He begged Toko, pleaded with him to come closer to the water's edge, but the sea was empty. Under the crags it was empty, too.

Joy was beginning to turn into worry and fear: What had happened to them? A shipwreck? But surely someone, even a single man, must have survived?

Slowly, almost by touch alone, and sensing the open water, the dogs nosed their way forward. The shouts of those who'd run after the sled were growing louder:

"Come back!" the people were screaming after them. "The ship is long gone! Nothing there, come back!"

Toko looked at John. But the other, not understanding the Chukchi language, was scanning the empty black stretch of open water in desperation. When his eyes met Toko's, he shuddered.

"Is it true?" he asked Orvo, who'd made his way forward.

"Yes," said the old man, head bent low. "They sailed on the very first day, as soon as the sea was clear of ice. They were in a great hurry, and didn't even come down to make their farewell."

"It can't be! It can't be!" cried John, and facing the sea, he howled: "Hugh! Hu-u-u-ugh! Why don't you answer me? Have you abandoned me? Oh God, but it's impossible!"

He jumped off the sled and ran for the edge of the fast ice.

"Hold him back, he'll fall into the water!" Orvo shouted fearfully.

Toko caught up with him and grabbed him from behind.

John was struggling, kicking, but Toko held him close.

"Hugh, come back for me! Don't abandon me here, don't leave me with these savages! Oh, Hu-u-u-gh!"

John fell to his knees, and then forward, prostrate. He couldn't speak at all now. His body convulsed with sobs, and his throat produced a drawn-out, animal howl—the cry of a man betrayed by his own tribe.

The Chukchi, observing the white man's grief, stood motionless; not one of them had made a sound until John went quiet, pressed flat against the ice.

All around, silence reigned. And the people imagined that they could hear the rustling draperies of the Northern Lights overhead.

Toko approached John cautiously. The other's eyes were wide open and gazing straight ahead into the distance. It seemed that he was seeing something far away, something that neither Toko nor any of his kin were ever to see. Yellow foam adhered to the corners of his mouth, and his face had taken on a strange aspect. It was as though a countless number of years had flown over his head, and it even seemed to Toko that there was a glint of gray in the hair escaping from underneath John's fur-lined hat.

"Take him back to the yaranga," Toko heard Orvo's quiet voice.

Toko clasped John around the middle and prepared to lift him up. But John, though slowly, rose by his own effort and leaning on Toko, limped toward the yarangas, black against the snow and the spill of the Northern Lights.

And from the north, wordlessly, without wind or wave, with barely a rustle, came fields of ice—to shut up the wide waterway so recently opened by the storm.

THE NOVEL

Vladimir Voinovich (1932–2018)
Translated by Peter Morley

Yet another son of the repressed father among the writers born in the twenties and the thirties, **Vladimir Voinovich** became a gloriously Soviet Jaroslav Hašek with his banned novel *The Life and Extraordinary Adventures of Private Ivan Chonkin*, the humorous story of a small man facing the Soviet system, the first book to combine humor and the Second World War.

Copied and distributed in samizdat, *Chonkin* soon attracted KGB attention, Voinovich was followed and harassed, probably poisoned and in late 1980 deported from the USSR to Germany.

Written in Germany, his other novel *Moscow 2042*, a satire on Russia's future, today is considered to be a dark prophecy: while the West was welcoming Gorbachev's *Perestroika*, Voinovich bitterly predicted the collapse of the democratic transition and the comeback of the KGB as a new Russian ruling elite.

Not long ago I wrote a tragic novel about the life of émigrés. The novel is called ... Actually, I can't remember what it's called; I'll have a look at the manuscript and write in the title later.

Although it took me about two and a half years to write the novel, I can't say I pushed myself particularly hard. The work generally flowed easily. All I had to do was write one line, and another would immediately write itself in my imagination, and after that a third one. I experienced no difficulties in describing nature or the state of characters, while the plot unfolded as though of its own accord.

The storyline, incidentally, was extremely simple. A Russian émigré writer discovers that his wife has been cheating on him with his best friend, an artist. He kicks up a stink, and she has no other option but to leave him for the artist. As soon as she leaves, he realizes that he can't live without her for a single second. He calls her, and she immediately returns, because she cannot live without him. But once she has come back, she realizes that she can't live without the artist. The situation is made more complicated because the writer and the artist cannot live without each other. The three of them curse and swear at each other, and then declare their mutual love. They try various ways of resolving the problem. Either the writer throws the woman out of the house, or the artist does. Sometimes she leaves one for the other of her own accord. Sometimes the writer gets sick of both of them and goes away, but cannot hold out and returns. Another time, the artist goes away. Then they decide to live together, all three – and live suffering from jealousy and hatred. Then they realize that they should all actually split up. It ends with all three of them wearing formal evening attire in the artist's workshop. They put on a record of Schubert and drink champagne by candlelight. The champagne, of course, is poisoned.

That's the novel in a nutshell. I wrote the last full stop about a month ago, and straight away took the manuscript to my publisher.

Yesterday the publisher invited me round. We sat in soft, leather armchairs in his office, which is hung with portraits of his best writers (my portrait, of course, is among them). Between us was a coffee table, on which lay a book, title side down.

Before starting the conversation, the publisher offered me something to drink: coffee, cognac, whisky, beer ... I asked for a coffee. He poked his head round the door and gave an order. His secretary brought the coffee, then left us. Stirring the coffee, the publisher looked at me carefully and said:

"Listen, Vladimir, you've written a wonderful novel!"

"Yes," I said humbly. "I think so too."

"I cried while I was reading through it."

"So did I," I admitted.

"And the last scene, when they drink poisoned champagne by candlelight while listening to Schubert, is sublime. There's nothing like it in world literature."

"Yes," I agreed. "I thought so too."

"Now, Vladimir, listen to me carefully. The thing is, we already printed this novel two and a half years ago."

I was surprised. "You printed it before I'd even written it?"

"No, no. We haven't reached quite that level of sophistication yet. Two and a half years ago you wrote this novel, and we published it.

It was a huge success, it got rave reviews, you won an award for it and gave a marvelous acceptance speech at the ceremony."

"That's impossible," I exclaimed. "Do you really think I can't remember what I wrote?"

"I don't think anything," he sighed. "But here is your manuscript, and here is your novel in printed form."

He turned over the book lying on the table and held it out to me.

I felt ill. I saw that the printed novel, just like the manuscript, was called … Now I can't remember what it was called. I'll have a look later and tell you then. Confused, I put the book and the manuscript into my briefcase and went home, forgetting to say goodbye to the publisher. At home I pulled out the book and the manuscript and began comparing them. As I was reading, I wept.

Interestingly, not only had I written the same novel word for word with the same title and the same number of chapters and words, but even the punctuation marks were the same throughout. This was even more surprising, as I'm usually pretty haphazard with punctuation.

I cried all night. I cried over the awful misfortune that had befallen me. How, I wondered, could this have happened? I'm not yet old enough to be struck down by such total senility. For two and a half years, I had written this novel straight through, passionately and in a fit of inspiration. I had smoked thousands of cigarettes and drunk gallons of coffee. Everything had turned out so well that, by turns, I laughed at my creation, or showered myself in tears, or slapped myself on the back, exclaiming: "Way to go, Pushkin, you son of a bitch!" And what of it?

When it was nearly morning, I decided that I would go to see the doctor as soon as I got up. Of course, the illness was at an advanced stage, but even so, there must be some medicine for it – some kind of anti-sclerotic or whatever it's called.

It was already getting light when I finally fell asleep.

After waking up, I decided to postpone my visit to the doctor. Never mind, I thought. I've just wasted two and a half years for nothing. To hell with them. It's a shame, of course, but I'm not going to spend my time going to see doctors. I'll get started on a new novel straight away instead. Especially as I have a splendid idea that I've been nurturing for two and a half years. The plot is extremely simple. A Russian émigré writer discovers that his wife is cheating on him with his best friend, an artist. He kicks up a stink, she leaves him, various other collisions happen (I still haven't thought of everything yet), and it ends up with all three of them getting together in the artist's workshop, putting on a record of Schubert and drinking poisoned champagne by candlelight.

Actually, I've got everything all thought out already, and in about two or maybe two and a half years I'll probably finish this novel.

THE MONSTER

Nina Katerli (1934–2023)

Translated by Bernard Meares

One of the most important female science fiction authors of the late Soviet period, **Nina Katerli** (born Nina Farfel) was as a child evacuated from Leningrad where her mother stayed and worked as a journalist during the siege. Katerli started her career as a chemist, but in the mid-seventies switched to professional writing. Being published officially with more convenient texts, while circulating samizdat copies of less acceptable writings, Katerli avoided direct collision with the KGB, but was monitored and summoned for the usual prophylactic chat.

One of the founders and the leading figures of the Saint-Petersburg PEN club (now disbanded), Katerli shared her literary work with human rights activity, publicly defending whistle-blowers persecuted by the Russian state security forces. Katerli's granddaughter Evgenia Berkovich, theatre director and playwright, is currently being persecuted by Russian authorities for her oppositional views.

"If only things were the way they used to be," said Aunt Angelina, and wiped her eyes.

"The way they used to be? Thanks very much! That's all I need. 'The way they used to be.'" Anna Lvovna could be seen choking back her tears and sniffling. "All my life I've lived in this apartment and cooked soup on a single burner in my own room, and I scarcely use any gas at all. And until very recently I had to go to the public baths, even though we have a bathtub right here. I was afraid to go to the toilet too often, not to mention the way my personal life …"

"No, if only things were the way they used to be," Aunt Angelina repeated obstinately. "I simply can't look at him the way he is now."

* * *

I myself had gotten used to the Monster, and even as a child had not been very much afraid of him. I was born after he moved into our apartment, so for me there was nothing unusual about coming across a shaggy creature with a single crimson eye in the middle of its forehead and a long scaly tail, whether in the hall near the bathroom or in the kitchen. But why go in for descriptions? One monster's very much like another, and ours was no more monstrous than the next.

They say that before I was born the other tenants in our apartment had filed an application with some agency, requesting that the Monster be evicted and housed someplace else, even that he be given an apartment all to himself. But the application was rejected on the grounds that if all monsters were given individual housing, there would be nothing left for large families. The argument ran that there were too many monsters and too few apartments, and when our application was turned down, the reason given was: "Yours is not the most serious case: There has not been a single fatality or instance of grievous bodily harm."

The fact that Anna Lvovna's husband had been turned into an aluminum saucepan for a whole month did not constitute grievous bodily harm, apparently. They say that as soon as her husband had returned to normal after having had borscht boiled in him and meat stewed in him for a month, he immediately abandoned her for another woman. Anna Lvovna was left on her own and since then has never forgiven the Monster for ruining her life. But the Monster claimed, on his honor, that he had turned Anna Lvovna's husband into a saucepan only because the man had been sweet-talking his mistress every evening from the phone in the hall, and he would have left home in any case. That way, at least he stayed home one more month, even if he spent the time as a saucepan.

I don't know how the story would have ended—Anna Lvovna, they say, was threatening to drop a burned-out light bulb in the Monster's feeding dish—but at that very time the Monster set off to work as an exhibit in a long traveling exposition organized by the museum of ethnography and anthropology.

In time, the tale about Anna Lvovna's husband came to be forgotten, but as the Monster grew older, he began to turn nasty, and gave us no peace at all.

You'd go into the bathroom and the sink and bathtub would be full of frogs and newts; or suddenly all the refrigerators would begin to howl horribly and heat up, the milk inside them would boil and the meat would roast; or else poor Anna Lvovna's nose would erupt in a boil of amazing size that changed color with each passing day: One day it would be blue, the next day lilac, and the day after that a poisonous green color.

It should be mentioned that Aunt Angelina and the Monster were on somewhat more equable terms. If she found a tortoise in her cupboard instead of bread, she would exclaim with pleasure, "Look, a reptile! I'll take it straight to the kindergarten for their pet corner!"

I now realize that when I was little the Monster simply couldn't stand me because I annoyed him so much. Everything I did annoyed him: I clattered up and down the hall and I laughed too loudly and I loved peeking into his room at him. So he kept giving me tonsillitis. Not serious cases, but the kind that if you so much as laugh you lose your voice, and if you run you get sent to bed.

When I grew up, the Monster did me great harm for a time; whenever anyone called me up, he would always get to the phone before the others and hiss, "She's not in. She's gone out with someone else."

I live alone now. My parents are no longer alive, I have never had a family of my own, and Aunt Angelina, with whom I share the apartment, takes care of me after a fashion, but as for the Monster ... At least he's stopped tormenting me. Of course, if I come back late from the theater or from visiting friends, I'm bound to trip over the cat in the hall even though we've never had a cat. Or I'll tear my new dress on barbed wire. But that's nothing—mere trivialities. And recently even that kind of thing has stopped happening. Something's gone wrong with the Monster. You wouldn't recognize him: his eye has turned from red to a kind of dirty ginger color and his fur has gone gray; to put it in a nutshell, our Monster is getting old. He's stopped going to work and sits for days on end in his room, just hissing occasionally and sometimes sighing. And it was only today that Aunt Angelina said she'd prefer things the way they used to be because it broke her heart to look at the Monster, and she didn't have the energy to sweep up his scales after him.

"About those dreadful scales I totally agree with you, Angelina Nikolayevna," declared Anna Lvovna. "It's disgraceful! He must be made to do an additional week of cleaning duty. Nobody should have to wipe his dirt up after him!"

At this point the conversation came to a sudden halt because the Monster's door squeaked loudly, and a minute later there he was in the kitchen.

"Picking on me behind my back, eh?" he asked, and his eye reddened slightly. "Well, now I'm going to make you all freeze. You've never felt such cold!"

And the Monster began to blow so hard that his cheeks turned blue and his head started to tremble.

He blew and blew and suddenly I noticed Aunt Angelina shivering and jumping in place and knocking her legs against each other and rubbing her nose as if it had been frostbitten.

"It's so cold, oh, it's freezing!" she moaned dolefully, for some reason winking at me. Then she suddenly screeched, "What are you standing around like that for? Keep moving! Keep moving! Or else you'll catch your death of cold! Hands on your waist! Bend your knees! One, two, three!"

I wasn't that cold; in fact, I was even rather warm, all the more so because we were in the kitchen and all the gas burners were lit. But Aunt Angelina was winking and shouting so that I, too, put my hands on my hips and started doing knee bends.

"There you go! There you go!" shouted the Monster gleefully. "Now you're going to dance for me!"

I scarcely had time to think before Aunt Angelina grabbed me by the hand and began leaping about in a frenzied dance. I followed her lead.

"This is a nuthouse!" declared Anna Lvovna angrily and left the kitchen.

The Monster stared after her with a frightened look, then turned to Aunt Angelina as she danced and asked quietly, "Why isn't she dancing? Why did she go away?"

"She's stiff with cold!" shouted Aunt Angelina, gasping for breath but continuing to dance. "Can't you see?"

But the Monster had already forgotten what he had been asking. Dragging his tail and leaving a trail of scales across the floor, he went over to his refrigerator and opened the door.

"Where's my bone?" he said in perplexity, "I remember it was here yesterday, I bought it at the store!"

"Your bone? There it is, you made soup out of it this morning, don't you remember?" shouted Aunt Angelina, stamping away, but at the same time managing to pass the Monster her own white enamel saucepan with soup in it.

"I did? Oh ..." and the Monster looked uncertainly into the saucepan, "I never had a pot like this."

"But it really is your pot, I just cleaned it up a bit, that's all."

"Aaargh!" he roared, "You dare touch my pot?! I forbid you to! For that both of you will ... you will both ... turn to stone for thirty-five minutes!"

Aunt Angelina suddenly froze the way children do when they play Statues. As fate would have it, my nose started itching and I was about to rub it with my hand when she inconspicuously but painfully jabbed me in the side, so I froze, too.

The Monster glared at us triumphantly, then grabbed the boiled chicken out of Aunt Angelina's saucepan and ate it whole.

"A delicious bone!" he rumbled, licking his lips, and then took pity on us.

"You can go now," he said dismissively, and strode imperiously out of the kitchen, slurping soup from the top of the saucepan.

"Why did you give him your entire dinner?" I asked, when the door closed behind the Monster. "And where is his bone, anyway?"

"He didn't have a bone!" said Aunt Angelina, "He hasn't been to the store for a week."

"Then what's he looking for?"

"God knows! Maybe he forgot. Or maybe he's just being that way to show us that everything's all right. But he doesn't have any money, not a single kopeck, and he's going hungry."

"What about his pension?"

"He doesn't have a pension! He's an exhibition object, and ... he's been written off, dropped from the show." Aunt Angelina lowered her voice. "It's as if he doesn't exist. And now I'm afraid about his room. I'm afraid he'll be evicted. Just make sure you don't tell Anna Lvovna."

"I won't breathe a word," I said, also in a whisper.

* * *

Aunt Angelina and I began taking turns buying bones and chopped meat from the butcher and leaving them in the Monster's refrigerator. On one occasion she left two apples and a small carton of kefir.

"All this meat's very bad for him! It can ruin his digestion," she said. "I wanted to buy him a big bottle of kefir but he always immediately bolts any food he has, so I bought a carton instead."

"He's bound to throw out the apples," I said.

"We'll see. Maybe he won't realize. Lately his eyesight's been getting poor," and at that moment Aunt Angelina looked around at the door; Anna Lvovna was just coming into the kitchen.

"It makes me laugh just to look at the two of you," she declared. "All this undercover charity—do you think I'm blind? Such pretense—what a show! And for whom! If he was human, it would be one thing, but he's not, he's just vermin."

"You should feel sorry for him; after all, he's old," I said.

"My dear, pity's not a feeling you should brag about, pity's humiliating. And in this case," she said as she put her coffeepot on the stove, "in this case, pity doesn't enter into it. It was one thing when he was making himself useful in his ... in his freak show; we could put up with him then, but not now. Animals should live in the wild."

The Monster had crept into the kitchen so softly that we didn't even know he was there. He now stood in the doorway and his eye was as ruddy as it had been in the first flush of youth.

"So, I'm an animal, am I?" he said slowly and slumped onto a stool. "I'll show you."

His breathing was heavy and irregular, the sparse gray fur on his head and neck stood on end.

"I'll show you. ... Your ... legs ... will ... give way ... beneath you! ... Yeah! ... You will ... all ... fall ... on the floor ... and then ... One, two, three ... All fall down!"

Aunt Angelina and I collapsed simultaneously. Anna Lvovna remained standing, leaning against the edge of the stove, and grinned, staring the Monster straight in the eye.

"And you?" said the Monster. "What about you? This doesn't mean you, I suppose? Fall down, I tell you!"

"Give me one good reason why I should," she said, scowling.

"Because I've put a spell on you, that's why."

"Oh, you slay me," said Anna Lvovna, going right up to him. "What have we here, a magician? All you know how to do is leave your scales all over the floor and help yourself to everyone else's food! You're just trash and you're due for the dump! Just garbage. You've been written off!"

"Written off?" repeated the Monster in a whisper. "Who's been written off? Me? Written off? Not true, not true! I can do anything! Look at them! They fell down!"

"Ha! Ha! Ha!" Anna Lvovna burst out laughing. "They're just pretending. They're sorry for you, see. You've been written off. You've lost your job. I've been to the museum myself and I've seen the directive with my own eyes."

"No!" The Monster leapt up from the stool and rushed from the door to the stove, thrashing his mangy tail across the floor. "I'll show you. I'll turn you into a rat! A rat! Now!"

"Ha! Ha! Ha!" was Anna Lvovna's only reply, and suddenly she stamped on the Monster's tail with all her might.

The Monster screamed. One after another great tears streamed from his eye, which immediately turned pale blue and dimmed. Aunt Angelina and I jumped up from the floor.

"You ought to be ashamed of yourself! Let him go! An old man. Don't be so cruel to him!"

"A rat! A rat!" hissed the Monster, forgetting himself, and he poked Anna Lvovna in the shoulder with a dark and crooked finger. "One! Two! Three!"

"Ha! Ha! Ha!" sniggered Anna Lvovna.

But now Aunt Angelina and I began to shout. "A rat! A rat!" we screamed. "You're a rotten rat! Vermin! One! Two! Three!"

Suddenly Anna Lvovna was gone.

She had just been laughing in our faces, her shoulders shaking in her white blouse, when suddenly she was no more. She had totally disappeared, as if she had never existed.

The kitchen suddenly fell silent. Something live jabbed against my foot and immediately leapt away to the wall. I screeched and jumped onto the stool.

A large gray rat shot across the kitchen and scuttled under Anna Lvovna's table. The Monster was whimpering softly, his face turned toward the wall.

"See," said Aunt Angelina, "you did it. Don't cry. Now let's go and have some soup."

"It's you who did it, not me. And it's true, you know; I have been written off. There has been a directive."

"What do we care about directives," said Aunt Angelina, carefully stroking the Monster's fur. "Don't you be afraid of anybody. And if anybody touches you I'll give him … I'll give him ants."

"And so will I," I said. "Okay?"

The Monster didn't reply. Slumped against the wall, he dozed off, shutting his eye and wrapping his thin hairless tail around his legs.

RED CAVIAR SANDWICHES

Asar Eppel (1935–2012)

Translated by Joanne Turnbull

A poet and translator, who translated into Russian Bruno Schulz, Isaac Bashevis Singer, Wisława Szymborska, Vítězslav Nezval, Henryk Sienkiewicz and other great figures of Eastern European literature, awarded with the prestigious Italian Premio Grinzane Cavour for his translations, **Asar Eppel** was himself a short-prose writer, master of the illusory and magic resurrection of the past erased and distorted by 'Sovietness'.

In 2002 Eppel was granted the Kazakov prize as the best Russian short prose writer of the year.

As you approached Ostankino Park, coming from Mariyna Roshcha along wide Novo-Moskovskaya Street, on your right you would soon see the Pushkin student dorm, an accumulation of stuccoed barracks. A barrack is done fast and slapdash. And always for drastic action. Like a barricade, its direct predecessor. But a barricade may fall, and then be taken down, whereas a barrack will never fall, and never be taken down, witness that heir to the barricade, the Pushkin student dorm.

Having at some point performed its panicky mission, become a shelter for faceless working-class students, and cast the ones who finished out into the world of socialist achievements and rah-rah Soviet songs, it did not fall and was not taken down, but occupied: by the ones who never finished, by all manner of riffraff, and by good souls. Occupied permanently and in perpetuity.

I had various acquaintances there. Of the first, second, and third ilk. Take, say, of the third, the amazing Samson Yeseyich. But about him later. Not here. Instead I'll tell you about Aunt Dusya who took care of him. And not just about her. First, however, let's celebrate the barrack. The Pushkin student dorm.

The barrack is an oblong two-storey structure crouched low to the ground with two entrances along the front and two outside wooden staircases going to the second floor. It is a barely whitewashed construction under a black tarpaper hat inside which people walk, sit, lie down, and out of which they peer. I couldn't tell you the length of the barrack today, but we can easily establish the width. Since the plaster walls were nothing but timber inside, the barrack's butt-end could not have been more than twenty-four or twenty-five feet wide; or rather, that's exactly what it was, since that is the length of a timber. Said feet contained the lengths of two rooms plus the width of the corridor. Allow five feet for the latter, and that leaves eight feet for each room. That's right! Along the length you may fit a working-class student's bed (six-and-a-half feet) and, at the head or foot of the bed, a nightstand in which the working-class student may keep his Marx or his tattered little tome with the disturbing but trivial title *Without the Bird Cherries*.*

On each floor you have a corridor five feet wide and, on either side of this corridor, opening on to it, you have rooms stretched the length of their beds and, crammed into these rooms, people, children and belongings.

The corridor, which is also the kitchen, is absolutely endless, for beneath its ceiling burn only two yellow ten-watt bulbs, as sooty as oil-stoves, and in the smoke and steam the nightmarish chiaroscuro from many different objects creates countless screens and culs-de-sac, and all of this corroded by the rich, fetid, murky air.

Smoke and stench pervade. Along the walls loom washtubs, rags on nails, twig baskets, two-handled saws wrapped in dusty, brittle yellowed newspapers wound round with twine; the floor is a sea of trunks piled one on top of another, little padlocked cupboards painted white, and damp soapy stools supporting basins under small hanging washstands. There is no rule or rest from the dimly glinting buckets of water, the trash buckets, and the buckets of slops for the pig which someone's godmother is fattening in a nearby village, from the old-fashioned camp beds (canvas on crosspieces), from the sleds, the vats, the barrels, the bowls, from the shovels caked with yellow clay, the pitchforks and the rakes, for the ground-floor tenants

---

* A sentimental love story by Panteleimon Romanov (1884–1938).

have vegetable patches under their windows, and some keep rabbits or chickens. There are children's skis, faded and flat as boards, one ski shorter than the other for lack of means. And there are plain boards, also of different sizes, with crooked brown nails bowed down to their rough surfaces.

There are even some things – marvellous but unsuited to the needs of barracks troglodytes – that once belonged to the ruling class: a broken chair lined with cord on velvet upholstery, a stand for walking sticks, and a settee (facing the wall) whose rounded back in tandem with the wall makes a marvellous receptacle for storing potatoes.

A frightful corridor, a foul labyrinth, no end to it! But even its endlessness is not beyond reproach, for it is broken up by open doors, by the odd conversation, always more akin to an argument, or by the um-pa-ra um-pa-ra-ra of an accordion, and from one of the rooms comes the astonishing voice of a portable gramophone which goes on valiantly playing the same popular tune from the last war on the same dull needle (sad to say, the record cracked badly not long ago).

Aunt Dusya lives in the cornermost and most pitiful room. The eight linear feet abovementioned multiplied simply by five become forty square feet, and anyone who has occupied such a room knows that opposite the door is the window, that to the left you sleep and rummage in your trunk, while to the right you sit at the table and keep moths in the closet. A treadle sewing machine, if you have one, may stand by the window; if not, you may put, say, a stool there.

The bedding on Aunt Dusya's cot forms a hummock, since non-seasonal things and big bunches of torn brownish stockings, the raw material for darning heels, are stowed under the mattress. The stockings tend to contain flakes of the epidermis of the once-young Aunt Dusya; the stockings are all knitted, though an occasional exhibit is of lisle or even Persian thread.

The ceiling is low, six feet ten inches, but that doesn't bother anyone because people were short and stumpy then, like the Oryol peasants in Turgenev's novels. Turgenev's stately Kaluga peasants did not settle here and were found no closer than Grokholsky Lane, and that was miles and miles away.

So then, on the bed there was a hummock and this caused us – me, pressing against my girl, so as to die, and my girl, pressing against me, so as to restore me to life, my girl who, unlike me, knew wide beds and how best to use them – various (we won't go into it!) inconveniences frustrating the ancient and inarticulate rite of embrace.

The barrack, its corridor, Aunt Dusya ... My blindingly beautiful girl, who knew other – Oh God, I slid down again! – much wider beds, and I, who knew only trestle-beds – Oh God, you slid down again! – but who also knew that my blindingly beautiful girl, who knew other wider beds, had come to see me. Why all this together? Why did all this couple, combine, connect on the ground floor of a barrack, more specifically in its right-hand rear corner, if facing the barrack from the front? – oh God, we slid down again! – here's why.

Little, wheezing, old Aunt Dusya took care of my old friend, the never-married physics teacher Samson Yeseyich, who lived in the barrack across the road. But about him, as I said, later and not here. So now, Aunt Dusya, who considered friendship with me good for the brilliant Samson Yeseyich (about which also later and not here), and therefore respected me, had supplied me with the key to her tiny room through the kind offices of Samson Yeseyich. She was in the habit – for a little something or simply for a word of thanks – of loaning her key to friends of the physicist, probably because the carnal life of others excited pleasant thoughts in her.

People with good memories will never forget how hopeless it was in those days to find a corner in which to consummate the unbearable half-meetings begun in bushes, in building entrances, on park benches or in dormitories when the roommates had fallen asleep – as if they ever did! So to land on Aunt Dusya's lumpy bunk, while Aunt Dusya herself went to her employer's to tidy up or just dashed out somewhere, was a rare and welcome piece of luck.

Now about *her* – the girl for whose sake I had got hold of Aunt Dusya's key.

We were trudging, by now deeply chagrined, uphill – this climb up a rough, rutted road studded with round flat sea stones and shingle on which one's feet kept twisting, had been a very bad idea of mine, and it seemed that she, my new friend, a Calypso-like beauty with fear in her eyes, was on the point of rebelling and wanting to turn back, since even the pretext for our ascent had been unclear and unconvincing: either to survey the sea from on high or to see what the new fruit on a tangerine tree looked like.

But my companion did not rebel, though she could have turned right around, and I waited in dread for her indignation, for her acquiescence to cease: I was young then, but I knew that acquiescence could easily turn to indignation. After all, she suspected, or rather understood our secret, or rather my intention – my clammy and intolerable hope. Of course she, too, was party to our tacit compact. If not for that torrid climb! At first she agreed to look at the new fruit, then she changed her mind.

We sat down under a tangerine tree on the baked earth, on the dry hot clods, and my hand began to insinuate itself between her softish, slightly cool, but also slightly flushed thighs. My five-fingered touch was discovering the longed-for world tucked between those stunning buttresses; suddenly my wrist was creeping along the dry hot clods of cultivated earth under the tangerine tree, and my fingers were squeezing in between her thighs, now relaxed, now clenched, and burying themselves like pups in the damp, vast – after the closeness of her thighs – tangle of the thickets attained. My girl was quivering, twitching and protesting, 'Don't, or else I'll get a headache, a really bad one!' Yet she went on, with her slender, ringed fingers, squeezing whatever she liked. 'Let's wait,' she whispered, 'this isn't the place. People will see us, and the sun ... Let's wait!' She went on twitching, her knees now irrevocably parted, but she was right, and the arid incline under the wayside tangerine tree was wilting and dying under the sun.

Wait till Moscow? Which one of us was going away that day, I don't remember. Let's wait till Moscow!

We walked to Aunt Dusya's at the end of a warm summer afternoon past the barrack and the mangy little vegetable patches, fenced in, or rather off from one another, with all sorts of junk. Standing in the windows of the low ground floors were people and insipid indoor plants, growing out of cans either rusty or once gold, now peeling.

Note: Russian cans have always been the colour of tin, and it was only the war, on top of all its meagre miracles, that produced the gilt, black-lettered cans of stewed pork that were our salvation. And though the war was over, and though it was already so over that we had somehow decided to return the Dresden art collection to the Germans, once we had shown it to all comers, these cans still rotted in the windows of the Pushkin student dorm, though some were wrapped in pretty white paper cut-outs, now shrivelled from the sun, mildew and water.

We walked to Aunt Dusya's, past low buildings in the windows of which stood people who seemed not to know me, though my acquaintances might just as easily have been standing there. Our skilfully chosen route allowed us to avoid meeting anyone since, in the first place, I was with a woman and, in the second place, a woman utterly unheard of in these parts.

People's first and most correct thought would be that she was a spy, since she was dressed and adorned as no woman to this day has ever been dressed and adorned, save the heroine of that universal film favourite *The Girl of My Dreams*. Even I, whose fingers retained the memory of her bathing suit, wondrous for those days, heavy to the touch, like a portière, and phosphorescent beneath the stars of our night-tide swim, when everything was beginning and when she kissed me with a kiss unknown in my once and future life, well ... even I, who knew her sartorial means, was stunned by what I saw.

As I said, the war had ended to such an extent that it was remembered as a time of hunger, but hunger with stewed pork, as opposed to the hunger after the war without stewed pork. The wartime styles (noted for battlefield chic) varied with American gifts (by those who had them) had ended, and the captured finery – fabulous for its elegance, its shimmering linings, its neat seams, its lacy underthings, and the many possible ways of wearing all this even inside out if you liked – had faded. The wartime styles had ended for everyone, and everyone was arrayed in their own homemade clothes. But not my girl. She came to me in a fantastic guise, which one I no longer recall, though she had her own, very good reasons for her appearance.

Women came to Blok* wafting perfume and mist. This I learned later. She came to me sparkling with rings, earrings and necklaces. All this would become known as costume jewellery and over the years people would get used to it, despite their shame and prejudices,

---

* Alexander Blok (1880–1921), the symbolist Russian poet whose principal symbol was a beautiful and mystical female figure.

they would get used to wearing this stuff that made broads look like ladies. But where could it have come from when it wasn't supposed to exist yet? Where did she get it all: the strange dress, the shoes with golden clasps glittering with glass beads? Where? Here's where: she was with the occupation forces in the Eastern bloc, had lived a long time in East Germany, and recently come from there, where she worked as a staff translator and lived with her husband, an officer in the secret service.

She was deathly afraid of her spook. With his secretive way of life and omniscience he compelled her soul and flesh to suffer, generally treating the latter with an unbearable brittleness. And this flesh was not assuaged, neither beside the warm sea, nor under the tangerine tree, for fear of being seen by some acquaintance, a junior officer, say, dispatched by the spook.

Nor could we arrange a meeting in Moscow. Not for a long time. But now Aunt Dusya had given me her key, had gone out somewhere, and I was walking with my girl, a little to one side and a step ahead or, you could say, behind, along the little paths and backways around the Pushkin student dorm to Aunt Dusya's barrack. It certainly tests a man's mettle: trying to sneak a glittering woman in the door of a teeming barrack right on the main street.

As it is, people are lolling dumbstruck in every window, old women perched on banks of earth are combing out wisps of grey hair with fine-tooth combs, former classmates may appear, and then there's the man by the shed who has been fixing his bicycle for a year now.

The summer street is light and sunny, and behind another shed boys are mating rabbits. Girls huddle at a deliberate distance, but still see how the rabbit, raptly nibbling grass beside the doe one instant, rears up on her the next, one of the long-eared little beasts squeals, then both wiggle their noses, and resume eating. The boys insist that the rabbits are *fucking*. The girls, watching from afar, know what the rabbits are doing, but don't use the word *fucking*. The brazen boys, wanting the girls' attention, make circles with thumb and forefinger, then insert the other forefinger, and slide it back and forth. The girls walk off.

Thus I lead my girl through my childhood, but she neither sees nor cares; she walks beside me in silence, thinking only of how her spook may have had her shadowed.

She walks with amazing calm. She is simply numb and blind with fear. *Her* fear. *My* fear has made me monstrously sharp-eyed and, when we pass from the daylight into the barrack's pitch-dark corridor, I manage to make out someone's slummy laundry hanging at the far end and a man sorting maggots for bait in a tin can.

Some trouble with Aunt Dusya's key ... and we're in the room. I've brought sandwiches. Red caviar. Five of them. Cheap eats in those days. And she produces wine! She produces ... wine ... Never in my wildest dreams would I have expected such a thing. She produces a wine I don't know, the only wines I know (and those by hearsay) are Cahors and 'three-sevens' port, highly regarded by local experts in anything you like – but not *this*.

'Wait a moment!' she says when I, having drunk a little wine and eaten half a sandwich, begin aquiver to embrace her, freely fondling the heavy warm folds of her soft dress, in itself a voluptuous sensation.

'Wait a moment!' she says. 'I have to run out first!'

'Run out?'

'I have to! Or else I can't ...'

I am crushed. In the Pushkin student dorm they run out, here's where: for the entire barrack there are all of two barns, resembling, as it were, rural granaries. Each one is high and light on account of the chinks in the walls and a lone dormer window. The barns are bleached with lime which drools down the dingy boards to create a unique atmosphere of slovenliness and untouchability. Each granary is divided by a wall that would have reached the ceiling, had there been one, but above the wall is empty space, and higher still one can see the ridge of the gable roof.

On either side of the wall – in the male and female halves – there is a platform made out of thick boards in which a series of eight holes has been cut. The effect of another presence is total. First, because of the low partition; second, because if you stand slightly back from the platform, the product of the performer on the other side of the partition is visible in the pit.

As if this weren't enough, huge holes have been punched in the wall at different levels. Here and there the holes have been boarded up with whatever came to hand. But only here and there. Now I was not born in a palace, and I have visited my share of latrines, and that one is supposed to sit, not stand on a toilet seat, I figured out all by myself at the age of twenty-three, but I never ventured into those monstrous outhouses except in dire need, though on sultry days the stench in their simmering semi-darkness grew somehow languorous, and through the breaches in the partition one could observe the determined squatting and listen to intriguing bits of female conversation. But that was in summer.

As we know, our people are uncommonly careless and sloppy with regard to earth closets. It costs our people nothing, given their disdain for basic aiming skills, to foul the rim of the orifice, soak the floor and leave fingerprints on the wall. The boards absorb everything, everything sticks to them, deliberate sloppiness begets forced sloppiness, and it becomes harder and harder to position oneself over the hole. Puddles further frustrate one's approach to the sloping grey gutter, especially if one is in soft soles or slippers.

And now, the cold is upon us. Everything that has been absorbed begins to freeze and form layers. By late December, crossing the ice crust to a hole is out of the question. There is less and less room for manoeuvre. The visiting public retreats closer and closer to the door, fouling the floor higgledy-piggledy. The walls (inside only, so far) are caked with tall ice crusts the colour of whey, rising up out of the floor like stalagmites, interspersed with fossilized brown clumps. The hoarfrost on the boards, the yellow newspapers frozen in the ice, the yellow crystals forming under the roof: nothing deters our people – where else can they go? By mid-February, only by standing in the doorway may one celebrate the call of nature in the murk of the fossil world.

This circumstance decidedly alters the daily rhythms of the Pushkin student dorm. People put off going until dusk or after dark. By now the walls are caked even on the outside with turbid ice crusts, by now the expanse around the walls, if not covered with snow, is you can well imagine what.

But now spring arrives. Someone, cursing wildly, is cleaning out all this muck. Who, I don't know. For half an hour after it has been hosed down the granary looks human, then it begins all over again, and towards evening masturbator Mitrokhin walks in and takes a swift chisel to the rough-hewn wall's most promising hole. In no time at all, he is convulsing in a corner in response to the rustling behind the partition.

For this granary, then, my girl is calmly about to set out. In haste and confusion, I explain the long way round, unable to imagine how she will get there, and if she does, how she, wafting perfume and mist, will react to the shame, how she will ford the swollen floor in her velvet slippers.

I cannot take her there, for I simply cannot imagine how anyone could take a woman to that place, and so become unwittingly initiated into this utterly secret necessity, into this apotheosis of awkwardness and discouraged dignity.

She goes. I wait. I get it! Walking through the settlement, humiliated by the road to Aunt Dusya's, appalled by her forty-square-foot burrow – I'm used to it, but she's seeing it for the first time – by the musty humpbacked bed on which we *will*, by the table with the caviar sandwiches, red-and-white and sparkling beside the cloudy tumbler in whose putrid water a dirty swollen onion, now limp and splayed, has disgorged the repulsive greenish bud of an onion leaf ... seeing all this made her change her mind. She's gone. She's just up and gone! She took her purse, didn't she! True, she left the wine ... she brought wine ... It never ever occurred to me that anyone would bring wine for my sake. She's gone! And if she's not gone, then she's lost, and if she's not lost then somebody's picked her up: as I said, the neighbours might easily think she was a spy. Only recently, loyal and concerned citizens not far from here caught a spy, apparently American. Or even two.

'Hey, Kalinych, you mother, why'd you block my woodpile with your bicycle? Ain't you ever gonna be done with that thing?' the cheerful start of a friendly exchange by the shed can be heard outside the window. I startle, freeze, steal up to the window, and peek through the slit between the gauze curtain and the peeling wood.

A rivulet of tiny ants streams by my eye, skirting a stony tumour of oil paint on Aunt Dusya's window frame. They stream out of one chink and disappear an inch or so later into another. That's nothing! At this point, my eyes could make out an amoeba. My ears could pick up ultrasound.

'Kalinych, you fuck ...' the usual sounds from the vicinity of the shed and then my pounding heart stops as the door, just behind me, opens with a jolt. I jerk round and am amazed to see my girl slip quietly into the room.

'Here I am,' she says, and I fasten my sharp eyes on her velvet slippers, especially the delicate line of her pretty dyed-black sole.

'Where can I wash my hands?'

Oh God! It will never end! I don't know where Aunt Dusya's washstand is in the endless corridor or which shard of soap on which of the thirty-three shelves belongs to her or what sort of soap it is. Maybe it's the marble soap sold by weight and boiled by the Ruzhansky soap-boiler – though boiled out of what? About that in due course. What if the basin under the washstand is full and has to be emptied? And if it's full, then of what?

'*Unmöglich!*'* I say, because my girl speaks German beautifully and at the time I too could get along in this language fairly well which, incidentally, is largely what drew me to her there, where the tangerine trees bear fruit.

'*Unmöglich, weil ich weiss nicht wo ist der* Aunt Dusya's washstand *und Seife!*'† I play the fool, and she, smiling, takes a sparkling perfume bottle from her bag, then some cotton wool, and neatly wipes her fingers with the many magnificent rings, among them a thick band binding her to her spook – not the custom then and also a surprising thing.

She went to the window, glanced through the slit to one side of the curtain, then turned around, undid her dress, took it off, then took off some other mysterious underthings, then took off everything else, and for the first time I saw a woman who had undressed for me.

'Now you take everything off!' said this miracle when I went up to her, embraced her and dazedly pressed myself into this unbearably various nakedness so unlike my own uniformity.

'Wait a moment! Stop! Metal inhibits love!' And she began to remove the sparkling objects from her neck, from her wrists, from her fingers, from her ears, and put them on the oilcloth-covered table where there soon accrued a small heap of watches, earrings, bracelets, rings – one rolled away under the bed. By her exquisite legs I, like the young Actaeon, found the gossamer ring in the desolation under the bed, and as I pulled my head out, I saw, still on my hands and knees, that the exquisite legs had been tucked up out of my way – taken off the floor: she had sat down on the humpbacked bed, and

---

* 'Impossible!'

† 'Impossible, because I don't know where Aunt Dusya's washstand and soap is!'

then lain down. I quietly placed the ring on the oilcloth. The ring clung trustingly to the others, and I just as trustingly entered the land where they kiss strangers sweetly, caress them, enchant them and yet sob, clinging to these strangers – the land of ripening tangerines and dry hot earth, the land of two, along whose damp sandy shores the wanderer Odysseus bends his firm steps towards Calypso languishing in the tangled thickets of her hair.

This was free love. All my previous conquests – hurried, prehensile, greedy and pitiful – were under-love compared with what happened in the land of the tangerine sun. Outside it was getting dark, in the room it was twilight, and this dusk increasingly isolated the land I had entered over and again, always to the sound of muffled laughter, muffled sobs, muffled words, and where I suddenly sensed moist lips humbly kissing my regal hand.

This was a meeting of two people who, for different reasons, dearly needed each other. A woman who needed me, and I, who needed this woman most in the world. A meeting without shame, or rather *outside shame*, celebrating with muffled sobs our triumph over the foul surround and over the hero of these out-of-the-way places, the spook; a meeting joining experience of vast Pomeranian beds with the entertaining erotica of Russian suburbs, slaking Mitrokhin's unbearable reverie, and sanctifying the ancient gesture made by the brazen boys in front of the girls at the rabbits' wedding.

The weary tangerine sun was already sinking when we heard a polite little cough through the door.

'Your landlady! She's been sitting there a long time, I think!'

When we came out of the room, leaving as a token of thanks two whole sandwiches and one almost whole, as well as half a bottle of wine, we found Aunt Dusya slumped on a sack of bran in the now empty corridor. She was dozing and softly grunting. I touched her padded jacket, I had to return the key. She jumped up, grinned slyly and surprised us with this phrase worthy of Sumarokov:* 'Love is by nature inherent in people!'

On the benighted street, my girl and I quickly went our separate ways, because she might run into undesirable acquaintances at the

---

* Alexander Sumarokov (1717–1777), poet, dramatist, advocate of Classicism.

Ostankino tram stop, she said, scraping a fleck of red caviar off her teeth.

I walked away from the Pushkin student dorm and, by the last barrack, ran into Nasibullin, a shy and very modest Tatar boy who enrolled voluntarily in a secret service college after school.

'Good evening!' he said politely because he always strove to associate his cultivation, diligently acquired thanks to the concern of society, with my own innate cultivation and, by way of continuing this association, he asked shyly: 'Been to the Dresden show yet?'

'Na-a-ah!'

'Go, don't miss it!' And to pique my interest he glanced down the dusky alleys, looked terribly embarrassed and said: 'Lots of naked people!'

THE BALLAD OF THE WOODEN PLANE

Eduard Kochergin (1937)

Translated by Simon Patterson with Nina Chordas

After losing his parents to the repressions in Leningrad, **Eduard Kochergin** was forcibly taken to an orphanage, transferred with this orphanage to Siberia during the war, fled, lived the life of a street child and vagabond, and after Stalin's death returned to Leningrad, to his mother who had been released from the camps.

Kochergin graduated from the theatre institute and showed he was a talented painter and theatre decorator. Since 1972 he worked in the Tovstonogov Bolshoi Drama theatre, one of the leading theatres in Leningrad and Russia.

Starting to write very late, Kochergin created cycles of autobiographical short stories about the social underground of late Stalinism, as it was never described before: with the precision of the witness and with the imagery of a great painter.

I can't remember how I ended up in the orphanage right before the war. My Godfather uncle Janek took me there. Or perhaps I was taken away from him. I don't remember how the war began either. I remember that all of us little mites, as the adults called us, suddenly started playing at war. The other kids made me, who lisped and barely understood Russian, along with two others, a red-headed Tatar and a second large-eyed, blackhaired mite – Blackie – into Germans. We were attacked every day, and we surrendered. We were led around the rooms with our hands up, like enemies, and then, shot one by one, we were made to lie on the floor for a long time. I didn't like the game very much.

I remember how the portions of breakfast, lunch and dinner became smaller. And when it got cold and the snow started falling, the kids stopped playing at war.

Then something strange happened. In winter, some enormous Gulliver-like guys came to the orphanage in quilted jackets and earflap hats, and swiftly took away the nine most emaciated boys, four or five-year-old mites. The men had us lined up against the wall, examined us attentively, and ordered the teachers to dress us quickly in the warmest clothes. They hastily put clothes of various sizes on us and gave each of us a heavy woolen blanket. Then, dressed, we went downstairs and out of the building, where a large rumbling bus stood waiting. Two of the guys lifted us up into it in turns. There were a few more adults in the bus in quilted jackets and earflap hats. On the first two seats, seven boys were sat down, and the wall-eyed Snotty and I, the last in line, sat among the guys on the back seat. To my right sat the senior Gulliver. He was in charge of everyone, and everyone obeyed him.

Winter that year was early, snowy and very cold. The entire city was covered in snow. The mounds of snow by the road sides were three times taller than me. None of us knew where the bus was going. When a boy nicknamed Stinky asked where we were being taken, the guy in charge replied:

"To the plane."

"To the plane? That's great! So we'll fly in the air!" we said happily.

"Yes, you'll certainly fly! You'll fly over Lake Ladoga."

We drove through the city for a long time, slowly, without stopping anywhere, even after the sirens howled and the bombing began. It was starting to get dark when we drove out of the city into an enormous snowy expanse, which was crossed only by our road. Suddenly the guys started to get anxious, and the drone of a plane could be heard. The driver increased his speed, we began to be shaken around and thrown from side to side, especially on the back seat. The road turned out to be broken up under the snow. The drone of the plane approached.

"It's a 'Messer'" the driver said. "It's going to follow us."

"Put the children on the floor under the seats right now!" my neighbor ordered, and as soon as we had been pushed under the seats, the bus was riddled with machine gun fire. We probably didn't hear the shots, the motor was humming and growling so loudly that we only realized the Messerschmitt had attacked us by the holes in the roof.

The first attack did not claim any victims. The driver squeezed the last juice out of the motor, to get out of this damn field as quickly as possible. The 'Messer' returned and, at low altitude, it attacked us again. The guy standing by the cabin fell down, and one of the boys screamed horribly ... I instinctively looked out from under the seat, and suddenly the 'Messer' moved to the side of the bus and fired a round at the windows on the left side. We were literally showered with a huge amount of glass shards. One of them stuck into my eyebrow above the bridge of my nose. The commander who was sitting next to me immediately lifted me onto his knees and pulled out the shard. Gulping blood, I lost consciousness.

When I came to, I was lying on a bench in some wooden hut. Out of the window, I could see a large white field surrounded by forest. I looked at the world with one eye; my other eye, along with most of my head, was bandaged up.

At that time, I still didn't understand Russian properly. The fur-hatted guy in charge took me from the bench and sat me down next to him, closer to the burning stove, and said something to comfort me. Boys were grouped around the stove, and with serious adult looks they stared at the living flames. After a few minutes, a large copper kettle boiled on the stove, and a little later we were given a metal cup, a sugar cube and a piece of bread. A ferocious fellow with a moustache and beard poured tea into the teapot right out the packet, and stirring the boiling water with an enormous knife, he began pouring a little into our cups. When we had finished our tea, all the Lilliputian boys were told to get dressed, do their buttons up and go into the yard to answer the call of nature. Then each one of us began to be packaged up, wrapped in a wadded cotton state blanket, turning us all into babies stuck into pouches. There were seven of these pouches. Why not nine? Where were the other two boys? – I didn't know how to ask. Perhaps they were seriously injured, or killed when the bus was fired on.

In the darkness, the big guys carried us, like infants, to the plane that was waiting next to the forest. It was quite a large plane, so at the time it seemed to me, and a lot of guys were loading boxes into it, handing them to each other from trucks. The pouches containing us were also put into the plane in the same way, from one pair of hands to the next.

Inside the plane, we were placed in our wadded pouches on wooden benches with backs, attached to the two opposite sides of the plane, and with ropes were firmly tied to them. Between the benches, there was a shooting frame, resembling a stepladder. In the center of four wooden beams that stuck into the ceiling, there was a platform made out of boards with steps. Above it, there was a hole in the ceiling, into which a large machinegun was fastened. On both sides of this gun there were wooden frames, from the floor to the ceiling and from the right side to the left. Durable boxes were attached to them with ropes. All of the space, apart from the aisles, was filled up with these boxes. This plane had probably been hastily converted from a passenger plane to a cargo plane. The portholes in the form of ovular rectangles were covered with pieces of metal on the inside. The salon was illuminated with two dull flashing lamps. The same guy who had sat next to me on the bus was giving the orders. Everyone else, including the pilots, carried out his orders.

I was bundled up opposite the legs of the shooter, although from below I could only see his enormous black fur boots.

I recall everything that took place in the plane in fragments. Either I lost consciousness from my injury – the shard of glass in the bus had after all hit me hard – or like the other mites, I was given sweet tea with alcohol in it, to stop us from wriggling.

I don't remember our plane taking off. I was probably under the influence of the drink. I woke from the terrible shuddering and severe pitching of the plane, good thing that we had been tied up with ropes, otherwise we would all have slithered across the floor.

How long we flew, I can't say. A weak light was shining through the machine-gun hole – it was probably already getting light. Something was happening to the plane. The guys stood there holding on to the beams of the frames. The shooter was firing his machine-gun from the step-ladder directly opposite me. I didn't immediately realize that he was shooting at the enemies who were following the plane. The pilots, trying to evade attack, began to maneuver in the air, rolling onto the left side of the plane and then the right. At these moments, we dangled from the ropes in the air in our pouches. I don't know how long the unequal battle with the "Messers" lasted. I passed out again. After a while I saw with one eye, as in a dream, that the shooter's step-ladder was being colored swiftly with something dark red. Blood. But where was it pouring from down the ladder, I wondered in my delirium. And suddenly, following the blood, the soldier's body slid down the pine steps onto the floor, his head shattered by a bullet. It began to smell of burning in the plane.

This was the first death that I saw, and I saw it up close. Perhaps because of my injury I didn't really know what was going on. Or perhaps after two and a half months in the blockade, I had already got used to the concept of death. But for some reason I wasn't afraid for myself, or for others. I accepted the soldier's death as a fact. War stupefies people. After the strafing of the bus, and the sight of that blood, something broke off in me – I was stupefied. The only feeling I had was one of cold. My legs in the blanket pouch had turned into frozen drumsticks.

Our wooden plane had evidently been hit. It started burning from the tail. The guys were trying to put out the fire with fire extinguishers. Suddenly a terrible pain pierced my ears – we were descending headlong. I disappeared from the world once more, losing consciousness. I came to when my blanket pouch was torn from the cabin with a savage force. All of the men who had been putting out the fire tumbled to the floor, evidently hit. The plane sliced into the snow-covered bank of a lake, and began sliding across it on its belly. I even remember the strange squeak-hissing sound of the sliding. I remember cries (I didn't understand the words) that the guy in charge made to the pilots from the floor, when the plane braked. After this he got up, crossed himself, as it seemed to me, and started giving orders. He ordered some of his subordinates to quickly remove the pieces of metal from the portholes, break the windows and push us boys through them, and take us fifty meters or so from the plane. He ordered others to save the boxes, pushing them through the windows and doors, and others to put out the fire outside and inside, until the entire plane had been evacuated. He ordered the pilots to remove all the devices, and take the instruments out of the plane, along with the sheets of iron, the dry rations, alcohol and everything valuable they could. The people, like ants before a storm, bustled around the plane, taking boxes, instruments, food and other things out of its belly. I remember that the ropes with which we were tied to the benches were chopped through with axes, and the pouches holding us were pushed through the holes of the windows. I remember that we were all placed on the snow together, in a row.

As soon as the main cargo had been taken out of the burning plane, and dragged away from it as far as possible, the plane exploded. I lost consciousness again for a long time. I came to from the harsh smell of alcohol. In a hut made of boxes and tarpaulin, the adults were rubbing our frozen legs, arms and faces with alcohol. To warm us up inside, they ordered us to drink hot medicine – water with alcohol.

Throughout the day, all the adults built a camp in the snow, resembling a round fortress. In the center of the circle they built a fire, which on the next day was joined by a metal oven assembled by handy men from pieces of iron off the plane. They made spades out of the remains of the metal, and small doors for dugouts. Everything that remained from the plane was used. Around the fire and stove, there appeared five dugouts with walls made of boxes and a floor of fir branches, covered with tarpaulin. I remember that the adults crawled into the dugouts. The warmest dugout belonged to us kids. With each day, our camp improved, and became cozier and warmer. I don't remember how many days we lived in it, but it was quite a long time. Initially we got water from the snow, and then made a hole in Lake Ladoga. To get logs, a road to the forest was cleared in the snow. The guy who was in charge sent the pilots to the nearest villages. They were dressed more warmly and had maps. They had to force their way over ten kilometers through deep snowdrifts.

During the first days we ate the remains of the dry rations, made porridge from rye flour and seasoned it with egg powder. The food was delicious. On the third day, the pilots returned on skis, and brought potatoes, cabbages, carrots, onions and other tasty things on sleds from the village. In honor of them, a feast was organized. We also took part – we were put on benches that the guys cut out of pine trees, and were given a mug of the tea that came from the village. And a whole carrot for each boy, although not all of the boys knew what to do with it.

Not until several days later, two enormous covered vehicles on caterpillar chains came for us. We were packed into the blankets once more, and together with the tied-up boxes, we were put into the all-terrain vehicles. We drove away from the camp as it began to get dark, and we reached a railway station by noon the next day. I remembered that the guys were very careful with the boxes.

Later, at the station, or perhaps in the train, I heard that they contained the blueprints and calculations of our new destroyer plane, and that the guy in charge was the engineer who had created this plane. The engineer was called Sergey, and his surname was Yeroshevsky or Yaroshevsky.

But why did he collect us, state orphans, and not just normal children, in his plane, and take us from blockaded Leningrad? It was strange. Why did this kind Gulliver single me out from all the other Lillputs, and even bandage my head himself? Because I smiled at him with one eye? Or because I was wearing a cross?

We were taken by train to Kuibyshev, and put in the NKVD orphanage. The local teachers took the cross away from me, the only thing that I had left from my mother Bronya.

MILGROM

Ludmilla Petrushevskaya (1938)

Translated by Anna Summers

Playwright, singer, journalist, poet and writer, **Ludmilla Petrushevskaya** is both a mainstream and underground figure, an artist out of step with other artists. Her domain is somewhere in between the fairytale, science fiction and absurdist prose; her writing has an otherworldly quality. Lyrical and shamanistic, Petrushevskaya's writing reveals the archaic side of modernity, the ancient rhythms and rituals lurking behind daily life.

Probably it is not a coincidence that Petrushevskaya wrote the scripts for the masterpieces of the legendary director Yury Norstein, the animated movies *Tale of Tales* and *The Overcoat* (after Gogol's piece), with many critics considering Norstein's works the best animation of all time.

A girl is sewing herself a dress for the first time. She has bought three yards of cheap gingham (barely more than a ruble per yard), but it's surprisingly pretty, black with bright circles, like a nighttime carnival.

This girl is a penniless college student. She has broken out of her schoolgirl shell, literally so—she managed to make a new skirt out of her old school uniform. The skirt came out messy, crooked, and off-center, but that's the end of the uniform, anyway.

Nor did the skirt turn out to be fit for spring. It's May, the hottest spring in memory, and still there's nothing to wear.

So the girl, following the "Sewing Ourselves" page from a women's magazine spread out before her (chest measurements, front panels), tries to make the dress herself and fails utterly.

The dress is lost, as are three rubles' worth of fabric. Her monthly stipend at the college is only twenty-three rubles.

Here the mom intervenes. Her whole life, Mom relied on a seamstress, but then difficult times befell her; her girl turned eighteen, and she stopped receiving child support.

The seamstress is out, and Mom considers what to do, except here's the problem: there's no money.

There's no money, the girl is eighteen, it's a hot May (the kind you feel maybe once every hundred years), and there are exams to take. But her daughter can't go outside. She's lying behind the wardrobe—that's where her cot is—weeping and moaning like a puppy.

So Mom calls her wise older friend, Regina, a Polish Jewess from the clan of the Moscow wives (that is to say, the new wives) of the Third International. In the thirties this whole communist contingent left the countries where it lived underground, came to the USSR via mountains and seas, remarried in Moscow, and then went up to heaven from their labor camps. Regina had served her time in Karaganda, was rehabilitated after the war, got back her old apartment on Gorky Street. The girl's mother, who'd also seen some things in her time, latched onto her to learn about life. Regina was a good friend of the girl's mother's mother, who has also been serving her time and is expected to return this spring.

Regina always dresses with Warsaw chic. She's sixty now and still has suitors, and she listens with sympathy to the confused mother of the girl.

Regina has a houseworker named Riva Milgrom. Regina is a European lady; she has soft white hands like an empress, and her house is always in order, as Milgrom makes sure.

That's what she's called: Milgrom—her last name, according to the old Party habit. Milgrom has a Singer sewing machine. The girl walks with the bundle of material through the May heat in her brown wool skirt. We know where the skirt came from—the mother had a dress she wore down until the underarms had sweat stains in the form of half-moons, at which point the dress was bequeathed to the girl, who wore it to school but could never raise her hand in class, her elbows clinging to her sides like a soldier's; it was hell. Finally the top with the sweat stains was cut off, and though the mother protested that it could still become a nice vest, the girl ran out of the apartment and threw it down the trash chute. Still the crooked skirt remained, and that's the skirt she's wearing as she walks clumsily through the heat of May.

Over the skirt, to cover the tear, which was hemmed crookedly with the wrong thread—the hands sewing them were the wrong hands—the girl wears her mother's blouse, which also has sweat stains at the pits, so, again, elbows at her sides like a soldier's.

The girl walks like a draftee, head down, watching her green winter shoes with their thick soles, her elbows at her sides. She passes by Patriarch Ponds; there's a gentle May smell in the air; young men are marching by, observing proud young girls in their new summer dresses.

Milgrom meets her little customer in her room, which is high up, right beneath the scorching Moscow sky—it's practically the attic—and here is quiet Milgrom with her big moist eyes, very white skin, and total absence of teeth. Milgrom looks like an old lady—her nose almost touches her sharp chin.

She opens up her sewing machine, produces a tape measure, and as she records the girl's measurements Milgrom launches into a saga about her darling son, the beautiful Sasha.

Sasha was so beautiful, people on the street would stop and stare; once his picture appeared on a box of chocolates.

The girl looks at the photograph on the wall that Milgrom points out to her: nothing special—a little boy in a sailor's outfit, big black eyes, a thin, elegant nose. The upper lip protrudes like a visor over the lower one. A cute kid with curls, but nothing more. The lips are too thin for an angel's—he has the Milgrom mouth.

At this point in her life the girl not only has no thoughts of children herself, but she also doesn't have an admirer even, not a single suitor, despite all her eighteen years.

For her it's all work, exams, library, cafeteria, shapeless green shoes, and a horrible brown dress with her mother's pit stains.

The girl looks indifferently at the wall and notices another portrait, an enlarged passport photo of a scrawny young officer in an enormous military cap.

That's the same Sasha; now he's all grown-up. While they were measuring her waist and noting it all down and ruefully examining the cut-up fabric, Sasha got married and produced a granddaughter, Asya Milgrom.

Old Milgrom pauses to console the girl and tells her she's not the only one who's clumsy, that she herself couldn't do anything when she was young- boil an egg or hem a diaper—and then she learned. Life taught her.

At some point during the long and bragging tale of Sasha it's time to go, but the dress stays; it will be finished tomorrow.

Three days later the girl—who wouldn't leave the house in her awful outfit, but who doesn't know how to wash, or iron, or sew anything; all she can do is read through tears in her corner behind the wardrobe—finally pulls herself together and says to her mother, "I'm going to Milgrom's."

"That poor thing," her mother says. "What a miserable life she's had. Her husband dumped her, literally kicked her out of the house, and took away her child, a little boy. First he took Milgrom out of her Lithuanian village—she was a rare beauty, sixteen years old, but she didn't speak any Russian, just Yiddish and Polish—and then he divorced her; you could do that then—with total freedom, he went and divorced her. And he brought another woman to live with him, and told Milgrom to leave. So she left. She was eighteen years old. She nearly went crazy; she spent all her days and nights on the street across from her old window so she could see her child. Regina found her half-dead, lying on the street—Regina being the protector of all the oppressed, of course. She put her in a hospital, and took her in as her maid—Milgrom used to sleep in the hall. When Regina was arrested, Milgrom apprenticed at a garment factory, earning herself a small pension and a room."

The girl listens to this absentmindedly, then goes to Milgrom's without really understanding what she's been told, and she sees the same little room just under the roof, where the smell of old woolen clothing chokes you in the heat.

Everything melts in the light of the setting sun as Milgrom produces some cups and a teakettle from the kitchen. They drink tea with black salted crackers, the luxury of the poor.

Milgrom once again brags about her son, Sasha, her shining face turned to the photographs on the wall, although the girl thinks, if her mother is telling the truth, where did she get those photographs?

Grown-up Sasha looks back from the wall with a cold, closed-off stare, his cap sticking up like a saddle over his big black eyes. Now he really looks like his mother.

With what tears, with what pleas did Milgrom get those photos from him?

Milgrom sighs contentedly underneath her wailing wall and then announces that little Asya has just lost her first tooth. All the things that everyone else has, Milgrom has them, too.

The girl puts on her dress; looks in the mirror; escapes from that sweet-musty smell, out into the street, the sunset; and walks by countless doors and windows, behind each of which, she thinks, live only Milgroms, Milgroms, Milgroms. She walks in her cool new black dress, and she is seized with happiness, filled with joy. It fills Milgrom, too, who is joyful for her Sasha.

The girl is at the very beginning of her journey. She's walking in a new dress, young men are already looking, and so on. In five years a boy will appear at her door with a bunch of roses he pulled out from a rose bush somewhere during the night. Milgrom is obviously at the end of her journey, but there might come a time when the girl will flash by at the end of Little Bronnaya Street, in a whole new form, carrying in her purse the photographs of her grown-up son, and bragging about him while sitting on a bench by the Patriarch Ponds—but she doesn't dare call him an extra time, and as for him, he's too busy to call.

The black dress shimmies down Little Bronnaya, which is wide and still filled with light, underneath the setting sun, and that's it now, the day is burning its last, and Milgrom, eternal Milgrom, sits in her little pensioner's room like a guard at the museum of her own life, where there is nothing at all but a timid love.

IT WASN'T ME

Svetlana Aleksievich (1948)

Translated by Richard Pevear
& Larissa Volokhonsky

A Belorussian writing in Russian, **Svetlana Aleksievich** won the Nobel Prize in Literature as a representative of Belarus, yet it is not possible to imagine Russian literature without her writings. Aleksievich relies on witnesses' accounts in producing her now world-famous texts about the human tragedies of the century: the Chernobyl disaster, the Soviet invasion of Afghanistan, womens' participation in the Second World War, the long-lasting legacies of Soviet authoritarian rule. But she creates symphonies of voices, where the drama rises from the harmonies and polyphony, giving, as she puts it, 'a voice to the speechless'.

Forced to leave Belarus under pressure from the dictator Alexander Lukashenko, after she was awarded the Nobel Prize she returned, and played a crucial role during the peaceful revolution of 2020 and was again forced into exile in Europe.

What do you remember most?
You remember most the quiet, often perplexed human voice. The woman feels astonished at herself, at what happened to her. The past disappeared, it blinded her with its scorching whirl and vanished, but the human being remained. Remained in the midst of ordinary life. Everything around is ordinary except her memory. And I also become a witness. A witness to what people remember and how they remember, to what they want to talk about and what they try to forget or remove to the furthest corner of memory. Curtain off. How they desperately seek for words, yet wish to reconstruct what is gone in the hope that from a distance they may be able to find its full meaning. To see and understand what they hadn't seen and understood then. There. They study themselves, meet themselves anew. Most often it is already two persons—this one

and that one, the young one and the old one. The one in the war and the one after the war. Long after the war. The feeling that I am hearing two voices at the same time never leaves me ...

At that time, in Moscow, on Victory Day, I met Olga Yakovlevna Omelchenko. All the women were wearing spring dresses, bright scarves, but she wore an army uniform and an army beret. Tall, strong. She did not talk and did not weep. She was silent all the time, but this was some sort of special silence, which implied more than could be said, more than words. It was as if she talked to herself all the time. She no longer needed anybody.

We became acquainted, and afterward I came to see her in Polotsk.

Before me yet another page of the war opened, before which any fantasy will fall silent ...

Olga Yakovlevna Omelchenko

MEDICAL ASSISTANT IN AN INFANTRY COMPANY

Mama's talisman ... Mama wanted me to be evacuated together with her. She knew that I was eager for the front, and she tied me to the cart on which our things were being transported. But I quietly untied myself and left with a piece of that rope still on my arm ...

Everybody was on the move ... Fleeing. Where was I to go? How to reach the front? On the road I met a group of girls. One of them said to me, "My mother lives nearby, let's go to my place." We came at night, we knocked. Her mother opened the door, looked at us, and we were dirty, ragged. "Stay there in the doorway," she ordered. We stood there. She brought enormous cauldrons, took all our clothes off. We washed our hair with ashes (there was no soap anymore), climbed on the stove,* and I fell fast asleep. In the morning this girl's mother cooked cabbage soup, baked some bread from bran and potatoes. How tasty that bread seemed to us and how sweet the cabbage soup! And so we stayed four days, and she fed us up. She gave us a little at a

---

* Russian tile stoves are elaborate structures that include "shelves" for sleeping.

time, otherwise she was afraid we'd eat too much and die. On the fifth day she said, "Go." And before that a neighbor came. We were sitting on the stove. The mother put her finger to her lips, so that we'd be quiet. She hadn't told her neighbors that her daughter had come back; she told everybody that her daughter was at the front. This was her only daughter, but she didn't feel sorry for her. She couldn't forgive the disgrace of her coming back. Of not fighting.

During the night she woke us up, gave us small bundles of food, embraced each of us, and said, "Go …"

She didn't even try to keep her daughter home?

No, she kissed her and said, "Your father's fighting, you go and fight, too."

Back on the road this girl told me that she was a nurse, her unit had fallen into an encirclement …

For a long time I wandered from place to place and finally wound up in the city of Tambov and found a job in a hospital. The hospital was good; after going hungry for a long time I ate well, I became plump. And then when I turned sixteen, they told me that, like all the nurses and doctors, I could give blood. I started giving blood every month. The hospital constantly needed hundreds of liters, there was never enough. I gave a pint of blood twice a month. I was given a donor's ration: two pounds of sugar, two pounds of farina, two pounds of sausage, to restore my strength. I was friends with a floor attendant, Aunt Niura. She had seven children, and her husband had been killed at the start of the war. The oldest boy, who was eleven, went to the grocery store and lost their ration cards, so I gave them my donor's ration. One day the doctor said to me, "Let's attach your address, in case somebody suddenly turns up who has had a transfusion of your blood." We wrote out my address and stuck the label to the vial.

And a while later, two months, not more, I finished my shift and went to sleep. They came and roused me. "Get up! Get up, your brother has come."

"What brother? I don't have a brother."

Our dormitory was on the top floor. I went down, looked: there stood a handsome young lieutenant. I asked, "Who wants to see Omelchenko?"

He said, "I do." And he showed me the label the doctor and I had written. "Here … I'm your blood brother."

He brought me two apples, a bag of candy—it was impossible then to buy candy anywhere. My God! How tasty those candies were! I went to the head of the hospital: "My brother has come …" They gave me a leave. He said, "Let's go to the theater." It was the first time in my life I went to the theater, and with a young fellow, at that. A handsome young fellow. An officer!

He left several days later. He had orders to go to the Voronezh front. When he came to say goodbye, I opened the window and waved to him. I couldn't get a leave: just then a lot of wounded arrived.

I had never received letters from anybody; I had no idea what it was—to receive a letter. And suddenly they handed me a little triangle. I opened it, and there was written, "Your friend, commander of a machine-gun platoon … died a hero's death …" It was my blood brother. He was from an orphanage, and probably mine was the only address he had. My address … When he was leaving he kept asking me to stay in this hospital, so that after the war he could easily find me. "It's easy to lose each other during the war," he said. And a month later I received this letter, that he had been killed … And I was so frightened. I was struck to the heart … I decided to do all I could to go to the front and avenge my blood; I knew that my blood had been spilled somewhere there …

But it wasn't so easy to go to the front. I applied three times to the head of the hospital, and the fourth time I came to him and said, "If you don't let me go to the front, I'll run away."

"Very well. I'll give you an order, since you're so stubborn."

The most terrible thing, of course, is the first battle. It's because you don't know anything yet … The sky throbs, the ground throbs, your heart seems about to burst, your skin feels ready to split. I never thought the ground could crackle. Everything crackled, everything rumbled. Heaved … The ground heaved … It was more than I could take … How was I to live through all that … I thought I couldn't endure it. I was so terribly frightened, and then I decided: so as not to turn coward, I took my Komsomol card, dipped it in the blood of a wounded soldier, put it in my pocket over my heart, and buttoned it. And by doing that I made myself an oath that I had to endure, and above all not to turn coward, because if I did it in my first battle, I wouldn't be able to take a step afterward. I'd be removed from the front line and sent to the medical battalion. And I only wanted to be at the front line; I wanted sometime to see at least one fascist face-to-face ... Personally ... And we advanced, we walked through the grass, and the grass was waist high. Nothing had been sown there for several years. It was very hard to walk. This was at the Kursk Bulge ...

After the battle the chief of staff summoned me. It was some sort of ruined hut, with nothing inside. There was one chair, and he was standing. He sat me in the chair.

"I look at you and think: what made you come to this hellfire? You'll be killed like a fly. It's war! A meat grinder! Let me at least transfer you to a medical unit. It's all very well if they kill you, but what if you're left without eyes, without arms? Have you thought of that?"

I reply, "I have, Comrade Colonel. And I ask you one thing: don't transfer me from the company."

"All right, go!" he shouted at me. I even got scared. And he turned to the window.

Heavy combat. Hand-to-hand ... That is a horror ... Not for a human being ... They beat, they stab with a bayonet, they strangle each other. They break each other's bones. There's howling, shouting. Moaning. And that crunching ... That crunching! Impossible to forget it ... the crunching of bones ... You hear a skull crack. Split open ... Even for war it's a nightmare; there's nothing human in it. I won't believe anyone who says that war isn't terrifying. Now the Germans rise up and advance; they always march with their sleeves rolled up to the elbows. Another five or ten minutes and they attack. You begin to shake. To shiver. But that's before the first shot ... And then ... Once you hear the command, you no longer remember anything; you rise up with everybody and run. And you no longer think about being afraid. But the next day you can't sleep, you're afraid. You remember everything, all the details, and it dawns on you that you could have been killed, and you're insanely frightened. Right after an attack it's better not to look at faces; they're some sort of totally different faces, not like people usually have. They themselves cannot raise their eyes to each other. They don't even look at the tree. You go up to someone and he says, "Go a-way! A-way ..." I can't express what it is. Everybody seems slightly abnormal, and there's even a glimpse of something bestial. Better not to see it. To this day I can't believe I stayed alive. Alive ... Wounded and shell-shocked, but whole. I can't believe it ...

I close my eyes and see it all again in front of me ...

A shell hit the ammunition depot, and it caught fire. The soldier who was standing guard next to it got scorched. Turned into a black piece of meat ... He kept jumping around ... And everybody watched from the trench, and nobody budged, they were all at a loss. I grabbed a sheet, ran over, covered the soldier with it, and lay down on him. Pressed him to the ground. The cold ground ... Like that ... He thrashed about till his heart burst, then grew still ...

I was all covered with blood ... One of the older soldiers came up and embraced me. I heard him say, "The war will end, and if she's still alive, there'll be nothing human left of her anyway, it's all over." Meaning that I was in the midst of such horror, and living through it, at such a young age. I was shaking as if in a fit; they took me under the arms to the dugout. My legs wouldn't hold me up ... I was shaking as if an electric current was running through me ... I can't describe how it felt ...

Then the battle began again ... At the Sevsk the Germans attacked us seven or eight times a day. So that day I also carried the wounded with their weapons. When I crawled to the last one, his arm was completely smashed. Hanging by little pieces ... by the sinews. He was all bloody ... His arm had to be urgently amputated and bandaged, otherwise it was impossible to bandage him. But I had no knife or scissors. My kit was loose on my shoulder, and things had fallen out. What was I to do? I bit his flesh off with my teeth. I bit it off and bandaged him ... I was bandaging, and the wounded man said, "Make it quick, nurse, I'll go and fight some more ..." In delirium ...

A few days later, when the tanks came against us, two men turned coward. They fled ... The whole line wavered ... Many of our comrades were killed. The wounded that I had dragged to a shell hole were taken prisoner. An ambulance was supposed to come for them ... But when those two turned coward, panic set in. The wounded were abandoned. Later on we came to the place where they lay, some with their eyes put out, some with their guts ripped open ... After I saw it my face turned black overnight. I was the one who had gathered them in one place ... I ... It frightened me so much ...

In the morning the whole battalion lined up, those cowards were brought out and placed before us. The order that they be shot was read. Seven men were needed to carry out the sentence ... Three men stepped forward; the rest stood there. I took a submachine gun and stepped forward. Once I stepped forward ... a young girl ... everybody followed me ... Those two could not be forgiven. Because of them such brave boys were killed!

And we carried out the sentence ... I lowered the submachine gun, and became frightened. I went up to them ... they lay there ... One had a living smile on his face ...

I don't know, would I have forgiven them now? I can't tell ... I don't want to lie. There are moments when I want to weep. But I can't ...

I forgot everything in the war. My former life. Everything ... And I forgot love ...

The commander of the scout company fell in love with me. He sent me little notes through his soldiers. I came to see him once. "No," I said. "I love a man who was killed long ago." He moved very close to me, looked straight into my eyes, turned, and went away. There was shooting, but he walked on and didn't even duck his head ...

Later—this was already in Ukraine—we liberated a big village. I thought: "I'll take a stroll, look around." The weather was clear, the cottages white. And outside the village—graves, freshly dug earth ... The graves of those who fought for this village. I didn't know why, but I was drawn there. On each grave there was a photograph and a last name on a plank ... Suddenly I saw a familiar face ... The commander of the scout company who was in love with me. And his last name ... And I felt so uneasy. Such great fear ... as if he saw me, as if he was alive ... And just then his men came to the grave, from his company. They all knew me; they had delivered his notes to me. Not one of them looked at me, as if I wasn't there. Invisible. Later, too, whenever I met them, it seemed to me ... so I think ... They wanted me to die, too. It was hard for them to see that I was ... alive ... I sensed it ... As if I was guilty before them ... And before him ...

I came back from the war and fell gravely ill. For a long time I went from one hospital to another, until I happened upon an old professor. He began to treat me ... He treated me more with words than with medications; he explained my illness to me. He said that if I had left for the front at eighteen or nineteen, my body would have been stronger, but since I had just turned sixteen—it was a very early age—I had been badly traumatized. "Of course, medications are one thing," he explained. "They may treat you, but if you want to restore your health, if you want to live, my only advice is: you should get married and have as many children as possible. Only that can save you. With every child your body will be reborn."

How old were you?

When the war ended, I was going on twenty. Of course I didn't even think of getting married.

Why?

I felt very tired, much older than my peers, even simply old. My friends went to dances, had fun, and I couldn't, I looked at life with old eyes. From another world ... An old woman! Young fellows courted me. Mere boys. But they didn't see my soul, what was inside me. Here I've told you about one day ... The fighting at Sevsk. Just one day ... After which I had blood flow out of my ears during the night. In the morning I woke up as if after a grave illness. A bloody pillow ...

And in the hospital? In the surgery room we had a big tub behind a screen where they put the amputated arms, legs ... Once a captain came from the front and brought his wounded friend. I don't know how he got behind there, but he saw that tub and ... fainted.

I can go on and on remembering. I can't stop ... But what is the most important thing?

I remember the sounds of the war. Everything around booms and clangs, crackles from fire ... In war your soul ages. After the war I was never young ... That's the most important thing. To my mind ...

Did you get married?

I got married. I gave birth to five sons and raised them. Five boys. God didn't give me girls. What surprises me most is that after such great fear and horror I could give birth to beautiful children. And I turned out to be a good mother and a good grandmother.

I recall it all now and it seems that it wasn't me, but some other girl ...

I was on my way home, bringing four cassettes (two days of conversations) with "yet another war," having various feelings: shock and fear, perplexity and admiration. Curiosity and bewilderment, and tenderness. At home I retold some episodes to my friends. Unexpectedly for me, the reactions were all similar: "Too frightening. How could she stand it? And not go out of her mind?" Or: "We're used to reading about a different war. In that war there are clear distinctions: us and them, good and evil. But here?" But I noticed they all had tears in their eyes, and they all fell to thinking. Probably about the same things as I. There have been thousands of wars on earth (I read recently that they've counted up more than three thousand—big and small), but war remains, as it has always been, one of the chief human mysteries. Nothing has changed. I am trying to bring that great history down to human scale, in order to understand something. To find the words. Yet in this seemingly small and easily observable territory—the space of one human soul—everything is still less comprehensible, less predictable than in history. Because before me are living tears, living feelings. A living human face, which the shadows of pain and fear pass over as we talk. Occasionally a subversive hunch even creeps in of the barely perceptible beauty of human suffering. Then I get frightened of my own self ...

There is only one path—to love this human being. To understand through love.

HERBS FROM ODESSA
Elena Makarova (1951)
Translated by Helena Goscilo

Writer, poet, Holocaust researcher, art curator and art therapist, **Elena Makarova** has lived in Israel since 1990. She is the daughter of poets Inna Lisnyanskaya and Grigory Korin, and the adopted daughter of the poet Semyon Lipkin. Both Lisnyanskaya and Lipkin were dissident authors.

Makarova writes non-fiction books about art in the Nazi concentration camps, especially in Teresin, and about Jewish educators who worked in those camps, trying to create a human sphere in the inhuman conditions.

Her prose derives from, or is guided by, research – the search for archives or witnesses, the hunt for an illusory yet real truth.

T he gentle voices of women growing plump jingled in the darkness like rattles.

"A room?" The receptionist burst out laughing. Turning to the empty foyer of the hotel as if there were stalls full of spectators in front of her, she repeated, "A room. ... Be satisfied with a bunk!"

"I was sent by Liusia Smertonosnaia. ..."[*]

"The excursion office!" exclaimed the receptionist in the resounding voice of a circus manager.

She traced out the number 48 on a card and placed the piece of paper on the smooth, glassy surface of the counter.

"You should be grateful!" could be heard behind me.

* * *

---

[*] *Smertonosnaia* means "death-bearing" or "fatal," the first of many motifs used to create an atmosphere of ominous mystery. Others include the name Skazka (Fairytale), the bathhouse (in Russian folklore traditionally associated with the devil), the cat, metamorphosis, the "magic" potion, the Gothic story (of death and supernatural events) within the story, and throwing out the icon.

... It was a bathhouse from a painting by the Armenian artist Bazhbeuk Melikian. Darkness, illuminated from within by gold. Inside it overflowed naked women grown languid from the water and the heated stones. Water streamed down their chestnut hair like sunflower oil. ...

Or no. It was a bathhouse where my aunt took me when I was five years old. The horror of pink nakedness. Pink women sat on long grey benches, and when my aunt entered naked, she was infused with pink before my eyes. As I moved along, I covered myself with my free hand, and the women shouted with raucous laughter. One of them doused me with warm water from a small washtub. I burst into tears. I sobbed violently, and my aunt, who was dry, led me off into the changing room. I was cold and ashamed for my aunt's sake that she, who was always smartly dressed and smelled of perfume, had suddenly become shockingly naked and pink.

Or no. It was a boarding school, where everything happened in full view: a bathroom without doors, and a secret diary stolen by the girls and read aloud in class. ...

"Shut the door! Can't you see we're naked?" said a woman. "Here's your bunk."

The steamy air billowed around the lusterless nightlamp. An old woman stroked her hair with a comb as she speared the number 48 with a dry, crackling sound. The bunk shook and creaked under the shifting bodies.

"Lady, take your passport!" The attendant tossed the passport on the glassy surface of the counter.

Varvara Semionovna Skazka.

The rasp of a chain. Then the door opened only as far as the chain allowed, and a face appeared with deep-set, gimletlike eyes, as if they were hidden in a pit. A mouth covered with husks from sunflower seeds uttered:

"Y-y-yes?"

It was the voice of a child who's barely started to speak.

The door closed and opened again. The old woman-infant gazed as pleadingly as a child, like the neighbor's daughter Zareta, who in the evenings would wait for her dissolute mother. When the latter finally arrived, Zareta wouldn't throw herself at her, but would look at her with a long, happy gaze.

Having gazed her fill, the old woman-infant in a cone-shaped dress (almost like a nun, yet not a nun; the dress grey and patched—you couldn't even call it a dress, but precisely a cone with slits for arms) moved forward.

After turning the key in the door, Skazka entered a big room. Above a tall, snow-white bed hung an antique clock mounted on dark wood. And on the piano with a white cover stood two photographs, of a man and a woman, in cardboard frames, with a statue of Buddha between them.

"These are my f-father and m-mother. They took F-Father during the Ezh-zhov purges,* and M-Mother recently d-died in the hospital."

She burst into tears but, regaining control of herself, wiped her eyes with a plump hand.

"Your mother's Varvara Semionovna Skazka?"

"Yes, yes," nodded Skazka. "Are you from Z-Zoinka? D-don't be afraid of me, I'm not all h-here. But I can p-play the p-piano. ..."

Skazka nimbly unfastened the button of the cover and ran her hand over the shiny surface of the piano.

"Z-Zoinka always used to s-stay with us. Our place is c-clean, and there isn't room in the h-hotel. Do s-sit down, you must be tired from traveling."

Her voice vibrated, faltering on the consonants and resting on the vowels, as if she felt pleasure in pronouncing the drawling sounds.

"Since M-Mama died, I c-cry and sing all the time."

She raised the lid, and, lowering her cone-shaped body into the swivel chair, she touched the keys with both hands.

"L-Lord, keep M-Mama," she sang, and glanced at me as if asking me whether it had come out coherently.

---

* The ghastly purges of 1936–1938, headed by Nikolai Ezhov the chief of the NKVD (secret police, now KGB), which entailed a wholesale elimination of personnel in various walks of life (e.g., the army, navy, etc.).

Encouraged by my praise, she sang her song a couple of times more and lowered the lid.

"Are you on v-vacation?" asked Skazka.

She heard out my brief story without blinking. Her light eyes were indeterminate in color, like a newborn's, with transparent lids in the white fluff of her eyelashes. All this colorless lightness was sunk in the darkness of her sockets, which were almost black.

"L-Lord, keep G-Grandf-father," she sang with gentle compassion.

… On the kitchen table stood a box from which protruded bunches of colored thread.

"You s-sing, and I'll w-work a bit."

She took a skein of the tangled thread and like a virtuoso pulled out a red thread, then another. She placed them side by side, took a thick sheet of paper out of the table drawer, tore an even strip off, and rolled it into a little tube.

"I bought it at the f-flea market. Pretty th-threads, and only ten kopeks for the l-lot. I have s-sugar and j-jam, too. Mama used to cook it."

The old woman-infant drank tea from a saucer. She rejected the cheese, but took a cookie and beslobbered it like a toothless child.

"Wh-while M-Mama was still alive I was treated to a pastry with r-real cream. W-without eating it, I brought it to M-Mama, but the cream dripped out.

"And M-Mama said I was clumsy. I'm so c-clumsy and ug-gly, no one will m-marry me.

"And I'm th-thirty.

"I b-bought a red d-dress with a white c-collar at the flea market, can I sh-show you?"

She minced into the room, returning quickly with the dress. She held it against her; it was twice the size she needed. She stood rooted to the spot, holding the dress at her throat with one hand, with the other at her barely defined hip.

"I d-don't look old in it, do I?"

"Of course not! It really suits you. You look twenty years old in it."

She blushed to the tips of her protruding ears and gave a giggle. She had only her front teeth, with black gaps yawning along the sides, which made her face seem even thinner.

"I'll t-tell you s-something later,"* she whispered, hanging the dress on the back of the chair. "No, I'll rumple it like this," she said and took the dress into the room.

On the back of the sheets of paper on which she'd wound the thread were some portraits. After she came back and sat on the chair, she tore a blank space with eyes and the tips of ears from a sheet of paper and wound the red thread around it.

"It's b-brand new, not at all rotten," she said and added mysteriously, "I'll tell you s-something later."

Every fifteen minutes the clock at the head of the bed chimed a short tune, similar to "L-Lord, keep M-Mama." I got out of bed in the hope of finding something light to read. In the bottom drawer of the oak sideboard lay a cookbook.

Its cover boasted a plump woman from the fifties with padded shoulders. She was smiling as she gazed at a frying pan with cutlets. Above the frying pan, in uneven handwriting, was inscribed the word "margarine." Evidently this was the late Varvara Semionovna's reference book.

Almost every page contained marks made in an indelible pencil: "butter" was crossed out, and on top was inscribed "margarine." The amount of sugar was halved everywhere, and instead of "roast" was written "braise." But the chapters entitled "Sauces," "Dressings," and "Vegetable Canning" had been left untouched by the late Varvara Semionovna's hand.

The tranquil smoothness of the pages with red bilberry and cranberry dressing, with sauces and anchovies, plunged me into drowsiness, and only in the morning did I hear above my head, "L-Lord, keep M-Mama."

Liusia Smertonosnaia stood on the street outside the dining hall where they'd arranged to meet and smoked a Prima. Her group was

---

* The promise becomes a leitmotif that contributes to the aura of uneasy mystery permeating the story.

having breakfast inside the massive walls of the dining hall, and Liusia chewed nervously on the tip of her cigarette.

"They're inside eating, while I'm freezing! And the bus is standing idle!"

Liusia's luxuriant hair escaped from beneath her mohair hat. In the hat, with her small figure, she looked just like a little chick.

"Every day these nerve-racking situations, every single day!" she complained, shifting from one slender foot to the other. "Give me a light!"

Lighting her cigarette from a passerby's, she shook her head and calmed down.

The excursion participants, their stomachs filled, now surrounded Liusia in a circle.

"Hurry up! Hurry up!!" she rushed them. "Who's the leader of your group?"

The group pushed forward a dumpy woman in a heavy black overcoat with a fur collar, and Liusia gave her a rundown of the excursion schedule.

In the cab she ranted against her work, complained that she couldn't stand it at school, the children drove her crazy, and Liusik[*] had to give her some valerian drops. This work wasn't any easier. For eighty-two rubles she was completely worn out.

"And did Aunt Vera graduate from an institute?" I interrupted Liusia.

"The circle of the intelligentsia is shrinking," she replied, indicating with her cigarette to the driver where to stop.

A yellowish-grey dust covered the houses and the asphalt. There was sun and wind, added structures protruding from balconies, staircases connecting the houses, the aroma of roasted seeds alternating with vanilla. ...

---

[*] Liusik is the husband of Liusia, and the nearly identical names make for puzzling confusion.

"Liusia!" cried a freckled woman with a thick black braid. "Look at our visitors!"

Wiping her hands on her padded jacket, she covered Liusia with kisses, and looking past me, she dragged Liusia into the elongated house, which resembled a coach.

"Sit on the bench. I'll be right back."

"Aunt Ver, don't fuss," said Liusia, but Aunt Vera had already disappeared.

A black cat was rumbling on the bunk. Something was cooking on the electric stove, filling the platformlike room with a sweet smell.

A tall old man in a padded jacket stole past.

"Aunt Ver, why'd you send him. ..."

Aunt Vera banged the saucepans without saying a word. The old man returned with a half-liter of vodka.

"Uncle Sasha." Liusia gave him a somewhat different, new smile. "Now, Uncle Sasha. ..."

"If Uncle Sasha gave his word, that means he gave his word. We've got our eye on a two-room place. But you have to wait."

Liusia nodded quickly and took off her hat.

"You've dyed it different again," said Uncle Sasha and went out.

"Turkey!" Aunt Vera had exchanged her padded jacket for a black wool dress with a mother-of-pearl brooch on her bosom. "None of this 'I don't want any.' Eat and make yourselves at home."

The room was full of rugs and figurines: reindeer and mermaids, Galina Ulanova[*] in a tutu, Oleg Popov,[†] Carmen,[‡] and four roosters with crimson combs.

---

[*] (1909/1910)—renowned ballerina transformed by the Soviet government into a living icon for her contributions to the department of classical Russian ballet. At the Kirov Theater in Leningrad (1928–440 and the Bolshoi in Moscow (1944–1960), she worked up an extensive repertoire of roles which she executed with lyricism and simplicity of means.

[†] A circus performer who has entertained millions with his antics on the highwire and his routines as a clown. The "Sunny Clown," as he is called, has traveled abroad frequently with his act.

[‡] The carefree protagonist of Prosper Mérimé's tale "Carmen" (1841), on which George Bizet based his famous opera by the same name. The latter, in turn, inspired Rodion Shchedrin's meretricious *Carmen Suite*, conceived explicitly to showcase the dancing skills of his wife, Maia Plisetskaia.

"I just saw out* a man from Novosibirsk." Aunt Vera arranged fat pieces of turkey on the plates. "His wife's thirty-five. Cancer. Has the circus left?"

"No. The bear bit Misha the trainer. Today's his first performance since the accident! It'll be sold out!"

"Is he the one?" asked Aunt Vera meaningfully, and Liusia nodded.

"You did a good job of dying your hair. It looks natural." Words had pooled in Uncle Sasha's Adam's apple as in a reservoir, and he had to push them out by force.

"We drink slowly, we live slowly." Aunt Vera raised her glass. "Even children aren't born in a hurry."

"My grandfather has cancer. He doesn't eat anything and has trouble urinating," I said, and accidentally met Liusia's disapproving gaze.

"Let's sit a while and get to know each other." Aunt Vera placed a moist hand on my arm.

"I have to be home in two days," I insisted dully.

After the vodka that had been forcibly poured into me, I'd grown limp and sat quietly. The fat turkey wrapped around my hungry stomach like a vacuum cleaner. The soft rugs absorbed the monotonous conversation interrupted by Liusia's exclamations.

"Sold out!! Sold out!!!"

"It's time!" rang Liusia's voice in my ear, and I came to.

"Tell me all about it and make it simple," said Aunt Vera and climbed up onto the berth.

"... I'll cure him," she concluded upon hearing the whole story of Grandfather's illness. For a long time she jotted down figures on a piece of notebook paper, added, multiplied, and divided in a column. "Two hundred," she totaled the conversation. "My price is your price. And so you'll have no doubts, take this book. I'm going to say the names, and you look for them in the book. There'll be no cheating."

... The stupefyingly sweet smell of the potion† boiling on the electric

---

* The verb contains a pun, for it means both "saw out" and "cheated."

† Another instance of paronomasia, for the noun means both "potion" and "poison," an ambiguity that intensifies the menacing overtones of the story.

stove, the Latin names of the herbs that Aunt Vera would repeat and, immediately forgetting them, would ask to have read out syllable by syllable, the rumbling cat, the warm stove, the vodka I'd drunk. ...

On top of everything, there was Aunt Vera's granddaughter in an embroidered jacket. She clambered up to join Aunt Vera on the berth and, waving her suede boots in the air, she said:

"A woman on our street was getting married. They dressed her up in a wedding outfit, married her off, and said, as usual: 'Exchange rings as a token of conjugal fidelity.' The groom started to put the ring on her finger, and she—dropped dead! They buried her in her bridal veil, in her wedding dress and with the ring. The gravediggers spotted the gold and came at night with spades. They dug up the grave, took off the lid, and—she was alive. She was in a lethargic sleep. One of the gravediggers suffered an instant heart rupture, but the other didn't get scared. He grasped her hand and took her to her parents. When her mother saw her she gave such a yell: "A ghost! Ah! Ah!" Her father merely opened his mouth wide, swayed, and—dropped dead. They took her mother to the psychiatric ward. And the gravedigger said to her, 'If that's the way things stand—I'll marry you. And if you won't, I'll put you back and bury you.' Well, what choice did she have? She married him. While her mother's undergoing treatment, the young couple's living in her house."*

"What about the first groom?" asked Aunt Vera, stirring the boiling potion.

"Who on earth knows?! He either took to drink or went crazy. Where are you from?" asked the granddaughter, scratching the cat behind the ears, which caused him to rumble even more violently.

"Moscow."

"Send us a velvet-bound photo album. A woman from our block got one in Moscow; it's a pleasure to look at."

The granddaughter jumped down from the bunk with the cat.

"I'll give him some bones so he won't turn into anything," she explained. "Black cats turn into witches at night."†

---

* This story within the story combines elements of folklore with the Gothic, as does the girl's observation that at night black cats metamorphose into witches.
† The capacity to alter appearance is a standard feature of the devil and of other spirits in Russian folklore.

Aunt Vera was rereading the notations syllable by syllable, lifting her brown eyes, shot with gold, to me after each word as if checking to see whether she was reading them right.

"It'll be ready the day after tomorrow," she said. "Or there's another possibility: we could use another herb, but you have to go a long way to get it, and it costs a lot. Do you want to get it? No, I'm not insisting. I don't have the time to go get it."

"I want to get it."

"Then it's three hundred."

I wilted.

"My price is your price," said Aunt Vera. "Two hundred fifty."

"I only have two hundred with me, but I'll get it," I said, realizing belatedly that I should have haggled from the beginning.

"What j-joy!"

The old woman-infant was wearing the red dress. It hung like a sack down her back and chest.

"I wore it for you," she explained, poking her finger at the crimson material. "I l-like you so much. ... You're not nasty, and you don't make fun of me. We have a n-neighbor. I used to visit her to watch t-television, and she used to make fun of me. I didn't n-notice, but M-Mama said: 'Don't go to her, she makes f-fun of you.' And I didn't n-notice that. I want to w-watch t-television so badly, but I haven't been going since Mama told me that. M-Mama kn-knows best. ..."

I offered her a pastry. She took it carefully, as if asking whether it really was for her.

I nodded. She took it over to the sideboard in her outstretched hand.

"They really fleece you," she sighed upon hearing how much the herbs cost. "When M-Mama died, our neighbors gave me ten rubles, and social services twenty, and my p-pension brought in t-twenty-one rubles. It wasn't even enough for the f-funeral. I really c-cried, and they said: 'We'll bury your mother for n-nothing.'

"Th-they're kind. ..."

"L-Lord, keep M-Mama," sang the old woman-infant, making the sign of the cross at the empty corner of the kitchen. "Before, when I was I-little and h-healthy, an icon used to hang here. But when they t-took Daddy, M-Mama th-threw out the icon. But I keep th-thinking it's still h-hanging there. ..."

"Do you want to unravel the thread?" she asked, apparently sensing that I was getting ready to leave.

"I'll w-wait for you," said Skazka, opening the door for me. "And then I'll tell you s-something. ..."

Liusia, accompanied by a white poodle, met me at the main entrance.

"I was just taking Charlik out," said Liusia, and I was sorry that I'd left Skazka.

Keeping Charlik on his leash, Liusia rushed about the Vorontsov Gardens.

"What's happening is awful," she reported when Charlik finally calmed down and raised his leg at a tree trunk. "The circle of the intelligentsia is shrinking."

Running around the apartment, she complained about the handyman; he'd put in a defective tap for the umpteenth time.

"See that Charlik doesn't get out," she ordered, disappearing behind the door. "Have a seat!" Liusia returned with a floor rag. "Because of that creep I'm late for the circus," she said, wiping the tile in the bathroom.

In panties and brassiere she sailed to the other room, and in a second she emerged in a close-fitting brocade dress.

"The style of '69! That's what I've come to!" Liusia was tearing at her hair with a massage brush. "You stay here a while, look through some art books."

"But can't I go to the circus with you?"

"It's sold out today! Sold out!!" shouted Liusia in answer to the impertinent query. "Misha's had an accident! The bear bit him!"

Someone knocked on the latticed window.

"Here she is again!" Liusia raced to the door.

The woman who burst into the apartment looked as if she was Liusia's mother: the same voice with a touch of hoarseness, the same luxuriant hair, and an overall petite appearance, through which one could clearly discern Liusia in her declining years.

Brushing Liusia aside with a shoulder encased in beaver lamb, the woman ran into the room. Liusia followed. Their loud, excited whispering swelled into a shout.

"Take it all! There's nothing to reproach me for! Nothing!! I haven't needed anything from you for a long time!! Not anything!! And especially your gold! Especially that!! Especially that!!!"

Charlik thrust his paw into the opening and slipped into the room.

"Take it!" Liusia dashed into the corridor, shaking a wedding band in the air. "Here! Here!! I can't stand the sight of it!!! Together with your Liusik!!!"

"You should see a shrink! You're crazy!!" The woman knocked the wedding band out of Liusia's hands, and it rolled with a clatter along the corridor. Charlik leaped toward the ring.

"He'll swallow it!!!" Liusia rushed toward Charlik, trying to get it out of the dog's mouth.

"I hope he chokes on it!!!" shouted the woman, slamming the front door with all her strength.

After getting the ring out of Charlik's mouth, Liusia collapsed on the kitchen couch.

"I'm late! Late!! Late!!!" Liusia had hysterics. "And that Liusik …," she sobbed, stressing "that." "All he cares about is his icons. It's sickening enough without them. Ha! That's what having a man in the house means! The tap leaks, the plaster's falling down. And I've got to do everything, everything, everything myself!

"What a bore!

"The circus is the only safety valve in this drab existence.

"The only one!!!

"You should see Misha!

"Grace, grace, and more grace!

"And we fools can't wait to get married. … We don't look around, expand our minds a bit. … And it's all Mother: Liusik loves you, Liusik's cultured, Liusik's this, Liusik's that. … Ugh!" Liusia crushed her cigarette with her index finger.

Charlik started to bark.

"And I'm stuck with his Charlik, too! If he'd only walk him once in a while! Here, gorge yourself!" Liusia threw him a sausage. "And you call this life?!

"You only live once, and there's no joy in it at all!

"You can't buy dresses! You pay double for crummy panties!

"Oh, to be an acrobat! Misha thinks I've got all that it takes.

"Playbills everywhere!

"A sell-out!

"Rehearsals all day!

"And how wonderful circus marriages are! You're always together, day and night! But as things are. ... What do I care about his icons, and what does he care about my tours!

"It's all hopeless.

"And Liusik has a heart condition besides.

"Have a smoke," said Liusia, not having noticed until then that I wasn't smoking. "You've caught me at a bad time.

"Now I want to live just for the circus.

"Misha has charm.

"And Liusik is vapid, dull, with his eternal 'you can't do this, can't do that,' and those icons. ...

"Oh, how I want to live! To wake up and feel free! Independent!!!"

Liusia glanced at her watch as if to check whether she'd gone over the time limit.

"It's time to go! Maybe I'll make it for the second part!"

I found Skazka reading the same cookbook.

"I wanted to m-make you an omelette and just c-couldn't find where it's d-described how to do it. M-Mama underlined everything f-for me, but I'm so s-stupid. ..."

The old woman-infant was clearly upset over something. She drawled more than usual, stumbling over each consonant.

She calmed down as we worked on the thread. She untangled it, and tearing off strips of newspaper ahead of time, I wound the thread around them.

"Do you l-love anybody?" asked Skazka. I dropped a finished skein. "A m-man," said Skazka more precisely, blushing darkly all over.

The thread from the fallen skein got tangled. Noticing that I was struggling with it, Skazka carefully, as she'd done with the pastry with the real cream, took the skein from my hand and in an instant tidied the thread.

The clock in the room chimed out "L-Lord, keep M-Mama." In the ensuing silence the alarm began to ring, and the drops of rain drummed louder on the roof of Skazka's house.

Anxiety flared in the eyes of the old woman-infant. Pressing her nose against the window pane, she seemed to be on the lookout for someone outside.

"I'm in l-love," muttered Skazka.

After a silence she rose, and with the small steps of a Chinaman she minced into the other room. I could hear her singing in a thin voice, "L-Lord, keep M-Mama." She seemed to know nothing besides this phrase.

"I'm ash-shamed," she uttered, gazing at me with her infant's eyes.

I sat down at the piano and asked whom she was in love with.

Skazka's plump hands slid along the faded material of her cone-shaped dress.

"With a th-thief," sighed the old woman-infant. "He l-lives here. He calls me D-Dusia.

"He's on t-tour now, in N-Nikolaev. I lined his w-wig for him, and he kissed me on the ch-cheek and s-said: 'D-Dusia, you're the best of women. And if you keep qu-quiet, I'll b-bring you p-presents.'

"He goes on t-tour wearing the wig, and he st-sticks on a beard, a really b-bushy one, b-black.

"'D-Dusia, you keep quiet and d-don't let anyone in at n-night. I'll l-love you for that.'

"P-poor M-Mama! She w-warned me: 'K-keep out of his way, he's n-no good,' but I l-lock my door to him and am in l-love with him anyway."

Clasping her hands at her sunken chest, Skazka prayed to her "M-Mama's" photograph.

"His M-Mama lives here, too. She s-sells seeds. She doesn't l-like me. 'I'll get you taken off the list of tenants,' she says, 'and I'll s-send you to an insane asylum.'

"And he d-defends me. 'Don't you t-touch her, Mother, she's a c-cripple.'

"And she says, 'This cripple w-will get it f-from me.' If it wasn't for him, she'd s-send me to the insane asylum."

I told Skazka that she had no right to send her to an insane asylum, that she was frightening her out of malice.

"She says, 'When I look at your m-mug, I k-keep tossing and t-turning all n-night.' She can't f-fall asleep," explained the old woman-infant.

"She envies you," I said, "because you're so young and nicely shaped."

Skazka got up from the chair and pulled her dress tight over her puny little body, showing how nicely shaped she was.

"I sh-should f-fix my h-hair somehow," she said, pulling her comb through her hair.

I tried to give Skazka something resembling a hairstyle. But her hair was unmanageable. Like a coil, it sprang out from beneath the hairpins and hung along her neck like icicles.

"Do you have a ribbon?"

"I d-do, I d-do!" Rummaging in the drawers of the sideboard, Skazka pulled out a narrow pink ribbon, the kind used for tying gifts. "It's M-Mama's."

I tied the ribbon around her head.

"P-pretty!" rejoiced Skazka, touching the ribbon. She was as happy as a first-grader decked out in snowflakes for a New Year's pageant.

We drank tea. She held her pastry with two fingers, evidently remembering the whole time that the cream could run out of it.

"Wh-what j-joy," she kept saying.

We went to bed late. I dreamed that Charlik was suffocating me; Aunt Vera was holding out some herbs to me, and right before my eyes they turned into pillow down. Grandfather called me in a strange voice; the face was Grandfather's, but the voice was someone else's.

I opened my eyes, but the voice didn't disappear. I listened intently. It wasn't one voice, but several. A velvety baritone and a treble kept interrupting each other.

"Sing, Dusia!" demanded the baritone.

"No, dance!" insisted the treble.

"'If I had mountains of gold … '" the baritone broke into song.

"'… And rivers filled with wine,'" the treble picked up the next phrase.

"'I'd give it all up for your caresses, and glances, and you alone would be mistress of all,'" they sang in chorus.

Someone turned the key in the lock. I hid behind the sideboard. Fortunately, it was Skazka.

"They're asking f-for you," muttered Skazka bashfully, handing me the panties and brassiere that I'd hung up on the radiator in the bathroom. "They won't t-touch you. ..."

In the kitchen three men were sitting at the table. Two of them were identical, small, with receding hairlines and sharp little eyes, twins, or perhaps made up to look like each other; Skazka's beloved was an enormous husky fellow with a narrow forehead and a beard.

"*Kinder*, that's too much!" he droned into his beard. "We don't touch children. 'We're happy-go-lucky mates, we're called the Octobrates,'"* he sang, and poured out the remaining vodka into the glasses. "Sing, Dusia!"

"No, dance!" said the twins in unison.

"Dance and sing!" decreed the fellow with the narrow forehead. "How does your song go: 'L-Lord, keep M-Mama!'"

One of the twins twanged a guitar string, and the old woman-infant started marking time.

"Why aren't you singing?" the fellow with the narrow forehead banged on the table.

Skazka struck up, "L-Lord, keep M-Mama!", her vapid infant's eyes staring at the empty corner.

Soon they started yawning.

"Dusia I adore, I take her by the tail, and see her to the door," said the fellow with the narrow forehead, and getting up. He chucked Skazka under the chin.

"Finally!" Aunt Vera enfolded me in a warm embrace. "We didn't sleep all night. Why did I let you go?! I had a vision, you know!"

---

* Russian *oktobriata* are schoolboys in the first to third grades who belong to a politically based organization that prepares them to make the transition to the older group of similarly indoctrinated representatives of social consciousness, the Pioneers.

I was stupefied, and suddenly, all at once, I believed in her and her healing herbs.

After she'd heard out my story, Aunt Vera told me to get up onto the bunk where the cat lay.

"Sleep," said Aunt Vera. She covered me with a sheepskin and left.

The cat didn't take its bright yellow eyes off me. "He turns into something else at night. ..." I covered myself completely, head included. The cat clawed at the skin. Aunt Vera's speckled golden eyes gazed at me. "What kind of devilry is this!" I said out loud, and the cat jumped aside.

I got down off the bed and sat down beside the stove.

"Can't you sleep?" asked Aunt Vera, thrusting her head through the door. Her speckled yellow eyes glittered like a cat's.

To the accompaniment of the cat's rumbling, we packed the herbs in cellophane bags. Aunt Vera recited spells, combining some roots with others and sprinkling herbs on top of them.

"We get letters every day." Aunt Vera took a little case out from under a cushion. "Read any of them."

And it was true. All the letters called Aunt Vera a healer and a savior; there wasn't a single letter that didn't contain thanks.

"The most important part will be ready tomorrow," said Aunt Vera, indicating the bottle with the brown liquid. 'It'll turn black by morning. Your grandfather will feel dizzy from it at first, but then he'll get an appetite. The main thing is for him to start eating."

"And what if he doesn't?" I felt some doubt. He'd eaten nothing the last two weeks, nothing.

"He will," said Aunt Vera firmly, "You've simply got to have faith. Without faith it's impossible."

Liusia wasn't home, but Liusik was. He plied me with tea, put woolen socks on my feet, and ordered me to take some aspirin.

Puffing away at a pipe, he kept looking at his watch, from time to time taking medicines.

"I live off chemicals," he kept sighing, meticulously stuffing the cotton into the next vial.

... Liusik and I talked about art, and I thought about the fact that, if it came to that, they could set up a fold-out bed in the kitchen.

At midnight Liusia burst into the room in a whirlwind of yellow.

"Did you take Charlik out?" she asked, imprinting a red kiss on Liusik's bald head. "Misha was in fine form! And the bear almost bit him again!" she said, putting the leash on the peacefully dozing Charlik.

The sleepy Charlik barely dragged himself along, stopping at every tree.

"How do you like my husband?" asked Liusia, getting a light for her cigarette from a passerby. "A nincompoop!" Liusia answered for me. "Misha, now!!!"

Because of Misha I couldn't get a word in edgewise about spending the night, let alone about Aunt Vera.

"Come on, Charlik, let's see our guest to the hotel." Liusia turned to the dog, who was sleeping where he stood.

"Can I spend the night at your place?"

"Only if you sleep on the floor," said Liusia, probably hoping that such an option wouldn't appeal to me, but I agreed quickly.

Aunt Vera packed my knapsack herself. She wound rags around the precious bottle of black liquid and placed it in a bag labeled "Foreign Trade Beriozka."[*]

We had a farewell drink. Aunt Vera's freckles were lost in the glow on her cheeks.

"Your cost is my cost," she kept repeating, and Uncle Sasha echoed her.

* * *

---

[*] A foreign currency store, where the best Soviet and imported goods are reserved for sale both to the Soviet "privilegentsia" and to foreigners for foreign currency. The average Soviet citizen never gains access to these items.

"You're h-here?" muttered Skazka, as if asking whether I'd come. "They're not here, but they c-could come," she said, her cone-shaped body blocking the way.

I held out a five-ruble note.

"Too m-much, that's too m-much." The old woman-infant refused it, but I dropped the money in the slit of her pocket.

"How k-kind you are! I'll h-hide it. His M-Mama's there," she indicated the kitchen.

With her red dress and the pink ribbon, the old woman-infant recalled a mad angel, if there is such a thing.

"L-Lord, keep G-Grandfather," she sang in farewell.

I triumphantly carried the glass with the infusion into the room, which was permeated with the smell of medicines. From the precious bottle I poured a tablespoon of the viscous black liquid into a wineglass and held it out to Grandfather.

His eyes darkened with pain, Grandfather looked at the faceted wineglass that promised him salvation.

"Lift me up," he ordered, and I pulled him by the arms, helping him sit up.

"God," whispered Grandfather, and frowning, he took the glass from my hands. "I'll do it myself," he said and touched the herbal concoction to his lips. "Poison! It's poison!" he shrieked, and flung the glass away.

He wouldn't touch the herbs again. He was fading quickly and horribly. In moments of lucidity he would look at me with inflamed, guilty eyes:

"Such bitter stuff, Lenka, such bitter stuff; such bitter stuff cannot cure a person."

A TALE OF THREE HEADS

Irina Ratushinskaya (1954–2017)

Translated by Diane Nemec Ignashev

Soviet dissident, poet and writer, **Irina Ratushinskaya** (1954–2017) was born in Odessa and later moved to Kyiv. After long harassment by the KGB, she was arrested in 1982 and accused of 'anti-Soviet agitation and propaganda', sentenced in 1983 to 7 years in a penal colony and 5 years in internal exile.

She served her sentence in a special camp for political prisoners in Mordovia and described these years in her best-known prose, her autobiographical novel *Grey is the Colour of Hope*.

She was released in 1986 during the summit between Ronald Reagan and Mikhail Gorbachev. Forced to leave the country, she lived in the UK and the US until 1998, when she regained Russian citizenship and returned to Russia.

Once upon a time there lived a dragon who was very, very lazy.

Normal dragons, as we all know, have from seven to twelve heads, but this one could grow only three, and those just barely. All in all, though, the three managed quite well over a bottle, stealing their drinking glasses from public soda water dispensers.

One fine Thursday the dragon sat down to dinner. As usual, there were three servings of the first course, three of the second, and three of the cherry compote for dessert. The First and the Third heads were smiling and licking their chops, while the Second was wondering, "Just look at all those dishes to wash." And grew downcast.

The Head didn't say anything for a while, then suddenly it burst: "Listen, we should collectivize the dishes. Throw all the food just as it is into a single bowl!"

"Even the compote?" the Third Head gasped in horror.

"Even the compote," insisted the Second, although it hadn't thought about the compote. There was no other way: can't start by compromising the initiative.

So they collectivized and started eating. Here the Second Head showed its mettle: chomp, chomp, and it had gobbled everything up. The other two were left with only cherry pits. But the Second Head was quick to point out that those pits contained all the vitamins. And as the dragon got up from the table the other two heads automatically thanked the Second. At first the clever head was amazed, but later it drew its own conclusions.

So the next day it said, "Listen, we should organize a cell. There are exactly three of us here and we're still not consolidated."

"Why do we need to be consolidated?" timidly inquired the First Head.

"We should," answered the Second with conviction (it had already figured out that one should always answer with conviction).

"Well, if we should, we should," agreed the First, "but what are we going to do?"

"We'll do what we're supposed to do," answered the Second. "Don't worry. Together we'll get things moving around here."

"I don't know how to move things," the First began, then stopped short.

"What you don't know, we'll teach you, and what you don't want to. ..."

"I want to, I want to!" the First Head answered quickly, by now afraid to find out what would happen if suddenly it didn't want to.

"That's the spirit," bellowed the Second with obvious gusto.

"You're with us too, of course?" it winked at the Third Head.

"Well, no, actually, I uh. ..." mumbled the Third Head, ignoring the wink. This time two heads sprang to the attack: "So you think you're too good to join the collective, do you?"

"Well, I'll think about it," the Third countered feebly, clearly weakening its stand.

"Think about it, think! You want to be smarter than the rest of us, do you? Think about it real hard!" said the Second Head, changing its tone, and with that put an end to the discussion.

All that night the Third Head sighed, and sniffled, and wiped away the tears with its long ears. The next morning it said that well, it still didn't really quite understand the whole thing, but it guessed so and wouldn't stand in the way of the collective.

A cell was organized.

Slowly they began to make things move, though the Third Head understood no more now than earlier. All the other dragons, even those with twelve heads, would bow from the waist whenever they met the three-headed dragon. And anyone who out of habit tried the old firebreathing trick was gone in a single gulp.

And so it went, and went, until the Third Head finally began to understand a thing or two. And the Second Head got nervous.

"That Third Head's getting awfully damn smart these days," it said to the First Head. "It's also got a distinct slant to the right. ... What if it starts bogging us down with needless discussion."

In short, they put their heads together, whispered back and forth for a while—and ate the Third Head.

Everything would have gone just fine after that, but the First Head started twitching and calling out in its sleep, which was most awkward, especially now that it controlled half of the vote.

The Second Head had no choice but to wait for nightfall and to eat the First. To their shocked acquaintances it said that for reasons of poor health the First Head had been retired to a sanatorium, all expenses paid.

Well, after that everything went quite well. The seven-headed dragons kept on bowing from the waist, and those with twelve heads simply disappeared.

Until one day our dragon got lazy and caught its remaining head in the train door at the last metro stop and was carted off to parts unknown.

And so it should be, for what sort of fairy tale would this be without a happy ending?

THE SWIM

Vladimir Sorokin (1955)

Translated by Brian James Baer

The leading Russian post-modernist, **Vladimir Sorokin** was trained as an engineer, but for a long period earned his money as a graphic designer.

His early works undermined Soviet cultural taboos and the sovietized, emasculated Soviet-Russian language itself, revealing its emptiness and dementia, the inflation of meanings and of the words themselves.

Already in the nineties Sorokin's name became a symbol for the whole new era of Russian literature, re-emerging from the years of captivity with a new energy and a new understanding of writing.

Recipient of numerous prizes, in his late dystopian novels Sorokin was quick to predict the return of authoritarian rule, yet in a new mode, postmodern, monstrous, as laughable as it is dreadful. Russian readers soon started to share the meme *Stop Sorokin from writing*, since all his predictions were coming true.

"Quotation number twenty-six, at my command!" The diminutive marshal of the River Agitation Corps hoarsely inhaled the night air, then yelled out: "Light the torches!"

A long column, consisting of muscular naked bodies lined up along the embankment of the City, swayed, then came to life with a barely perceptible movement—a thousand hands darted to a thousand shaved temples, snatched a thousand matches from behind a thousand ears, and struck the matches against a thousand bare thighs.

Tiny flames leapt upward all at once, and a moment later the marshal was convulsively squinting his eyes, which had grown accustomed to the darkness. The torches flared up and tongues of flame flung themselves toward the deep purple sky.

The marshal meticulously groped the rows of naked people with his eyes and once again opened his mouth: "Staying in formation and maintaining your distance, en-*ter* the water!"

The column, which was assembled in a particular order, moved and, marching silently in bare feet, began to glide swiftly down the granite steps of the embankment toward the black, still water of the River. The water parted, allowing the entire regiment in. The soldiers carefully lowered themselves into the icy September water, pushed off from the stone bottom, and swam in the same formation, holding the brightly burning torches above their shaved heads. A moment later the column had swum out into the middle of the river where the fast-moving current caught it and carried it downstream.

The most onerous condition of these agitational swims for Ivan was the prohibition against switching hands.

He could swim in the icy water for a long time, but holding a thirteen-pound torch with a fully extended arm for five endless hours was truly difficult. And no matter how he prepared for these swims, no matter what kind of training he subjected his right arm to, all the same, by dawn his arm would be seized by a slight trembling, and he would be powerless to curb the cursed tremor. Injections, liniments, and electromagnetic therapy were of no help.

Nevertheless, Ivan was considered the finest swimmer in the regiment, and for six years now he had been entrusted with the most responsible positions in the quotations.

Today he was swimming as a comma, the only one in the long quotation, of the highest difficulty rating, from the Book of Equality:

ONE OF THE MOST IMPORTANT ISSUES IN MODERN
SPECIAL PURPOSE BOROUGH CONSTRUCTION
WAS, IS AND WILL BE THE ISSUE OF THE TIMELY
INTENSIFICATION OF CONTRAST

There was no period at the end of the quotation, and so the only punctuation mark was the comma born of the flame of Ivan's cone-shaped, thirteen-pound torch.

Synchronized swimming came easily to Ivan. He had grown up by the sea and long felt at home in the water. After four years of MAAT (Military Aquatic Agitation Training), he simply couldn't imagine his life without those long nights that smelled of the River; without the dark water that broke up the flashes of flame; without the leaden pain that would gradually take over his arm holding the torch; and without the predawn breakfast in the spotless regimental cafeteria.

Service, like the River, carried Ivan along swiftly and smoothly. At first, as a rookie, he was placed in the middle of large, solid letters, like *M*, *W*, and *H*. Later, when they were convinced of the accuracy of his swimming, Ivan was gradually moved to the edges. Two years later he was already swimming as the left leg of the letter *A* or, together with the pockmarked Tatar Eldar, as the tail of the letter *Q*.

A year later Ivan was assigned to swim in dashes and exclamation marks, and after receiving the honorary tattoo "Swimmer Agitator of the First Class," he was entrusted with commas.

After seven years of service, Ivan had earned the rank of corporal, the State Swimming Medal, a great deal of verbal praise in front of the regiment, as well as a certificate of merit "For Exemplary Service in the Aquatic Transport of Chapter VI of the Book *New People* by Adelaide Svet." (The chapter was transported over the course of four months, and every night Ivan swam as a comma.)

He took more air into his lungs and slowly exhaled into the water, which smelled of silt. The torch tilted, but his fingers instinctively clenched the metal handle, straightening it.

His body had already warmed up, his teeth had stopped chattering, and his legs were cutting through the water with obedient kicks. Up ahead, the two shaved heads of the left foot of the letter *I* gleamed white, and beyond them the fiery mass of the column's torches quivered and undulated.

Ivan knew exactly where his place was—six meters from the left-most head; and he was swimming at a calm, measured pace, controlling his breath. He mustn't stray either to the left or to the right; he could not lag behind, neither could he rush ahead or the comma would attach itself to the *I*.

His torch was burning brightly, and the flame frequently leaned to the side, reaching down toward the turbidly moving water. The flame would dance just above the water's surface and then straighten up again.

During these swims Ivan liked to look at the stars. At the moment they were hanging especially low, shining cold and prickly.

He turned onto his back, felt the water burn the shaved nape of his neck, and smiled. The stars were standing in place, motionless.

He knew that it was dangerous to look at the stars for too

long—he might not notice the belly of the *S* drifting toward him, and the shaved heads would bump with horror into the lagging comma. Ivan looked back. Behind him, swimming in the crescent moons of the *S*, were his comrades Murtazov, Kholmogrov, Petrov, Doronin, Sheinblant, Popovich, Kim, Borisov, and Gerasimenko. Their faces were calm and focused. Ivan understood that with his comma he was dividing this long but very important sentence in two, and that without his torch the sentence would lose its great meaning. Pride and a sense of responsibility had always helped him fight off the cold. Once again he easily defeated it, and the autumn water now seemed warm.

He looked once more at the stars. Most of all he liked the constellation that resembled the ladle used by the regiment's cook to pour tasty turnip soup or to plop some thick barley porridge with margarine into the soldiers' bowls. And although he'd known since childhood that the constellation was called the Seventh Path and that the prickly star at its end bore the name of the Great Reformer of Human Nature Andrei Kapidich, it wasn't the golden obelisks of the Temple of Overcoming that rose up in Ivan's memory, nor the twisted horns of Kapidich, but rather the image of a large, shiny ladle.

He turned and began to swim on his right side. He could already feel a slight fatigue in his right arm. And it was no wonder—the tin handle of his torch had been filled with six liters of fuel. Few individuals were capable of swimming five hours in cold water while carrying a torch above their head. Ivan had understood this from the very beginning of his service in MAAT. After seven years his right arm had become almost twice the size of his left, as was the case with all the soldiers in the regiment. As his muscles expanded, his tendons bulged, and his skin turned a purple hue, inside Ivan there grew a proud self-confidence, and the feeling of superiority over his fellow citizens who did not have such a right arm intensified. From early spring until late fall he would wear short-sleeved shirts, showing off his powerful arm. This felt very good.

Soon the monolithic granite embankments narrowed, the First Bridge sailed by above the quotation, and the faint whisper of unseen onlookers could be heard. After the bridge the embankments soared upward and began gradually to crawl over the strip of river.

Ivan gripped his torch more firmly and raised it higher. One thousand and eighteen times he had swum through this place, through this awe-inspiring and solemn orifice, but every time he was overcome by a tremor of excitement for beyond the bridge lay the City, where the River became the Canal of Renewed Flesh, which intersected the City, and there on the embankments of the canal, like thousands upon thousands of times before, were gathered the most venerable representatives of the City.

An hour later the whispering grew stronger and now an uninterrupted beelike buzzing hung over the canal. The granite embankments squeezed the River to such an extent that when he was lying on his back, Ivan could see the heads of the City residents looking down. Here below there was no wind at all, the water was like a black mirror, and the flames of the torches calmly cut through the damp air.

His right arm drew attention to itself when a pain in his shoulder began to stir and stretch in a loose spiral toward his fingers, which were now white from the strain. Eventually the pain would reach them, and the tin handle would seem like cardboard, icy, greasy, burning, downy, and rubbery, and then his fingers would be tightly grasping a void, and Ivan would lose his right arm until the very end of the swim. And the end would come as usual, down to the smallest detail: in the dim, predawn air two sleepy instructors would lean over Ivan and unclench his white, cramped fingers, which had no desire to part with the extinguished torch. Ivan would help with his left hand.

He turned and exhaled several times into the water.

The noise above intensified, somewhere an ovation broke out, and the twenty-meter-high granite banks smashed it into a sustained echo.

"Just wait until we reach the Principal Neighborhoods!" Ivan thought, thrilled as he recalled the thunder of that endless heart-stopping ovation. Workers just don't know how to applaud like that ...

He looked askance at his arm. Pain had already seized his forearm, and it was now impossible to stop it. True, he still had one final remedy, an illusion of resistance, a naive palliative, which helped for an instant: if he suddenly squeezed his fingers and tensed the muscles of his entire arm, the pain would disappear. For a second.

Ivan clenched his teeth and squeezed the handle of the torch with all his might. A sound could be heard like the cracking of an egg, and something oily flowed down his arm.

Ivan looked and turned deadly pale: a barely noticeable piece of tin along the seam had come undone, and fuel was now leaking from the handle of his torch. He took his left hand out of the water and pressed his palm against the opening; the torch tilted and an orange flash touched Ivan's face. He recoiled, disappeared beneath the water, then resurfaced amid the swirling fire. Greedy yellow flames burst from his body, and around him spread a fiery patch. The swift-moving fire forced Ivan to utter a drawn-out cry. He went under, resurfaced in the middle of the *I*, burst into flames, screamed, and started thrashing his arms against his comrades and against the surface of the water until the moldy granite split open his flaming head.

When the comma, squeezed up against the vertical face of the *I*, burst into flames, the onlookers on the embankments realized that this was the Third Hint about which the winged Gorgez had spoken at the last Congress of the Renewed. A powerful ovation hung for quite some time over the canal.

At that moment the comma disappeared, resurfacing and breaking the *I* into yellow pieces. Having destroyed the *I*, the comma found itself in the upper window of the *S*, and that letter too was complaisantly torn apart; the *W* then moved up from behind, but, catching hold of the comma, it caved in and broke apart; the next *I* by some miracle swam through the mass of flames and safely caught up with ONE OF THE MOST IMPORTANT ISSUES OF MODERN BOROUGH CONSTRUCTION WAS.

The ovation continued, and on the black mirror of the River the subsequent events of that fateful night began slowly to unfold.

AND, having edged its way into the thickest patch of fire, began to turn into an accordion, transforming itself into a complex figure, reminiscent of the transom of an unusual window; in an act of self-destruction, BE THE swam over, replenishing the swarm of torches; the more cautious ISSUE tried to avoid the danger zone but was flattened against the granite wall; the long INTENSIFICATION turned out to be more stable than the previous words and to the very last made every effort to survive, coiling itself up like a caterpillar in an anthill; the remaining letters at the end of the quotation perished one after the other.

During the collapse, a thunderous ovation sounded and never waned. Only when the last word had broken apart did the embankments gradually fall silent. The crowd of nocturnal observers froze, held their breath, and looked down.

There was frenzied activity below: the fires were tossing themselves about, crowding together, trying to re-create the second part of the quotation, but the strips of words immediately broke down into yellow beads. When ONE OF THE MOST IMPORTANT ISSUES IN CONTEMPORARY SPECIAL PURPOSE BOROUGH CONSTRUCTION WAS I swam safely past the Second Bridge, the iron body of which divided the social classes, the Principal masses greeted the fiery words with such a thunderous ovation that the flames in the torches shuddered, threatening to go out.

IT'S NICE TO BE DEAF

Anna Politkovskaya (1958–2006)

Translated by Alexander Burry
& Tatiana Tulchinsky

She never wrote pure fiction and never presented herself as a writer. Yet, **Anna Politkovskaya** was never just a journalist in her texts. She wrote from Chechnya, from the 'small corner of hell', as it was called in one of her book's titles. And she always wrote stories, the human stories: those of refugees and fighters, Chechen and Russian mothers searching for their children in the horror of a war zone, old and ill, lost, abandoned; kidnapped by the state security, tortured and thrown into the pit. She was the Nemesis of the generals and state officials and the last hope for people without hope, and her dispatches from Chechnya were widely read around the world.

Politkovskaya was poisoned by an unknown substance in 2004, during the hostage crisis in Beslan, and mercilessly murdered two years later in the entrance to her own house in Moscow on the day of Vladmir Putin's birthday.

The person who ordered the assassination was never found.

The war began the way wars usually do, with the bombing of villages and cities, which led to torrents of refugees. Thousands of people, grabbing their children and elderly, fled wherever their feet would carry them. They were coming and going every which way, a trail of people many miles long following the main highway of Chechnya, the Rostov-Baku Federal Route. But this trail got bombed too.

September 1999. We are lying on withered autumn grass. To be more precise, we want to lie on it, but for most of us all that's left is the dusty Chechen ground. There are too many of us—hundreds, and there are not enough amenities for everyone.

We are the people caught in the bombing. We didn't do anything wrong; we were just walking toward Ingushetia along the former highway, which is now all torn up by armored vehicles.

Grozny is behind us. We run as a herd from the war and its battles. When the lime comes, and you have hit the ground face down, assuming a fetal position, trying to hide your head, knees, and even elbows under your body—then a kind of false, sticky loneliness sneaks up on you, and you start to think: "Why are you crouching? What are you trying to save? This life of yours that no one but you cares about?"

Why is it false? Because you know perfectly well that this isn't really true: you have a family, and they are waiting and praying for you. And it's sticky because of the sweat. When you're clinging to life, you sweat a lot. Some people are lucky, though. When they feel that death is near, all that happens is that the hair rises on their heads.

Still, there is loneliness. Death is the one situation where you can never find companionship. When the diving helicopters hover over your bent back, the ground starts to resemble a death bed.

Here are the helicopters, going for another round. They fly so low that you can see the gunners' hands and faces. Some say that they can even see their eyes. But this is fear talking. The main thing is their legs, dangling carelessly in the open hatches. As if they didn't come to kill, but to let their tired feet get some fresh air. Their feet are big and scary, and the soles almost seem to touch our faces. The barrels of their guns are squeezed between their thighs. We're frightened, but we all want to see our killers. They seem to be laughing at us crawling comically down below—heavy old women, young girls, and children. We can even hear their laughter. But no, this is just another illusion; it's too noisy to hear that. Automatic weapon fire whistles in the air around us, and someone always starts to wail along. Has anyone been killed? Wounded?

"Don't move. Don't raise your head. That's my advice," a man next to me says. He dropped to the ground right where he was, in his black suit with a white shirt and black tie.

My neighbor Vakha starts talking nonstop. This is a good thing; it's better to talk now than to be silent.

Vakha is a land surveyor from Achkhoi-Martan, a big village not far from Ingushetia. In wartime Chechnya, everyone is afraid of everything. This morning, Vakha left his house wearing his suit and carrying his folder as usual, so as not to attract attention, as if he were going to work. In fact, he had decided to flee.

"Every time," Vakha mumbles, because you can't help mumbling with your mouth pressed to the ground, "every time the helicopters come, I take my folder, get out some paper, and pretend to write. I think it helps."

People nearby start to laugh quietly.

"How can paper help? What are you talking about?" a tiny, skinny man to his left mutters in a loud whisper, spitting out dirt.

"The pilots see that I'm working, that I'm not a terrorist," the land surveyor retorts.

"And what if they think just the opposite? That you're taking down their license plate numbers?" a female body in front pipes up, gingerly shifting a bit. "I'm all numb. When will this all end?"

"If they think that, then you're done for." We can't see who says this. He is behind us. And it's a good thing: his words are tough, sharp, and pitiless, like an ax.

"There you go again. Enough of that." An old man's voice cuts the tough guy short. Then he asks Vakha, "Show me your folder, please. I'll tell the others."

The bodies, who have been silenced by the tough guy, are eager to clutch at straws again, to enjoy an unexpected gift of momentary happiness, the last for some.

"Go ahead, show us ..."

"We'll all get these folders ..."

"The Russians will run out of them ..."

"Putin will wonder, why are all the Chechens running around with folders during the war? They should be carrying automatic weapons ..."

"And he'll give out folders to the Feds* too. All of Chechnya will be carrying folders ..."

"Vakha, what color should the folders be?"

The helicopters don't stop circling around. The children's crying shakes the ground that is studded with people, machine guns are

---

* Representatives of Federal troop units and military departments. The term is used both by them and by civilians. In Chechnya, the term is synonymous with "Russians."

shooting—why don't they shut up for just a moment?—and the explosions of falling mines croak the whole time, introducing a banal note into our stay on the death bed. That's all we need!

Still, people joke around. Vakha defends himself meekly.

"It's all in Allah's hands," he says. "But say what you want, I've never been wounded with this folder. Not in the first war, and not in this one. It's always helped me."

"So you had the folder in the first war too?" someone bursts out laughing, in a kind of nervous spasm. "Then why are you lying on the ground, man? Why don't you get up?"

Vakha is tired of that.

"Everyone's lying on the ground. Why should I be the one to get up? Why should I make myself into a target?"

"But you have your folder." It's the old man who cut off the tough guy, who, by the way, has been silent ever since. The old man laughs somewhere behind us, if you can call body movements and raspy sighs against the ground laughter. "You don't know how lucky you are, man; they might think you're counting us. And that means you're on their side."

Vakha is silent now; it's no time for jokes. Everything in its place. He starts blowing dust from his dirty black sleeves, breathing from somewhere under his body. After all, this is the only thing he can do in the fetal position we've been forced to assume.

In twenty-four hours, Vakha and his magic folder will be destroyed, blown up by a mine about a mile from where we are now lying. He'll take just a few steps away from the road, into an untidy, unharvested field from that first wartime autumn. There were already too many mines to count, and everyone to a man, including soldiers and militants, was wandering around Chechnya without a map of the minefields. It's like playing Russian roulette.

Vakha walks to that side not because he has to, but simply because he's exhausted from waiting. The line to the passport checkpoint was too long. It consisted mostly of us jokers, the new family he'd been prepared to die with the day before, lying on a different field.

Now dead, Vakha lies on a field again, but this time fearlessly, with his wounded face looking up and his hands spread wider than they've ever been in his life. The left hand is about ten yards from his black jacket, which has been torn to pieces. The right hand is a bit closer, about five steps away. And Vakha's legs are quite a problem: they disappear, most likely turning into dust at the time of the explosion and flying away with the wind. His folder with its blank sheets of paper meets the same fate. It saved him from the helicopters, but it can't save him from the mines.

Then two soldiers carefully approach Vakha from the checkpoint with the long line. One of them is young and scrawny; he looks like he's fifteen years old, and his helmet and boots are too big. The second is a bit older and bigger, well-built, with his hands in the pockets of his camouflage pants. The first starts crying softly, dirtying his face as he wipes his tears, and turns around, not having the heart to look. The second smacks him on the back of the head, and the first soldier shuts up immediately, like an alarm clock that's been turned off with a slap of the hand so that a person can continue sleeping in the morning. The Chechens in line buy an "emergency reserve" big black plastic sack for "Cargo 200"* from these soldiers' lieutenant. Then they gather Vakha's remains and spend quite a while discussing where to bring them. To his mother, wife, and children in the camp at Ingushetia? Or to his empty house in Achkhoi-Martan? Reason prevails—the body should be brought to Achkhoi, of course. It will be buried there anyway, in the family cemetery. So why waste money lugging it to Ingushetia? You need to bribe a lot of people to get there. At the Kavkaz checkpoint, the border between this war and the rest of the world, you need to pay twice, once each way. And you'd have to pay two or three times as much for a corpse, depending on the commander's mood that day.

... But for now, Vakha will be alive and well for twenty-four hours. And we continue to lie on the field on the outskirts of Gekhi, hoping to get away from the helicopters, and almost believing in a happy future. After all, it's only the beginning of the war, the first days of October 1999. It seems to us that the fighting won't last too long, and that the refugees will soon be able to return to their homes. All we have to do is survive this day, and things will straighten themselves out.

At one point, Vakha becomes bolder—after all, when there is danger for too long, everything gets to be dull and boring. Ignoring

---

* Army jargon for a corpse. "We have a Cargo 200" means that there are dead people.

the helicopters, he suddenly turns over onto his side. And in a normal, human way, without earth in his mouth, he begins to talk about his family—his six children, who had left Achkhoi a week ago for Ingushetia along with his mother, wife, and two unmarried sisters. They're the ones he's trying to make his way to.

Off to the side, Gekhi is being bombed. Probably as fiercely and continuously as Königsberg was in World War II. Vakha turns face down again.

"There were so many refugees from Grozny gathered there—a real nightmare," he says, distracted from the topic of his family and engrossed in the rhythm of the attackers' mounting, irrational bombing of their own people. "Thousands, probably. In the last bombing, a week ago, a hospital was destroyed, and the sick and wounded were taken away. Where will they take the wounded now?"

The women are quietly wailing, and shushing the children so they don't wail, as if the children weren't people too. The splashing sounds emitted by the weapons swarm around us from all sides, not letting our minds rest. Although it's been only about half an hour since the beginning of the helicopter attack, it seems like half a day, enough time to recall most of your life. People gradually start to lose their self-control. Cries of desperation can be heard; men are sobbing. But not all of them. Among us are some thirteen- or fourteen-year-olds. They are excitedly and joyfully discussing which weapon is being used at a given moment. And what else can they do besides demonstrate their thorough knowledge? They've been learning modern weapon terminology their whole conscious lives, since the Chechen war began, for nearly ten years.

Between the teenagers and us, a little boy is quietly crawling around. He is probably six years old, thin and sad-looking. He isn't screaming, crying, or grabbing his mother, but looking around thoughtfully and saying "It's nice to be deaf" in a simple, calm, even everyday voice. As if he were saying "It's nice to play ball."

Right then the "hail" overtakes us. There is no greater torture for a person's hearing, not to mention life, in war. The hail comes from the late twentieth-century version of the Katyusha* rocket launcher.

---

* An artillery rocket launcher with high striking capacity. It was actively used during the second Chechen war. Its fire was commonly called "hail."

It whistles and hisses for a long time. But if you can already hear it, that means it's past you, and death, though it was nearby, has chosen someone else for the time being. And you laugh about this. The hail turns you into an inhuman beast that has learned to rejoice in someone else's misfortune.

The boy, who is lying comfortably on a grass bush pillow despite the circumstances, sums it up this way:

"The deaf can't hear any of this. And so they're not afraid."

Vakha quietly pulls the boy closer, hugs him, and gives him some candy from the pocket of his black jacket.

"What's your name?" Vakha asks, crying softly.

"Sharpuddin," the boy answers, surprised to see a grown man crying.

"It would be even better, Sharpuddin, if we could become blind, mute, and stupid." Vakha's eyes dry up under the boy's gaze. "But we're not. And yet we have to survive anyway."

The helicopters fly away after about five minutes, and the hail falls silent. The raid is over. People begin to pick themselves up at once and shake themselves off. Someone praises Allah. The field becomes lively. The women run to look for trucks for the wounded, and the men carry the dead to one place.

A day and night pass. The boy, Sharpuddin, goes up to the men who are collecting Vakha's remains in a black bag, and silently begins to help them. They sternly shoo him away like a dog, for his own good, but his mother objects. She says that her son was the last child that Vakha caressed in his life. And then Sharpuddin is allowed to help.

OF SAUCEPANS AND STAR-SHOWERS

Mikhail Shishkin (1961)

Translated by Leo Shtutin

Living in Switzerland, **Mikhail Shishkin** is inevitably compared with Vladimir Nabokov, the great émigré. The comparison makes sense, since as a novelist Shishkin is definitely one of the most exquisite stylists in modern Russian literature.

He finished a course in German studies and writes Russian and German, taking lessons from both literary traditions. Shishkin is the only author to receive three major Russian literary prizes: The Big Book, The National Bestseller and the Russian Booker Prize.

All winter long I fantasized about spending the summer in Valais and roaming the mountains every day. I pored over the map and plotted out various routes. I'd be mountain-bound bright and early and homeward-bound come evening, tired and happy after a full day's ramble.

But then summer came, and I landed up in hospital with a bilateral hernia. There was no escaping postoperative complications, either— inflammation, high fever, antibiotics. As soon as my stitches were out I went off to Brentschen. But I had to kiss goodbye to all my wonderful plans. No hours-long hikes in the mountains. The first few days I ventured only as far as the table on the lawn in front of the chalet. I gazed at the Weisshorn and rejoiced at life.

The mountains in this vicinity have inspired so many descriptions that they seemed like quotations emerging suddenly from beyond the clouds.

I thought, too, about how, as the years go by, taking genuine delight in something becomes possible only when you can share that delight with somebody else. My son had promised to come and visit for a couple of days, and, watching the Rhône valley change colour in the twilight, almost as if it were pulling on a lilac stocking, I so wished I could enjoy this spectacle in his company rather than alone.

But he could never seem to find the time to come.

As I waited for his visit, I gradually started getting out and about, venturing further and further from the village each day, now taking the level road towards Jeizinen, now the mountain track in the direction of Leukerbad, and every time I imagined how we'd stroll around these parts together. I walked at a leisurely pace, often stopping. The stitches itched unbearably—I wanted to pick the plaster off and tear at the scars with my nails.

Then my son emailed to let me know he was already on his way. His short message ended with the following riddle: imagine a saucepan big enough to hold anything you like—a chicken, a whole bull, a house, the entire Earth, even the entire universe. Yet what can such a saucepan never hold?

Let me explain. The thing is, his mother and I divorced when he was seven. I became a pop-in father. And, later, a fly-in father. Things were probably better that way, for everybody and for him first and foremost. When his mother and I fought—undignifiedly, inanely, smashing crockery and slamming doors—he didn't cry, just threw himself now at her, now at me, his hands clenched into little fists. Living like this was impossible. My leaving home did us—my son and myself—a world of good. Had we continued to live together, I would have only shouted at him: put your shoes away! Or, Do your homework! Or, Stop badgering me, can't you see I'm writing! But because I'd left, our get-togethers throughout his childhood were about him and for him only, and I never told him to stop badgering me. Not a single time. It was worth leaving home for that alone.

In periods away from one another we'd exchange letters. About anything and everything. I thought up various charades for him, crosswords, riddles. In each letter he'd pose tricky questions of his own, such as: If steam is lighter than water, then why is ice not heavier than water, but lighter?

He's all grown-up now, but he still rounded off that email with one of his riddles.

He's twenty-three now, an adult.

By the age of sixteen I already knew everything about myself. I knew what I wanted from this life: to write books and to travel. And

I knew that this was impossible. Because I was born into a country where whatever I might write would never be published, and beyond whose borders I would never be allowed to travel. This was a slave-country, and my slave-parents had birthed me into bondage. I knew exactly what I wanted, but it was all impossible—and I felt like a disconsolate wretch.

My son, in contrast, has it all within his grasp: he's already travelled half the world, he writes, makes films, gives concerts of his own music. But he still doesn't truly know what he wants from this life. Which makes him feel wretched, too.

Happiness, most likely, is conditional neither on liberty nor on its lack.

There I was, strolling along the track in the direction of Leukerbad, the air laden with the sharp aromas of the warm sunlit forest, of pine resin and wild strawberries, and I pondered what it was that wouldn't fit into a saucepan big enough to hold the Milky Way, all the galaxies, and the entire universe from beginning to end?

And then I encountered my father. He was walking towards me, a rucksack on his shoulders, sturdy mountain boots on his feet, sun-bronzed, healthy, young. This was my father, but not as I knew him in his final years, a grey-haired, gnarly guzzler. This was the father I remembered from my childhood. I stopped, astounded, while he strode over to me, nimbly and vigorously, as does a weary traveler at the conclusion of a whole day spent on mountain paths, with the end of a long, splendid hike finally in sight.

Drawing level with me, he smiled and said, *"Griiezi!"*

"Griiezi!" I replied.

And he strode on towards Brentschen.

The fact that my father had spoken to me in Swiss German brought me back to reality. Needless to say, this young man, many years my junior, could not be my father, delivered to the flames of a Moscow crematorium in his sailor's uniform seventeen years previously.

During the war my father had been a submariner in the Baltic, and a photograph of his Shchuka hung on our wall. That Daddy had a submarine was a source of great pride for me as a child, and I'd constantly be making drawings of the photo in my school exercise book, carefully inscribing the number Shch-310 on the submarine's nose. Every ninth of May—Victory Day—my father would get out his sailor's uniform, which he was always having altered to accommodate his ever-growing belly, and pinned on all his badges. Later I grew up a bit and realized that in 1944 and 1945 my father helped sink German ships which were evacuating refugees from Riga and Tallinn. Hundreds if not thousands of people met their deaths in the waters of the Baltic—for which my father was decorated. I've long since ceased being proud of him, but nor do I condemn him. There was a war on, and my father won in that war. He was avenging his brother.

My father went off to war as a volunteer at the age of eighteen—to avenge Boris, he would tell me. His older brother was killed in the summer of 1941.

As a child I'd spend every summer at my grandmother's, in the holiday village of Udelnaya near Moscow. A wall in her room was hung with old photos. One showed her sons: two teenage brothers sitting in embrace, head to head, floppy ears touching. Nowadays everyone always smiles on photos, but these two gazed seriously into the camera as if they had foreknowledge of everything that would soon happen to them. Another snapshot showed a youth in headphones: a ham-radio aficionado, Boris was training to be a telephonist.

I remember Grandma unfolding the frayed old sheet of paper marked "NOTIFICATION," kissing it and wiping away tears. He was twenty. Looking at my son today, I find this simply impossible to imagine. He's just a boy still, no more than a kid. But back then, Boris seemed like a big grown-up hero to me.

My grandfather was a peasant from down Tambov way. He was arrested in the midst of collectivization in 1930. Grandma would tell me about how, when requisitioners arrived at their yard to take away the cow, he became indignant at being left with nothing to feed two little children. He was arrested and sent off to Siberia to build the Baikal-Amur Mainline. He managed to pass on two short letters before vanishing. When Grandma was dying, aged ninety-five, her mind started going a bit, and everything that happened to her in 1930 began resurfacing. I'd phone her, I remember, and at first she'd speak to me as normal, but then she'd suddenly start asking, "Who is this? Misha? Who's Misha?" And I'd tell her, "It's me, Misha!" Her husband, my grandfather, was also called Mikhail, and she'd scream down the phone, "What are you doing? Leave him be! Don't take him away! Let him go! Misha, where are they taking you?" She had been transported back to that year, and her husband was being arrested all over again. To avoid dying of hunger, Grandma had to flee the village with her two children, my father and Uncle Borya. She found a job as a cleaner near Moscow before spending the rest of her life as a kindergarten nurse.

On every form he filled out, my father held back the fact that he was the son of an enemy of the people, and he lived his whole life in fear that this would come out into the open. It's so important for a son to be proud of his father. But it was fear, not pride, that dwelt in my father's soul.

That frayed and yellowed document Grandma kissed and cried over wasn't actually a notice of death, but a notification that Boris was missing in action somewhere in the Kandalaksha area. Such an odd word that it stuck in my memory. This is a small town in Karelia. Now I realize she was forever hoping that he hadn't perished, that he was still alive somewhere. "Missing in action"—what does this mean, exactly? Could mean anything. And she thought, What if he's still alive, what if we're to meet again? And my father harboured the same hope about his brother.

Grandma died in '93, my father in '95. And then, in 2010, something happened—the sort of thing that normally happens in films or books, not in real life. I was in Norway. A translation of my novel *Maidenhair* had been released there, and I was invited on a tour of speaking engagements across several cities. My Norwegian translator Marit Bjerkeng and I were strolling around Tromsø, a town in the country's far north, and we popped into the small local museum. Two diminutive rooms housed an exhibition about Soviet POWs in Norway during the war years. The retreating Germans evacuated their camps from Finland to the Tromsø region. And all of a sudden I remembered that word from my childhood—Kandalaksha. That was where the notification had come from! Kandalaksha was somewhere in Karelia. And I thought, what if my Uncle Borya had been captured there, and was then transferred to Norway in 1944 together with the other prisoners? Marit helped me make an enquiry to the Norwegian archives. A copy of the registration card of POW Boris Shishkin was found immediately and sent to me by email.

POW'S PERSONAL CARD. ISSUED AUGUST 29, 1941. STALAG 309. All their camps were called Stalag—a contraction of Stammlager. This number designated a network of camps in Finland. Every POW was given a metal ID tag, and his number was 1249. SHISHKIN, BORIS, BORN DECEMBER 30, 1920, IN THE VILLAGE OF NOVO-YURIEVO. NATIONALITY: RUSSIAN. PRIVATE, MILITARY UNIT NUMBER. CIVILIAN PROFESSION: RADIOMECHANIC. TAKEN CAPTIVE AUGUST 27. IN GOOD HEALTH. FINGERPRINT. SURNAME AND ADDRESS OF KIN IN POW'S COUNTRY OF ORIGIN. MOTHER: LYUBOV SHISHKINA—my grandmother.

Reading this, I came into a sharp realization of what it was to be resurrected from the dead. This person, my twenty-year-old uncle, now thirty-three years my junior—this boy had suddenly come back to life! And it hurt so much that neither my grandmother nor my father had lived to see this day.

I went straight off to the Internet, and you can find everything there, including information on this Stammlager 309. Photographs, investigations, documents. Stories of people who were imprisoned there and survived. There were even photographs of firing-squad executions taken on the sly by a German soldier. POWs were predominantly employed in construction—they built railways. I read about POW telephonists—and realized: of course, that was him! He must have been given work within his profession!

On the reverse of the card was a note: ES BESTEHT DIE VERMUTUNG, DASS DER KRIEGSGEFANGENE JUDE IST, LAUT AUSSAGEN EINES VERTRAUTEN MANNES. WURDE AM 25.7.1942 DER SICHERHEITSPOLIZEI ÜBERGEBEN. Which means he was shot.

In the course of my Internet research on Stalag 309 I came across a photograph of executed POWs in a big pit. Perhaps one of them was my father's brother.

How can I convey this feeling? My uncle Borya has just been resurrected—and he's been killed again. It's a good thing after all, I remember thinking, that Dad and Grandma didn't live to see this!

That he was killed as a Jew is, of course, astonishing. He was of Tambov peasant stock, going back generations. Evidently someone had got square with him: the slightest denunciation might get you shot.

I set about tracking down that photograph from my childhood.

Our family archive was destroyed ten years ago when my brother's house near Moscow burnt down. I got in contact with my father's last wife, Zinaida Vasilievna, but after moving house numerous times she had nothing left. It's extraordinary: I see it right before my eyes, that prewar snap of the youth in headphones, but it exists nowhere except within me.

Every document, every photograph, everything that should be kept in the family from generation to generation—it has all perished. But it all still survives in what remains of that machine of death. Why? How on earth can this be?

I was also struck that a Russian translation had been written onto the card in someone's hand. Who did the translation? What for? When? There was a Russian stamp, too: PERSONAL REGISTRATION CARD AMENDED, REFERENCE NUMBER 452. 1941. And a handwritten word: NOTIFIED. Meaning that Boris's mother, my grandmother, had been sent the paper she was to cry over for so many years.

It turned out that all these archives were transferred to Russia after the war and are held to this day in Podolsk, near Moscow. My grandmother and my father lived so many years in ignorance of their Boris's fate, and it was their own country, for whose sake Boris had died, that held the truth back from them. Only after Perestroika were the archives opened temporarily, and Western historians made copies of them. I received Uncle Borya's card from the Norwegian archives within a single week, yet Grandma and Dad received no news of him from their own state in a whole lifetime.

Information concerning POWs was kept secret because in reality the state was waging war against its own people. My relatives, my loved ones lived out their entire lives in a prison nation which used them for its wars and despised them.

When Perestroika began, my father made an enquiry to the KGB about the fate of his father. All the victims of Stalin's repressions were being rehabilitated. He showed me an official letter confirming the rehabilitation of his father, my grandfather. Charges were being dismissed for lack of *corpus delicti*. Dad had been tanking up since morning and would only bellow, "Bastards! Bastards!"

After the war he drank his whole life through. And all his submariner friends, too. They probably couldn't do otherwise. It was the disease of their generation. Aged eighteen, he spent months on end immured in a submarine, haunted by the constant fear of drowning in an iron coffin. An experience like that can shackle you for the rest of your life.

Under Gorbachev, when the really hungry years began, my veteran father received food parcels containing produce from Germany. In his eyes this represented a personal humiliation. He and his friends had seen themselves as victors their whole fives, and now he was forced to feed from the hand of the vanquished foe. He regarded the collapse of the USSR as defeat in a war he had waged together with the rest of the country. My father hated Gorbachev.

I didn't like Gorbachev either, but precisely for the reason that he did everything in his power to prevent the collapse of the USSR and the entire Soviet system. My father and I viewed the history being made around us from opposite vantage points. There was an unbridgeable gulf between us. We had long since ceased to be close to one another. And this, of course, had little to do with politics.

The final straw leading to our estrangement came at my wedding. Inviting him, I remember, was a conciliatory gesture on my part. Dad got drunk, started a punch-up, and I had to restrain him with the help of a friend and pack him off home in a taxi. It was hard for me to forgive him such things.

It's so important to be proud of one's father. But I was ashamed of mine.

I started communicating with him again only shortly before his death. He spent his last years simply destroying himself with vodka. Denied his drink, he'd start smashing up everything in the house. Zinaida Vasilievna stopped fighting for him—she herself would buy him his bottles so he'd get sozzled and quickly pass out. He drank so much it seemed strange his body was still holding up. All his submariner friends had long since drunk themselves into the grave. My father must've been in a hurry to rejoin his war buddies. Out of their whole boat he was the last man standing.

At the funeral feast Zinaida Vasilievna told of how my father died:

"He's fallen off the bed and he yells, 'Zina! Zina, I can't see anything! Turn the light on! The light! I need more light!' It is light, Pasha, I say, it's sunny outside!"

It was odd that my bibulous veteran-submariner father should have uttered the same dying cry as Goethe.

For as long as I can remember, my father always said that, upon his death, he must be laid in the coffin wearing his sailor's uniform. And at the morgue a grey-haired swabby was wheeled out to us in an open coffin. Lately his whole body had been quaking and shaking, but now, arms folded on his chest, he had an air of serenity, as if mollified by the thought that he wasn't being cremated just any-old-how, but in his striped sailor's jersey.

The coffin turned out to be too short. His head wouldn't fit—it was wedged up against the coffin wall, his chin pressing into his chest—and his face wore a strange, lively expression which betrayed mild annoyance. Can't even put me into the coffin properly, it seemed to be saying.

Zinaida Vasilievna went off to remonstrate with the morgue authorities, but they just jabbed a finger at the receipt: You ordered 180 cm, we put him in 180 cm. A woman in a grubby white coat and rubber gloves came out and started explaining that coffins must be ordered with room to spare because dead bodies tend to stretch:

"Were you unaware of that or what?"

Zinaida Vasilievna waved a hand, loath to get involved:

"Do whatever you want! I've no strength left to deal with this."

We had to go to the crematorium at Mitino. A bus was laid on, caked with dirt to the very windows. I made to close the coffin. Nails had already been hammered into the lid, but I only noticed this when it wouldn't shut properly. I took a look: a nail had lodged itself right into the top of my father's head. Something reddish-blue had oozed out of the ripped skin and into his grey hair. The coffin was left open.

As I sat in that screechy, clapped-out bus—clutching the seat for fear of being sent flying by a pothole, my leg keeping the coffin from sliding away—I remembered the bike rides to Ilyinsky Forest Dad and I went on every August before school started. Time and again he'd shoot off ahead on his heavy trophy cycle. "Dad, wait!" I'd yell, and I'd try and catch him up on my Orlyonok, hop-skipping over tree-roots: there were pines all around, and weaving along the paths would've been better. At times you'd come across sandy areas, and your tires would sink.

In the crematorium, when the time had come to close the coffin, I bent the nail to the side as best as I could so Dad would be spared more pain.

Shortly before he died, my father resolved to have us photographed together.

"What for?" I said.

He tried to convince me:

"I'll pop my clogs, Mishka, and you'll look at the photo and maybe you'll think back to your old man the sailor!"

"All right, old-man-the-sailor, let's go!" I said, just to get him off my back.

We went to a photo-studio near their house just outside Strogino. We sat down in front of a Lumiere-brothers-era camera. The photographer, a young girl with a boyish hairdo, said, pulling a strand of gum from between her teeth, "You could do with a smile!"

Our attempt to produce one couldn't have been too convincing: "Say cheese, now!" laughed the girl.

Just recently I was looking for something or other, going through old papers, and suddenly there it was—that very photo. Dad and I, earlobes touching, both with cheese in our mouths.

My son phoned in the evening, when he was changing trains in Brig, and I drove down in my old Golf to pick him up at the station in Leuk.

He came out of the train with a massive backpack—that's how he travels the world. We hugged. Every time I see him these days, I marvel at how grown-up he's become—a whole head taller than me now.

On the way back I pestered him with silly pointless questions about his studies, about university, about his flatmates. He studies in Vienna. *Historisch-Kulturwissenschaftliche Europaforschung*. He told me about his amusing professors, whom he loves for their love of history, and I listened enviously. I studied foreign languages at the Lenin Pedagogical Institute, but the principal subjects there were history of the Communist Party and scientific communism. And I hated the professors. How strange that slavery should be known as a science.

While he took a shower and unpacked, I got supper ready: fried potatoes with onion and sausages.

"Mmm, smells good!" he shouted from his room.

We ate at the table by the window, looking on as the Weisshorn glowed pinker and pinker in the sunset. *Alpenglühen*. I told him about my encounter with my father on the mountain path.

"I barely remember Granddad. Tell me something about him! What can you remember from your childhood?"

And I started telling him about what I could still recall. About how, when he was drunk, my father would always start belting out the 60s hit "Mishka, Mishka, Where's Your Smile?" and, wrapping his great big arms around me, a preschooler, he'd make me sing along, but I tried to struggle free—his drunken stench was horrible. And about how we'd go cycling in Ilyinsky Forest. And about other odds and ends. Suddenly it transpired that the long years of my childhood had been distilled into a mere handful of recollections.

One involved a trick my ex-submariner had once shown me. I see it clearly: we're going for a haircut on a Sunday, and I'm whingeing—I'm scared of the hair-clipper and I hate the barber's. He's pulling me by the arm, and look, he says, look at this trick! And, miraculously, Dad's become a giant, and he's holding out on his palm a tram that's pulled in to a stop.

My son laughed and said that I'd shown him that same trick when he was a kid. Only it wasn't a tram I had on my palm, but the high-riser on Vosstaniya Square.

We started reminiscing about his own childhood. About how we went off to meet his mum at the station one day, and it was so heaving with people we were scared we'd lose her, and then I sat him on my shoulders, and he saw her and yelled at the top of his lungs, "Mummy, mummy! We're here!"—and was dead proud later on because he thought that, had he not spied his mum out in the crowd from the height of my shoulders, she'd never have found us.

"Tell me," he asked, "what's the happiest childhood memory you have of your father?"

I remembered the haymow. Born in the countryside and into a peasant family, my father lived his whole life the wrong way—as a city-dweller, spending years in some office—but he yearned to be a peasant, to work the land that had been taken away from them. And so, come summertime in the dacha, he loved working with the soil, planting apple trees, crafting, digging, building. He always dreamt of sleeping outside, on a haymow, rather than in the house. Once he brought a whole haycock over from somewhere and fixed himself a bed right under the open sky. I was about seven or eight, and I cajoled him into letting me sleep with him. It was such a delight to lie on that prickly bed, nuzzling into my father's shoulder and breathing in the overwhelming fragrance of the hay! It being August, stars were falling. We lay there, the universe looming above us, and looked on as meteors streaked across the sky.

We sat and talked, my son and I, until it was completely dark and the stars had risen over the Valais. And suddenly he said, "Let's go!"

It was cool outside now. We wrapped ourselves in blankets and settled down into armchairs on the lawn in front of the chalet. Lights shimmered in the valley. The last of the day lingered in the western sky, and the Milky Way hung low overhead. It was uncannily quiet, even the breeze had fallen silent. Just us and the stars. But not one deigned to fall.

Sitting like that, heads jerked skywards, was uncomfortable, so we lay ourselves down on the broad, sturdy table. Head to head, ears touching. We talked about anything and everything. Reminisced some more about childhood. Then he told me about his girlfriend. About how much he loves her. Though she no longer does.

Later it got seriously cold, but we were loath to head back into the warmth: we still hadn't seen a single star fall over Brentschen.

Finally we headed back inside to sleep, it was really late now.

Before going to bed I popped into his room to say good night.

"You know, Dad, if I ever have a son and he asks me to recall some happy moments with my father, I'll definitely think back to tonight—to how we lay on the table under the night sky here in Brentschen, watching stars fall."

"But not a single one did."

"What difference does it make!"

We were silent for a while. Then I said, "It's late. Good night! Get some sleep! We'll talk plenty more tomorrow."

"Good night!"

And then I remembered what I'd been meaning to ask him the whole day, but kept forgetting:

"Oh yes—tell me, what doesn't fit into that saucepan that's big enough to hold everything?"

"Oh come on, Dad," he laughed, "it's simple! That would be the saucepan lid!"

The lid!

But of course! How didn't I twig at once!

FRIEDMANN SPACE

Viktor Pelevin (1962)

Translated by Anastasia Lakhtikova

A man who only on rare occasions gives an interview and hides his private life from the public, **Viktor Pelevin** is one of Russia's most commercially successful prose writers. He emerged in the nineties as a prophet of the new post-Soviet world, twisted, surreal and absurd for many of those who were born and raised in the USSR.

Pelevin's distinctive pattern is a play with reality and a play within this play; omnivorous, he mocks, derealizes and laughs at every new concept, item or idol of modern life, Russian and Western, transforming it in his texts to what is nicknamed *pelevinschina* – a turned upside down universe of its own, where nothing is what it pretends to be, and the author is the demiurge of uncertainty and chaos.

Experts agree that a sizable portion of contemporary popular culture functions according to a principle they've dubbed the "windmill": the merely comfortable selling the poor fantasies about the lives of the rich, the very rich, and the fabulously rich. Often this pattern varies by way of some colorful true-life detail coming out: one of these merely comfortable individuals showing the tabloids around his actually rather modest house in the opulent Rublev neighborhood of Moscow, for instance, all the while parroting some legitimate example of a famous oligarch's conversation that he's managed to overhear (like the sacramental phrase such powerful men always repeat on arriving in London, fresh from visiting their goldmines in the far north: "Why, the Siberian winter was really quite mild, this year!").

This rather consistent and, in its own way, beautiful mechanism has, however, one dangerous shortcoming—not infrequently, the rich themselves want to find out how the rich live, and thus are forced to study the existing literature on the subject, without fail produced by these same, merely comfortable arrivistes, who are, by comparison, if not entirely destitute, then still rather close to this condition. This is the only way to explain the Babylon of mansions in the Rublev neighborhood, or the frightening number of Maybachs stuck in Moscow traffic.

So, is there any truly reliable and scientifically proven method of seeing into the world of the megarich?

To this question, we would like to present a firm reply in the affirmative.

But we have to begin our story in the distant past, going back to the nineties of the previous century. It was in those days of primitive accumulation that it suddenly occurred to one Chinghis Karataev, a particularly energetic figure of this era (who, aside from business, was also a big fan of the Strugatsky Brothers' science-fiction epics) that the proverb "money attracts money," found in nearly every language in the world, could be taken literally.

It was easy to substantiate such a theory in those wild days. Karataev took a big shoulder bag, put three hundred thousand dollars into it, and, having given his Chechen guards the day off, set out for a stroll around the city. His hypothesis was that the fairly large amount of cash he was carrying would somehow attract even more money to itself. He spent about three hours wandering the Moscow streets. During his stroll, he found two wallets—one only had a few thousand rubles in it, small change at the time, while the other one contained four hundred-dollar bills. In addition, Karataev found a gold ring with a topaz in it, as well as a schoolbag holding a stamp album, which, as it turned out later, held two rare "Straits Settlements" stamps from the British colonies. His total take for the day equaled about three thousand dollars—not itself a massive sum, of course, but clearly exceeding the threshold of the statistically significant, as far as a brief walk around Moscow went.

Two days later, Karataev repeated the experiment by putting five hundred thousand dollars in his bag. This time, the result was much more impressive—aside from wallets, coins, and jewelry, Karataev found a plastic bag with forty thousand dollars in it hidden under a bench on Gogol Boulevard (an ultraviolet light revealed that the word "bribe" had been written on the bills, but this in itself didn't alter the implications of the find).

Thus, his strange, even absurd supposition had been confirmed in practice. This frightened even Karataev, and he decided to figure out exactly how it all worked.

A few days later, in a Moscow suburb called Dolgoprudny, Karataev tracked down a certain Professor Potashinsky: a theoretical physicist who had fallen on hard times, and who had once worked for one of the classified space programs. After Karataev scrubbed down and fed the professor, he told him about his findings and demanded an explanation: for one thing, he wanted to know why nobody else had ever noticed this effect. The professor answered that from the point of view of experimental science, this particular question was simple: during the transportation of a large sum of money, an ordinary person would only be thinking about delivering it to its destination along the safest possible route; it was unlikely that he would push his luck by wandering up any dark alleys.

—Besides, added the professor, what do you mean "nobody else ever noticed"? How do you think the proverb you were testing out got coined in the first place?

Then the professor gave Karataev a short lecture.

—The effect that you have discovered, Chinghis Platonovich, he said, can only be explained by analogy with gravity. First of all, one has to keep in mind the fact that money in its essence is a social mediator: it does not exist in and of itself, separately from the people whose behavior it affects. In this particular case, it was probably not your money that attracted more money. It's more likely that the huge social magnet represented by the sum you were carrying influenced your consciousness in such a way that you started perceiving the world slightly differently from how others see it. It was you, not the bag on your shoulder, who discovered the wallets and the plastic bag under the bench—just you! You out of the hundreds of people passing by!

Karataev had to admit that this made sense. What Potashinsky said next, however, stunned him:

—We've observed, said the professor, that sums of money behave like gravitational masses. The only difference being that the source of the financial gravity is not money in and of itself, but the consciousness of its owner. The behavior of large gravitational masses has already been studied by contemporary physics in great detail. It is not difficult, therefore, to deduce the financial corollaries to these discoveries. Have you heard about black holes?

Karataev said that he understood the general idea—they are, they say, stars that have collapsed under their own weight into tiny invisible points; science doesn't really know much about them.

—Precisely, said the professor. In the vicinity of a black hole, all the properties of space and time as they're known to us become distorted. But there are certain things we do know about them. If you, Chinghis Platonovich, were falling into a black hole, everything would end rather quickly as far as you were concerned—your body would cross the event horizon, beyond which even light can't escape; then, torn into particles, it would be sucked into a singularity. But for an external observer, it would look like you'd approached the boundary of the black hole and then frozen there forever. From the point of view of an external observer, you would never cross that boundary—time, for you, would have stopped. It's impossible to fully comprehend this paradox: it can only be accepted.

Later, the professor would remember that Karataev was simultaneously inspired and frightened by what he had heard.

—Well, he said. Well, let's continue the experiments then.

First they decided to see how Chinghis Karataev's subjective time would be altered when the sum he was carrying was increased to a million dollars. The cash was divided into two identical red Puma bags. Their straps crisscrossed over the entrepreneur's chest like bandoliers (he was outfitted in this fashion not only for convenience, but also to the even distribution of financial gravity). Professor Potashinsky also hung an electronic chronometer, borrowed from his old lab, on Karataev's chest. An identical chronometer was synchronized with the first and kept in Karataev's office. The goal of the experiment was to compare the readings of the chronometers after a three-hour walk around the city. Potashinsky was supposed to walk ten meters ahead of Karataev in order to find out whether he would be able to spot—before Karataev himself—whatever valuable things would be attracted by his employer's financial gravity.

Unforeseen circumstances, however, interfered with the experiment. When Potashinsky and Karataev left the office, a bomb went off in a nearby trash can. It killed Karataev on the spot and threw Potashinsky aside, damaging the professor's spine. Potashinsky saw a masked man come running up to Karataev's body, grab both bags, throw them into the trunk of a parked car, and drive away.

A few years later it turned out that the attack had been carried out by a professional hit man from the Vyborg criminal syndicate named Sasha "*Der Soldat*": the gangsters had found out that a significant sum of money was about to pass through Karataev's office. But in the first days following the tragedy, suspicion fell on Potashinsky.

While the Department of the Interior was investigating, Potashinsky had a hard time of it: sleepy Moscow cops failed to comprehend any of what he told them about the planned experiment, and even began to suspect that the professor was feigning insanity. Later, however, in view of the enormity of the sum that had been stolen, the Federal Security Service joined the investigation, and there, the professor found a very attentive audience indeed. The legendary General Slipa, who at that time headed FSS department #6, dedicated to paranormal and neo-scientific affairs, got personally involved. After his discharge from the hospital, Potashinsky was taken on staff as a consultant for a project that Slipa poetically dubbed "The Green Corridor."

In the late nineties and at the beginning of the new millennium, work on the project was moving very slowly, and was basically limited to repeating the experiments already conducted by the late Karataev: there was a shortage of money in the country, and it was only whatever cash happened to be seized as material evidence in criminal cases that allowed the research to continue. The experiments were conducted on young volunteers from among the FSS officers, who with Slipa's blessing became known as "lucrenauts."

It was finally determined that "the Karataev effect" did indeed exist, and that large sums of money had the ability to transform reality. Two additional points were clarified as well, at this time. First, said transformation took place only in cases where the money in question had actually become a lucrenaut's own property, however briefly (a convoluted plan was developed to provide temporary cash flow through their accounts—but we need not concern ourselves with its intricacies). Second, the effects of the money were entirely internal to a given lucrenaut, and couldn't be registered by any scientific device. For instance, in the experiment that had led to Karataev's death, the chronometers would not have shown any difference, no matter how long he had walked the streets. But Potashinsky refused to believe that the entrepreneur's death had been in vain.

—His glorious sacrifice was like those of the heroes of our

childhood, he said in a video-recorded memorial speech, the characters in *Andromeda Nebula, The Magellanic Cloud,* and *The Country of Crimson Clouds*. Romantics like him are the ones who once made our country great...

As their scant financing didn't allow them to conduct any serious experiments, Potashinsky devoted himself passionately to theoretical issues during those years—and made several important discoveries, as they say, on the tip of his pen. Some physicists still consider his calculations to be pure fraud, though even they agree that the mathematical approaches he brought into play were witty and unconventional. His attempts to connect the theory of relativity as well as quantum mechanics to such fields as the neural mechanisms of perception are still considered highly dubious: "like an iron and beef sandwich," as one imaginative specialist put it. Nevertheless, the conclusions the professor reached are astounding.

But let's turn the floor over to Potashinsky himself (here the professor is trying to speak in simple terms, so that even you and I can understand him):

A simple parallel with black hole theory allows one to see that there must be a certain sum of money, the personal possession of which would lead to something resembling a gravitational collapse within the boundaries of one's consciousness. By analogy with the Schwarzschild radius, which is the radius a given mass must be compressed to in order to generate a black hole, let's call this particular sum of money the "Schwarzenegger threshold." Its amount can be calculated on the basis of the nonsteady solution to Einstein's field equations, as put forward in 1922 by A. A. Friedmann. In memory of the great mathematician, let's call the mysterious dimension entered by a person whose holdings exceed the Schwarzenegger threshold, the "Friedmann space."

The nonsteadiness of the solution means in this case that the sum total of the threshold has to be recalculated every year due to a multitude of economic indicators. Its exact value is classified at the moment. I can only say that many Russian businessmen have managed to cross the Schwarzenegger threshold.

Our calculations indicate that, after crossing this threshold, it is impossible to acquire any factual information about the inner life of a superrich subject, though an external observer will still think that the subject is capable of initiating contact and, indeed, discussing a broad range of subjects, from soccer to business. It may be hard to grasp this from an everyday perspective, but it is nonetheless true that, in such cases, the external observer will be dealing with a relativity illusion, similar to the seeming cessation of time at the boundary of a black hole; except that in this case, everything will be reversed: time will stop in the lucrenaut's consciousness (American physicists call this effect "the end of history"), but not the observer's. Moreover, beyond the Schwarzenegger threshold, all lucrenauts perceive one and the same singularity—Friedmann space is the same for everyone! But what exactly a lucrenaut sees while there, we, most likely, will never find out. And here's why.

A superrich person can, of course, lose all his money and once again become just like you and me. But here another paradox awaits us: when his consciousness returns to the normal human dimension, he, no matter how he tries, will be entirely unable to tell us about his experiences in Friedmann space, because he won't remember a thing. A lucrenaut crossing the Schwarzenegger threshold in the opposite direction, returning to earth, as it were, will retain only the so-called "false memory" that corresponds to the illusory trajectory of his life as recorded by the external observer. The symmetry of the space-time continuums—financial and physical—remains intact, in this respect, and all the fundamental Einstein-Friedmann equations are still valid. In practice, this means an absolutely amazing, not to say terrifying, thing. That is, only a lucrenaut personally present in Friedmann space can see what happens there—and he'll only be aware of it as long as he remains there. He can never bring this information back and share it with the rest of us ...

A few years later, the first opportunity to check Potashinsky's theoretical propositions arose. Two undercover researchers were placed into the cell of a former oligarch serving his sentence in a prison camp (out of compassion, we won't mention his name). Their goal was to find out what, if anything, the prisoner remembered about his past. The researchers insinuated themselves into the former oligarch's confidence and soon determined that he retained no memories of Friedmann space—just as the theory had predicted. Potashinsky's assumption regarding the existence of a "false memory" turned out to be valid as well: the oligarch's recollections coincided with the external pattern of his biography, as an observer would have recorded it, in every detail. Thus, one of the cornerstones of Potashinsky's hypothesis was confirmed. After this, the highest state authorities took an interest in the scientist's experiments.

At that time, even the most audacious dreamer couldn't have imagined that scientists would soon have the ability to see into Friedmann space. It happened, of course, thanks to rising oil prices. And yet, the primary factor in this achievement was the technological progress of humanity.

By 2003, a group of Japanese scientists succeeded in developing a set of microprobes that, implanted directly into the brain, allowed them to objectify human perception, if imperfectly. The Japanese equipment couldn't determine what its subject was feeling or thinking, but it could generate a multicolor (though blurry) image of what the subject was seeing at a given moment—not only while awake, but also in the active phase of sleep. This was possible because the signal was received directly from the areas of the brain responsible for unmediated representation, rather than from the optic nerve. This equipment was immediately purchased by Potashinsky's team.

The probes could transmit wirelessly, which allowed a lucrenaut to carry on with his daily life unhampered by his participation in the experiment. The only requirement was to keep relatively near a signal receiver, which transmitted all information to the laboratory computer in real time.

Potashinsky's experimental procedures could be summarized as follows: First, a set of test electrodes was implanted into the brain of a lucrenaut-researcher (for this role, as usual, volunteers were selected from among the young officers of the FSS). After this came the launch, fueled by a tractive network of offshore accounts all working according to the recoilless financial principles invented by Potashinsky: the volunteer's private property was augmented until it reached the sum guaranteeing that he would pass beyond the Schwarzenegger threshold.

Many of the large transfers of capital that have been noted by international currency regulation committees over the last few years—all of whom were at a loss to account for them in any coherent way—were associated precisely with these experiments. Similar to how ballistic missile launches can be detected from all over the world, the lucrenaut launches conducted by FSS with the aim of studying Friedmann space were registered by all sensitive economic sensors, of course. But the majority of observers peering into the financial universe mistook these tremors for the redistribution of wealth after the privatization of Soviet property. This isn't surprising, however—the launches were conducted in absolute secrecy, and there was no way for anyone not directly involved with the project to tell which members of the pleiad of new superrich might be one of the FSS research vessels.

Now it has been revealed who they were, of course—not all of them, but the first pair. The first ever controlled leap beyond the Schwarzenegger threshold was made by Russian lucrenaut Yuly Kropotkin. A month later he was followed by Sergey Timashuk. The payload sent with the second launch was more or less the same as the first—approximately six hundred million dollars (of course, in the "real world," these new financial stars rose into the stratosphere under cunning pseudonyms).

The lucrenauts led the lives of rich sybarites—flitting from continent to continent in Boeings refurbished as flying palaces, drinking rare and expensive wines, yachting, playing cards, transferring their genetic material to gentle creatures who sold themselves so expensively that the transaction already resembled love—in a word, they denied themselves nothing. And all this time, the signal relays registered the transmissions coming from the probes implanted in their brains, sending these to the FSS computer center in Moscow, where they were gone over as thoroughly as possible.

When this first expedition into Friedmann space came to an end, the lucrenauts' accounts were closed, and the process of returning them to the human race was initiated. Yuly Kropotkin successfully touched down at Domodedovo Airport. But Sergey Timashuk was not so lucky.

When making his approach to terminal 2 at Sheremetevo Airport, he entered a semi-comatose state onboard his Global Express XRS, which was making its final flight at his expense. The welcoming party decided that he'd simply had too much to drink, but the lucrenaut's condition did not improve the following day. He was practically incapable of communicating with anyone around him, and was heard to be muttering the same mysterious phrase over and over again: "The moon is the sun for the poor!" (Scientists suggested that this might have had something to do with the unknown visual phenomena that he might have observed during his passage through the Schwarzenegger threshold—similar to the apparent distortion of heavenly bodies in close proximity to a black hole.) It proved impossible, in the end, to return Sergey Timashuk to normal life. But his sacrifice—made in order to acquire this unique scientific data—was not in vain.

For the first time in history, Friedmann space had been photographed by means of two probes, absolutely independent from one another, completely eliminating the possibility of error. As a result of this unprecedented breakthrough, the project scientists acquired the second experimental confirmation of Potashinky's theory.

If you recall, the professor's calculations had established that, having crossed the Schwarzenegger threshold, all lucrenauts would start perceiving one and the same reality. The very first telemetric data showed that this was true: the video signals from Kropotkin's and Timashuk's brains coincided completely. Moreover, Potashinky's theory had predicted that time in the Friedmann space must come to a stop. This too was confirmed: the image from both video probes was static and hadn't changed during the entire experiment. Thus, Professor Potashinsky's hypothesis was vindicated. Theoretical science hadn't enjoyed a similar success, perhaps, since evidence of black holes—which had also been discovered on the tip of someone's pen—were actually found in space.

Not everything went so smoothly, however. The very first photographs of Friedmann space astonished and amazed the researchers: the flickering screen of their monitor displayed a blurry, washed-out image of ... a corridor.

No single image from the surface of Mars, no radio telescope image of the galaxy ever underwent such intensive analysis as these images. Unfortunately, the low resolution supplied by the first-wave neuro-optical implants precluded study through magnification. But as far as they could tell, using every possible reference point, it was a typical institutional corridor—with linoleum tiles and walls in chrome green up to two meters (above two meters they were white). A few meters ahead, the corridor turned right, into some sort of unlit area; it was difficult to tell what might be over there.

Viewing the image using infrared or ultraviolet didn't add much to their initial impressions; all they could establish was that there was something very hot around that corner.

So-called scientific journalists immediately started printing guesses as to what kind of a corridor it was and where it led, but the serious scientists strongly disapproved of this approach.

"None of this actually indicates that there is any such corridor or source of heat," writes one of the researchers. "All we know for certain is that the received video image of Friedmann space looks *similar* to a corridor. If you thought you saw a human face made up by geological features on the surface of Mars, this would not imply that it had been carved by Martians. It would just be your own interpretation of a natural geological formation."

To settle everyone's mind, Professor Potashinsky at last consented to a long interview. The camera framed him with Chinghis Karataev's recently opened monument in the background: it is a light aluminum structure, featuring two swan-like red Puma bags with crisscrossed straps, and, soaring over them, as though suspended in the air, a sandglass, reminding future generations about this brave man who gave birth to a new form of science at the expense of his own life.

—Why a corridor? asked Potashinsky, a gawky, shriveled-up giant with an enormous shock of gray hair (sitting in a wheelchair: the consequences of the old explosion bother him more and more often, these days). "You know, the so-called 'anthropic principle' in contemporary cosmology helped me to understand this. Why is the universe around us exactly as it is, and not different? Why are we living on this strange globe half-covered with water? It is because, my friends, that if our universe was some other universe and did not contain this strange, wet globe, we ourselves wouldn't be here either, asking this very question. The world is what it is because we are in it. And if it was different, we would not be us, and it's not certain that any such question would ever come into anyone's head—or whatever they'd have instead of heads. So: why does Friedmann space look like it does? There can only be one answer: because it does! We can't know what's there in reality. But for some reason we see it precisely as we do—in the form of a half-darkened corridor.

—You don't have any idea at all? begs the interviewer. Not even the slightest guess?

Potashinsky sighs and smiles.

—Possibly. The problem is that, from the quantum point of view, the question itself determines the result of the experiment. The first name given to our project was "The Green Corridor." They ask me every day: Professor, what's there, around the corner? As a scientist I can only give one reply—from the scientific point of view such a question doesn't make any sense in the first place ...

—It is, certainly, he continued, difficult to come to terms with the now scientifically proven fact that all multifaceted creative activities of all the individuals populating the summit of the human pyramid is simply an illusion of relativity, and that, in fact, the consciousness of every one of these individuals is nothing more than a static peephole, peering into the dimness of a corridor leading who knows where.

—Most likely, it is precisely our psychological repugnance to such a thought (or else the resulting intensification of our struggles for power) that stands behind the rumor so persistently spread by the tabloids: that a simple computer error led to the telemetry received from our lucrenauts getting mixed up with the input from the security camera in the secondary boiler room of the Metropol Hotel (under which, as is well known, the secret FSS computer center was located). Well, we can all believe what we like.

—One only hopes that new expeditions beyond the Schwarzenegger threshold—which our civilization, lost in the unimaginable stretches of the universe, anticipates with baited breath—will help to clarify this question once and for all.

THE CRY OF THE DOMESTIC FOWL

Maxim Osipov (1963)

Translated by Alex Fleming

Continuing the Russian tradition of doctor writers, like Chekhov and Bulgakov, **Maxim Osipov** for many years lived in the small provincial town of Tarusa, closely connected with Marina Tzvetaeva's family and providing a refuge for many authors, including Konstantin Paustovsky. He writes short stories while practising as a doctor and the head of the local hospital. Ironical and attentive, Osipov's stories introduce the reader to the human types and faces of the Russian provinces, where surprisingly not so much has changed since the time of his great predecessors. Even though the medical techniques are new, the illnesses of body and soul are as tragic as they were for Asclepius. After the full-scale invasion in 2022 Osipov left Russia.

The provinces as home: warm, grubby, ours. But there's another way of looking at them—an external, superficial point of view, yes, but one shared by the many who didn't choose to end up here: the provinces as sludge, the doldrums. That the locals are pitiful is the most flattering thing one can say about them.

The cry of the domestic fowl drives out the dark thoughts that take hold through the night.

Morning at the hospital. On the bed lies a skinny, smoked-out man—a bus driver who's had a heart attack, a bird of the wild. For him the worst has passed, so he watches the medics treat the patient next to him, a trampish-looking old man whose wrist bears the blue sun tattoo of a prison-camp guard. An electric shock, his heart rhythm returns to normal. "Old fella's still ticking," the driver chuckles from behind the screen. He and I exchange glances. Will they let him drive his bus again? And the more burning issue: What if his wife runs into that other woman—the one who brings him shashlik—at his bedside? But this driver could also tell you a thing or two about me. These wild birds are very perceptive.

We're compelled, clearly, to love not only those we are close to—our fellow domestic birds—but our wider surroundings, too: the people and the place. And to do this one must notice, recall, invent.

And so, from my childhood: my father and I are walking somewhere, it's far away, the day is hot. We're out in the countryside and I'm desperate for a drink. My father knocks at a stranger's house, asks for some water. The woman says there is none, but she brings us some cold milk. We drink and we drink, a lot—probably three pints. My father offers her some money, but she just shrugs and asks, straight-faced: "You out of your mind, dear?"

The place could be anywhere with its own kind of appeal—particularly Central Russia. You can fall for this place just as easily as a woman can fall for a loser. "Yes, we love this country, as it rises forth," goes Norway's national anthem. We also extol the virtues of our geography, which, considering our size, is hardly decent. Our anthem was written by our authorities—by *others*—not by little birdies like us.

Another memory: I'm eighteen, driving an old Zaporozhets, when suddenly in the back—where the engine is—I see a cloud of smoke. I'm expecting the worst, an explosion. There are people on the pavement—get back, it's going to blow! "Pop it open," says a man, about thirty, walking by. He takes out a rag and—calm, unhurried—smothers the flames. Then he walks off. Another bird of the wild.

Of cars, of travel more generally, the memories come thick and fast; domestic creatures are prone to trouble on the roads. This is where they cross paths with wild and predatory birds. Such encounters make their mark, through unexpected goodness, through evils previously unimagined. "Killers, they're just your average people," the police chief will say, and then all of a sudden you—you chicklet, you domestic little thing—you'll accept it, you'll get it; it'll become part of you.

While on the subject of the police: the doctors here enjoy their own special relationship with the force. Whether it's getting a patient up the stairs when the elevator's broken down, locking up the drunks till morning so they don't brawl in the wards, or even towing an ambulance out of the mud, they have the police on speed dial. They too wear a uniform and give the local populace the illusion of security.

Just outside the casualty ward there's a policeman with a man in handcuffs. The man is young, a little roughed up, must have done something serious; around here they don't cuff just anyone. "If you'd just played the wife-and-kids card straightaway ..." the policeman berates him, "but no, you had to go on about that lawyer of yours and your Moscow thugs."

Suddenly, alongside the guy who put out the flames in my car, I remember a sweaty, unkempt ice-hockey player. "You must be doubly pleased to have beaten the nation that invented the sport in their own backyard?" an interviewer asks. The ice-hockey player smiles a toothless grin, "Like I give a shit!" With an income like his, he could afford some new teeth, but clearly this man can still chew his meat perfectly well, thank you very much. The impression is resounding.

What else? A sermon once heard on the Intercession of the Theotokos: the day on which our pagan forefathers were defeated is now one of our most respected holy days. There's no easier pastime than bad-mouthing the church. Much like bad-mouthing Dostoyevsky: it's true, of course, all true, but it also misses the point. The church is a thing of wonder, Dostoyevsky is a thing of wonder, and the fact that we Russians are still here—that, too, is a thing of wonder.

You out of your mind, dear?

That could easily have been one of our grannies in ward one. *Grannies* is no insult here; it's what they ask to be called. The one who's in the worst health hears and sees things: "Yuri, that you?" she'll ask the patient next to her.

"Nope, not me," she'll reply.

"So who are you?"

Granny.

"Then who's this—Yuri?" she'll ask the patient on her other side.

"No," Granny Three will reply, "I'm Granny, too."

To these women, there's nothing insulting about the word *granny*, even if they don't in fact have any grandchildren; they view themselves not as sharp-witted ladies of advanced years—like their city-dwelling avian contemporaries do—but as *grannies*.

In the afternoon, two of the orderlies have a loud argument. One of them works here so that she can pocket the food the patients don't eat and take it home to that swine of hers, while the other owns several hectares of land, holidays by turns in Turkey and Europe, and became an orderly just to find a place for herself in society. Apparently it gets messier: Orderly One went on holiday to Europe, and, poor as she is, put it on credit. The bailiffs have already paid her a visit.

Around here, the private comes before the public. A tax official, a twenty-something kid, does our auditing. "Oh," he'll say, "good thing you're a doctor ... as it happens, the army have ... I'm trying to ... you know?" It's not hard to catch his drift. *On compassionate grounds* is a reliable turn of phrase—we're all in one another's hands. But where *Moscow doesn't believe in tears*, as they say, around here tears are the only things we do believe in. When the need is great, we make an exception.

It's ugly—we shouldn't allow ourselves to be touched by it—but this happy-go-lucky collective deceit unites the nation just as well as any good law. Electricity, gas, phone bills unpaid? In the capital, a lack of money is something to be ashamed of; here, it's pretty much the norm. The utility-company employees try to help us out here and there: "These meter readings look way off. Why don't I reset a few values for you here ..."

"Thank you, that's just what I thought. And if you or your family ever need a doctor ..."

Uncles, goddaughters, nieces; water, electricity, gas. It's familiar, comfortable, benign. And though it may have its drawbacks, as a way of life it's pretty stable. Here nobody has any secrets. Just like in heaven.

The orderlies and the grannies are the afternoon's affairs, and by evening it becomes clear that far too much time and energy have gone into one of the day's tasks, while many are left undone. Twilight sees the return of cruel, exasperated thoughts, specifically: Where did all the bright people go? When we were young there were enough of them around. What, did they all emigrate? One thought latches on to another—it's a vicious cycle. Night and its fears make the spirit more vulnerable to evil. To make matters worse, swallows and tits often fly into the house—a very bad omen. But there's nothing you can do; you can't live your life with your windows closed: either move, if you're afraid, or let go of these superstitions. Such are the thoughts that churn in the mind until dawn arrives, with its brief respite of sleep.

Life is scary, whether you're in Moscow, Saint Petersburg, or the provinces. We can say as much—it *is* scary. There are things in life of which it is impossible to write: the deaths of innocents, young people, children. The terrifying, unnecessary experience of their deaths stays with us. That can't be cried away; no cry can drive it out.

But then day will come, and the birds will still be there—fowls of the air, fowls domestic, wild, all of them. The world doesn't break, no matter what you throw at it. That's just how it's built.

THE LITHUANIAN HAND

Julia Kissina (1966)

Translated by Brian James Baer

>Performance artist, poet and writer, **Julia Kissina** was engaged in the unofficial artistic scene of the late Soviet Union and published her works in *samizdat*. Later she moved to Germany, changing performative genres, organizing artistic happenings, teaching photography and writing prose.
>
>Autobiographical, mystical, drifting through history, Kissina's writing explores various undergrounds and spaces of its own, cultural and national, in the margins of the mainstream, mapping and probing the boundaries of the artistic sphere.

I went to a flea market, and there were wives selling mummies of their husbands—veterans of the Great Patriotic War.[*] And the mummies weren't lying down; they were standing up, leaning against polished wooden boards. Almost all the mummies were in military uniforms. One was a lieutenant, another a major in a rotting high-collared jacket, and a third a simple soldier. One woman had a dried Tajik dressed in an Indian costume—he'd been an actor in Dushanbe before the war. And the mummies were all richly decorated. Some even had gemstones in place of their eyes. And these poor, indigent old women, with their last ounce of strength, were boasting, vying with one another in praise of their goods, and haggling with the customers.

"My Vanyok was sent to the front when he was seventeen. That's why I'm still a virgin. But I don't regret it. I've kept my love for him through the years like a nail. My room is filled with portraits of him! After his contusion, he suffered. He couldn't be a man. He cried all the time. But toward the end of the war, we got married all the same.

---

[*] The Great Patriotic War is the official Russian designation for World War II.

I waited for him to be cured and to give me children. The war ended and everyone was happy, but in December of '46 he died in the hospital. It was cold there and he froze to death. He'd been kind to all the crippled people, and for that the government decided to give him a medal after he was dead. And they gave me some money to have him mummified. But the first mummifier I came across was such a bastard. He was a non-Russian, a foreigner (probably a Jew)."

"Oy, how I suffered. Our apartment was very damp—the windows faced West—and in the early fifties my sister and I began to notice a strange smell. It smelled until 1956. And our apartment was so small then. For six years I looked all around, and then I found out what it was! Sergei was moldy. He'd been standing near the balcony and his hand caught a draft. So I called the doctor, but he balked: 'Why would you want me to treat a corpse?' I told him, 'That's my husband, Sergei Afanasievich Petrenko, a war hero, not a corpse.' Then the doctor asked: 'Why is he mummified like an Egyptian pharaoh?' 'The government ordered it,' I said. Evidently, the doctor was a Communist. 'We have only one mummy,' he said, 'Vladimir Ilyich Lenin. I'm going to report you.' 'Who are you going to report me to?' 'To the appropriate authorities,' he said."

"Yes, we had a lot of troubles after the war," lamented another old woman. She leaned against her mummy and sighed. Then they caught sight of me and broke into radiant smiles and began to scurry about.

"Come here, dearie, we'll tell you about our goods. We'll let them go for cheap."

"I'm afraid I don't have enough money."

"What are you saying, dearie? You can pay in installments. I wouldn't have put my Indian up for sale for anything. I would have admired him my whole life long and then left him to my grandchildren, but, oh, you know what times these are."

The other old women began to hum and buzz.

"There's nothing to eat and we have to feed our grandchildren."

"We need money for bread—does that make us traitors to our husbands?"

"We're not angry widows ..."

"I'll put a gold ring on his finger and you, young foreign lady, you can sell it and buy a computer."

"But how will I get it home?"

"Take a taxi. We have boxes—strong ones, three millimeters thick, with cotton wool for padding."

"You won't regret it. He'll make a nice decoration for your apartment."

"Go on, take it," the old women began once again to hum.

"He's not rotten is he, your Indian?"

"What are you saying? We had him completely restored in 1960. Now he's ready for your Munich art gallery.

"My son helped me reinforce his father. He's a scientist. When he was a child after the war he'd go digging around inside his dear father. He didn't sleep at night—he was always exploring. Such a curious boy. And then he up and became a biologist. And the neighborhood kids were amazed: 'Hey, you're lucky. Where did you get that mummy of your dad?' And he was so proud of it—the government ordered it and so it happened. And everyone envied him. So take the mummy, put it next to the sideboard in your living room, and everyone will envy you too."

"You should take my Andrey Petrovich instead. He has magical powers—he cures people. A priest blessed him for ten rubles a long time ago. Then he started to bring people luck. One time a neighbor stopped by. She told me she had stomach cancer and cried, the poor thing. So I told her: 'Spend a night in the room with our Andrey Petrovich—and it will go away like that.' And can you imagine, it went away like that. Now she runs around like a goat. She's in her sixties and she runs around like a goat. She kept asking if she could have Andrey Petrovich, or at least a finger. 'It'll be like a relic in a church,' she said, although that pig wasn't even religious. But then the hard times came and one black day I sold her a finger. Then *he* got mad at me for having cut it off. I got so sick. My daughter, Katya, nursed me back to health. But now she's dead and I have no one but Andrey. I have nothing to live on, but I'm sad to part with him." The old woman embraced the mummy and broke into tears. The others rushed over to comfort her, telling her she'd spoil her mummy, and they hissed at me.

"Why are you just standing there, staring? Either buy something or go away. You'll jinx our business."

I spit three times and trudged over to the edge of the market where less pushy women were selling only heads. They didn't brag as much about their goods. And the heads weren't even their husbands'; some were purchased at one time or another cheap, others were brought back after World War II, or from Afghanistan—those were a little fresher. You could even find imported heads, from Yugoslavia.

I went up to one of the saleswomen. She was perched on some wooden crates and was selling a woman's hand on a board. A heart had been painstakingly embroidered onto the hand, and on the heart there was a cross—all of it sewn right on the hand.

"Buy the hand," she said. "It's from Lithuania, a Lithuanian hand. I stuffed it and embroidered it myself. And I had it blessed. I'll give it to you cheap, dearie. Just fifteen dollars."

"Ten."

"Thirteen."

I bought the Lithuanian hand from her, although I suspected it was all lies and that she'd purchased it in some Moscow morgue or hospital. You can't take a hand across the border. It wouldn't make it through customs. And what did I need it for there, when I could do a good deed here, in Moscow. I'll bring it to Nastya's. Her birthday's this Friday!

SOMETHING LIKE THAT

Linor Goralik (1975)

Translated by Ainsley Morse,
Maria Vassileva, & Maya Vinokour

Computer scientist, poet, translator and a prose writer, **Linor Goralik** (1975) is one of the most frequently quoted authors in the Runet because of her absurd cartoon series *Bunnypuss and His Imaginary Friends: F., Sch., Hot Water Bottle, and Pork Steak with Pea.*

But her prose, which has the irregular, anonymous, chaotic and impulsive character of an online post, is an important and fruitful attempt to marry the offline and online hemispheres of the Russian language and to explore the new narrative possibilities of the digital age. After the 2022 full-scale invasion, Goralik established ROAR (Resistance and Opposition Arts Review); the most important platform for Russia's cultural anti-war movement.

(A WAR STORY)

I

—... We also had Aunt Lusya, Lyudmila. She was a good swimmer before the war, a world-class athlete. They evacuated her factory, like moved the whole thing out near Ashkhabad, workers and all. The factory wasn't top-secret, but it was important: they made stove parts there, which were somehow important to the war effort. And some parts needed to be moved from the factory to the warehouse across the bay, but you couldn't do it all at once because some of the parts couldn't be transported near the fuel, and also the fuel couldn't be near the cleaning cloths, or something like that. Well, they figured out how to transport the parts, but they had to move them across the bay, back and forth all the time, it couldn't be done in one go. And for this they used people who were not very important to the factory, like my aunt. Two women and my aunt. On this little tiny motorboat. And at this time they were evacuating the top brass from Ashkhabad because there was a rumor that the Germans had some kind of plane capable of bombing the city. So they put all the brass on a cruiser and sent them off, promising to move the factory later. And this cruiser crashed into the little motorboat, hard. And didn't even stop. And these women started to drown. But Aunt Lusya was a super swimmer and she tried with all her might to swim to the surface, but she was trapped under the motorboat and the wet cleaning cloths were clinging to her. And then she realized: Okay, this is death. She opened her eyes to die with dignity. And there in the water she sees all the sea creatures watching her, all of them. Just standing there watching her. Creatures beyond what she could have imagined. Well, there were fish, of course, but also other creatures she couldn't even have imagined. And they're watching her calmly, not like they're going to eat her, but like they're children. And suddenly there's some movement among them, like they're moving aside, and a gigantic octopus appeared. And this octopus chucked my aunt to the surface, over to the other side of the bay. And she never went back to the factory, but stayed there, and Grandma kept receiving letters from her for a long time.

II

—... Grandpa's dad worked in a top-secret lab, they were making this stuff you could throw into the water from a parachute, and it would make the water stiff like jelly. That got Grandpa's family an apartment in Moscow.

III

—... I remember my great-grandpa a little bit, he had a horsey, a horse. They lived on the left bank with a garden gone completely wild, but regular stuff still grew there, and my cousin and I used to pick the cherries and currants. These cherries were tiny, really just pits, but, you know, for a city kid to be picking cherries from a real tree, you understand ... And Great-Grandpa was a proper carriage driver, with a horsey. He mainly moved furniture, and he'd take us for rides. My brother and I called each other *cousin* and *cousine* in French, we liked that kind of thing, in general we put on airs and graces, plus getting to ride around in the carriage, you understand. Bookish kids. And Great-Grandpa himself was quite a reader before the war, during the evacuation he reassembled his library and dragged it back to Sevastopol on his own back. But they called him up again and made him a driver to drive the brass around in an armored truck. And this one time, he was driving without any passengers through a village, very angry that they'd made him go at all, and so he was driving through an empty village, everyone had already run off, and he was driving really fast. And then wham, and the car swerved, and he thought: I ran over a chicken. This happened a lot, in the villages people would ditch chickens, turkeys, and they'd go wild. But it was a little girl. So, he ran her over. And afterward, he started to feel that instead of legs he had rooster tails to the knees. He walks normally and when he looks down he sees legs, but when he isn't looking, he is dead sure there are feathers, springy ones. Like they're curved. Now there was a Tajik serving with him in the army, and he promised Grandpa that he would cast a spell that would make everything go away. Grandpa lay down on the ground, the Tajik started whispering, going on and on, and suddenly Grandpa started to choke, and right out of his stomach, as if it were his guts, all this crap started climbing out—some binoculars, rags, then the wheels of his truck. Grandpa's blue, choking, and the Tajik's whispering. And then right behind the wheels the little girl climbed out of him, and Grandpa—I mean, Great-Grandpa—starts screaming: "There she is, that bitch, the scum that threw herself under my wheels!" And then everything climbed back into his stomach and his stomach slammed shut, and there was nothing more the Tajik could do. How do I know this? I mean, I don't know it exactly, my *cousin* told me about it like it was a terrible secret. How he knew about it, I have no idea, probably overheard it.

IV

—... Grandpa used to tell Dad that the scariest thing is the way the Germans pronounce "Kalashnikov." There was something about it ... we just can't understand now.

V

—... So they didn't even know where they were, and suddenly they're told: a musician is coming. And for some reason they decided that it was Lyubov Orlova, who was this actress, a star, a blonde, like a Soviet Marilyn Monroe, only respectable. Well, so for some reason they decided this, wishful thinking probably; they joked about it for a few days, and so on. Now this was somewhere in a neighborhood of Budapest, they didn't know where exactly, but it's already clear that victory's coming, spirits are high, it's springtime. And these guys weren't dog shit either, they were all fighter pilots, even though they'd been transferred to the new base without airplanes, just brought over in trucks, the airplanes were supposed to arrive later, once they were repaired. And in one of the empty houses Great-Grandpa and his friend found an easy chair, only really wide, like super comfy. And they fitted it with truck parts, like a motor, so that this chair could lift a person into the air. Not make them fly exactly, but it could lift them pretty high and hover there in the air; true, it rattled an awful lot, but understand—they were real pilots, they could fix anything, they could take a plane apart and put it back together, they knew everything about mechanics. Well, so they were riding around in their chair, boozing it up there in the air, it was boring and everyone had fled the city, it'd all been bombed to smithereens. And the brass tells them: a musician is coming. So they decided that it was Lyubov Orlova and then they're told: she's on her way. Grandpa—I mean, Great-Grandpa—went up in the armchair and instead of a lady he sees two American convertibles, it's the Allies. And they had some Negro with them. Anyway, it was Jimi Hendrix, can you believe it? Back then they were constantly sending all kinds of singers and performers to the front to cheer up the troops, the Allies, so they sent Jimi Hendrix. And there was a concert. Well, of course, they showed him the camp, partied all night long. Now my grandpa was sort of a translator, he knew English like a native because of that story with my grandma—I mean my greatgrandma or whoever she is to me, anyway with his mom, I mean—I told you that one already. So he drank with Hendrix until late at night, and then they showed him the armchair, sat him in it, and lifted it like twenty feet up in the air. And all of a sudden Hendrix says from up there: someone's coming, but in the dark I can't tell who it is. So, just in case, they all got their guns—there were local partisans living in the ruins, in the city, and street children, who were attacking and killing our guys. And whoever it was out there was now afraid to get any closer because the armchair's making such a racket, and they also can't see in the dark, can't tell what it was. And then Hendrix says: pass the guitar up here and I'll sing. If it's our guys, they'll sing along, and if they stay quiet, then shoot. And he started singing, and the answer is silence and some shouting in the local language. So they had to start shooting, but you can't really shoot in the dark so they hit hardly anyone at all.

VI

—... Grandpa tells this story about how the older kids would swim in ice holes, this was the cool thing to do in their village. They'd get naked in the snow, stretch one arm out, shout "Ooooo!" then take a running start and jump in. But when the war started someone snitched on them that they were making the *Sieg Heil* sign, and they were all taken away.

VII

—... Grandma and her sister, they're real, real old, my mom was a late-in-life child, and me and my sister too: when mom gave birth to us, she was thirty-two. She wanted one boy and got two girls instead. Grandma and her sister were still little during the war, like seven or eight years old. Their dad left for the front, he was disabled, had a limp, but he was a doctor, and by then they were taking every doctor they could get, so they took him too. And their mom began weaving these big mats out of rope, very beautiful, she weaves one and then undoes it—she's doing that all the time, doesn't feed them, doesn't even talk. And they ran away, and this was in Vologda, actually, we're all from Vologda, and the war was already there, the Germans were very close. So they decided to be daughters of the regiment and ran to the forest where the soldiers were, they barely made it. And they said: we want to be daughters of the regiment. Well, they were these two little squirts, maybe eight or ten years old, all funny-looking and super skinny, it was wartime, after all. So the colonel yelled at them, of course, and got a soldier to take them home. The soldier took them to the city and then says: you're on your own from here, I have to get back. He left, and then Rita—that's Grandma's sister—says: look at all the shell casings lying here on the road, this is where our side was retreating. And it's true, the entire road to the city is covered in shell casings. And Rita says: whoever walks along here can count the shells and figure out how many soldiers we have. So they went back and started to collect all those shells in their aprons. And then Rita said to Grandma: "Zina, someone's breathing." And they looked into a ditch and they see a wounded man lying there. He had apparently rolled there, and then everyone had left. They took off his uniform jacket, braided the sleeves together to make a bag, and gathered the shells into this bag, and the next morning they dragged the full bag of shells to the regiment. Can you imagine? Two little squirts, like seven or eight years old. Well, of course they still didn't take them into the regiment, just gave them some canned food and sent them home.

VIII

—... My mom remembers the beginning well, Grandma used to take her along to the hairdresser, but in the days before graduation everywhere was packed with schoolgirls and Grandma couldn't get a manicure. Mom was only three, but she says: "I remember it all—we walked in, and there were all these good-looking boys in suits waiting for their girls to get manicures, but Mom was feeling really sick, so we didn't wait and left. I was really sad about it, there was a brocade curtain there, and while Mom was getting a manicure I would pretend to be a queen, and then they'd paint my pinkie nail."

IX

—... When they started evacuating everyone, my grandpa had just gotten very sick. He was little then, like six years old, I think. And the neighbor lady kept coming around and shouting at his mom not to take her sick child on the train because he'd infect everyone. And Grandpa was really scared that everyone would leave and he'd die, he had a really high fever, and he kept thinking that the train was going to leave. And Mom kept trying to persuade him that he wasn't contagious, that it was just a case of salt-sickness. And she would tell him that once when she was little she'd seen a salt-sick nanny goat at dawn, all shiny. Mom thought that the goat was made of something special, she ran up to touch it, and she sees that the goat is barely moving. So that was salt-sickness, and if you don't drink hot liquids, you'll gradually get covered in little salt crystals, get sick, and die. She was saying this to get him to drink lots of hot liquids because they couldn't get ahold of a doctor, all of the doctors had been sent to the front, even the disabled ones. There was only the hospital director, the only one in the entire city, and everyone was trying to get him, and Mom couldn't get ahold of him. And Grandpa kept touching his right temple 'cause there were little crystals there, and he was really scared and didn't tell Mom and tried to cover it up with his hair. And she went and stood under that doctor's windows until he came out. He came out and asks: What's his temperature? And Grandpa, when they took his temperature, he barely squeezed it because the thermometer was chipped at the top and that thin tube of mercury stuck out and he was afraid his fever would make the thermometer burst. So the doctor asks: How many days has he been in bed? And Mom says: Seven, and the doctor asks: And what's his temperature? She says: Ninety-nine-point-seven. He turned her towards the streetlamp, looked at her face and says: "Looking at you I wouldn't say he's a ninety-nine-point-seven, let's go." They got there and the doctor says: Put some music on the gramophone for me, I can't work without music. But Grandpa and Mom—that is, his mom—only had these happy-go-lucky records, and the doctor was pretty peeved. Then he took Grandpa's temperature and, of course, it was one hundred and four. He started to dig around in his hair, and his whole head was already covered in these little crystals. So they never did get evacuated.

X

—... They lived somewhere where the revolution started late and the war came right after. So Grandpa told Dad that behind the city there was this little hill used for execution by firing squad, and they would go there to watch: the Whites, the Reds, the Whites, the Reds, then the Germans, the Partisans, the Germans, the Partisans, each in their turn. Almost every day.

XI

—... She's probably like forty already, not much older than me, but she has like a grandma name: Musya, Musya. Her name's actually Mustafa, but you can't call a girl that, so it's Musya. Three months ago, I was going home after surgery, Dad was driving me home, and I was still, like, blerg. And then Dad, he wanted to entertain me, and he knows that I love history—him, not so much. So he tells me: did you know your grandfather was responsible for the relocation of the Meskhetian Turks during the war? They were deporting them and relocating them somewhere, Beria wrote to Stalin that they didn't respect Soviet authority. And your grandpa was involved in this. Dad sees my eyes pop out of my head and quickly says: no, no, he wasn't the one evicting them from their homes! Somebody else was in charge of that. He was only in charge of the relocation. That's when I started to think: if ever I meet one of these Turks, I must confess. So Musya and I met in Prague, she was working there as a translator at some mission. We got to talking about where we're from, who our people are, and she goes: Meskhetians. I tell her: you know, my grandfather resettled you. And she's like: yeah, well, mine signed off on the lists, so where does that leave us?

XII

—... Great-Grandma didn't let her husband back into the house after the war, wouldn't let him in for three days. She knew what day his train was arriving and had been toiling since morning. She worked in the mines, would fall into bed just as she was, wouldn't wash her hands for three days at a time—that's how they lived, it was wartime. Now she took a bath, started curling her hair. She had nothing—a single suitcase, but she looked after it well. She always found ways to do things, come up with something elegant, even during all the Soviet crap—like, she would curl her hair on a fork like it was a curling iron: clamp the hair with a cloth, heat the handle, and then twist. That's how she was. And she got out her pre-war clothes, silk lingerie, a dress, a necklace. She even knew how to look made-up, even though there was nothing. She did her makeup. She started at six that morning, and the train was arriving at five in the evening. And he comes knocking, but she doesn't open up. Well, the women came running, it was a dorm, everyone knew everything, eight people to a room in bunk beds. Her people, the ones in the room with her, are like: "Raya, open up!" No response. So they broke in. And she was standing in front of the mirror, wearing heels, a scarf on her shoulders, all that. They say to her: "Raya, why won't you let your husband in?" And she says: "What for?"

XIII

—... You don't have to tell me about this stuff—my uncle, Grandpa's older brother, has been telling me about it my whole life. Their research institute was being transported somewhere on a barge, away from the Germans, there were like two hundred of them. And all of a sudden planes are flying overhead, usually they'd dock and hide, but this time they see that it's our guys. Usually they'd dock quickly and run to hide, but this time they stayed put. And suddenly there are bombs, they're being bombed by their own guys. One woman got knocked out, and he was hit somehow too. He came to in the water, she's lying on a board, unconscious but still alive. It's September, the water's cold, he realizes that he has to swim, so he grabbed on to her board and started pushing both himself and her. He's pushing and pushing and suddenly he sees that the water's blocked off, like with a fence, but there's a way through. He swam to this passage and pushed her through, but on the other side the whole river had been transformed into a fine labyrinth made of all these iron gates, basically, no boat could get through, that's the whole point, someone unfamiliar wouldn't be able to get out. Well, he was a mathematician and kind of understood part of it, and he decided—I'll keep trying until I freeze to death. And he got out, but how he doesn't remember—all he remembers is that he would leave the woman, swim out to explore, and then come back and push her, and that the going-back part was the scariest. And do you know where it was that they swam out? In Petersburg, during the siege. So you don't need to tell me about all this stuff.

THE AGENCY

Anna Starobinets (1978)

Translated by Hugh Aplin

A star of Russian science fiction and horror, **Anna Starobinets** (1978) worked as a journalist, wrote scripts and children's literature, but became famous for her novels and short stories.

Her genre is an illusive and agile mixture of fantasy, gothic fantasy and fiction, driven by her sixth sense for the unknown and otherworldly.

Starobinets also wrote an autobiographical text *Look on him* – unique for the Russian culture, society and literature, a female account of the trauma of a lost pregnancy. She condemned Russia's invasion of Ukraine and left the country in 2022.

I walk down a narrow, smelly path between some sheds. The sheds are all green for some reason, only occasionally are there dark brown ones. I try not to catch their walls with my shoulder: they're covered in yellowish slime and bird droppings, with chicken and pigeon feathers stuck on top of it. My shoes and trouser legs are covered right up to the knees in whitish mud. Out of inertia, I look where I'm going all the same: I try not to step in a puddle or a pile of dog's stuff.

A small, spotted mongrel with a bloated belly and filthy eyes is lying across the path gnawing a chicken bone. I take a step forward. The mongrel shows its yellow teeth and growls quietly. I stop. Ahead there are only four sheds and then – the way out of the labyrinth. I raise a foot – the mongrel switches to yelping, and the black and white fur on its back stands on end. My shoe kicks it in the face. It jumps back a metre, but then runs up to me again and breaks into piercing, squeaky yapping. I kick it once more and press it to the ground with my foot, a rumbling comes from its belly and its face is right up against the chicken bone. I press harder. The dog falls silent. Something gives a crack – I don't look to see what. I walk quickly to the end of the path and find myself in a children's playground. I give my shoes a good wash in a puddle.

* * *

In the centre of the yard is a sandpit in which there are two backward boys pottering about with buckets. Squat swings, a rotten wooden table. Children are clustered by the table, examining something closely with their mouths wide open. I go closer. I see her.

In the photograph in the newspaper she looked different – a bemused, dribbling doll with frightened eyes and an idiotic yellow bow on her head. In the flesh she was nothing special: an unprepossessing five-year-old child, sniffing and breathing hard as she concentrated on something. I squeeze my way through between the children until I'm standing next to her. She stares at me silently in astonishment. She continues poking enthusiastically with a bit of green bottle glass at something lying on the table. To her right is a murky mayonnaise jar, and crawling around at the bottom of it are some earthworms, orange and black soldier beetles and a huge May-bug.

She pulls a soldier out of the jar and puts it down on its back on the table. She has dirty, chubby hands with black streaks under the nails. Poking her tongue out with the effort, she cuts the insect in two down the stomach with the bit of glass. The children examine the two kicking halves with curiosity. She delves into the jar once more and pulls out an earthworm. Hanging from her finger, the worm wriggles convulsively for a certain time, then surrenders and goes compliantly limp. She picks up the bit of glass.

I pull a stern face and ask menacingly:

'And what's going on here?!'

The children run off giggling. She turns to me sharply and drops the worm onto the ground. She looks. Dully, without any expression. Her gaze crawls absent-mindedly over my clothing.

'What is it you're doing?' I ask very quietly.

She lowers her head. Sniffs. The worm lies motionless on the ground in the same place that she dropped it.

'We were playing hospitals.' She gives the worm a little kick with the toe of her boot. 'I'm the doctor.' The worm curls nervously into a spiral. 'I'm doing an operation.'

I say to her:

'Look what you've done. Killed a beetle. Its mummy will be very upset.'

I remove my dark glasses and look her in the eye. Sadly and a little reproachfully. Her face finally wrinkles up in crying. Tears drip onto the table. She screws up her eyes.

I say to her:

'Do you know what you have to do now for its mummy to forgive you?'

'What?'

'You have to swallow the bit of glass.'

Rule number one. No foul play, no physical intervention. Only the natural order of things, corrected slightly by us. If you simply want to get rid of someone – find a hit-man. Our work is different. We do accidents. We do coincidences.

We have everything. We have top-floor apartments with balconies in bad condition. Winning lottery tickets. Our own casinos. Our own schools. Our own shops. Our own aeroplanes. Our own hospitals. Actors who play the roles of lovers over any period of time – from a couple of hours to a couple of decades. Actresses who play devoted women. Actresses who play debauched women. Actresses who play actresses. More than five hundred kinds of fatal poison. Defective step-ladders. Tens of thousands of morbific bacteria. And vaccines against the illnesses. We have one-eyed kittens. Pure-blooded Dobermans. Foodstuffs past their sell-by date. Condoms with holes in them. Faulty cars. Feature films whose existence is suspected by no one: for the time being neither the director nor the screenwriter is indicated in the credits – an entire film library, works of genius awaiting their 'creators'. Gigantic stacks of books written by anonymous authors – one day they will become bestsellers ... We have everything.

I came to the Agency through an advertisement: 'Wanted: editors, sound men, screenwriters, assistant directors, actors.' The interview took place in an empty room: I was examined by a quiet, nasal voice which oozed from a speaker in the ceiling.

'How old are you?' asked the Speaker.

'Thirty-five.'

'What is your occupation?'

'I'm a scriptwriter. I write scripts for TV serials.'

'What are your interests?' asked the Speaker.

'I don't have any. In the evenings I watch TV. I play Counter-Strike.'

'What position do you sleep in?'

'What?!'

'What position do you sleep in?' the Speaker repeated impassively.

'Well, on my right side usually. Sometimes on my back.'

'Do you have a wife?'

'No.'

'Do you have a sex life?'

'What difference does it make?'

The Speaker remained silent.

'No,' I said.

'A lover? Female or male?'

'No,' I said.

'Pets? Plants?'

'No.'

The examination lasted about five hours. I described in the greatest detail my childhood, my favourite guinea pig, the guinea pig's fall from the sixth floor, my parents and my parents' funerals, my adolescent spots, my adolescent nocturnal emissions. I listed the names of the glossy magazines that help me masturbate. That used to help. I looked patiently at idiotic pictures and told the Speaker what they reminded me of. I even thought up rhymes for various words that the Speaker dictated.

The result was that I was taken on to work for the Agency. Because I'm a nobody, I think. I have no friends or relatives. My appearance is unprepossessing, unmemorable. Average height. Average weight. I can be confused with anyone at all. It's impossible to remember me. If I rob somebody in broad daylight, the victim won't recognise me at a confrontation. I have no birthmarks, moles or scars. I have thin lips, an entirely unremarkable nose, dull hair, small, inexpressive eyes, a small, soft member. I'm impotent. I have no interests. I can invent endless miserable stories about orphaned children, parted lovers, amnesiac beauties and grasping, perfidious fiances. I wear dark, plain clothing – usually grey or dark blue – and dark glasses. I lead a boring life. I'm exactly the man they need. The ideal Agent.

* * *

There are flowers growing there. They twist and stir in the wind. Revolting, fat, graveyard flowers – almost the height of a man. They have powerful, glossy stems and garish yellow heads. And there are nettles as well, gigantic too, and ordinary grass – thick, crisp, moist. That's absorbed juices from under the ground.

There are very few people. The Writer, stooping, has frozen in a fixed pose, looking at the ground, not stirring. His wife cries all the time, but neatly, without hysterics. And there are several more women crying.

I stand at a certain distance from them, leaning against a tree. Quite close, but not so as to attract attention. I'm wearing a long, grey raincoat. It starts to rain, and I pull the hood over my head. I think: how amusing. I've already described all this a number of times – before, when I was writing scripts. Be it in the first episode or the hundred and first – sooner or later in a serial there's a funeral. And in a funeral scene it has to be pouring with rain. And someone's solitary figure is standing a little way off. In a grey raincoat, behind some trees.

The rain gets heavier, and soon everyone starts to disperse – with a little more bustle than there should be under the circumstances. One woman lingers by the grave: she has an umbrella.

I draw the hood down a bit tighter, in such a way that practically nothing can be seen of my face, only the tip of my nose and my glasses, and I head towards her. I didn't put on my usual dark glasses today – I chose different ones, with round, reflective lenses. I don't want her to remember me, but there's nothing to worry about, I can go up really close to her. She'll look, but will remember only herself – her reflection on my face.

She has a kind, round physiognomy with three trembling chins. Stupid blue eyes study themselves in my mirrors as I quietly ask her to give me the Writer's address. Who am I? Just a great admirer of his talent ... Such a tragedy ... I have children too, it's dreadful to imagine ... No, I don't mean to be a nuisance paying visits, I simply want to send a letter of condolence, that sometimes helps, you know. I'd restrict myself to a telephone call, but of course, they don't have a phone.

She nods trustingly and dictates the address.

* * *

To begin with I very much enjoyed the work. I was actually called in to the Agency extremely rarely – once in three months, no more than that. I was presented with an apartment and I worked from home. Every morning in my post box I found a large stiff envelope with no inscription whatsoever and, inside it, the next script. Not once did I see the courier who – evidently in the middle of the night – brought the envelopes. Because there was rule number two. Under no circumstances and under no pretext should Agency staff know one another either to look at or by their voices. No meetings or corporate parties: each Agent works completely autonomously. We receive our tasks over the phone from the Co-ordinator – a nasal, electronic patter without life and without intonations.

Every morning I ate a couple of yoghurts and a beaten raw egg, drank tea with milk in it, washed myself quickly with cold water and immediately set to work. I read carefully through the scripts and made pencil notes in the margins. After which I still had about an hour and a half to get on with things of my own before the Co-ordinator rang.

The Co-ordinator was unswervingly polite. ('Good day, how are you today? I'm glad everything's all right with you – so now let's get down to business. A Client will be coming to see you today at about five – please discuss the details of the script with the Client – ensure that the script conforms to the Agency's requirements. All the best, good luck in your work.')

The Agency is a secret organisation. It has branches in every country. Only the chosen few know of its existence.

Our clients can invent their own scripts, or they can use a readymade story – from a book or a film. The greatest popularity is enjoyed by Stephen King: several times I have had commissions for *The Shining, Misery, Dreamcatcher*. A sad young man brought a printout of a very short story by King – I don't remember what it's called now – about a finger that came to life and set itself up in a married couple's bathroom. The young man wanted us to let two clockwork rubber fingers loose for an evening in the washbasin and toilet bowl in an apartment belonging to two nice, educated pensioners. He had been saving the money for this commission for ten years. The educated pensioners were his parents.

A half-crazy old millionairess once came to commission an episode from *Pet Sematary* for the noisy family living next door to her. Screwing her eyes up dreamily, she said:

'And so, you arrange an accident, their cat goes under a car and dies. They bury it, but a day later the dead cat comes back and frightens …'

'I'm sorry, that's not possible,' I replied patiently.

'Not possible – but why?' the old woman asked in wonder for the umpteenth time.

'The dead cat can't come back. But we can make an effigy of the cat. It'll be an artificial, clockwork cat. Synthetic. Quite dead to look at. Or simply a live cat, made up to look like the dead one.'

'No, no, if the cat comes back alive the whole point is lost. And I want their cat to go under a car and die. Them to bury it, and then, a day later …'

Apart from that, clients simply adore *Titanic*. Rounding up everyone who's antipathetic to you onto one gigantic vessel and sinking it triumphantly in one go is an option that is seductive, expensive and vulgar. The Agency accepted such a commission only once, in 1912, when somebody – I won't name names – did actually *come up* with it all. Then the script was considered striking and challenging. But to repeat a trick over and over again is the lot of people who are utterly lacking in imagination. We propose to such clients that they make do with a plane crash. As a rule, they agree. And some are satisfied with just a train or coach crash.

Original scripts are, as a rule, worse than wretched. For example, billionaire daddies like to commission practically the whole of the lives ahead of them for their precious little ones. Born – educated – made a fortune – got married – died in their sleep. I myself come up with all kinds of details, and at least some sorts of twist in the plot for such bare outlines. It's deadly dull. But what's to be done: every day, the richest people on the planet, and others who are simply very rich, bring their money here. Such huge sums of money that they suffice for the upkeep of our Agency. Such huge sums that we have everything.

The Writer walks to the railway station to buy tickets to go back. Naturally, they can't stay here any longer. The little town is too small, and what happened is already common knowledge. What's more, the provincial quiet is of no use now: the Writer isn't likely to continue working on his new novel. To return to their big, roaring, amicably indifferent city is the only thing they want right now.

He walks with his head drooping low. I follow him.

He is wearing a bright-red scarf, a foolish joyous blot on his black clothing. I've been watching him for more than a week now, but it's the first time I've seen this scarf. Perhaps he just picked it up somewhere by chance and attached it to himself without thinking: the Writer usually dresses tastefully. Or maybe he put it on deliberately – so that sympathetic looks would affix themselves to this loud piece of cloth and not to his face.

He buys the tickets. Trudges back slowly along the narrow, empty platform. I follow him. I feel sorry for him. He doesn't hear my footsteps behind his back: they are drowned by the noise of the approaching train.

Of course, I didn't mean to be content with the position of a simple script editor for the whole of my life. It's not that I'm a careerist, and unfulfilled ambitions have nothing to do with it. It's simply that I'm a creative individual. I always dreamt ... yes, I always dreamt of testing myself in the Agency as a director.

One morning the Co-ordinator rang me, and after the customary little nasal recitative, he added one more phrase: '... Please discuss the details of the script with the Client – ensure that the script conforms to the Agency's requirements – from today you are entitled to implement commissioned scripts independently.'

I was ill at ease. In expectation of the Co-ordinator's call, I had already been staring senselessly at the television for more than an hour. Only two channels were working for some reason, and by turns I had been shooting the TV's remote control at the participants in a talk show on one, and some suspicious-looking, smiley medical workers on the other. When I'm fretting, I always channel-hop. It calms me down.

'The door was open.'

Someone else was in the room. Someone was talking to me in a vile, hoarse voice. On the screen, a fat woman in a miniskirt was fidgeting in a huge leather armchair and getting ready to cry. I aimed the remote control at her, pressed the green button, and she dissolved with relief in a square of darkness. I continued to watch. The darkness was filled with my reflection – mine, and that of the person standing behind my back.

'Be so kind as to leave that channel on. My favourite talk show.'

I moved a finger and the woman was resurrected. The long-legged presenter was holding out a glass of water to her and gloating. The fat woman was wiping her tears with disposable paper handkerchiefs and mournfully shaking her head. I know for certain that the door could not have been open. I always close the door.

I looked round.

With this Client, everything was strange, very strange, right from the start. Firstly, I wasn't brought a script that day – I waited in vain all morning. Secondly, I wasn't warned about his coming. He came himself. And thirdly, he seems to have had a key to my home. How could he have got in otherwise? I always close the door.

Onto my desk he put a folder with the inscription 'Script' and a big newspaper cutting – almost an entire page.

The article had a title that was very grand and senseless somehow: was it 'The New Voice of a Generation', or 'The Voice of a New Generation', or 'The Generation of a New Voice'? ... Something of the sort. Paraded directly beneath the headline was a gigantic photograph depicting a happy family: a husband, a wife, a little daughter. He looks into the camera over the top of his glasses – a little ironically, rather wearily, all in all, benignly. She smiles and looks at him with pride: the smile is at one and the same time silly and false. In one hand she holds a sheet of paper of some sort – an official document, seemingly – while the other arm is just lightly around the child.

The photograph was framed by a skimpy text, in which it was announced that the popular Writer, the winner of several prestigious literary prizes, was leaving the capital with his family for a small provincial town in order to devote himself entirely, far from the bustle of the capital, to writing his latest book.

There followed an interview with the Writer. He said that the idea for the new novel had been gestating for many years. That the most pressing problems of modern society would again be broached in the new novel. That the first reader of the new novel would, as always, be his wife. And that in the new apartment they had bought in the little provincial town there would be no telephone: they had no use for superfluous links with the outside world.

I was about to reach for the folder with the script, but he stopped me.

'Later. That's later. The next time I come.'

He moved towards the door. The script and the newspaper cutting stayed lying on my desk.

Looking at his back, I asked:

'When?'

'Soon.'

'All the same, I'd like to know a little more precisely.' I was intending to say this harshly, but it came out more ingratiating. 'After all, I do have to do a certain amount of planning ... of my affairs.'

He said:

'Don't worry. You won't have any other affairs in the near future. Apart from this one.'

This was my first serious commission, and I decided to prepare thoroughly. First of all, I set off for the bookshop.

The Writer's books are on display on the central stand under the sign 'Bestsellers'. Two novels (all he has written so far) are laid out in neat piles. Hands reach for them – with pink nail varnish, with green nail varnish, without nail varnish, with bitten nails, with hairy fingers, with wedding rings. When the piles are getting very low, a sluggish salesgirl appears, dragging her long, bowed legs on huge heels, and brings some more. I reach a hand out too, pick up both novels and join the queue at the till. Standing in front of me is a girl with sparse yellow hair holding the same books in her hand as me. She examines the covers indifferently. One is bright green, with an indefinite, blurred profile. The other is a dirty red, and there are endless rows of cans and bottles of sauce on it. I almost hate the Writer already.

Next to the till stands a saucer of caramel sweets. The yellow-haired girl stuffs several into her mouth at once and chews them, making a crunching noise. She looks round at me and immediately turns away.

It's stuffy in the shop and there's a horrible smell of glue. I already hate the Writer. I can't bear caramel.

I read all evening and most of the night. They were quite short, those books, but they irritated me too much for me to deal with them quickly.

The first novel was called *Death at the Supermarket*. It told of a single, elderly woman who went to a supermarket to buy a dressing for some fish dish that she intended to cook for dinner. Naturally, however, she didn't limit herself to buying just the dressing, since supermarkets are specially laid out in such a way that customers rake as much food as possible off the shelves, and there she is, wandering among the sausages, the cheeses, the sauces, the packs of broccoli and bottles of Coca-cola, and remembering her childhood, her youth, the whole of her life. Unhappy love affairs, abortions, parties. At the same time she is reading the inscriptions on labels. She walks around, remembering and reading, and she can't stop, and gets lost in a labyrinth of food. Her head is spinning, and then she is already staggering and calling for help, but the clatter of trolleys drowns the weak voice of an old woman. And when a well-schooled shopping consultant finally approaches her to sing out his standard 'how can I help you', she falls down and – see the name of the book – dies.

Appended to the novel was an ecstatic afterword – there it was explained that in his 'bold and savage works' the Writer was battling with the cult of consumption.

It was unendurably dull.

The second book – about a manic serial killer, a member of the Greenpeace movement, which was destroying everyone who didn't love nature enough – I didn't even bother reading, I only looked through it. Nothing special either.

The Co-ordinator stopped ringing me. The Agency gave the Client a key to my apartment, and he would come when he considered it necessary. He would appear without warning, steal up ever so quietly and say, 'Tell me about it. I want to have a report. I need all the details.'

And I would tell him, trying to stand with my back to him. Looking him in the face was impossible. But not looking was almost impossible too. It called, hypnotised, mocked you, that face did. It enticed, bewitched and sucked out your soul – and then rebuffed it. It was hideous. A parody of a clown.

One half of that face – the right – always remained motionless. But the other gave a weird half-grimace when he spoke, the mouth twisted to the left, the left eyebrow now rose in amazement, now knitted in malice, pulling up and down with it, as if on an invisible thread, a trembling, twitching cheek and a mockingly winking eye. But the most dreadful thing about that face was his other eye. The one on the dead half, with red, inflamed lids. It never blinked. And it was round. The perfectly round eye of a bird.

The Writer falls. Gazes around in surprise. In front of his eyes there are apple cores, empty plastic Coca-cola bottles, seedhusks, broken green glass, squashed beer cans caught under the sleepers. He looks up and says feebly: 'Help!' but the roar of the train drowns his voice.

'No one will be surprised. No one will suspect anything,' says the script. 'Writers, like all creative individuals, are psychologically unstable. And it's common knowledge in the little town that he had a motive for suicide.'

I stand on the edge of the platform and look down. The blood-red scarf is indistinguishable now against the general background.

Then I go to the post office, buy a postcard of Father Christmas (I don't like it, and it's not the season either, but the pictures on the others they are selling are even worse: a revolting tilting doll and gold roses), I check the script and, trying to copy the hand in which it's written, I trace out carefully and neatly, 'You see, I can after all.' It comes out looking similar.

I fill in the address that the woman with three chins gave me and send the postcard to the Writer's wife. The Widow.

When the Client came the second time, he picked up the script from my desk, reached it out to me and said, 'Read it out loud.' I read, and he moved his repulsive lips soundlessly and sometimes smiled. Twenty pages of typed text – he knew them off by heart. For the first time while working at the Agency, I began to feel afraid. So much hatred.

* * *

There – I've done almost everything the Client wanted. Almost. The last page of the script is lying in front of me.

Only the Widow remains. I ought to have done away with her today, but I couldn't. I feel something's not right. Basically, of course, it's all the same to me, it's none of my business, it's simply my job, but … Something's not right. I'd already arrived at her house, with a huge bouquet of tulips ('Good day, flower delivery – a bouquet sent by admirers of your late husband – please accept my condolences.'). But she yelled so … Yelled so horribly … I left.

Yes, I know, I know. She's not been in her right mind for a long time – after what we've done to her. She opened the door to me and stood on the threshold – almost naked, her dirty, matted hair covering her face, holding a large frozen fish in her hand and sucking its head, as though it were a lollipop. She stuck her lips into the icy open jaw, she licked the fish's dead eyes. She looked at me for a long time, senselessly, dully. I reached the bouquet out to her and she took it with her free hand, examined it for a minute or so, then dropped it. And suddenly began yelling wildly, wailing. I expect lunatics often yell like that. But she … something in her yells put me on my guard.

And I left. Before doing away with her I have to clear something up. I've got a number of questions for the Client.

Why doesn't the Co-ordinator ring me any more? Why did she yell like that? But the main thing is …

'Where does such hatred come from?' I surprised myself by daring to ask after all.

He's silent.

I'm too fretful – so much so that my hands are shaking. And my whole face seems to be burning. I go to the bathroom to have a wash with cold water. He follows me in silence.

I have a wash, and I feel better. I dry my face with a towel and hear him locking the bathroom door from the inside. I start to feel scared. He's standing right behind my back. He's mad.

I raise my head. In the mirror above the washbasin is the reflection of his deformed face. I suddenly notice there are tears flowing down his cheek.

'Are you crying?'

In reply he smiles – his left half smiles. He says:

'Lagophthalmos.'

'I don't understand.'

'Lagophthalmos. Hare eye. The circular muscles of the eyes are paralysed, and so the lids don't close, which leads to the breakdown of tear circulation.'

I ask:

'Have you had it since you were a child?'

He shakes his head:

'A car crash – just over five years ago. Multiple fractures of the extremities, a fractured skull, damage to the facial nerve. Half of my face is paralysed. I spent three months in intensive care. Then six months more in a surgical ward, and a couple of years in a psychiatric one. In a certain sense I began my second childhood. I'd forgotten how to chew …'

I have absolutely no desire to listen to him any more.

'Why are you telling me all this?'

'… and now I can take only liquid nourishment … Every morning – over a period of several years – my doctor has rung me and, like a caring mother, has asked me how I feel and given me instructions for the whole day. And he would have continued ringing – I think he would have rung me all my life, if …'

'Stop it!'

'… if I hadn't cut the telephone lead. I can't appear in the street without dark glasses. I have fifteen scars on my face, and at times they're terribly painful …'

I screw my eyes up.

'… the only thing that helps is icy water.'

Almost in a whisper I ask once more:

'Where does such hatred come from?'

In the mirror I see him smile with one side of his mouth:

'Try and remember. It's all very simple.' He looks at me with his round, dead eye. I look at myself with my round, dead eye.

'Where have you been?'

I speak in a vile, high-pitched voice. Not my own at all – or perhaps I've only just noticed what my voice really sounds like. My T-shirt is disgustingly wet under the armpits: pungent black stains are spreading across the blue synthetic material. I smell bad. I've got a stomach ache. After my every phrase something gurgles inside me – loudly and tragically.

She is silent. I pour myself another glass, knock it back in one, and follow it with another cigarette, making sure that the hand with the lighter doesn't tremble too much. I feel sick. I take a deep breath of air and cough, squeakily and disgustingly somehow too. I take another breath and say:

'Perhaps you'll explain to me what's going on?'

She studies an invisible object on the floor carefully. Then raises her eyes to look at me – and there is nothing in them apart from sloth, apart from a brazen, unceremonious desire to sleep.

'In the morning, OK? We'll talk in the morning.' She leaves the room.

'No, now!' I scream in her wake, but I don't run after her, I restrain myself.

I hear the bathroom door closing and the hissing of the shower. I drink straight from the bottle. Then I say out loud: this won't do, a sense of dignity, what about a sense of dignity; I pour myself a glass, and mutter something else under my breath like a madman, like an imbecile. Then I start crying.

She goes to bed.

My hysterics. My night. It doesn't matter any more now, everything's allowed now, I behave like a woman, ha-ha, I slam doors, I run around the apartment, I sob, I shake and writhe. I rehearse a speech. I make threats, I argue a case to the mirror. I drink. It runs out, and I emerge from the building into nauseatingly spinning space and buy more, and I drink.

I crawl in to her towards morning.

All those months – when she was trying to leave early and come back late, and sometimes didn't come back at all, or suddenly escaped at an ungodly hour under some utterly idiotic pretext (her parents have been struck down with back pains – what, both of them? – well yes, both of them ... – and their poodle needs to be taken for a walk urgently; her girlfriend's love-life has gone wrong – and she has to go and console her at once), and stopped touching me, and almost stopped talking to me – all those months I couldn't bring myself to ask her that question. I don't want to ask it now either – but I'm drunk, and the words tumble out of my mouth by themselves somehow, slowly, inexorably, in big, stinking lumps.

'Do you want me to leave?'

Her gaze roams around the room – scattered behind my back there are evidently dozens, hundreds of fascinating, invisible little things. Finally she notices me too. Is going to say something. I get scared, very scared.

'Yes.'

That's it. I feel as if someone's cold paw, having imperceptibly overcome the layers of skin, fat, and whatever else there is inside, has grabbed my stomach firmly and squeezed with all its might. And I've died.

For a time we talk, if it can be called that. From some-where in the next world I ask all these questions – unnecessary, tedious and vulgar. I don't have to think about their formulation, I do everything on auto – I've made the useless heroes of my useless scripts say these words a million times. Do you have someone else? So it's all over between us? Who is he? She answers, clearly trying to look guilty, but she can't manage it. She's like a diligent schoolgirl reciting a poem she has learnt by heart, but without having gone into the meaning. False intonations. Emphases in the wrong places. Yes, it's all over. Yes, there is someone else. He's a writer. She obediently makes her report to me, she tells me everything – more, even. He's so talented. He's so interesting to be with. He hasn't published a single book yet, but everything lies ahead, because he's so motivated. True, he's poor, and he doesn't even have an apartment, but that's not important …

So where are they going to live? What do you mean, 'where?' here, of course.

For her I'm already a ghost.

The final touch – and how did those damned scripts contrive to get out of their inoffensive parallel world and clamber into my loathsome reality? – she seems to be pregnant. By him, naturally. Maybe she's pregnant, but maybe she isn't – she's not yet completely certain. But she feels a bit sick in the mornings, and she wants to sleep all the time. Talking about this, she becomes noticeably more animated, she confides in me as in a girlfriend. For her I'm already a ghost.

I turn completely into one of my ridiculous characters. I shout that I'll kill him. And I'll kill her as well. And their disgusting offspring – if it appears.

She is evidently following one of my scripts as well, and so guffaws in reply – loudly and unnaturally. And squeezes out through her laughter:

'Y-you? Come on then, kill me ... kill me ... You can't do anything to me ... you can't even ...'

And while the car is slowly, cinematographically toppling over, wheels uppermost, and before my head bangs into the side window and hundreds of splinters of glass sink into my face, I have time to reflect upon a lot of things. And to understand why everything has turned out the way it has. Why she has treated me this way. Because I'm a nobody, I think. I have no friends or relatives. My appearance is unprepossessing, unmemorable. Average height. Average weight. I can be confused with anyone at all. It's impossible to remember me. If I rob somebody in broad daylight, the victim won't recognise me at a confrontation. I have no birthmarks, moles or scars. I have thin lips, an entirely unremarkable nose, dull hair, small, inexpressive eyes, a small, soft member. I'm impotent. I have no interests. I can invent endless miserable stories about orphaned children, parted lovers, amnesiac beauties and grasping, perfidious fiancés. I lead a boring life. I'm exactly the man ...

... I'm exactly the man they need. The ideal Agent.

SULFUR

Dmitry Glukhovsky (1979)

Translated by Marian Schwartz

Probably the most famous writer of Russia's younger generation, **Dmitry Glukhovsky** gained international recognition for his post-apocalyptic fiction series *Metro 2033*, *Metro 2034* and *Metro 2035*. The series, describing a dark Russian future after a nuclear conflict and using an image of the Moscow underground system as a metaphor for the disintegrating Russian Federation, procreated the whole array of copyists and has been transformed into a highly successful computer game universe.

After Russia's full-scale invasion, Glukhovsky condemned Russia's aggressive war and quite soon was sentenced in absentia by a Russian court to 8 years in a penal colony for 'spreading false information about the Russian army'. He currently lives in exile.

"Lieutenant Valentina Sergeyevna Skaredova. So, I'm recording, bear that in mind. On my phone, here. I've been given your case. Hello."

"Hello."

"All right. This is for the recording. The case concerning your husband, Maksim Aleksandrovich Petrenko, born 1973. With whom you resided in civil matrimony at 21 Leningradskaya Street, apartment 5, micro-district 8, Central District, Norilsk."

"Yes."

"On December 26, 2018, Maksim Aleksandrovich Petrenko, employed by the Copper Plant as the equipment tooling foreman in the sulphuric acid shop, did not report for work at the appointed time. In a call to you from an employee in the Nornikel administration's personnel office, you informed him that your husband, Maksim Aleksandrovich Petrenko, was home ill, specifically, from intoxication. Correct?"

"Yes."

"The next day, Maksim Aleksandrovich Petrenko did not go to work again, which provoked another call from the administration, which you answered once again. You stated that Maksim Aleksandrovich was still in his sickbed due to intoxication or infection. This was repeated on Wednesday. Am I stating this correctly?"

"Perfectly correctly."

"Later, at your own initiative, you contacted the Copper Plant's personnel office, informing them that Maksim Aleksandrovich would continue his absence from work until the New Year's holiday, after which there would be the holiday in connection with New Year's."

"Yes."

"On January 7, the municipal garbage collection crew, namely, D.K. Kovalchuk, informed the First Police Department of the Norilsk Department of Internal Affairs of the discovery on his assigned route of a plastic bag from the Magnit store containing the head of a middle-aged man."

"DisCOvery."

"What"

"DisCOvery, not DIScovery."

"It doesn't matter in a document. It's letters."

"I'm just telling you. Everyone here says DIScovery. I used to say DIScovery, too, before I went to training school, but then I got used to it."

"Excuse me."

"That's all right."

"… containing the head of a middle-aged man, who was identified as your husband, Maksim Aleksandrovich Petrenko."

"That must be professional lingo for you."

"What?"

"DisCOvery. Here people say SULPHURic instead of sulphuric, for instance. (Coughs.) I'm sick of fighting."

"Is this what worries you most of all now?"

"No. I was just saying, just by the way. Sorry. You go on."

"Just a minute. You made me lose my train of thought. Oh, right. Who was identified as your husband, Maksim …"

"Yes. That's right."

"The identification was made by an employee of the personnel department of … Right. After a lapse of … After a lapse of … After about two weeks. All this time you told your spouse's place of work he was indisposed."

"Correct."

"When a task force arrived at M.A. Petrenko's place of residence, you informed them that Maksim Aleksandrovich was at work."

"Yes."

"At that time, a human hand and foot, which forensics established as being body parts belonging to M.A. Petrenko, were discovered in the freezer of your Candy refrigerator. You don't deny this?"

"No."

"When they identified the victim's head in the morgue, you stated, and I quote, that the dead induced you to commit this crime and they were to blame for M.A. Petrenko's death."

"Exactly."

"Police Captain A.P. Sergeyev, who carried out your arrest, reports that you had, and I quote, 'a calm and focused look.'"

"I don't know. He knows better."

"Elena Konstantinovna …"

"Yes?"

"Did you kill your husband Maksim Aleksandrovich Petrenko?"

"I already gave my confession."

"Did you dismember the victim yourself or with the help of someone else?"

"Physically?"

"What?"

"Do you mean physical or spiritual help?"

"Physical."

"Myself."

"And … and spiritually?"

"I was led."

"By who?"

"I was led by the dead."

"What dead?"

"The dead among us. I don't know any names. The dead. The ones buried near the mountain."

"Near what mountain, may I ask?"

"Schmidtich Mountain. We have this mountain. Shmidt Mountain."

"It's ... Who do you have buried there?"

"You just moved here, right? Everyone who built the city. Norilsk's founders, so to speak. The political prisoners. The zeks. You should read a little."

"And it's the dead who demanded you commit a crime against your husband under Article 105 of the Russian Criminal Code?"

"They don't have articles. I just understood what they needed, for my husband to die, too. They'd been calling to him, but he balked and wouldn't go. I just helped."

"Right. Wait a minute. Let me double-check." (Writes something down.) "Now who else died?"

"What?"

"You say they needed him to die, too. Too—who is that?"

"The ones like them."

"And you ... There was no one else you happened to ... kill?"

"No."

"But how did the dead ... how did they tell you they needed you to kill your husband?"

"They whispered. Chanted."

"Be more precise."

"Well, this is a dead city, Valya. Dead. It's hard for the living to hold on here, for long anyway. Can I call you 'Valya'?"

"You should call me 'comrade lieutenant.'"

"You only just moved here, right?" (Coughs.)

"What does that have to do with this?"

"I can tell you're not from here. So pink. And fresh. You were assigned here, right? As an investigator. How long for? A year?"

"So this is how I see it. I think you're faking. That you're trying to avoid responsibility. That your goal is to get off by playing the fool. You're not crazy at all."

"I didn't say I was crazy. It was your captain who said that. I'm not trying to play the fool, Valya. I'd rather go to prison."

"We're going to schedule an examination for you with a psychiatrist. You can play your little game with her."

"All right, then. Is that all? Can I go back to my cell?"

"No, you can't. Can you tell me, for the recording, exactly how you killed him?"

"With a knife. A kitchen knife. I stabbed him in the neck."

"Did he resist?"

"No. He was drunk. Asleep."

"There's no trace of blood in the apartment. Where did you ..."

"In the bathroom. I dragged him to the bathroom, as usual. Laid him out there. And that's where."

"And after that ... also by yourself? Without accomplices?"

"What?"

"Well ... his head. His hands."

"Of course. Who was going to help me?"

"It's just that you ... you look ... ordinary. Well ... although it's possible. But how?"

"I got the hacksaw from our shed and did it. It doesn't take a lot of intelligence. It just took a long time. Is that all?"

"No. You have cigarette burns on your chest. And old scars."

"Yes."

"I want to understand. Did he beat you?"

"Yes."

"Is that why?"

"Of course not. Who doesn't get beaten? You can understand him."

"Meaning?"

"How can I put it? You just try living here as long as us. Have you been to the works yet?"

"Not yet."

"You should go. Go. Stop by the sulphuric acid shop. The nickel shop. Just take a walk around the complex, tell the guard it's for a case. Go down into the mine. See how they work. What they work with. Men sit underground for all those hours at a time. Breathing that. They come out up top—and it's dark. A whole winter without sun. And their wages—you know what they get? You've seen our prices. And a wife at home. You have to drink here. You can't not drink here. The pressure here is crushing. It squeezes the life out of you. And the dead sit there calling to you."

"Right. Fine. Did you know Stanislav Antonovich Prokhorov?"

"Who's that?"

"He was discovered with stab wounds in the area of the neck on a beach at Lake Glinyanoye."

"So?"

"I was just asking. Similar signature."

"You never know who's going to be killing here. There, didn't you read the news? This fellow, married, with a kid, goes upstairs to his neighbors' and beats the whole family to death with a metal rod. (Coughs.) The woman, the man, and their three-year-old daughter. Beats them to death with a steel rod. Google it."

"I know."

"They convicted that other one there. The pensioner. Who slit his wife's throat on her birthday. Both, what, sixty years old?"

"Yes."

"Any idea why they kill each other?"

"Why?"

"Because they don't have a real life. Because there's so much death around, death outweighs everything else. People are happy to kick the bucket themselves and to kill others. To end it already. It's in your Moscow or wherever you're from …"

"Moscow."

"It's in your Moscow that life seems real. But here, it's like a dream. It's easier to kick the bucket. Death's so close here. As for that one, at the beach … (Coughs.) Addicts maybe."

"We're working on—"

"Addicts hear the dead better. Hear and see."

"You're back to that? You don't have to try so hard. You'll get your psychiatrist."

"Go on, have your psychiatrist. A psychiatrist's all well and good. Will you let me go? It's four-thirty in the morning, you know. I'm not resisting. I'm not refusing to talk."

"We still aren't done."

"Psychiatrists. At Nornikel, before they hire someone, they make him see a psychiatrist twice. And fill out a questionnaire with eighty questions, too. And what, does that help? A psychiatrist is beside the point here."

"What isn't?"

"You haven't been here long enough, so you don't hear them. Stay a little longer—you'll start picking them up. You'll start picking them up, believe me. And you'll hear them calling for you. Calling and calling. There's lots of them here, lots … lots. Near the mountain. So … at home, why do you think we're on piles instead of foundations?"

"So the permafrost doesn't thaw."

"I thought that, too, when I got here. No, Valya, it's to keep the dead as far away as possible. We need the air cushion because of the cold, not the warmth. Because of the whispering. See, as it is you can't tell the dead from the living. Even you understand that the dead don't decompose here. And the living walk around all gray. It's easy to make a mistake. You don't feel the difference between life and death. It's easy to confuse them. And people do."

"It's written here that you've been diagnosed with a tumor."

"Yes."

"Of the mammary gland."

"What of it? Lots of people here have that. We're breathing sulphur. The women are one thing, but you feel sorry for the little ones."

"Two years ago. Did you have an operation?"

"Yes. I took the boat to Krasnoyarsk that summer."

"And so?"

"It'll keep growing. There's no getting cured here. Once they get a hold of you, they never let you go. Like a fish on a hook, you know? A strong fish jerks and pulls, tries to swim to the bottom—but one day its strength runs out, even when you're strong."

"'They'—you mean the dead again?"

"Yes. They're the strong ones here, you know? They can reel you in no problem. There's so many of them over there. More than us. A chorus of them whispering."

"Did they ask you to kill your husband?"

"Yes."

"And dismember him?"

"No. At that point they don't care. I came up with that. I freaked out. At first it was scary. Then I pulled myself together. I had to do something with him. Because he was lying there talking. And the others were chipping in, too." (Coughs.)

"What did you do with the other parts?"

"Dumped them somewhere. You think I remember? It was a blizzard there, a black blizzard. Have you been in one of our black blizzards yet?"

"Not yet."

"Have you seen the wires stretching from entryway to entryway? It's so you can get where you're going in a black blizzard and not get lost. Otherwise they find you afterward. People set off to see their neighbors, or to the shop ...and get found the next summer. Especially old people, if no one notices in time. You can't see your hand in front of you. The drifts go as high as a bus. Buses get stuck. The passengers get out and push the whole bus. Just hope it gets stuck in town. The wind carries off dogs. I didn't have to hide anything especially. I'd just throw out a package and go home for the next."

"Another question. Did you notice anything strange at his workplace?"

"They had vacation, too. The holidays."

"I mean, you sat through all the holidays that way ... with him?"

"What else could I do?"

"And after the holidays you went back to work."

"Yes."

"And don't you have ... on staff ... a psychologist or something?"

"Who needs that? It's a kindergarten, Valyush, not a mine."

"Did you return to your duties? As a teacher?"

"What was I supposed to do? Sit on my hands at home? The blizzard died down, school opened up, and I went."

"Right. Fine."

"Don't you think ... I love my little ones very much."

"Fine. I didn't mean anything by that."

"God didn't give me any of my own."

"I know."

"What do you know?"

"That you don't have any."

"Well no. I don't. Sometimes you get to thinking, what if you had? What it's like for them here in winter in the pitch dark. Without any sun. Grownups are one thing, but there are the little ones. No sun of any kind for six weeks. Do you understand? Darkness and more darkness. And then it starts the tiniest bit, little by little. For a little while. (Coughs.) They're all so frail. We draw the sea for them on the walls in our kindergarten, and palm trees. Draw them. We use a blue light on them ... the old-fashioned way. They're all such tadpoles here. Transparent."

"Why?"

"Why do you think? No sun. And what are they breathing? The sulphur in the air is twenty-eight times higher than the limit, and cobalt is thirty-five. Have you seen the clouds over the city? That's all from the smokestacks. Those aren't real clouds. It's the sulphur. Your eyes—don't you feel them stinging? It's the sulphur."

"And how about for pregnant women here in general?"

"Well, that's how it is. That's exactly how it is. You think what? That he and I had nothing between us? We did, only ... only it's the same every time. You wake up in the night. You think you dreamed it. But it's all over. Blood and more blood and it's all come out."

"But you ... How long have you been living here?"

"You have that in the file. We arrived in 2005. From Lipetsk. Novolipetsk. We thought it would be better here. Easier."

"Thirteen years? That's a long time."

"Eighty for salary. We let ourselves be bought, idiots. Eighty ... for all of it, for everything."

"Eighty-thousand?"

"Eighty-thousand. A good salary, by the way! We'd never come close to that. That was for them, in the sulphur shop, or the mines. That's what they're paying for, for their health. For their life, for their years. The men live to fifty. Compare that to your own years. But a ticket home is sixty! And the prices in stores ... You can't save. You get trapped on a wheel—so go on, run."

"And so ... does this happen to people often?"

"What's that?"

"Well ... aborted pregnancies."

"Miscarriages? Everywhere you look."

"You probably have to live here a while, though. Not right away."

"Yes, live here a while."

"Right away probably nothing's going to happen."

"Right away ... but you ...what about you? Did you come that way? Did you bring it here? (Coughs.) Oh, lordy me. What did you agree to come here for?"

"You think I had a choice? You go where they send you."

"Where they send you. Where's your fella?"

"In Karaganda."

"Oh."

"Fine. Fine. That's all. I think I've heard everything. I'll come again tomorrow. We'll have to record the whole thing from the beginning."

"Fine."

"Yes. That's all. Do you want a smoke?"
"No. Can I have some tea?"
"Yes. I'll bring some. I'll go get it now."
"Thank you."

"Did he beat you badly?"
"You saw."
"But why?"
"Why? Because you have to get it out. You get slapped around there in the shop and you bring it home. The shop ... have you seen photos of it? Did they show you?"
"Well, yes."
"After he got burned?"
"I saw his head."
"Ah. Well yes. Well, it was after the burn. After the burn things got really bad. A day didn't go by he wasn't plastered. They said they'd fire him. But he didn't care. They can talk all they like, but they were never going to fire him. Who else was going to go to the sulphur shop? For eighty? The young aren't fools. The young go back to the mainland. They want to live and there's nothing but the stench of death here. Nickel, copper, sulphur. And them, near the mountain. (Coughs.) You have to understand. They were sent here, too. The motherland decrees ... There are probably more of them here than us. Calling for you."
"I added a splash of brandy."
"You won't get in trouble, will you?"
"It's night. Who's going to find out?"
"Good. Your whole insides smooth right out. Unknot. Thank you."
"Well ... basically, you have to say all this at the examination then. Talk about your dead, fine. And I'm going to ... I'll write, well ..."
"I don't give a shit anymore. Write whatever you want."
"In terms of what?"
"I had to. I should have a long time ago. Fool that I am, I wouldn't have gone through all that and he wouldn't have suffered. One way or another. I wanted to poison him, but I didn't know what to use to be certain. And then I just lost it. When he hit me in the belly again. I could barely wait for him to fall asleep."

"You tell them about the dead, at the examination. Talk about the dead. You've got experts here like ... They'll believe you."

"I don't give a shit. I'm confessing."

"Why do that?"

"I can't take it anymore. I don't want to. In the colony, the end will come sooner. The end can't come soon enough."

WHOOOO

Sergei Lebedev (1981)

Translated by Antonina W. Boius

Sergei Lebedev (1981) was born in Moscow. Both of his parents were geologists who worked in the remote areas of the USSR. Following their path, from the age of fourteen Lebedev worked eight seasons as a field worker in expeditions to the Far North of Russia and Central Asia.

Later Lebedev became a journalist mainly focused on historical and educational issues. He also contributed as a criminal investigator and forensic correspondent.

Since 2010 Lebedev has written six novels dedicated to the theme of the Soviet hidden past, to the impact of Stalin's repressions and its consequences in modern Russian life. The novels are written through the lens of the family's history. He currently lives in Germany.

Kasatonov's guardhouse stood in the middle of the steppe pitted with indistinct sinkholes. Kasatonov liked it: it was as if during a war here, artillery had been fired from a distance. War had in fact passed through here in 1942, but it left no visible traces. A column of German tanks had driven through, throwing up clouds of chalk dust, but nothing more. Nothing more had happened here since time immemorial. If not for the sinkholes, there would be nothing to catch the eye. Besides the guardhouse and the semaphore, of course.

The limestone covered with steppe grasses was unstable. Rainwater seeped in and undermined it. The embankment was prone to collapsing or sliding sideways, which would make the rails crooked and the switch jam. That meant supervision was needed. An attentive human eye was needed.

A post at any other switch would have been removed long ago. A team would arrive on a dilapidated, oil-stained repair trolley, oil the mechanism, regulate the automated settings, and that would be it. The watchman would have been sent off to the city to retire and do crossword puzzles.

But here, Kasatonov had a special switch.

An H-hour switch.

One day, multistarred generals in underground bunkers would break open special seals, or whatever it is they were supposed to open, they wouldn't tell Kasatonov what, and military siren alarms would blare throughout the country, in all the barracks. Armies would move into staging areas to escape the enemy's missiles. And then Kasatonov's switch, which connects the single track with the main one, would join the points to the mainline rails. They would connect, without question. Trains carrying tanks and armored personnel carriers would pass over it.

It's far to the cities from here. Even to the stations. Barren hillocks, you wouldn't even run into a gopher, there was something they didn't like here, the bastards: maybe the chalk in the ground was wrong. Sometimes in the distance, at the boundary of your vision, a deer would flash by in the haze of overheated air. But you couldn't get it with a carbine, you needed an optical sight.

It was far, remote. That was why Kasatonov was stationed there, a skilled and proven man. He was repairman, lineman, and sentry. The guardhouse was an old freight car taken off its wheels. Post No. 4367STR.

Water was stored in a cistern, hauled in by a shunting locomotive once a month, along with food. In the winter, snow could be melted. There was never a lack of snow here.

Kasatonov tried planting potatoes, but they wouldn't grow. And it wasn't really suitable, it's not a summer house, it's a guarded site, and Kasatonov had the right to take the first warning shot, and then to shoot. He was given an SKS, a self-loading carbine, the weapon of the Soviet rear guard, military builders, warehouse watchmen, and prison guards. Kasatonov had asked for an automatic rifle. Still hadn't gotten one, they kept dragging their feet, saying it wasn't in accordance with the rules.

The rules called for two men to serve here, alternating twelve-hour shifts. One would rest, the other staying by the communications console, going out every two hours to check the switch and do the rounds. Those were the instructions written on a steel plate. Neither fire, nor water, nor a distant shell explosion could harm it. The instructions, embossed in metal, would survive a fallen watchman and be used by the next one.

Kasatonov respected that steel plate affixed above the console. He wiped it carefully to keep the paint from peeling. It was no toy, it was factory-made, stamped. Yet it seemed to speak to him directly: be on guard, Kasatonov, transmitting directives from the top, from the very towers of the Kremlin.

He was from a faraway forest region, forever beyond the reach of the railroad. They kept extending it, both tsars and the Soviet regime, but they couldn't overcome the swamps. At the southern edge they established the Zelenoe station, but from there you had to transfer to river transport. It was there at Zelenoe that he saw his first train, when he was a conscript.

Yes, there were supposed to be two men. In the first few years they kept promising that his partner would be sent any day. They've already selected him, he's coming, being trained, filling out forms, getting access, obtaining clearance for access to the instructions on the steel plate that Kasatonov put into the fireproof cabinet when the train engineer came for tea in the winter. It was a special post, and that meant the man assigned to the switch had to be checked up and down and inside out by the authorities.

He took inordinate pleasure in the words *register, record, document*. Registering meant seals and signatures, papers filled out, involving a person who was proven, trusted, verified, unassailable, subject to the Code and secret clauses of secret statutes, entered into the staff roster, allocated a salary, assigned to a numbered post, attached to a unit, a military unit, and through the unit to the whole, to the army, subordinate to command, required to maintain loyalty to his oath, guard the post, and be given a personal weapon—with the right to use it, *if*.

Except that no one was registered, no one was dispatched, even though Kasatonov had truly waited at the ready in those early years. He imagined his partner as a younger brother, the one he had never had. He would teach him the ropes, make sure he didn't laze around, went out on time to check the switch, and memorized the instructions perfectly, because there could be a surprise inspection, which happened sometimes.

Then that passed. Instead he developed a suspicious, worried fear—don't let them send someone, some slacker, some dolt who will need to be taught how to swat flies, while they pension off Kasatonov.

"You're joking!" he would say to an imaginary fat lieutenant in the personnel department. "That won't work. Kasatonov will continue serving." And self-assured and relaxed, he would go out to the switch, his steady companion, and sit on a piece of the wooden tie. He would sit looking at the distant mountains beyond the steppe. The peaks matched up, snowy, jagged battlements; the Caucasus.

Kasatonov did not like mountains. You might think, what were they to him, let them just be, they're beautiful. But they infuriated him. Who set them there across the flatness? The mountains didn't let railroads through. They didn't make room for trains. They had power over space.

Kasatonov would sit until twilight, and then pick up the long-handled hammer used at stations to check train wheels and brake boxes. He hefted it and eyed the spot and carefully beat out a ringing rhythm on the switch, gradually accelerating like a train.

Overwhelmed by loyalty and delight, he could feel the iron body of the railroad awakening, the railroad that exists in all parts of the country and in all its time zones. He struck one little railway joint, one hard bone sticking out, yet the response was from the whole, as if his insignificant tapping pleased it and he was allowed to place his ear on the rail as a reward. The echo of his hammer receded in the metal and then returned, transformed, from afar, having run thousands and thousands of kilometers across the great country created and bound by rails. The rails sang to him about everything that is and was.

About trains of soldiers that traveled from all regions to the west. About trains of prisoners that traveled from all regions to the north and east. About how you couldn't trust land. It was cunning and unfaithful and that was why you had to load its back with heavy embankments, rails, and ties, and drive spikes into the ties—only then could the land truly be conquered.

In the cursed August of 1991 the radio informed Kasatonov that there was a state of emergency in the capital. Then it fell silent, as if the receiver had broken.

He spent three days at the communications console, waiting for the green call key to light up, for the bulbs on the train map to blink, for the trains to start rolling, for a surge of the power that had been accumulated over decades and written about in newspapers and celebrated in songs.

The air rustled with the frightened whispers of mainline dispatchers. Three times the apparatus came to life, the yellow key lighting up: expect a call. But the green never turned on. The order did not come. The military trains did not roll.

On the third day Kasatonov, disillusioned and desperate, barely able to stand on his feet from exhaustion but not allowed to sleep, pushed the call key himself. For the third time in his life.

Twice before, the blizzards had blown snowdrifts the height of a man across the line and he needed a snowplow train. Kasatonov—following the instructions—had made the call, and a clear voice responded instantly.

"Duty officer. I'm listening."

Now, there seemed to be contact, the connection was on, but no one said anything.

"This is four-three-six-seven, over," Kasatonov repeated.

On the other end, it was as if kids were fooling around: picking up the phone and breathing into the receiver. Someone seemed to be walking, breathing, smoking, sighing heavily, unhappily.

Kasatonov could not believe this kind of negligence was possible. He decided it was an error, the signalmen had messed up, and there was no connection with the control point at all. He ran his eyes over the metal plate with the instructions. If there is no connection with the control point, you must sound the alarm. He tore off the stamped lead seal from the red key and pressed with all his heart.

Jiggle, jaggle, and then nothing.

The sound in his earphones was harsh, like a strong wind blowing over an empty bottle.

"*Whoooo ...*"

Kasatonov tried again: *crack, clack, snap.*

And in the earphones, "*Whoooo.*"

Third time: *click* and *pop.*

He shouted: "This is four-three-six-seven, come in!"

There was that sound again: "*Whoooo.*"

Kasatonov suddenly realized that in many thousands of guardhouses and cabins, booths and compartments, cipher posts, offices, and bunkers, frightened servicemen were shouting into microphones, zero one and zero two, sixty-nine and eight slash seven, secret and super secret, all trying to shout their way to the top. And the response was the monotonous, terrifying "*Whoooo* ..."

Kasatonov flew out of the guardhouse. Silence.

In the distance were the mountains bathed in light, their broken lines, crooked battlements, battlements, battlements.

Far in the distance, space sang along with the airwaves, the wind playfully roaring among the stones: "*Whoooo* ..."

Oh, how he wanted to kill, shoot that *Whoooo*, tear it apart with explosions of shells, cut it to shreds with sprays of automatic fire! He grabbed his carbine and shot into the air.

"Bang! Bang! Bang!"

From the steppe the thrum settled around him: "*Whoooo*."

He dropped the carbine, picked up his hammer, readied himself, and then banged out a melody on the rail, the secret code.

Nothing. The railroad was silent. Dead.

Kasatonov threw the hammer aside. Rushed to his bed, covered himself with his military coat, and stuffed cotton from the first aid kit into his ears so he could not hear "*Whoooo*."

Only on the fourth day did *Whoooo* disappear from the airwaves. The voices of his superiors returned. But they no longer had their previous power.

Their military service was put under civilian command. He still served: wearing the insignia of a nonexistent country, with its military ID, with its bullets in his carbine. Kasatonov sensed that he could leave his post and nothing would happen to him for that. Many left; no wonder the rails were silent and did not respond to the hammer.

But where would he go? What did he have besides the guardhouse, besides the instructions on the steel plate?

Kasatonov believed that one day, not tomorrow, not in a month, but maybe in a year or two, the green call key would light up on the dead console, and a firm young voice would say, "Four-three-six-seven, do you hear me? Over!"

"Loud and clear, control point, over," Kasatonov would reply, straightening his uniform.

"Check the points, four-three-six-seven," the control office would order. "Readiness for twelve oh-oh. Tomorrow special trains will pass through you."

"Will check the switch, over," Kasatonov replied.

He would adjust everything, oil everything. In the morning, he would connect the side rail to the main line. The consists of trains would roll, the army would return, and the cheerful soldiers under the red banner would catch wind of *Whoooo*, chase it into the mountains, and kill it in the dark ravines.

During the day, Kasatonov hunted, setting snares in the steppes. In the evening, in the cooling twilight, he smoked the dried steppe grasses and stared at the distant city at the foot of the mountains.

They spoke a foreign language there, related to the language of mountain rivers, avalanches, and landslides. Even the dogs barked differently than in Kasatonov's homeland.

Long, long ago, when he was a young conscript, a soldier in a railroad convoy, Kasatonov transported those local residents to the hot deserts, from the Caucasus mountains to Asian Kazakhstan, to a place where there was nothing taller than a camel. Hundreds of train consists traveled east, leaving the dead at wayside stops. The engines' black smoke covered the rails. Kasatonov sensed that this was forever, there would be no return. That was what made convoy work magnificent and terrible. Not just a few Chechen prisoners here and there, but an entire nation, from young to old, was in its grasp.

And with this disorder—they were back. Once again, they were drinking the waters of their rivers, breathing the air of their mountains, when they were supposed to have rotted in the sands.

Before, when the highest command was in power, Kasatonov did not let himself ask why they had returned. Who let them? Now he began pondering: How was this possible? By what right? Was this how the disintegration of a vast empire had started? Were the mountains beyond the city, the alien and insubordinate mountains, the source of that devilish sound? *Whoooo*.

Kasatonov expected the call keys to light up in spring, when the snows melted. He remembered what he was taught: war sleeps in winter, the troops burrow into their dugouts, the weapon lubricants freeze. In spring, the roads open up and the generals lay out fresh maps atop their desks.

The keys lit up in the final days of November, in a snowless period when all steppe creatures, now in their white winter coats, were helpless before hunters.

Kasatonov brought a white hare into the guardhouse, a huge one. The console was ringing, buzzing, *ding-dong*. His first thought was that it would freeze, just a click, and then nothing.

The green key was lit up.

Kasatonov turned it on cautiously, afraid he would hear that horrible *Whoooo*.

There was a loud voice: "Four-three-six-seven, respond!"

No *Whoooo*. He could hear other command voices, dispatchers calling other posts.

Kasatonov barely managed to respond, almost mixing up his own number, "This is four-three-six-seven, over!"

The speaker barked: "Battle ready! Four-three-six-seven, the password is APATITE! repeat, password APATITE! Do you read me, over?"

"Confirming APATITE, over," Kasatonov gulped and answered firmly.

The connection broke.

The instructions Kasatonov had showed the passwords BIRCH, TORCH, CORRIDOR, CORDON. No APATITE. He didn't even know what apatite was. Maybe they meant appetite? Did his nerves make him mishear?

He could have honestly replied that he did not know this Apatite-Appetite. He had not been informed. They had not updated his code tables. But what if the dispatcher had hung up on him? Sent the trains through a different switch?

"Battle ready, battle ready," he said to himself, tapping and greasing the switch. "Battle ready!"

His heart rejoiced.

"Apatite! Appetite! Appatite! Apetite!"

He wanted to stay up all night awaiting the signal, but fell asleep, exhausted, right at the console.

* * *

A horn blast woke him in the morning.

Kasatonov ran out of the guardhouse.

At the semaphore, at the switch, stood a consist of trains. Its end was invisible in the gray morning mist. His eyes scanned the cars and platforms: one, two, seven, eleven, twenty-two, he couldn't see beyond that. A regiment, maybe even a brigade. All its tanks, armored personnel carriers, trailers, tech vans, antiaircraft installations, camp kitchens, tankers, tractors, repair shops—in one formation.

Wrapped in tarps, the tanks and armored personnel carriers poked at the fabric with their gun barrels, as if they had a soldier's morning hard-on. The soldiers smoked and pissed from the train doors, the steam of urine mixing with cigarette smoke.

Kasatonov, moving the railway points, prayed for the diesel locomotive, rails, tanks, and cannons to depart, to pepper them with TNT over there, shoot, mutilate, clobber, wipe them off the face of the earth; crush them, bomb them out, so that the whole world would be brought to life by the shooting, and no one would ever dare say *Whoooo* on any speaker again.

The consist started moving heavily, crawled onto the main line, and set off in the direction of the mountains.

Days passed: as if the trains had not been there.

The communications console was silent again.

There still was no snow, as if winter was not prepared to come down from the whitened mountains to the plain.

Kasatonov began to think that it had been a dream: platforms, tanks, machine guns, quadruple barrels of antiaircraft guns, the evening call, the password APATITE or APPETITE.

Yet he knew definitively that the military trains had not been a mirage. The ties in the places where the zealous soldiers had urinated copiously still stank. He walked there, like an old hound around new markings, sniffing, where were they, the dogs, where did they go, why weren't they raising their voices?

On New Year's Eve, bare, black, terrible, the sky cracked open over the city in the distance, at the foot of the mountains. Pounding, roaring, yellow explosions, and red lightning bolts raced across the sparse clouds. He recognized the voices of tank cannon, the voices of artillery, and he danced in the icy wind and shouted into the darkness, laughing and mocking: "*Whoooo! Whoooo!*"

In the morning he was felled by a fierce fever, and the guardhouse was snowbound for days by blizzards. He didn't hear them. Then Kasatonov began getting up. He had strength enough to heat the guardhouse and boil water. His ears were swollen, as if from the shelling, and he could not hear the sounds of the world, the inflamed echo of the nocturnal cannonade traveling through his body.

One icy morning, as if to restore his hearing, a diesel locomotive sounded at the guardhouse.

Kasatonov crawled out, dragging a shovel to dig out the snow-covered railway point.

The train was on the main line.

There wasn't a single person on its platforms.

Only tanks and armored personnel carriers, dead, smashed, illuminated by the sun rising from the winter darkness.

They were poorly cleaned, like discarded tin cans. Like tin cans, they stank even in the bitter cold, reeking of rotted meat and cinders.

He stared in disbelief at the fractures of split armor, scorch marks, cuts, dents. At the black, human cracklings stuck to the slopes of torn turrets.

He heard the mountain wind howling in the dead metal, blowing into the blasted hatches and twisted barrels: "*Whoooo.*"

MOM

Natalya Meshchaninova (1982)
Translated by Fiona Bell

Popular screenwriter, author of films and movie series, laureate of the Nika prize (Russian Oscar) for the best script in 2018, **Natalya Meshchaninova** published one book of prose, the collection of short stories called simply *The short stories*.

For the Russian public, still used to the idealization of childhood, Meshchaninova's texts, describing her early experiences of family violence, the hardships of growing up, and teenage dramas, were a real lesson of understanding and compassion.

It is not a coincidence that Meshchaninova wrote (together with others) a script for the TV series The School. The authorities severely criticized it for damaging the reputation of the educational system, while teachers and pupils were arguing that for the first time they could see on screen the real schools they taught and studied in.

Every comment, every sentence of yours drives me fucking nuts. But I'm sitting here, keeping a straight face, being patient. In reality, I'm about a second away from bursting into tears at our incompatibility. I've been a millimeter away from that for years now.

We're sitting in a restaurant. I take you to a restaurant every time you visit me in Moscow. You expect an act of generosity; I come through. Actually, maybe you don't even expect it—but I come through.

I look at you. You've got a lump of potato salad on your fork and you're swaying to the beat of a song some random guy is performing live … He's singing especially for you, this Armenian singer. His voice is godawful. Unbearable.

But you're swaying, oblivious to how godawful this performance is. The blood is draining from my ears, but you're A-OK.

I feel the urge to flip the table, but you've come for a week. I can survive a week without flipping tables, with some teeth-grinding.

Mom.

I love you.

I say this to myself once every minute, so I don't turn into a monster. I say these words—"I love you"—as if to absolve myself a little. I try to balance the scales unconsciously with these words.

"I love you, Mom." It's a spell that keeps me from turning into a werewolf when the sun goes down.

I close my eyes and remember how you smelled when I was a kid. I remember how I'd hug you and smell your pillows furiously whenever you had gone away. How I'd wait for you to come home from work and, after spotting you from the window, I'd start running around the room and singing. How I'd climb under the table at dinner. It was dark down there and I could only see your knees and I'd feel a surge of happiness, seeing them. I'd crawl under the table knowing your knees would be there with me. I remember your voice, your hands, rough from something, but still nice, when you used to stroke my hair hard. It hurt a little, I had sensitive, thin hair, but still. It made me happy that they were your hands, your hands, Mom.

Our conversations before we fell asleep, when—lo and behold—I ended up sleeping in your bed, and you told me about your job, about sheep and goats and ostriches. And how I'd squint with pleasure and fall asleep sweetly.

The way you adored me, worshipped me, when I worked myself into a frenzy and grimaced while doing impressions of Philipp Kirkorov, Kuzmin, all the performers you liked. When I put on ridiculous rags and you applauded me like a real fan: "A star is born! A star is born!" Your hugs so tight, your aggressive kisses, like in Soviet movies when they bruise each other's cheeks. Your presents: a Cinderella doll with a change of clothes and Karlsson, whom I always punished for disobedience—like you did me—with a willow switch from the tree that grew outside our window and always turned green before the other willows in spring ...

I open my eyes. Now I have the strength to smile and speak with you more gently.

I preserve these feelings inside myself artificially, these feelings that I don't have the right to give up. That I don't want to lose.

But it doesn't last long. You'll say something stupid again and I'll explode. No one in the world can drive me over the edge like you.

We're sitting together in the kitchen and you say:

"You know, you're so fat, and I can't figure out why ... We were all so skinny ... I was skinny till I was forty. Everyone told me I looked like Thumbelina. I'm fat now, of course, but that's understandable. On the other hand, now that I'm fat, I look like Catherine the Great! Me—Catherine the Great! I've always wanted to be Catherine the Great. In fact, as Empress Catherine the Great, I've brought the nice Krasnodar weather to Moscow. Otherwise you'd freeze here. But I brought warm weather. See?"

"You know, Leonid told me I should donate my *sarafan*. Honestly, it ages me. Nooooooo, Leonid doesn't know how old I am. Are you serious? God forbid! That's why I'll never call an ambulance, even if I'm in real trouble. The first words out of the lady's mouth will be, 'How old are you?' I don't *think* so ... I'll never call an ambulance in front of Leonid. Besides, I've collected and dried so many herbs, they're like my very own ambulance. One time I took some aloe and honey and, to be fair, my body broke out in an allergic reaction and I ended up having to call an ambulance anyway ... I have such a great aloe plant on my windowsill. If you come home, I'll cut some off for you, you can bring it back to Moscow and then you'll be healthy as a horse."

"You know, I bought you a sheepskin coat, an extra-large. What? You won't wear it? But it's nice, look, so warm. It's brown, even. I remember you always liked brown suede jackets. What? Why are you yelling? Well, give it back ... somebody will wear it. Calm down, I didn't waste my money. I didn't buy it. This woman gave it to me. You know her, she's nice, she's a poet, too.

"Did you know that St. Basil's Cathedral was built before Christ? But what does it say on Wikipedia? What is Wikipedia, anyway? Who cares what they write there! Ivan the Terrible? I'm so sure. It's a pagan temple, I'm telling you, our ancestors built it before Moscow even existed. It's a pagan temple in honor of the god Ra! Seriously, that stuff on Wikipedia is horseshit! I'll give you a book to read, it's got the real story."

"Did you know that dolmens cure cancer? I know a woman who drank a calendula tincture and sat by a dolmen for three full months, and her cancer was cured. Do you get checked for cancer? I don't. I know what to do if something comes up. The dolmen cure. They cured a woman of sterility. People go there to jump over fires, too. But not close to the dolmens. You can't have fires there, it's just a treatment area. You build fires by the river, at the foot of the mountain. I walked on coals, it was so exciting, Natasha! Of course, I got badly burned … You need feet with calluses on them, so you don't get burned. You know, it's like those silicon gloves you use to take pans out of the oven. People with lots of calluses on their feet can walk on coals all day without feeling anything. I have calluses, too, but for some reason they didn't help. My feet really hurt that time. Maybe if I do it again, my feet will have some sort of immunity to fire."

"Here's a picture of Stepan sitting with some girl, look, she's so beautiful! How could he not be in love with her? Look at her cute little nose! I don't know, she's just gorgeous. An actress? Yes, an actress … remember, you used to want to be an actress, too? But with your looks … Of course, a director has power. It's good to be the boss. Though that'll never help you keep a good-looking man. You know what my mom told me: a good-looking man is never yours alone. Understand? Be careful! But really, this girl, she's incredible. Very beautiful."

"Look, you're obviously very high-strung. When you were little, you were so sweet, you listened to me. Such a sweet- heart! Always hugging me! How come you're so rude now?"

"MOM, I'M GOING FOR A SMOKE AND THEN TO BED."

Mom, I'm going for a smoke and then to bed, and I'm also gonna get drunk. You're saying the most ridiculous bullshit, I can't listen to it unless I'm drunk.

I just can't while sober, I'm sorry. My blood starts to boil. It's not healthy. I also have medical conditions: one's migraines, the other's alcoholism. Your monologues are triggering them both. Mom, please stop talking. Why can't you just appreciate a quiet evening!

Mom.

I'm not willing to make sacrifices anymore.

Although neither are you …

"Mom, what if you stayed a few more days? It's been a year …"

"What are you talking about? My dog- wood's in bloom, I need to water my tomatoes, I've got my garden, my onions …"

"Mom, will you come visit this summer?"

"What do you mean, 'summer'? My tomatoes and cucumbers will be ripe, I've got my bees at home, my chickens …"

Well, Mom, this summer I've got my shoots, casting, scouting, rehearsals, editing, footage, all that bullshit …

So, Mom.

The point is, we don't need each other.

When did it get like this, you making me crazy and me scaring you?

When was that critical moment when a good psychoanalyst would've concluded: these are two separate people now?

You probably think all this started the moment I got on that plane and flew far away from you. The day I crushed your careful plot for me: the youngest daughter, staying by your bedside and bringing you glasses of water. Best-case scenario, we'd die on the same day. Worst-case, I'd survive you by a year, tops. But no matter what, at least I'd be with you until you died.

But!

In fairy tales, younger daughters go looking for the scarlet flower. So did I. I left, up in a puff of smoke. This traitor was as good as gone.

That's not the point, of course. The point is, right now we're sitting here on the couch, two strangers. You're touching my shoulder and I'm trembling in protest.

How, when, why did this happen? This blind, inconceivable, bleeding love, for which I would have killed without batting an eye, turned into hate. As if I've crossed over to the dark side of the moon.

No way you have the courage to admit to yourself that you haven't loved me for a while now. For you that would be blasphemy, breaking a taboo. You're only capable of loving strangers. Your family is just an obligation. And I want so badly—so badly—to judge you, to rub your face in your own lying, your indifference, your selfishness.

Every time we see each other I waste all our time on this stuff. And once you leave, I sob. I'm so lonely. I miss you. I cry myself into a stupor and give myself stomach cramps. And later I have night- mares where I lose you forever …

"Mom, why don't you stay three more days …"

"I can't do that! I have my chickens at home, Leonid's starting a new job, there's no one to feed the chickens, and the seedlings are sprouting already …"

Mom.

How's this. What if this were it. What if we never saw each other again. First of all, you've got high blood pressure and a bad heart. You're already seventy-two.

Second, I'm an alcoholic, and bad shit could happen to me, too.

In this web of impending deaths, where exactly do chickens and seedlings fit in, Mom? What sort of pedestal have we put them on?

Where do shoots and editing fit in? Or money problems, or the producers' voices descending on me from the skies?

Why the fuck do we make an effort to meet once a year, so you can spend a week watching me stress over work and I can have conversations with you about chickens and other stupid shit?

But whatever. Even if we threw the chickens and the producers out the window (they're basically the same—both need tending, at the expense of all human dignity). Imagine we had all the time in the world. What would we do?

I can answer that with almost 100 percent certainty.

I'd get upset at all the sentences that came out of your mouth, because of their unbelievable stupidity.

You'd be offended and then you'd fake, if not fainting, then dizziness, until I felt sorry for you.

It's the same thing every year.

Maybe if we lived together, some sort of catastrophe would've happened already. But as it is ... we're a mother and daughter living in forced separation.

I shrink from physical contact. You instigate it.

You try to preserve my younger self, the gentle, zit-ridden, energetic girl who sang and danced Indian dances in the rain with you. The girl who cried at the top of her lungs when she found out the cat had eaten a mouse. The girl who hugged you and talked to aliens in her sleep to impress you, to shock you, to get attention, to let you know in this stupid way that she was special, not like everyone else. The girl who wrote scandalous stories with explicit sexual details so you'd notice she was mature.

And later that already-grown girl who guarded you, never letting you make mistakes, always staying close, beating up your men, protecting you, giving liters of blood to save you, always with you. Always on your side, no matter what. Basically, you've always needed that girl—the one who still doesn't completely understand you.

I, on the other hand, am trying to pull away from this new, unwelcome, distorted you. Because that's exactly how I see you now. Because I've come to understand. And now, at my mature age, I can't fucking believe this is how things turned out.

You try to resurrect the past. All we had together, that solidarity, that feeling of us against the world. Against all my fathers, all our relatives, all our neighbors, and everyone who gave us side-eye at the store.

Our songs in the grass. Me and you, Mom. We sang nonstop, like crickets, as the sun went down. We loved going to the field to watch the sunset. I loved that … We walked in the blossoming apple orchard. You were always singing or coming up with poems. I sang along and also thought up things about spring and snow- drops. We loved each other fiercely, and I always—listen—I always felt your heart, your warmth.

And now you try to resurrect the past. You're always trying to remember things: what did I care about before my enlightenment? And I …

I'm trying to set aside the present.

I'm sorry. I can't call today. I get upset as soon as I do.

It's such a nice evening, my husband's here, I want to spend time on Facebook. I'm not calling. I'll do it tomorrow.

Tomorrow comes. It's a beautiful morning. I need to make breakfast for Sasha, write my screenplay, and then I have a meeting. Friends come over, I get drunk. Then it's evening again, and I still want to keep things peaceful, not painful. But as soon as I call, that's what it's going to be. Because of your helpless voice, because of my idiotic irritation. Because I'm not there with you (even though I didn't want to be). Why is everything so painful, anyway? Oh, because I'm not there …

You're scared of me and my short temper, so you lie a lot. Lying is your new thing. Even though you're—let me repeat—seventy-two years old, and you've started to lose your memory, so you mix up your own statements. That's why your lying isn't even lying. It's a personality quirk. That's all.

That's why almost all our conversations are pointless. You rip them out of your memory like turning the page of a newspaper.

I remember a scene from this great documentary, where the granddaughter comes to her grandma with important questions, but the grandma isn't totally there anymore. Or she's pretending not to be. She doesn't remember anything, doesn't give a single answer.

That's how you are, never really answering any of my painful questions. And I get it. It's not easy, answering adult children's questions about why things were the way they were during their childhood.

Why, Mom, why did you always go around acting like a friend or a classmate, able to listen and cry with me, but unable to protect me?

I'll never get an answer. Impossible. All you have in response are tears and pursed lips.

And you say:

"Come on, sweetheart, we're all alive and well, come on!"

"Come on, sweetheart, you've always been so independent, I trusted you."

"Come on, sweetheart, remember, you said you didn't want to go to school anymore, we bought you a certificate, at the market, remember? And our whole family went crazy, they thought you'd become a cleaning lady, but you became a director, see?"

"Come on, sweetheart, remember, when you were thirteen I left you alone at the beach. I trusted your good sense. You've always been more mature than me! It's like you were born that way ..."

"Come on, why are you screaming again?"

I scream, Mom. I scream at night, too. I'm a screamer. Yes, I'm rude. Sometimes I scream swear words at you, at your tomatoes and your bees. I'll never get an answer. No matter how much I torture you, no matter what revelations I share.

None of this has anything to do with your current life. Or mine. Now I'm Sasha's mom, and some nights I don't even scream with hatred. And (guess what?) I don't even want an answer that badly anymore. There just isn't one. That's life, we're alive and well, what more do you want. Everything's sinking down—good, let it drown in the dirty Anapka River. You won't even be able to see what's lost.

Don't reopen your wounds, don't talk about, remember, or touch what's scary, don't wake the bear, don't draw your swords. Let's put it aaaaall to bed, Mom, in our vineyard valley where the stars shine so brightly. I'll never forget that valley, Mom. Like that classic paradox about love and blindness.

And when you die (if I'm still alive), I'll scream at myself for having screamed at you.

Whenever I think about you, I tremble, Mom. Your childlike weakness, your helplessness—they're my greatest heartbreak.

I can accept you, I can accept you. But—I can't. I'm too disappointed.

I often dream about our house, the one I hate, the one that pulls me back like a magnet. Our stuffy, mosquito-y apartment with creaking wooden floors and cockroaches, and that balcony ... I often dream I'm down below on the street, looking up at our balcony, and I see the light on and I think, as long as the light's on that means you're there, you're alive. But I can't go into the building and walk upstairs. I'm standing there in my dream like an idiot, watching. And in my dream, I wonder whether I even want to go upstairs and see that place again, supposedly my home, but not really mine at all.

And the grass around it is so green, so tall.

You and I used to lie in that grass. I wanted to lie like that forever.

I wished our grass had never seen Uncle Sasha, your sleepwalking indifference, your heart attacks, your yellow cowardice, or my red hatred.

Mom.

Let's lie a little longer in our green, green grass and look at our balcony, where the lights are on, where you are. And let's sing this song together—you in your open-mouthed Kuban style, me in my out-of-tune falsetto:

"We have mountains, we have plains,
We have windiness and wilderness.
We are children of the stars
But more than any other,
We belong to you, we're yours,
The eaaaaaarth is our mooooother."

THERE IS NO NIGHT

Ksenia Buksha (1983)

Translated by Anne O. Fisher

Journalist, copyrighter and biographer of Kazimir Malevich, **Ksenia Buksha** won the National Bestseller prize for her text *Freedom Factory*, an industrial novel set in the post-industrial and post-Soviet era, a collection of military plant worker's monologues combined in an Alexievich-style massive canvas.

Buksha's short stories are full of humour and tender absurdity. 'In the big novels you always fabricate something', says Buksha. 'So to write a short story is my way not to lie to the readers'. She currently lives in exile.

At the end of a dead-end street in the outskirts there stands a little maternity ward. It's next to a huge overgrown park where birds do sing, but the only light's from stars, not streetlamps. There are crumbling buildings along the edge of the park, hangars or something, garages. The wild apple trees in this park let their fruit fall before its time. People from the neighborhood amble through the park with strollers and dogs; they sit on fallen trees and make fires; children gather acorns. Out past the park the highway rustles, and the river glitters.

The little old maternity ward hasn't been renovated in a hundred years. The window frames are black with age. It's green outside the ward windows, but inside, it's bitter brown splotches on faded white. This is the little maternity ward where all the women in the city without papers or registration are brought to give birth. And this is also where, if you pay, you're guaranteed the attentions of a doctor and a midwife, then R-and-R in a two-person room. Maybe the ward isn't really as little as it looks at first glance. Three floors: the second floor is labor and delivery, the third floor is pre-labor, and the first floor is recovery and the private examination room. There's also a wing, but we're not going to talk about the wing, or about what goes on inside it.

It's here, in this little maternity ward, that women give birth day in and day out. In this elderly, shabby, warm little ward, where white paint coats the doors and freckles the windows, and round glass globes dimly light the halls. This is the place, the second floor of the maternity ward, where Vernik, the head of the labor and delivery section, and his assistant Virsavia do the deliveries. First thing in the morning there's already a line to see them. A lady doctor in the examination room shouts at the women in labor, takes their information, gives them their enemas, and distributes clean gowns with unbleachable brown stains and holes from years of washing.

Sergey Ivanovich Vernik is an OBGYN. Of all the medical professions, this one stands out for dealing with pathologies and normalities alike. No matter where Vernik goes, anywhere on ward territory, he's followed by a long train of Indian and Russian students. They need practice, so sometimes Vernik has them do the delivery instead of him.

"Am I handsome?" Vernik asks a pregnant woman lying down for her ultrasound. "Now who do we have here, a boy, is it? Come on, move your hands, show me what you've got there ... that was to the fruit of your womb, not to you ... All right ... A boy. A good-looking guy. Looks like me. So then, am I handsome?"

"Very," says the pregnant woman.

"You're darn right," Vernik nods, satisfied. "I am handsome. Sure am." He walks on, and the students make their way after him, hoping for some practice.

Vernik is always joking and bragging. He thinks it's part of his job to make women who are nervous, and about to give birth, feel more upbeat. He's right.

Vernik's assistant, the midwife Virsavia, says, "Wow, you're so round!" as she guides yet another frightened future mother by the elbow down from the third floor to the second. "You sure you've got twins in there, not triplets?"

"Oh, no. Not triplets. Triplets would be over the top! Well, but you know better than me."

"Don't worry. We'll get you delivered quick as a wink. We get everyone delivered here."

"Oh, don't make it too quick! You've got to have time to take the ring off."

"Vernik will come and he will personally take off all your rings, and bracelets too. Your contractions are still pretty mild, dear. He'll be right here to take it off. He's the one who put it on, so he's the one who'll take it off, nice and easy. He's already on his way. He'll be right here, and he'll take it right off."

"That's right, he's the one who put it on, so he can be the one to take it off."

"That's right. Now let's just give you a nice little Actovegin drip. That's it, just lie back. Yes, those are contractions … he'll be right here … oh, there he is right there, here he comes!"

Vernik comes in. A little flock of Indian students trails after him.

"Aha!" Vernik exclaims. "So now it's our very own Marina Igorevna who's come down to the second floor! There she is, she's gone into labor, isn't that just wonderful. We'll get you delivered quick as a wink," he murmurs. "Right this way, over here, please. Oh, how wonderful. The cervix is just perfectly ready for labor. Everything's ripe, and everything's … wonderful. Yes, Virsavia, hand me a flashlight please … why is it always so dark inside you women … mmm-hmmm … yeess s …"

"Who is that, the anesthesiologist?"

"Marina, don't get in the way or I'll tie up your hands. What do you need an anesthesiologist for? Cervical incompetence makes it easier to give birth."

"Oww-ww … something's not … right … I think something's not right down there."

"And how many years have you been delivering babies?"

"None … I do PR … used to …"

"Just what I thought. Now, I deliver babies, and I've been doing it for thirty years. It's your second birth, what are you so jumpy for?"

"I'm not jumpy … it's just …"

"Turn your voice off! And don't you go jumping around on me! No jumping around! Hold tight right here and try not to move, or else I'll … There! That's it. Now your contractions will come faster, my dear. You'll have the baby by morning."

"By when!?"

"By morning. You can get up and walk around the corridor a few times. That might make everything go faster. Should I leave you the ring as a keepsake? For your personal collection? Ha ha!" Vernik jokes. "Want me to wrap up the placenta for you too? And the wire, to display in your personal museum?"

"No, that's okay ... thanks ..."

"Because I could ... all right, then, you'll have the baby by morning, so just relax for now ... There seems to be quite a lot of you today, quite a few ... Atmospheric phenomena, eh? I love thunder in early May ... Yes. Virsavia, blow up the ball. Everything's ready for the delivery. We'll get you delivered quick as a wink. We get everyone delivered here. Here's a watch for you, time your contractions. When the contractions double, shout my name so I wake up."

Vernik heads off, whistling "Victory Day" to himself.

There's an ominous somnolence in the delivery room. The radio is just audible. Women walk carefully down the corridor, stopping short along the painted walls and waiting out their contractions. A little flock of students whispers at the window. It's a regular workday for them. There are lindens and poplars in the yard.

Marina Igorevna remembers how she and her husband went to a warm country on vacation. She still smoked back then, still wore her heels tall and her hair long. She lay around on the beach, tanning to a crisp. Then they went to see a holy elder monk in a monastery. He husband had to keep asking her to go, since she didn't want to – going across the steppe, in the heat, and so on and so forth – but he said, we're going and that's the end of it. He said: there's a little stream that flows right there, right on the monastery property, and if a woman drinks from that stream, then a little baby will grow in her belly. Marinka doubted this: what, it just grows, out of nowhere? Her husband, embarrassed: okay, so not out of nowhere. Of course not. The partner has to be in possession of the appropriate genital organ. Let's go for it, Marina. What if it works?

Marinka started thinking about it. She'd wanted kids for a long time. She'd already gotten to where she made that same wish every New Year's Eve: Lord, please just stick a baby in my belly already. And now this: some monk, a stream ... Well, why not, she said, let's ask, and she made her way through the heat to the monastery.

The monastery was pretty. Flowers were in bloom everywhere, even on the walls. Cultured monks were weeding the flowerbeds and repairing the path, covering it with bright gravel. The little stream flowed right through, with flowerbeds along the banks, and it turned out that you couldn't just go up to it and have a drink without first obtaining a ticket and receiving the elder monk's blessing. The line to see the monk was an enormous mass with several ends. Marinka decided to take some pictures of the cathedral with her new digital camera while her husband waited in line for the blessing. No matter how she tried, she couldn't get anything: the sun was in the wrong place, the cathedral didn't fit into the frame ... Marinka took a few steps back, then a step to the side, then another one to the side, and then another step back, and then she lurched over and stepped squarely into a flower bed, and from there (not far to fall) she and her camera both plopped right into the stream.

"Oh, dammit!" Marinka said, really loud, so everyone in the monastery heard. The sightseers burst out laughing, the monk weeding the flowerbed shook his head reproachfully, and her husband ran out of the line to help her get back on shore. They did get their blessing, eventually, and so Marinka ended up gulping river water once more, this time legally.

After they got back from their vacation, Marinka found out she was pregnant. Nine months later she had a girl. A year after that, she concieved twins.

Her husband said, "Clearly our official inquiry got bogged down in processing for a while up there in heaven. But your first prayer, the one you said unconsciously, got there faster."

"But I cursed!" objected Marinka.

"The Lord knows what he's doing," her husband said.

Marina stops short, a shadow at the wall. The pressure from inside is getting heavier and heavier. A green "down" arrow blinks invisibly on her belly. Her belly has turned into a hard clot, it's squeezing taut into itself, holding itself up. Eight dusty yellow lightbulbs get in line and start dancing in a circle.

"Ooohh ..." she hears. "Ooohh. ... oooohhh. ..."

An old lady stands in the doorway of the next delivery room. No, really, an old lady, it's no exaggeration. She's as old as the hills. And pregnant. She holds her belly with both hands and looks at Marina without blinking.

"Ooohh, sweetie, I'm so scared," she lisps, tears brimming in her eyes. "How'd I ever get into this? I stopped getting my period, it was the fifth month … they don't do abortions in the fifth month …"

"Everything's going to be all right," Marina says.

"Oh, nothing's going to be all right," says the old lady, and waves her hand in angry resignation. Then, again: "Ooohh … oooohhh …"

Marina is struck with fear. The white night begins. The students have all gone off somewhere and the halls of the labor and delivery ward are almost empty. Sometimes the contractions get worse, other times they fade away again.

Vernik arrives.

"So, my dear Marina Igorevna. I can see it in your eyes, you're …"

"I'd love an epidural."

"Get along with you now. What do you mean, an epidural? Lie down. Good. Virsavia, we're going to do an amniotomy."

"One or both?"

"Just one." Vernik holds up one finger.

"With your finger?" Marina asks, raising her brows, horror distorting her face.

"With a needle!" Vernik looks reproachfully at her and shakes his head, like she'd asked him to do something dirty. "With this needle right here. The main thing is for you to not be afraid. And don't yell and carry on, that's the main thing. You'll yell all right, when you're pushing."

"What's my name?" asks Virsavia.

"Virsavia …"

Virsavia approves. "Good. I wish everyone could have a labor like yours." "Really?"

"Really."

"I'll bring you a ball," says Vernik. "You'll give birth on the ball. The contractions will be strong at first, then they'll become less painful."

Here comes Virsavia, lugging a ball, blown up taut. Marina is planted up on top, right on the north pole, and ordered to rock back and forth and bounce up and down. Immediately her contractions get sharper, longer, she has to pick out her breath like the end of a ball of yarn. Drops of dirty bordeau trace down the sides of the ball Marina's sitting on. Gradually, millimeter by millimeter, she is turned inside-out.

There's a cell phone right in front of her, on the white bedsheet. She dials her husband's number, again, for the nth time. Her husband is two thousand kilometers away, in Krasnoyarsk. It's well past midnight. No one picks up, and the phone goes to fax.

Marina remembers her first pregnancy. She had cervical incompetence then, too, and they also put a ring on it, a so-called therapeutic pessary, which supports the cervix and doesn't let it stretch apart. And the thing was that it all came out of the blue: she started feeling bad one day at work, they called the ambulance, and she spent a week under observation. At the time she wasn't thinking about much of anything, but later, it would often make her shudder: if the pregnancy hadn't stuck that time, she would've had to forget about ever having children of her own.

Marina did public relations back then. She liked the work, although she often caught herself thinking that it was all nonsense. Should've been a doctor. Ever since she'd gotten pregnant the second time, she'd had a sincere appreciation for the medical profession. No one in her hometown would take her pregnancy on: cervical incompetence, thirty-three, twins. The only thing they suggested was abortion, with a discount for medical conditions. She had to go to Saint Petersburg. And it was only here, it was only him, this Vernik guy, with his giggles and gimmicks, who agreed to help her. There are people out there, after all, who do what matters. But her? A flabby little fattie, not that much younger than that scary old lady in the ward next door … worked in PR, now she'll be stuck at home for the long haul … would she have been a good doctor? Probably not, no …

Thoughts flash into existence, then wink out. Her face doesn't have any look at all, her eyes are blind, turned inward. A wet lock of hair dangles in front of her face.

Vernik and Virsavia are running up, and the pediatric nurse, too, who's always there when twins are delivered.

"All righty now," says Vernik, rubbing his hands together. "Go ahead, lie down real quick, I'll have a look at you."

"There are so many of you," Marina said. "The first time I was in labor … ooow! Ooooww!"

"Move your hands!" shouts Vernik. "Virsavia, hold her hands! What is this now! Marina, you should be ashamed of yourself!"

Everything around her is covered in brownish liquid. Marina shoves the doctors away. It's impossible to lie down.

"I'm standing up!" she shouts. "Let me stand up! Do something, now, or I'll fucking ..."

"Oh, so it's 'I'll fucking ...' now, is it," murmurs Vernik, doing something carefully between Marina's legs.

"It hurts, I'm going to faint!" weeps Marina.

Virsavia says, "Shout on the exhalation. Hold your legs like that ... turn carefully onto your side ... Anya, hold her leg up ..."

As if she's dreaming it, Marina sees her own leg, bent at the knee; the lady doctors are holding her hips while she hisses and spits and bugs her eyes out from the pain, and above them all the glass of the door, painted to halfway, with yellowish dregs spreading over it.

The phone rings at five-thirty in the morning.

"Marisha!" She hears her husband's distant, high-pitched, vibrating voice. "So, has it started?"

"You got that right."

"Oh, darn it! And there I was asleep! I was asleep, and then I went to the bathroom, and get this, a light bulb exploded, and then I went over to wash my hands like a good little boy, and then a light bulb exploded there too, and I thought, something's going on! And I look and there's twenty unanswered calls on my phone! How are you?"

"I'm in labor. Is Katyusha asleep?"

"She's asleep!" He abruptly lowers his voice. "Grandma's there with her ... well, just hold on! I won't sleep any more! I'm keeping my fingers crossed! Go on and ... and give it your best shot!"

"Best shot, coming up."

Meanwhile, things are not going swimmingly. The contractions have died out. Vernik has stopped cracking jokes, now he's just encouraging her. Outside, dawn came a long time ago; bright rays of sunshine are pouring into the maternity ward, there are stripes of light and shadow in the park out the window. But to Marina, everything around is transparent and indistinct. She's floating away with no strength left, not even for fear. Suddenly it hits her with utter clarity that she might die now, along with the two little boys who are pushing and shoving in the dark inside her.

"Now we'll inject some oxytocin. It will stimulate contractions."

Vernik bends over to her. "Almost fully dilated. You just have a little more to go. You'll have the babies in half an hour."

The delivery room fills with doctors: Vernik, Virsavia, the neonatologist, the pediatric nurse, and somebody else, and the students – Indians, Russians, Chinese ...

She's carried over to the chair. They lift her up high, and tell her to pull on the iron pipes so her pushing is more effective. She grabs the prongs and hunkers onto her spread legs, reminding herself of one of those chickens skewered on rotating spits, ready to be grilled.

"Okay, listen now, on the next contraction you're going to push," Virsavia says. "Push like you're pooping."

She tries to push, but the only thing she feels is terrible, splitting pain. The idea that she has to finish this soon, right now, drives her on.

"Good job!" Vernik shouts. "Let's go, let's go ... Stop! Let's go, let's go, let's go ..."

Virsavia joins in: "Come on, come on, co-ome on ..."

She pushes diligently and suddenly starts feeling something beatifically right, as if her body had figured out what to do all by itself. Exhale, uncontrollable push, another, and a sturdy, blotchy, slippery bean slides out of her. The first newborn.

"Why isn't he squalling?! Slap him, bring him back!" says Marina, trying to raise her head.

"Now where am I going to bring him back from, when he's right here with us?" says the neonatologist, from somewhere in a green gloom pierced with the rising sun's rays.

She lifts the newborn higher and puts him on the scale: "It's a boy. Three kilograms two-fifty."

"O-ho!" Vernik says. "Not bad for twins," but he's not looking at the baby, he's looking at Marina. He takes hold of her belly with two fingers like a pillowcase and shakes it roughly, so that her second child, a slowly suffocating clot, bounces around. The cervix is already stretched out. No contractions. Now Vernik, Virslavia, and Marina are giving birth together, the three of them: one shakes and pushes her belly, trying to stimulate contractions, another one tries to dig the baby out while shouting "come on, come on, come on!" and Marina herself grips the black, slippery, sweat-soaked iron prongs and pushes with all her might, which gave out a long time ago.

The second baby is born alive and mostly well. They put him straight in the incubator, to get some oxygen.

After giving birth to the placenta, Marina lies back on the chair. She's shaking, and there's a tic in one eye. Virsavia brings a blanket. Marina asks for her cell phone and presses "redial" with an unbending finger, to call her husband.

Later, the very next night, just before dawn, the milk comes in.

The heat overtakes you, your breasts swell, the sweet white droplets ooze and drip. You take the younger boy and unwrap him so he's all naked. You lay him down on your stomach. The hungry little thing sticks out his tongue, finds the nipple, and latches on, greedily, hastily, lips turned inside out. He eats, and swallows your milk noisily, he sucks you, he worries your nipple with his little tongue, and he falls asleep on you, with his ear to your heart, and you feel his little smackings and snufflings.

Vernik and Virslavia's indistinct shouting drifts down from the second floor: "come on, come on, come on!" and "let's go, let's go, let's go!" It's a white midnight out the windows of the maternity ward; the old park rustles in the twilight, and the Neva splashes.

On the wild apple trees hang clots of sour, hard, unripe apples.

ALESHA'S HOMECOMING

Liza Aleksandrova-Zorina (1984)

Translated by Natasha Perova

Coming from the northern mining town of Kovdor on the Kola Peninsula near the polar circle, the remnant of the Soviet's ambitious attempt to colonize and industrialize the North, **Liza Aleksandrova-Zorina** hews to the long-lasting Russian literary socialist tradition in order to focus on a small man, a person lost among the tectonic movements of history and crushed or expelled by the rigid and anonymous structures of state and society.

Currently living in Sweden, Aleksandrova-Zorina is also engaged in journalism and human rights defence. She worked as a spokesperson for Team 29, the group of lawyers providing juridical help to accused civil rights activists (recently the group itself became a target of state persecution and was shut down).

From Donetsk to Moscow Alesha travelled by bus. At the checkpoints the militants – just yesterday he had been one of them – took him outside and searched him: they stripped him to his underwear, threw everything out of his knapsack to check if he had any weapons, and took his cash. "Bloody scammers," whispered a woman who had agreed to carry Alesha's package among her own things unaware that apart from his money and a few personal belongings she was carrying a hand grenade wrapped in a piece of cloth. From Moscow Alesha took the train to his home town on the Kola Peninsula. He spent all thirty hours of the ride sleeping on the upper bunk while flowing past the train windows were deserted villages with huts leaning to one side like some lumbago-broken old women.

"Where you've been?" asked the driver who gave him a ride from Murmansk for as far as he was going his way, to the exit from the highway leading to his village.

Alesha waved him off: "Over there ..." and stroked his grenade secretly. But the driver knew right away what "over there" meant.

The village streets were empty and the sun was hanging over the houses as if stuck on the chimney of the closed factory. Alesha lost track of time and couldn't figure out if it was day or night and whether people were sleeping or had abandoned the place. Many years ago the coal mine was flooded here, there were plans to resettle the villagers to town because there were only about a hundred people left and no children were born for quite some time.

An old APC was parked in the yard of their house. It had been decommissioned from the nearby border-guarding detachment some thirty years ago. Alesha's father bartered it at the time for his buggy which must have been taken apart for scrap long ago while the APC was still as good as new. The villagers clubbed together to buy enough gas to go for cloudberries to the forest swamp near the border, or to the market in town; in the summer they dried mushrooms on its armored sides, aired rugs and blankets, and in winter they used it as a storage for venison and fish safe from the dogs.

Alesha pressed his face to one window, then another trying to make out if anyone was inside. He knocked quietly and then louder. His mother was the first to wake up, she saw his nose flattened against the glass and cried out, but then recognized him and cried, "That's Alesha!" A minute later the house came alive with shouts and noises, doors banged, his mother unlocked the door and threw her arms around his neck. Alesha pushed her off lightly. "C'mon, Mum. Don't!"

Mother hastened to prepare some snacks: she sliced some bread and salted fish in big chunks throwing the fish tail to the cat in the yard, and Father brought a bottle of vodka.

"I don't drink, Dad," Alesha said when Father moved a glass of vodka towards him. Father gulped down his own glass and then his, exhaled noisily, put a slice of fish in his mouth and licked his fingers. He made a move to embrace his son but Alesha jumped and grabbed his side where he used to carry his gun.

"Easy, easy, son, relax. What's wrong?" Father raised his arms in surrender. "Sorry, Dad. I haven't come to myself yet."

His knapsack was sitting next to him on the floor as if Alesha had just dropped in for a minute to have a quick snack and be on his way. He had one hand in the pocket holding his grenade all wet and slippery from his sweaty hand. From time to time, when no one looked, he took it out under the table to change hands, and chuckled.

For the wedding neighbors and classmates, those who still remained in the village, came over. They brought home-made salads in deep bowls, cooked potatoes, fish, and pies. Tables were brought out into the yard and put in a row, stools and chairs were placed around them. Lena stood aside in her long wedding dress rented for the occasion. In embarrassment she put a hand over the cleavage of her low neckline. "Have a drink with us, Alesha," the guests called to him.

"I don't drink."

"He doesn't drink. Don't mind him. We'll drink to him." Father waved him off. Alesha was loved in the village, he used to laugh and joke all the time, it was never dull in his company. But now he hardly ever smiled and was silent most of the time. "Alesha, tell us a story," people begged him. "Something to make us laugh. You know how to cheer up people."

"A friend of mine got his fingers torn off. So we put them in ice and carried them to Donetsk. A doctor sewed them back in place."

"Bullshit," someone said.

"The doctor was drunk though and mixed up the fingers. But they got stuck anyway. Very awkward for the boy, and not good for shooting: instead of the index finger he has a pinkie now."

The guests laughed. Alesha watched them intently without as much as a smirk, and finally forced a semblance of a smile.

He'd never laughed once since the day two years ago when he went to Moscow to find a job. He worked at various construction sites where they often cheated him of his wages. He spent nights at railway stations or wherever he could find a shelter, and then he heard of this job. The pay was low but they hired anyone who'd done their army service. He came to the designated place on the ice-clad river where one bank was Russian and the other bank was Ukrainian. He cut a hole in the ice, watched his fishing line sink down and began to wait. Several hours later, when he was already stiff with cold, a man, his face wrapped in a scarf, came for him from the opposite bank and led him away.

Alesha saw his first death when a woman with her little daughter stepped aside from the road to let their car pass and was blown up on a mine. The little girl continued to hold her mother's hand, because she had nothing else to hold on to. He quickly got used to death, the war became habitual and predictable, and after the ceasefire downright boring.

Then a fighter appeared on the other side. The frontline passed along the river and on the opposite bank, beyond the meadow, a group of Ukrainian fighters whiled away the time. Occasionally they opened fire on each other, rather to amuse themselves and remind of their presence, because you couldn't really hit anyone at this distance, perhaps only accidentally. So that fighter started coming for a shit each morning, right when Alesha was on duty. He pulled down his pants and squatted with his bare bottom turned to the other side to show his contempt. Alesha shot at him, sometimes gave a short burst but missed each time, he was out of luck – he wished he were at least 200 meters closer. For the first time in a long time he laughed again.

They went to the registry office in the APC, so they could take a shorter route across the swamps. They decorated the armored sides with painted hearts, draped the vehicle with net curtains, and put dolls representing bride and groom on the top, though the dolls got lost on the way. As they drove through the village the guests sat outside on the armored sides singing songs, but when they entered the forest everybody went inside where there was a smell of gas and grease mixed with half-rotten fish. There were not enough seats for everybody, so some people had to ride standing clutching at one another.

The town was small: from the central square you could see the forest on the right and the mining plant on the left. But for the remaining residents even this small town became too large. The abandoned houses with dark eye sockets stood side by side with still inhabited houses. The deep cracks on the old roads looked like wrinkles. Just then a blast came from the quarry making glass panes rattle. Sticking his head out of the APC tower Alesha felt as if one war had replaced another.

* * *

The marriage ceremony was short: Alesha and Lena were invited into the registry office while the rest of the group were told to stay outside; they were asked if they were marrying of their own free will, then their passports were duly stamped and they were let go to the four winds.

The way back home took longer and they only arrived towards evening. They bumped into a rusted kiosk on the way and nearly ran over two old women who dived into a ditch as the APC drove above it. At some point Alesha got outside pulling Lena with him; he lifted her in his arms and jumped down on the move twisting his ankle a bit. The APC drove on leaving a trail of squashed shrubs.

They walked in silence along a path leading deeper into the forest. Lena was admiring the ring on her finger.

"Talk to me." Lena asked him.

"What's there to talk about?" Alesha shrugged his shoulders and adjusted his knapsack.

Alesha used to crack jokes all the time making Lena laugh till her sides split. But now he kept silent. Last year when he came for a vacation she asked him all sorts of questions: whether he had to kill, and how he felt hiding in basements during bombings, but he just mumbled something inarticulate and so she hesitated to pester him with questions now.

"Have you come for good? You won't go away again?" She asked him.

Instead of an answer Alesha just shook his head. Lena stood on tiptoe and kissed him. They turned into a forest path and soon reached an old rusted gate of the abandoned forestry, the gate was closed but there was a hole in the iron fence where two bars had been removed. Alesha squeezed through the hole and offered a hand to Lena; she pretended she was of two minds about coming but then followed him lifting her wide skirt to avoid tearing it on the prickly shrubs.

"Do you love me?" Lena asked as she undressed hanging her underwear on the fir branches.

Alesha nodded.

"I love you too."

Alesha got out a raincoat from his knapsack and spread it on the ground. Lena laid down on it immersing into the soft damp moss.

"Wait a bit. I'll have a smoke."

He lighted a cigarette, took several long deep drags and put it out on a boulder. Lena watched him from down below covering her breasts and lower abdomen with her hands, she was shivering in the cool wind but waited patiently.

Alesha did not take off his clothes – he was embarrassed for his shabby unclean underwear – he just unzipped his pants. He fell on top of her, made a few sharp jerks, gave out a sob and fell quiet. She lay under him and stroked his back. Then he rolled off her and lighted another cigarette. He put her head on his breast and kissed her nape.

"Am I pretty?" Lena asked and turned the wedding ring on her finger.

"Uh-huh."

Lena picked some berries and put them in her mouth.

"When a person dies his eyes drain out," Alesha said suddenly. It took Lena a while to grasp what he was saying. "And his belly swells with all his insides rotting: heart, stomach, spleen, kidneys, they all become liquid and mixed up, so you can't make out what's what. His blood oozes out under his back, if he's lying on his back or it collects under his belly, if he's on his belly. Then his face turns blue as if someone had bruised it all over. His tongue falls out and he's drooling. As if he's alive. Except that he's stinking terribly. You can get used to anything but not that stench, you can't get used to that stench."

Lena was too terrified to budge.

"And if the corpse has been there for a week it begins to move as if it came alive. The body shakes, its arms and legs jerk, its head shivers."

Lena felt nauseous and spat out the berries from her mouth imperceptibly.

"That's the worms eating the body from inside, that's why it's shaking." Alesha laughed.

A gust of wind tore off Lena's slip from the branch. She shrieked heartrendingly and covered her face with her hands. Alesha jumped up and rushed to catch the slip, but he only managed to overtake it when it got caught in the shrubs. When he got back Lena was crying noiselessly wrapped in the raincoat, her shoulders were shaking. "What are you crying for, silly?" Alesha laughed and embraced her lightly. "I'll buy you lots of such slips and panties. Don't cry."

When Alesha and Lena got back home the guests were already pretty drunk and no one paid attention to Lena's tear-stained face.

"Let's drink to the newlyweds!" His father shouted.

"I don't drink, Dad. I told you."

"Aren't you Russian?!" People laughed. "Let's drink to the newlyweds anyway." Mother opened the window, put out a TV set on the windowsill and made the sound louder. They showed a new film about WWII interspersed with adverts. Alesha looked at the famous actor playing a soldier in the trench and smiled wryly. On the screen a detachment went on the attack, and so the guests shouted: "To the Motherland! To Stalin!"

Picking at the meat jelly on his plate Alesha recalled the fighter on the other bank. When one day he failed to appear Alesha was worried if he was alright, and when finally he reappeared Alesha was happy and got his gun ready. The lad pulled down his pants and squatted while Alesha shot at him again and again, but both of them knew he'd miss – the lad was lucky that Alesha was not a good shot. Alesha even liked the lad, and when the latter demonstratively wiped his bottom with plantain leaves Alesha laughed heartily. At times he felt he'd enjoy having a drink with him and talk: they had much to talk about, but the boy was too far, you couldn't get him with a gun and his voice wouldn't carry that far either.

"Tell us a funny story," the guests asked Alesha. "You're sitting there like a stranger. Make us laugh. You used to be good at it."

But he could only force a wry smile squeezing his hand grenade tighter in his pocket. Their house was old, built for the first settlers, who came here after the war to dig a pit-mine. The toilet was in an outhouse in the yard. Alesha went inside, locked himself in and lit a cigarette to ward off the stench and the fat flies. Sitting there with his head resting on his fists he could hear the shouts, arguments, and laughs in the yard, then the guests sang "Katyusha" and his dad banged on the bottle with a spoon wishing to give a toast. His toast was long and from the toilet it was hard to make out the words. Alesha could only hear the shout: "To world peace!" which was picked up by the others.

"Come join us, Alesha! We're drinking to peace." The guests called to him.

Alesha did not respond. He took out his grenade and a roll of fishing line from his pocket, pulled out the pin and tied some line around the grenade, then lowered it in the cesspit. Keeping the fishing line tight he unwound the roll so that it was long enough to reach the house. There he sat down on an upturned bucket, lit a cigarette and started waiting. He let out rings of smoke and examined his blood-stained fingers cut by the fishing line.

Finally his father got up from the table and walked towards the toilet on his shaky legs. He had trouble closing the door which kept evading him, but finally he managed to lock it. Alesha counted to ten and jerked the fishing line.

There was a loud blast, the guests dropped down shrieking. Shit went flying around. The blast sent the roof flying off the rickety plywood shed and the walls fell apart each on its side. Father stood upright for a while shaking and feeling the air with his hands like a blind man, and then he collapsed.

"Oh, he's dead!" Mother cried out and rushed to him crouching down.

Father rolled on his back and stared at the sky not grasping what had hit him.

"I'll be damned! What was it?" Father wailed. "I can't hear, not a sound. I'm deaf." The guests were scattered on the ground around the table covering their heads with their hands, they were scared stiff. Suddenly Alesha burst into a loud laugh.

"What's with you?" Mother whispered. "What's come over you?"

"Isn't it hilarious?" Alesha laughed. "It's super, isn't it? I was thinking on the way home what a funny joke it'd be."

Lena broke into tears hiding her face in the grass, first she wept quietly, then louder and louder, almost hysterically, and they could not calm her down for a long time. They sat around the table again looking down into their plates sullenly. Lena gave a light sob from time to time or sighed audibly. If any of the guests started a story they'd fall silent in the middle.

"It was really funny, wasn't?" Alesha mumbled through his teeth. "Why don't you laugh?"

Mother washed Father pouring water from the hose over him.

She brought him dry clothes, sprinkled some scents on him, but the smell of shit still prevailed and people grimaced. Father, who lost his hearing temporarily, just looked around completely dumbfounded.

The heavy silence got so dense you could almost feel it with your hand. Alesha reached for the bottle. He filled his glass, gulped it down and sniffed his sleeve instead of a snack, then filled his glass again.

"It was hilariously funny," he said enunciating each word. "Really funny. I was thinking all the way home how funny it'd be. Why don't you laugh?" He gulped down another glass and banged his fist on the table.

"It was funny, it was. Go on, laugh! I said laugh!"

Alesha recalled how risky it was to bring the grenade all the way from Donetsk. If they found it on him at a checkpoint they'd shoot him on the spot, and if they found it on the Russian border they'd arrest him. He had carefully calculated everything so that Dad would not get killed – he only wanted to play a little practical joke on him. But no one laughed and he couldn't understand why. The soldier from the other bank would have appreciated the joke: that was his stuff. Alesha recalled how the boy pulled his pants down, confident that he was practically unreachable for his gun, maybe a stray bullet could get him, but he was always in luck. And he was surely laughing his heart out as he wiped his bottom with plantain leaves. Alesha couldn't see his face but he was sure the soldier was laughing.

"It's funny. Laugh, c'mon!"

One of the guests looked at his watch, cleared his throat and said he had to leave. And then the others started getting up too and leaving in a hurry. Alesha jumped up and grabbed an axe stuck into a wooden chunk. The guests scattered in all directions. "C'mon, laugh!" Alesha ran after them.

Some people ran out of the yard and hid behind the house, some others dived into the APC and locked themselves in, and those who did not manage to escape crawled under the table.

"Laugh!" Alesha shouted overtaking his father who was gasping for air as he was running for his life – he did attempt a laugh but it came out more like a sob.

His mother hid in the house afraid to go out, she was crying through the vent window: "Alesha, sonny, don't kill your father, have pity on him! Have pity on the people!" Father reached a tree from which clothes lines with laundry stretched to the lamppost. With unexpected agility he started climbing the tree till it creaked dangerously under his weight. Alesha started chopping at the tree trunk.

"It was funny," he repeated in a hoarse voice. "Funny!"

The tree began leaning to one side slowly and his father wailed in terror. His mother clutched at her head and rushed away from the window. The tree crashed on the APC, Father fell on the ground and rolled away.

"Funny!" Alesha shouted and dropped the axe.

He woke up in his room. He was lying across the bed with his knapsack for a pillow. He tightened his belt, put on his jacket, opened the window, sat on the windowsill and lit a cigarette. The sun was lingering above the horizon blinding his eyes. A mangy stray cat was furtively eating leftovers from the plates on the table. Some guests slept right on the ground under the table or slumped against the front door. Wrapped in a rug, his father in a torn shirt, his face bruised and puffy, was snoring on the APC. Alesha went out into the yard, drank from a can with rainwater and splashed the remains on his face. His mother, still sleepy and disheveled, went out after Alesha to give him a parcel with some food for the road. Lena watched him from the window with her face pressed to the glass.

"Take care of yourself, sonny." She embraced her son.

"And you keep an eye on Lena."

"Don't worry. I won't let her out of my sight."

Alesha stepped over a guest sleeping on the ground and quickly walked away from the yard. He was eager to get back to the frontline and see the soldier on the other bank. He knew now what he was going to do with him to take him down a peg or two, and he was already planning the details. First he'd appear as usual on his morning duty. When the soldier squatted with his pants down he'd shoot at him lazily a couple of times, and miss as usual. The boy would laugh wiping his behind and leave, only to return the next morning. Alesha had never seen his face but he knew for sure that the boy was laughing as he wiped his ass and pulled up his pants.

But then at night, which was always pitch dark in the steppe on summer, Alesha would crawl on all fours to the river, swim to the other side, the current would carry him downstream and he'd have to walk back, then he'd crawl across the field to the pit. He had long located that pit overgrown with grass – it was a former common grave from which the bodies were removed to be buried properly in the cemetery. The fighters on the other side must have known about the pit, but they had long forgotten about it. That was where Alesha was going to hide till morning waiting for his man to come for a shit. Alesha would ask a friend to take his place at his usual post, so seeing a sentry there the boy would turn his back and pull down his pants. At that moment Alesha would pop up from the pit and shoot him in the ass, right between his buttocks. He imagined how stunned the boy would be as he was hurled away by the shot, and then he'd fall with his face down squirming with pain. He'd be slithering like a worm, trying to turn round to see who had finally hit him. His comrades would rush to his aid. Meanwhile Alesha would try to escape by swimming back to his own side, if he was lucky. Visualizing the surprised face of his soldier, who would surely burst out laughing if he had time, Alesha laughed too and picked up his pace.

ZAINA

Polina Zherebtsova (1985)

Translated by Irina Steinberg

A writer and painter, **Polina Zherebtsova** was born in Grozny, back then the capital of the Chechen-Ingush Republic. Having witnessed the Russian war against Chechnya as a child and being wounded herself, losing her grandfather in a Russian air strike, she began writing a diary, which she later published as a documentary account.

She also lived through the second war (beginning in 1999) and was only able to leave Grozny later on. Since 2013, she has been living in Finland, where she was granted political asylum.

One of our neighbours from the apartment block next-door was a woman called Zaina. She was a woman who sold her body, although she didn't necessarily charge money. In times of trouble, she would have rebel fighters over. An Ichkerian flag hanging in the window of her apartment signalled her availability.

It was a beautiful flag—rich green, with a fluffy white wolf lying across the middle. Zaina didn't charge much for her services—a jar of pickles and enough flour to fill a bowl.

Then, after her visitors had left her abode, Zaina would cover her bright red curls with a headscarf and hurry out to share the food she had earned with her neighbours, especially the elderly and families with children.

When the enemy—in the shape of Russian military forces—advanced, and the rebels were forced back from their territories, Zaina offered the same level of hospitality to the invaders. The Russian men gave her tinned meats and tiny jars of jam. And after they'd left, Zaina would do what she always did—share the food with the sick and the young.

This is why, despite referring to her as a "whore" behind her back, gossiping mercilessly, and generally refusing to treat her as a fellow human being, the whole neighbourhood was nevertheless tolerant of Zaina.

Most of the male population used Zaina's services. Women like her are a true rarity in Chechnya, since the standard punishment for such behaviour is death. It's the Muslim woman's brother, uncle or father that kills her. And nobody will ever condemn the murderers. Quite the contrary—people will honour and respect them, and policemen will come to shake their hands, roaring: "Peace be upon you!"

But Zaina didn't have a family. She didn't have a father or a mother, or any sisters or brothers who could have killed her or, indeed, shielded her from this life. All we knew was that she was born in the mountains of Dagestan, spoke Chechen, and switched the flags hanging in her window in accordance with the territorial changes of the Russian Federation. We didn't even know how old she was.

Righteous local women in their long dresses and housecoats would cast an expert eye over her and judge her to be over forty.

"She's beautiful because she doesn't have any children!" they would say spitefully. And their faces would contort as if reflected in cracked glass—glass that couldn't withstand the repeated impacts of a man's fist and had fractured all the way across and all the way down.

Zaina wore trousers. She was one of the only women in the city to do so. That too was shameful.

Zaina would not have been allowed to have children—local tradition dictated that such a woman was not fit to carry a child in her belly.

In any normal family, a woman was old at forty. It could hardly be helped—she'd have eight or nine children by that age. Married off at fifteen, by the time she was thirty-odd, she'd be a grandmother.

This was a different perception of time and youth. These were different cultural norms—straight from the mountains.

The beautiful Zaina had managed to survive even the strict Sharia persecutions. Other women like her would have been shot of course, stoned, or beaten to death with sticks, but not our Zaina. Strict Muslim preachers would come to our neighbourhood to dish out punishments, but when confronted with the blue-eyed, laughing Zaina, they would smile back at her and then disappear into her tiny apartment for several hours at a time.

Slight and slim, like a miniature statuette, the beautiful Zaina cast a spell over these men the moment they set eyes on her. She loved dancing and music. She was a skilful cook of eastern dishes.

On leaving the fallen woman's apartment, the preachers would try to make a quick getaway so that people wouldn't spot their long beards and start making crude jokes at their expense.

"Everyone knows everyone's business here!" our neighbour Auntie Mariam once said to me. "Where you've come from, whom you've cast your eye over, and why …"

"How did Zaina come to live here?" I asked, as I observed her red curls and smiling face outside the kitchen window, where we were making pilaf with Auntie Mariam.

"Ramses brought her here. He'd picked her up somewhere. She was so happy back then—she thought he might marry her. But his family forbade him from even thinking about it. And without the family's blessing … well, nobody would go against their family's wishes!"

Ramses was Chechen. He lived upstairs on the third floor. He kept Zaina as his mistress for a while and then he passed her on to his friends, like one passes round a pack of cheap cigarettes.

Zaina was put up in someone else's apartment—one that belonged to a Russian family that had fled when times got tough. She lived in this apartment as if she owned it. Ramses would occasionally say hello to her if he was sure that none of the neighbours was watching. But of course that's unheard of in Chechnya—everyone has eyes in the backs of their heads.

Traditionally, people in Chechnya keep their front doors unlocked. Even if the door has a lock on it, it's pointless trying to keep it shut. People don't even knock, they just walk straight in. And why ever not? They're your neighbours after all!

"Auntie Mariam, we need to borrow the iron!" That's the Avari girls from upstairs. They don't even wait for an answer before grabbing the iron and running back up.

No sooner has the door slammed behind them than we hear:

"It's me! I've come to get some water!" Old Ahmed makes his way past us to the bathroom, the metal pails in his hands clanking together.

"Mariam! I'm just going to leave a bag here in the corridor!" We can't see who this is. "My brother will come pick it up in an hour!"

We recognise the voice—it's Zalina from the apartment block opposite.

And so on and so forth, the whole day long.

"When we first moved here," my mother reminisced, as she sliced onions for the pilaf, "we never locked the door. Well, only if we were going out to the shops and nobody was staying in. It would drive you mad—having to keep on locking and unlocking it—someone would come knocking every five minutes. Children and adults! Either they're coming by for a chat, or bringing some food to share, or asking to borrow something. I've never lived anywhere so friendly! I've grown to love this way of life with all my heart."

To be honest, I didn't share in my mother's delight. I thought that everyone has a right to live peacefully, in their own space, but, afraid of getting a smack, I kept my thoughts to myself.

The pilaf turned out beautifully on that summer's day, and the grown-ups decided to invite Zaina, who was sitting in front of her apartment block, to come and share it.

In other peoples' homes, Zaina was always very quiet. She'd only speak if someone asked her something, and then she'd tell brief, funny stories as if her life was one long party and it was everyone else who was living in sorrow and war.

"What a fool I was back then!" Zaina would say with a smile. "When I was younger, I'd forget to lock the door sometimes. So just as my guest was getting ready for earthly pleasures and taking his pants down, a neighbour would walk in, without even knocking, to borrow some sugar or some salt or some such. One esteemed gentleman from the ministry was so shocked when he saw his auntie come in, that he fell backwards onto a table. Something cracked in his back. The poor man's friends came to take him away on a stretcher, as his auntie ran alongside it, flogging him with his own socks."

"How did you end up like this?" my mother would muse. "Someone must have betrayed you. Some scoundrel. You must have married, then got divorced, and then your family wouldn't take you back?"

But Zaina would just laugh in reply and wouldn't reveal anything about her past life.

During the Second Chechen War—which was actually the Third—Zaina hung the flag with the wolf back up in her window. Shell fragments had shredded the flag in late autumn of that year, but she kept it in place because she didn't have another. Shells used to explode in the communal yard, right by the front door of our building. We'd have to wait for a lull long enough to allow us to run out and collect snow for water.

One time, the shelling was so violent that it seemed like munitions were raining down on our neighbourhood with enough force to reduce all the buildings to dust, and us along with them. What does it feel like to be the person trapped inside, choking on the plaster flying off the walls and ceiling? Explosions exert the force of an earthquake measuring six on the Richter scale. The building shudders like a dog that's just been kicked. And all the while, you're lying inside of it, face down on the floorboards, recollecting moments from your life, trying to remember enough to fill the gaping black void that's swallowing up everything around you.

This bombardment happened when Old Ahmed the Chechen and his Russian wife Irina were living on a neighbouring street where all the houses were privately owned. They'd been together for thirty-five years. In the beginning, before the First Chechen War, nobody knew what their nationalities were—nobody even thought to ask such questions back then. All we knew was that their only son had died in a car accident.

And then it came to light that Old Ahmed's wife was Russian. When word got around, some of their neighbours started spitefully enquiring whether he was going to turn her out now. But, after being on the receiving end of Old Ahmed's walking stick or his slop bucket, they bit their tongues and went back to greeting the couple respectfully.

The street their little house stood on kept changing hands. The rebels, with their small, mobile artillery gun, had retreated behind the garages, while the Russian troops had advanced in armored vehicles and opened fire from all manner of weapons. The old couple couldn't put out the fire raging in their house and were sheltering in the corridor, where the walls were thicker.

Zaina was lying flat in the snow. She hadn't managed to make it to the door of the cellar, where she would have taken shelter, and now she didn't dare lift her head enough to crawl the rest of the way, so heavy was the gunfire. She could see that the old couple's house was burning, but it was futile calling out for help with the shooting as loud as it was. Nobody could hear themselves think.

Irina suddenly appeared in the doorway. Her housecoat was on fire. She waved her arms in the air and shouted something before disappearing back into the burning building.

The Russian armored vehicle rotated its gun and trained it on the house. Soldiers jumped out and, presuming they'd located the rebels, started firing machine guns in the same direction.

Everyone in the cellar froze. They were watching these events unfold through a small hole in the wall and it was now clear that the old couple were about to die. That was the moment when Zaina suddenly jumped to her feet and ran at the Russians, not heeding the shells exploding all around her.

"Stop! There's people living there!" she shouted. "Don't shoot!"

Glued to the hole in the wall, the remaining population of our neighbourhood couldn't believe their eyes. In her ubiquitous trousers, in a light jacket that wasn't even done up, with her headscarf lost in the furore, Zaina was shielding someone else's burning house with her body.

Curls of her red hair fell around her slender shoulders. Her blue eyes shone brightly. Her beauty was breathtaking in the surrounding hell.

The Russian soldiers were so taken aback, they even stopped shooting. And behind the garages, the rebels with their small gun also fell silent.

Zaina ran into the house and led out Old Ahmed, who was choking from the smoke, and then his wife Irina, who had managed to throw off her burning robe and was now wrapped up in a shabby, dark-green coat.

"Are there really people living here?" the astonished soldiers kept asking.

Then one of them walked up to the old couple and shouted, "Show me your papers!"

"They're in there!" Irina pointed to the charred remnants of their house. "If you want to go look for them, be my guest, you can go straight through!"

Taking advantage of the lull, Old Ahmed, Irina, and Zaina quickly made their way to the cellar. Nobody tried to stop them.

The Russian soldiers and the rebels continued fighting.

With time, word of the fallen woman's heroic deed made its way round the whole neighbourhood.

"You're so brave!" People would say to her face, but behind her back they still whispered. "It doesn't matter; everyone knows what she is. One good deed won't make up for her past."

But Zaina sang songs and laughed out loud, just like she always did. Then one time she came to see my mother and have her cards read. My mother hadn't told anyone's fortune for a long, long time, but Zaina managed to talk her into it. She said it was very important—a matter of life or death.

"Tell me, will I die young? I don't want to live to old age!" Zaina kept saying. "An old woman lives out her days surrounded by grandchildren. What kind of old woman would I make? It's not going to work! I can't do it!"

My mother fanned out the cards and studied them carefully.

"I can see you've had a tough life. But that will pass. Things will change. You'll meet a good man. You'll have a house and you'll grow old. You'll have grandchildren and great-grandchildren too."

"That can't be true!"

"It is! The cards never lie. I've broken a vow for you. I swore I'd never read cards again."

"Will there definitely be grandchildren?" Zaina was thoughtful.

"Definitely. I can see a small boy. But he's not your son, he's your grandson. He loves you very much. You're going to play with him. And a little girl, in a pink dress. She's still a baby ... Hold on a minute, are you pregnant?!"

Zaina reached down, picked up a biscuit, and bit into it. That's when we noticed that she was crying. But she started smiling through her tears straight away, so we wouldn't think ill of her, and hid her face behind a glass of water.

"Would you like to hear a poem I wrote?" I asked.

Zaina nodded.

Noise cuts through the silence.
Time is no more.
Someone thought up a war,
To last a hundred thousand years.

Someone thought up names,
And sliced up the centuries.

In a world of everlasting war,
The clouds are cursed.

All who were born drew lots,
And all of us will die.
You can decide to go into the light,
Or to fall on the ice.

For a minute, everyone was silent.

"Make yourself scarce!" my mother suggested. "The Russian poets lived and wrote better than you and yet they all died in poverty. Nobody needs your poems here." "I just wanted to ..."

"Thank you!" Zaina said and smiled. She added quietly, "I was married off at thirteen. That was no life. I was always trying to please my elders. They beat me. My husband broke my ribs for disobeying him. The neighbor spoke to me and he didn't like the way I answered him. I ended up in hospital. I lost a child ... I remember my husband kicking me, while his mother and sisters sat in the next room. Nobody came to help me. I just kept screaming: 'I don't love you! I never loved you!' Then I passed out ...I didn't go back to my family after the hospital, I ran away. I never forgave them. I've been hiding ever since. My real name is Aminat."

"We won't tell anyone!" my mother said quickly, looking pointedly at me.

"It doesn't matter. Nothing's going to change now anyway. I've lived my life."

"Things will change! The cards say everything will turn out well for you. The second part of your life will have light, even though the first had darkness."

Zaina stayed with us for a while longer and then she left. Weeks passed. Neighbours asked each other—"have you seen our Zaina?" But nobody knew anything. We had our own worries and had almost forgotten her red curls and blue eyes, until we ran into Old Ahmed and Irina at the market one day. They had moved away to a village, to live with distant relatives, and rarely came into the city any more.

"Zaina's gone missing!" we announced.

Old Ahmed sighed and changed the subject, but his wife couldn't help herself and said, "Zaina has changed her name. She's had a baby.

These are difficult times, but it's not all bad—a person can disappear and start a new life. We helped her as much as we could."

With that, the old couple wished us a safe journey home without any shelling, and then they turned to go back to their car.

A VILLAGE FEST

Alisa Ganieva (1985)
Translated by Will Firth

Born in Dagestan, one of the Russian republics of the North Caucasus, **Alisa Ganieva** won the Debut prize for young prose writers under the male nickname *Gulla Hirachev*, playing with identities and the local dialects.

Ganieva writes mostly about the Caucasus, which since the early 19th century was a magnet, inspiration and terra incognita for Russian culture, the representation of closeness and otherness, the source of romanticism. But she writes about the modern Caucasus, stuck between colonialism and postcolonialism, affected by Soviet deportations and post-soviet wars, and the emergence of religious extremists and deep corruption.

She is also a literary critic, politically engaged journalist and currently lives in exile.

The village began coming up in telltale wormholes straightaway, in February. First, an irksome slogan appeared on the square with a sickening portrait of the commander-in-chief; then, dirty symbols of death began flitting past—in black-and-orange stripes, like cannibalistic caterpillars. Our protagonist, Akhmedov, pretended to go on living as before; he studied the faces of the villagers to try and discern secret despair, suppressed anger, and horror hidden in cowardice. Yet the faces showed only emptiness and the acquiescence of hired criminals.

The village had turned into a slave market, a trading hub of live meat and dead conscience; it lived recklessly, loudly, and with festive abandon. The mountains he had so loved since childhood met him in the mornings without their former grandeur, and it seemed they no longer towered up but lolled around in pillows of cloud, like raped and insulted prostitutes who were already old hands at the brothel. On the gray, rocky ridge behind the administration building, for the whole village to see, another symbol of death three times the height of a man jutted out and sullied the beauty of the sweeping vistas: the semi-swastika Z.

Masses of tourists trudged by. Excursions from central Russia trickled into the village museum, and there was Akhmedov. Despite occasional funerals featuring dead young soldiers, the village buzzed with laughter and merriment. That day, too, they were expecting a celebrity arrival from Moscow. Akhmedov, the director of the museum, was therefore summoned to the administration and ordered to prepare a patriotic speech.

"We will honor our soldiers who have returned from the denazification mission," pronounced Yakhya Yakhyayevich, uttering the D-word with a guttural cough. "Concoct a momentous little address for us, brother: about the historical connections, our ancestors, and the struggle against neo-fascism; you know, short and sweet. We're to be assigned funds for the indigenous peoples' festival, so this is a rehearsal, you see. It's crucial we show we've got grit."

"It needn't be me. I mean ... I ... I'm not much of an orator," Akhmedov stammered, but Yakhya Yakhyayevich resolutely turned away toward the patchily painted wall that sported an icon of the commander-in-chief—from back when he was young and not puffy. No, he would hear no objections.

That was a week before the celebration, and Akhmedov had spent the whole week as if in a pestilential haze. So far, he had managed to stay out of things. Whenever there were questions, he replied that he was old and not on social media, and therefore did not take part in any flash mobs to the glory of cruise missiles, and that the tremor in his hands did not allow him to wave flags at public events in the name of the expansion of the empire. He had thought of calling in sick that day, but he was summoned to the school in the morning because of his teenage nephew, who had come from a small village beyond the mountain pass to complete his certificate.

"He's shameless!" the teacher shouted. "We have good education and teamwork here, but your Ibrahim is growing up a terrorist."

Akhmedov's bowels trembled, and he yelled back.

"What's he done wrong? Nothing!"

His nephew sat at a desk in the empty classroom with his shaved head lowered. It was flat at the back from lying in a wooden crib.

"I said I don't want to march at the fest today," he muttered softly.

"See? He's undermining our good work!"

"We were told to carry a portrait of Imam Shamil. I don't give a flip."

"Why not?" Akhmedov wondered. "He's our national hero."

"Then why are they chucking him in with this diabolical bazaar in Ukraine? He stood for freedom—so we wouldn't be conquered. And now it's us who are blitzing and bombing …"

"See what I mean?" the teacher winced. "I'm not going to the top yet because they'll call in state security straightaway."

Akhmedov felt a churning inside him that went cold again. He waved his arms and spoke ardently, but without understanding what he said. He had to keep his nephew out of this; he would call him a fool, promise to give him a belting, and deal with him himself. But suddenly his nephew jumped up and spoke in a rasping, breaking bass:

"And this singer … he sings in leather shorts. I don't want to bow to him and march in front of him. Mahomed doesn't want to either, or Ilyas. He's a devil, not a star."

"We'll deal with you later," the teacher moaned. "That's traitorous stuff. You provoke the class. If your uncle weren't director of the museum you'd be under interrogation by now, sonny!"

Akhmedov flailed his arms, explained, justified—all in a flurry—and escorted his nephew out of the classroom.

"He's to be well away from the fest today! And then we'll show him!" the teacher repeated, red in the face.

Akhmedov ran out of the school in anger, almost despair. His nephew, waiting for him at the exit, had felt the heat and wanted things to simmer down, yet soon he went on again about how absurd the endless fanfares and celebrations were, where he was expected to stand with other children. Akhmedov grabbed him by the shoulders and shook him wildly, in rage:

"Do you want to share the fate of my son? Is that what you want?" he shouted in their native Avar.

But then he realized there were people about and someone was probably watching them from the terraced gardens and porches clustered around; he waved to the boy not to dally and strode off home.

His brooding nephew hopped along after him over the crumbling stones of the streets, muttering his many objections. Muffled old women descended in the opposite direction with their hands behind their backs, attracted by the cooing noises from the square. The sound system was being tested and occasional balloons burst.

Akhmedov's wife was out; she had probably gone to return the milk separator to the neighbor. He ordered his nephew to stay in his room, then he locked himself in another and paced from wall to wall with agitation. The teacher's threats caused him physical pain. An old pang raised its head and crawled along the arteries to his heart, gnashing its maw. Akhmedov went to the bookshelf and took his son's photograph—a young face cut by the black band of mourning.

Five years earlier, his son had just finished school and, since he did not reach the college admission score, he had remained in the village to work as a hired builder. Akhmedov reproached himself many times that if he had traveled to the capital and slipped the dean the customary amount, his son would have been accepted at the faculty and grief would have been avoided. But five years before, Akhmedov took a stance and avoided such fuss, and early one September morning his son set off for the neighboring village, where a stone layer was needed.

About three hours later, he called his mother to say he had snacked on the khinkal dumpling and cheese he took on the trip and was almost at the highway; and then he disappeared. After dinner, people from around the area went out in search of him, and soon they found Akhmedov's son in the bushes, riddled with bullets and forever cold. He was in strange clothes and a huge, oversized coat, and an old machine gun lay next to him. The police officers who arrived at the scene immediately surrounded the body and dragged it off to the station for investigation.

A fight ensued for the body. A heated crowd of villagers and relatives joined Akhmedov and his wife to demand that the boy be handed over for burial before sunset. The police resisted, gave confused accounts of events, and ultimately produced an official statement claiming that Akhmedov's son was a militant who had been hiding in the forests and carrying out sabotage for months, including an arson attack on the TV tower. They claimed he was armed to the teeth and had opened fire on the police, who had been conducting a reconnaissance operation in the mountains.

All this seemed like a nightmare and utter nonsense. Dozens of people knew Akhmedov's son—he lived in sight of everyone, loved football and computers, and dreamed of enrolling in university. It was blatantly obvious that the police shot the boy by mistake, and then, in an attempt to conceal the crime, planted one of their machine guns on the boy and dressed him up absurdly. One sharp-sighted eyewitness even spotted an inventory number on the machine gun.

Everyone's nerves were at fraying point that evening. The police locked the gates, but the crowd demolished them and enraged women even managed to storm the building and carry the body out. Then men in different uniforms caught up with the procession, fired salvoes into the air, and Akhmedov's dead son was soon in the grips of the government hydra again, to disappear forever in its dark labyrinths, to remain branded, calumniated, mutilated, and buried far from his relatives, under a number, in an unmarked grave, like an accursed terrorist. Every night, Akhmedov remembered the grimace of surprise on his white young face and his arm with the broad, hard-working hand that hung down from the stretcher.

For five years, he and his wife went from one government institution to another, seeking recognition of the mistake, and at times the hope of justice glimmered and grew. No one believed Akhmedov's son was guilty, and the police continued to blather, now claiming he was shot dead when their colleagues—whom they adamantly refused to name—returned fire in self-defense, now backing down and declaring that no reconnaissance operation had been carried out that day and no one could say who had killed the unfortunate boy. And who knows, maybe they would even give permission for him to be reburied in a humane way, in his native village. But just as permission was about to be given, the war that was not allowed to be called a war broke out. The commander-in-chief ordered his ragtag army to invade the neighboring country and raze its cities in a hail of rockets, and the mustached, fat metropolitan chief, who was in charge of his son's case, told Akhmedov:

"Do you know how many people the cops shoot in America? And they go scot-free. Here, any trifle and you get hauled up by the scruff of the neck. This is going no further. Such are the times—we need to be watchful. Our country is surrounded by enemies, and here you are undermining it with your petty petitions. We need to stand together now, not sue each other. It's the times we live in ... All the more because you're director of the village museum. Responsibility lies with you."

Akhmedov felt the threat in those words and could see the museum being taken away from him, and the case would still not be resolved. He prepared to wait until the war was over, but it dragged on, drawing all of those involved into an unknown abyss. Several young men from their mountainous region had disappeared without a trace—no funeral, none of the payments promised by the state.

"She's crying," his wife told him after a condolence visit to her third cousin, whose beloved first-born was among the missing. "'How many more of our boys have to die? No one asks where they go, and what they die for,' she says."

Festivities were necessary to find some shred of meaning in this whole senseless butchery, in the vile atrocities and omnipresent lies. Meaning was found in the distant past, in mothballed slogans from the Second World War, in the exhumed specter of Nazism, which they were taught to believe in with the same awe as they learned in mosque to believe in fables from the time of the prophet.

"Fascists at every turn"; "If we hadn't attacked, they would have"; "secret American laboratories"; "there are no civilian victims, it's all staged"—these phrases became mantras, talisman tales that saved the minds of millions from the terrible truth. And Akhmedov had to go up to the black microphone that day and repeat those tales in his own words. To concoct a spiel about the historical connections and their glorious ancestors, as Yakhya Yakhyayevich ordered. The wardrobe door creaked, and he looked for a suitable shirt. Burgundy was too pretentious, checkered indecorous. He chose a white one, slightly yellowed at the elbows. He had worn it to the last court session for his son's case.

When Akhmedov went back onto the street, he felt a heavy weight moving slowly in his right eye. It bounced upward with every step, hitting blood vessels and capillaries. By the time he reached the square he was completely exhausted, and nothing resembling a festive speech had formed in his mind. There was a bustle already, and he tossed habitual "salaams" to a few people and even laughed at the odd joke, but he did all this mechanically, while inside, in his aorta that was abundantly coated with dangerous plaque, there huddled a small and caustic sense of shame—for his laughter, timidity, insignificance, and confusion, and for his resignation to this savage reality, which had bent him into an ignominious and slavish pose.

"They say he's coming up the switchback now, he'll be here soon," chirruped the clerk of the village bank, who they sometimes played shesh-besh with in the evenings.

Akhmedov did not immediately realize that this was the same singer, a celebrity who it seems often went on stage in skimpy shorts and eyeliner. His image in no way suited the belligerent mood of the event or the local patriarchal ways, but his fame redeemed everything. The square brimmed with people.

Sure enough, a few minutes later the cortege appeared—a white Mercedes pulled up behind the traffic police car after viewing the village, and the guest of honor darted out, fully clad, in trousers and a pinkish shirt unbuttoned at the top. Zurnas blew, a drum beat, and a chain of dancing mountain women in cheap synthetic dresses supposed to depict national costumes formed a ring around the radiant singer. Colorful bunches of wildflowers sailed into the throng and Russian tricolors flew.

The singer grinned with his white teeth as he bashfully parodied the movements of the Lezgian dancers. He was happy with the mission entrusted to him, the inebriating mountain air, and the rapture of the natives. The head of the administration with his entourage waddled swiftly toward the guest to place a large sheep's-wool hat on his head and present him an ornamental dagger. A roar of applause went up, mixed with cries of One of us! and women's laughter. The officials began their speeches, and Akhmedov, not listening, fitfully gleaned words for his impending address. The weight in his eye grew heavier.

"Zaripat Musaevna is first, then our veteran of the special operation, and then you," Yakhya Yakhyayevich told him, creeping up from behind. Sweat streamed down Akhmedov's red cheeks.

Zaripat Musaevna was the school principal. She spoke confidently, loudly, and with a fanatical twang. Her long, shining shawl boasted a decorative fringe.

"I tell the kids at morning assembly: our grandfathers won a victory for us, and now it's our turn. As our president said, we are all different nationalities, but we are all Russians. Together we are a force. I am proud that our children know who they are. They are warriors of a huge country, which is fighting alone against global fascism, against the insidious designs of NATO, against the destruction of the brotherhood of Slavic peoples …"

Children in military uniforms, including the youngest elementary school students, were lined up at the back of the platform like life-size puppets, trembling as they held flags and portraits of dead soldiers from the region. Black-and-white photographs from the forties alternated with modern ones in color. A black-and-orange banner blared the numerals "1945–2022." Old tsarist cannons, which had been standing there almost since Shamil's capture, gleamed on either side of the banner in the blazing sun.

Akhmedov shielded his eyes, rummaging in his memory for seemly historical parallels—his museum, the village's past, today's camarilla. But it just did not jell.

High above the slate roofs of the village, where a fast river ran through a rock-cluttered bed, there once nestled the former village, now in ruins. It was besieged for almost three months, with 4,000 Dagestanis surrounded by an Imperial Russian army of 15,000. The defenders left almost no descendants because all of them were killed by cannonballs and bayonets or died of disease and hunger. Only Shamil, wounded in the leg, escaped with one of his wives. When the victors approached the towers and entered the village, the women who were still alive grabbed the children and flung themselves from the cliffs so as not to fall into the hands of the enemy. The ravines stank of corpses and the river ran red with blood.

Since then, no one had lived on the site of the burnt village. A garrison was built on the site of the current one, which gradually expanded and took in inhabitants of the surrounding small villages. At the beginning of the twentieth century, Akhmedov's grandfather, the owner of a rare herd of horses, also moved here. The horses were confiscated, of course, and his grandfather perished in Siberia. All he left behind was a fine silver dagger belt and a few books written in Arabic script, which miraculously survived destruction. Akhmedov donated the family relics to the museum.

"How are things? All set for the speech?" a stocky, broad-shouldered villager with black birch gum in his teeth tapped him on the shoulder. It was Nabi from the sports committee, who supervised the freestyle wrestling club. When Akhmedov's son disappeared, Nabi was the instigator and main wrangler with the police, and since then Akhmedov had warmed to him. But when the occupation of the neighboring country began, Nabi suddenly became a keen supporter of this mad danse macabre; he was so eager to advance on Kyiv that Akhmedov could not help asking why he had not enlisted and gone to fight. "If only I were younger!" Nabi grunted and avoided a straight answer. After being appointed to the sports committee, he soon acquired a piece of forest in a nature reserve and became complaisant and as soft as butter.

"My cousin's son disappointed me," Nabi continued through a new burst of applause—the officials were presented the veteran of the special operation.

"What happened?"

"He refused to go to war. He and two hundred others, they say. All from our republic."

"Were they set free?"

"Certainly not! They're being kept in a shed without food or water until they see sense. They're lucky—they should be turfed into jail! Likewise, my cousin says to her son: 'Why are you disgracing me? You coward! Go, and don't come back,'"

"They don't want to kill?"

"I don't know why they're so chicken," Nabi grimaced. "They just don't like the uniform. There are no bulletproof vests, apparently, and no boots—only an assortment of sizes and broken ones. They complained at the beginning, and they froze whenever it was cold. Like women, basically. I also say: just let them try and come back!"

"They went there for the money, didn't they?" Akhmedov felt the urge to ask.

"Huh? Where'd you get that from?" Nabi snorted, glancing at him sharply and even with a certain alarm. He shook his head as if he could not believe his ears, then waved and hurried off to greet a person who had just arrived.

Akhmedov now drifted closer to the microphone. Smells of cheap women's perfume mingled with those of burnt sugar—they were sure to be selling cotton candy somewhere in the crowd. His head was still empty, his temples rang and burned, and a ball of unknown murk gathered in his chest. A bemedaled soldier with a symbol of death on his lapel waited at the microphone, shifting from one foot to another. An ugly scar stretched across half of his face.

"His jaw fell out when the tank exploded," a woman said at the back of the crowd. "He picked it up, put it back on his face, and kept fighting."

"Wow, what a hero …"

"All his comrades were killed, and he alone survived. His mother had no word from him for two months and was afraid he wouldn't be coming back."

"O Allah, may this war end soon."

Akhmedov closed his eyes and hoped it would make him feel better. Noises multiplied and seethed in his ears. An invisible tormentor thrust pliers into his graying head and began to twist and jerk, searching for a nerve to seize. The young veteran's voice came to him in broken waves:

"Thanks to God, I returned … Inshallah, we shall continue to defend our Motherland … Our filial duty … The forces of neo-Nazism …"

I must send a lad to bring me an Analgin, Akhmedov thought and opened his eyes wide. Spirals of color swirled before them. The square was in a festive mood. The veteran looked small and ugly, almost frightened. Another came to mind, ninety years old, who had lived on the outskirts of the village. Once a year, on May 9, he was dressed up in a ceremonial jacket with medals and exhibited on the square as an idol to be honored with bouquets.

He fell into frailty a few years earlier and his impoverished daughter applied to the administration for a wheelchair so that he could move around the house a bit and go out into the garden for fresh air, but despite all efforts a wheelchair was never found, so the veteran farewelled life from the captivity of a sagging sofa. Shortly before his death, administration staff finally got round to paying him an unannounced visit. They brought a loaf of bread and a bag of short-grain rice. Photographs from the occasion soon adorned all the region's official websites—ladies in mink coats at the bed of the dying liberator.

"We were there to help the civilians," the veteran spoke. "Why? Because who else would, apart from us? An old lady lay on the ground, and I helped her to her feet …"

His voice was replaced by another, hoarser one, and the name

Akhmedov rang out. He realized they were calling him and he needed to go to the microphone right now; he had to appear before the whole village against the background of the children at attention in army caps, against the backdrop of the glowing orange symbol of death on the mountain ridge, and to merge with the shroud of darkness that covered them all. Electricity coursed through Akhmedov's calves; they trembled, and the pads of his fingers clung stickily to his wet palm. He headed for the microphone with a slight sway.

The famous singer emerged from behind the loudspeakers, surrounded by his entourage; he had been able to partake in the gifts of the village during the speeches. His hit song was coming up and his smile vanished in the woolen curls of his new hat. The sight of the singer made Akhmedov feel a hundred times hotter, his head ached inexorably like in a vice; his intoxicated gaze slid over the heads of the multitude and snagged on a portrait of Imam Shamil. A toad began to squirm in his throat.

"Up this way, please," the host from the district administration beckoned him.

Akhmedov grasped the microphone with one hand, fixed his troubled gaze on the crowd, made a nondescript sound, then doubled over and vomited loudly and relentlessly. There were gasps of fright, and after a hasty moment the song started.

OY OY OY

Alla Gorbunova (1985)
Translated by Elina Alter

Acclaimed and widely translated poet, laureate of the prestigious Bely prize for her lyrics, **Alla Gorbunova** won the 2021 Russian NOS prize for a collection of short stories, her first book of prose.

These stories, closely linked with the rhythms of poetry, explore the intertwined and mixed worlds of the Russian millennials, the first generation to be free from the distinctive stigmas of the Soviet past – but to be exposed to the swirls and traps of the new Russia, slowly turning to its dark and perilous future.

> There's a man lying down in
> a grave somewhere /
> With the same tattoos as me
> —Coil

In the bathroom of the Krasnoyarsk airport, pop starlet Amanda, passing through on her tour, happened to glance at the cleaning schedule and froze: the cleaning woman's signature corresponded precisely to her own, Amanda's, signature. Every crook, every curl—it was all identical, as though Amanda herself had signed there. Amanda couldn't understand how such a thing was possible, and that very same day she hired a private investigator to find out every detail about this cleaning woman. The following morning, the investigator told Amanda that the cleaner's name was Lyudmila Pashkevich; she was forty-four years old, uneducated, lived alone in workers' housing in the Sovetsky neighborhood of Krasnoyarsk, and there was nothing special about her, and on top of all that she had a harelip. Starlet Amanda had just about calmed down, but then the investigator produced copies of all of the cleaning woman's documents, including some job application she had written out by hand, and to her horror Amanda saw that Lyudmila Pashkevich's handwriting was precisely the same as her own. All of this made Amanda somehow uneasy.

Like a thorn in her heel, this cleaning woman tormented her. After all, she'd been doing just fine, recording songs, visiting her cosmetologist and her tanning salon, dating her boyfriend and knowing no woe—and now there was Pashkevich. Amanda tried to put the woman out of her mind—no, no, I have nothing in common with her, what's a signature, what's someone's handwriting? It's only a coincidence. It happens—she told herself. Her concert went well, though she hadn't yet performed her newest song. No one in the world had heard it yet; Amanda had written it only recently and intended to return to Moscow and record it in the studio. It went like this: "I love you and you love me / we're together finally / you're my joy / oy oy oy!" Amanda was going to dedicate the song to her boyfriend. Waiting for her return flight after the concert, Amanda decided to go into the airport bathroom. You don't scare me, Pashkevich, she thought, though at the idea of the bathroom her heart began beating strangely. I know everything about you, you're a poor lonely woman with no education and a harelip. The bathroom was sunk into a glimmering twilight, and when Amanda entered, all the noise of the airport faded away. In the bathroom, a woman with a harelip was stooped over washing the floor, and she was singing "Oy oy oy!" to the tune of Amanda's song as she dragged her rag across the tile. "What's that you're singing?" Amanda mumbled. "Oy oy oy!" sang the woman, almost viciously, then looked up at Amanda with cloudy gray eyes: "It's a song, see," and went on scrubbing the floor. Amanda flew to Moscow. Life lost its colors for her: recording, performing, trips, clubs, her boyfriend, the cosmetologist and the tanning salon, shopping and whatever else she had loved—all of it had turned out to be a trick, a lie, because somewhere in eastern Siberia there lived a woman with a harelip and Amanda's handwriting, her signature, her song. Amanda's entire life was ruined, poisoned, revealed to be a hoax, someone's cruel joke. Soon Amanda threw herself out of a window, nobody knew why. At her funeral there was a woman with a harelip whom no one recognized. She stood there for a while, then went away.

We are grateful to the following for permission to reproduce copyright material:

Svetlana Aleksievich: 'It wasn't Me' translated by Richard Pevear and Larissa Volokhonsky in *The Unwomanly Face of War* by Svetlana Alexievich, Penguin Classics, copyright © Svetlana Alexievich, 1985, 2017. Translation copyright © Richard Pevear and Larissa Volokhonsky, 2017. Reproduced by permission of Penguin Books Limited;

Liza Aleksandrova-Zorina: 'Alesha's Homecoming', translated by Natasha Perova. Reproduced by permission of the author; and the translator;

Isaac Babel: 'The King' translated by Boris Dralyuk in *Odessa Stories*, Pushkin Press, 2018. Reproduced by permission of the publisher;

Ksenia Buksha: 'There is no night' translated by Anne O. Fisher in *Chtenia 23: Women Writing: Readings from Russia*, Vol 6 (3), Issue 23, 2013, pp.15–25. Reproduced by permission of the translator;

Mikhail Bulgakov: 'The Steel Windpipe' translated by Michael Glenny in *A Country Doctor's Notebook* by Mikhail Bulgakov, Harvill Press, translation copyright © Michael Glenny, 1975. Reproduced by permission of The Random House Group Limited;

Yuly Daniel: 'Hands' translated by Brian James Baer in *Short Stories in Russian: New Penguin Parallel Text*, translation, introduction and selection copyright © Brian James Baer, 2017. Updated 2024 for this edition. Reproduced by permission of Penguin Press, an imprint of Penguin Publishing Group, a division of Penguin Random House LLC; and the Estate of the translator. All rights reserved;

Georgii Demidov: 'The intellectual (The Cauchy principle)' translated by Diane Nemec Ignashev in *Five Fates from a Wondrous Planet*, Vozvrashchenie, 2015. Reproduced by permission of the translator;

Leonid Dobychin: 'Kozlova' translated by Richard C. Borden with Natalia Belova, in *Encounters with Lise and Other Short Stories*, Northwestern University Press, 2005. English translation copyright © Northwestern University Press, 2005. All rights reserved;

Asar Eppel: 'Red caviar sandwiches' translated by Joanne Turnbull in *Russian Short Stories from Pushkin to Buida*, Penguin, 2005. Reproduced by permission of the translator;

Alisa Ganieva: 'A Village Fest' first published in *The Missing Slate*, 2017, translated by Will Firth in *Words Without Borders*, February 2023. Translation copyright © Will Firth, 2023. Reproduced by permission of the author, translator and Words Without Borders. All rights reserved;

Gaito Gazdanov: 'The Mistake' translated by Bryan Karetnyk in *The Beggar and Other Stories*, Pushkin Press, 2018. Reproduced by permission of the publisher;

Vladimir Gilyarovsky: 'Tankard with Eagle' translated by Brian Murphy and Michael Pursglove from *Memoirs of Old Moscow in the years before Lenin and Stalin*, 2016. Reproduced by permission of the translator;

Lidya Ginzburg: 'a Siege Day' translated by Angela Livingstone in *Notes from The Blockade,* Harvill Press, copyright © The Estate of Lydia Ginzburg, 1995. English translation © The Harvill Press 1995. Reproduced by permission of The Random House Group Limited;

Linor Goralik: 'Something Like That (A War Story)' translated by Ainsley Morse, Maria Vassileva, and Maya Vinokour in *Found Life. Poems, Stories, Comics, a Play, and an Interview*, Columbia University Press, copyright © 2017. Reproduced by permission of Columbia University Press;

Alla Gorbunova: 'Oy Oy Oy' translated by Elina Alter in *Ings & Oughts*, Deep Vellum Publishing, 2021. Reproduced by permission from the publisher; and the translator;

Dmitry Glukhovsky: 'Sulfur' translated by Marian Schwartz, copyright © Dmitry Glukhovsky, www.nibbe-literary-agency.com. Reproduced by permission of the author; and the translator;

Ilya Ilf and Yevgeny Petrov: 'Blue Devil' translated by Anne O. Fisher in *Interview at Praça Rosefielt*, Bauer Verlag, Frankfurt. Reproduced by permission of the translator;

Valentin Kataev: 'Knives' translated by Alec Brown in *Soviet Anthology*, Cape, 1943, copyright © Estate of the author. Reproduced by permission;

Daniil Kharms: 'The Fate of the Professor's Wife' translated by Matvei Yankelevich in *Today I Wrote Nothing: The Selected Writing of Daniil Kharms*, translation copyright © Matvei Yankelevich, 2009. Reproduced by permission of The Overlook Press, an imprint of Harry N. Abrams, Inc., New York. All rights reserved;

Vladislav Khodasevich: 'Pompeii' translated by Bryan Karetnyk in *Russian Émigré Short Stories from Bunin to Yanovsky*, Penguin Classics, translation copyright © Bryan Karetnyk, 2017. Reproduced by permission of Penguin Books Limited;

Julia Kissina: 'The Lithuanian Hand' translated by Brian James Baer in *Short Stories in Russian: New Penguin Parallel Text*, translation, introduction and selection copyright © Brian James Baer, 2017. Reproduced by permission of Penguin Press, an imprint of Penguin Publishing Group, a division of Penguin Random House LLC; and the author. All rights reserved;

Eduard Kochergin: 'The Ballad of the Wooden Plane' translated by Simon Patterson with Nina Chordas in *Christened with Crosses*, Glagoslav, 2012. Reproduced by permission of Wiedling Literary Agency on behalf of the proprietor Vita Nova Ltd;

Vyacheslav Kondratiev: 'At Freedom Station' translated by Louis Wagner in *The Wild Beach & Other Stories*, edited by Helena Goscilo and Byron Lindsey, copyright © Ardis, 1992. Reproduced by permission of Ardis/The Overlook Press, an imprint of Harry N. Abrams, Inc., New York. All rights reserved;

Andrei Bely: 'The Yogi' translated by Anthony Kroytor, https://aanatolivich.files.wordpress.com/2008/06/bely_yogi.pdf. Reproduced by permission of the translator;

Sigizmund Krzhizhanovsky: 'Quadraturin' translated by Joanne Turnbull in *Russian Short Stories from Pushkin to Buida*, Penguin, 2005. Reproduced by permission of the translator;

Mikhail Kuzmin: 'Father Gervasy's Secret', https://dalspace.library.dal.ca/bitstream/handle/10222/21661/toc_e.html. Reproduced with permission;

Sergei Lebedev: 'Whoooo' translated by Antonina W. Boius in *A Present Past: Titan and Other Chronicles*, Head of Zeus, 2023. Reproduced with permission;

Nikolai Leskov: 'The Small Mistake' translated by Richard Pevear and Larissa Volokhonsky in *The Enchanted Wanderer and Other Stories* by Nikolai Leskov, Vintage Classics, translation copyright © Richard Pevear and Larissa Volokhonsky, 2013. Reproduced by permission of The Random House Group Limited;

Elena Makarova: 'Herbs from Odessa' translated by Helena Goscilo in *Balancing Acts: Contemporary Stories by Russian Women,* Indiana University Press, 1989. Reproduced by permission of the author; and the translator;

Nadezhda Mandelstam: 'The last letter' translated by Max Hayward in *Hope Abandoned*, Harvill Press, copyright © Atheneum Publishers, 1989. Reproduced by permission of The Random House Group Limited; and Peters Fraser & Dunlop (www.petersfraserdunlop.com) on behalf of the Estate of Max Hayward;

Natalya Meshchaninova: 'Mom' translated by Fiona Bell in *Stories of Life* by Fiona Bell, Deep Vellum, 2022. Reproduced by permission of the publisher;

Vladimir Nabokov: 'The Return of Chorb' published in *Details of a Sunset and Other Stories*, McGraw-Hill, copyright © Vladimir Nabokov, 1976. Reproduced by permission of The Wylie Agency (UK) Limited;

Irina Odoyevtseva: 'Epilogue' translated by Irina Steinberg. Reproduced by permission of Literary Agency Galina Dursthoff; and the translator;

Yury Olesha: 'Liompa' translated by Aimee Anderson in *Three Fat Men: Complete Short Stories* by Yury Olesha, copyright © Ardis, 1979. Reproduced by permission of Ardis/The Overlook Press, an imprint of Harry N. Abrams, Inc., New York. All rights reserved;

Maxim Osipov: 'The cry of the domestic fowl' from *Rock, Paper, Scissors*, originally published in English with a translation by Alex Fleming, New York Review Books, 2019, translation copyright © Alex Fleming, 2019;

Mikhail Osorgin: 'The Flora of Penza' translated by Donald M. Fiene in *Selected Stories, Reminiscences, and Essays* by Mikhail Osorgin, copyright © Ardis, 1982.

Reproduced by permission of Ardis/The Overlook Press, an imprint of Harry N. Abrams, Inc., New York. All rights reserved;

Viktor Pelevin: 'Friedmann Space' translated by Anastasia Lakhtikova in *Best European Fiction 2010*, Dalkey Archive Press, 2009. Reproduced by permission of FTM Agency Ltd; and the translator;

Ludmilla Petrushevskaya: 'Milgrom' translated by Anna Summers in *There Once Lived a Girl Who Seduced Her Sister's Husband, And He Hanged Himself: Love Stories* by Ludmilla Petrushevskaya, Penguin Classics, copyright © Ludmilla Petrushevskaya, 2013, translation copyright © Anna Summers, 2013. Reproduced by permission of Penguin Books Limited;

Andrey Platonov: 'Nikita' translated by Robert and Elizabeth Chandler and Angela Livingstone in *The Return and Other Stories* by Andrey Platonov, Harvill Press, translation copyright © Robert and Elizabeth Chandler and Angela Livingstone, 1999. Reproduced by permission of The Random House Group Limited;

Anna Politkovskyaya: 'It's Nice to Be Deaf' translated by Alexander Burry and Tatiana Tulchinsky in *A Small Corner of Hell: Dispatches from Chechnya* by Anna Politkovskaya, The University of Chicago Press, 2003. Permission conveyed through Copyright Clearance Center;

Mikhail Prishvin: 'The Blue Banner' translated by Lisa C. Hayden in *1917: Stories and Poems from the Russian Revolution*, Pushkin Press, 2016. Reproduced by permission of the translator;

Irina Ratushinskaya: 'A Tale of Three Heads' translated by Diane Nemec Ignashev in *A Tale of Three Heads: Short Stories* by Irina Ratushinskaia, Hermitage, 1986. Reproduced by permission of the translator;

Yuri Rytkheu: 'A Dream in a Polar Fog', translated by Ilona Yazhbin Chavasse in *A Dream in Polar Fog*, Archipelago Books, 2005. Reproduced by permission of the publisher;

Varlam Shalamov: 'Major's Pugachev last battle' from "The Left Bank" published in *Kolyma Stories. Volume 1, Book 2*, originally published in English with a translation by Donald Rayfield, New York Review Books, 2018. Translation copyright © Donald Rayfield, 2018;

Mikhail Shishkin: 'Of Saucepans and Star-Showers' translated by Leo Shtutin in *Calligraphy Lesson: The Collected Stories*, Deep Vellum Publishing, 2015. Reproduced by permission of the publisher;

Mikhail Sholokhov: 'Shibalok's family' published in *Selected Tales from the Don*, Elsevier, 1967. Reproduced by permission of Elsevier through PLSClear;

Vasily Shukshin: 'Tough Guy', translated by Laura Michael and John Givens in *Stories from a Siberian Village* by Vasily Shukshin, a NIU Press book, copyright © Northern Illinois University Press, 1996. Reproduced by permission of the publisher, Cornell University Press;

Fyodor Sologub: 'The White Dog' translated by John Cournos in *The New Statesman*, 1913, copyright © New Statesman Ltd. Reproduced by permission of the publisher;

Aleksandr Solzhenitsyn: 'La main droite' published in *Zacharie l'Escarcelle*, translated as 'The Right hand' by Michael Glenny in *Stories and Prose Poems*, Farrar, Straus & Giroux LLC, 2015, copyright © Aleksandr Solzhenitsyn, 1970, 1978. Reproduced by permission of Les Editions Fayard;

Vladimir Sorokin: 'The Swim' translated by Brian James Baer in *Short Stories in Russian: New Penguin Parallel Text*, translation, introduction and selection copyright © Brian James Baer, 2017. Reproduced by permission of Penguin Press, an imprint of Penguin Publishing Group, a division of Penguin Random House LLC; and Literary Agency Galina Dursthoff. All rights reserved;

Anna Starobinets: 'The Agency' translated by Hugh Aplin in *An Awkward Age*, Hesperus, 2010. Reproduced by permission of the author; and the translator;

Nadezhda Teffi: 'Solovki' translated by Robert Chandler and Elisabeth Chandler in *Other Worlds: Peasants, Pilgrims, Spirits, Saints*, Pushkin Press, 2021. Reproduced by permission of the publisher;

Yury Trifonov: 'A Short Stay in the Torture Chamber', translated by Bryon Lindsey in *The Wild Beach & Other Stories*, edited by Helena Goscilo and Byron Lindsey, copyright © Ardis, 1992. Reproduced by permission of Ardis/The Overlook Press, an imprint of Harry N. Abrams, Inc., New York. All rights reserved;

Vladimir Voinovich: 'The Novel', translated by Peter Morley in *Life Stories: Original Works by Russian Writers*, Russian Information Services, 2009. Reproduced by permission of FTM Agency; and the translator;

Polina Zherebtsova: 'Zaina' translated by Irina Steinberg. Reproduced by permission of the author; and the translator;

Mikhail Zoshchenko: 'A victim of the revolution' translated by Jeremy Hicks, originally published in *The Galosh and Other Stories*, Angel Books, 2000. Reproduced by permission of the Pushkin Press; and the translator.

In some instances we have been unable to trace the owners of copyright material, and we would appreciate any information that would enable us to do so.